CALIFORNIA

From the Golden State Come
Four Modern Novels of Inspiring Love

D0616124

KRISTIN BILLERBECK
DINA LEONHARDT KOEHLY
SALLY LAITY
KATHLEEN YAPP

BARBOUR
PUBLISHING, INC.
Uhrichsville, Ohio

To Truly See © 1998 by Barbour Publishing, Inc.
A Gift from Above © 1996 by Dina Leonhardt Koehly.
Better than Friends © 1994 by Sally Laity.
Golden Dreams © 1996 by Kathleen Yapp.

ISBN 1-58660-261-6

Cover design by Robyn Martins.

All Scripture quotations, unless otherwise noted, are taken from the King James Version.

Scripture quotations marked NIV are taken from the HOLY BIBLE, NEW INTERNATIONAL VERSION®. NIV®. Copyright© 1973, 1978, 1984 by International Bible Society. Used by permission of Zondervan Publishing House. All rights reserved.

Published by Barbour Publishing, Inc., P.O. Box 719, Uhrichsville, Ohio 44683 http://www.barbourbooks.com

ecpa Member of the
Evangelical Christian
Publishers Association

Printed in the United States of America.

CALIFORNIA

From the Golden State Come
Four Modern Novels of Inspiring Love

To Truly See

Kristin Billerbeck

Dedication

To my precious children who must deal with MS's effects every day.
Trey—for your discerning and humorous spirit,
Jonah—for your compassionate and sensitive nature,
Seth—for your God-given charm and disarming personality, and
Elle, my princess—for just being a light in this home.
I love you all.

Chapter 1

Brenda Turner stood in the empty examining room, buttoned her pale green silk blouse, and tucked it into her straight ivory skirt. Slipping her feet into her sling-back heels, she sat to await the doctor's return. A familiar muffled ringing sounded from the brushed leather briefcase at her feet. She reached for the tiny cellular phone, grabbing her hairbrush at the same time.

She pressed a small button on the phone. "Brenda Turner." After listening for a moment, she impatiently interrupted. "Tell the printer, they *must* be finished by Thursday. If I don't have those brochures in my hand *on time*, Atlas Printing will be a memory. I'll make sure of that."

She listened for a few seconds before interrupting again. "Take charge, Katie! They may conveniently forget that Star Digital is their most valuable client, but it's your job to remind them! Look, Katie, my appointment is here. I'll see you in the office soon." Brenda folded the small telephone quickly and slammed it into her briefcase. Frustrated, she wondered whether she would ever find an administrative assistant who could handle the pressure. She tossed her blond hair and looked intently at the doctor as he entered, her work momentarily forgotten.

A short, stocky man in a white lab coat, Dr. Wilhelm wore a solemn face and carried an oversized file envelope filled with X-rays. "Miss Turner, these are the results of your latest MRI, and these are the results of your first one two years ago." He clipped the two negatives on a lighted board and Brenda's brain loomed brightly before her. She walked toward the pictures, fascinated by the images.

"Wow, look at those wrinkles—she must have an incredible IQ," Brenda joked, trying to make light of the situation.

Dr. Wilhelm smiled thinly and proceeded with his clinical diagnosis, but he avoided looking his patient in the eye. "Miss Turner, these white spots on your brain here represent what we call plaquing, indicative of demyelination. Your double vision, loss of balance, and dizzy spells are the result of a demyelinating disease."

Brenda looked at the doctor inquisitively. His ridiculous double-talk irritated her. Noting her angry confusion, the doctor continued, "Your central nervous system is made up of many wires insulated with a material called myelin, just like real wire would be insulated with a rubber coating. Something is attacking your myelin, replacing it with scar tissue. Judging from your symptoms, I'd say this is a brain stem attack, which is sending strange messages to your eyes and ears, affecting your equilibrium."

"Look, Dr. Wilhelm, I'm a bright woman, but you're not speaking English. In laymen's terms, please—do I have a brain tumor or what?" Brenda stepped closer to the doctor, using her five-foot-ten-inch stature to try to intimidate him.

"Miss Turner, I am diagnosing you with multiple sclerosis." The blunt response hit Brenda like a freight train. Her shoulders dropped as her breath left her. She looked pleadingly at the doctor for a smile, anxious to share in the joke, but his face remained grave. She found the chair behind her with her hands and slowly sat down, trying to absorb the information. The young executive had been taught to keep her cool amidst troubling news, but this had thrown her.

She remained seated and spoke after regaining her composure. "Meaning?"

"Myelin can repair itself, and it already has once before. You see your old films show these white spots." The doctor pointed to two small white blurs. "But in the latest MRI, the old spots are gone. What you have is very likely relapsing-remitting MS, which means you may fully recover from the symptoms you're experiencing. . . just like you did last time. There is the possibility you may not, although my guess would be that it would continue on a remitting course for quite some time." The doctor finally looked her in the eye.

"Doctor, I can barely stand up with this dizziness. People at work are beginning to think I had one too many at lunch. How can I possibly work like this? There must be a pill or something—you know, to speed things up."

"Miss Turner, there are lots of medications to help minimize your symptoms, even a few that may slow the progression of the disease, but there is no cure for multiple sclerosis."

Brenda fumed at the negative answer. She couldn't abide such powerlessness. Somebody had to have a better answer and she was determined to find it. She began roughly pulling the film down off the lighted screen.

"Very well, Dr. Wilhelm, I can see I'm going to need a second opinion on such a serious diagnosis. Thank you." Brenda's mind was racing, anxious to find the neurologist who would tell her what she wanted to hear. She placed the negatives under her arm and walked decisively from the room, slamming the door behind her.

The doctor craned his head cautiously around the corner and called tentatively after her. "Miss Turner, those MRI results belong to the hospital."

"It's my brain. I'd say they belong to me. My insurance paid for them, correct?" Turning quickly to storm away once again, Brenda stumbled and careened into the wall. She reached desperately for support and managed to salvage her balance, if not her dignity. She exited using the wall as her guide. The stout doctor shook his head sorrowfully and returned to his office.

❧❦❧

Brenda turned up the volume on her surround-sound stereo while a motivational speaker preached the art of negotiation. No matter how loud she turned the tape, Dr. Wilhelm's forceful words echoed louder: *multiple sclerosis.*

She drove her shiny, black BMW convertible as if it were on autopilot and soon arrived at her office. She hastily squealed the sports car into her reserved parking space and collected the X-rays from the passenger seat. She folded them once carefully, hiding them in the large side pocket of her briefcase. Worried that she might lose her balance again, she removed her taupe heels and replaced them with bright white running shoes.

Brenda eagerly approached the mirrored-glass high-rise that felt like home. She pressed her name badge to the electronic security panel and the door clicked for her entry. The familiar steel gray lobby felt like a warm arm around her.

Katie Cummings, Brenda's secretary, rushed past the rows of cubicles, frantically waving her arms, "Brenda, you're here. The VP of engineering has been looking for you all morning. Are you ready with the campaign? He says hardware has completed the prototype today, and software will be ready by the weekend. He's been screaming 'where is marketing?' for an hour. You turned your cell phone off." Katie's face was anguished, and when Brenda didn't speak, she continued. "Brenda, I wish you would delegate more authority. Your staff has been yelling at me all morning. I'm not a punching bag."

"Katie, I'm sorry you had trouble, but how often am I ever out of the office?" The tall blond sat calmly behind her large mahogany desk and allowed her eyes to wander confidently over the sketches and copy changes in front of her. Brenda knew she would meet the impossible deadline; she always did. That's how she had become vice president of marketing at only twenty-seven. Her secret was time; she devoted all of it to work. Outside her door, she watched middle-aged engineers banging on their keyboards, stuck in their tiny cubicles while she sat comfortably in her spacious office overlooking the man-made lakes and waterfalls outside the building. A corner of her mouth lifted smugly as she recalled her accomplishments.

"Katie, tell engineering and software to worry about engineering and software; the marketing's ready to go—as always." Katie smiled and strode assuredly toward the engineering department, "Oh, and Katie, before you go, I'm doing a little research project. Would you please find me the best neurologist in town? And I'm having dinner with someone from Cyreck. His name's on my calendar. Find out about him."

"Absolutely." Katie made mental notes and left.

Brenda's head was spinning. She tried to read a report, but her eyes would not focus. The lines jumped from on the page like a vertical hold on a television set gone berserk. She closed her eyes and opened them again, but the results were the same. She rummaged through her purse for a mirror and looked at her reflection. She closed one eye, concentrating on the bright blue of the other. It didn't appear to be moving, but the sights in front of her continued to jump. She closed her left eye and peered at the right. It also remained motionless while the mirror appeared to leap relentlessly. *What is going on?*

Instantly, Brenda recalled the doctor's ugly words. *It can't be multiple sclerosis,* she thought. *That's when people can't walk. My legs feel fine. I just feel so tired and dizzy. Why today, when I have so much to do?* She rubbed the back of her neck and kicked off her bulky athletic shoes underneath the desk. *Caffeine. Of course! I haven't had any coffee today.*

Brenda leaned across her desk and buzzed Katie on the intercom. "Katie, would you mind ordering me a mocha and making it a double shot? I'm just falling asleep today, and I can't explain it."

"Perhaps if you went home once in awhile and used that device called a bed, you might feel more awake," Katie said sarcastically as she came to the door.

Brenda had grown very dependent upon her new assistant since she had started six months earlier. Although Katie was younger, she acted with a wisdom that Brenda failed to understand. "Katie—your poor husband—do you nag him to death too?"

"Nope, he knows the way home. Besides, you're much easier to irritate." Katie said the words sweetly, and Brenda knew she was sincere. Katie leaned against the door frame. "Seriously, Brenda, I worry about you. I've never seen you eat a meal that didn't involve a sales pitch or leave early to do something fun. And meeting your physical trainer upstairs in the gym doesn't count!"

As usual, the slender, young executive ignored the prodding from her secretary. "Just get the mocha, please." Brenda picked up the phone to return her calls. She had tried to answer her E-mail and finish her reports, but her eyes simply wouldn't focus; they seemed to be getting worse. She knew she would have to delegate some things if she was going to make the deadline. Failure was not an option.

෨෯෫෬

"Brenda, here's your double mocha. I added whipped cream today—maybe we'll put a little meat on your bones. I took the liberty of arranging an appointment with Dr. Luke Marcusson, noted neurologist, researcher, and neurosurgeon at Stanford." Katie deepened her voice to sound impressive. "He can see you next month." Katie brought in the coffee, iced, as her boss preferred, and watched as Brenda scooped the white topping off the drink and into the garbage below. Katie just shook her head, expecting it.

"Next month? No, Katie, I can't wait until next month. I need this research as soon as possible. Never mind. Just get me his number." Anticipating the request, Katie stepped forward and handed her the number.

"Brenda?" Katie dropped her voice to above a whisper.

"What is it, Katie?" Brenda glanced up impatiently.

"Your blouse is misbuttoned," Katie whispered discreetly, closing the door behind her as she exited.

Brenda rolled her eyes, disgusted by her carelessness. She strained to focus on the number in front of her. She fumbled with the buttons on her blouse and screamed at the door in frustration, *"Katie!"*

The secretary's face was white when she opened the door, "What is it?"

"Get this quack on the phone. My phone's not working," Brenda barked. *How can I possibly work with everything jumping like this?*

Katie's soothing voice came over the intercom. "Dr. Marcusson's nurse is on the phone. Brenda, be nice. Not everyone understands you the way I do."

Brenda picked up the phone. "Who am I speaking to?"

"This is LeAnne, Dr. Marcusson's nurse. Dr. Marcusson is booked for new patients until next month. Can I help you?"

"Are you a neurologist?"

"No, I'm Dr. Marcusson's nurse."

"Then you can't help me. I want to talk to the doctor. Tell him it's his sister Brenda." Elevator music floated through the phone, and Brenda tapped her foot impatiently during the wait.

A rich, deep voice came over the line. "Since I have no sisters, I'm going to assume you have something important to tell me." Brenda could sense the smile in his voice and was suddenly embarrassed by her forwardness.

"I'm sorry, Dr. Marcusson. Dr. Wilhelm diagnosed me with multiple sclerosis today. I'm anxious for a second opinion, and I understand you're quite renowned."

"Dr. Wilhelm's a very competent neurologist. Nevertheless, I understand your need for a second opinion with such a serious diagnosis. Why don't you tell me a little about your symptoms?"

"Well, my head feels as though it's buzzing, like I'm slightly tipsy with alcohol. My eyes won't focus. Everything appears to be jumping, and I'm seeing double when I look to the left. My hands and feet are always freezing, while the rest of me is hot, and I'm inexplicably exhausted."

"I'll tell you what, since you are 'family,'" he paused to let her hear the chastisement, "if you can meet me in my office at six-thirty, I'll go over your MRI results with you. I assume you managed to get a copy of your films." Once again, Brenda flushed with embarrassment. Apparently, Dr. Marcusson had a full understanding of her boldness.

"Six-thirty. . . ? Uh, I have an appoint—no, I'll be there." Brenda knew she couldn't turn down the appointment when she had been so brash. Dr. Marcusson seemed to have a sense of humor, but Brenda didn't want to push it.

"I have surgery scheduled for this afternoon, so if I'm a few minutes late, relax for a few minutes, and *don't* read a magazine. Give your eyes a rest. And bring a list of questions you may have. I'll put my nurse on the line and you can give her your phone number just in case."

"Thank you, Doctor." Brenda spoke sweetly to the nurse, trying to make up for her earlier rudeness. LeAnne wasn't appeased and gave Brenda a slice of her own coldness. After the phone call, Brenda packed her briefcase with reports.

She agonized over how long it had taken her to get the appointment with Cyreck but knew she wouldn't be of any use this evening, anyway. Brenda delegated the meeting to one of her product managers, then made a beeline for Katie with final instructions.

Katie's cubicle was always filled with flowers, thank-you cards, and smiling photos that looked like ads for diversity training. Brenda often wondered how anyone had time for so many friends but chalked it up to the petite brunette's constant cheerfulness and bubbly personality. *People are just attracted to women like her.* She was talking on the phone, intermittently typing on the keyboard of one computer and navigating the mouse on another. When she saw Brenda in her cubicle, she lifted a short forefinger to tell her boss she'd be only a second and quickly hung up.

Katie addressed Brenda, "Your dinner meeting—"

"Don't worry about it. Mike's going to handle it. It's his problem now. I'm going home for the afternoon. If you need me, just call."

"Brenda, are you all right?" Katie looked deeply concerned.

"I'm fine, just fighting a little flu bug, I think." Brenda balanced herself against Katie's gray laminate desk and pretended to trip over a shoelace to hide her balance woes.

"Well, I'll say a prayer for you tonight," Katie stated easily.

Brenda threw Katie a condescending grin. She thought her secretary's naïveté and penchant for prayer was sweet.

Chapter 2

Brenda spent the afternoon in a deep sleep. She awoke with just enough time to make it to her appointment. Amazingly refreshed after her nap, she noted that her eyes and balance were nearly normal. She rushed down the front steps to her BMW and raced to Stanford University Hospital. Her appointment was in one of the small buildings next to the main hospital.

Dr. Marcusson's office was elegantly decorated and smelled of new carpet. Burgundy wing-back chairs filled the corners of the waiting room, and a long, supple leather sofa was placed between them. The walls were finished with a gray marbled wallpaper, and a single, colorful painting hung over the sofa. On the coffee table were the latest issues of *People, Newsweek,* and *Reader's Digest.* Brenda's eyes were drawn to a large plaque that stated, "I can do all things through Christ which strengtheneth me." Immediately she wanted to flee. *Katie!* She clicked her tongue. *I should have known she'd find me some religious doctor.*

Katie had repeatedly invited Brenda to church. Right now it seemed like her secretary's search for the best neurologist went as far as a Sunday social. *He's affiliated with Stanford Hospital, so he must be qualified.* Brenda searched the office until her eyes lit upon a diploma. *Stanford University Medical School.* Brenda was encouraged to know that Dr. Marcusson had indeed been educated at the world-renowned school.

"Brenda Turner?" It was the deep-toned voice Brenda remembered from the phone. Feeling guilty for seeking clues to his credentials, Brenda jumped slightly. She turned to extend her hand and was completely taken aback.

Dr. Luke Marcusson stood well over six feet and for once, at five foot ten, Brenda felt petite, even in heels. His light brown hair was parted to the left and shaped in a short, conservative style. His eyes appeared to be brown, but under the receding lights they showed a hint of green. A warm smile crossed his face, and Brenda thought she'd faint at the sight of it, leaving her uncharacteristically speechless. He was casually dressed in a pair of khakis and a forest green golf shirt that wrapped loosely around his wide, muscular shoulders.

Brenda was overwhelmed that a man's mere presence could render her silent. Her next thought was to keep her medical issues quiet, especially after noting that his left hand was free of a wedding ring. *He looks more like a fireman than a physician!*

Brenda stumbled as she tried to recover herself, "Yes. . .Dr. Marcusson, I assume." She reached out and lost control of the oversized negatives in her arms.

The slippery film tumbled clumsily onto the gray tweed carpeting. Brenda felt her face flush red, and she bent over quickly to pick them up, knocking heads with the already kneeling doctor. She fell to the floor and closed her eyes in despair.

Dr. Marcusson held out his hand, apologized, and lifted her gently to her feet. He led her to the sofa before returning to gather the MRI results. He arranged the negatives in order and held one up to the light to study it.

"Miss Turner, your MRI shows a great deal of plaquing. Much more than normal, especially around the brain stem area. With what I know of your symptoms and after seeing these negs, I'm afraid I would have to agree with Dr. Wilhelm. This definitely appears to be multiple sclerosis. We look for either multiple symptoms or multiple occurrences. In your case, each MRI shows both, making a diagnosis fairly straightforward. I'm sorry." He handed her back the film images, but she refused to take them, as if they were the disease itself.

"But I walk fine—well, except for my balance. And I don't feel like this all the time. Most days I jog three miles on the treadmill." Brenda unconsciously smoothed her hands along her hips.

"There is no shortage of symptoms for MS, Miss Turner. And there are no two cases alike. There's the possibility that you will completely recover tomorrow, without treatment, and never see these symptoms again. There's also the small possibility that your symptoms could worsen. Relapsing-remitting MS is usually marked by full recoveries, such as you've had. If the course changes to worsening gradually, that is what we call chronic-progressive MS. Everything here points to relapsing-remitting disease, which is good news. I can't make you any promises, but there are a great deal of new treatments available. Seventy-five percent of all patients will never even need a wheelchair."

"A wheelchair?" Brenda was incensed. "Look, Dr. Marcusson, I am a very busy woman. I put myself through college and made it to vice president of marketing at Star Digital. I own my own home in Palo Alto. I don't have time to be sick—I'm on a deadline! So, what can I take?"

"Miss Turner, this disease doesn't care about your credentials. Your best defense is to take some time off and sleep this flare-up away."

"Sleep? You mean during the day?" She looked up at him in disbelief.

"I mean whenever you can. You must reduce the stress in your life. I imagine your job can be stressful, but a little time off might do you well."

⟨჻⟩

Luke ached for the beautiful young woman before him. He had diagnosed MS in many young patients, and it was always difficult, but it had never before affected him in such a personal way. Her large blue eyes gazed up at him, pleading for a report he was unable to offer. There was something different about the confidence she placed in his ability to immediately heal her. Her apparent faith forced him to take a certain responsibility he didn't want but couldn't forfeit.

He rationalized that his deeper feelings probably stemmed from her being alone. To receive a serious diagnosis was trying, but to do it without support nearby seemed utterly devastating to him. He longed to pull her close and tell her that God loved her, and that with Him she would be fine, but he kept a professional distance.

He tried to avoid noticing her long, shapely legs and the toned body that appeared gym-earned, but for the first time in his career, his physician's eyes failed him. This woman had clearly affected him. His cousin Katie had told him of Brenda's harsh personality and he found himself mystified. Knowing she wasn't a Christian, Luke tried to shake the tempting feelings that stirred within him and forced his mind back to her medical condition.

"What are my options? Drugs? Vitamins? A vacation is not possible." Luke noticed how Brenda approached the subject without emotion, as though she were dealing with someone else's illness.

"Well, I would need to review your history and symptoms, but most likely we'd give you steroids to reduce the inflammation that's causing your symptoms."

"Steroids? Am I going to look like Arnold Schwarzenegger?"

"No, I'm afraid these steroids turn muscle into fat." Luke went over a list of symptoms with her and stopped midsentence when his patient appeared to look through him. "Is this too overwhelming to think about right now? I understand if you'd like to read a few books or get further information, but I really don't advise that you wait too long before starting on meds. The earlier in the bout, the better our chances for fighting it quickly."

Brenda's voice shook, and her casual attitude left her, "I–I can't see a thing anymore, just flying colors. My eyes won't focus at all, and I'm so dizzy and disoriented." Luke could see the fear that filled her eyes and could hear that she struggled with the sudden blindness.

Brenda began to cry openly, not for her health, but for her seemingly ruined plans. "Doctor, I've known what I wanted since I was ten years old. I'm twenty-seven, and I'm two years ahead of schedule—already a vice president. I never planned for any detours. Illness isn't plausible." She paused for a moment, and her tears stopped quickly. "I did allow for a sabbatical next year," she said eagerly. "Do you think this will last longer than two months?"

Luke tried to remain calm and kept his voice soothingly quiet, even as he reached for her elbow to guide her, ignoring her career-related questions. "It's all right, Brenda. It's probably just the stress of the diagnosis. It can leave as quickly as it comes. We're going to get you to the hospital right now. With your permission, I'm going to get you on intravenous steroids tonight."

"How long until I'm fat?" Brenda asked weakly.

Luke saw that Brenda Turner had it all in the world's eyes. Educated, successful, and beautiful. Of course, her appearance was important to her; it was probably a valuable asset to her success. He looked with a man's eyes at the shapely woman; her conditioned calf muscles were flexed sexily in her high heels, and her tightly fitted cream skirt caressed her hourglass shape easily. "You shouldn't be on steroids long enough to gain weight." Catching himself he added, "Although, you can watch what you eat. And that does *not* mean diet. These medications will make you feel famished." He smiled at her, and she returned a grateful grin.

"Thank you, Dr. Marcusson." Brenda's voice shook, her distinguishing confidence shattered.

"Do you have family or a friend who could bring your things to the hospital?" the doctor asked in his business tone, trying to sound unaffected by her answer.

"I'm not married, and no one has a key to my home. How will I—" Brenda's anxious voice mounted with each statement. "Don't you understand? I don't have time for friends. I'm the vice president of marketing for Star Digital," she cried.

"So you've said." This woman baffled him with her devotion to a job, even for a nonbeliever. *If this woman would put her efforts toward God's work, who knows what she might accomplish?*

"Doctor, one day you will have video on demand. Any movie, anytime from the comfort of your own home. VCRs will be dinosaurs! My job is integral to making that dream a reality in America." Brenda's voice lifted with exuberance. Luke saw how her sales pitch had taken on a life of its own, and her blindness seemed instantly forgotten.

"Since I don't own a television set, I'd say that dream is a little farther off for me than you might think. Now, I want you in the hospital tonight. Will you agree to steroid treatment?"

"Seeing as how I can't see to drive, I'd say I have little choice. Would you mind calling me a cab?"

Luke knew by her request that her independence was past the point of healthy. He surprised himself by offering, "How about if I took you home? I know it's unorthodox, but I'd like you to start treatment as soon as possible." It wasn't one of his better ideas, but he wanted her to concentrate solely on getting better. He told himself to wrap himself in God's armor, for he was not blind to her appearance. He prayed silently for God's strength.

"Really? I just live here in Palo Alto, on Harding." Brenda placed her trust in Dr. Marcusson, allowing him to guide her toward his car.

❧❀❧

Brenda wasn't surprised by the doctor's offer. Men often went out of their way for her initially. Rarely, however, was she honored by a second invitation. Although her eyesight was now hopelessly blurred, she had a clear mental picture of the striking young doctor in his dark green golf shirt and his long legs in casual khakis. Dr. Marcusson guided her gently with large, refined hands. *Those of a surgeon,* she thought, marveling at his chivalry.

Once in the passenger seat, she fidgeted and felt her nylons catch on something. She moved and felt her stocking unravel down her calf. Seeing her confusion, the doctor apologized. "Oh, I'm sorry about that. I usually put a towel down when I'm expecting a passenger. The seat is ripped."

"What kind of car is this?" Brenda asked, her eyes unable to focus on the make.

"It's a '79 Pinto, complete with faux wood paneling exteriors, although they're pretty faded."

"You're kidding, right?" Brenda could not believe that someone with Luke Marcusson's credentials would drive a Pinto by choice, and she laughed out loud at the notion.

"Just like television, cars aren't very important to me," he said seriously. With a certain horror, she realized he was telling the truth.

"I gather you're a single man, Dr. Marcusson," Brenda said with mirth in her voice.

"As a matter of fact, I am. And the woman who takes me will have to love the Lord and my car," he stated playfully. "By the way, where on Harding?"

Brenda gave him directions and leaned back in her seat. She was intrigued. Surely, this man cared more for material items than he let on. *Doesn't everyone? Why would someone take the time to become a neurosurgeon when he apparently has no regard for possessions? On his salary, he could afford just about anything. Maybe he's some kind of monk. Why else would a man with a medical degree from Stanford believe in God? This guy does not compute.* Brenda found herself longing to know what made him tick.

"What do you do for excitement, Doctor? I take it you don't race this thing on weekends, and if you don't own a television, I guess you're not a couch potato." She knew by his sleek athletic build that he wasn't one to sit around. Brenda felt lighthearted. While trying to decode her driver, she had completely forgotten that she was sightless. It almost made her game more fun. Blinded to his handsome profile, she wasn't intimidated by his clean good looks, and it was easy to forget that he was a distinguished neurosurgeon.

"When I get a chance to get away, I generally work with my church's youth group. We take trips to the beach, mountain bike, and sometimes go camping. I haven't been as active lately, though. I've had additional surgeries and a new research detail added to my schedule."

"No, I mean *fun*. What do you do for fun?" His angelic answers were beginning to annoy her, and she felt trifled with by his eternal optimism.

"What do *you* do for fun, Miss Turner?" The question threw Brenda, who didn't have a valid answer herself.

"I don't really have much spare time, I'm vice—"

"president of marketing. Yes, I know." The doctor's voice was agitated, and

Brenda knew what she was up against now.

"I see. You're threatened by successful women. I don't see why you would be. You are a brain surgeon. I would think your ego could handle it." Brenda crossed her arms and rolled her blinded eyes.

Luke broke into uproarious laughter. "You pegged me."

His mocking laughter infuriated her and she persisted. "That's why you're religious, right? You're one of those radicals who uses the Bible to keep a woman in her place. Home and pregnant! My parents were just like you, telling me all I needed was Jesus and a husband." Brenda could almost feel the steam coming from her ears. This man and his antiquated ideas caused her to fume. She thought these ideas were extinct in Silicon Valley.

"Now, wait a minute," Luke stated calmly. "You can say a lot of things about me, but I would never use God's Word to do evil. Miss Turner, you may think God is a joke, but I assure you He is real. He loves you enough to have sent His only Son to die for you. Laugh at me all you want, but do yourself a favor: Read God's Word before you turn Him away."

Brenda shrank in her seat and felt her nylons rip up to her thigh. She told herself she shouldn't feel chastised by this zealot, and yet his words cut her to the core. She stubbornly crossed her arms, knowing full well she had gone too far in her accusations. "I'm sorry, Dr. Marcusson. That was very rude of me," she said coldly. She wouldn't admit she was wrong, though; she still felt justified in her charges.

"You certainly seem to like a good fight, Miss Turner. Why don't you turn some of that energy toward your disease?"

Brenda was livid, but she knew he was right, which only made her angrier. He had pegged *her*—she did love a good fight. When she attended business meetings, she could debate anyone within shouting range, but she hadn't learned where to draw the line, the point where her words became weapons. Although men were quick to approach her, she rarely dated. When she did, most were quickly put off by her opinionated manner. Brenda couldn't remember when there had been a second date. Fairly often, she was home by eight-thirty after the first one. She decided to try to put on her best behavior for the doctor. After all, Dr. Marcusson had graciously brought her home; she owed him her gratitude.

Luke pulled the car into the driveway and marveled aloud at her stylish Victorian home. "This is your house? It's pretty big for someone who lives alone. Well, I can't say environment has ever been too important to me. My nurse made me hire a designer for the office. She said she didn't want to spend all day in a place I designed. Imagine that," Luke joked, obviously trying to lighten the mood.

"I bought the place before the market took off. I've almost tripled my investment in five years. My mentor helped me get in, but I paid back every penny and my mortgage is quite reasonable, thanks to my bonuses. When Star goes public, I'll probably buy another house or duplex as an investment. I love real estate."

Brenda couldn't imagine why she had allowed so much information to come tumbling out. Usually, she was quite particular about what she shared.

"That's wonderful. If I ever buy a place, I'll know who to—"

"You don't own a home?" Brenda was incredulous. "Dr. Marcusson, why don't you just hand the government your paycheck?" She stared in his direction, but between the looming darkness and her fuzzy eyesight, she couldn't even make out his imposing form. She imagined it, though.

"During my residency at Stanford, I moved into the campus housing and just never moved out. It's such a hassle to move. Besides, I spend so much time at the office and hospital, it's convenient living just across the street."

"Forget about convenience—we're going to find you a house. Even in this up market, I guarantee you'll be better off to purchase a home. I would imagine at your salary, you would need at least one tax shelter, probably more. When I have my eyesight back, we'll go house hunting." Brenda was shocked by her own forwardness and covered her mouth unconsciously, as though someone else had put the words there. Why had she so blatantly offered to spend time with him? No matter how attractive he was, his outdated morals made him clearly off-limits.

"Are you a real estate agent?" Luke asked innocently.

"Agent, in this area? Are you kidding? Everything's negotiable, Dr. Marcusson. Don't forget that. Do you know what six percent of a six hundred thousand dollar house is? A ridiculous amount of money for filling out a few forms, that's what. This market is too expensive for a double Realtor deal. Your closing costs would be outrageous."

Dr. Marcusson remained quiet, and Brenda thought he didn't believe her. "I'm good at this, really, Doctor. I'll find you the best house in your price range, guaranteed. You're right that an agent is best if you're unsure of yourself, but when you've done it over and over again, they become obsolete. I can scan a contract faster than any agent I know. I guess it's kind of a hobby of mine. I just seem to have a sixth sense. I know what's out there and what's a good price." Brenda realized she must have sounded full of herself, but the fact was she did understand the real estate market, and she loved house hunting. She had already helped several of her coworkers purchase homes.

"So that's what you do with your free time."

"I guess it is." Brenda delighted in the realization that she did have a hobby.

"If I decide to buy, you'll be the first to know. I'm trying to get a research fellowship at Baylor University in Texas right now. It's one of the best programs in the country, and they may be close to the cure for multiple sclerosis."

Brenda had no idea why the thought of Luke Marcusson moving out of state bothered her, but it definitely did.

"Do you want help inside?" the doctor offered.

"No, I'll pack a few things and be out shortly." When Brenda fumbled with the car door, Luke reached across her and opened it. She felt his arm across her, and her stomach fluttered at his touch. She wished he weren't so handsome, and she found herself trying to concentrate on his chauvinistic attitudes. She stepped out onto her familiar driveway and the ground flew up to meet her with a hard bump.

❧❧❧

Luke watched her step from the car and disappear. He rushed out his door and ran to find her crumpled body on the driveway, her face looking shocked. "Are you okay?" he asked.

"I'll take that hand after all, Dr. Marcusson." As Luke lifted her from the concrete, her warm scent filled his senses. He closed his eyes and allowed the moment to overwhelm him before he remembered that she was his patient. He had no business being at her home, but how could he have allowed her to go alone in a cab? He might have called his cousin Katie, her secretary, but that would have broken patient confidentiality.

Clearly, God had led him here, and now he would have to be worthy of the call. He straightened and took a step back while still holding firmly onto her arms to help her balance. Walking backward, he led her up the steps to her wide front porch. Proverbs 31, where God describes a godly wife, suddenly popped into his mind, along with a new insight. A desirable woman that needed him was certainly more temptation than he was capable of handling alone. He remembered the verse about beauty being fleeting and now fully understood its meaning. This woman was truly captivating.

Luke had always imagined his future wife would be the sweet, gentle soul that relished being a wife and mother. Surely, Brenda Turner held no stock in such values, and he found himself annoyed that he didn't know better than to be attracted to her.

Brenda reached into her soft leather briefcase and came up with a set of keys. Luke took them from her and unlocked the door, "Where's the light?"

"To your right, there's a switch on the wall." He reached in, and soon the front porch and living room were awash with light. Brenda stumbled in before him, a pleasant smile crossing her face. "Home at last."

Luke breathed deeply to take in the scent of vanilla. He was surprised at the warmth of Brenda's home. Luke had expected her home to be filled with cold, modern furnishings. He was fascinated to find her entire home Victorian in theme. A traditional, white crown molding lined the walls at both the ceiling and the floor. The room was painted a deep muted lavender, and the sofas were white tapestry with dark, Queen Anne legs that matched the hardwood floors throughout the home. "I feel like I've stepped back in time. Lavender. . .hmm. It's really very nice."

"Ralph Lauren," she said, while placing her keys back in her satchel.

"Lauren Bacall."

"What?" Brenda missed his joke.

"Aren't we naming famous people?"

"No. I was telling you the designer of the paint color."

"Ah, so it would have been more appropriate for me to say Sherwin-Williams?"

"You have a strange sense of humor, Doctor. Make yourself at home. I'm going to crash into the bedroom and get my things. Open the armoire there, and you'll find a big black box. It's called a television. On the coffee table, there's a little box called a remote. There are sixty different channels waiting to entertain you."

"Channels? I thought the future of television was that I get to choose anything."

"Only if you make me well, so I can implement it. In case no one informed you, I'm vice president of marketing." She winked at him and felt her way into the bedroom.

Luke looked around the room with interest. The focal point of the room was a large marble fireplace, surrounded by a white mantel on three sides. The marble continued onto the floor in a splash of gray. On the mantel were two antique, silver frames, and Luke walked toward them to study the contents. He noticed immediately to his satisfaction that there were no men in the pictures.

"Who's this little girl?" Luke called toward the bedroom. He kept his voice low, because everything echoed over the hardwood floors.

"On the mantel? That's my niece, Kaitlyn. I've never seen her in person. She lives back East with my brother and his wife."

"That's too bad. You certainly put some thought into decorating. Are these all antiques?"

"Not all of them, but I take my vacations down South to purchase antiques and furniture. For some reason, it's just easier for me to take a vacation if I have a goal in mind." Brenda emerged from the hallway with a small overnight bag that matched her briefcase.

She was charmingly adorned in a fitted pair of jeans and a white T-shirt. Luke could not remember when he'd seen such justice done to a pair of Levi's. His doctor's eyes failed him once again, and he knew that having Brenda Turner as a patient was playing with fire.

"Dr. Marcusson? Are you there?" She asked anxiously, a worried frown crossing her beautiful, full lips.

"Over here, Miss Turner." Luke walked toward her as he spoke, giving her a general idea of his location. "You certainly look more relaxed. How on earth did you get ready so fast?"

"I'm not very patient, so I know how to do things quickly. I keep an overnight bag packed at all times. I never know when I'll be called away on business. I have a suit and a pair of casual clothes packed. I just took the suit out."

"Very organized; I'm impressed."

"Dr. Marcusson, what if these steroids don't work? I've got to work to support myself. It's not only my life; it's my livelihood we're talking about."

"We'll deal with each problem as it comes, okay? In the meantime, I think we're going to have excellent luck with the corticosteroid therapy, and there are many new therapies becoming available that help to prevent new exacerbations, and the cure gets closer every day. Let me take your bag, and you hang on to my arm. Is there anyone you need to call before we go?"

"Just my secretary, Katie. She'll need to know I won't be in tomorrow. This is such bad timing—I've got a deadline. I have all the necessary files with me—the office will be at a standstill." Brenda shook her head, clearly disturbed.

Luke quickly changed the subject. "I think it's only fair to tell you that Katie goes to my church. She's also my cousin." Luke spoke in a quiet whisper now that Brenda was on his arm.

She looked at the floor and shook her head. "When you started talking religion, I had an inkling you two knew each other."

Luke ignored her comment and continued, "I'll call her after you're checked into the hospital and let her know you will be out for awhile with doctor's orders."

"But I don't want her—"

"I wouldn't tell her of your condition without your approval."

⇘❧⇙

Dr. Marcusson checked Brenda into her room, and a nurse started an IV immediately.

"Miss Turner, this may give you trouble sleeping, and I noticed you brought your briefcase with you, but I want to make it clear: No reading. Do you understand?" Brenda just nodded in reluctant agreement. "I'm not telling you this to punish you—"

"You have no idea what you're asking me to do. My eyes are my life. I am successful because of them. I—"

He cut her off quickly, "Hopefully, that won't change after therapy, but you must allow yourself to get better, or you may not fully recover. Okay?" Luke felt like he was talking to a child, but he also knew this was one obstinate woman. The way she looked at him so expectantly with her tropical blue eyes sent his emotions soaring. He shook the thought. As much as he found himself attracted to her, he found himself equally exasperated by her intense preoccupation with her job.

"Yes, Doctor," Brenda sang in a sarcastic tone.

"I'll have the nurse get some books on tape from the hospital library. What do you like to read?"

"The classics."

"You're determined to make my day tough, aren't you?"

"Don't you mean night?" Brenda asked. "It must be well past nine by now."

"You're right. I need to get something to eat and turn in for the night. I'll see you in the morning during my rounds. If you need anything, your call button is right here." Luke took her hand and placed it on the button. Her warm touch electrified him. He held her hand a moment longer than necessary and pried himself away from her bedside. "Good night, Brenda," he whispered.

"Good night, Luke," she answered quietly after he'd left.

Chapter 3

Brenda awoke the next morning after a few hours of restless slumber. The medicine had made falling asleep nearly impossible, but the drastic fatigue of MS finally prevailed. When she opened her eyes, a whirlwind of colors whizzed by, and she instantly dissolved to tears. Her eyesight had not returned, and for the first time, Brenda realized she might not recover. Her first thought was of her beloved Victorian home. *I must get better,* she vowed. With renewed determination, she thought about the campaign she had to complete. She rang for a nurse to dial her direct line at Star Digital.

"Katie, this is Brenda." She struggled with her emotions. Dr. Marcusson had said the drugs would cause her to be overly sensitive.

"Brenda, I'm so happy to hear your voice. Are you all right? Luke. . .I mean, Dr. Marcusson called me last night to let me know you weren't feeling well. Is there anything I can do?"

"Katie, I'm fine. I'm just having a little trouble with my eyesight. Dr. Marcusson is wonderful. Thank you for recommending him."

"He's not too bad on the eyes either, huh?" Katie joked, and Brenda felt her stomach turn.

"They've got different patches and things on my eyes all the time, so I'm afraid his looks are lost on me." Brenda lied without the slightest hint of guilt. She had managed to keep her blindness under wraps, as well as her attraction to the handsome doctor.

"Can I bring you anything? A mocha and a Balance bar perhaps?" Katie asked, and Brenda laughed at the reference to her normal morning snack.

"The breakfast of champions? No, thanks. They're treating me fine here."

"Now I know you're ill. When *you* consider hospital food fine treatment, something's not right."

Brenda ignored the comment. "Katie, I need you to do something for me. I need you to take the campaign on my desk to Mike Wilcox." Brenda cringed with the words. Mike had been her fierce competitor since she started in Star's marketing department three years ago. She had won the coveted vice president's position, but Mike was always lurking, waiting for her to fail. She knew this was his opportunity, yet there was nothing she could do about it. She was of no use without her eyesight, but she couldn't allow Star Digital to fail at such a crucial time. She took solace in having the most pertinent files in her briefcase stashed safely under the bed.

"Mike Wilcox? But, Brenda, he'll take credit for everything you've done."

"I know, Katie, but he's also the only one who can meet my deadline." Brenda began crying suddenly. Relinquishing her responsibilities made the loss of her eyesight a stinging reality. A flood of tears followed and she sniffled loudly into the phone, unable to maintain decorum. "Oh, Katie, I have to go now. They want to do more tests." Before Katie could respond, Brenda hung up the phone and covered her face while she sobbed.

"Miss Turner?" Dr. Marcusson's familiar voice was soft and low, and Brenda felt his consoling hand on her shoulder. Unconsciously placing her hand on top of his, she sniffled, hiccuped, and continued crying.

"I can't see!" she wailed.

"I know—I know, but that's why you're here." He slipped his hand from beneath hers, and she knew he must be looking at her. She must have appeared a sight. She squeezed her eyes shut, as though that would make her invisible.

"I love to read. I read *everything*. How will I live without it? Or drive? Or work. . .what if I can't go back to work? I could lose everything. My entire life feels over."

Dr. Marcusson didn't respond at first, and Brenda reached with her hand to make sure he was still there. "Miss Turner, the chances of you losing your eyesight permanently are very remote. We're doing everything we can, and once you can see again we'll talk about options for reducing future episodes. Open your eyes and look toward me."

Brenda pulled back to look up at the doctor but grasped firmly onto his hands to secure his presence. She saw a flurry of color pass by and the mere act of opening her eyes made her stomach nauseous again. "You're wearing white and you're on the ceiling and floor." She laughed through her tears, and she felt him squeeze her hands gently.

"You're right—I am wearing white. It's a lab coat. Since you can't read right now, I'm going to tell you some of the basics of MS. Bouts typically last eight weeks at this stage. Let's just look at that as our deadline for now, okay?"

"Eight weeks, right," Brenda said aloud, mentally counting the days.

"Miss Turner, I can't promise you what course your disease will take, but I've talked to a friend. She's agreed to dictate a book on the subject onto a cassette tape. I'm picking her up at the airport tonight, and she promised to have it done by the end of the weekend."

Brenda missed the message regarding the book. All she heard was that Luke was picking up a woman at the airport. Jealousy shot through her like a bolt of lightning, and instinctively she asked to know more.

"A friend?" she asked slyly.

"Actually, she's my ex-fiancée. We're still good friends. She's just getting back from the mission field in Africa." Dr. Marcusson's tone told her he admired his ex-fiancée's work, and Brenda felt overwhelmingly empty. If Dr. Marcusson liked women who did charity work, Brenda had nothing to offer. Everything she did in life was based on a return for her investment, both for her time and money.

"Why didn't you get married?" Brenda tried to sound casual but feared her interest was altogether transparent.

"We just felt God was leading us in different directions."

"You think God talks to you?" she asked honestly.

"I know He does. That doesn't mean He calls my name out loud or that I hear voices. It means He speaks to me through prayer, the Bible, the church, my close friends, and in circumstances. Understand?"

"No." Brenda shook her head. She wanted to say she did. She was sure his ex-fiancée heard God too, and her competitive nature wanted to lie to him, but somehow she couldn't.

"Dr. Marcusson?" A nurse appeared in the doorway. Brenda sensed a white outline in the lighted hallway, and it angered her. She knew Luke would be called away.

"Yes," he answered.

"Wyatt Ross is on the line for you. She says her plane will be in early. This afternoon at two. If you can make it, great. Otherwise, she says she'll grab a taxi."

"Thank you, Nurse. I'll be there. Would you mind giving her the message?"

"Certainly, Doctor." Brenda saw the doorway darken, and she relished once again being alone with Dr. Marcusson. She wondered why he could leave in the middle of the day to pick up an old girlfriend at the airport but couldn't see new patients for over a month. She glared at him warily, envying the woman that wielded such power over him.

"Is my car safe at your office?" Brenda wanted to kick herself. His selfless ex-fiancée was returning from the deserts of Africa, and here *she* was asking about her BMW.

"Of course it's safe, but I can store it at my place if it makes you feel better."

"Would you mind?" Brenda liked the idea of her car being at the doctor's house. It made her feel she was more than just his patient.

"I want you to forget about things like your car. They're unimportant. Your assignment today is to listen to a soap opera, Oprah, or something equally brain-draining and tell me what happened, okay? They'll be starting your IV earlier today, so I hope it won't affect your sleep as much. I've prescribed a sedative if you need it. 'Til tomorrow. . ."

"You're not coming back today?" Fear filled her voice.

"I have a full set of rounds to make and other patients to see. Let me know what Oprah has to say." He patted her shoulder and walked from the room, leaving Brenda feeling utterly abandoned.

Luke had crammed all of his appointments into the morning to accommodate Wyatt's arrival at the airport. His present surgery and patient schedule felt like his residency, and it was beginning to take its toll. He had already spent far too much time with Brenda Turner, but he couldn't help himself. He wanted her to know that no matter how bad things got, God would be there for her, and so would he. However, he knew his own emotions were becoming entangled, and he longed to discuss them openly with Wyatt, his confidante.

He arrived at the airport and parked close to the terminal. He was glad she had chosen to fly into the San Jose airport, which was far more accessible than San Francisco International. He found Wyatt's flight number on a screen and rushed to meet the on-time flight. When he approached the gate, Wyatt's tanned face, under an untamed mane of light brown hair, beamed with a welcoming smile.

"Luke, I'm so glad you could come. I can't wait to tell you about my trip. We treated and healed hundreds with the medicine that was provided. What a blessing." Wyatt's enthusiasm was obvious, and Luke felt a tinge of envy. "Luke? What's the matter with you?"

Luke laughed. Wyatt was always so perceptive, and at times it unnerved him. "The patient I told you about on the phone last night."

"Brenda? I've been praying for her."

"There's something more. I'm drawn to her like a magnet, even though she's not a Christian," he confessed. "As a matter of fact, her only religion seems to be financial success."

"Do you think treating her is too much of a temptation?" Wyatt put a concerned arm around him.

"She's gorgeous, Wyatt, but her heart is so hardened. I wish I could help her myself. I see this scared little girl that I just want to rescue and care for. She doesn't seem to have any friends, and her only concern seems to be for her work and possessions. I'm embarrassed to admit how attracted I am to her. How much I want to be there for her. We're nothing alike—she loves the things of this world, while I love the people in it. Still. . .there's something in her eyes that speaks to me."

"Don't be too hard on yourself, Luke. Maybe you see something deeper. If it were just her looks, I don't think you'd spend so much time thinking about her welfare. After all, a pretty, blind woman in love with *things* doesn't sound all that attractive. Perhaps God has given you a special calling regarding her. Some of the hardest hearts are the easiest to crack open with His unconditional love. Have you prayed about your feelings?"

"Constantly, but so far, God is quiet. Pretty comical, considering I just told her today how God speaks to me. I've only known her two days, but her case just consumes me."

"Maybe if you allow others to take on some of the burden, you'll feel less passionate about the case. I finished dictating the book for her on the plane." Wyatt held up a cassette tape.

"How could you possibly—"

"Your voice sounded pretty urgent last night, so I borrowed a book from the medical library in Kigali. I can't sleep on planes anyway. My neighbors didn't exactly appreciate my constant talking into the tape recorder, but if anyone they know gets MS, they'll be prepared."

"You must be exhausted. Let's get you home. Besides, Brenda probably will take to the steroids and be out of my life for good within a week. When's Barry arriving?"

"He's coming Saturday. He managed to rummage some additional meds in town and stayed to administer them. He's speaking at our church on Sunday, trying to drum up some more support so we can go back soon. We want to try to stay for good this time, so funding will be more difficult."

"I've got to hand it to you, Wyatt. You and that husband of yours sure have hearts for the sick and needy."

"So do you, Doctor. Your calling just pays better." She laughed an infectious giggle. "Luke, God has you here for a reason." She paused for a moment. "Perhaps Miss Brenda Turner is that reason."

Luke smiled at the mention of the name and lifted the string-wrapped boxes that served as Wyatt's makeshift luggage. He had driven Brenda's car to pick up Wyatt and now was embarrassed at the showiness of the vehicle. Wyatt was awestruck. "You got rid of the Pinto?"

"I'll get rid of the Pinto when one too many parts has to be scraped off the pavement. This is Brenda's. She was worried about leaving it in my parking lot, and I told her I would park it at my campus apartment. I figured my car would be safe in the parking lot."

"Unless they tow it as an abandoned vehicle." They laughed together and Luke's heart lifted. He was truly glad he had remained friends with Wyatt Ross. They had been schoolmates since childhood in Christian school. They had always talked of marriage, but when it came down to actually going through with it, they realized the love they shared was not for marriage. It was always more of a mutual admiration.

He had been thrilled when she married his fellow neurologist Barry Ross. Now the couple came home twice a year for funding and supplies. Then it was back to Africa to treat the ill. He crossed his arms and lifted an eyebrow at Wyatt. "Listen, smart alec. That vehicle has picked you up many a time. You and Barry should be grateful for my faithful chariot," Luke chastised.

"Yeah, well, that 'chariot' has also left us stranded on many a street, or have you conveniently forgotten?"

"Always looking at the negative." Luke clicked his tongue.

Wyatt's tone turned serious. "Luke, I'm going to drop by and meet Brenda tomorrow. It sounds like she needs a friend. I'll let her know I'm a nurse—would that be okay?"

"That'd be great. I'm anxious to hear your opinion. Perhaps you'll see that same special spark that I see."

The two sped off in the BMW while Wyatt filled Luke in on her latest mission trip.

Chapter 4

Brenda awoke early to the sound of her roommate's blaring television set. *Is this woman deaf?* She roughly pulled the sheet over her head and turned over, but it was no use. A news anchor's peppy voice boomed with authority through the thin curtain separating the two beds.

"Brenda? Are you in here?"

"Katie?" Brenda recognized her secretary's voice, and its familiarity made her want to cry with joy. She had been in the hospital for three days now, and she was lonely. No one had come to visit, which was no surprise, but in her shattered state, it cut deeply. Brenda's only living relatives were her brother and grandparents in Connecticut, and they wouldn't care. "What time is it?" she asked groggily as she sat up in bed.

"It's seven-thirty on Saturday morning. I brought you a mocha and a Balance bar." Katie's thoughtfulness proved too much, and Brenda's eyes began watering. She felt Katie's arms around her, and she cried softly into her shoulder.

When she finally was able to speak, she began slowly, "I can't see anything but flying colors. Dr. Marcusson says I have multiple sclerosis." It was the first time she'd said it, and the admission made it a stark reality.

"It's okay, Brenda. I'm here, and God is here." Katie placed her hands on Brenda's slender, elegantly manicured hands while she talked. "Jesus healed a blind man in the New Testament. I brought my Bible if you'd like to hear about it," Katie said brightly.

"I don't think so, Katie. Thanks." Brenda shook her head, but Katie seemed undeterred.

"He has the power to heal you, Brenda, but even if He doesn't heal you, He will give you the strength to go through it. Lean on Him. You won't be alone. I'm here, and you've got the best doctor in Silicon Valley—I made sure of that." Katie's easy reference to God was unusually comforting to Brenda. Usually, the young executive balked at Katie's insipid prayer talk, but today it was soothing and even seemed to make sense. Still, it left her with more questions than answers.

"I bet Mike Wilcox was drooling over being handed the campaign. I've worked so hard on this stupid project. I just want to hurt something." Brenda hit the bed dramatically, startling the woman in the next bed.

"Brenda, let it go. Concentrate on getting better. Mike Wilcox sees the void he's been waiting for. No offense, but you would do the same thing."

"Ouch," Brenda said, chastened by her assistant's candor.

"Well?" Katie said, her arms crossed, anticipating the answer.

"Okay, you're right; I would." Brenda quickly added, "But that doesn't make it right."

"No, it doesn't, but you've played this game long enough to know business sometimes has nothing to do with what's right. I want you to stop worrying about work. It's only a job, and you'll be back before you know it."

"When Star Digital has its initial public stock offering, I'll be rich!" Enthusiasm rippled through Brenda's voice. "That opportunity doesn't present itself at every company, you know. I started on the ground floor of this company. I deserve that money."

"You own a million-dollar house in Palo Alto, and it's full of antiques. And you have a BMW convertible. What more do you need?"

The question threw her for a moment. "Katie, the house is worth nine hundred thousand dollars, and I *could* own two, or maybe three, as investments." Brenda was boggled by Katie's lack of understanding. Surely, everyone wanted more; that was the Ameri-can way.

"Brenda, just for your benefit, I'm nodding my head and crossing my arms in disgust. Since you can't see me, I want you to know how sick you sound, and it has *nothing* to do with being in this hospital. God has already given you so much—"

"God gave me this stupid disease, and now all the money I earned is just slipping through my fingers." Brenda said.

"Disease?" Katie said sharply. "Brenda, how dare you blame God for this disease and not thank Him for everything else. Life is not always perfect, you know. If you're going to acknowledge God, you need to remember His goodness first. You've never thanked Him for all His provisions, but once a tiny spoke gets thrown in your wheel, it's all God's fault."

"Tiny spoke?" Brenda snorted. "I have *multiple sclerosis*, a chronic illness that is *attacking* my body. I may be like this forever. I have no husband to support me, no one to pay my mortgage. I'm all I have—I make it happen."

"Brenda, I know you don't feel well. And I know it's scary that your eyes aren't functioning, but your real sickness is inside. God has provided for you all along. Even now, He's given you a survivor personality, a hospital and doctor providing the best of care, and people who *want* to help. So stop concentrating on what you don't have and start concentrating on what you do."

Katie had always been blunt with Brenda but never this candid. The executive flinched as though the words were daggers. All Brenda wanted was a little compassion, but her assistant seemed oblivious. Just like her mother always had. *Religious people just don't get it.*

"Katie, you don't understand. You're one of those people that life comes easy for. You see the best in all situations, no matter what. I'm not built to be content.

That's why I'm so good at what I do." *You probably don't even care about a nice house,* she thought. *You can't understand, because material possessions aren't important to you. If they were, you would have gotten a better education, and you'd be more than just a marketing assistant.* Brenda crossed her arms and leaned back on her pillow like an angry, spoiled child.

"How's my favorite patient?" Luke Marcusson's lighthearted voice broke the tension in the room, and Brenda grinned widely at his presence, instantly forgetting the confrontation.

"Tired and grumpy," Katie replied.

"Steroids can certainly bring out the best in a person." Luke laughed at the remark, but inwardly Brenda was grateful for the diversion.

"Thanks for the excuse, Dr. Marcusson, but I'm afraid Katie knew me before the steroids," Brenda reluctantly admitted.

They all shared in the joke before the doctor began asking about Brenda's vision. "Brenda, can you look in my direction?" Brenda looked toward the deep voice, and for a fleeting moment saw the gorgeous man she remembered. His tall stature and rugged jawline immediately had her full attention.

She watched him move his clean, flawless hands to rub his face and immediately began to dream of them. She always noticed a man's hands, and Luke's were seemingly perfect, large and masculine, yet sleek and graceful enough to perform surgery. Brenda found herself swept away in her thoughts before she realized she was actually *seeing* the dream before her.

"I see you!" she said excitedly. "You're still jumping toward the ceiling, but I can see your features—and your hands," she added shyly, as though he might read her thoughts. Dr. Marcusson held his finger above her head and asked her to track it. She tried, but it made her eyes hurt with the strain, and she closed them tightly.

"Brenda, the steroids seem to be working. Tomorrow, I'm going to switch you to oral steroids and send you home. I'd rather you not be alone, at least for a few days. Do you have someone who can stay with you?" Again, Brenda cringed at the thought that she had no friends. She certainly didn't want to admit such a thing twice to Luke Marcusson, and her mind reeled for an alternative.

"I can hire a nurse. I wouldn't want to put anyone out."

"Nonsense, Brenda. You'll stay with Jacob and me," Katie offered in her perky voice.

Brenda felt trapped. If she said yes, Dr. Marcusson would know she was fresh out of friends. What would he think of her? If she said no, she had the added stress of finding a nurse quickly. "No, Katie, I couldn't. I wouldn't want to impose." Brenda longed to go home alone, but she knew without her complete eyesight and faculties, she needed help. Brenda's lack of friends left few alternatives. She felt the doctor looking at her, probably wondering what kind of woman would be so pathetically alone in the overpopulated Silicon Valley.

"Impose? In our house? There is no such word. I'll pick you up, and we'll go by your house first and get your things. When can she go, Dr. Luke?"

"This afternoon, right after her IV treatment. I'll release her about one-thirty instead of waiting until tomorrow," Luke said decisively. Brenda couldn't help but wonder whether this had been planned, but knowing Katie's inability to lie, she doubted they could have pulled off such an elaborate ruse.

"Great; we'll get home in time for Oprah," Katie joked. Luke and Katie planned the next few days, while Brenda sat idly by, relinquishing control of her life.

Chapter 5

Brenda kept her eyes closed on the ride home, which saved her from the constant blur of the passing sights. She relished the warm sunlight and smiled at the thought of home. When she arrived at the stately Victorian, the wild jumping in her vision was beginning to settle down; she was definitely getting better.

Once inside, her beloved dining room set from South Carolina came into view. She walked toward it and gently touched her precious English china displayed on the elaborate mahogany sideboard. Seeing her treasures made her eyes water. *These are my friends*—the perfected surroundings she had worked so long and diligently to create. She ran her fingers along the table, grateful to be home.

As she stood in the entryway between the dining room and the living room, she heard Katie come up behind her. "Brenda, do you need help?"

"No, no. Just thinking about a few friends." Brenda knew she related better to objects than to people, but her elegant furniture was of little use to her now. *Katie is the only one here for me, and maybe that's because she fears for her job.* Brenda's eyes welled up. "These medications have me on a roller coaster," she said, by way of an excuse.

"You'll be home to stay in just a few days. I know our home isn't yours, but we'll love having you." The petite brunette craned her neck to look into her boss's eyes.

Brenda nodded and took new courage as she walked further into the house to gather her things. The message light blinked on the answering machine and she tentatively pushed the button. "Yeah, Brenda. Mike Wilcox here. Looking for the prep sheets on the campaign for the set-top boxes. Call me." Beep.

"Miss Turner. This is Wells Fargo Bank calling to inform you that you are qualified for our new platinum Visa card. We'll call later." Beep.

"Hi, Brenda, it's Chris at Slatterly Antiques. Just found a beauty of a Queen Anne buffet. Looks just like you, and I won't put it on the floor until Monday. Call me if you're interested." Beep.

Painfully, it was true. No one cared that her eyesight was precarious. She slowly packed her things and walked gloomily out to Katie's car.

"Is everything okay, Brenda?"

"This disease has opened my eyes about a few things," Brenda said cryptically.

"Nothing like slowing down to discover our true selves," Katie offered discerningly.

The ride to Katie's house was mostly silent, each woman lost in her own thoughts. When Brenda realized where they were headed, she spoke up loudly. "Where do you live?" she asked nervously.

"EPA."

"East Palo Alto? *Murder capital of the United States, East Palo Alto!*"

"That was a long time ago. Not since 1992, in fact. Things have calmed down a lot since then. There was heavy gang activity that year, a lot of retaliation gunfire."

"Uh, Katie. We're talking death here. Surely, you make enough to live in a decent part of town."

"My husband and I have a ministry here. Jacob's a lay pastor, been working with some of these kids for nearly ten years. Long before we were married. Now some of them are grown and married themselves."

Katie's romantic reminiscence was lost on Brenda. "Don't you know what people think about this city? How can you possibly live here?" Brenda was truly frightened to be heading into such a notorious place. She had lived in the Bay Area for a decade and never once driven through the dangerous neighborhood.

"That's perception, not reality. This is a very tight-knit community and people really care about each other. I have no fear for my safety here. Neighbors look out for one another. Of course, there are certain areas I don't wander into that are known gang turf, but our neighborhood is perfectly safe. Besides, my fate is secure in Christ."

Brenda remained unfazed by the romanticized description. After all, she read the newspaper and she knew what went on in East Palo Alto: drug deals and murders. Katie drove deeper into the shabby neighborhood. Brenda strained to see the worn-out houses with their unkempt yards and discarded cars where there should have been lawn. Her fearful eyes were drawn to the black iron bars guarding each window and doorway. People of all descriptions stood on the street corners and in the front yards; their sheer number was enough to intimidate a passerby.

"See what I mean, Brenda? It's Saturday and everyone is out socializing. Up here on your right, this local church has a barbecue every weekend to raise money. Can you smell it?" Katie was her usual upbeat self, and Brenda stared at her as though she were crazy.

"Katie, I don't think these guys are socializing. They're probably organizing a drive-by shooting or something."

"Brenda Turner, you watch too many movies. Just because people are poor does *not* mean they're criminals. I know for a fact they are socializing. Usually on Saturday, I'm out here with them. Stay with us a few days, and you'll learn to look beyond someone's outward appearance or the car they drive."

Brenda rolled her eyes at Katie's naiveté; her religious lifestyle surely clouded her judgment. The car pulled into a driveway and Brenda was shocked at the darling house that fluttered slowly in her gradually returning vision. It was blue and white with a picket fence in front and flower boxes hanging from each window. The porch had a white wooden swing dangling contentedly from its roof and a tiny, child-sized rocking chair beside it.

"Stay in the car. I'll come around and get you," Katie demanded. Brenda wanted to say there was no way she'd leave the car without a bulletproof vest but decided it was better not to offend her hostess any further.

The car door opened, and a tall, mustached man with light, wavy hair stood above her with his hand extended. He had a certain sweetness in his face, and his smile was warm and genuine. "I'm Jacob Cummings. It's such a pleasure to finally meet you. Katie just goes on and on about you. I feel like I know you already."

Brenda took the extended hand and unfolded herself out of the vehicle. Katie came and stood next to her husband and peered up at him with admiring eyes. Brenda envied the love Katie so obviously felt for Jacob. *Will I ever find a love like that, where I can look at a man with such awe and respect?* She snapped back to reality; certainly she wasn't the type for dreamy-eyed looks and romantic fantasies. "Jacob, I can't thank you enough. I'm sure Katie's told you that I can be difficult. I appreciate your taking me in anyway."

"On the contrary, Brenda. Katie has nothing but praise for you. You're always welcome in our home." An African-American boy with big, full cheeks peered between Jacob's tall legs and looked up at Brenda. "This is Daydan, he's three, and he lives here with us." The boy smiled a wily grin and held up three small fingers.

"I didn't know," Brenda said absently.

"You never asked, I guess." Katie hadn't meant the words as a reprimand, but Brenda rarely took an interest in others. She was simply too busy at work for idle chitchat.

"Let's get you settled so you can rest. I understand you have orders to watch Oprah." Brenda laughed and allowed her things to be taken to a bedroom in the rear of the house. Daydan followed behind Katie and Jacob, leaving Brenda alone in the living room.

The interior of the house was quaint and warm. French blue carpet provided a country feel, and Katie's many crafts filled the walls: homemade dolls, patchwork quilts, and several tole paintings which left little room for future projects.

Brenda smiled to herself because her eyes were slowly returning to normal and she could see the simple decorations. Their presence took on added meaning as she saw things she would normally have ignored for their lack of elegance. The furniture was simple and functional with heavy oak pieces taking up the bulk of the room. A boxy, dark oak armoire stood in the corner with a television. The sofas were a dark blue check, and a country red rocking chair completed the grouping.

Brenda stretched her worn frame. Her body ached from fatigue, and her eyes stung from wearied dryness. The medication made it impossible to relax, although she shuddered with exhaustion. Even though she was slowly regaining her eyesight, she was beginning to wonder at what price.

Katie returned to the living room with Daydan in tow and sat on the couch. "Can I get you anything to drink or eat? I stocked up on Balance bars and Diet Pepsi, but I'm assuming you eat real food too."

"Momma Katie, I hungry," Daydan replied.

"He talks?" Brenda asked.

"Of course he talks. He's three years old," Katie answered incredulously.

"I've never really spent much time around children," Brenda shrugged.

"I'm sorry, Brenda. That was rude. I just spend so much time around them that I forget it isn't obvious to everyone. Daydan, Daddy went out back. Why don't you go see if you can help him in the yard? Then I'll have a snack for you when you come back."

"Okay, bye-bye." The boy waved at Brenda, and she returned the gesture with a smile.

"Brenda, about Daydan—he is our son. His mother was a teenager in our weekly Bible study about four years ago. Tasha was her name. She dropped out of the class but returned after Daydan was born. She was obviously on drugs but asked if she could leave Daydan for an afternoon while she went to see about a job." Katie's eyes began welling up with tears, and Brenda felt helpless at the sight, wondering if she should do something for her friend; but she remained in her seat like a wooden doll. "Anyway," Katie continued through her tears, "that was two and a half years ago. We've raised Daydan as our own since he was six months old. His grandmother, Ruth, helped us get temporary custody because she was too old to watch him all the time. Ruth takes him during the day while we work. We've just been notified that Tasha has completed a drug treatment program and may be allowed to regain custody within the next few months." Katie was choking over her sobs now. "I know you have enough to think about, Brenda, and I don't mean to bring you lower; but I love that boy as if he were my own flesh, and I am going to fight for him with everything I have. I'm telling you this so that you know that Daydan doesn't leave with anyone. Okay?"

"Of course, Katie. Absolutely." Brenda's heart ached at the story of her assistant's plight. Katie had never brought it up or had an outburst at work. Brenda hadn't even known the child was Katie's, although the dozens of pictures on the secretary's desk would have made it clear to anyone who had bothered to inquire.

The fact that Katie would take Brenda in at such a difficult time seemed unreal. *Why would anyone take energy reserved for a custody battle and throw it away on me? She seems to have complete self-control. I wish I could approach work in such a quiet manner; that kind of poker face is worth millions.* Brenda longed to know Katie's secret but knew it wasn't the time to ask. She placed her hand awkwardly on Katie's back and began to pat it softly.

Luke rubbed his tired eyes with the palms of his cramped, postsurgery hands. He cradled his head while he bent over a plate of dried meat loaf and instant mashed potatoes in the hospital cafeteria.

"Luke?"

The young doctor looked up to see Wyatt Ross standing over him with a small, clear plastic bag filled with tapes. "I came for Brenda, but it seems she's checked out. I have all this MS information for her."

"Of course, Wyatt. Sit down. I released her today after treatment." Luke motioned with his hand for Wyatt to sit as he stood up. "Do you want a cup of coffee?"

"I don't need a thing, Luke. Please sit down. You look half-dead."

"I feel half-dead. I've had so many surgeries scheduled this past week and dozens of research patients to see before tomorrow. I ought to have that fellowship at Baylor within three months."

"How is Brenda?" Wyatt asked.

Luke's heart jumped at the mention of her name, but he maintained his even physician's voice. The image of Brenda's beautiful, deep blue eyes and tangled blond hair danced in his mind's eye. "She's slowly regaining her eyesight. I think within a few weeks she'll be back to normal."

Wyatt wasn't fooled by his casual answer. "I guess what I meant was how are *you* and Brenda doing? Have you had a chance to reconcile your feelings?"

"I've had a few days to pray over the matter, and I've decided to transfer her case to another neurologist." Luke looked away.

"I think that's the right thing to do, Luke," she said placidly.

"I'm handing her case over because I can't see her with physician's eyes. The sooner she's on her way, the better," he said, trying to convince himself. "She may help me with finding a house," he added quietly.

"I thought your future was in Texas at Baylor. Sounds like you're grasping at straws, Luke," Wyatt lowered an eyebrow and crossed her arms.

"Bay Area real estate is a good investment, regardless. I could always rent it out," Luke offered weakly. Deep in his heart, he knew it wasn't a good idea to spend time with Brenda. It would only allow his feelings for her to deepen, but he also didn't want to think about never seeing her again. There was just something about her, something about *them*. "Besides, I didn't ask if it was a good idea. I need a tax write-off, and she's going to help," Luke snapped, cutting off further discussion.

"Okay, fine." Wyatt raised her palms in surrender. "Let's change the subject, shall we? This one is becoming a little volatile for my taste. Where is Brenda? I'd like to get her these tapes."

"She's at Katie's," Luke grumbled.

"In East Palo Alto?" Wyatt asked in disbelief.

"Yes." Luke knew he was being cold with Wyatt, but he also knew their friendship could withstand the temporary freeze. He wasn't in the mood for explaining himself. All he wanted to do was find a doctor's cot and lie down.

"See you at church tomorrow," Wyatt said kindly.

Luke realized Wyatt's feelings were hurt. As she walked away, he added, "Thanks, Wyatt. I'm sorry I snapped at you."

"Barry and I only want what's best for you, Luke. You know that."

Luke just nodded.

❦❈❦

"Will you read me a story?" Daydan asked, his huge brown eyes open wide in anticipation.

Brenda looked down at the tiny boy that appeared by her side on the sofa. "I can't read today, Honey. I'm sorry."

"That's 'kay; we watch a wideo." The little one headed for the armoire and opened it, then installed a videotape all by himself. Brenda marveled at the boy's independence. Soon, Mickey Mouse was singing a happy tune, and Daydan placed himself cozily at Brenda's side, snuggling into her with a wide grin.

"Dinner's almost ready, Brenda. We'll eat in the living room tonight. I'd rather you sit in a comfortable seat, 'cause I know your body hurts from the medicine." Katie appeared in a cutout area that led to the kitchen, wiping her hands on a kitchen towel.

There was a knock at the front door, and Brenda found herself hoping it was Dr. Marcusson, even unconsciously retouching her hair at the possibility. Katie walked purposefully toward the entryway, removing her apron as she went.

"Wyatt!" Katie exclaimed, hugging the woman at the door while jumping excitedly. "You're back. How long are you staying?"

Wyatt. Slowly the name began to register upon Brenda's mind and she realized this was Luke's ex-fiancée. Brenda's eyes narrowed warily; an unconscious, but apparent, expression of loathing crossed her face. Wyatt was short by Brenda's standards, probably about five foot three and plain. Her hair was long, desperately thin, and a natural mousy brown. She wore no makeup and a pair of loose-fitting army khakis with an ill-matching plaid shirt. She possessed a flawless, tanned complexion and full, bright green eyes. Still, there was nothing spectacular about her. *What did he see in her?* Brenda wondered.

"Katie, I've missed you," Wyatt replied in a meek voice, reaching down to stroke Daydan's cheek, as he skipped to their guest. "I'm here as long as it takes to raise funds for next time. Barry's home tonight; his flight was late. He'll be speaking tomorrow at church, probably through glassy eyes."

Turning toward Brenda, Katie suddenly seemed to remember her. "I'm sorry. Where are my manners?"

Brenda stood, partially facing the wall, as though she were invisible. Upon hearing the approaching introductions, she rotated and produced a counterfeit smile.

"Wyatt, this is Brenda Turner."

"Brenda, it's a pleasure to meet you." Wyatt reached out her hand and Brenda reluctantly reached for it, nodding as a response. "I'm actually here to see *you*."

"Me?" Brenda hoped it wasn't true. She wanted nothing to do with this woman. This image of Luke's past.

Katie broke in. "Come on in; sit down, Wyatt."

Wyatt took Brenda's unwilling hand and led her back to the couch. "Brenda, I'm a nurse. I used to work for Dr. Marcusson." *So, that was what she called it.* "I know you have nystagmus and ataxia." She spoke quietly and, Brenda thought, condescendingly.

"What?" Brenda said curtly. She didn't have those things at all as far as she was concerned. And Miss Wyatt Ross could take her highfalutin words elsewhere.

"I'm sorry. Nystagmus is the double vision and eye problems you're having, and ataxia is the dizziness."

"Yes." Brenda knew she was shooting daggers from her eyes, but she couldn't help it. Luke had been in love with this woman, and no matter what the nurse had to say, Brenda hated her. "I can't read, you know." Brenda knew her tone sounded like that of a wounded cat but found herself unable to be cordial. Jealousy coursed through her body. Unmerciful jealously for a man who had never given her more than his duty as a physician.

"Brenda, I think what Wyatt is trying to do is explain a few things about the disease for you," Katie intervened, trying to take the edge off Brenda's tone.

"What's to know? I have a disease, there are drugs to manage symptoms, end of story. When I can read about it, I will." Brenda began to walk toward the guest bedroom without excusing herself. Much to her surprise and dismay, Wyatt determinedly followed her and shut the door to the bedroom behind her.

"Brenda, I know this is frightening, and you don't know me from Adam. But I'm a good friend of Dr. Marcusson's, and I've had a lot of experience treating MS. At least let me explain some of the basics to prevent future attacks, okay?" Wyatt's tone was pleading. She placed the tapes on the desk near the bed and pulled on her hair nervously. "First of all, you need to keep your body cool. Heat only exacerbates your symptoms. No lingering baths or hot tubs. If you exercise, I'd recommend an air-conditioned gym, or swimming. You want to make sure you don't get to the point where you break a sweat."

"Then what's the point?" Brenda asked sarcastically.

Wyatt ignored the comment, concentrating on her task. "Secondly, you need to keep yourself stress-free. Now I know you're in a very high-profile job, so you might want to consider taking another position that has fewer responsibilities or possibly shortening your hours at the office."

Oh, you'd love that, wouldn't you? Brenda eyed her opponent suspiciously and challenged the nurse by her very expression. She could tell Wyatt was uncomfortable with her, and she took pleasure in her uneasiness, pushing her farther away. "I have managed more at twenty-seven than most women accomplish in a lifetime. Do you think I'm going to give it all up for a stress-free life? I'm sick, not crazy. I've worked too hard."

"Brenda, I didn't mean to suggest you give up your life. I only meant—"

"Never mind. I'm really tired, but I guess you and your books know that. I'd like a nap before dinner, if you don't mind." Brenda held the door of her bedroom open and waited for Wyatt, who stood stunned, to leave the room.

"Brenda, I've left a tape player with some multiple sclerosis books on tape. Please listen when you get a chance. You may be able to keep from ever getting ill again, and you won't have to worry about your job, okay?" Wyatt was visibly shaken by the encounter and picked up her purse from the bed and left quickly.

"Katie, I'm sorry I must hurry, but I've got to pick up Barry at the airport. I'll see you tomorrow at church."

Katie saw the tears in Wyatt's eyes and immediately focused on Brenda, throwing her arms up in exasperation. "Brenda!"

"I didn't do anything! I just told her I needed a nap!" Brenda replied before shutting her door to end any further reprimand.

Chapter 6

Sunday morning came quickly. Luke would have preferred to remain leisurely in bed, but the early sun pulled him from his sleep at his normal hour. He staggered the few steps to the kitchenette in his studio apartment and poured himself a bowl of cornflakes, smelling the milk before pouring. It had been awhile since he'd visited the grocery store. He would have to include that on his "things to do" list for his one day off.

After breakfast, he walked out to the attached garage and found his beat-up Pinto missing. In its place was a sleek, black BMW convertible. "Brenda's car. I totally forgot." He slapped himself on the forehead. Luke had transferred Brenda's chart to Dr. Wilhelm along with a written explanation to Brenda that his practice did not allow for her therapy.

After listening to Wyatt, he had decided that the house-hunting idea was only an excuse to be near Brenda, which could only bring heartbreak. But there was the matter of the car. He would have to see her and, inwardly, he worried that his eyes would give his true feelings away. It had been a cowardly thing to do, transferring her charts without consulting her. Clearly, God was making him face up to his feeble actions. *Lord, give me strength.*

Behind the racy sports car was Luke's prized possession and sole extravagance: a $1,500 mountain bike. Wyatt and Barry had laughed unceasingly when he showed them the bike, telling him he was the only man they knew with a bike worth more than his car. The thought of the scene made him smile, and Luke was anxious for his day of worship and recreation. He put on his bicycling shorts, covered them with loose-fitting khakis and a chambray shirt and strapped a picnic lunch of scraps to his bike. He rode the two miles to church and figured he would gather a few teens from the youth group to accompany him for his weekly mountainside ride following service.

☙❦☙

Katie was frantic after one night with Brenda in their home and shared her concerns with her husband. "Jacob, she can't stay here anymore. She's scared to death. Last night when the gunshots went off, she threw herself on the floor. She didn't sleep at all. I heard the television on all night. It's obvious it bothers her to be here. We can't just let her live in anxiety. She'll never get well." Katie beseeched her husband with the facts in their bedroom, while he dressed for church.

"Did you explain to her that gunshots go off every night at eleven? That it's just somebody fooling around?"

"Jacob, she's never heard a gunshot before. As far as Brenda was concerned, they were coming for her. She's not going to get any better if she fears for her life. We've got to respect her doubts. East Palo Alto is not for everyone."

"I realize that. I'm just concerned you haven't given her enough time to feel safe here."

"Jacob, how do you explain to someone that gunfire doesn't mean anything? That it's just a part of the night here. We've been here so long that we don't even realize how strange some things are anymore."

"You're right, Katie. But I don't want you to abandon her when she needs us most. And you can't stay with *her* right now. What if Child Protective Services comes by about our request to keep Daydan permanently? We've got to maintain as normal a routine as possible."

Katie's eyes widened suddenly. "I think I have an idea."

"I don't like the sound of that at all." Jacob swayed his head back and forth while he finished buckling his belt. Katie whispered something into her husband's ear and he sighed loudly. "I wouldn't get too attached to *that* idea, but I'll do my best."

❧❀❧

Luke relished the warm spring morning air in his face, partaking in his own worship as he rode his bicycle toward church. The sky was the bluest of blue with only a hint of one tiny cloud that served as a strong contrast against the rich azure. He breathed deeply, and the spice of eucalyptus trees and freshly cut grass filled his senses. He kept a leisurely pace to keep himself cool for service and found himself at the sanctuary before he was ready to relinquish his bicycle.

"Luke!" Barry Ross's balding head and generous frame came rambling toward him with burly arms outstretched. Luke grabbed his old schoolmate and hugged him fiercely. The shadows from the historic church provided a parklike setting, and the men sat beneath a sweet-smelling jasmine vine, anxious to catch up on their latest news. "I suppose Wyatt told you we ran out of funding in Africa. She's in talking with the deaconesses about further support now." Barry shook his head in despair, "I tell you, Luke, sometimes I have to wonder what God expects. He tells us to go to Africa, then it feels like we're on our own."

"I know what you mean. . ." Luke dropped his chiseled jawline, immersed in his own thoughts. "I feel like God is taunting me with this woman by showing me what I can never have."

"Wyatt told me about Brenda. I'm sorry for her, Luke, and you too, of course. I thought it was all over, though. Wyatt said you'd transferred her case."

"Unfortunately, I still have her car. What did Wyatt think of her?" Luke asked eagerly, feeling like a high schooler. "I thought she might call and tell me last night, but I guess you two were busy at the airport."

"Actually, Luke, I know Wyatt would never want to hurt your feelings, but she's pretty concerned about your emotions over this woman. Says you're going to keep seeing her on a personal level." Barry's friendly gray eyes were warm and concerned.

"I told Wyatt I was going to have Brenda help me house hunt, but I think I have ulterior motives."

"Luke, when was the last time you went out on a date?"

"With a woman?" Luke laughed.

"Yes, with a woman. You're thirty-six years old. It's about time you started thinking about settling down. Maybe you're just lonely. Have you been to the singles' group here?"

"Barry, you know I hate that stuff. As soon as someone's mother hears I'm a doctor, they're sending out wedding invitations. If God wants me to have a wife, He'll bring me one."

"Right to your doorstep, huh?" Barry asked. "Maybe you could steal your best friend's girl."

Luke laughed at the reference to Wyatt and Barry's shaky start. "You and Wyatt were meant to be. She and I never loved each other that way. I want what you and Wyatt have, but I'm happy single if that's God's plan for my life. I'm just frustrated right now, but I'll get over it."

"That's the right attitude. I just wanted to know where you stood. Wyatt sounded pretty upset over her encounter with Brenda yesterday. I feel better knowing you're standing on solid ground."

"Did Wyatt mention what happened? I know Brenda's personality can be a little harsh, but it's all an act. She's really vulnerable and sweet inside. Her business exterior is all a front. As a matter of fact, Katie says she listened to the gospel yesterday and didn't even roll her eyes." Luke heard himself and knew he was justifying Brenda's bad behavior. He wanted to believe she was the woman destined for him, the woman God had hand-chosen to marry him and live out the rest of his days. But if she didn't dedicate her life to Christ, she was not the one. Barry and Wyatt were only trying to reinforce that fact. "You're right; I'm not thinking clearly. Oh, and chalk me up for a twenty percent increase in my African mission support. Wouldn't want you two hanging around too long." The two men laughed and hit each other on the back roughly as they walked into the sanctuary.

꿍

Brenda paced back and forth in the guest room like a caged animal. The bedroom was pleasantly decorated in a blue and white floral motif with cranberry red pillows accenting the bed. Brenda had to admit that Katie's home was homey, even if it was in the ghetto.

Katie entered suddenly. "Brenda, you've got to quit worrying about work." Katie carried a load of laundry in her hands and tossed it onto the bed.

"You could have gone to church. I wouldn't have wilted in two hours' time," Brenda chastised.

"I know. I was more concerned about your fears about being in our fair city."

"Katie, I'm sorry. I don't mean to be ungrateful, but I don't understand why you live here. You're nothing like these people. They shoot their guns off for fun, for heaven's sake. Doesn't that concern you? If not for yourself, for Daydan? I mean if you have to have a Bible study here, can't you rent a place for a day or something? I know you and Jacob mean well, but you don't have to be martyrs."

"Actually, Jacob did rent a garage when he first came here. He commuted for nearly a year before he felt like his home in Palo Alto wasn't home anymore. *This* was his home and where he felt God calling him to be."

"I don't get that at all. He lived in *Palo Alto*. Do you know what people will pay to live there today? God should love you no matter where you live."

Katie sat down with Brenda on the bed amidst the pile of clean-smelling laundry. "God does love us no matter where we live, Brenda. I know this is hard for you to understand, but God makes His wishes known to His people. He wants us here, and nothing makes us happier than fulfilling His will for our lives. If I didn't live here, I wouldn't have Daydan, and he's the best part of my life."

"Even if I did what God wanted, I would never live here," Brenda stated emphatically. "No offense, Katie, but this place is scary. Don't you notice all the bars on the windows? That is not the sign of a healthy neighborhood."

Katie laughed and nodded. "I suppose you're right about that. You know what? If you did commit your life to God and you honestly *couldn't* live here, God wouldn't require it from you. He gives us each special gifts and calls us accordingly, so don't let that deter you."

"Yeah, okay."

"Listen, the reason I came in here is to tell you I have an idea. I know you have the campaign files that Mike Wilcox is looking for, and I know you're not likely to part with them. I have a compromise for the sake of *all* our jobs. And if you're not up to it, you'd better tell me."

Brenda sat on the edge of her seat, exhilarated at the possibility of working again.

"I'm listening!"

"Tomorrow, rather than go in to the office, we'll just drive there. You can wait in the car while I get what we need, and then we'll go to your house to work. I can dictate the copy and you can edit it out loud. How does that sound?"

"Like sheer heaven!" Brenda clapped her hands together like a child at a birthday party, tossing her blond hair happily.

"You are a strange woman, Brenda Turner." Katie's sweet smile broke through, and Brenda felt immense fortune by having the support of the petite brunette who cared so deeply for people.

Brenda bent her statuesque frame and hugged her petite assistant tightly. "Thank you!"

"Now, wait a minute, that was the easy part. There's a condition."

"Name your price," Brenda said without thinking.

"First, you don't read anything after I leave your house, understood?"

"Agreed. What else?"

"I know you're uncomfortable here, and I'm concerned that it will affect your health. Jacob is talking to Wyatt Ross as we speak, about becoming your personal nurse for the next two weeks. I know money is not an issue for you, and she could really use the salary for her ministry in Africa. You'd be doing each other a favor—you each have what the other needs," Katie said enthusiastically.

Immediately, Brenda began shaking her head. "No, Katie. You have no idea what you're asking of me. Anyone but her, please." Brenda thought of the sweet-tempered missionary that Luke had once loved, and all rational thinking left her. She felt an envious loathing rise within her.

"I've never met anyone who didn't think Wyatt was the crown jewel of people. We're only talking about two weeks. Even the lamest of your secretaries has lasted that long, so I know you have it in you."

"You wouldn't understand. You get along with everyone," Brenda argued.

"It has to be her, or I won't help you. Wyatt's mission works with thousands of sick and dying children every year." Katie shook her head defiantly. "No, it definitely has to be Wyatt. I never met anyone who didn't absolutely love her, and you will too if you just give her a chance."

Brenda knew Katie wouldn't give in. She was generally so easygoing, but when there was something she felt strongly about, there was no use disputing.

"Fine."

Katie broke into a winning grin and began folding her laundry.

✿❧✿❧

"Absolutely not, Jacob. She hates me!" Wyatt cried. "No, she hates me with a vengeance, and I have no idea why." Barry and Luke stood still, unwilling witnesses to the ugly scene.

"Wyatt, are you sure you're not reading a little more into this situation?" Luke asked innocently.

"Honey, you might be overreacting just a little bit," Barry added gently.

"You men are all the same. You see a blond with shampoo-commercial hair, and your brains go right out the window. You have no idea who she really is! It's all an act; can't you see? To us women, well, her charms are quite transparent. We see the truth," Wyatt cried. The men all looked at her quizzically. Noting her out-of-character behavior, she calmly added, "I'm sorry, but I *don't* want to work for her. Not for two weeks, not even for two minutes. I can't think of anything I'd want to do less."

Luke stepped forward, wearing his most humble and disarming smile. "Come on, Wyatt. If she hires a nurse, we don't know what kind of care she'll get. You love the Lord! And you've worked with so many MS patients, you know the disease. Besides, just think how many children this salary might save in Africa." Luke saw Wyatt's face soften, and he knew he was getting somewhere. It was then that he threw the final punch. "Please, Wyatt. Do it for me."

Wyatt closed her eyes in defeat. "All right, Luke. I'll do it, for you," she whispered.

Barry hugged his wife with pride. "That's my girl!"

"Great," Jacob said quickly, not giving her a chance to change her mind. "You'll start tomorrow evening at six o'clock. Brenda'll be on her best behavior, I promise. Gotta run; Daydan's waiting in Sunday school," Jacob said happily.

Wyatt stood defeated while Barry and Luke both beamed. "Thank you, Wyatt. I know God's love will shine through you. I can't think of anyone I'd rather have share the gospel with her than you. Your life is a living example, and it will mean a lot to her, you'll see." Luke had all the confidence in the world in his friend. He knew her gift of evangelism and her all-encompassing love for humanity. Luke simply wasn't willing to give up the idea that God had handpicked Brenda to be his future wife. He tried to take Barry's earlier words of caution to heart, but something about Brenda had gripped him and wouldn't let go.

"Luke, I hope you're right, but I'm afraid she's going to see the worst example of Christianity in me. I can't help it; something about her brings out the worst in me," Wyatt admitted.

Luke knew Brenda could be severe, but he had never seen such a violent reaction in Wyatt. She *always* saw the best in people. He honestly wondered what Brenda could have done to upset her so but figured ignorance was probably best.

"We'll have prayer behind you, Wyatt. You'll do fine. And remember, you're working for God, not Brenda Turner," Barry said with his bulky arm still tightly woven around his petite wife. "Join us for lunch, Luke?"

"No, thanks. I'm taking the youth group for a bike ride this afternoon. They've been calling me an old man lately, so I'm going to take them up Skyline today and show them who's old."

"Take it easy on them, okay?" Wyatt said sweetly.

"Of course I will." Luke winked at Barry.

≈❀❀≈

Brenda packed her bags, made her bed, and perched on the edge, ready for home. She was so anxious to return to her old routine that she wished it were Monday already instead of early Sunday afternoon. Working gave Brenda a purpose in life, and with this dreaded disease hanging over her head, she needed more than ever before to feel valuable. She scuffed the toes of her shoes impatiently on the rich country-blue carpet and tapped her fingers on the old rolltop desk beside her.

Katie walked by the doorway with yet another load of laundry and noticed the antsy inmate waiting to pounce. "Brenda, I never would have told you about working tomorrow if I thought you wouldn't rest. You know what Dr. Marcusson said about getting some sleep. Anxiety isn't good for you."

"I'm resting. See, I'm just sitting here." Brenda looked up with innocent eyes.

"Why don't you listen to some of the tapes Wyatt made for you? I would think you'd be interested in staying healthy. The healthier you are, the more money you can make," Katie said flippantly.

The incentive worked, and Brenda reached for the untouched cassettes. "You're right, Katie. That will chew up some time," Brenda said enthusiastically, and Katie rolled her eyes.

"The boys will be home soon, so I'm going to close your door so they don't interrupt you. Lie down and take it easy while you listen."

Brenda lay back against her pillow and clicked the recorder on. The first thing she noticed was Wyatt's voice. There was concern in it that Brenda couldn't quite describe—a gentleness that Brenda would never own. She knew Luke must have been attracted to that sweetness, something Brenda had tried to copy in the past, only to have her brusque personality come tumbling out shortly thereafter. She sighed loudly and began concentrating on the words rather than Wyatt's soft voice.

Brenda heard for the first time some of the many statistics that describe the average MS patient. It was as if they had hand-selected her for the disease. *Why didn't someone tell me I was a candidate for such a devastating illness?* Brenda made a mental checklist as she listened.

Then came a seemingly endless list of symptoms that accompany the disease, and she was thrilled when she had only three of the top ten. This was one competition she was willing to lose. Wyatt's voice listed the courses that several MS patients had followed: One had recovered to nearly normal after each and every episode; another was confined to a wheelchair shortly after the second episode. The best and worst cases. Brenda took solace in the fact that her bout sounded most like the woman who had recovered fully. There was no guarantee, of course, but the comparison gave Brenda hope.

After her lengthy recitation about the disease, Wyatt addressed Brenda personally. "Know that I will be praying for you, and I know Luke is praying for you. I have all the faith in the world that you will fully recover. Remember, you'll be feeling the effects of the drugs as well as your symptoms, so take heart—it will get better. I promise."

Brenda didn't know what to make of the personal note or why it touched her. Wyatt said she would be praying for Brenda. Even after her own rude behavior toward the missionary, she knew by the sincere voice that Wyatt would make good on her promise. She saw Wyatt in a new light, but her heart still burned with insecurity over the woman who had shared a special part of Luke's life.

Brenda emerged from her room with a new attitude. She found her empty place at the dinner table and sat. "I'm so excited about getting back to work. I can finish the campaign by Wednesday, present it to corporate on Thursday, and pitch it to the client next Monday. Star Digital ought to be public within two months."

Katie took Brenda's plate and loaded it with meat, mashed potatoes, and steamed vegetables. "Brenda, I'm glad you're excited about getting back, but remember, your body will probably not hold up under your old schedule."

Brenda ate her steamed vegetables quickly, the adrenaline of impending work giving her speed. "I know, I know," she said with a mouthful of food. "But do you think Mike Wilcox has been taking it easy while I've been gone? I've been out of work for two days, four, if you count the weekend. I can assure you he's done everything he could to undermine my authority in that time." Brenda swallowed, took a quick sip of water, and stabbed another bite of meat. She was famished from the medication and felt like she couldn't shovel the food in fast enough.

"Let me put this in perspective for you. You were *blind* yesterday!" Katie fairly yelled. "You've got at least six weeks of vacation stored up, months, if you count your sabbatical. Relax!"

Jacob intervened with a calm voice. "Brenda, I think what Katie is trying to say is that Star Digital's initial stock offering is secondary to your health. If you have to give that dream up, God will replace it with something better. It may be difficult to see in the midst of the trial, but God always works for the best."

Brenda stared at him questioningly. "No offense, Jacob, but if God is out there, He rewards those who work hard, don't you think? You can see I've been rewarded quite well in my career, and I don't think it was by chance, do you?" she challenged, her jaw discreetly chewing rapidly.

"No, Brenda, of course I don't. But you're looking at success through the eyes of the world. God doesn't see people as we see them. He sees them on the inside. Take Wyatt Ross, for example. Wyatt was a successful nurse in the world-class Stanford neurology department when she got the call to go to Africa and treat the poorest of the poor. She left one of the most respected hospitals in the country for a mission where she must beg for funding. She has pleaded with every major pharmaceutical company worldwide to get the supplies she needs just so a few children will make it through the night. The world may not see her as successful, but I'll tell you what, I bet God does." Jacob lifted his voice for emphasis.

"You're comparing Lee Iacocca with Mother Teresa. It's apples and oranges," Brenda said through a mouthful of potatoes. She felt her face flush red at the comparison between her and Wyatt.

"Point taken, and you're right. God does give each of us different gifts. That wasn't a good analogy. But my point still stands. God doesn't see success as the world sees it. Since we all have different personalities, we all have different struggles."

"I don't see success as a struggle," Brenda replied curtly.

"Maybe not, but you seem willing to sacrifice your health for it, so maybe it's a bigger struggle than you think." His words touched a nerve. Jacob smiled at her graciously and reached for the bowl of potatoes, changing the subject. "Would you like more potatoes?" he asked while passing the bowl to her.

"No, thanks," Brenda replied sheepishly. *Why do all religious people seem to have such a problem with success?* Her own parents had always discouraged a career for her, but she had shown everyone. She had amassed investments that no one could take away from her.

Chapter 7

Brenda was dressed in a fitted, navy Chanel suit, complete with pumps, tapping her fingers nervously on the nearby desk. Katie had to dress Daydan, make the family lunches, then dress herself. Brenda thought she might faint from the wait.

"Okay, Brenda. It's seven-thirty, time to go," Katie called from the kitchen.

Brenda bolted up, bags in hand, then fell back onto the bed for not allowing her balance to catch up with her. Jacob took the suitcases. He led her outside, and Katie met her in the car with a Balance bar. "We'll stop at a drive-thru and get you a mocha. I wouldn't want you to suffer from caffeine withdrawal symptoms. It's been nearly two days," Katie joked.

Jacob hugged Brenda good-bye graciously while she self-consciously patted him on the back. "You're always welcome," he said.

"Thank you, Jacob." Brenda buckled herself in, and Katie started the car.

When they stopped to drop Daydan off at his grandmother's, the mischievous toddler hopped into the front seat and planted a kiss on Brenda's cheek. "I miss you, 'kay? You come my house again." Daydan nodded for recognition.

"I sure will, you little cutie. You take care of Grandma today, okay?"

Again the boy nodded and ran up to the house. Brenda opened the window, and a light breeze filled the car. She closed her eyes in peace until she felt someone looking at her. She opened her eyes wide and saw a large, dark outline beside her. She sat stone-faced, blinking her eyes for assurance that she was seeing a burly African-American teenager standing next to the car. She dropped her hand, freezing in panic. If she rolled the window up, she would appear prejudiced and he might hurt her. If she left the window down, all he had to do was grab her. She quickly determined that he was too close for her to do anything. She produced an instant smile, hoping he might just go away. If he wanted money, she was prepared to give it without a struggle.

The brawny teen reached into the car and held a piece of paper in his hand. He wore a broad, inviting smile and spoke pleasantly. "Excuse me, Miss. Did you lose this paper? I think I saw it fly from your car."

"I—uh, thanks." Brenda reached frantically for the page, still concerned he had ulterior motives.

"No problem. You have a nice day, now." The teen waved his large hand and ran to join a group of kids who were waiting for the bus.

Brenda dropped her hand, closed her eyes, and exhaled deeply just as Katie returned to the car. Knowing Katie wouldn't understand her obvious prejudice toward the poor, Brenda kept the incident to herself. The women stopped at the nearest espresso drive-thru, and then continued on to Star Digital. Brenda sipped on her mocha to settle her anxious stomach.

"Brenda, stay in the car. If you start to think you can do better than me in there this morning, just think about what Mike has probably told the staff about your time off. It won't do you any good to go fumbling into your office, agreed?"

Brenda only nodded, wishing she could jump out of the car and get back to her desk. She could crank out the rest of her campaign tactics in less than a day. She swallowed her morning dose of oral steroids and fidgeted while she waited.

❧❀❧

It was after one o'clock when Luke finished in surgery. He scrubbed down and returned to his cuffed slacks and dress shirt for the office. After lunch in the cafeteria, he headed for the exit.

"Dr. Marcusson, yoo-hoo, Dr. Marcusson." A high-pitched voice called to Luke from across the room. He recognized the voice and turned to wait for Eve Moore to catch up with him. Eve was a petite beauty who knew her way around the hospital halls. It was common knowledge that she had her sights set on marrying a doctor, and today Luke seemed to be the grand prize in the bachelor game.

"Nurse Moore, how nice to see you," he said.

"I heard you performed groundbreaking brain surgery this morning with Dr. Olgilvy. The whole department is just buzzing. I wanted to be the first to congratulate you. It's not just *anyone* he asks to assist him." Luke opened his mouth to speak, but Eve beat him to the punch. "I also saw you finally traded that heap of yours in for a real car. I never imagined you in a BMW and a *convertible* too. Why, you must be hiding a real tiger in there," she said flirtatiously, poking him in the ribs.

"Actually, the car belongs to my girlfriend. She's ill right now, and I've been using her car." *I can't believe I said that outright lie.* Although Luke chastised himself, he had no intention of straightening out the truth.

"Girlfriend? You must support her in grand style to drive a car like that. If you ever get tired of her. . ." She dropped her chin but kept her eyes on his.

Luke clenched his teeth to avoid a thoughtless response. "Actually, she bought it herself." *There, that's a true statement.* "Have a pleasant day."

Luke walked out into the bright blue sunlight that made living in California worth the trouble of traffic and high prices. He sniffed the clean, eucalyptus scent and crossed the street, entering his office by the back door. A quick glance through the reception window showed a waiting area full of patients. His nurse, LeAnne, greeted him with a pile of phone messages in her hand.

"Luke, Mr. Townsend has been trying to reach you this morning. His wife disappeared from the nursing home again. He says he's ready to increase her dosages now and wants to discuss it with you. The police have been looking for her, but it's been four hours now."

Luke took the written message from her. "Thank you. Let me know if you hear anything further. I think we might need to look into a different care home for her, one that specializes in physically healthy Alzheimer's patients. I'll call him back shortly. Just let me get caught up."

"Mr. Montgomery is in room two. His chart's on the door. You've got a full schedule today, so I'll do my best to keep it moving. You've got a long list of doctors calling to confer with you about the surgery this morning, and I told them you'd get back to them after hours. Also, Baylor called about your clinical trials. They're interested in talking in detail and wanted to see you at next month's conference. And Dr. Wilhelm called about Brenda Turner."

"Is everything okay?" he asked anxiously.

"Yes, he just wants to confer on her dosages." She gave him a quizzical look in response to the intensity of his voice.

"Thanks, LeAnne. It's too bad there aren't two of you. If I had you at home, I might have fresh milk in the fridge."

She smiled. "I hear there are a few nurses vying for the honor."

"Get back to work," he teased. "Keep it up, and I'm going to tell your husband you're gossiping again." She grinned even wider.

⥲❧⥲

Brenda's picturesque Victorian house came into view, and Katie pulled into the driveway. Katie's expression turned to one of a serious nature. "Brenda, I don't know an easy way to tell you this, so I am just going to blurt it out. I don't want you to stress and I've considered not telling you, but I can't do that either, so here goes: Mike Wilcox had human resources bypass the password on your computer. He stole the files you created for the newest set-top box products, and he's been working on the campaign since Thursday."

Brenda remained unfazed, flipping her long blond hair casually over her shoulder. "Katie, Mike couldn't write his way out of a paper bag. He may be a good salesman, but he's a terrible marketer. Most of the staff hate him, so who would help him?" Thinking about her statement, she continued, "But I guess a fair number of them hate me too, huh?" She crinkled her nose.

Katie reluctantly nodded. "He's got four days on you, Brenda, and you're still not one hundred percent. Please let it go. It's not worth it. Your stock options are vested regardless of who pulls off the deal."

"I have managed this product since its infancy. It has to be me! I've got twelve companies making an inferior knockoff and one week to sell these set-top boxes to the best satellite providers in the business. Then *we'll* get the credit, Katie! Star's stock will make us millionaires! Do you trust that success to Mike Wilcox?

We're talking one week. It's now or never. Tell me you're with me," Brenda said with full confidence, her competitive nature reveling at the challenge.

"I don't want to be a millionaire if it means sacrificing your health. I'm not sure I want to be a millionaire at all," Katie argued. "Dr. Marcusson told me if you continued at this pace, your health would pay the price. He doesn't want that on his conscience, and neither do I."

Brenda paused at the mention of Luke but went on, "I'm going to do it with or without you. It will be ten times easier with your eyes, but I'll find a way regardless. Dr. Marcusson would do the same thing for his precious Baylor fellowship!" Brenda spat.

"Fine, I'm with you, but only because I'm worried about you."

They spent the day surrounded by data, charts, and outlines of their prospective company and its executives. They studied each aspect of the campaign with painstaking detail; the only breaks they took were when Brenda's eyes sent her to the rest room to battle an overwhelming wave of nausea. Katie kept her fed and rationed her antifatigue pills throughout the day. All in all, the patient seemed to be doing well, surviving on pure adrenaline.

Wyatt Ross knocked at the door three times, each time more aggressively, before entering the hurricane of paperwork uninvited. The living room was strewn with a flurry of graphs, and Wyatt followed the paper trail to a bedroom office down the hall. It took her a moment to pick a pathway into the room, where she found Brenda and Katie in the midst of an animated conversation on a tapestry sofa against the wall.

"What on earth is going on in here?" Wyatt asked.

"Wyatt, welcome to campaign headquarters. It's a shutout game, and we're in the final innings," Katie said. The two women, punchy from the long day, laughed themselves into hysteria while Wyatt stood by, flustered by the surrounding chaos. The women continued to laugh, tears streaming down their faces, until Katie glanced at her watch. "Oh my! It's six. I gotta go."

She made a hasty exit after promising Brenda that she'd be back at seven the following morning. "Wyatt, I left prescription instructions on the counter. Don't give her any more caffeine or antifatigue stuff. She needs to sleep." Katie slammed the door and was gone.

Luke saw his last patient at eight in the evening. Mrs. Townsend, his runaway Alzheimer's patient, had been found at four in the afternoon, nine hours after disappearing. Luke had gone by to check on her condition, which delayed his other appointments. Knowing his cupboards were bare, Luke decided to treat himself to dinner away from the hospital cafeteria.

He ate at a nearby salad restaurant, deciding to return Brenda's car after he finished. He mulled over various explanations of why he'd transferred her case without consent and rehearsed them in his head. He knew he couldn't tell her the truth; it would make him appear weak and unmanly. *I can't control myself around you, so I had to give you back to an old man who can handle it.*

When he arrived at the perfectly manicured Victorian on Harding Street, he was glad to see Wyatt's rental car parked outside. She would provide a buffer for his plan.

Luke knocked quietly on the door in case Brenda was sleeping, and Wyatt answered immediately. A continuous, high-speed clicking sound came from the front bedroom and Wyatt motioned him in. "How are things going?" he asked.

Wyatt looked up at him with big, sorrowful eyes. "Fine. She hasn't said a word to me. She's in her office." Wyatt led him to Brenda's home office.

The young vice president of marketing sat behind a custom-designed, built-in cherry wood desk, typing frantically on an oversized computer. Luke shook his head, exasperated. "Ahem. I know that's not Miss Turner at the keyboard, because I specifically told her to stay away from the written word. And most certainly that would include the computer."

Brenda turned and faced him, her blue eyes blinking rapidly. She grappled with the black, elastic pirate patch she was wearing to prevent double vision. Luke raised his eyebrows, but his cool demeanor belied his true feelings. His stomach churned at the sight of her, and he stood speechless, drinking in her beauty. He forced his thoughts aside.

"Miss Turner, did you hear me? It looks like you're reading, and I'm certain I shared my concerns with you about its possible ill effects."

"I. . .I'm on deadline and. . ." She looked at Wyatt, but Wyatt simply avoided her stare and headed for the living room. He studied her again.

"Brenda," Luke came toward her and knelt beside her. He tried to avoid her intense eyes, but he took her hand, feeling the now-familiar electricity pulse through his system. His deep voice was quiet and filled with sincerity. "I'm not trying to punish you. If you damage your eyes, they might never return to normal. Do you think I'm telling you this again and again for fun?"

Brenda wet her lips and answered slowly, "No, Doctor, but my future depends on this week. It's everything I've worked toward. I know it's bad timing, but it can't be helped. I'll be able to relax in one week. I'll go to Hawaii if you want— lie on the beach—whatever you say. Just let me have this week."

"It's not up to me." He squeezed her hand tighter and moved closer, willing himself not to kiss her. "I don't have control over the disease, but in many ways, Brenda, you do. Do what I ask—it's for your own good."

Brenda blinked in quick succession, and he knew she was willing to promise him anything, but could she keep such a promise when her financial future seemed to depend upon this week? Her mouth opened, and she started to speak but stopped. Then her apparent true emotions tumbled out. "I. . .I can't. I'm sorry." Brenda pulled her hand away and turned toward the computer. "You won't earn your ticket to Baylor from me."

"Is that what you think?" Luke rose from the floor. "You don't know me at all Brenda—not at all." He looked up and saw Wyatt standing once again in the doorway. He shook his head and walked sullenly toward the door.

"I've been trying for two hours. Your plea was more heartfelt but certainly no more effective," Wyatt explained as they entered the living room. "Do you want a cup of coffee?"

"That sounds great."

"Have a seat. You look exhausted again. Brenda probably senses you're the proverbial pot calling the kettle black when you say stop working." Wyatt didn't look at him, concentrating instead on pouring the coffee.

"I know I'm working a lot. But I've had this incredible opportunity. I've been assisting on computer-aided neurological surgeries. Patients will come from around the globe to have it done. Do you think Baylor will be able to ignore that kind of experience?"

"Full-time research at Baylor would take you away from a lot of personal contact."

"I know, but it's what I always *planned* to do. They may be close to the cure for MS, and I want to be a part of that. Not just helping a few patients with the available drugs, but creating new ones, perhaps even the antidote. This oncology surgery will put me on the map. They filmed the surgery today for teaching purposes and sent it to fifty different schools and hospitals around the world. My phone rang off the hook with surgeons wanting to confer. I'll be able to go anywhere," Luke uncharacteristically bragged.

"Help! I'm surrounded by twisted workaholics." Wyatt threw up her arms and ran for the kitchen.

❧❦❧

Brenda appeared in the hallway from her office, holding on for dear life while the world spun around her. Continuously staring at the computer had finally led to an equilibrium revolt, and Brenda wasn't sure which way was up. She swayed like a willow in the wind and clutched the doorway to hold her steady. Luke heard her grasp for the wall and turned to face her.

Brenda tried to maintain her upright position, "Aha! You do use technology. And you gave me that line about not watching television. Your surgery was seen around the country because Star Digital compressed the pictures into data that could travel over phone lines. That's because *I* was able to perform my job two years ago. You see?" Brenda's face beamed before she nearly fell over from the vertigo. Luke ran to her side.

Afraid that if she reached for his hand she would be on the floor, she held her place. He must have sensed her trepidation because he pulled her toward him, gently embraced her waist, and brought her to the couch, where he sat next to her. *He is so gorgeous,* she thought while trying to focus on his chiseled, masculine features as they whirled before her. *Like a great painting,* she thought, *something about him demands attention.* A wave of anger shot through her because she was unable to see him clearly.

"Brenda, your car's in the driveway. Wyatt's going to drop me at home. I should have told you sooner, but I've transferred your case back to Dr. Wilhelm." He paused, but Brenda remained silent. "If that's a problem, I can recommend another neurologist that might better suit your needs. I know that some patients have a difficult time seeing the doctor that diagnoses them."

Brenda lifted her chin defiantly, holding her tongue. *He's not here to check on me; he's here to discard me. My case might harm his chances for his beloved research career.* "No problem at all. Dr. Wilhelm will be fine. I appreciate your personal attention," she said coldly while rising from the ivory silk sofa. "I really must get back to work. Congratulations on your surgery, Dr. Marcusson. It's very exciting to begin a new venture. I wish you the best of luck with it. I'm sure Baylor will be calling soon," she said airily.

Brenda walked slowly into her office, widening her stance to avoid walking into the wall. She settled into her ergonomically correct chair, dropped her face into her hands, and cried.

Chapter 8

Brenda worked straight through the night with only one short nap. She lay down shortly before dawn and wondered whether Wyatt minded that Luke had visited her. *Does she still love him?* Brenda suddenly remembered her own status. Even if Luke were available, he'd seen enough devastation by multiple sclerosis to know better than to get involved with someone who had it. Luke's future didn't involve her, and it was time she faced facts.

Wyatt awoke around six and made coffee for the two of them. She came in wearing a dark blue terry cloth robe with a tray in her hands. "You haven't slept at all, have you?"

"A couple hours, maybe." Brenda paused for a moment. "Wyatt, do you mind if I ask something personal? You don't have to answer if it makes you uncomfortable."

"Go ahead. I've got nothing to hide." Wyatt shrugged.

"I know about you and Luke. Did you ask him to stop seeing me as his patient? Are you two getting back together?" Brenda wasn't coy. She played her cards freely at work and saw no reason to do it differently in her personal life. If Luke and Wyatt were together, she wanted to know. If that were the reason she was being forced from his life, she would understand. If it was the MS, there was little she could do about that.

"Brenda, I'm a married woman! For nearly ten years now! Luke and I had a puppy-love thing in graduate school, that's all. My husband Barry is Luke's best friend. They went to medical school together at Stanford. I love Luke like a brother." Wyatt rambled off her excuses quickly, as though she were ashamed that Brenda would think such a thing.

Brenda's face warmed. "Oh, Wyatt, I'm sorry."

"You didn't know I was married? What did you think this ring meant?" Wyatt held up her left hand.

"I never noticed it, and I probably would have assumed it was from Luke if I had," Brenda admitted. "It seems I've developed a childish schoolgirl crush."

"Brenda, you're Luke's patient," Wyatt reasoned.

"I know—I'm sick, I don't believe in God, and Luke's moving to Texas. Is there anything I've forgotten?" Brenda cried. Noting Wyatt's fearful, furrowed brow, Brenda continued. "Don't worry. Luke's never offered me anything more than his medical expertise. I haven't had much experience with men, and I read his concern as romantic interest. That's why I was so mean to you. I was jealous. I'm sure you'll all have a good laugh over this." Brenda stood to leave the room, but she swayed back into her bed instead. Wyatt sat alongside her easily, like an old friend.

"Brenda, I don't know what to say. When I first met you, I wondered what it must be like to have a face or figure like yours. It reminded me of yearning to be like my Barbie dolls all over again. I guess I was a bit jealous myself. So, what is it like to have men knocking down your door?" Wyatt grinned, taking the edge off the conversation.

Brenda's blond hair dropped in long straggles around her shoulders. "Wyatt, I wouldn't know. In case you didn't notice, I have this little problem with tact. I say what I think, usually before I've thought about it. Men don't seem to take too kindly to it. I don't exactly ooze warmth. Still, Luke took it all in stride. But I'm not just jealous of you because of Luke. With both you and Katie, I'm so envious of that gentle quality you seem to have. And I wondered, if God made *me* like that, soft and gentle, would I believe in Him too?"

"Brenda, Katie and I are just two examples of God's women. There are lots of women in His kingdom who are not gentle or servants by nature. They've got to work at it. God has a place for everyone in His church. It's not an exclusive club."

"That's what Katie says, but my mother always told me that no Christian man would marry a woman with such a mouth. That's all my parents ever wanted for me—to find the right husband. If they could know how successful I am now, they would still see me as a failure." Brenda used the back of her hand to wipe a tear away.

"Your mother probably wanted that for you because it made her so happy. Were your parents happy together?"

"I guess they were, but my mother was a doormat. She did whatever my father asked—waited on him hand and foot. I never wanted that! That's why I was so attracted to Luke. He was the first man that was interested in my *job*. The first one that seemed to understand my need to succeed. You saw last night—he asked me to quit working on the computer, but he never *forced* me. He allowed me to make my own choice. Now I know it's because he doesn't really care, since I'm not his concern anymore."

Wyatt smiled with warmth. "I'm going to confide something in you, because I think it's important for you to understand the kind of man Luke is. He's a Christian, and the Bible tells him he is not to be involved with a nonbeliever. God calls it being unequally yoked. God is number one in Luke's life, and he needs to be with someone who has that same commitment. Trust me, without it, you'd both be very unhappy. It's not a reflection on you, Brenda. You weren't wrong about Luke. He did think of you as more than a patient. In fact, he thought you were the most beautiful woman he'd ever seen. He loves your free spirit and your commitment to success and your outlandish sense of humor in the midst of such a difficult trial. I'm telling you this because I want to you know that Luke is not abandoning you. He's doing what he must to follow God's will."

Brenda was more confused than ever. Luke wouldn't see her on a personal basis not because of another woman or his job change, but because she didn't have a relationship with a God she couldn't see. She was helpless in that situation, and it seemed so unfair to her. Everyone told her it wasn't an exclusive club, but no one told her how to get into it. Katie had tried to pray with her, but there had to be more to it than that. Perhaps if she found out what this God wanted, there would be a chance for her and Luke.

She looked at Wyatt hopefully when Katie came bounding in. "Let's get to work."

"Katie, I'm exhausted. I'm going to bed. I left the slide graphics and logos on my desk. Would you get them made this morning?" Brenda asked sweetly. "I'm done for today—come back tomorrow." Every part of her ached. She felt as if she had fallen asleep, and someone had kicked her in every joint of her body.

"A day off?" Katie replied as Brenda closed the door to her bedroom. "What's with her? She's a little cheery, wouldn't you say?"

"I think she's making a concerted effort to be more pleasant," Wyatt answered.

"That oughta last about a minute. Tell Brenda I'll take care of these slides. She'll be worried when she wakes up and comes back to her senses. I'll be back in the morning, and we'll practice her presentation. She could do it in her sleep. I've never met more of a natural. I've got an appointment about Daydan's adoption, anyway. See you tomorrow."

❧❦❧

Brenda woke from a hard sleep at 2:04, according to her alarm clock. The shades were pulled, and she didn't have the slightest idea whether it was morning or afternoon. "Wyatt?"

The nurse appeared in the doorway. "Brenda, are you hungry?"

"I'm starving. I want prime rib and a Diet Pepsi," Brenda laughed. She lifted her worn frame from the bed and immediately fell to the floor.

Wyatt came immediately, lifting her from the rose-colored area rug covering the hardwood floors. "You have to remember to get up slowly. Let your equilibrium catch up with you. I'll get you a bowl of soup. Sorry, but we don't have any prime rib on hand, and with all that prednisone in your system, I don't think you need a heavy meal."

"The slides—did Katie take them?"

"She told me to tell you they're done. She'll be by tomorrow to help you practice. You know, it's obvious there's a very important piece of Thursday's presentation that you've forgotten," Wyatt said cryptically as she left the room.

Brenda quickly talked herself through her checklist. "No, I've got the demographics, the psychographics, the company principle information, the slogan, the campaign outline, and the best product in town. Everything."

Wyatt came back into the room with a cold, wet towel and wiped Brenda's brow, "It's not a fancy marketing component; it's the simple fact that you can't walk alone. How do you expect your CEO, or worse yet, your buyers to take you seriously when you walk like a drunk? Are you willing to walk with a cane?"

"Absolutely not. They find out I'm sick, and it's over for me."

"Legally, they can't fire you, Brenda."

"Maybe not legally, but they can demote me to a job I can 'handle,' and put an end to my career like that." She snapped her long fingers.

"I can teach you to walk with your affliction. God didn't give you those big feet for nothing," Wyatt teased.

Laughing, Brenda answered, "My dad used to tell me to take my skis off in the house." She shrugged her shoulders since thinking of her father brought tears to her eyes. Everything brought tears to her eyes when she was on these medications.

Wyatt took Brenda's hands and stood in front of her. "When it's really bad, you'll need a walker. You've got to face that. But if you take it easy and you're having a good day, we can teach you to walk without assistance. All you have to remember is that your brain is not sending the right message to you, so we're going to reprogram your legs. We're going to learn to overcome what your brain is telling you by reacting first, before you receive any message. Trust your feet, not your head. Let your feet feel for you. If one foot starts to lose the floor, use the other to guide you." Wyatt walked with Brenda for nearly two hours.

Brenda was feeling extremely confident by the end of the lesson. "Now, let's try it in heels. I think I can do it."

"No heels—you're going to wear flats. It's not worth risking it, Brenda. If you fall, you'll look ridiculous, and your campaign's shot. Flats are in style, and it's not like you need the height." Wyatt craned her neck to look into Brenda's eyes.

"I don't even own flats. I like towering over people, especially little weaselly men like Mike Wilcox," Brenda smirked.

"You take far too much pleasure in that man's pain. Go get your sneakers. We're going to the mall. You can practice walking while you buy a pair of flat dress shoes.

Brenda did as she was told and came running out of her bedroom, showing off her new skills. "Can we take my car? Please, please, please? I miss it so much, and you'll look great driving it! Come on! I know you loved it last night when you took Luke home."

"What would the missionaries back home think?" she joked.

"Probably that you sold out in style!" Brenda had missed being outside and enjoyed the ride to the mall immensely, taking pained efforts to focus on the familiar drive. She lowered the top on her car at a stop sign and laughed aloud when

Wyatt gave her a stern stare.

Once at the mall, Wyatt pulled a cane out of the trunk and handed it to Brenda.

"What do you expect me to do with it?"

"I want you to walk with it," Wyatt said enthusiastically.

"I don't want it. Put it back."

"Brenda! It's not just for you. It's so people around you know you need a little extra space."

"I'm not going in until you put it away. I'm not an invalid, and I don't need that thing."

"You will be an invalid if you don't take care of yourself. You pull one more all-nighter and you'll find yourself needing more than this cane."

Brenda proceeded walking toward the store and relied on her ears to get her safely across the parking lot. Her eyes had indeed become worse since she had spent so much time on the computer, but she wasn't going to admit it. Brenda saw the curb coming up, but her leg didn't anticipate the height; and she fell to the cement, stopping herself with her hands and forearms. She got up slowly so as not to anger her spinning brain and wiped the gravel from her scraped palms.

Wyatt made no mention of the incident, and Brenda entered Bloomingdale's without further trouble. "Mommy's home, Honey." She turned around for Wyatt's reaction, and the two women laughed together, their earlier spat forgotten.

A bright white counter loomed, equipped with mirrors, cosmetics, and perfume. "Do you need makeup, Brenda?"

"Sit down, Wyatt. I'm giving you a makeover."

"A makeover? I don't think I'm the makeover type."

"Don't be ridiculous, with green eyes like that? And porcelain skin a model would die for? Your complexion is just so dry from the desert. Wouldn't you love to show up looking like a supermodel tonight for Barry?"

"Quite frankly, no."

"Come on, all men want their women to be glamorous once in awhile. At least that's what the magazines say."

"The magazines that make their money off cosmetic ads."

"Now you're just being a stick in the mud. Sit down!" Brenda pushed her onto a chrome and white leather stool and proceeded to throw orders at the nearest salesgirl. "A light moisturizer, something she could wear on the plains of Africa." Brenda closed one eye and tried to concentrate on Wyatt's face.

"Are you going on a safari?" the salesgirl asked, intrigued.

"No, I'm a medical missionary in Kigali," Wyatt said brightly. Noticing Wyatt's old, ill-fitting khakis and ancient plaid shirt, the salesgirl pulled the makeup trays behind the counter.

"If you two just want to play dress-up, maybe you could go to Wal-Mart.

Some of us have to work for a living."

Brenda's lighthearted mood snapped. "Excuse me! This woman is the wife of the prominent neurologist *Dr*. Barry Ross, and I am *vice president* of Star Digital. Well, Missy, not only have you lost out on a nice commission, but I will be sending a letter to your manager, telling her of your unspeakable behavior. I don't think she'll be too pleased to know how you treat your customers."

"Brenda, please. . .it's okay, really," Wyatt said, trying to calm her down.

"No, it's not okay. This woman spends her day making frivolous women into Barbie dolls while you give up the life of luxury to help the poor. Who is she to make my friend feel like dirt? I won't stand for it!" Brenda was incensed and continued to berate the clerk, who apologized profusely.

Wyatt watched the whole thing as though in a trance. It took several moments before she focused on Brenda. Brenda bit her lip at the sight of Wyatt's concerned brow. "Brenda, please. Let me talk to you, please!" Wyatt pleaded, and Brenda finally relented, following her across the aisle into the shoe department. "Brenda, that woman tried to hurt our feelings, but Jesus tells us to turn the other cheek."

"Turn the other cheek? Do you want to get walked over your entire life? That's ridiculous. Besides, Jesus didn't have to deal with snotty salesgirls."

"Brenda, that woman probably makes six dollars an hour, eight dollars at best, in a town where the average home costs half a million dollars. She watches wealth displayed before her every day. She probably gets walked on day in and day out by rich socialites. Please give her a break. She's just trying to make a living. She only wants what you have but has no idea how to go about it."

Brenda looked at the salesgirl and suddenly saw her as she herself had once been, desirous of a lifestyle that seemed only a dream. She now felt compassion where the anger had been. She nodded at Wyatt, using her assistance to get back to the counter. "Excuse me. I'm sorry I was rude. May we please try another shade of eye shadow?"

The clerk looked at the women warily, nodded, and brought the color palette out onto the counter. Brenda asked politely for each product she wished to try and purchased an entire skin care and color system for Wyatt. Wyatt begged her not to, but Brenda would have none of it. The two women paid for their purchases, selected some shoes, and walked to the car without a word.

Once inside the car, Brenda spoke. "I'm sorry I embarrassed you, Wyatt."

"Money is only temporary, Brenda. Right now, it may mean success, but it'll mean nothing in the end."

Brenda thought about Katie's earlier explanation of seeing people as God sees them and thought Wyatt must have perfected that ability. It was still something that eluded Brenda.

❧❦❧

"Brenda, I really wish you hadn't bought all these things. Now I'll feel positively compelled to use them. I might become downright vain!" Wyatt lifted their packages from the car and helped Brenda into the house.

"Don't be silly. I bought them as much for that salesgirl as I did for you. All that religious guilt my mother programmed into me. I never realized before how much differently. . .better. . .I'm treated because I have money. That situation just caused me to remember I never want to be without the power money brings. It only confirmed that I'll never live under other people's control again! I just get so frustrated with the poor that they don't try to better themselves. You know, get an education or a job with promotion opportunities. I think it's their own fault." Brenda tossed her blond locks unconsciously.

"When your father was alive, what did he do for a living?"

"He was an accountant. A very successful one. He worked a lot. Sometimes he didn't come home until after I'd gone to bed." Brenda boasted.

"So that explains part of your work ethic. Think about the child who has spent his life on welfare with only a mom to raise him. He's probably never seen anyone go to work. How does he learn what is expected behavior?"

"It's just the American way. Everyone knows that," Brenda said without compassion.

"No, *you* know that. You've seen it put into action."

"I'm still mad at them for being poor. I can't help it. If they'd just do something about their situation, they wouldn't be that way."

Wyatt changed the subject. "I was really proud of you with that gal today in Bloomingdale's. It took a lot of character to go back to that counter and apologize—and even more to buy the makeup. You were a star today."

Brenda smiled widely. "I did do that, didn't I? Maybe some of your gentle nature is rubbing off on me. Do you think?" Brenda took pleasure in being able to humble herself for someone else.

"Brenda, I think God has special plans for you, and I think He's working on them right now." Wyatt hugged her suddenly, and Brenda self-consciously hugged back.

❧❦❧

Luke put off his hospital rounds until late afternoon. His patient load had been overwhelming with his newly added surgery and research schedule, and it kept him at the hospital continuously.

"Luke!" Dr. Olgilvy called from down the hall. Luke was surprised to be on a first-name basis after a mere six surgeries with the legendary oncologist. Frederick Ogilvy was a distinguished man of about fifty. He was still athletic for his age and not even winded after jogging to catch up with Luke. "The wife's having a dinner party. Just a small get-together with some of the area's cancer surgeons. You know the drill. Eight o'clock at my house. Here's the address. Is there a significant other?"

"No, just me." Luke took the calling card.

"Great, the wife'll get someone. You know how women are about an uneven number at the dinner table. Heaven forbid we dine with an odd number," Dr. Olgilvy said sarcastically while he slapped Luke on the back. "See you tonight."

Luke sighed, looking at the card in his hand. *Atherton. Of course, Dr. Olgilvy would live in Atherton, the most exclusive city on the Peninsula. What have I gotten myself into this time?* Luke wasn't comfortable in elite social circles, and he cringed over situations like this.

It was 7:30 before Luke left the office, and he was thankful that LeAnne had stayed late to sort out the many charts he had left in piles on his desk. "I'll be on the beeper. Would you let the service know?"

Not waiting for an answer, Luke dashed out of the office and ran full speed to his Pinto for the short drive to his apartment. He dug deeply in his closet for the one suit he owned and selected a tie that was least likely to be outdated. He checked his reflection in the mirror and buttoned the double-breasted suit Wyatt had made him purchase for her wedding. It had been an expensive suit at the time and displayed Luke's tall, lean physique well. But now he wished he'd taken the time to improve his dress wardrobe. Certainly a doctor should own at least one fashionable suit.

He hopped into the Pinto and found himself wishing he'd kept Brenda's car one day longer. Before long, he was on a shaded Atherton street, lushly canopied by the mature trees of the old-money neighborhood. The mansion rooftops were barely discernible through the extensive greenery and iron gates. Luke located the address and turned onto a brick driveway that wound for a short distance through the trees. In awe at the auspicious display of wealth, Luke found himself wishing that Brenda was by his side. "She would handle this like a pro, and she'd let me know which fork to use," he said.

A tuxedoed man met him at the end of the drive and motioned with his white-gloved hand to stop. "I'll take it from here, Sir. Dr. and Mrs. Ogilvy are waiting." For the first time in his life, Luke winced at the sight of his battered vehicle. He had to give the hired valet credit, though; not so much as a snicker crossed his face. He hoped there was a nice big tree to park the car behind.

The estate was a brick Tudor masterpiece that seemed to stretch on forever. Luke climbed several brick steps to a set of double glass doors. Another tuxedoed man answered. Luke couldn't avoid noticing that the help was dressed better than he was. The butler took his name and led him into a spacious living room, filled with half a dozen people. "Dr. Luke Marcusson," he announced. A small round of applause followed, and Luke felt utterly out of place.

"Doctor, let me see those prizewinning hands I've heard so much about." The approaching redhead took his hands and examined them before her audience. "I'm Gloria Ogilvy. Such a pleasure to finally meet you." Luke guessed her to be about fifty, with flawless makeup and no wrinkles whatsoever. Seeing Dr. Alto, a noted plastic surgeon, Luke guessed where they had gone. "Luke, I'm sure you know everyone. Dr. Alto and his wife, Miriam." Gloria Olgilvy pointed them out and Luke shook hands with each. "Dr. Wrightly and his wife, Jennifer, and I believe you're acquainted with Nurse Moore."

Eve Moore, the nurse with her eye on Luke, appeared from amid the small gathering. Gloria Olgilvy took each of their hands and melded them together in her own before letting go. "Don't they make an absolutely divine couple? My husband always says I have an eye for matchmaking."

Frederick Olgilvy piped in, "I never said any such ridiculous thing. Gentlemen, will you escort the ladies into the dining room? Dinner is served."

Luke offered his arm to Eve and smiled pleasantly. "Eve, you look very nice this evening." His tie felt tighter by the minute.

The dining room was a grand affair, swathed in ivory sheers that hung from the cathedral ceilings for an artistic, dramatic effect. The table, a great masterpiece of fine carved walnut was decorated for a feast. Tiny gold bowls filled with water were placed at each setting with a floating votive candle for atmospheric light.

Gold name cards sat atop gilded ivory plates. Luke held Eve's chair before finding his own beside her. She smiled easily, as though such luxury came naturally to her, and Luke found himself wondering whether Brenda would enjoy such a scene. *She would probably be forced to hold back her contagious giggle.*

As if reading his thoughts, Eve began the conversation. "So I noticed you had your old car back. Girlfriend feeling better, I hope? Or did you two have a little falling out?" she asked, batting her long eyelashes and looking at him from an angle with her chin dropped coquettishly.

The hostess overheard the conversation and barged right in. "Frederick, you told me he was single. I'm so sorry, Dr. Marcusson. I hope I haven't placed you in an awkward position. No offense, of course, Eve; you're always welcome here." Luke looked at his dinner companion, wondering how often she'd been called upon to fill an empty seat for a bachelor doctor. He smiled and proceeded to answer Mrs. Olgilvy.

"No, not at all. Brenda's quite busy with a deadline." Luke felt his web of deception getting more tangled but kept up the front easily after sensing a suspicious Eve Moore from the corner of his eye.

"What does she do? No, wait, let me guess. She's a surgical nurse," Gloria said loudly. The entire table erupted into polite laughter.

"Actually, she's not in the medical field. She's vice president of marketing for a technology company." Luke prayed silently over the bowl of lobster bisque that seemed to appear from nowhere. He began eating immediately, hoping to divert the topic.

"How on earth did two such opposites attract?" Eve Moore probed.

"Pardon me?" Luke asked, hoping for a reprieve from the personal question he didn't have the answer for.

"You know women, old boy! She wants to know how you met," Dr. Olgilvy said. "Women are always so nosy," he mumbled, but his attention remained on Luke.

"We, uh, met at a conference on multiple sclerosis." *A very private conference,* he added silently.

"You won't have much time for those anymore. Not with a pair of skilled hands like yours," Dr. Alto said. "Frederick's got big plans for you."

"I'm not sure my future is in surgery—I'm partial to research," Luke admitted.

Luke had shocked the table, and everyone stopped eating to look at him. Now more uneasy than ever, he felt like the centerpiece at the table and hoped the meal would end quickly so he could make a hasty exit. When a spring salad mix arrived with unrecognizable vegetables and a bitter taste, Luke knew his evening was only beginning.

Dr. Olgilvy sat and contemplated the comment during the cessation of conversation. He crossed his arms and finally replied in a jovial tone, "Very noble of you, Luke. Very noble, indeed." The young doctor had only succeeded in impressing the famous surgeon. It was clear that Olgilvy still had plans for Luke, and the young doctor's own dreams were simply small obstacles to the wishes of the distinguished surgeon.

Chapter 9

Brenda left her shades open for the night and awakened to bright sunlight. *It's finally Thursday! And just look at that blue sky. It's got to be a sign for my presentation.*

Brenda started running a bath for herself. She found that she couldn't stand up in the shower, so she had learned to wash her blond locks in the sink before getting into her antique claw-foot tub.

Brenda lathered quickly in the bath and used extreme caution by crawling out of the tub gingerly. The combination of hot water and her dizzy spells had sent her to the hard tile floor several times. She didn't want fresh bruises for her important appointment this morning.

She applied her makeup carefully, using her pirate patch loosely over one eye to do one side of her face and then shifting it to the other side. She blotted her lipstick with a tissue and emerged from the bathroom in her burgundy red tailored suit with dynamic gold buttons and opaque hose to hide her recent falls. "Well, how do I look?"

"Brenda, you look the picture of health. No one would ever guess," Wyatt answered.

"I know, and that's given me an idea. I'm going to take the cane with me today. If anyone has the nerve to ask, I'll just explain I had a little running incident or something. It's not worth breaking my neck to keep up appearances. Lots of people need canes for leg injuries and other things. It doesn't announce that I have multiple sclerosis."

"Just don't lie, Brenda. If you have to conceal the truth, that's fine. But please don't lie. God won't honor that."

"Very well, Wyatt. If it's important to you, I'll come up with something that isn't a lie." Brenda didn't know why Wyatt's opinion meant so much to her. After all, the two women had only known each other for a week. For some reason, however, it was important, and she wouldn't break her promise. Brenda seemed to be growing a conscience with Wyatt around, and while it confused her, there was something about it that felt right.

Katie had taken Wednesday off in addition to the Tuesday Brenda had given her. It was so unlike her secretary to be off near an important deadline. Brenda knew there was something crucial happening in her home life, but to allow Katie her privacy, she hadn't asked for the details. In Katie's absence,

Wyatt helped Brenda practice.

Katie opened the front door without knocking and had her hands full of iced mochas. "Caffeine all around. Get yours here!" Katie sounded happy, but her red face and swollen eyes told reality. She had tried to cover her eyes with makeup but had only succeeded in bringing more attention to their rosy puffiness.

"Katie?" Wyatt came forward, taking the drinks and setting them on the coffee table.

"No, please don't ask. Just be praying. Daydan's custody trial is Tuesday. Our lawyer doesn't think we stand a chance, and that's all I can say without breaking into tears again, okay?"

Brenda and Wyatt nodded.

"We've got a big day ahead of us, Brenda. Let's just concentrate on the presentation. God will take care of us. God will take care of us," Katie said it twice, as though trying to convince herself.

Brenda noticed that Katie was unsure of her statement, and for once she felt like affirming the godly words. Katie had always seemed so confident in her faith, but today she seemed certain of nothing. It shook Brenda.

"Katie, go home. I can do this alone. I'm taking the cane, so I won't fall. I'll be fine." Brenda was wondering where her sudden concern for Katie came from; usually she only cared about what suited her, even if it was inconvenient for someone else.

"No, we're going to be millionaires; do you hear me?" Katie said, trying to muster enthusiasm. "And I'm going to hire the best custody lawyer in California!"

"I hear ya! Okay, Wyatt, say a prayer for us. It couldn't hurt," Brenda said breezily as they dashed out the door.

"I'll be on my knees," she promised.

❧❦❧

The beaming sunlight was too much too soon for an exhausted Luke. His patient load was wearing him thin. When he awoke, he grabbed his Bible from the nightstand and headed for breakfast at a nearby restaurant. It had been nearly two weeks since he'd been to a grocery store. He also took the newspaper to check out car ads. The Pinto had broken down on the way home from Dr. Olgilvy's dinner affair, and that was the last straw. As a doctor, he had to have something more reliable.

Dr. Olgilvy had asked him to accompany him to Connecticut on Friday night to speak on their latest techniques at a weekend conference, so he didn't know when he could scrape the time to buy a car. Luke had arranged to have his patients seen by his partner, Dr. Byer, during his brief time away, but inwardly he worried about how long he could keep up this schedule. His research was beginning to fall behind. Two high-profile careers was one too many. A decision would have to made soon, but if Baylor didn't come through with an offer, the decision would be made for him.

Barry Ross was coming along to speak with some pharmaceutical companies at the conference about medications for his mission. Luke hoped that he and Barry would have a chance to talk.

⚜⚜⚜

Brenda listened smugly while Mike Wilcox made his presentation. She took mental notes on his many mistakes and reformed her presentation in her mind to challenge each of his main points. She could tailor a presentation to fit anyone's needs at a moment's notice.

This was Mike's first audience with Star Digital's CEO, and Brenda almost felt sorry for him at how inept his concepts were. She watched CEO Dan White, and he didn't seem to notice. It wouldn't become clear to him until Brenda spoke.

Mike finished and threw Brenda a condescending grin, as if to say, "Top that." She smiled broadly at him and stood before her company's executives, using her cane to lead her to the head of the conference table.

"Gentlemen, such a pleasure to see you this morning. As you can see by my cane, I've had a little trouble jogging lately, but I can assure you, you'll see me in the executive gym soon." The men laughed politely and she proceeded, assuming her business tone.

"Mr. Wilcox has a very good point about our product belonging in America's homes. Our set-top boxes are the best the satellite industry can provide for its customers. It allows the largest amount of choice to a consumer with the touch of a finger. However, we're a latecomer in the industry. What would make a satellite provider change its set-top box now? A cheaper, better alternative? Absolutely. Gentlemen, I have taken this opportunity to contract a field service team available for Day Graphics' use.

"The set-top boxes in today's market have a failure rate of 40 percent. Yes, nearly half of all their present set-top boxes will fail in the field—in their customers' homes. And those numbers don't take into account the lack of field engineers able to fix the problem." Brenda pointed to her graphs to bolster her point, while the CEO nodded his head diligently. "Gentlemen, this should be Star Digital's new sales pitch." She unveiled her masterpiece and explained every detail in rapid succession.

When she was through, the men erupted into applause and came to congratulate her on a job well done. A job they knew would not go unnoticed by potential buyers. She saw Katie smiling proudly in the corner.

Brenda noticed Mike Wilcox angrily staring at her. "I know there's something wrong with you, *Miss* Turner! When I find out what you're hiding, and I will, there won't be a company in Silicon Valley that will even look at you. Then, the real vice president will stand up," he threatened under his breath.

Brenda mustered every bit of remaining strength and remained expressionless while she calmly replied, "Mr. Wilcox, I think we all know who the *real* vice president is. If you'd like to remain a product *manager*, I suggest you stick to your supporting role, where you belong." Brenda smiled condescendingly.

Katie took her hand and led her quickly to the car. Brenda took no satisfaction in her successful coup. For some reason, the thrill she had always experienced with success was gone. "This stupid disease is removing the very life from me. I accomplished everything I planned today, and I feel nothing! What's wrong?"

"Perhaps you're finding out that people are more important than money." Katie's voice cracked.

"I doubt it," Brenda grunted.

"Brenda Turner, I may lose my son on Tuesday. I'd give every cent of those millions to be able to raise him! Quit feeling sorry for yourself," Katie chastised.

Brenda sobered, thinking back to her own deceased parents. All the money in the world wouldn't allow her to tell them she was sorry. *Money may not be as important as people, but it sure can numb the pain,* she thought.

❧❦❧

Luke was happier than he'd been in a long time, being on research detail. As he sat down in the hospital cafeteria for lunch, he was almost disappointed to see Dr. Olgilvy coming toward him.

"Luke, my boy. You don't eat this slop too often, do you?"

"Enough to think it actually tastes pretty good," Luke replied facetiously.

"Oh, you *are* spending far too much time in here. Why don't you meet the wife and me at *Il Fornaio* this evening and bring your little vice president along. My wife is dying to see your taste in women. Just a casual little get-together where we can discuss the upcoming medical conference. What do you say? Gloria will keep your girlfriend busy while we talk business."

"I'd be honored, but I'm not sure about Brenda. She's been very busy at work. I don't even know if I could catch her," Luke lied, amazed at how much easier it was getting.

"Surely that little filly carries a cell phone. Give her a call, and we'll see you at seven tonight. I want you to be rested for our big trip to Connecticut tomorrow. I'm going to head downtown and get some real lunch. This stuff will rot your stomach."

Luke groaned. His lies were catching up with him, and now he was forced to produce a girlfriend that didn't exist. He thought about asking Wyatt to pose as Brenda but quickly deserted the idea as more trouble. Besides, Wyatt would never support his lying, but Brenda might. Luke would have to tell Brenda the truth and pray that she'd go along with it. He regretted now that he had transferred her case.

He sauntered back to his office and sank into his chair. LeAnne brought in a stack of messages and patient charts that needed his signature. She looked at his defeated expression. "Why the long face?"

"If you only knew. LeAnne, would you get me Brenda Turner's number?"

"My favorite patient?" she said sarcastically.

"What is it about you women and Brenda Turner?" he called after her as she left his office.

She reappeared in the doorway a few seconds later with the number. "What a chauvinistic thing to say! You've been hanging around Olgilvy too long. But since you asked, I'll take great pleasure in telling you what *my* problem is with Brenda Turner. She's got the charm of a viper. Fortunately for her, it's wrapped in a blond, blue-eyed, supermodel package. I pity the man who enters her lair." LeAnne handed him the number with a wily grin.

Luke closed the door to his office and dialed the number three times before finally pushing the last digit. He felt like an awkward teenager calling his crush for the first time. She answered immediately but groggily.

"Brenda? This is Luke Marcusson—the neurologist," he added nervously.

"I know who you are, Doctor."

"Did I wake you?" he asked gently.

"Unless you call at three A.M., you're likely to wake me. I do a lot of napping these days. Especially now that my deadline is complete until Monday when I make my presentation to our buyer. Wyatt's been helping me a lot with walking and keeping track of the plethora of pills you prescribed." *Brenda, you're doing it again.* Why she ran off at the mouth at every opportunity with Luke Marcusson was a complete mystery to her. "How is everything going with you and your new surgical career?" Brenda had missed the sound of his voice and wanted to hear him speak.

"That's actually what I'm calling about. I'm afraid I wasn't quite honest with you about my career change." Brenda thought about what Wyatt had told her about Luke being a man of integrity.

"Not honest? You?" she said softly.

"It's a long and detailed story, but it has to do with your car being in my possession. I told someone at work, stupidly, I might add, that it belonged to my girlfriend. I used your name, and now I'm being asked to bring you to a private dinner party with the chief oncology surgeon. It's tonight and if you tell me no, I would hardly blame you. But if you find it in your heart and you're not too tired, I would love to have you accompany me tonight. Frankly, it would save my hide with my new boss."

Brenda remained speechless. Was Luke Marcusson really asking her to pretend to be his girlfriend after he had dumped her as a patient? Her foolish pride told her to say no and let him handle his mess himself, but inwardly Brenda would give anything to be with Luke Marcusson, even for only a momentary charade.

"Brenda, are you still there?" Luke asked tentatively.

"Yes, I'm still here," Brenda whispered, still having trouble finding her voice.

"It was a stupid idea, and I'm sorry I bothered you."

"Luke, no, don't hang up!" she cried desperately. "What time do I have to be ready and how would you like me to dress?" She sat up in her bed, throwing her rose coverlet to the side.

"Really? You'll do it? Brenda, I would be so grateful. Dr. Olgilvy is watching me closely, and I don't want him to know I lied. I did it to save someone's feelings, but there's no excuse for it. Is six-thirty okay?"

"Only if you promise to take my car. I'm not sacrificing another pair of ten-dollar nylons to that sock-eating Pinto of yours."

Luke laughed. "Listen, that Pinto—"

"I know, I know. Wyatt told me all about your loyalty to that car. It still owes me a pair of nylons!"

"A nice dress, not too fancy, okay? And Brenda, I'm really looking forward to tonight."

"Me too, Doctor. Me too." They said good-bye and Brenda held the phone for a moment. Luke Marcusson had asked her out. Maybe it was only to help him in his ruse, but she was thankful for any opportunity to see him. After her long nap, Brenda's eyesight was really quite good. She could see clearly, although objects still seemed to spin relentlessly. She decided she would take the cane in the car with her but use Luke for her crutch if he would allow it. That way, she would look like a doting girlfriend rather than an invalid.

Brenda stood slowly, but decided she was still too fatigued to get up. She called for Wyatt. "I'm sorry I didn't get the phone, Brenda. I was unloading groceries."

"That's fine, Wyatt. It was Luke Marcusson, and I'm going to help him out on a business meeting tonight. Would you mind waking me up in an hour so I can get ready?"

"Sure. Anything else I can do?" Wyatt asked with concern in her voice and Brenda knew the cause of it. She also knew that Luke probably wouldn't want his lie shared, especially with a pillar of righteousness like Wyatt.

Brenda looked down while she spoke. "I'm just helping him out as a friend. Okay? You've been platonic friends for twelve years now; you said so yourself. That's all this is." Brenda cowered under her sheets, hoping to end the conversation.

"Luke *never* looked at me the way he looks at you, Brenda." Wyatt closed the door, and Brenda was filled with elation by her last comment. *Does he look at me differently?* Brenda stared at the ceiling with a romantic, dreamy smile.

Chapter 10

Luke arrived promptly at 6:30. Wyatt gave him a wary look as she opened the large, white door.

"I know what you're going to say, Wyatt, and you can just save it. We're friends. I explained everything to her." He stepped in and sat on the plush ivory sofa.

Wyatt followed him, pointing her finger and whispering loudly, "Luke Matthew Marcusson, that woman has just been diagnosed with multiple sclerosis. Everything in her world has just changed. Games can get out of hand and innocent people get hurt. People that can't afford to be hurt! If this job is causing you to question your values, you better step back and question this job." Wyatt calmed her angry voice when she heard footsteps. Luke knew Wyatt to be a sweet and gentle soul, but when people she cared about were involved, she was as fierce as a mother bear protecting her cubs.

"Brenda?" Luke stood immediately, unprepared for what he saw. Brenda was an astonishing vision in a fitted, deep navy dress, cut well above the knee to showcase her long, shapely legs. The tightly finished bodice was a scooped neckline with wraparound straps that bared her sexy, rounded shoulders, but kept her chest discreetly covered.

Her long blond hair flowed easily over her shoulders, and the tropical blue of her eyes lit up against the navy backdrop of her dress. A simple strand of cultured pearls hung from her elegantly sculpted neck. Luke found himself wondering whether anyone would believe that this gorgeous woman was his girlfriend. "You look absolutely beautiful," he said breathily. It was all he could manage.

"Thank you, Luke. You look very nice yourself."

Wyatt interjected, "You can thank me for that. That suit was from my wedding. You two are a sight. Let me run and get my camera." Wyatt left the room, and Luke searched for something to say.

"I can't thank you enough for doing this for me, Brenda. I should warn you that Mrs. Olgilvy tends to be a little nosy. Just so you know, I told her we met at an MS conference."

"Well, that slipped around the truth a bit. But I admire your creativity," Brenda giggled. Sharing in his charade made Brenda feel she had been let into his life. Not just his professional life, but his private life as well. She wanted to share in his triumphs and failures. She wanted to know more about who this strikingly good-looking man was inside.

"I didn't tell them about your MS. Of course, you can tell them if you like, but I wanted it to be your decision."

"Our friends are the only ones who know, and I'd just as soon keep it that way. I don't want to be defined by a disease."

"That's fine," Luke agreed.

"I may need your help getting around in the restaurant. I don't do well in public situations. Too much activity for my eyes, you know? They don't know where to focus, and I get confused easily. It was like that in the mall the other day. I think the neon lights bother me as well."

"I've heard that from some of my patients. A few of them have nicknamed it 'Wal-Mart syndrome' because it happens in stores with fluorescent lighting. I don't think you'll have to worry about that tonight. We going to *Il Fornaio*, and it has soft, dim lights for atmosphere."

"I take a lot of clients there. I'll be right at home."

Wyatt reentered the room with a small Instamatic camera in her hand. "Move over here against the fireplace." She used her hand to wave them toward the back wall. "The marble will complement your navy attire perfectly. You two look like you went shopping together. Actually, you look like Barbie and Ken," she laughed.

Luke placed his arm around Brenda's slender waistline, and the touch forced them to look into each other's eyes. The attraction was magnetic, and Luke wondered whether he would ever pry his eyes from her. The spell was broken by Wyatt's abrupt cough. The two looked up and smiled eagerly for the camera. The hunger they felt for one another was painfully obvious. Luke kept his arm around Brenda's waist and led her to the door. She selected her cane from a brass umbrella holder near the door and folded it up, placing it in her clutch purse. Luke smiled at her obvious trust in him and vowed silently that he would never let her fall.

Wyatt followed them to the door and pulled Luke back at the last minute. "I'm warning you, Luke. Watch your step," she cautioned in a small, but threatening, whisper.

❧❀❧

The buzz of whispered conversation increased in the trattoria as the radiant Brenda and imposing Luke entered the restaurant. Their height alone was enough to capture most people's fascination, but combined with their stunning good looks, eyes simply followed them. Frederick and Gloria Olgilvy stood when they entered, thrilled to be seen with the attractive couple.

Luke kept his arm protectively around Brenda's waist, as much to steady her balance as to establish ownership for all the gawking men. Brenda greeted Dr. and Mrs. Olgilvy with the utmost combination of friendliness and professionalism, and Luke marveled at her allure all over again.

"Luke tells me you're very *personally* involved at the hospital, Mrs. Olgilvy," Brenda said smoothly. Luke laughed inwardly at her translation of Mrs. Olgilvy as a busybody.

"Well, I feel a certain responsibility for my husband's staff, you know, to see that they are fulfilled personally as well as professionally," Mrs. Olgilvy droned, completely taken in by Brenda. "I'm so glad Dr. Marcusson has found someone. I can't be everywhere, you know. And I do feel such a responsibility for my husband's staff," Gloria said.

Brenda gazed at Luke dreamily and stroked his arm, taking hold of his hand, sending shivers through his body. "I'm so relieved to know someone protects him from all those beautiful nurses." Brenda smiled easily, and Luke had to look away to keep from laughing.

"My dear, you don't know how lucky you are to have such a man. Professional, ethical, and I daresay he gives Mel Gibson a run for his money." Mrs. Olgilvy threw Luke a flirtatious grin.

"Enough of such frivolity. Luke tells me you're a vice president for a high-tech company. Which one?" Dr. Olgilvy asked.

"Star Digital, Dr. Olgilvy. We make set-top boxes for home entertainment satellite systems."

"Call me Frederick, please. Are you public yet?" he asked, obviously hoping for a stock tip.

Frederick? In all the years Luke had worked in the same hospital as Dr. Olgilvy, no one had ever been invited to address him as Frederick. Dr. Olgilvy hadn't even mentioned the upcoming medical conference and, somehow, Luke doubted he would.

"We're not public yet, but that may change soon," Brenda said with a smile.

She made polite and endearing small talk throughout the entire meal. She ate daintily, but managed to polish off a Caesar salad, a plate of *Penne al Forno,* and tiramisu for dessert, without an obvious break in the conversation. Truly, she had elevated her wiles to an art form, and Luke was beginning to understand why perceptive women despised her. Luke didn't see her as deceitful, though; he saw her as a beautiful chameleon able to change colors for her particular audience. He was fascinated by her but relished the thought of being alone with her later to have the *real* Brenda Turner return. The Brenda who would giggle endlessly over their triumph, the woman who fought her chronic illness with dignity and style, ignoring the MS when possible and accommodating it when necessary.

After dinner, Luke escorted Brenda to the car slowly, careful to let her overworked eyes and equilibrium adjust. They had left after the Olgilvys so that Brenda could wobble out of the restaurant without being noticed. Luke was enraptured by the return of the natural, fun-loving Brenda that relished every moment of their game.

"I enjoyed the dinner. Thank you so much for inviting me. Dr. and Mrs. Olgilvy are quite charming. I think you were a little hard on her. Her heart's in the right place." Brenda laughed lightheartedly, and Luke listened with pleasure.

"Tell me she's not annoying after she sets *you* up on a date!"

"Now why would she do that? Apparently, I already have the most eligible, handsome brain surgeon at Stanford," Brenda teased. "By the way, I hope you didn't have your eye on any cute nurses. I daresay Mrs. Olgilvy will be watching out for me."

Luke couldn't take it anymore. He stopped in his tracks along the populated University Avenue and pulled Brenda into his arms, searching the tropical blue of her eyes. "Brenda, a man can only take so much temptation." He drew her closer still and kissed her deliberately, his desire overwhelming him. He felt her kiss him back, and he embraced her tighter still, closing his hand firmly around the back of her long, elegant neck. The two became lost in the moment, kissing each other freely, unconcerned with the bustling life around them. Luke ran his hands through her silky long hair, engaging the nape of her neck with both hands to keep her locked in his fiery embrace.

A passing car honked, and Luke suddenly realized where he was and who he was with. He separated immediately, getting a hold on his consuming desire. "Brenda, I shouldn't have. I–I don't know what to say." Luke watched her blush and look away under the golden streetlight and knew he'd said the wrong thing. Of course he wanted to kiss her. Of course he knew what he was doing. Of course he wanted more. *More lies.*

"No, it's quite all right, Luke. Apparently, we got a little caught up in our one-act play. Let's just get home, shall we?" Luke recognized her standard cold response, the way she acted when hurt. He remembered it from when he had transferred her case. He wanted to hit himself for being the one to lose control. Wyatt had warned him. God had used Wyatt and Barry to warn him, but he hadn't heeded. Inwardly, he'd always known he wouldn't be able to handle the temptation of Brenda Turner.

Now that he had traveled too far down his dark path, he would have to desert her, for her own sake as well as his own.

God had commanded that a couple not be unequally yoked, but for the first time, Luke had questions. His passion spoke with a deafening fanfare, while God's voice seemed but a whisper.

≈❀❀❀≈

Brenda banished the simple front-step good-night from her memory and concentrated on the earlier passion of Luke's kiss. His memory filled her with warmth, and she knew that *this* was the man for her. Surely, his God would never keep two such compatible people apart. What kind of God would do that? She lay awake in bed and contemplated the thought. Her body ached from MS exhaustion and pain, but her mind was filled with pleasure. She closed her eyes, unable to believe that she, such an active, athletic woman only two weeks ago, would be worn-out from a simple dinner.

She heard the front door shut and knew that Wyatt must finally be home. The nurse came to check on her and found her dreamily lying awake next to the soft light of a single, rose-scented candle.

"Brenda, did you have fun?" she asked cautiously.

"We had a wonderful time, Wyatt. He was an absolute gentlemen and he kept a tight hold on me. I looked the picture of health. He was charming and handsome and attentive. . .and he kissed me. He kissed me like I've never been kissed before. It was seductive and sweet and romantic and exhausting. I've never felt this way about a man before." She looked up at Wyatt, whose face was ghostly white. "I know how you feel about the religious thing, but God wouldn't want to deny our happiness. I know He wouldn't." Brenda smiled happily. "I think I love him. I know that's naive—I hardly know him, but I feel like I've known him forever."

Wyatt sighed loudly and somberly sat down on the edge of the bed. "Brenda, you're right. God wouldn't want to deny His people happiness. And that's why He's set up rules for us to live by. Just because something *feels* right doesn't mean it is. The most important thing to Luke is God, Brenda. You will never be number one. Will you be able to deal with that? Being second to a God you don't believe is really there? I know you don't have much experience with men. I want you to understand that as women, we tend to be more emotional, letting our feelings run away with us. Many times, men let their emotions run away as well, in the name of sexual desire. Brenda, I'm not trying to say Luke's kiss didn't mean anything. I'm just trying to prepare you, in case he ends it. Remember, he's got his heart set on that job at Baylor."

"Wyatt, don't look at me that way with pity in your eyes. Luke *wants* to be with me. I know he does. I know by his kiss. I may not be very experienced with men, but this goes beyond experience. It's something I feel in the deepest part of my heart."

"I'm not saying he doesn't *want* to be with you. I'm just saying it wouldn't work out. Without a spiritual compatibility to build on, there's no basis for a relationship. Luke knows that. And when he thinks about it, he'll come to his senses. Brenda, I know that sounds harsh, but you'd truly have a life of pain after the excitement of courtship wore off. Barry, Katie, Jacob, and I—we're all just trying to protect you. We all love you, both of you."

"You're jealous, aren't you? You've always been Luke's confidante, and you're afraid I'll get in the way, aren't you?" Brenda spat, tears streaking freely down her cheeks.

Wyatt clung tightly to Brenda's hand, "Brenda, I would never do anything to hurt you or Luke. I love you both, and I would like nothing more than to see you come to know Jesus in a personal way. That's what God and Luke both want too.

Let me get something for you to read. Are your eyes doing okay?" Wyatt relinquished Brenda's hand and left the bedroom. She returned shortly with a small tract in her hand and, when Brenda refused to take it, she set it on the nightstand.

After the door was closed, Brenda threw the tract across the room and sobbed herself to sleep.

Chapter 11

L uke packed his suit in a garment bag and wished he had time to go shopping. He hated to spend the money, but this would be the third time in a week that Dr. Olgilvy would see him in the same suit. In all Luke's tenure at Stanford, he'd never once worried about his appearance, but suddenly his suit was outdated and his car decrepit. This job was definitely forcing him to make some changes in his attitudes, and Luke hoped it was for the better. *Certainly there's nothing wrong with a doctor owning a reliable car and a decent suit.* He zipped the garment bag and shaving kit and set everything by the door while he waited for Barry.

Luke took the quiet moment and knelt down to pray. He found himself begging forgiveness for his lying and the kiss he'd stolen from Brenda the previous night. Then he thought about her warmth and the curve of her body and found himself asking for forgiveness again in the middle of his prayer. *Lord, You know my thoughts. Please, Lord, let her accept You and become an acceptable wife for me. I don't want to think of the alternative, but Your will be done.*

The young surgeon got off his knees just as the doorbell rang. Barry Ross stood at the door, an unhappy frown crossing his full face. "Wyatt's mighty angry at you, and I can't say I blame her." Barry's lumbering frame filled the doorway, and he walked past Luke without shaking his hand.

"Nice to see you too," Luke said dejectedly while he motioned toward the simple, beige couch that was centered in the colorless room. "Have a seat." No paintings graced the walls and the off-white carpeting and white walls provided a sense of blankness. The same way Luke felt. He started to explain, "I thought I could handle it. She would impress the Olgilvys and I would get rid of Nurse Moore and be off to Baylor before anything came of it. It started out as a simple plan, but you've seen Brenda. It's not just her looks either. I'm not *that* shallow. In all my years of practice, I've never met anyone like her. It's her inner strength—the way she handles everything with such grace and ease. She makes me laugh, and I want to know more about her. Every time I learn something new, I want to know more. Her appeal is captivating and infectious. You should have seen her with Olgilvy. That man didn't talk a word of medicine last night. He sat utterly entranced."

"Luke, I'm not blaming you for being attracted to her. I'm blaming you for allowing things to progress to a point where you're both going to get hurt. What happens when Wyatt and I leave? You and Katie are all Brenda has, Luke. Have you seen anyone else around since she was diagnosed? When you finally realize that Brenda does not share your salvation, who's left to pick up the pieces? Do you expect her to handle this alone?"

"I'm not going to abandon her, if that's what you're worried about."

"So that means you're not moving to Texas if Baylor calls?"

Luke knew he was caught. He hadn't thought it through. "I don't know. . .but I'm buying a house here. Brenda's right. I'm paying too much in taxes; so for now, I guess, I'm staying put. Brenda's going to help me house hunt," Luke offered.

"I thought you decided that wasn't a good idea," Barry challenged.

"Well, I changed my mind. I'm getting too old to live in this unadorned abyss. I still live like a college grunt instead of a practicing neurologist." Luke knew he was justifying his time with Brenda. He knew God wasn't condoning his actions, yet he couldn't leave her while she needed him. House hunting seemed the perfect ruse.

"You've got three days to exact a plan that makes sense, and I hope you find your answer in prayer!" Barry paused and looked around. "What is up with this apartment? This place looks exactly like it did five years ago. Aren't there furniture stores around here?"

Luke looked around at his bare walls and his desertlike environment and laughed. Barry grimaced. "You're one of a kind, my friend. Maybe you ought to hang that expensive bike on the wall for decoration! Come on, or we'll miss our flight."

~ ❈❊❈ ~

Brenda slept until noon, her tired body aching from her evening out to dinner. She dreamed of coffee but found herself unable to lift her body from the bed. Staring at the clock, she tried to make out the time, but her overworked eyes were like wild little boys on a play yard. She closed her eyes, willing the accompanying nausea to go away. She didn't even have the energy to yell for Wyatt but thanked her lucky stars when the young nurse appeared.

"Last night too much for you?" Wyatt asked with concern, placing coffee on the marble-topped nightstand.

"Ooh, my aching head is swimming. I feel like there are bees buzzing in the back of my brain, and my eyesight is gone again. Just jumping colors, and I'm sick to my stomach. I just want this moving to stop. . .oh, please, just make it stop." Brenda clutched her temples and gripped her hair, pulling it in frustration.

"So, I take it you'll be staying in today?"

Brenda's speech was slurred, and her words slow; her symptoms were worse than ever. "I don't have a choice. It's too bad I don't drink alcohol. I could save a lot of money!"

"Someone seems to be forgetting a major presentation on Monday," Wyatt said, while trying to help her patient sit up. "The most important part of your career. Or was that just an exaggeration for my benefit?"

"No, I'm just resting so I'll be able to go through with it. I've learned a valuable lesson. I can't push my body like I used to. It just doesn't work that way. Instead of working overtime, it just shuts down and says no. Even my mouth feels like it's coming off novocaine. You know that feeling after the dentist? Oh, my whole head is buzzing." Brenda held her head in her hands and prayed that her head would stop spinning.

"Then we agree you're spending the day in bed." Wyatt lifted the floral coverlet over Brenda's shoulders and felt her head for a fever. This was no bug. It was all multiple sclerosis. Brenda had allowed her constant activity to further the intensity of her present bout with the disease.

Brenda moaned. "Trust me; you'll get no arguments from me." Motivated by the coffee sitting on the nightstand, she forced herself to sit up, but as she reached for the cup, her body slid sideways toward the center of the bed. Wyatt fluffed the pillows behind her and lifted Brenda to an upright position, but it was no use—she had lost her equilibrium. All she could manage was lying down. "You were right about overworking this body."

"The fewer exacerbations you have, the more likely you'll always fully recover. That's why we've been nagging you to slow down. Would you like to live with this permanently?"

Brenda grabbed her head again. "I don't want to live like this for one more minute!" she exclaimed. "Wyatt, what have I done? I can't beat this thing. This isn't some pushover client."

"You've got the whole weekend to recover. I'll go rent some movies, and we'll *listen* to the classics until the weekend is over." Wyatt held Brenda and steadied her cup to give her a sip of coffee. "Here, take your medications."

"I can't drink any more until I visit the ladies' room," Brenda confessed. Wyatt helped her out of bed, and Brenda sank to the floor on her hands and knees. "Don't mind me—it's just easier this way. I have more of an idea where the floor is." She laughed at her own appearance and proceeded on all fours to feel her way to the bathroom.

Wyatt called after her, through the closed door. "I think we should call Dr. Wilhelm about another corticosteroid run. You have an appointment this afternoon anyway."

Brenda's demeanor changed instantly and terror filled her voice. "No, Wyatt, not that. The pills are bad enough; I don't want to do another IV. Please, let me just see if I can sleep the damage off this weekend with the steroid pills. Change the appointment. I don't want to get dressed today. If I'm not better by Monday, I'll tell Dr. Wilhelm to go ahead." Brenda pleaded through the door.

"What about your presentation?" Wyatt asked, hoping to provide the necessary encouragement Brenda needed to fight her symptoms.

"Whatever happens, happens. I don't care."

"That statement elates me and worries me at the same time. Brenda? Talk to me." Wyatt rapped gently on the door.

Brenda opened the bathroom door, and Wyatt adjusted her eyes to the floor where she came crawling out. "What's the difference? What use am I to anybody like this?"

"Listen to me. Depression is a big part of this disease, and I see you sinking into it. You've got to live victoriously, do you understand? If you can't do it on your own, then I'm going to get you a prescription. I won't let this disease take your will."

"No more pills! I can't take it anymore. Pills to fight inflammation, pills to fight fatigue, pills to fight dizziness, pills to fight ulcers from all the medications, vitamins for the holistic route. No more! What good is a happy invalid? I *want* to wallow in it! Do you think Luke would want me if he could see me crawling to the toilet? I'm just one of his pathetic patients now. No neurologist is stupid enough to get involved with a disease he knows that well."

"Brenda, your life is not futile because you have multiple sclerosis. Luke knows you have MS, but that didn't stop him from thinking you were the one to impress Stanford's chief of neuro oncology."

"Do you think he'd still ask if he could see me today? And what about my CEO? Do you think he'd trust me? Entrust the future of Star Digital to a woman who can't stand on two feet. I'm useless like this, and I *want* to be miserable, so leave me alone!" Brenda crawled into bed and pulled the cover over her head, hoping Wyatt would get the hint and leave. Wyatt remained, seemingly ready for a battle.

"So you're just going to feel sorry for yourself?" Wyatt asked gently and without malice.

Brenda peeked out of the covers. "Yes, I have that right, you know. Not everything in this life is rainbows and gumdrops like you and Katie see it. I was perfectly healthy two weeks ago. Why shouldn't I feel sorry for myself? You have your health, a husband, and a life. I have this house and my job. And who knows what will happen now that I'm completely blinded by this stupid disease or now that I can't stand from dizziness. I may lose everything I have, so pardon my anger! Luke doesn't even think I'm good enough to be on his research project, much less in his life! He knows I'm not getting any better, doesn't he? It has nothing to do with your God!"

Wyatt's sweet demeanor took on a hard edge. "You may mock Katie and me for our optimism, but, Brenda, I've had children die in my arms from lack of money for a simple inoculation. Katie has had teens from her Bible study shot dead in the street, and now she may lose her son to a system that doesn't care about that child! We're no strangers to suffering, Brenda, but I'll tell you what. My God is bigger than all the suffering in the world! You're just as diseased in your soul as from MS. And the sooner you wake up to that fact, the better off you'll be. I suppose life looks bleak right now, but if the worst thing that could happen to you is losing this house, consider yourself fortunate." Wyatt slammed the door and left Brenda wallowing in her self-pity and anger.

"That's supposed to make me feel better? Somebody's got it worse, so count my blessings! That's easy to say when you're standing up!" She shouted at the closed door, but her comment was answered only by the sound of the front door slamming. Suddenly, Brenda was alone and scared. *Wyatt wouldn't just leave without saying good-bye, would she?* Brenda allowed herself to give way to tears and soon she was sobbing hysterically, both for herself and the possible loss of her new friend.

She wanted to call Katie to come and stay with her in her present darkness, but there was no way she could find her phone number and dial it herself. Brenda just continued to cry. *They don't care about me anyway. If they did, I'd still be Luke's patient, not a reject he knows won't get him that promotion. He's just making Wyatt do his dirty work, so he can be through with it. I was right to vow never to get married. Men only complicate matters. I've got to concentrate on this sale at work and forget about Luke Marcusson.*

⤙❦❧⤚

Wyatt slammed the front door of Luke's waiting area, and several startled patients looked up at the commotion. She looked around and apologized, "I'm sorry; the door got away from me," she explained, but her frustration showed in her pained expression.

LeAnne came to the reception window and grinned. "Wyatt Ross, what a pleasure! But I'm afraid only Dr. Byer is in today. Luke isn't here. He's in Connecticut at a conference."

"I know. Barry's with him. I'm actually here to see if I can borrow a wheelchair."

"A wheelchair? Certainly. Do you know when you might be able to return it?"

"I'm not sure. If my patient continues to need one, I suppose we'll have to buy one. In the meantime, I'd rather not spend her money if it's not necessary. I'm leaving next week, so I suppose we'll do something about it before then."

"This isn't for Brenda Turner, is it?"

"Please don't get me started, LeAnne. It's been a very trying day, and I'm struggling to understand God's will," Wyatt confessed.

"I'm sorry, Wyatt. Just a second, and I'll get the wheelchair for you." LeAnne disappeared for a moment and reappeared with a silver wheelchair, an ancient relic that looked like it weighed a ton.

"I should have known Luke's wheelchairs would be prototypes," Wyatt joked, and LeAnne laughed out loud. "Well, I suppose it's better than nothing."

Wyatt needed to cool down after her confrontation with Brenda, and she allowed herself the luxury of lunch at her favorite salad bar. She bought a magazine and spent a relaxing afternoon walking around Stanford Shopping Center, the kind of expensive place she could only afford to window-shop. It was after four before she returned to Brenda's home and found the patient in a hard sleep.

※※※

Brenda finally awoke at five o'clock and was thrilled to hear Wyatt moving about in the kitchen. "Wyatt?"

She rushed to the room. "Brenda, how are you feeling?"

"Hungry. What else is new? They might as well give you a twenty-pound roast at the drugstore when you pick up these steroids. I just want to eat everything in sight."

"It'll get better. You won't be on those high doses forever. I called Dr. Wilhelm today. He wants me to keep a close eye on you in case your depression gets worse. He says you're probably still dealing with the reality of onset."

"Constant spinning, blinding darkness. That sounds a little depressing, doesn't it?"

Wyatt left the room and returned with the big, ugly wheelchair. "Get up. We're going out to dinner."

"I don't want to go out to dinner. I don't want people feeling sorry for me."

"Don't worry, where we're going no one's going to pity you. Get up or I'm leaving and you can find a new nurse," Wyatt threatened. Brenda was astounded at the show of force from such a normally meek character.

Convinced Wyatt was serious, Brenda pulled herself out of bed and crouched down to the floor. Wyatt pulled a pair of loose-fitting jeans from the closet and grabbed a company T-shirt from Brenda's drawer. Brenda felt the clothes. "I don't want to wear this."

"Get them on—now," Wyatt said, leaving no room for argument.

Brenda did as she was told and crawled out the front door. She watched the outline of Wyatt struggling with the heavy wheelchair down the front porch steps. Brenda gripped her way down the stairs and felt her way into the wheelchair. She brushed off her soiled knees, trying to salvage some semblance of pride.

Brenda fell asleep in the car and awoke as her BMW came to a stop. "Where are we?" she asked groggily.

"We're at the restaurant. Stay here until I get the wheelchair."

Brenda just nodded, hoping they were somewhere she could get a huge steak. While on the prednisone, Brenda had been craving red meat, something she hardly touched otherwise. Wyatt came around to the passenger side with the bulky chair and helped Brenda maintain her upright position while she got in. Wyatt then placed two pillow on each side of her. "These will keep you from slipping." Brenda looked up with innocently fearful eyes, but Wyatt was unmoved.

Brenda willed her eyes to focus on the single-story building in front of her. There was a line out the door and no other businesses around. Everything she saw was in fuzzy, outline form; there was no clarity in anything. They seemed to be in an industrial part of town; that was obvious by the oversized barrels stored behind cement fences. Wyatt parked the wheelchair behind the last person and slowly inched it forward as the gathering moved. "Where are we, some kind of buffet?" Brenda asked snobbishly.

"You might say that." Wyatt's tone gave nothing away and Brenda wondered when her beloved, sweet-hearted nurse would return. Or had she ruined this relationship too?

Brenda could hear the laughter and giggles of children. She heard people walk past her and say hello. She lifted her chin in greeting in case they were talking to her. Once inside the building, the lack of sun helped Brenda's eyesight and she finally concluded where Wyatt had taken her. "This is a soup kitchen!" she gasped.

"It's a Christian homeless shelter for families in transition," Wyatt corrected. "I suggest you keep your voice down so you don't offend anybody."

"Why on earth would you bring me here?"

"You told me the worst thing that could happen to you was that you might lose your house and your job. Well, here we are. These people have all been there. None of them has a home or a well-paying job. Do they look defeated?"

Brenda fought her eyes to focus, finally covering one to avoid the double vision. She saw smiling families sitting at the tables, praying over their meals, laughing at each others' jokes, and enjoying the hearty meals in front of them.

"Most of these people trust the Lord, and I can tell you that they are living victoriously. It may not look like it to you because you see them from the steps of a Victorian home in Palo Alto. But look closely at their faces. Do they *look* poor?"

Brenda was incensed; her body shook with anger that Wyatt would stoop so low. "So are we going to Bob Cratchett's house next to have a look at Tiny Tim? Maybe then, I'll repent and understand the evil of my ways."

"Brenda Turner, you are no better than these people. You *think* your money separates you from them, but God may take that wall away, so you might want to wipe that smug attitude from your personality," Wyatt said with an uncharacteristic sting in her voice.

A stout Mexican woman approached them with a tray in her hand. She bent over to look Brenda in the eye, reminding her she wasn't invisible. The Hispanic woman spoke in broken English, "I see you in chair. Very hard to get close to server, tables so tight, so I bring food." The woman placed the tray on a table and moved the regular chair from around a table to make room for Brenda. She then pushed Brenda's chair toward the plate. "If you need anything, yell for Yolanda."

There was nothing for Brenda to say but "thank you."

"You get used to system. Everybody friendly here—we trust Christ our Lord for His goodness. No worries." She said as she hobbled away with a limp. Wyatt followed after her and got a plate for herself before sitting across the table from Brenda.

"What has God done for these people? What do they possibly have to thank Him for?" Brenda was exasperated how people in such horrid conditions could praise a God they couldn't see for things He hadn't provided.

"They have a roof over their heads, food in their stomachs, and their families together. What more is there?"

"Life!" Brenda exclaimed.

"You mean a BMW, a stately home in the right neighborhood, that type of thing?"

"Yes, I guess I do. What's wrong with that?"

"Those things will all burn and the people that trusted in them along with it. The things these people are investing in, their God, their families, their assets, are eternal. Your investments could be wiped out with the next big earthquake." Wyatt let the affront sink in for a moment, then added, "We're here, so enjoy. This is what God gave us today. Brenda, these people all have a thousand times what any of our patients in Africa have. God has blessed them richly."

Brenda ignored the God talk. If Wyatt wanted to belong to the God squad that was her choice, but Brenda knew better. She knew that relying on God was something that weak people did to give themselves comfort. So be it. She wasn't going to change Wyatt's mind. Wyatt had invested her whole life in believing in the invisible crutch just like Brenda's own parents had done.

"This tastes great! What is it?" Brenda was shocked by the quality of the food on the plate before her. She ravaged the meal, unable to control her ravenous appetite from the steroids.

"It's homemade tamales. The woman that runs the shelter is an expert Mexican chef," Wyatt replied.

Brenda was famished and finished her plate before Wyatt had even eaten one tamale. "Can I get more?" Brenda, though embarrassed, held up her empty plate. Who would have thought a homeless shelter would serve such an excellent meal? *No wonder these people don't bother looking for work.*

"I suppose you can have more now. The line is gone. That means anything remaining is free for seconds." Wyatt screeched her chair as she got up to get Brenda more, but before she left, Yolanda appeared with another plate of food.

"Thank you so much. How did you know?" Brenda stammered.

"You like my daughter. She skin and bones, but she eat like a horse."

Brenda laughed aloud and suddenly forgot where she was. She looked around her again and noticed no one was staring at her. When people had finished eating, they cleared their plates and stacked them on a corner table. Brenda was amazed by the organization of it all, like a well-oiled machine.

Following dinner, Brenda motioned to Wyatt to come close. "If these people can follow this system so easily, why can't they follow society's system and keep a job?"

"In Silicon Valley? How many well-paying jobs do you think there are for uneducated, unskilled workers, most of whom have never learned the language?"

"That's their fault. There must be fifty different trade schools in the area. Just about anyone could learn to be an electronics technician or computer repairman, and English programs are a dime a dozen."

"What about tuition?"

"The government offers hundreds of grants. They're all over the Internet."

"Well, you're right. We'll just tell them when they're finished here at the homeless shelter to run home and check their computer for the proper grants to get their education and when they're through with that, they can hire a nanny to watch their children while they get trained."

"Okay, I'll give you that, but anybody could get a job at a fast-food restaurant, and Congress just upped the minimum wage, so where's the problem?"

"First of all, Brenda, five dollars an hour isn't going to support a family and secondly, all the minimum wage hike will do in most of these people's cases is reduce the number of hours employers can hire their workers. What's the first thing you ask on a application, Brenda? Where a person lives. What's the first thing you look at? Their appearance. Since these people don't have access to an address or proper interviewing attire, their prospects are nil. It's a big, negative cycle. Stop and look at the facts, Brenda. You think you have all the answers, but until you've walked a mile in their shoes, you have no idea what they face." Wyatt seemed personally offended by Brenda's belief system, and the young executive could not understand it. It wasn't Wyatt she was talking about.

Chapter 12

By Saturday morning at the medical conference, Luke was ready to clobber his fellow Stanford surgeon. Dr. Olgilvy had made a career living off his reputation and ultimately acted as though the entire neurological community should bow at his feet. Luke was expected to follow at a respectable distance and remain handy in case the proud doctor needed any support backing up his claims.

Luke had an hour before his next forum was scheduled to begin, and he set about searching for Barry, a lunch companion he could stomach. He saw his distraught friend coming toward him and knew by the expression that Barry had not fared well with the pharmaceutical companies. "No luck?"

Barry shook his head in defeat. "They've got me figured out already. One sales rep told another, and now they all run when they see me coming. Sort of like you *working* doctors do to them."

"It'll happen. Let's go have lunch away from this ritzy hotel. Preferably someplace downtrodden that Frederick Olgilvy would never think to enter." Luke exited the hotel quickly, so as not to be noticed by Olgilvy.

They walked across the busy street to a diner named Fat's Place and sat down at the counter. An older waitress with jet-black hair stood silent, holding her pad in expectation. Luke ordered a turkey on wheat with an iced tea, and Barry ordered the meat loaf special and milk. The woman tore off a page and placed it on a wheel above the steel opening.

Luke lifted his tea toward Barry and cheered, "Here's to job misery!" The two glasses clinked and both men looked straight ahead into the steel kitchen. "So who's next on your pharmaceutical hit list?"

"I'm done for the day. Perhaps they'll be more generous on Sunday," Barry said halfheartedly.

"I'll listen to a few pitches this afternoon and see if I have any luck. If they think it will get them closer to Olgilvy, we may have an advantage."

"That'd be great. I'm losing momentum. Besides, I promised Wyatt I'd look up Brenda's brother while I was here. He lives around here somewhere, and the ride will do me good. It'll give me something else to think about. Poor girl doesn't have any family out West."

"You're seeing Brenda's brother?"

Barry nodded. "Why?"

"I thought Brenda didn't want him to be bothered with her disease," Luke said. "She said he had enough to worry about with his family." He was astonished that Brenda would encourage such a visit. She always seemed so confident and self-assured about life on her own. He couldn't imagine her wanting someone to contact her family for her; it just didn't seem in her character.

"I'm not going to tell him about the MS. I'm just going to tell him Brenda wanted me to look him up. He can take it from there, if he chooses to."

"And *does* Brenda want you to look him up?" Luke asked warily.

"That's what Wyatt tells me. Although, something tells me I probably should have asked Brenda myself," Barry said doubtfully.

"Where Wyatt's concerned, that probably wouldn't have done you any good, anyway." They both laughed at Wyatt's gentle manner for getting what she wanted.

"Why don't you sit in on the forum this afternoon, and I'll join you? I'd love to meet Brenda's brother," Luke suggested, anxious to know more about Brenda.

The two men finished their meals and left a sizable tip before crossing the street and entering the elegant hotel once again. Luke was accosted by Dr. Olgilvy as soon as he entered the lobby.

At Luke's afternoon forum, Dr. Olgilvy, truly a pioneer in his field, engaged his audience of doctors. Luke began wondering whether this experience was worth working with the arrogant Dr. Olgilvy. *Perhaps Baylor will have called by the time I get back,* he hoped.

Luke snapped to attention when he heard his name. "And in conclusion, I would just like to extend my congratulations to Dr. Luke Marcusson, Stanford's new assistant chief surgeon in our neurosurgery department." Luke shot his head around to make sure he'd heard correctly. With everyone staring at him in the room, he knew he had. Olgilvy had given him the sought-after promotion in front of all of Luke's peers.

Luke didn't know whether to be elated at the boost to his career or infuriated that Olgilvy hadn't bothered to tell him beforehand. He just knew he wanted to escape and pretend he'd never heard it mentioned.

Luke stood up and went to the podium, shaking hands with the man he equally admired and despised. He tried to see him as God did, but try as he might, he was disgusted by his aggressive, tactless, grandstanding behavior. Would Baylor even consider him now that he was the "property" of Frederick Ogilvy? Luke prayed silently for God's peace and began, "I am deeply honored that my surgical skills have been recognized by such a talent in the field, and I hope that our collaboration will eventually rid this world of fatal neurological tumors forever." Luke knew his speech was banal at best, but he was so thrown by Frederick's announcement, he was at a loss for intelligent communication.

Their collaboration. In his short, ill-prepared address, he had accepted the position. Was there really a choice? He had been offered a dream position in front of his peers, any one of whom would have taken the job in a heartbeat. Declining would have been career suicide. Was God telling him to stay put or was Luke being corralled because of his own lies? Thinking back to Brenda's Oscar-winning performance and the steamy kiss they'd shared, Luke knew that this was his own doing.

Luke headed quickly toward Barry. "Follow me and act like we have somewhere to go. I need to escape." He and Barry smiled at well-wishers while jogging casually toward the exit. They soon dashed into a waiting yellow taxi at the curb.

"Where to?" the driver asked.

"Just drive; I'll have an address for you in a minute." Barry fumbled through his pockets and came up with the crumpled pink Post-It that Wyatt had given him. "It's 127 Briar Lane, in Kent."

Luke gazed at him inquisitively. "Where are we going?"

"Brenda's brother's. It'll get your mind off it. Besides, we have nearly an hour's drive. That'll keep you out of Olgilvy's path for the night, until you figure a way out of this mess."

"An hour's drive? Whoa, my friend. It would be a whole lot less expensive to rent a car. Hey, driver, pull over here, please."

The cab driver eased to the curb in front of the Hilton. After paying the fare for their three-block-long adventure, the two men stepped into the lobby of the hotel. Although they were not guests at this hotel, the concierge was able to make arrangements for a rental car, and within a half hour they were on the road to Kent.

"It's a good thing I brought my Visa card along," said Luke. "I don't like to use it, but I carry it for emergencies like this." He steered the Ford Taurus onto the turnpike. "They didn't have any Pintos left, so I had to settle for this one," he joked, but Barry didn't laugh.

"Luke, there's something I need to say," Barry began soberly. "I've watched you change since you started working with Dr. Olgilvy, and I don't like it. I never thought you enjoyed this job, and when you dressed Brenda up and paraded her in front of Olgilvy like some type of trophy, I knew you weren't thinking straight. This is a good job, Luke, but it needs to be right for you."

Luke nodded defeatedly.

"You're not arguing with me? Are you ill?" Barry asked.

"I miss my patients and the research. I've been so involved in their lives, involved in making advancements in their quality of life. I don't get the same satisfaction with the surgery. Of course, I love seeing them beat the cancer too, but just my hands are involved, not my heart. At least, not the way it is with my neurology patients, who count on me so personally. Being there to have the same conversation every day with an Alzheimer's patient may sound routine, but the day their true personality comes back, there's nothing like it! It's why I became a doctor."

"There's the spark, Luke. Neurology is your answer."

"Do I have an answer? Do you think Olgilvy will accept my resignation without destroying my career? And what will leaving say to my peers? That I couldn't hack it, that's what. Quitting will make me a failure in neurology too. I've got no choice."

"I never thought about it, but I think you're right," Barry stated simply.

Luke rubbed his hand across his forehead. "Got any room in Africa?"

"Look at the bright side. You no longer have a huge decision dangling before you."

Luke kept his head bowed, trying to figure a way from the web he had tangled around himself.

Arriving in Kent before the evening sun had dropped, they approached a quaint New England farmhouse and knocked on the door. A teenage girl with a remarkable resemblance to Brenda answered the door, followed by her father.

Barry stammered, "We were looking for Doug and Kelly Turner." He looked again at the address on the Post-It and compared it to the house number.

"I'm Doug Turner, and this is my daughter, Kaitlyn. How can I help you?"

Luke and Barry looked at one another in shock as if they had stepped into a time warp. "Again, Mr. Turner, I'm sorry. We were under the impression that your daughter was five. I'm Dr. Luke Marcusson, and this is my associate, Dr. Barry Ross." Luke rarely attached his doctor status before his name, but he was hoping to add to their credibility to cover for their vast confusion. "We're friends of your sister Brenda and we were out here on business. We were hoping—" The door slammed in their faces and the doctors gazed at one another in wonder.

The door quickly opened again and Doug Turner stepped out onto the porch. "Look gentlemen, I'm sorry to kill the messengers, but as far as I'm concerned, I don't have a sister."

"Your daughter looks remarkably like her aunt. Does Kaitlyn know about her?" Barry asked hopefully.

"Like I said, I don't have a sister, and there's no sense dragging my children though the ugly scenes of the past."

"Your sister's ill," Luke offered as an olive branch, hoping to reach her brother's heart.

"Even if she were dying, there isn't a breathing relative who would attend her funeral," Doug replied curtly.

"Mr. Turner, I don't know what's happened in the past, but Brenda still has your daughter's picture on her mantel. She obviously cares."

"You know nothing about it. And if my sister was so concerned about her family ties, she'd know that Kaitlyn is now thirteen and she'd stop living in the past. She'd know that Kaitlyn has two brothers, nine and eight. I wish you the best of luck with her, but she has no family as far as I'm concerned. Good evening." He stepped back inside the house, leaving Luke and Barry staring at each other on the front step.

"Apparently, Wyatt did not clear our visit with Brenda," Barry said as they walked back to the car.

"Apparently." The two men clambered into the car to begin the long drive back to the city. "I'm afraid Brenda's lack of friends extends to family as well." Luke looked at his hands set firmly on the wheel. How he ached for Brenda. Beautiful Brenda, without God, without her health, and without her family. Luke wished he could go to her and help crumble the cold exterior she used to protect herself, but he knew only God could do that.

Barry broke into his thoughts. "No wonder she's a workaholic."

❧❦❧

Sunday morning seemed as bleak to Brenda as the day before. The sunshine invaded the darkness of her closed eyes, and she mourned the beautiful weather she couldn't see clearly. *Will I ever leave this wheelchair? Will I ever see Luke's handsome face clearly again?* Brenda's soft sobs began. Her face was red and her nose swollen from her many tears, but still they persisted unabated.

"Brenda, why don't you come to church with me this morning?" Wyatt's voice invaded the blindness. Brenda shook her head violently. "Come on, just to get out. No one will know you. What's the difference if they see you in a wheelchair?" She paused for a reaction. "I'll buy you breakfast afterward," she added.

"Hobee's?" came the meek but hopeful reply.

"Hobee's it is," Wyatt agreed.

Brenda crawled out of bed and over to her Georgian armoire across the room. She pulled out lingerie and crawled humbly to the bathroom with the unmentionables in her mouth.

"You're getting good at doing things yourself. I'm proud of you."

"Well, if you ever need a pet, I'm quite good at fetching things."

"I wouldn't take you. You eat too much. I'd be better off with a Great Dane," Wyatt cracked. Noticing the tears again, Wyatt immediately apologized. "Brenda, I was just trying to lighten your mood, Honey. I'm sorry I hurt your feelings. You're in the depths of this bout, but you'll pull through; I know you will."

Brenda climbed to her feet, using the bed as a ladder and threw herself into Wyatt's arms, weeping with all her heart. "I hate this disease! What kind of disease takes away your abilities and self-respect within two weeks? Who ever heard of being so dizzy you need a wheelchair? If somebody told me that a month ago, I would have said they were crazy! I would have said they needed a psychologist, not a neurologist. I didn't even know what a neurologist did!" Brenda's deep, heart-wrenching sobs broke her sentences into syllables.

"Go ahead and cry." Wyatt felt her own tears coming on, and the two women locked in a weepy embrace.

When Brenda felt better, she pulled away. "Wyatt, I'd give anything to have my health. I'd give my left arm if the room would only stop spinning and I might see life again. I worked so hard for all this furniture and the right wallpaper, and it means nothing to me, nothing at all." They embraced again before Brenda slid to the floor and crawled into her closet, concentrating on finding clothes that matched.

"It's kind of hot for that blouse. Would you like me to pick something for you?" Wyatt offered.

"No. My arms look like I've been beaten from all my encounters with the walls. I think I'd be more comfortable in long sleeves." Brenda looked down while she spoke, her trademark confidence gone.

"If you're overheated, that'll only make your symptoms worse. Please wear something without sleeves. Your arms are only bruised below the elbows. You can just keep your arms on the wheelchair, okay?" Wyatt was learning the art of negotiation.

Brenda nodded and allowed Wyatt to bring her a pale pink silk tank top. She wore a pair of simple navy strap sandals and nodded when she was satisfied with her ensemble. Wyatt applied some powdered foundation and a pale berry lipstick for an added touch. "You look as beautiful as ever. The only difference is people will have to look down instead of up to see your lovely face. Now, you'll get to see how the short half lives."

Brenda relied on Wyatt for everything. The fear of her nurse leaving was growing. *What will I ever do without her?*

After Brenda's torrent of emotions, the women were late to church. Wyatt pushed Brenda's wheelchair into a darkened corner near the rear of the church. Brenda appreciated the anonymous seating and listened to the hymns with intensity, allowing the music of praise to fill her senses. Childhood memories invaded, but Brenda forced them back.

The pastor's sermon focused on unconfessed sin, and Brenda felt she might explode from her own guilt. She imagined that everyone around her could see inside her and they *knew*. She thought of her mother and father and their tragic deaths. How she wished she could have made things right before they died. If only she'd put her foolish fears aside. Hot, stinging tears rolled down her cheeks uncontrolled.

The pastor's concluding words spoke with power to her. "Unconfessed sin is a living, breathing germ that breeds in our very soul, making us sicker and sicker until we can no longer function in our own carefully arranged world. If you have unconfessed sin in your life, or if you've never allowed Jesus to carry that burden for you, I urge you to come forward today and allow His blood to wash you clean.

He can take it all away. Jesus came to save the lost, my friend. He loves you regardless of your past. Let Him free you. Come here, and leave your cross at the altar of Christ."

Brenda felt her wheelchair move forward as if of its own volition. At first, just a few inches and then more. Her hands went to the silver guide wheel and she maneuvered the chair forward through the aisles, miraculously without so much as a bump into any obstacles. Once she neared the altar, she felt a warm hand placed on her shoulder. *What am I doing?* But as soon as the doubts rolled in, something dissipated them. Someone took control of her chair and she was wheeled slowly out of the sanctuary.

She heard a warm voice that told her how to pray for God's forgiveness and ask Jesus to come into her life. Brenda repeated the prayer, confessing silently. A warm peace washed over her, and Brenda knew it was finished. She finally felt free. Free of the terrible, ravaging guilt that had plagued her for years. Brenda finished with a good, cleansing cry. Not the fearful, anxious tears that had plagued her for days but a release of emotions that had been pent up inside her for years.

The same gentle woman who taught her to pray told her about a new believers' Bible study, gave her a Bible, and pushed her back into the now-quiet sanctuary. "Did you need to go somewhere?" she asked softly.

"No, Mary, I've got her." Wyatt's familiar voice filled Brenda's heart. If it hadn't been for Katie and Wyatt, Brenda would have never felt God's touch in her life. She knew that God's love had been shown through His people, unconditionally and consistently. It was as though He had given her a new family. When Brenda had nobody, they were there.

"Now I really owe you breakfast, huh?" Wyatt teased, and both women laughed through their tears. They now shared a new bond that was stronger than the distance that would soon be between them.

Many church members stayed to offer Brenda their support in the upcoming months, offering her their congratulations for her new commitment. If she needed help reading her Bible or being driven somewhere, several women gave a name and offered a phone number. Outside the sanctuary, Wyatt placed the ancient wheelchair in the back seat of the convertible. When the summer season ended, Brenda would either have to invest in a smaller wheelchair or a car with a bigger trunk. In the meantime, Wyatt kept the top down and the wheelchair in the back.

"I feel like I could take on the world today. I feel free!" Brenda lifted her arms and let the breeze fill her senses. Wyatt placed her hands on Brenda's as she tore out of the church parking lot in the BMW. "You're beginning to like this car, aren't you?"

"I love it!" Wyatt surprisingly admitted.

"Wyatt Ross, you sound positively materialistic." Brenda laughed hysterically, while Wyatt wore a mischievous grin.

"It's ending soon. I'm going to enjoy the sporty life while God allows it."

"We'll enjoy it together! Let's drive to the beach after breakfast," Brenda said enthusiastically.

"I should have known you wouldn't go before food! What about your presentation tomorrow?" Wyatt asked cautiously.

"Forget it. Are we at Hobee's yet? I'm going to have a huge eggs Benedict with tons of hollandaise and a steaming cup of tea. I can taste it now."

"We'd better get you off those steroids soon, or you won't be able to afford to feed yourself."

"You're buying today, remember?" Brenda said enthusiastically.

"I wouldn't have it any other way, Miss Turner. My new friend in Christ, you have so much excitement ahead of you. It won't be an easy transition, but it'll be the thrill-filled ride of your life."

"Doesn't God have an easy cruise version? I've had enough excitement for one year."

"I'm afraid not, so just sit back and enjoy the ride." Wyatt accelerated the BMW and Brenda relished the momentary rush.

⋙⋘

Word spread quickly that Luke was Olgilvy's new assistant chief of neurosurgery. The promotion allowed him to get Barry the required medications for Africa. There wasn't a pharmaceuticals rep present who would turn down Olgilvy's new protégé. Dr. Ogilvy was flying on to Baltimore to consult at Johns Hopkins, so Luke and Barry were spared the ordeal of traveling back to California with him. Both men were exhausted by the events of the weekend, and they slept most of the way home on the red-eye flight. Luke arrived home to find an eviction notice in his mailbox. "These units are reserved for the exclusive use of physicians who are completing their residency at Stanford University Hospital," he read before crumpling the letter and throwing it across the room. He was exasperated. *Lord, what's next? First a new job, now a new house. What else?*

Chapter 13

Brenda nearly collapsed at the BMW following her big presentation for Day Graphics. She had given every ounce of energy she had to the meeting, which she attended in her wheelchair. It was abundantly clear that she would not be able to work for some time. "Katie, in my briefcase are my sabbatical papers. Would you see that they are turned in and approved by the CEO? I'm going to take a vacation and spend some time getting well."

"I'll see to it this afternoon. And, Brenda, you can't be fired now," Katie stated emphatically.

"Katie, of course I can. At my level, they call it corporate downsizing. They'll say they're eliminating the position, hire Mike Wilcox as corporate marketing manager instead of calling him a vice president, and it's done. They do it every day. Trust me; this is best. I'm going to need that initial public stock offering money if I can't work for awhile. A sabbatical will take me through until we're public."

"Brenda, I hate to hear you talking like that. Have faith that God will heal."

"He may, but I still need the break."

"I won't be in the office tomorrow. It's our court date." Katie said the words without tears. Brenda thought she had probably cried every last one she had for the possible loss of her son, Daydan.

"Wyatt and I prayed for your family last night, Katie. I know everything will work out. I just know it." Brenda had all the confidence in the world that God would come through for the Cummings family.

"How do you think we did in there?" Katie asked, ignoring the subject of Daydan's court date.

"I think we'll be millionaires within the next year. They'd have to be stupid to turn down our offer. We'll have our initial public offering, and then we can both quit worrying about work for awhile."

"Brenda, are you planning to leave Star Digital?"

"Not a chance. I'm just thinking about taking it easy for awhile, that's all. Maybe allowing Mike Wilcox to take on some of the burden."

Katie shook her head. "I never thought I'd see the day."

Brenda arrived home without a care. Her obligations for work were over, and now she could concentrate on beating her disease. She had bought several books on the subject of multiple sclerosis, including a special diet book that worked for some. She had approached work with a full frontal attack, and now she would do the same for her disease.

Katie assisted her up the porch steps. Once on the oversized front verandah, Brenda slumped back into the chair. She thought she heard Luke's pleasant, low voice, and her heart skipped a beat at the mere possibility. She quickly opened the door.

Using the doorjamb to guide her, she stood up and took a half step into the house. Luke's voice raised in anger as soon as she stepped across the threshold. "Brenda Turner, why are you in the wheelchair? Why didn't you keep your appointment with Dr. Wilhelm? Do you have any regard for your health at all?" He chastised her without listening for answers.

Brenda's excitement about seeing him turned immediately to anger. "Dr. Marcusson, I told you the last time I saw you that I had a deadline. I'm not the kind of person who drops a major business deal just because I don't feel well. Would you let a patient suffer because you had a minor inconvenience at home?"

"That's a ridiculous analogy! You're coming with me for more corticosteroid therapy *now.*"

Brenda sat firmly back in her wheelchair and crossed her arms. "I'm not going anywhere. There are alternatives, you know. You doctors always want to pump us up with drugs." Brenda pointed to the armful of books that Katie was carrying to show the doctor what she meant.

"You want alternatives? Let me just give you the rundown of your current choices: The vitamin route, which I understand Wyatt already started you on; there's bee sting therapy, where some quack stings you twenty or so times for the bee venom; there's magnetic therapy, where you put magnets in your shoes; oxygen therapy, and an abundance of surefire cures readily available for purchase on the Internet. And you can try any one of them *after* you complete conventional therapy, which has a proven track record for bringing back your eyesight!" Luke came toward her.

"Luke, it's *my* treatment." Brenda used his first name, hoping to appeal to his emotions.

"There is no reason for you to be in a wheelchair right now. If you wanted to be in charge of your own health care, you should have thought about it during that work marathon that stressed your disease to this level." Luke gently tugged on her hands, but she opposed him.

"Luke, you can't make me—"

"Wanna bet?" Luke swept her out of the chair and into his tightened, firm arms. "Wyatt, call the hospital and tell them we're on our way. Have them page Dr. Wilhelm." He struggled to control Brenda's long, flailing limbs and kicked the wheelchair away from them.

"My wheelchair!" she squealed.

"You won't be needing it." Luke remained calm, finally subduing her thrashing with his muscular arms.

"Luke, how do you know none of those alternative therapies work? You'd never believe in something unless it involved your paycheck!"

"Brenda, you're heartless sometimes. Like I said, you can try anything you like, *after* we get your eyesight back."

She had never heard him talk so intensely. Brenda was mere inches from his face, and suddenly the memory of his powerful kiss filled her mind, completely eliminating her rising anger. His warm features subdued her temporarily. "I just want to be healthy," she said in a soft, vulnerable voice.

"Who do you think sees more MS patients cured, a neurologist or a traveling salesman? Have I ever given you reason not to trust me?" Luke opened the BMW and gently seated Brenda in the passenger seat. "Give me the keys."

"No," she declared.

"Give me the keys, or we'll take the Pinto," Luke threatened and immediately Brenda tossed the keys, hearing the jingling stop as he caught them. The car started, and Brenda knew she was destined for more IV steroids. *Oh, Lord, no.*

"Luke," she tried pleading, "this stuff makes me feel awful. At least when I'm on the pill form, I can manage some form of control in my life. I don't want to act like that again. I don't want to be out of control anymore. I've given my life to God. I don't want to be that monster again."

"Brenda, I heard about your conversion and no one could be happier for you." *Or me,* he thought. "But God uses medicine. All those alternatives are aimed at keeping you in remission. I'll even help you if that's what you want, but first you need to achieve remission. Besides, I have my own reasons for wanting your eyesight back. I'm getting kicked out of my campus housing. The complex is for medical residents only, and I'm long past that stage. I've got a month to find a house. You said you'd help, but I doubt you'll be much good without your eyesight."

"Why don't you just hire a Realtor?" she shot back.

"In *this* area?" he said lightly, using her own words. "Do you know what six percent of a six hundred thousand dollar house is?"

The two laughed together, and the present tension was broken. Brenda finally relented her will to Luke's, at least for the moment.

"Brenda, I'm not trying to control you. I'm trying to make you better in the best way I know how. If you won't see Dr. Wilhelm, I feel compelled to take over your treatment."

"I thought you didn't have time for me." Sadness enveloped her voice.

"Brenda, I lied to you. It was never that I didn't have time for you, although my schedule *was* beginning to squeeze out new patients. The real reason I transferred your case was—"

"I was too opinionated. I know; I've heard it before. It's the same reason I don't have friends. I'm trying! As a Christian, I am really trying to think of other people's feelings before I blast them with vicious opinions."

"Brenda, that has nothing to do with why I transferred your case."

She felt him looking at her and didn't know what to say. "I'm trying to be sweeter to people. If you put me on those high dosages of steroids, I know I won't be able to control myself. I want to be like Wyatt and Katie. Sweet and gentle, the kind of godly woman that people want to be around," she admitted openly.

At the next stoplight, Luke leaned over and looked directly into the sky blue eyes that couldn't return his gaze. "Brenda, God wants you to be the best possible Brenda you can be. He doesn't want another Katie or Wyatt. He wants us all to be servants, but that doesn't mean that you will serve in the same capacity. Do you understand?" Luke asked.

"No."

"Brenda, you have a combative personality. I'm sorry to say it that way, but you know it's true. Perhaps God wants you to be a lobbyist in Congress or fight for the poor to purchase housing. I'm not saying God wants you to be mean to people, but Brenda, He designed your skill set for your *own* ministry, not Katie's or Wyatt's. You have an incredible ability to handle confrontation. If you can do it lovingly, God will use that skill."

"Does that mean you'll take my case again?" Brenda asked.

"You never let me finish. I didn't transfer your case because I didn't like you. I transferred your case because if I looked into those incredible blue eyes to examine them one more time, I wouldn't have been able to control myself."

Brenda's face broke into a blushing smile while Luke raced toward the hospital.

Chapter 14

After two days on intravenous steroids, Brenda's eyesight was restored to the point that she could focus on everything around her. This time she vowed to stay away from all books, computers, and eyestrain until she was fully recovered. Luke visited her every day of her stay in the hospital, not as her doctor, but as her friend.

During her three-day stay, Luke and Wyatt brought their pastor in and anointed Brenda's head with oil, praying for healing. Brenda felt uncomfortable at first, with the many hands being placed on her head; but eventually she sat back and relented to her new friends. Following the prayer, Brenda had Wyatt read the Scripture that ordained the anointing of oil, and afterwards, she knew it was God's will.

"Brenda?" Luke entered her hospital room carrying a huge bouquet of pink tulips and yellow roses. "I didn't know what type of flowers you liked."

"Pink tulips and yellow roses are my exact favorites," she replied with a happy smile and a wink. "How did you know?"

"I see your eyesight is holding, and you haven't lost your marketer's knack for saying the right thing. Dr. Wilhelm has released you. I'm here to take you home. I brought the real estate section. I thought I might read you a few entries. Are you up to it?"

"Since I won't be sleeping for a couple days, I say we give it a try. I don't feel nearly as achy this time." She paused a moment before adding humbly, "Thank you for forcing me to come. I'd like to return the favor. Let's go house hunting." Luke signed Brenda's release papers and took her hand, lifting her from the wheelchair.

"Say good-bye to the wheelchair," Luke said.

Although she was able to see quite clearly, Brenda held firmly onto the muscular forearm of the handsome neurologist as he led her to the car. His touch warmed her heart, and she took full advantage of the opportunity to be close.

"Your chariot awaits, Madam." Luke swept his hand and opened the door to a brand-new, midnight blue Toyota Camry.

"Luke! You didn't!" Brenda gasped incredulously.

"I did. Bought it yesterday. I thought it was kind of tacky to court you in your own car. Well, that, and the Pinto died on Highway 101 last Tuesday, leaving me little choice. I bought the blue because it complements your eyes." Luke saw Brenda seated comfortably and headed for the driver's side.

Brenda waited for him to climb into the car. "I'm so proud of you. This was a big step!"

"I figured I'll have a new job, a new home—I might as well finish it off. Get rid of everything!"

"Not everything, I hope," Brenda said flirtatiously.

"No, not everything," Luke said softly, looking intently at Brenda. "At least until you find me a house!" Luke laughed, and Brenda swatted his leg.

"Have you thought about what you want? A condo, town home, house, mansion."

"Mansion?"

"Just seeing if you were paying attention. Do you want a yard? How many bedrooms?"

"Okay, okay. One thing at a time. Yes, I want a yard and a house I can stay in forever. I don't want to have to move again, unless God takes me on a mission or elsewhere. Oh, and I only want one floor. I've seen too many patients have to leave their homes because they can't get up the stairs. I don't want that ever to be an issue."

Brenda looked at the solid, muscular man beside her and doubted that frailty would ever be a problem for Luke. He pushed a button and the sunroof peeled back, allowing rays of sunlight to shower on Brenda's golden blond hair. "Now you're just showing off."

"I was trying to impress you."

"Consider me impressed." Brenda smiled, looking away in uncharacteristic shyness. This man made her feel like a silly schoolgirl. "What city did you have in mind?"

"Any suggestions?" Luke shrugged his shoulders. "I want something near the hospital."

"You'll pay for a Palo Alto address, but you'll never have to worry about resale value." Luke shot her a look. "Oh, that's right, you're not going anywhere. What about Menlo Park? It's close. the weather's perfect, and you can find a house as low as two hundred fifty thousand or as high as over a million. Do you want to start there?"

"Menlo Park, yes. A million dollars, no," Luke answered.

"Okay, I have a few rules for my house-hunting services. First, never act like you love a house. There is always something wrong with it! That attitude will help you in negotiations. You don't want to put the owners down; you just want to let the Realtor know it's not exactly what you had in mind. It makes them work harder for the sale, thus lowering the price, but like I said, with all the competition, you're still going to pay asking price."

"Is that all?"

"No. Secondly, don't get attached to a house until it's in escrow. That will save you unnecessary heartache when someone comes in and tops your offer."

"Deal. Is that it?"

"No, this is the most important part. No Eichlers, the flat-roofed houses."

"Okay. Should I ask why?"

"Of course. Because they are seriously ugly, hard to sell, and I would have to question your taste."

"Okay, are those all the rules?"

"Yes."

"Then Menlo Park, here I come with the best-looking non-real-estate agent anywhere."

Brenda blushed red at the compliment. She wasn't used to receiving them, and Luke seemed to offer them so easily. She thought it was one of his finest attributes.

⁂

Luke maneuvered his new sporty coupe quickly. He hadn't realized how much fun driving could be until he'd unloaded the Pinto. It was actually a pleasure instead of a constant prayer to get to his destination. Brenda's mood was gay, and her health was extraordinary after her days on the intravenous steroids. Luke hoped the day wasn't too much for her. He glanced at her to make sure she was up to the task. *She is so beautiful, such perfect features. Lord, I can't thank You enough for calling her to Your kingdom.*

"Brenda, I've made a decision," Luke said, trying to keep her awake.

"Two in one week? You wouldn't be straining yourself, would you?" Brenda quipped. She knew how hard change was for Luke. She hoped her lighthearted treatment would help him move out of his comfort zone. At least long enough to get him a new home, something that was now a necessity after his eviction.

"Miss Turner, who's working for whom here?" he said lightly, his hazel green eyes sparkling with mischief.

"That depends—we haven't discussed salary."

"Of course. Dinner at the restaurant of your choice?"

"Great. I want the Lodge."

"The steak place?" he asked skeptically.

"Yes. I want a big salad, a huge prime rib with tons of horseradish, and I'll top it off with a mud pie. Doesn't that sound great?" Brenda's eyes were wide with anticipation, and she rubbed her hands together in pleasure over the thought.

"I'd better find a house soon, or I'll be too broke to buy it."

"You're the one who insisted I take the intravenous steroids. It's only fair you take on a few of my increased grocery bills. It's the least you can do."

Luke took a sharp right turn down a lush, oak-lined cul-de-sac. The houses were well-spaced with extensive, manicured front lawns that would be ideal for a pickup football game after Thanksgiving dinner. Spring flowers lined each long walkway, and the house for sale had a mature sequoia tree that shaded the entire yard. The house was a remodeled rancher with several white French windows and an elongated set of double front doors that marked its dramatic entrance. "How much is this neighborhood?" Luke asked, knowing it was probably above his self-imposed price range.

"Just look at it first. The moths won't get out of your wallet if you just look. I promise." Brenda giggled under her breath.

"I am not cheap!" Luke exclaimed passionately.

She turned serious. "I know, Luke. You're very generous. However, I think you're looking at this house thing in the wrong light. You've got to realize a house is an investment. In your income bracket, you're probably paying forty percent in taxes right now. By sheltering some of that income in a house, you'll have more to spend where you want to spend it: missions, the church, wherever. Not sheltering income is bad stewardship."

"Bad stewardship. Where did you learn that?"

"Wyatt asked me where I thought I might have trouble with sin—you know, besides my temper. I told her with money, so she taught me about stewardship. You know the parable about the men who each receive money for investing? Each of them increases their boss's money, except the one who buried it. God has plans for your salary, Luke."

Exiting the car, they were greeted by a friendly real estate agent dressed in an ivory suit. The agent's dark bob and big brown eyes were highlighted by the light color she wore. Her impeccable, professional appearance caused Brenda to feel self-conscious in her simple jeans and short-sleeved sweater. She wished she'd gone home to change after leaving the hospital. The agent handed them an information sheet, and Brenda stole it from Luke's hands before he could see the price.

"Just look at the house first," she cautioned.

"I'm Jessie Morgan," the Realtor said. "If you have any questions, please feel free to ask. Make yourselves at home. Are you two getting ready to start a family?" she asked innocently. Luke and Brenda looked at one another guiltily, and both were at a loss for words. "I'm sorry. The reason I asked is that this house is perfect for a growing family. The house was redesigned casually, with children in mind. The backyard is completely self-contained with an included swing set. There are lots of preschoolers and infants on the block, and you're in a wonderful school district here. It's part of the Menlo-Atherton district."

"Atherton? Brenda, we're—"

"In Menlo Park still, and it doesn't cost anything to look," she whispered, pulling him away from the agent.

❧❧❧

Luke was captivated by the house, every last crevice. He loved the sunken living room, the cream carpet, the French doors, the oversized tub in the master bathroom, and especially the parklike backyard. He could just imagine playing baseball with his future sons under the great oak tree. There was a trickle of a running creek in the back as well as a basketball court and the swing set. Watching Brenda wander around the house, he imagined her entertaining their friends in her casual, take-charge manner. This is where he wanted to grow old with her. Catching her eye, he snapped out of his reverie and followed her into the kitchen.

Brenda clapped her hands together and moved toward him. Her eyes sparkled with excitement. "Luke, look at this kitchen. It's perfect! Look at these huge countertops and the country French cabinets with the plate racks. I couldn't have designed it better myself. These hardwood floors are just gorgeous!"

"What about not getting attached to a house before escrow? And what was all that stuff about there always being something wrong with a place?" Luke chided jokingly.

"Why do you think I told you all that? Because those are my weaknesses. I never can seem to control my emotions where the perfect home is concerned." She covered her mouth to contain a laugh.

He grimaced at her while shaking his head. "This is the perfect home, isn't it?" She nodded. "This is it, Luke."

Luke knew it was the right home and that he wanted to take Brenda as his wife and move in the very next day, but he had to pray. This wasn't like him. He couldn't just purchase a house at the drop of a hat. He had to think about it, stew over it. He didn't even know what it cost. A new job, a new house, possibly a wife—it was all too much. "Thank you," he said to the Realtor and raced out the door, pulling Brenda by the hand.

"Luke, what are you doing? Don't you want to talk to the Realtor and maybe make an offer?"

"I can't work this way, Brenda. I have to pray about it. It's my home! You may go off and spend a wad of cash readily, but I don't!" he barked. Brenda broke away from his grip, an expression of pain coming crossing her face.

❧❦❧

Brenda was so hurt by Luke's uncharacteristic outburst that she feigned fatigue, rather than have to eat dinner with him. She couldn't go through an entire meal pretending; her medications would make that literally impossible. They made her so much more transparent, and right now she hated such a blatant side effect. Luke drove her home. He walked her to the door, but once she was safely on the porch, he turned and hurried back to his car. When Brenda entered the house, she found Wyatt and Barry watching a movie on the couch. Wyatt was in tears with a wadded-up tissue in her hand.

"Wyatt, what's the matter?" Brenda ran to her, looking at Barry suspiciously.

"Nothing, Brenda. It's this movie. It's so sad!" she wailed.

Brenda looked at the screen and saw they were watching *Jurassic Park*. "Wyatt, you're watching a movie about dinosaurs."

"I know," she wailed.

Barry grabbed the remote and flipped the television off. "I think that's enough television. What Wyatt's trying to tell you, Brenda, is that she's pregnant."

Wyatt broke into loud sobs. "Can you believe it? We've been trying for ten years, and all of a sudden, God decides to bless us when we least expect it. Oh, Brenda, I *need* a job," she cried.

"You're staying here? Oh, Wyatt, that's the best news I've had in months!" Brenda forced herself in between the close couple on the couch and threw her arms around them both. "We're going to have a baby!" She jumped from the couch and began skipping through the living room. She turned when she realized what this meant. "Of course, you'll live here. I won't take no for an answer."

"Brenda, you may not want to offer us that when we tell you what we did." Barry looked at his wife. "Go ahead, Wyatt. Tell her what *we* did. You've kept it to yourself long enough."

"This really isn't a good time, Honey." Wyatt patted her husband's knee, but he remained unfazed by her gesture.

"Wyatt!"

"Okay, okay. When Barry and Luke went to Connecticut, I had them visit your brother," she blurted, turning away from Brenda's gaze.

"My brother? Doug? They saw Doug?" Brenda was baffled.

"We didn't know you two were estranged, and we thought it would be a nice surprise to have him call you."

Brenda sat slowly. "I haven't seen him for more than nine years." She tried to comprehend what this meant. Possibly this was the reason for Luke's sudden outburst at the open house. "Did Doug tell you?" Brenda closed her eyes in despair.

"No," Barry answered. "And we didn't ask. He just said you weren't on speaking terms. He also mentioned that Kaitlyn is thirteen now and has two younger brothers, nine and eight."

"I have nephews?" Her voice cracked. Brenda walked numbly into her floral bedroom and dropped onto the rich, cherry pedestal bed. *My sins have finally caught up with me. Forgiven. Maybe by God, but never by my family and now Luke too.* She focused intently on the ceiling fan before finally falling asleep.

Chapter 15

Luke didn't know what to say to Brenda after the open house. He wanted to tell her was that he was falling in love with her, that his thoughts were filled with spending his days in the *perfect* home in Menlo Park with her. Instead he'd panicked over the many changes taking place in his life and let down the one person he cared about most. Why couldn't he have lost his temper with Olgilvy or the university's housing office? Why did it have to be Brenda?

Luke was shamed by his behavior and too embarrassed to go to her and tell her his feelings. He wallowed in his work, taking on more new patients and more surgeries at the same time. Two weeks passed, and he still hadn't called. The longer the time that passed, the worse he felt about calling her.

❧❀❧

Star Digital would be public on the stock exchange within the month. Upon hearing she would soon be a multimillionaire, Brenda called Jessie Morgan, the Realtor, and inquired about the house she and Luke had visited together.

"Right, you were the attractive couple, very tall. I wouldn't have remembered you, but you two are hard to miss."

"Thank you. I'm calling to find out if you've had any offers."

"It's the oddest thing, but no, we haven't. Such prime real estate too. Are you and your husband interested in making an offer?" the woman asked expectantly. Brenda had hoped that Luke had bought the house, that Miss Morgan would unhappily say it was sold. She hoped that she hadn't heard from him because he'd been so busy with escrow. *This is best*, she thought. *I don't ever want to be the kind of woman who counts on a man for anything. Why would I expect him to buy that house? And even if he had, it wouldn't mean anything to me.* He hadn't made any commitments and by now, it was obvious he wasn't going to. *Not even a phone call.* Brenda shook her head sadly.

"Miss Morgan, you have the wrong impression. I'm not married. My name is Brenda Turner, and I'd like to submit an offer. I'll have it to you by tomorrow."

"Who's your agent? I'd be happy to arrange—"

"I'm not using a Realtor. When can we meet?" Brenda could tell by the extended silence that the Realtor was thrown.

"How's ten? My office is—"

"Actually, I live in Palo Alto, and I'm unable to drive right now. Can you

107

come here?" Brenda's question was pointed, and the Realtor was quick to agree. The woman took down her address and promised to be there at ten.

"My other line is ringing. Please feel free to call if something comes up." Brenda buzzed her other line. "Brenda Turner."

"Brenda, it's Luke." Her heart quickened at the unexpected sound of his voice. It had been three long weeks since she'd heard from him, and his call sent a flurry of emotions through her, but anger prevailed. "I'm sorry I haven't had a chance to talk with you. It's a long story, but I'm very busy as chief assistant surgeon." Brenda remained stoic as he continued. "I finally had a chance to look at the information sheet on that house. They wanted seven hundred thousand dollars for it," he said incredulously.

"I know," Brenda said as guilt heated her body.

"Buying that house just represents everything I didn't want to become as a doctor. Besides, four bedrooms is far too much for me after my studio. I hope you're not upset I wasted your time," he said apologetically. *Her time—that was all he cared about. He'd wasted her time.* "Brenda, are you still there?"

"I understand the house being too big of a commitment for you," Brenda said solemnly.

"I'm sorry, I've just been feeling so much pressure to pursue things I don't want yet, and I took it out on you. Will you forgive me? I still owe you dinner."

He was feeling pressured to pursue her, so that was it. "Luke, why don't you get settled and call me then?" Brenda wasn't ready to spill the news about her stock option fortune or the perfect house she planned to buy with it. She stared longingly into the photograph Wyatt had taken of Luke and Brenda on their first date. His generous smile and laughing eyes, combined with his roguish jawline and build, sent all her rational thoughts sailing.

"Brenda?"

"Yes, Luke," she said hopefully, hating herself for it.

"I love you. The real me will be back soon." Luke hung up the phone, and Brenda stared into the receiver, unsure if she'd dreamt the words or actually heard them. *He loves me? What does he mean? Oh, Luke, I don't care. I love you too.*

❦

Brenda hung up the phone and heard Barry enter the house. His voice was clearly excited, and she ran toward the living room.

"I have a job! I start on Monday." Barry's full face widened with a proud grin.

"Barry, already?" Wyatt asked.

"I'm practicing neurology again. I'm going to be assisting Luke with his practice."

"Luke?" Brenda asked, her interest piqued.

"Yes, he's decided to stick it out with the neurosurgery for at least another six months. He's tried to tell Olgilvy about Baylor, but feels this is best for awhile.

With me, he'll be able to get the surgery experience he wants without abandoning his research patients."

Brenda knew she wouldn't be hearing from Luke anytime soon. Hoping to change the subject, she spilled her news bluntly. "I'm buying a house tomorrow."

"Brenda, you have a house." Wyatt looked stunned.

"I'm buying *another* house in Menlo Park. The country French house I saw a few weeks ago. I'm putting an offer on it."

"I don't understand," Wyatt stammered.

"I'll be wealthy beyond my wildest dreams next month, so why not?" Brenda rationalized.

"Because you don't need a house, that's why not. Do you plan to spend everything you've made in the next week?"

"It's an investment, Wyatt. This way, you, Barry, and the baby will have this house, and I'll be out of your way. It's completely rent-free until you go back to Africa. My gift to you for all your love and care."

"Brenda, are we bothering you? I thought we'd make a nice threesome. Do you want us to leave?"

Barry, seeing the nature of the discussion, left the two women alone.

"Of course not. The furniture's staying. The new house is French styling, so I'm buying all new furnishings. Light wood, ladder-back chairs, that type of thing. A relaxed, casual elegance. I don't feel well. Please excuse me." Brenda dashed into her room and closed the door, ending any further reprimands. She leaned against the door, listening to Wyatt's quiet footsteps just outside. This was clearly best for everyone. Wyatt and Barry would be alone with their baby, and Brenda would just be alone. Again. For the first time, the thought filled her with a cold, empty sensation.

✥

To Brenda's surprise, Luke called every day for two months. He hadn't bought a house but was renting a small condominium near the hospital. He never visited Brenda nor asked to see her, but he called every evening at nine and asked about her day, her health, and her walk with the Lord. Brenda, against her better judgment, shared everything and wished with all her heart that he was there to hold her. They would talk extensively and when the call ended, Brenda would feel lost, aching for his touch. He finished each conversation by telling her he loved her.

Once a week at church she would see him, but he never acted as more than a casual acquaintance. Occasionally, he would join her, Wyatt, and Barry for lunch after service, but they were never alone. Their phone calls provided the only intimacy in their relationship. Brenda was confused. She had fallen intensely in love with him, but he kept a distance between them that she couldn't cross, and she kept her own. She still hadn't told him about the house.

She was scheduled to move the following week, and she still hadn't mentioned it to Luke. She felt she had betrayed him by buying it and hadn't found the courage to tell him.

Tonight, when he calls, I'll tell him, she vowed. She dressed for her first day back at work, looking at her once-again slender appearance in the mirror.

"Brenda?" Wyatt came to the bedroom door, her rounded belly just beginning to bulge under her loose-fitting T-shirt. Brenda looked at her expectantly. "Barry and I have come up with an amount we'd like to pay you for the house for rent."

Brenda shook her head vehemently. "Absolutely not. Anything you pay me is money that could cure an African child. Besides, it's a write-off for me. Just think of it as the Lord's provision." Brenda waved a hand, dismissing Wyatt and concentrating on her reflection.

"No, Brenda, this is very important to Barry. If you decide to donate the money we pay you, that's your business, but we cannot in good conscience live off you while we're both working. I have no choice. Barry has spoken, and he is the leader of our household."

The final words sent an eerie chill through Brenda's spine. Remembering the disturbing acts that her mother had termed biblical submission, Brenda's respect for Barry swiftly deteriorated and she couldn't hold her tongue. "How can you say that? You've been the breadwinner all summer. Now he suddenly has a job, and he's boss?"

"Brenda, it wouldn't matter if I earned *all* the money. It's not like Barry's lazy. He's been gathering missions support." Wyatt's tone was persuasive. "That takes a lot of effort to raise finances and gather medications. Besides, the Bible says the husband is the head of the household."

"My mother always threw that in my face! Every time my father belittled her in front of her friends or screamed at her for buying a roast that was too expensive, I heard those ridiculous words, 'The husband is the head of the household.' My mother would meekly apologize to her friends for *her* insubordinate behavior, then slink back to the store and return the meat that was thirty cents over budget! I'll *never* let that happen! No man will ever tell me how to run *my* life. Just because I'm a Christian doesn't give a man the right to walk all over me!"

"Brenda, there's a lot in the Bible that's hard for a new believer to understand. But everything there has a purpose, and God placed it there for good reason." Wyatt spoke softly and sat down beside Brenda at the foot of the bed. Brenda kept her back stiffened, unwilling to bend on the subject. "I want you to read that passage tonight in Ephesians five. There is far more responsibility placed on the husband. I think when you see God's intentions for the husband to care for his wife as Christ cares for the church, you'll see it differently."

"*This* is the very reason I haven't spoken to my family in years."

Wyatt looked intrigued and continued prodding. "I don't mean to disparage your father, especially when he's not here to defend himself, but Brenda, his way worked for your mother. She quietly submitted to his leadership. Possibly, you considered it too harsh, but your mother was happy. Wasn't she?"

"She pretended to be happy, but I heard her quiet sobs when Dad left for work. I saw her mortification when she was left to entertain friends after my father had cut her to shreds for wasting precious coffee on 'a bunch of freeloading gossips.' She may have loved my father, but she wasn't happy."

"You've got to allow God to take that burden from you, Brenda. Hanging on to that anger, not leaving it at the altar for Christ to carry, that's sin." Wyatt surrounded her with loving arms. "Tell me what caused the terrible rift in your family. I think you'll feel better if you do."

Brenda longed to lift the heavy burden from her soul, to share it with Wyatt and allow God to take it away, but she couldn't part with it. She sat gazing into Wyatt's understanding green eyes, wondering if she could let go, knowing she couldn't. *Not yet.*

❧❀❧

Brenda returned to work happily after her two-month hiatus. Entering her familiar office brought tears to her eyes. Katie was there to greet her with flowers and a balloon bouquet. "Welcome back!" Katie's sweet brown eyes sparkled with her smile. "I left a Balance bar and a mocha on your desk."

Brenda came forward and hugged her assistant fiercely. "I've missed you so much!"

"I'm sorry I haven't seen much of you. We've been so busy with Daydan's birth mother and her visitation rights, I just haven't had the energy."

"Please, Katie, don't worry about me. I'm sorry things are still rocky with Tasha's visitations. I'm praying."

"We appreciate that. God's will be done," Katie said coldly, unable to muster any true feelings of warmth. "Try as I might, I can't resent Tasha for wanting the same thing I do. I just keep hoping that God has a plan that will work for all of us. How are you feeling?"

"Great! I'm off the steroids and back to running. I bought a treadmill and put it right under the air-conditioning vent. It's like running in a cold arctic snow!" Brenda laughed. "I'm only on one medication. I give myself a shot every other day, and I feel almost normal. Just a little dizzy when I'm tired or hot."

"Have you heard from my cousin?" Katie smiled with mock innocence.

"I hear from him every night, but that's as far as it goes—just a nice, solid friendship," Brenda said casually. She sat down proudly at her huge mahogany desk, running her arms across it. "I missed this place."

"I bet." Katie held a pad of paper and rattled off statistics for Brenda's schedule.

"Great. Thanks, Katie, for holding down the fort."

"That's my job. By the way, the stock just hit ninety dollars a share." Katie smiled brilliantly and exited.

Brenda leaped from her desk and kicked her heels together. It had happened: She was now worth nearly four million dollars, including real estate. How she wished her mother and father could see her now. Would they be proud? Or would they still say poor Brenda just couldn't find a man?

Brenda returned home just before nine. She had so much to catch up on at work, and her fatigued body couldn't gather the energy to run her treadmill. She could barely manage eating the dinner Wyatt had prepared. The phone rang at precisely nine o'clock, and Brenda warmed to Luke's rich voice.

"Hi, Sweetheart. How'd things go today?" Luke asked.

"Great, I think I sold the engineering department on my application ideas for the next wave of digital television. On-demand television is closer than ever."

"I can't wait," Luke joked. "What else is happening?"

"That involves a little confession."

"To me?" Luke questioned.

"Kind of. I haven't been fully honest about my recent activities. I bought the Menlo Park house. The one we looked at together." She waited, hoping for a positive answer.

Luke sat down on his kitchen stool, unprepared for the news. "You mean you put an offer down?"

"No, I mean I move in on Saturday. Don't blame Wyatt or Barry. I swore them to secrecy."

Luke looked down at the sparkling engagement ring in the small black box he held. The woman he loved had deceived him and for the life of him, he couldn't understand why she would allow this to go unmentioned. "I don't understand, Brenda. Didn't you think I'd be happy for you?"

"I didn't want you talking me out of it. I wanted the house and paid for it with my own money, so it didn't concern you. I had air-conditioning installed and I'm thinking of putting in a pool. There are no stairs—it's completely conducive to MS life."

Luke remained quiet. Brenda was planning a life alone, a life that didn't include him. It was clear she was capable of life without him. That's why he was so attracted to her in the first place. He dropped the ring box dejectedly onto the counter.

Go to her.

God's words were clear, and before he had a chance to think, he asked impatiently, "Are you available for dinner Saturday?"

She waited a moment before speaking. "I—uh. . .guess so. So what about the house?"

"What about it? Are you available Saturday or not?" he asked curtly.

"Yes," she said simply.

"Be ready at six. Dress nicely. I'll see you then."

"Wait a minute. Do you remember how to get to the house?" Brenda inquired.

"I'll pick you up in Palo Alto." Luke hung up the phone, thoroughly annoyed about Brenda's recent moves. *She's so blasted independent, but what good would it do her to live a wealthy, lonely life?* Moving away from Wyatt and Barry certainly wasn't a step in the right direction, and Luke was determined to set Brenda on the straight and narrow. Brenda had done everything in her adult lifetime alone, and Luke was determined to show her that two were better than one.

Chapter 16

After working all week, by Friday night Brenda could feel her body giving in to the disease. Her double vision returned slightly, and her left leg tingled with numbness. She had exceeded her limits at work, coming home each night later and later, sometimes even missing Luke's nine o'clock phone call. She fell into bed ready to celebrate the weekend and awaited Luke's call, which was punctual.

"Evenin', gorgeous." Luke's voice filled her senses.

"Hi, Luke."

"Are you ready for the big move?" It was the first time he'd mentioned the new house, and Brenda rejoiced at the possibility that he was happy for her.

"Not really. I'm afraid I overdid it this week. The movers can handle it. I don't have much, just my office and a sofa or two. I'll just rest at the new house and oversee everything."

"I had a feeling your job might continue to be an issue." Luke's voice was even, not showing the slightest hint of judgment. "Maybe God has something better for you," he said cryptically.

"It seems I'm stuck. I had always planned my own business, but I'd never get independent health insurance now. And who's going to hire me with MS? Even if it's in remission, I'd still have to disclose it on an application. With my meds costing nearly a thousand a month, I'm afraid I'm unhirable. Even with my excellent track record, I'm not worth the risk."

"Stop worrying. God has the answer," Luke said.

"I know, but I hope He speaks soon. These hours are killing me, and I don't ever want to be sick like that again. Not ever. I'll sell this house first and live off the proceeds. God has given me the financial ability to quit. I just don't have an answer to the health insurance problem. He will provide, though. I know He will." Brenda's voice was determined.

"Absolutely, He will. I love you, Brenda, and I can't wait to see you tomorrow." Luke knew how God would provide. Brenda would have Luke's health insurance as soon as she was his wife, and marrying a neurologist would most certainly be a benefit. She wouldn't have to work another day if she chose not to. Luke's plan was coming together nicely.

"I love you too, Luke," Brenda was finally able to say the words, and she felt immense relief at releasing her true feelings.

Luke arrived Saturday evening wearing a new pair of espresso brown slacks with a classic matching houndstooth check sport coat, "Luke Marcusson, I do believe you spent some money!" Brenda allowed Luke into the house and circled the doctor, investigating his new suit.

"Very funny. You look stunning, as usual," Luke replied, kissing her gently on her high cheekbone. She felt his touch pulse through her body. Brenda was wearing a dress she'd had custom designed for a work event. It was a muted aqua blue that matched her eyes, covered by tastefully placed beaded sparkles. The v-neck was cut deeper than normal for her, but a well-placed chiffon wrap preserved her modesty. Her hair was pulled up into a loose bun, with soft blond ringlets framing her face.

"Thank you," she said shyly. "Where are we going?"

"Somewhere I hope we'll never forget," he said mysteriously. "Where are Wyatt and Barry?"

"They spent the day away to allow the movers access. I guess they went out to dinner. I haven't had much rest. I hope I'll be good company tonight."

"You're always good company." Luke offered his arm and led Brenda to his sporty, yet practical, new car. They drove for nearly twenty minutes before stopping at a large gate surrounded by foliage on a remote roadside speckled with bicyclists. Luke got out of the car and unlocked the gates, drove in, and locked them behind him. Inside was a small, abandoned parking lot surrounded by large trees with a small dirt pathway between.

"Luke, where are we?"

"You'll see. Just be patient."

Luke assisted Brenda out of the car and opened the trunk, pulling out a huge wicker basket. They walked along the path, and soon the sound of rushing water invaded the stillness. The path soon opened to a clearing where a huge, white circular columned structure loomed above them. It was surrounded by a perimeter of small marble steps leading to a great pool below, which was enveloped in a sea of grass.

"Luke, it's so beautiful. What is this place?"

"It's the Pulgas Water Temple. This is where the water from the Hetch Hetchy River near Yosemite enters the Crystal Springs Reservoir."

"It's perfect." Brenda ran up the marble steps and marveled at the rush of crystal-clear water running through it. She pulled the clip from her hair and let her long, lustrous golden curls fall to her back. "I feel like a princess here."

"As it should be." Luke kept his eyes fastened on Brenda, delighting in her every movement as she skipped across the idyllic scene.

"Where is everybody? I would think people would flock here."

"It's closed most of the time. Vandals and drag racers on the road outside keep it off-limits. I have a friend who works for the water department. He gave me access. Are you hungry?"

"We're eating here?" Brenda's blue eyes brightened.

"Yes, I've packed dinner. I even shopped at the natural foods store. There's nothing on our menu with anything that violates the MS diet. No easy task, I might add."

"It's a pain, isn't it? And how I miss a good piece of prime rib."

"Not when I tell you our menu." Luke took her hand and climbed down the steps. Once on the grass near the shallow, elongated pool, he produced a red-and-white-checked tablecloth, snapping it smartly and laying it smoothly on the ground with a theatrical flair. On top of it he laid two matching chair cushions and set the "table" with real white china. He helped her to her seat and spread the feast before her. "First, we start with a fine appetizer; spinach-stuffed mushrooms, handmade by Wyatt. Next, we have our main course, lobster salad, followed by Raspberry Bavarian, courtesy of Dr. Swank's MS-approved recipes. Of course, we'll wash it down with a fine vintage." Luke lifted a bottle over his forearm and spoke in his best French accent, "Chateau du sparkling apple juice." Taking out two champagne flutes, he filled them.

"I don't know what to say. I'm so flattered." She looked at his warm hazel eyes and knew she didn't want to say anything. She wanted to show him, to feel the fire of his kiss and be beside him under the dwindling sunlight, amid the soothing sounds of flowing water. Luke lit a candle, and she shook the tempting thought from her head.

They ate without a word, searching one another's eyes and basking in their ever-growing love for one another. When they finished the meal, Luke hurriedly threw the dishes into the basket and came close. He lifted her into the canopy of the water temple and she squealed in surprise.

He placed her next to the well of rushing water and bent down on one knee. "Brenda Turner, I have waited so long for this day. I have stayed away for fear my physical attraction would prove too strong for us to bear. My heart's desire was to know you intimately, but I couldn't trust myself with you alone. That's why I've relied on the telephone so that I might learn everything about you without letting us both down."

Brenda was overcome by her own emotions, and happy tears filled her eyes at the revelation that he had stayed away so that he might pursue their relationship. The slight hint of green in his brown eyes mesmerized her, and she willed herself to allow him to continue talking, when she really wanted to bend down and make full use of his lips.

"I've watched you grow so deeply into your faith, becoming a woman of God that I know He delights in. I've watched you battle your disease with grace and dignity; and I know, Brenda, that my life will never be the same without you and I don't want it to be. Brenda Turner, will you marry me?" He held up the most magnificent ring she'd ever seen. It was a bright blue, brilliant-cut sapphire, encompassed between two smaller brilliant-cut diamonds and held up by a classic platinum band. It was obviously an estate piece; jewelers didn't make rings like that anymore.

Marriage? Brenda was stunned speechless, her blue eyes wide in shock. *Of course, a man like Luke would want to be married, but how can I say yes?* How could she when she'd watched her mother and her years of toil and pain? How could she, knowing she might not be healthy or able to care for his children? How could she when she already had everything she'd planned?

Brenda cringed. She was most afraid of Luke's careful spending habits. She had worked hard for her money, and she couldn't bear to hand control to a man. Not even an upright, godly man like Luke. She closed her eyes momentarily. Opening them, she looked into his expectant gaze and knew her lips would deceive her and reply yes. So she turned away, looking down at the rushing water beside her.

"I can't marry you, Luke. I'm sorry." She couldn't offer more, even at the risk of his feelings. If she did, she would certainly betray her true feelings. *Why couldn't we have continued the way we were? Why did you have to ruin it with a marriage proposal?*

Luke stood slowly and closed the ring box over the exquisite sapphire. "I see." Brenda had never heard a cold chill in his voice before. It was tempered and carefully restrained. He straightened to his full six-foot-three stature and squared his broad shoulders. "That ends the entertainment portion of our evening." Luke held his arm out, but Brenda just couldn't bring herself to grasp it. His touch would break her resolve. She walked swiftly to the car, waiting at the passenger door while he collected the picnic basket.

Brenda wanted to make things right, but words failed her. She could think of nothing that might offer an acceptable excuse to Luke. How could she tell him that she had always dreamed of true love but that had never included marriage? The fantasy always stopped before the altar. The silence in the car lasted for a painful eternity. Brenda's only request was that Luke take her to the Palo Alto house, because the Menlo Park home would only be salt in the wound to her beloved. She couldn't endure a night in an empty, lonely house tonight. Luke dropped her at the door and she scurried into the house, bidding him a quick, obligatory good night.

Brenda ran to her bedroom and threw herself on the bed, her whole frame quaking from her deafening sobs. She cried for over an hour before she heard the front door open. Brenda hurriedly sat up, wiping the tears from her cheeks and hugging her long legs to her chest.

"Brenda, we're home!" Wyatt announced, shortly before appearing in the

117

doorway. "Oh, you are here. I thought you might be at the new. . .what's the matter? You look a terrible sight."

"Luke asked me to marry him."

"Brenda, that's wonderful! Why are you crying?" Wyatt went to the bedroom door. "Barry, I'll be a minute." She closed the door and sat at the edge of Brenda's bed. "You said yes, right?"

"No." Brenda inhaled roughly, choking over her cries. She carried on for several minutes before looking Wyatt in the eyes. "It's not something you'd understand. I'm just not the marrying kind. I'm not like you or my mother."

"No, you're not, but I don't understand what that has to do with marrying the man you love. Let go of this before you lose the man I know you love! You owe me an explanation, and I'm not leaving until I get it!" Wyatt crossed her arms defiantly.

Brenda saw fire in Wyatt's green eyes, a wrathful intensity she'd never seen in her gentle friend. Brenda began slowly. "I don't know where to start." Seeing that Wyatt's demeanor hadn't changed, she went on. "My parents were strong believers in the Bible. They went to a strict, frightening church where I never saw an ounce of love portrayed. Their view of God was that He was vengeful and terrifying; He was never tempered with love, and I guess you could say that was how our home life was as well."

"Go on," Wyatt stated impatiently.

"My mother felt a woman's *only* calling in life was to get married and have children. They saved every extra cent to send my brother to college, but I wouldn't *need* college. When I didn't have a husband after high school, they finally relented and said they'd pay for community college. You can probably guess the rest. I didn't find a husband there either. Probably because that's the last thing I ever wanted."

"What about your brother?"

"Doug was raised to believe the man was the head of the household. My mom and dad were determined to see their pattern continue in our lives. I would be the submissive housewife and my brother the strong husband. Unfortunately, they did everything for Doug while they left me to my own devices. They figured I wouldn't need their help because a husband would soon manage everything for me. I learned to do everything for myself while Doug was left virtually reliant upon them. I earned a full scholarship and finished my MBA at Stanford Business School. Doug never did finish. He didn't have the least idea of how to manage for himself. Last I heard, he was a stay-at-home dad, and his wife works to provide for them. He was happy with the arrangement, and I don't fault him, but still it's ironic."

"That still doesn't explain why you're not speaking."

"My parents died of carbon monoxide poisoning while I was at Stanford. My dad was too cheap to replace the old furnace. It was during finals week, and I couldn't risk losing my scholarship to go back East. My entire family was morti-fied at my career goals, that they would take precedence over my parent's funeral. They all thought I was so driven because no man would have me. My grand-parents had arranged for me to meet a carefully selected man from their church. Going back, even for the funeral, felt like death to me. I didn't want to lose my freedom again. And I still don't."

"You can't possibly think Luke cares about your money." Wyatt's eyes had tears in them now.

"I know how carefully he spends it, and I won't stand for somebody telling me I can't buy boneless chicken because it's cheaper to debone it myself."

Wyatt began laughing and covered her mouth, trying to stop. "You're not going to marry the man you love because you think he might make you debone a chicken?"

Brenda also began giggling through her tears. "No, I'm not going to marry him because I love him more than anything on this earth. How could I ever say no to him? If he told me to buy the whole chicken and pluck it myself, I just might do it." The two broke into laughter again.

Wyatt soon became serious again. "Luke is not like your father. He relishes your independence."

"No, but he would be the head of the household, right?" Brenda asked sheepishly.

"That's what the Bible says, but Brenda, God's plan is for you to submit to Luke's will because he would act in the best interest of his family. The full respon-sibility of his household rests upon him. That's a huge sacrifice for a man to make."

"I don't want to submit to Luke," Brenda admitted stubbornly.

"You don't want to submit to God either. I know all this is new to you, but you've got to learn to trust in God and not your wealth. Money and material goods will all pass away. When Christ returns, do you want to be left with your stuff or lifted into the clouds with Jesus?" Wyatt patted her arm and left. Before closing the door behind her, she left her with one last thought. "Read the story of the rich young ruler in Matthew nineteen. God is giving you all His blessings, including a man after His own heart. Which will you choose? You'll never truly own anything unless you give it to God first."

Chapter 17

B renda continued to read her Bible and pray, but she skipped over any passages that spoke of money. *God doesn't live on earth. He doesn't understand the importance of a healthy bank account here in Silicon Valley. The Bible was written a long time ago; certainly some things have changed.* Her financial portfolio was her compensation for this terrible disease she endured.

Luke no longer called and Brenda only saw him occasionally at church. He never sat with her, spoke with her, or mentioned anything of his proposal. If pressed with unavoidable contact, he would simply nod and be on his way or ask rigidly about her health.

Brenda ached at his coldness. She longed to rush to him, but Luke never allowed her the opportunity. Worst of all was the knowledge that she loved him, and that she lived in *their* perfect home—alone. Brenda didn't feel the completeness in the Menlo Park house that she'd felt when buying the Victorian. As a matter of fact, she didn't feel anything about the big, sterile country home that once seemed as warm as a cold winter night in front of a roaring fire.

Only her time alone with God filled her with warmth. God had been faithful to honor Brenda's prayers of physical healing, but her soul still ached for something more she couldn't describe.

As winter neared, Brenda's discontentment grew, and her ability to keep up with the pressures of her job as vice president dwindled. After deep prayer, Brenda knew she would have to resign her executive post. One overcast October morning, she humbly entered the office of her general manager and asked for a smaller assignment. Knowing she wouldn't be able to handle the tasks of a similar position elsewhere, and in desperate need of health coverage, Brenda asked to be a marketing manager within her own department.

The first week of November, Brenda bid farewell to her spacious corner office overlooking the man-made lakes on the company campus, and moved into a simple, gray cubicle. Her new boss and former rival, Mike Wilcox, took over her old mahogany desk and sweeping water views.

Brenda had moved the last few boxes into her cubicle when Katie appeared. "I got Mike's old cubicle. It's the biggest one there is," Brenda said enthusiastically, while she fought back tears. Katie came forward and hugged her. "I won't have anybody to get me a mocha or a Balance bar."

"I'll still do that as long as I'm here. I did that because I was your friend,

Brenda, not your slave. In case you haven't heard, secretaries don't do those things anymore. We're administrative assistants now. You're supposed to get your own coffee."

Brenda broke into laughter.

"Seriously, you were a great boss. Who else would have gotten me such a huge share of stock? I'm nearly as rich as any of the managers in this place."

"Well, you did more work than most of them did," Brenda stated truthfully.

Katie pulled forward a chair and motioned for Brenda to sit. "Jacob and I talked to an architect last night."

"An architect?"

"We're adding on to the East Palo Alto house. We've gotten to know Tasha pretty well since she's been visiting Daydan, and we found out she dreams of being a nurse like Wyatt."

"I thought Tasha was getting custody of Daydan."

"She will have custody, but it seems we're getting custody of Tasha. She's going to live with us. We just agreed two nights ago. Thanks to you and our stock money, we can afford to build a new private room and pay for Tasha's college. I'm quitting my job, so I can be home with Daydan during the day while she attends school. Day's grandmother is getting too feeble to keep up with him all day long. He's got more energy than a speeding train. We've grown to love Tasha so much and being around us, she's seen how much we love Day, and it's made a huge difference. I don't think she wants him to lose that, especially with Jacob for a father."

"You're leaving?" Brenda was stunned, unable to fathom life at work without her Christian sister. Life appeared bleaker than ever. She was alone in her big empty house, and now she would be alone at work as well.

"Brenda, I'm only in East Palo Alto, and if you're afraid to come see us, we'll come see you. We'll see you every Sunday at church, like we always do."

"It's just not the same. It was so much easier to come to work, knowing you'd be here if I had an attack or needed support. I always thought I'd have financial freedom to leave, but now that I have the money, I'm stuck because of health benefits."

"Keep praying, Brenda, and stop putting your trust in money and start looking to Him." Katie looked upward.

⇜❧❧⇝

Luke had learned all he cared to about computer-aided surgery. He was yearning to get back to his first love of neurology and his patients. Barry and Wyatt had almost raised the needed support to get back to Africa, and they would be leaving within months after the new baby arrived. It was time to confront Dr. Olgilvy. Luke had prayed for a way out, but God had remained silent on the subject and his deadline grew ever nearer.

LeAnne, Luke's nurse, appeared in the doorway to his office. "Barry called.

Wyatt just had an eight-pound, seven-ounce girl and they've named her Grace. They're over at the hospital. Barry won't be in today, so your first appointment is at ten."

Luke ran to the hospital, anxious to see Barry's first child. He was breathless when he arrived.

Wyatt looked exhausted but radiant. She held the baby girl in her arms and her euphoria was apparent. Barry hovered behind her with a new father's pride. "Have you ever seen a more beautiful sight?" she asked, noticing Luke.

"No. A beautiful baby in your arms is probably the most precious sight God will ever grant me. I'm so happy for you both." Luke bent down and kissed Wyatt's forehead.

"We've waited so long for this, and it's better than I ever dreamed it would be. I feel more love for this child than I could ever put into words." Tears streamed down Wyatt's cheeks while she wore her widest smile.

"Wyatt, she's beautiful. Just like her mother." Brenda appeared by the bed with an extravagant bouquet of flowers and a huge teddy bear with a big pink collar. Under her arm, she carried a box wrapped in pink ribbons and bows, with a sterling silver rattle as a centerpiece of the wrap.

"How did you know it was a girl?" Barry asked, noting the pink.

"I didn't. I have the exact bounty at home in blue, in case it was a boy." They all laughed and watched the baby intensely. "May I hold her, Wyatt?" Brenda meekly asked.

"Oh, please do," Wyatt answered. Brenda sat in a nearby chair to avoid any unexpected dizziness and took the precious bundle from Barry. Tears filled her eyes, and Luke was torn by the scene, wishing he didn't have to watch the woman he loved cradle a baby. *She might have been ours, Lord.* Brenda inadvertently looked at him and the storm of emotion was too great.

"I've got to get back to the office. My partner's nowhere to be found today, and I've got a full load of his patients." Luke patted Barry on the back and kissed Wyatt's cheek. Luke exited as quickly as he could without a glance or remark toward Brenda.

⁓⊱❈⊰⁓

Brenda spent the entire morning with tiny Grace, until the newborn cried for her mother. As she suckled, Barry left the women alone. "I'll go check on a few patients while I'm here," he offered by way of excuse.

"Luke looks great, doesn't he?" Wyatt asked.

Brenda nodded. "My new job is going well, but by Friday night, I'm worn to the bone." Brenda's robotic conversation did not go unnoticed by her closest friend.

"You know we'll be leaving for Africa soon. I thought you might want to place an ad for the Victorian. We won't be needing it after the first of the year."

"I'll get that done. Thanks," she said absently.

"Why are you doing this to yourself? You love Luke. I know you love Luke. Brenda, tell him before he moves on with his life." Even with her strength depleted from childbirth, Wyatt remained steadfast in spurring Brenda.

"It's not that easy, Wyatt. Luke and I have different outlooks on the future. It's just like the reason he said you two broke up. Our lives are going in different directions."

"Do you think I wanted to abandon the cushy life of a Stanford doctor's wife to go live in a desert across the world, with critters I'd never heard of, and bugs the size of compact cars?"

"You're a nurse, Wyatt. You love people."

"I love people, but not enough to forfeit a fancy lifestyle for them. Only God could change my heart—and He did. Now I *want* my daughter raised in Africa, and I want to grow old, seeing thousands saved by the medical help we can provide. But none of it is from me. *I* couldn't have cared less. Without God's prodding, I would have never known that world existed. God restored your health, Brenda. Now ask yourself what you'll do with that gift."

"Everyone's leaving me. You and Barry, Katie and Jacob. I've lost you all in the blink of an eye." Tears of self-pity overcame her, but Wyatt was without sympathy.

"You haven't lost everyone. God is still here, and He's left you a man who loves you deeply. Did you see Luke's eyes when he watched you with Grace? For cryin' out loud, Brenda, go tell him you love him before it's too late. Is any amount of money really worth his feelings? Did you read about the rich young ruler yet?"

"I read it. A rich young man asked Jesus what he needed to do to gain eternal life. Jesus told him first not to murder, nor commit adultery, not to steal, nor to give false testimony, and to honor his mother and father, and love his neighbor as himself. Then he needed to go and sell everything he had."

"Why? Jesus said all we have to do is place our faith in Him, so why would He tell him that?" Wyatt persisted.

"Because he'd have no use for it. But we live in an expensive area, Wyatt. Obviously, I can't go sell everything I own."

"Jesus told the young man to go sell everything he had because the young man's sin was covetousness, and his riches were between God and him, keeping him from a true relationship with God. There's nothing wrong with having money, unless the money has you."

"But the Bible says he went away sad because he had great wealth, so maybe he did give it up! And he was sad because he had so much; that makes sense. If Jesus asked me to sell my houses or stocks, I would."

"The young man turned his back on Jesus! If he truly were going to follow Jesus, he would have left with joy and not thought twice about his things. He didn't sell them, and I don't think you'd sell yours either, Brenda."

"Are you saying I'm not saved? What about all that saved by grace business?"

"Brenda, you are saved. You've been washed clean by Christ, but you're holding back your possessions from Him, unable to take full advantage of what He offers. God doesn't need your things, Brenda. I'm just saying, until you offer them, you'll never own true freedom."

"Take care of Grace. I'll be back tomorrow. I love you, Wyatt, even though you're a nag," she added quietly. She smiled and kissed her friend's cheek and the baby once more.

"I love you, Brenda. I'll always be there for you."

Brenda walked into the hospital corridor and exhaled deeply. Wyatt was right; Brenda no longer received pleasure from her things. They were a constant reminder of what she didn't have: Luke, Katie, and soon Wyatt and Barry. God was slowly taking her loved ones away one by one, making her new home feel sparser and emptier with each passing moment.

"Miss Turner?" Brenda turned to see a handsome, middle-aged doctor approaching.

"Dr. Olgilvy, what a nice surprise. How are you?" Brenda took his offered hand and shook it sincerely.

"It's Frederick, and I'm fine. Are you here to have lunch with Luke?"

"No, I'm visiting a friend who just had a baby, actually—the prettiest baby ever," Brenda bragged like a proud grandmother.

"The best reason to come to the hospital," Dr. Olgilvy commented.

"No kidding. After those MS corticosteroid treatments, I didn't think I'd ever step into a hospital by choice again." Brenda realized suddenly that Dr. Olgilvy didn't know about her disease, and she felt like kicking herself.

"Brenda, you have MS?" Dr. Olgilvy asked incredulously.

"Yes, I thought Luke might have told you. That's actually how we met. He was my doctor until we began seeing each other on a personal level." Just being able to say his name freely felt like a victory.

"Have you had lunch yet?" he asked.

"No, actually, I haven't." Brenda could feel her stomach grumbling.

"Gloria's waiting in my office. Why don't you join us for lunch?"

Brenda wanted to say no, but how could she? Luke's boss was a man of prominent stature and more importantly, a man who had power over Luke's career. It was the least she could do for Luke, after she had so blatantly disregarded his feelings.

Entering Dr. Olgilvy's office, Brenda noticed a petite brunette chatting easily with Mrs. Olgilvy. She wore a pale pink nurse's uniform and it was cut tightly to show off her slender, young body.

"Brenda, what a nice surprise. This is Nurse Eve Moore. Have you two met?" Gloria asked. "Eve, this is Brenda Turner, Luke's girlfriend."

The pretty nurse came toward Brenda, extending a hand and producing a counterfeit smile. "So, Luke's into blonds now." The nurse looked Brenda up and down, eyeing her jealously. "Tsk, tsk, such a fickle thing he is." Brenda filled with rage, and she clenched her jaw tightly, at a loss to respond kindly. *How dare this impudent little nurse disparage Luke in front of the Olgilvys.* Sensing her anger, Eve continued, "Luke and I go way back. Hasn't he mentioned me? No? Isn't that just like Luke." She looked back at the Olgilvys, seeing if they were interested in her comments.

"A doctor that looks like Luke is bound to have a history," Gloria offered, by way of a white flag, hoping to dispel the obvious clash between the two women.

Brenda decided to put an end to the awful scene quickly. "Shall we go?" Brenda asked cheerfully, while looking down over Eve Moore's small frame.

The Olgilvys eagerly agreed, and they spent a delightful lunch discussing Brenda's favorite topic: Luke Marcusson. She learned so much about Luke's new surgical skills, and she was further impressed by each sentence. She had no idea the technique or abilities required to perform his latest job as assistant chief to Dr. Olgilvy.

The Olgilvys continued to talk of their latest stock deals and art purchases. Hearing them rattle off prices and money gains, Brenda heard the characteristics in herself that she hated most and wondered if God was trying to tell her something.

❦

After lunch, Brenda ran back into Wyatt's hospital room. "Wyatt! Wyatt!" she whispered loudly, rousing the young mother from her sleep. "Please wake up."

"Brenda, is everything okay?" Wyatt wiped her eyes with the back of her hand. "Is the baby okay?" she asked with a look of alarm.

"Everybody's fine!"

"Brenda, what—"

"You were right. Money hasn't helped me—it only stirs up my worst attributes. My father loved me. I didn't realize that until now. He would never have been impressed with my accomplishments, because they are all based on earthly things! He wanted me to know God, and a husband was secondary! I allowed my father to go without ever telling him I loved him. Now I'll have to wait, but I can't do that to Luke. I've got to tell him how I feel! I've been living on faith in my money, not God. I allowed myself to believe in God because I knew *I* could take care of everything! That's what you've been trying to tell me, isn't it?"

"Yes, Brenda," Wyatt said through tears.

"After we talked about the rich young ruler, God gave me a prime example in the Olgilvys. They have everything I thought I wanted, but their lives are so empty. Did you know they never had children because they'd interfere with her tennis game? After seeing Grace, I knew what I really wanted. I just pray I'm not too late. When I get home, I'm signing my stock over to your ministry. It's worth about three million dollars right now. If I'm going to trust in God, I need to trust Him fully."

"How——?" Wyatt was wide-eyed.

"I just heard two very wealthy people who sounded very poor in soul to me," Brenda said. "I need to do this."

"What about Luke? What changed your mind about him?"

"That was just simple, unbridled jealously. I heard this nurse talking about him like he was a piece of meat, and I knew immediately that I don't want him in anyone's arms but mine! I gotta go. Love you!" Brenda ran out the door in her excitement and straight across the street to Luke's office.

Wyatt looked up to the ceiling and mouthed, "Thank You."

Chapter 18

Brenda rushed into Luke's office and was met in her breathless state by Luke's unfriendly nurse. "Can I help you?" she asked icily.

"LeAnne, I need to see Luke. Will you please tell him I'm waiting? I know we've had our differences in the past, but please, this is very important."

"He's in his office. Go ahead," she said with a hint of a smile.

Brenda raced into his office before her resolve left her. She closed the door behind her and Luke looked up from his chair, confused. "Brenda, are you all right?" He stood to his full stature, and Brenda thought she'd melt at the sight of him.

"Never better. Would you mind sitting?" she asked shyly and he obediently sat back down. "I had lunch with the Olgilvys today. They think very highly of you." Brenda tried to catch her breath, but her chest pumped wildly.

"Did you come all the way over here to tell me that?" Luke asked briskly.

"No." Brenda walked toward him, keeping her eyes firmly directed at his. As she approached, he rolled his chair back away from the desk. Brenda sat suddenly and uninvited in his lap and gazed intently into his captivating hazel eyes. Stroking his rugged jawline gently with her long fingers, she began her unrehearsed speech.

"Luke, I know I can be hardheaded and exasperating, but worst of all, I can be extremely foolish. I thought we could continue without marriage, that I wouldn't become ensnared in what my parents planned for me. I know now that my father wasn't the best role model, but I also know that he did what he thought was best. What I'm trying to say is that I trust you, Luke. I trust you to do what's best for me. Just like the day you kidnapped me and dragged me back to the hospital. You brought me back my eyesight, and, more importantly, you showed me that sometimes you do know what's best for me, more so than I do."

"What is it you want, Brenda? My forgiveness? Consider it granted," he said coolly.

Brenda took his face in her hands and came mere inches from him. She could feel his warm breath and her own rapidly beating heart. She whispered softly, "No, Luke, I want you completely as my husband and my lover and the head of my household." Tears overcame her.

"Brenda Turner, you are exasperating!" He stood up to leave but moved her into the chair.

"Luke, I'm sorry. I didn't—"

"Just be quiet for five minutes, will you, please?"

Brenda crossed her arms in her lap, and Luke returned and knelt down beside her. "I am head of the household. I do the asking. Understood?"

"Yes, Sir!" She saluted.

He stood and began to walk out of the office once again. "Luke, that's just cruel. If you just wanted to play with my heart—"

"Brenda, what did I just tell you?" He looked back, his warm eyes smiling.

"I'm shutting up." Brenda used her hands to close the pretend zipper over her mouth.

Luke returned moments later and knelt beside her. "Miss Turner, I think you are the most beautiful, exhausting woman I have ever laid eyes upon, and I will do you proud as head of your household. Say you'll be my wife." Luke held up the tiny black velvet box with the familiar sapphire sparkling inside it.

"Yes, Luke. *Yes!*" She jumped from the chair and almost bowled him over. He stood awkwardly to his feet and they enveloped each other in a giant hug.

"I'm curious. What changed your mind?" He looked down and kissed the top of her head.

"I'm embarrassed to admit it, but this vixen, Nurse Moore, at the hospital."

"Eve?" Luke was dumbfounded.

"That's her. That conniving little tease implied in front of Dr. and Mrs. Olgilvy that you two had had an affair. I knew you had better taste in women, but it sure got me to thinking that I didn't want any better women coming along. The thought of you with someone else was more than I could handle. It was fine when it was you alone, but you with someone else—that did it. Besides, with Wyatt as your ex-girlfriend, I knew you were bound to find some sweet, gentle little thing, and then you'd know better than to come back to me."

Luke laughed uproariously. "I doubt that, Brenda. You've got a couple things in your favor. First of all, you're devastatingly beautiful, and more importantly, I'm head over heels in love with that opinionated, defiant, hardheaded, godly woman that lives inside. Remind me to send a bouquet of roses to Eve Moore. I owe that woman a great deal."

"Besides, I have one more alternative therapy I can't try without you," Brenda said sheepishly, her cheeks tinged with pink.

"What would that be?"

"Pregnancy. It seems the hormones have some astounding effect on multiple sclerosis that causes remission. So, next bout, we've got a date."

"Let's hope there won't be any further bouts, but that doesn't have to alter our plans." Luke kissed his bride-to-be again and broke himself away reluctantly.

"What were you doing with Olgilvy, anyway?"

"We had lunch with Gloria, of course. By the way, he would understand if you wanted to cut back on surgeries. He wasn't aware of my disease, but now he says he understands why you're so involved in multiple sclerosis issues," Brenda replied innocently.

"I've been trying to accomplish that for six months. How is it you managed to sign my partial resignation in one lunch hour?"

Brenda only shrugged.

"Seriously, Brenda. I owe you and the Ogilvys a big apology. Lying got me into that mess, and I'm going to come clean with Olgilvy and explain myself. I've asked God to forgive me, and I hope that you will too. That was a terrible example I set, telling others you were my girlfriend before it was true."

"I knew it wasn't typical of you, Luke. I could tell by how uneasy it made you, not to mention what Wyatt and Barry told me about your integrity."

The two locked in a kiss, resolving to leave lying in their past.

Epilogue

Dear Wyatt, Barry, and Grace,

Brenda has been in complete remission for nearly a year now. We're praising the Lord for His provisions and hoping we can claim victory over multiple sclerosis for good. Glad to hear your ministry is thriving. Brenda was delighted to hear that the money has helped to save so many lives already.

I finally relented and bought a "tax shelter" in the form of a business office for Brenda. She has started a new job in East Palo Alto, running a nonprofit program that equips the poor for the workplace. The biggest change in her is seeing the compassion in her heart for these people. I think she started the ministry with a chip on her shoulder, but God showed her the devastation caused by being unable to provide for your family, and her heart has changed.

We visited Brenda's brother last month. They had a rough time, but I think things will eventually work out. Brenda promised to visit again, and she delighted in her niece and nephews.

The best piece of news I have is that Brenda is pregnant with our first child. Please pray for her and the baby's continued health. As for me, I'm performing between one and two surgeries a week and keeping my practice full. Olgilvy wants to make sure I devote enough time to MS to ensure Brenda's future. Baylor finally called, but I turned them down. God has called me here.

In His Love,
Luke

KRISTIN BILLERBECK
Kristin lives in Northern California with her husband, an engineering director, and their four young children. A marketing director by profession, Kristin now stays home to be with her children and writes for enjoyment.

A Gift from Above

Dina Leonhardt Koehly

Dedication

This book is dedicated to my gifts from above:
Craig, Nicole, Madelyn,
my parents,
Drew, Lana, Blake, and Tanner.

*Every good gift and every perfect gift
is from above.*
JAMES 1:17

Chapter 1

Celine Hart stopped abruptly and glanced quickly in the window of Barton's Bookstore. Through the glass she could see a hazy reflection of herself, and she noticed that her hair was a tousled mess. She reached into her handbag and retrieved her hairbrush to tame her windblown hair. Her eyes then located what she had been looking for through the window—Celine Hart, the author's name, was boldly printed on the front cover of the best-seller romance novel. Celine Hart. . .her name. . .her book.

As she continued to stare at the book display, she touched the glass, and suddenly she was unable to move as the weight of terrible sadness grew inside her.

Darrell had left her because of this? She still couldn't believe it. Celine had thought that Darrell would have been happy about the success of her third novel, *The Winds of Love*. But when it had made the New York list of best-selling books, he had been livid with jealousy and then proceeded to give her an ultimatum—either give up her writing career or forget their wedding in the fall.

Celine had been completely startled and shocked by his reaction. She recalled their conversation.

"What does my writing career have to do with our wedding?" she had asked him.

"I will not have any wife of mine wasting her time writing books to fulfill other people's fantasies," he had replied sternly.

Celine shook her head sadly as she recalled his hurtful words. He had made her novels sound so cheap and dirty. In her opinion, as well as her fans', she wrote beautiful love stories to give people, as well as herself, an escape from their daily pressures and worries by whisking them away into a private world full of dreams, romance, and, most of all, love.

Her mind drifted back to Darrell. The real problem wasn't the book, she concluded. It was his self-centered attitude in believing that he was the only one in the relationship who deserved to have a successful career. How could she have been so blind to this obvious character flaw in him?

Celine was thankful for one thing, though, and that was that she had written *The Winds of Love* before the wedding and had found out what he was really made of before it was too late. Silently, she thanked God for watching over her. At one time, Celine would have done practically anything for Darrell, but now she realized that she had been blinded by love. And when Darrell had dared to ask, or rather demand, that she give up her writing career, she knew for sure that his definition of love was different than hers.

Celine's thoughts wandered off to some comforting words defining love. "Love is patient, love is kind," she said in an almost inaudible whisper as she recalled what she had learned from the Bible. "It does not envy, it does not boast. . . . It is not easily angered, it keeps no record of wrongs. Love does not delight in evil but rejoices with the truth. It always protects, always trusts, always hopes, always perseveres. Love never fails."*

Celine tore her gaze from the store window as she silently questioned, *Lord, will I ever find that kind of love?*

She walked over to her convertible parked by the curb and opened the door. At first, when Darrell had ended their relationship, Celine had wallowed miserably in self-pity, but now she was just plain furious with herself for falling for such a jerk. Celine threw her handbag into the car then slid onto the seat. Why did life have to be so difficult? Just when her life had been going so well, she had suddenly been thrown a curveball.

It had been over two months now since Darrell had walked out of her life without a second glance back, and Celine knew she had to let go of the hurt and get on with her life. Why was she still being so melodramatic about it?

She started up the engine and headed for home. The noonday sun was unusually warm for November in southern California, and she was looking forward to a long swim in the community pool. Maybe that would take her mind off Darrell. Yes, a good swim was what she needed.

⁂

The next morning, after hours of getting absolutely nowhere, Celine stared at the computer screen, reviewing her work. *What work?* she asked herself dismally, then looked down at the keyboard and punched a single key to erase the last sentence she had typed in.

"Brad, why can't you help your beloved Belinda straighten out her life?" Celine questioned the hero of her latest novel. Then she slammed her fist against the keyboard and groaned. Nothing was going right for her today.

The morning had begun with Queen Esther, her calico cat, knocking over her mug and spilling hot coffee on her white sweatpants. Celine had wanted to give Queenie her walking papers right there and then, but Queenie, with her big, beautiful, brown eyes, had looked up at her mistress and begged for another chance.

"Humph," Celine had muttered. "I've given that cat a million chances. Why should I give her another?"

---

*1 Corinthians 13:4–8 NIV

Then Queenie, sensing that her mistress was still upset, had given her best performance, playfully rolling over, softly purring, and looking up at Celine.

"Oh, all right," Celine had said as she threw up her hands in exasperation. "I'll give you one more chance." Celine's problem was that she was too much of a softy and Queenie, with her feline senses, knew that she could work Celine. Celine had to chuckle. Queenie was one smart cat.

The sound of the phone ringing brought Celine back to the present. In the past three hours, there had been so many distractions and interruptions that she hadn't even finished three sentences. Trying to complete a novel was hard enough without any interference, but this was getting ridiculous.

Just as the phone rang for the third time, Queenie, with her tail high in the air, sauntered back into the study. Celine threw her a pleading look. "You owe me one, Queenie. Would you answer the phone and tell the caller that I'm not available at the moment?"

Queenie meowed and cocked her head and, almost as if she understood the request, stared up questioningly at Celine. As Celine reached for the black desk phone, she sighed and wondered why she hadn't just put on the answering machine for the day.

"Hello," she answered in an abrupt voice.

"Celine, where's that sweet, cheerful voice of yours?" her mother, Samantha, asked.

"Oh, hello, Mom. I'm not in a good mood," she apologized. "I think I got up on the wrong side of the bed this morning, and let me add that Queenie didn't help much to make it better."

"I take it that Queen Esther is up to her old tricks again?" her mother speculated.

"That's putting it mildly," she grumbled.

Samantha laughed softly at her daughter's plight. "Changing the subject, how is your book progressing?"

"Don't ask," Celine moaned. "I'm going to have to call Edward to ask for an extension on the deadline, and I'm dreading it. He's not going to be very happy about it."

"What's the holdup?"

"I can't seem to get past chapter four. Belinda is an emotional mess, and she doesn't want to get any help, and then there's Brad, and of course he's head over heels in love with her, but she can't make a commitment due to the fact that she's so wrapped up in her own problems."

"Ugh, it doesn't sound too good. Might I make a suggestion?" her mother asked, then without waiting for a reply, she continued. "Why doesn't Belinda see a Christian counselor? That way she can get help with resolving her problems. I have a good reference, Dr. Andrea Carroll."

Celine couldn't help but chuckle at her mom's suggestion. Dr. Carroll was her mother's friend of twenty years. "Mom, thank you, but no thank you. You know I can't write something like that. Edward doesn't like any religious input in my novels. The books that make it to the best-seller list are the ones filled with intrigue, passion, mystery, high society, exotic locations, romantic cities—"

"Yes," her mother intervened before Celine could finish. "I know, it's the glitzy, glamour stuff. Remember that I've read all your books, Honey," she reminded. "I just happen to believe also that you could still be successful writing novels with an inspirational message."

"It's a nice idea, Mom, but it has one major flaw," Celine commented. "There's really not much of a market out there for that type of book."

"But have you really checked it out?"

"Well, no, I haven't," she admitted. "Maybe I will one of these days," Celine said, trying to placate her mother.

After they said their good-byes, Celine hung up the phone and then dialed Edward, her editor. She greeted him and chatted for a few minutes, then told Edward the bad news. His reaction was what she had expected; she held the phone away from her ears.

"Celine. . .Celine, are you listening?" he demanded.

She put the receiver back to her ear. "Yes, I'm here."

"Well, tell me when you can have it ready."

"I'll have it to you by the first of the next month," she said.

"Celine, I'm cutting you slack this time," he growled. "Don't do it again."

"Thanks, Edward. I really do appreciate it."

"I know, I know," he said, his voice softer. "Good luck with Belinda and Brad."

"I'll talk to you soon," she said, then hung up.

Celine sat back in her chair and pondered her mother's earlier suggestion. Writing an inspirational novel would surely be interesting and gratifying, but would it be as profitable financially as compared to what she was now earning with her secular novels for Pennington Publishers? Definitely not, she surmised without a second thought.

Celine massaged her forehead with her fingers; she had a tension headache, and the pain was getting worse by the minute. She decided to turn off her computer for the day, and she hoped that tomorrow would bring some fresh, new ideas her way.

Celine got up and walked over to the window. Outside, the neighborhood children were playing football in the grassy area. She loved the community in which she lived. After *The Winds of Love* had surprisingly made New York's best-seller list, Celine had decided to buy the town house in which she lived now. Her father, Chase, and her brother, Raine, had helped her out with all the financial details, since that area wasn't one of her strong points.

At twenty-eight, Celine seemed to have it all, or so her friends and family thought, but she felt that there was a certain void in her life—an emptiness that no material possession could fill or satisfy. It was more than having a man in her life to fulfill her. But what was it? She couldn't put her finger on it and that bothered her immensely. She grimaced as she turned from the window. "Why do I always have to analyze everything?" she muttered under her breath.

She walked into her bedroom and changed into her sweat suit, then laced up her sneakers. In the bathroom, she tied her hair back and stared back at her reflection in the mirror. She had high cheekbones, deep blue eyes, and blond hair that cascaded over her shoulders like spun gold. Her best feature, though, was her smile and, when her dimples appeared, it could melt anyone's heart, or so her father would say.

Celine headed for the park for her daily run. After her run, she noticed that her headache had disappeared. In fact, she felt so good that she decided to drive over to her sister-in-law's house for their weekly chat.

As Celine drove up the familiar palm-studded driveway, her eyes scanned the front yard for any signs of their dog, Peppy. As she parked her car, she didn't spot him, but she wasn't going to take any chances either. Quickly, she got out of the car, locked it, and was headed for the front door of the house when, without notice, Celine was propelled forward by a big fur ball placing huge paws on her back. Peppy was a gigantic English sheepdog with glacier blue eyes under the mass of his white and bluish gray hair, who loved to play with everyone, friend or foe. *He obviously isn't much of a guard dog,* Celine mused. Her brother, Raine, always argued that point, though, and would defend his buddy by saying Peppy would lick the burglar to death.

Celine reached down and ruffled Peppy's ears and gave his back a good scratching. Peppy playfully rolled over, wanting his belly rubbed, which Celine did without hesitation. When she saw that he was really relaxed, she bounced up and darted for the door. Fortunately, Lynette, her sister-in-law, had the door open when Celine reached it and, before Peppy could scramble for the door, Lynette had it closed. The front door shook under Peppy's weight. Celine giggled, looked at Lynette, and said, "You better check into getting Peppy's brakes fixed or one of these days he's going to come crashing through this door."

Lynette nodded, then smiled. "I'll have Raine look into it, since he's the mechanic in the family." Celine laughed as she followed Lynette out to the backyard to sit on the lounge chairs by the pool. It was a nice, sunny afternoon, and the sun's warm rays felt good against her skin.

"Ce, I hope you'll stay for dinner tonight. Raine hasn't seen you for awhile," Lynette said as she handed Celine a tall glass of iced tea.

"I'd love to stay," she agreed, willingly accepting the invitation. Since it was a Friday night and she didn't have any plans, she most certainly wasn't in the mood to go home and work on chapter four of her book. Celine definitely welcomed the diversion.

For the rest of the afternoon, the two women sat outside and talked about the news of the week, which included everything from world politics to a delicious new pasta recipe that Lynette had tried out.

At seven sharp, Raine walked through the door and marched straight into the kitchen. "What's that wonderful wife of mine cooking tonight?" Raine asked, then smiled when he spotted his sister, sitting at the table, peeling cucumbers and carrots for the salad. "Hey, Ce, what a nice surprise."

"Hi, Raine," Celine greeted him cheerfully. "I haven't seen you in the last few weeks, so I presume that you've been working hard at D.W.'s?"

Lynette glanced over her shoulder from the sink. "What's new? I've barely seen Raine in the last few weeks either."

"Hey, don't gang up on me," Raine bellowed. "You both know after all these years that my hours double at D.W.'s when it's around the holiday season."

"Well, well, aren't we grouchy tonight, Darling. But Ce and I will lift your sour mood with our fantastic home cooking," Lynette remarked lovingly as she went over and gave Raine a hug and kiss. "Now be a good boy and change for dinner. The meal will be ready in a few minutes, so hurry."

Raine grinned at his wife's attempt to lighten his mood, then replied in a high-pitched voice, "Yes, Dear."

The women laughed as he headed up the stairs to change. Celine set the dining room table while Lynette finished slicing the roast beef onto a large platter.

The dinner was delicious, just as Lynette had predicted, and so was the strawberry shortcake that followed for dessert. All through dinner, though, Celine had noticed that her brother had been unusually quiet, and she felt like something was troubling him. "Raine," she began, "are you okay? You've hardly said a word."

"Well, it wasn't one of my better days at D.W.'s. Two of my top sales managers handed in their notices today, which means I'll have to spend a great deal of time interviewing replacements, then training them before the Christmas shopping rush hits full force," he explained.

"Oh, Honey, that surely is unfortunate," Lynette sympathized.

"Don't worry," Raine said. "It will all work out."

D.W.'s was short for D.W. Buckley's, one of the nation's most prestigious department stores, where Raine had been employed for over five years. During that time, he had worked his way up the ladder to the position of head of operations. Celine knew that Raine had definitely earned his position due to the many hours of hard work that he had put in at D.W.'s.

Celine glanced at the antique clock on the mantel. "I didn't realize it was so late. I'd better be heading for home," she said as she stood up.

"Why don't you stay and watch some movies with us?" Raine suggested.

"Oh, I've got some work I have to catch up on at home, but thanks for the offer." Celine turned to her sister-in-law and said, "Thanks for dinner. It was great."

"Anytime, Ce. We enjoy the company," Lynette said as she followed Celine out to her car.

"Say good-bye to Peppy for me." Celine smiled.

"Hey, Ce, have you decided yet whether you are going to join us on the pre-Christmas retreat?" Raine asked as she climbed into her car.

"How can you go now with having to find and train new sales managers?" Celine questioned back.

"Phil, my assistant, is going to cover for me over that weekend," he explained. "So, are you going to join us?"

"I honestly don't know. To tell you the truth, I would feel like the odd man out with mostly all married couples there," she stated, expressing her reluctance to attend.

"Oh, no," Lynette interjected. "There will be as many singles as married couples. Remember, we've attended this retreat for a few years now, so we should know."

"Ce, you're coming because we've already paid the deposit for the three of us and have a cabin reserved, so you can't say no," her brother informed her, then grinned. "Besides, it will be a spiritual uplift that we could all use."

"Raine, you are getting to be awfully bossy in your old age," she remarked teasingly. "But since I happen to trust what you both have said, I'll go to the retreat."

"Great," Raine stated with a victorious smile and continued. "It's this next weekend, so we'll call you and give you the details on what to bring."

On her drive home, Celine was actually looking forward to the thought of getting away and attending the retreat with Lynette and Raine. The good Lord knew she needed a relaxing break away from the daily pressures of life. Yes, she was truly looking forward to it.

Chapter 2

After agonizing all night over a pathetic attempt to progress beyond chapter four in her novel, Celine finally went to bed. The morning, though, came too soon for Celine as she was in the middle of a glorious Hawaiian vacation when her dream was disrupted by the loud and obnoxious ringing of her alarm clock. She reached over and turned the alarm button off, reset it for fifteen minutes later, and rolled over, closed her eyes, and tried to catch up with her dream.

What seemed to be only seconds later, while Celine was sipping ice-cold papaya juice on the deck of a luxurious yacht, she awoke again to the noise of her pesky alarm clock. Grumbling, she sat up and yawned, then tossed back the covers and reluctantly got out of her warm, cozy bed. She walked over to the window, opened it, and inhaled a deep breath of fresh morning air. All was quiet except for a few finches, chirping in the trees. Hearing the birds, she was reminded that in a few hours she would be enjoying a weekend away, lost in the serenity of the mountain wilderness.

Celine pulled out her small suitcase and placed it on her bed. Then she rummaged through her drawers for some warm sweaters, pants, hiking shoes, and a few other needed items and threw them into the suitcase. After she had dressed and applied her makeup, she headed for the kitchen for her morning cup of coffee. When she entered the kitchen, she chuckled as she saw only Queenie's tail outside the open cupboard door.

"Queenie, what are you up to?" Celine demanded. At the sound of her name, Queenie peeked innocently around the door. Celine walked over to the cupboard and saw that Queenie had knocked over the cat food box. She picked up the box and poured some into Queenie's bowl. "The way you behave, people would tend to think that I don't feed you," Celine remarked as she patted Queenie's head.

When the sunny rays of morning peeked through the kitchen window, Celine grabbed Queenie and the box of cat chow and hurried out the door to her neighbor's. Mrs. Kay, the friendliest lady in the neighborhood, who also happened to be extremely fond of animals, had a Persian cat named Romeo and a miniature dachshund named Juliet. A strange combination, Celine had thought, but Mrs. Kay insisted that the two furry friends got along very well.

When Celine had decided to go on the retreat, she knew Queenie would have a place to stay for the weekend. "Queenie, Romeo, and Juliet," Celine repeated the trio's names with amusement. It sounded like the title to one of Walt Disney's movies.

When she reached Mrs. Kay's house, she knocked on the door while Queenie squirmed in her arms. Mrs. Kay opened the door and greeted her warmly. "Good morning, Dear," Mrs. Kay said and then reached out and scratched Queenie's chin affectionately. "And good morning to you, my furry friend."

Celine smiled. "Thanks again for taking Queenie for the weekend."

"No problem, Dear. You know how I adore animals." Mrs. Kay reached out and took Queenie from Celine's arms.

"I'll pick her up on Monday evening," Celine said.

"Okay, Dear. Have fun on your retreat."

After Celine said her good-byes to Mrs. Kay and Queenie, she made a bee-line back to her place so she could straighten up her abode before Lynette and Raine arrived.

When Celine heard the wheels of Raine's car roll down the driveway, she picked up her gear and headed out to meet them.

"Hi," she greeted them. "It looks like we are going to have beautiful weather for the retreat."

Raine nodded. "I called the mountain weather report, and they said there wasn't any snow in the forecast for this weekend. In fact, the weather is supposed to be quite mild for this time of the year," he commented as he opened the back hatch of the car to put Celine's gear in.

"I'm so happy you're coming with us, Ce," Lynette said as Celine climbed onto the backseat. "We'll all have a great time."

Celine nodded. "I'm glad you guys talked me into it."

☙❀☙

The retreat was located about three hours south of them, and half of that driving time was mountain terrain. Raine was an excellent driver, so Celine was able to sit back, relax, and enjoy the view out her window. It was a lovely time of year, especially in the mountains, and she was in awe of the majestic white pine and Douglas fir trees that lined each side of the road, making a green canopy covering.

As the car climbed the winding mountain road to a higher elevation, Celine saw traces of last week's snowfall still on the ground. When she rolled down the window, the fragrance of the evergreens filled the inside of the car. Celine took a deep breath and filled her lungs with the fresh, crisp air.

Shortly before lunchtime, they arrived at Pine Village, the town just outside their final destination. Raine parked the car near what looked to be a Swiss chalet carved into the side of the mountain.

"I hope you women are hungry because we are stopping for a lunch break," Raine announced.

"Ce, you're in for a real treat," Lynette remarked. "We come and eat here every time we attend the retreat. It has the best homemade cooking you'll ever taste."

"And you'll love Gramma Em, the proprietor," Raine declared. "She's eighty-five years old and is the town's matriarch. She's been running the restaurant alone ever since her husband passed away some twenty years ago."

"She sounds like quite a lady," Celine remarked as she followed them up the steps and into the restaurant.

When Gramma Em saw them enter, she flashed them a friendly smile and walked over to them. "Well, hello, strangers," she said, welcoming them with a bear hug. Then her warm eyes rested on Celine. "Who's the new addition?"

"This is Celine, my sister," Raine introduced.

"And she looks like you. She has the same beautiful blue eyes as you, Raine," Gramma Em said, then addressed Celine. "I hope that you are hungry, young lady, because today's special is my famous Swedish meatballs with egg noodles, freshly baked bread, and my five-vegetable garden salad."

Celine chuckled. "Boy, if I wasn't hungry before, I'm hungry now."

"Good." Gramma Em's smile widened. "Take a seat by the window, and I'll put three orders in for Swedish meatballs."

True to Raine and Lynette's word, it was the tastiest home cooking Celine had ever had the pleasure of tasting. The portions, though, were for lumberjack appetites, and the women could finish only half of their meals. Raine, as usual, cleaned his plate with ease, which pleased Gramma Em immensely. Before they left the restaurant, Gramma Em made them promise to stop by on Monday on their way home from the retreat.

Once they were back on their way to the retreat, Raine chose the scenic route and drove through the rest of Pine Village. It was a quaint, picturesque little town with one main road lined with the usual tourist shops and restaurants. Celine could just visualize how beautiful it would look covered in a fresh snowfall. *It would be much like a town in a storybook fairy tale,* she imagined dreamily.

At the edge of the village, the road forked off into two streets, and Raine took the road to the left that headed down a rocky road full of winding curves and led them to Pine Cove.

The Pine Cove retreat area was much larger than Celine had anticipated; it was like a town in itself. As they drove along the leaf-covered road inside the grounds, cabins of all sizes lined the road on both sides. To Celine's surprise, it even had a small general store. The main lodge sat on a small knoll, surrounded by tall evergreens.

Raine parked the car by the front entrance and walked up to the lodge's office to register and check in. He came back with the cabin keys in hand. Their cabin was a short way up the road, and they almost drove right past it because it was camouflaged by a small forest of trees. It looked so cozy and inviting, and reminded Celine of the storybook house that the seven dwarfs lived in.

Inside, the cabin was charmingly decorated with rustic furnishings and accessories. It was small, though, with two bedrooms, a bathroom, and a tiny, comfortable-looking living room. Since every one of the guests dined at the lodge's dining hall, the cabins weren't equipped with kitchen facilities.

After they all brought in their gear, unpacked, and changed, they headed promptly back down the road to attend the welcome meeting at the lodge. To Celine's surprise, a large crowd had turned out for the retreat. With the holidays around the corner, she had figured that most people would be busy with other plans and be getting ready for the festivities of the season.

A hostess led them to a table and gave them each a copy of the schedule of the classes and activities that were available to them over the weekend. After they were comfortably seated and settled in, Celine's eyes scanned over the schedule of classes. The last retreat she had been to was when she was in her early teens. It had been at a Bible camp and was one of the best weekends she had ever spent away from home as a teenager. She had met lots of wonderful kids her age who had shared her love for the Lord.

As Celine continued to look over the schedule, she stopped abruptly when she read, *Stephan James,* the name of one of the guest lecturers.

"No way," she said out loud as she stared at the name on the printed page.

"No way what, Ce?" Lynette looked at her in question.

"Oh," Celine said, pointing to the schedule, "I saw a familiar name on the list of speakers, but it couldn't be the same person I knew by that name."

"What's the name?"

"Stephan James." She paused in thought. "I went to high school with a boy with the same name, but he was a rebel with a capital *R,* so it couldn't be the same person," she reasoned, then her attention was drawn to the front of the dining hall to a gentleman who was introduced as the coordinator of the pre-Christmas retreat.

The noise in the room quieted down as the man began to address the crowd. "Welcome to Pine Cove. We are pleased to inform you that God has provided us with many gifted speakers for this year's retreat. We hope that your weekend with us will give you a spiritual lift for the holidays." He then held up the schedule and continued. "Now I will go over the classes and activities. If any of you have questions, please see me or a hostess before you leave."

The speaker reviewed the schedule and when he came to Stephan James's name, Celine's ears perked up attentively. "This will be Stephan's second year with us, and I recommend that you don't miss his class tomorrow morning and his Sunday afternoon class."

When the speaker finished, he went on to the next speaker, but Celine wasn't listening. She couldn't help but wonder if that was the same Stephan James. Well, she knew one thing for sure: With God anything could be possible.

"Ce," Lynette repeated for a second time.

"Huh?" Celine turned to her sister-in-law.

"Do you want to go horseback riding or hiking this afternoon?"

"Horseback riding sounds fine to me," Celine expressed without reservation.

"Then it's settled. We'll all go riding," Lynette stated gleefully.

❧❀❧

An hour later, after they had all changed into their riding clothes, they walked over to the stables. When they arrived, they noticed another group coming in from a ride and couldn't help but laugh when the riders walked strangely after they had dismounted. Celine knew she would probably look the same way. It had been ages since she had ridden a horse.

Joe, the stableman, saddled a couple of Appaloosas for Raine and Lynette and then saddled Pronto, who looked to Celine to be a half-pint pinto. When Celine mounted Pronto, she gathered up a handful of mane and patted the side of his neck.

"Hello, Pronto," she said softly as she leaned toward his ear. "Are you going to be a good boy?"

Pronto snorted.

"Does that mean yes or no?" She chuckled as she grabbed the reins and gently tapped Pronto with her heels.

Pronto promptly moved out at an easy walk, falling in behind the leader's horse. Raine and Lynette's horses brought up the rear. There were seven other riders in the group and, to Celine, they all looked more experienced at riding than she.

The path the leader chose weaved its way up a steep slope behind the lodge and led them through a forest thick with trees. Celine hadn't done much riding, but whenever she had gotten the chance, she had thoroughly enjoyed the experience.

The weather was perfect for the ride. The mountain air was brisk and cool but not cold. When the group was halfway through the ride, the leader's horse took off in a canter through a clearing, and the leader called out for the others to follow. All the horses followed the lead, except one—Pronto—who ignored Celine's command and kept an even pace walking. When Celine couldn't see any of the other horses and riders ahead, she slapped Pronto's hindquarters a few times with the reins to get him to speed it up, but it didn't faze Pronto in the least. A few paces more and Pronto veered off the trail, lowered his head, jerking the reins out of Celine's grasp, and began to graze.

She was starting to wonder if this stubborn animal called Pronto was a mule hiding in horse's clothing. Quickly, she pulled at the reins, but Pronto fought her and kept on grazing. By this time, Celine's thoughts were running wild. What if she got separated from the group and became lost in the mountain wilderness? It was going to be dark soon. What happened if she was stranded there overnight and. . . ? Her panicked thoughts were interrupted by the sound of horses' hooves in the distance, and suddenly Raine came into view. "Oh, thank You, Lord," she exclaimed out loud in relief. "Raine, I can't get this mule to budge," she called to him.

He chuckled as he rode up next to her. "Yeah, it looks like you've got yourself a real stubborn one. Did you try giving that pinto a few slaps on the rump?" he asked.

"Of course I did," she sighed in frustration, "but he simply ignored me."

"Well, we will see about that," Raine said as he steered his Appaloosa close to the back side of Pronto. He then gave the pinto a smack so hard on the rump that it could be heard echoing through the forest.

Fortunately, Celine had a tight grip on the reins and was firmly planted in the saddle, for the half-pint pinto took off like a flash of lightning. Pronto ran so hard and fast that Celine had to do all she could just to stay in the saddle. Only a few minutes ago she couldn't get Pronto to budge; now she couldn't get him to stop. She pulled back on the reins hard and yelled, "Whoa, Pronto!" But Pronto galloped on, ignoring her commands once again.

In no time at all, the pinto caught up with the rest of the group and sailed right past them with Raine hot on Pronto's hooves. Celine's heart was racing as fast as Pronto was galloping, and the fear in her was starting to escalate when Pronto started to descend the steep slope that led back to the stables. She started to pray quickly, sending out an SOS to God for help. Then she yelled out again in a firm voice, "Whoa, Pronto, whoa!" To Celine's relief, Pronto finally slowed down and then stopped.

Raine steered his horse next to Pronto and looked at Celine apologetically. She glared back at him, her eyes afire. "The next time we are out riding and you decide to slap my horse's rump—*Don't!*"

"I'm so sorry, Ce," Raine apologized. "I had no idea that little mule would take off running like that."

"Well, it's only thanks to God above that that crazy animal stopped before I broke my neck," she huffed, still upset by the incident.

Lynette and the leader of the group rode up beside them and asked Celine simultaneously, "Are you okay?"

"Yes, now that Pronto, the sprinter, has decided to behave," she remarked sarcastically.

"What do you say that we've had enough action and adventure for one day." Raine turned to Celine and winked at her.

"Let's head back to the stables then," the leader motioned.

Celine nodded wearily and gladly followed the leader's horse down the steep path to the stables.

Chapter 3

That night Celine decided to skip dinner at the lodge since she was still full from the hearty lunch at Gramma Em's restaurant. Tomorrow's schedule was filled with numerous classes and activities, so she thought she could use the free time that evening to complete chapter four of her book. Celine had once read and had also been told by other writers that the best way to cure writer's block was to change your surroundings. She felt certain that the retreat weekend and the atmosphere of this beautiful wilderness would lift her out of her writing slump.

Celine went into her room, pulled out her writing material from her duffle bag, and went back out into the tiny living room. She settled herself on the cozy couch that was facing the front picture window, giving her a view of God's magnificent opalescent splendor as the sun set through the wooded forest. In a matter of minutes the sun disappeared, and the outdoor lights that lined the road immediately illuminated the lush forest, creating a magical and romantic effect. Raine and Lynette appeared from their room, dressed for dinner, and threw Celine a puzzled look.

"Why aren't you ready?" Lynette asked.

"I thought I would stay in tonight and work on my book," she explained.

"Well, it's okay if you miss dinner, but don't skip the camp sing-along at the outdoor amphitheater later," insisted Raine.

"I'll try to be there," Celine said as she shooed them out the door. "Now scat, so I can get to work."

After they left, Celine snuggled back into the soft couch and began to think about Brad and Belinda. She had to give Belinda more emotional stability before anything could work out between her and Brad. With hesitancy, Celine pondered Belinda's character and sighed. She remembered her mother's words of wisdom: what Belinda needed was the Lord. Then she frowned as she imagined Edward's reaction. He would yell, then demand a rewrite. She felt stuck.

After an hour of staring out the window, she tapped her pen rapidly against her notebook, not having written down one lousy word. Angrily, she scribbled two words in capital letters on the blank page—WRITER'S BLOCK.

"Oh, well," she muttered as she stared at the words and cringed. While thinking that she might be forced to call Edward and ask for another extension, she moaned. What was she going to do? A cold chill ran down her spine. She didn't understand her inability to write even one word down. She had changed her surroundings, so why was she still having problems? Nervously, she started tapping her pen again and felt panic rise within her. The due date was just around the corner. What was she going to do?

Celine dropped her pen and lowered her head into her hands. She needed answers, and there was only one person she trusted to give her the right ones. She cried out in frustration, "Lord, I don't understand why this is happening. Please lift this pressure off my shoulders and help me with this problem. I trust You, Lord."

Celine knew that nothing more could be accomplished sitting there, so she grabbed her coat, hat, and gloves, headed out the door, and followed the posted signs directing her to the amphitheater.

Along the path, the lights fell through the pine trees, the light chipping into little sparkles like in a pretty fairyland. Celine wondered if she could work these mountains into her novel. *What novel?* she asked herself dismally.

As she continued along the path, she heard a rustling noise in the trees and she stopped, frozen in her tracks. It sounded like an animal. Celine finally got courageous enough to look in the direction of the sound; and she breathed a sigh of relief when she saw above her, nestled on a pine branch, a momma raccoon with her little baby raccoon. Celine didn't linger to chat with momma raccoon because she knew raccoons weren't exactly the friendliest of animals, especially when it came to protecting their young from strangers. So she quietly but quickly moved on down the dirt path.

When she arrived at the sing-along, it was so crowded that she gave up all hope of finding Raine and Lynette, so she sat down on a bench in the back. The music that the group was playing on the stage was soft and melodic, and it had an instantaneous calming effect on Celine. As she focused her eyes on the band, she noticed the main vocalist, but from where she was seated, it was hard to see his face clearly. He was dressed casually in jeans, a colorful pullover sweater, and a baseball cap, and his voice was deep, with a rich-sounding quality. She could listen to this kind of music all the time, she decided as she relaxed back against the bench.

The band sang a half-dozen songs and when they finished, the crowd gave them a standing ovation. After the group left the stage and the applause quieted down, the emcee addressed the audience. "Stephan James and his band, Voices in the Light, have come a long way in the last few years, as most of you probably already know. God is using this group to minister to the young people across America, so keep these fine young men in your prayers," the emcee said, then paused. "Remember, Stephan will be teaching a class tomorrow morning, so be sure not to miss it."

As Celine digested this information, she knew that the Stephan James she saw on the stage only moments ago *could* possibly be the same boy with whom she had gone to school. This man didn't look like him, but then again it had been many years since she had last seen him. As she remembered, the Stephan she had known was also musically inclined and had been in a rock and roll band, which was a far cry from the contemporary Christian music that was being played this evening. *It probably wasn't him after all,* she concluded.

The sing-along lasted about another hour. The audience joined in singing songs of worship along with the praise singers on stage, and the last chorus they sang was a reprise of the song, "Hallelujah." Celine was caught up by the heartfelt praise from the audience as their voices drifted toward heaven.

The evening air was turning chilly, sending shivers through Celine's body, so she tightly wrapped her coat around her and pulled down her wool cap around her ears. As she continued to sing "Hallelujah" with the crowd, she tilted her head back and gazed up at the clear evening sky. The moon was full and bright, and the stars sparkled like tiny diamonds that God had scattered across the sky. *The night had turned out to be a perfect evening,* Celine thought to herself happily as she silently thanked God.

Before the song ended, Celine headed back to the cabin. She didn't wait to find Raine and Lynette, for she was afraid she would risk getting a cold if she stayed outside any longer. Celine welcomed the warmth of the cabin and wasted no time in changing into her nightgown. Then she slid into the bed and pulled the blanket up under her chin. She fell asleep minutes after her head touched the pillow, but not before she had said good night to the Lord.

❧❀❧

The next morning, Celine awoke to the sound of tapping on her door. "Ce, are you awake?" Lynette called through the door.

"I am now," she replied in a groggy voice. "Come in."

Lynette opened the door a fraction and peeked around it. "Breakfast is going to be served in a few minutes. Can you be ready quickly?"

Celine stifled a yawn. "No problem. I'll be ready in a jiff."

"Okay," Lynette said as she closed the door.

Celine jumped out of bed, grabbed her toiletries, and headed for the bathroom. When she finished, she quickly shed her bathrobe, got dressed in jeans and a pink wool sweater, then brushed out her long, tousled hair.

"Hey, where were you last night?" Raine quizzed Celine as she entered the living room. "I thought you said that you'd come to the sing-along."

"I did, Raine, but I sat in the back since I couldn't find you both."

"It was great, wasn't it?"

Celine nodded. "I'm glad I went."

"Well, I'm starved," Raine said as Lynette entered the room. "Let's head for the lodge."

When they arrived at the lodge, the breakfast buffet bar in the dining hall was crowded with hungry-looking people, but Celine noticed that the line was moving fast. She was starved. *The wilderness atmosphere creates a healthy appetite,* she mused. Once the three of them filled their plates, they found an empty table and sat down. To Celine's surprise, the food was tastier than she had anticipated for retreat cooking.

"Ce, Raine and I are going to attend C. S. Bently's class after breakfast. Have you decided which class you're going to go to?" Lynette asked.

"I decided on Stephan James's class," she said, then took a sip of her orange juice.

"You'll enjoy him," Raine remarked, then turned to Lynette. "Do you remember him? We took his class last year."

She nodded. "I remember him now. He sang last night at the sing-along. Oh, he's very good-looking," Lynette remarked as she grinned at Celine.

Celine ignored her comment. The last thing she needed now was to get involved with a man. She was still slowly getting adjusted to Darrell's abrupt and harsh departure from her life.

"After class is over, I'm going to scout around a bit," Celine informed them. "I'll meet you back here at lunchtime."

As Celine was heading down the narrow hallway toward her class, a man came barreling around the corner and ran right into her. The Bible and purse in her hands went flying through the air, hitting the side wall. When Celine regained her balance, she saw the man bending to retrieve her belongings.

"I'm sorry—are you okay?" the man asked as he turned to face her.

She nodded politely. "I'm fine," she said as she straightened her clothes. "It's a good thing you weren't running around that corner or I might have lost a few teeth." She grinned.

The man chuckled and handed her the Bible and her purse.

She looked at him closely. "Is it really you, Stephan?" she asked incredulously.

The man blinked and looked at her for a split second, then shook his head in disbelief. "I can't believe this. Celine Hart, Whitman High," he marveled in astonishment.

"You've really changed. I barely recognized you," she said.

"It's the short haircut instead of the long-haired hippie look I had back in high school." He grinned. "How long has it been since the last time we saw each other?" Stephan asked as he tried to recall.

"It has to be graduation day," Celine commented, "which was almost ten years ago."

"Ten years, wow. No wonder we barely recognized each other." He paused and gazed at her admiringly. "The years have treated you great, Celine. You look fantastic."

She blushed slightly at the compliment and replied, "And so do you, Stephan." Then she changed the subject. "I saw you singing last night, but I still had my reservations that you were the same Stephan James from Whitman High."

"I've changed so much since then. . .and it's all for the better." He glanced down at his watch. "Hey, I've got a class to teach and I have to go, but perhaps we can meet after my class is over."

"Sure, that sounds great. I was heading for your class anyway, so I'll walk with you."

When they entered the classroom, Stephan gently touched her arm. "I'll talk to you right after class."

She nodded, then took a seat in the back of the room.

As Stephan took a few minutes to organize his notes, he couldn't help but think of Celine Hart. In high school, they had shared a few classes together, but they had never dated. Not that he hadn't wanted to, but Celine had been out of his league. She had dated the top athletes and hung out with the most popular people of the school. Although she had always treated him kindly, Stephan had been termed a "rocker" and didn't mix with her crowd. *Oh, how I have changed since then,* he thought to himself.

In school, he had heard from his friends that Celine had come from a wealthy background, and that had placed another wall between them as friends. At least that was what he had thought at the time, since he was from the poor section of the city. Back then he had really liked Celine, yet at the same time he had struggled with feelings of jealousy and dislike for her because she had seemed to have it all—a family that was together, the comforts and status of wealth, and, to top it all off, she was the prettiest girl in the school. He knew, though, that she had a caring heart and wasn't vain or empty-headed. Celine definitely had brains that backed her beauty.

Stephan brought his mind back to the present and said a quick prayer before addressing the class. "Good morning, everyone. I'll start off by briefly sharing about some events that happened in my life that will lead into my topic entitled, 'A Gift from Above.' "

He leaned forward against the podium and continued. "At the age of four, I lost my father in a tragic car accident. My mother was left to support my two sisters and me by working two jobs for many years. We lived in a one-bedroom apartment, which was tough on all of us. When I was fifteen, my two older sisters got jobs, so we were able to move into a two-bedroom apartment.

"During my high school years, I got involved with the wrong crowd, and I was constantly in and out of trouble. About that same time, I joined a rock and roll band in which I sang the lead vocals." He looked back at Celine briefly, and their eyes met. "To this day, I'm still amazed that I even graduated. I guess you could say that I just passed by the skin of my teeth.

"A year later, my mother quit her night job because she didn't seem to have the energy to keep up the pace of two jobs anymore. As the months went by, my sisters and I noticed a dramatic change in Mom's health. She always looked pale and run-down, but now she had lost a lot of weight. Finally, we got her to go to the doctor for a routine physical. The results of the tests taken that day shattered my world." Stephan inhaled a sharp breath as he recalled that day.

"The doctors said that my mom had terminal cancer, and she had only six months to a year to live."

Celine's eyes grew misty as she listened to him recount that moment. The pain must have been unbearable, and her heart reached out to him.

"That day, my sisters and I brought Mom home from the doctor's and we sat down on the couch, holding her hand, as Mom wept uncontrollably, devastated with grief. My mom was a gentle, God-fearing woman who gave her all to her children. She was too good to die so young," Stephan said as he looked down briefly, then continued. "I had saved some money from playing gigs in clubs with my band and, a few months down the road, I asked Mom if I could take her to the mountains for the weekend. She agreed, so we packed up our gear and headed for the mountains. In fact, the place we camped at was only a couple of miles down the road from here." He gestured with his hand. "It was the best time my mom and I had ever shared together. I didn't want it to end.

"On the last day of our campout, we hiked for awhile, then rested by a stream. We sat down in the long grass along the bank, and that's when my mother took my hand in hers and told me that I shouldn't fear her death because God had given her a peace and that she was ready to be with the Lord."

Celine sat in amazement at the faith and trust that Stephan's mother had in the Lord. *What a remarkable woman she was,* she decided, and then her attention went back to Stephan as he continued.

"When I heard those words, I thought she had flipped her lid. I couldn't even begin to comprehend what she was saying to me. How could a person have a peace about dying? It sounded absolutely crazy.

"The words that my mother said to me next changed my whole life. She went on to share with me that when my dad died, her world fell apart, and the only thing that had helped her to go on for my sisters and me was the presence of the Lord in her life. She said that God had given her the strength to work those two jobs for all those years so we wouldn't have to go on welfare.

"At the end of our talk, she said that she had one request of me before she left, and that was that I would give God a chance. She told me that the peace she had about her death was a result of accepting Christ as her Savior many years ago and knowing that she would spend an eternity with Jesus in heaven, and she wanted the same for me."

For a moment, Stephan glanced around the room, collecting his thoughts, then went over and sat down on the corner of the desk. "When Mom finished, tears rolled down my face because I knew she was speaking the truth. I wanted to be with her someday in heaven. The last thing my mom told me that day was to use my talent for the Lord's service. She said that my ability to sing was a gift from God and that I shouldn't waste it. I surely questioned that because, at the time, rock and roll was my life. But I kept quiet because I wanted my mom to be happy and to think that I would change.

"A month later, my precious mother passed away. Since that time, Mom's dying wish came true. I asked Christ into my heart, and I joined the church my sisters attended. Then I joined the youth group at church," he chuckled. "At that moment, I knew Mom was in heaven, rejoicing. Soon after that, the Lord convinced me to start singing for Him. It was so hard to make the first step, but eventually I did. I quit the rock group because they didn't appreciate my newfound faith and had no intentions of sharing it. I then joined the youth group choir, which eventually led to getting my own Christian band together.

"This awesome change in my life was a direct result of many prayers and God's power working through me. There was no way that I could have made that change on my own, which finally leads me to the topic of my message."

Stephan scooted off the desk and walked back to the podium. "God has given all of us gifts to use for His glory. Right now, I want everyone in the class to write down at least one gift or talent that you know God has blessed you with. After you write it down, ask yourself—and be honest—if you are using your talent to honor God. If the answer is no, pray and ask God how you could turn it around so that your gift would glorify the giver. I'll give you a few minutes to meditate on this, then the class will be brought to a close."

In the back of the room, Celine stared at her blank piece of paper that one of the class members had previously passed out. She knew if she had been in Stephan's place, losing both her mother and father at such a tender age, she could have easily become bitter and angry at God for taking her parents from her. But Stephan wasn't bitter in the least. Instead, he was better as a result of his giving his life over completely to the Lord.

Celine picked up her pen and wrote down a single word that came to mind— *novelist*. She was a writer, and suddenly it all became clear to her. That was the special gift that God had given to her. All along, God had been urging her in subtle ways to start using her talent for His work.

She felt like shouting out in relief. No wonder she was having writer's block—God had been trying to wake her up so she would listen to His voice and follow His direction for her life. No wonder she was feeling an emptiness and void in her life. She had put her relationship with the Lord on the back shelf while she did what she thought was right for her life, following her own dreams and blindly shutting out God's voice of guidance. *No longer will I be deaf to God's voice,* she shouted with joy inside her mind, then glanced upward and whispered, "Lord, I'm all ears."

Chapter 4

The whole room was quiet as Stephan's gaze drifted curiously over the class. His eyes rested on Celine, who was writing on a piece of paper. Immediately, his thoughts switched to Angela, his fiancée of two years. He had met her backstage at one of his concerts. She was a friend of the wife of one of the band members. When they were introduced, they instantly liked one another; ever since that time, they'd dated steadily. A few months prior to the retreat, they decided, or at least Angela did, that it was time to set a date for their wedding. Stephan hadn't been totally convinced that he was ready for marriage, but Angela had given him an ultimatum—either marry her or she would start dating other men. He was almost sure she was bluffing, but he didn't want to test it.

Stephan's focus was drawn back to the petite blond sitting in the last row of desks. He was anxious to talk to Celine; there was so much catching up to do. He glanced down at his watch, then addressed the class. "I don't want to disturb all of you, but it is time for the class to end. I pray that you received something from my class, and if any of you have any questions, I'll be up front for the next few minutes."

As Celine waited for a few people to finish talking to Stephan, she stayed seated and took a long look at him, marveling at how much he had changed. In his high school years, Stephan had looked quite different. There hadn't been a day that went by that he didn't wear his faded blue jeans, black boots, and a T-shirt with his favorite rock and roll band imprinted on the front of it. Mostly everyone who knew him in school, friends and acquaintances alike, called him by the name of Rebel Rocker, or R.R. for short. Celine had been drawn to him because she had felt that behind that rough exterior was a person crying out for attention. Many times she had helped him with his classwork, but that was as far as the friendship went.

Stephan had never talked about his personal life, nor did he ask Celine anything about hers, but he was always kind and polite to her and appreciated the help she had given him with his class studies.

When she saw that Stephan had finished talking, she picked up her things and walked up front. He smiled as she approached him. "Stephan," Celine began as she placed her hand on his arm, "I feel so privileged to have had the opportunity to hear your testimony and the message God gave you to share with the class."

"I'm the one who felt fortunate to have you in my class," he acknowledged with a warm smile. "Say, I was wondering if I could help you with your class-work?"

"You remembered?" she exclaimed as her eyes widened in surprise.

"Celine, I'll never forget it. I'll bet you didn't even know that you were one of the major reasons why I graduated," he announced gratefully.

"You're kidding."

"No, it's true. I wouldn't joke about that matter," he commented as he gathered his papers from the podium. "Celine, we have more than an hour before lunch will be served. Would you like me to show you the prettiest spot in all of Pine Cove?"

Celine's diamond blue eyes sparkled at the prospect. "Need you ask? Of course I would, Stephan."

"Great," he said as he took her arm and led her to the back door. "Let's go and change into some hiking clothes and meet back here in fifteen minutes."

"Okay." She nodded, then disappeared out the doorway.

Stephan practically ran to his cabin, which was located on the opposite side of the grounds from Celine's cabin, and a twinge of excitement stirred within him as he changed his clothes. He couldn't seem to get his mind off of that sweet, little friend he had known so long ago. Just looking at Celine's deep blue eyes and beautiful, captivating smile was enough to set his heart pumping a little too quickly.

Suddenly he caught himself. What was he thinking? He examined his reflection critically in the mirror as he combed his sun-streaked brown hair. Had he already forgotten about his engagement to Angela? What was wrong with him? This was so unlike his character, and he was definitely puzzled by his thoughts of just moments ago.

Feeling quite guilty, he tried to think of Angela as he laced up his hiking boots. Soon she would be his wife and, as the story goes, they would live happily ever after. Or would they? He kicked the wall and was angry for even doubting it.

His thoughts strayed back to Celine, who was probably waiting for him. He picked up his keys and headed out the door. As he walked up the leaf-covered road, he saw Celine, sitting on the front steps of the lodge. She was truly a vision of loveliness. Dressed in fitted black jeans and a deep red pullover sweater, her soft blond hair cascaded gently over her shoulders and her small hands were folded gracefully in her lap. To an artist's eye, she would be a dream girl to sketch.

Stephan inhaled a deep breath. *Why is she affecting me this way? It's ludicrous,* he told himself.

As Celine watched Stephan out of the corner of her eye, she noticed his fine masculine build and the confidence in his step as he strode toward her. Gone was the boyish-looking face of the past; now, maturity was etched upon the features of his handsome face. His wavy hair was lighter than she had remembered it to be, probably a result of his being out in the California sunshine. When their eyes met, her heart skipped a beat.

He grinned broadly. "Are you ready to go?"

"You bet," Celine said as she stood up and dusted herself off. "How far is it?"

"Fortunately, not too far. It's less than a mile from here." His eyes softened. "It was the place where my mom and I had our special talk."

Celine looked at Stephan with compassion and gently touched his shoulder. "I'm so sorry you lost your mother when you were so young."

"So am I, Celine. I still miss her greatly, but I have the memory of her locked in my heart to keep me company when I'm lonely for her."

They walked along the path leading to the stream and used the time to reminisce about their younger days. Stephan could not believe how for one so small, Celine could keep up with his brisk pace. She had a definite bounce in her step, almost as if she were skipping along like a little girl would. She hadn't changed in that area. He smiled to himself. She was still full of energy, with life radiating from every part of her.

As they approached the stream, Celine's eyes lit up. "Wow!" she exclaimed. "You weren't kidding when you said that this was the prettiest spot in all of Pine Cove."

"It is, isn't it?" agreed Stephan as he took her hand to help her down the grassy slope and over some rocks. They found a flat boulder that jetted out over the stream and sat down on it, dangling their legs over its side.

On each side of the stream, the canopy of trees was so thick that they almost blocked out the light of the noonday sun. Celine leaned back on her elbows and listened to the peaceful sounds of the water rippling downstream, while a squirrel chattered in the treetop. She directed her attention back to Stephan. He was sitting so close to her that her skin began to tingle. When Darrell had left her, she had thought that she would never again be interested in a man, or at least not for a very long time. One broken heart was enough for a lifetime. Yet, here she was with Stephan only for a short while, and familiar emotions were stirring inside of her.

It has to be the place, she decided. *It can't be the man.* Then Celine stole a quick glance at him and a smile hit her lips. Yeah, who was she trying to kid?

"A dollar for your thoughts?" Stephan ventured when he saw her smile.

"A dollar?" Celine grinned. "You're a big spender."

"No, that's what they call inflation," he remarked wryly.

"Well, my thoughts are free to you. I was silent because I'm overwhelmed by the beauty and serenity of this place."

"I know what you mean. I could spend hours at a time here doing absolutely nothing but staring at God's awesome handiwork called nature." He leaned back and propped himself up on his elbows.

"Tell me more of what you've been doing over the years," she said with interest.

"The last few years really consist of me and my band doing concerts across the United States and also speaking engagements like the one here at Pine Cove."

"How exciting," she commented. "It must be wonderful to travel across the country sharing the gospel in word and song."

"I like the traveling, but the most enjoyable time I have is when I'm doing concerts right here in California," he admitted.

"I agree there's no place like the Golden State. Please tell me more, Stephan," she urged. "Do you have a wife and children?" She silently hoped, for a reason unknown to her, that his answer would be no.

Stephan chuckled at her directness. "No children and no wife, as of yet. I am engaged, though."

Celine's heart dropped, but outwardly she showed elation. "Oh? When is the big day?"

"We haven't set an exact date yet, but Angela wants it to be within a year's time." Stephan felt a knot develop in his throat as he thought about his fiancée. For some reason, he didn't feel like talking or thinking about Angela at that moment.

"How did you meet?" Celine continued her quizzing.

Stephan cleared his throat. "It was about two years ago at one of my concerts."

"Love at first sight?" she asked with curiosity.

"No, I wouldn't say that. But we did like each other instantly." Stephan sat up on the rock and Celine followed suit.

"Is Angela here with you at the retreat?" She persisted with the questioning and, at the same time, was startled with herself for being so inquisitive.

Stephan hesitated before replying. "No, Angela doesn't care too much for the mountain retreats."

"That's too bad. I would have enjoyed meeting her," she commented, then glanced down at her watch. "It looks like it's almost time for lunch."

"I guess we'd better be heading back then," Stephan said somewhat reluctantly as he got up and extended his hand to help her up.

She placed her hand in his and felt the warmth of his touch penetrate through her. As they walked along the wooded path, she struggled for words and remained silent, lost in her thoughts. She enjoyed walking by his side while silently appreciating the quiet beauty of the luscious forest that surrounded them.

When they entered the noise-filled dining hall, Celine spotted her brother and Lynette seated in the far corner. She turned to Stephan. "Would you like to meet my brother and sister-in-law? They are the ones I came with."

"Of course I would." He smiled at her. "I was wondering who you came with."

She chuckled. "You know, Stephan, that doesn't seem to surprise me. You never did ask many questions."

Stephan chuckled as he followed her. "I guess I haven't changed much in that area."

They approached the table and Celine made the introductions. "Hi," she greeted them. "I want you both to meet an old school friend of mine, Stephan James."

Raine stretched out his hand and shook Stephan's hand. "Hi, I'm Raine and this is my wife, Lynette."

"Glad to meet you both. Have you been to the retreat before? You look familiar."

Lynette spoke up. "Yes, and we've attended your classes, and we've also enjoyed your music."

"Thanks," Stephan said as he shifted his attention back to Celine. "I'm happy you joined your brother and sister-in-law in coming to the retreat or we would never have had this reunion."

"Let me tell you," Raine interjected, "it was like pulling teeth to get her to come with us." He smiled at Celine. "But I think she's glad we were so persistent."

"You're right," Celine admitted. "So far I've had a wonderful time here, with the exception of the ride on that stubborn mule," she said as she rolled her eyes, and Raine and Lynette laughed.

A puzzled expression appeared on Stephan's face. "I didn't know they had any mules at the stables."

Celine chuckled softly, feeling in a giddy mood. "Let's get some food, and I'll tell you the inside info on the mule I rode yesterday."

Stephan nodded, then turned to Lynette and Raine. "I hope to see you both later."

As Raine watched them go, a smile crept on his lips, then he turned to Lynette.

She was already smiling mischievously. "Honey, are you thinking what I'm thinking?" she inquired.

"Yes, on one condition, though, and that's if he's single."

"He wasn't wearing a ring, Dear," Lynette informed.

"What else did you notice, Sherlock?" he teased.

"Well, didn't you notice that Ce was more bubbly than usual and that there was a definite sparkle in her eye?"

"Hmm, yes, I think you are right, Sherlock. What's our next step?"

"Clues, Watson, clues," Lynette jested. "I think tonight I'll find out the scoop from Ce."

"Sounds like a plan, Sherlock," he whispered as his eyes searched the room, as if looking for spies. "I trust you explicitly to find the answer before the clock strikes midnight."

Lynette leaned over and hugged Raine tightly. "Watson, you are so much fun. I love you," she whispered.

Raine kissed her tenderly, then gazed into her eyes with deep love and affection. "And you, my dear Sherlock, are the love of my life."

☙❈❧

Celine and Stephan were filling their plates at the buffet table while Celine shared the story about her wild mule ride. Stephan couldn't help but laugh as he envisioned Celine, riding wildly through the mountain terrain. He couldn't even begin to imagine Angela going through a similar experience and staying on the runaway pinto. In fact, he couldn't imagine Angela even wanting to ride a horse. She wasn't the outdoors type at all, and that was the major reason why she wasn't here with him now. It had disturbed him greatly, but he let it slide and didn't push Angela into doing anything she didn't want to. Stephan thought of Angela's parents. Her father was a real estate mogul who owned shopping malls across the state and had numerous other real estate holdings. So whatever Angela wanted, Angela got.

Retreats and campouts were unheard of in Angela's household. Instead, it was weekend trips jetting off to exotic places like Paris, London, and Rome. Stephan had always enjoyed the simple things in life like strolling along a sandy beach just before sunset, hiking through the mountain wilderness, or biking along the Pacific coast highway at sunrise. *But Angela*, he thought sullenly, *doesn't share my passions.* But then again, it was only a small difference, and love would cover over those differences. Angela would make him the perfect wife.

Stephan felt his stomach tighten. Why was he feeling uneasy when he said or thought the word *wife?* Before this weekend, he had had no doubts in his mind about eventually settling down with Angela. But now he felt unsure about making a lifetime commitment to her.

As Stephan followed Celine to an empty table, he glanced down at his plate full of food. With his confused thoughts of Angela, he didn't feel much like eating.

As Celine sat down, she could see that Stephan's thoughts were elsewhere, and it looked to her like he was a little bit stressed out. "Stephan, are you all right?" she asked with concern.

Stephan tried to shake off his feelings of confusion concerning his relationship with Angela. "I'm fine, Celine," he stated, then smoothly changed the subject. "Will you be at the Nativity play tonight?"

"I wouldn't miss it. What time does it start?"

"At six o'clock," he said between mouthfuls.

"Will you be a part of the play?"

He nodded. "And it won't be hard to spot me. Just look for the man leading Mary on a mule." He grinned sheepishly.

"You're playing Joseph?" He nodded, then she asked, "Tell me, will it be a real mule that Mary will be riding?"

His eyes lit up with amusement. "No, we were going to settle for a pony from the stables, but now that you've uncovered a mule hiding in horse's clothing, I could suggest that we use him instead." Stephan's eyes sparkled as he chuckled softly.

Celine giggled merrily. "And that would be the last we'd ever see of Mary."

With great delight, Stephan laughed at her sense of humor. "You are marvelous company, Celine. I hope I'll be able to see you after the play tonight."

"I'd like that. How about if I meet you backstage when the play is over?" she suggested.

"That's perfect," he agreed as he ate the last bit of his buttered roll. "I don't mean to rush, but I have to meet with the other actors in the play to review the script one last time before tonight." He stood up and reached out, touching her arm. "I'll see you later then."

"Okay." She smiled up at him, then watched him disappear out of the dining hall. She glanced down at her plate and noticed that she had barely touched the food. She had been so consumed with Stephan's presence that food was the last thing on her mind. She picked up her plate and walked over to Raine and Lynette's table. They were busy chatting when she pulled out a chair and sat down.

"Hey, Ce. Are you going to join us for a little swim later?" Raine asked.

"That sounds fine. I could use a good swim after I finish consuming all these calories," she said and resumed eating.

"You should have seen the calorie-laden plate that I just inhaled, Ce." Lynette sighed and patted her stomach.

"Well, it looks like you and I will have to swim a vigorous one hundred laps, minimum," Celine commented with a grin.

Raine rolled his eyes as he listened to the girl talk. "Women, women, women." He groaned loudly. "Why do you always worry so much about calories and weight?"

"Honey, if Ce and I had our metabolic rate cranked up as high as yours, we wouldn't have to worry. So hush up and count your blessings you don't have to watch your weight," she scolded.

"My lips are sealed," he said dryly. "Ce, where is Stephan?"

"He went to study his script for tonight's Nativity play."

"You'll enjoy the play," Lynette mentioned. "When the weather's nice, it's performed outside, under the stars. Last year we had snow flurries, so the play was held indoors."

"Getting back to Stephan," Raine began. "How did you like his class earlier?"

"I'm glad you brought that up," she said, then hesitated slightly. "As a result of attending his class, I want you both to be the first to know the good news."

Lynette and Raine exchanged looks, then Lynette asked, "What news?"

"As of today, I will not be submitting any more of my work to Pennington Publishers."

"What?" Raine and Lynette exclaimed in unison.

"My decision came when the Lord spoke to me through Stephan's message in class. Stephan talked about using our gifts for the Lord's work and, as Stephan changed from singing secular music to Christian contemporary music, so am I changing my writing from secular to Christian fiction novels," she explained quickly, anxious for a response.

"That's fantastic!" expressed Raine.

"What are you going to do with the novel you're working on now?" Lynette asked.

"I'm going to follow Mom's advice to me earlier and allow my characters, Brad and Belinda, to have a born-again experience." Celine giggled.

"Good idea." Raine chuckled and then reached for his glass of water. "Now I suggest that we make a toast." Celine and Lynette joined Raine in raising their glasses.

"To Ce's new adventure in writing. May the good Lord bless you with many inspirational ideas for your books."

Their glasses chimed together, and a flood of happiness washed over Celine. She silently thanked God for His voice of direction and His gentle correction.

Chapter 5

As Stephan walked toward his cabin, his mind drifted to the brief time he had spent earlier with Celine by the stream. He was absolutely mesmerized and captivated by her and, if it had been his choice, he would have spent the rest of the day with her. He definitely wanted to know more about Celine, the adult. She was so different from anyone he had ever met, and he knew that if he weren't extremely careful with his emotions, he could easily fall head over heels for her. His pulse quickened just thinking of her smooth, silky voice and her innocently sensuous smile.

In the long run, Stephan knew it was best that they hadn't stayed longer at the stream. For one thing, he could barely handle sitting that close to her. She had the ability to turn his emotions inside out and upside down in a matter of minutes. All his life he had been proud of his ability to keep his emotions under tight control. But now this little blond just whisked her way back into his life again, and his controlled emotions flew out the window in one swoop.

He shook his head in disbelief. This couldn't be happening to him. He raked his fingers through his hair. "You're not supposed to feel this way," he reprimanded himself. "You're engaged to be married, you fool."

He kicked some small stones on the dirt road. "What a mess." He scowled and threw open his cabin door and marched in. "Well, Man, you've really done it this time, haven't you!" he practically shouted as he tossed his keys onto the table and walked into his bedroom and flopped onto his bed.

He simply wished that Celine was married, then he wouldn't—or rather couldn't—allow himself to be affected by her. But at lunch he had noticed that she didn't have a ring on her finger, so he concluded that she probably wasn't even engaged.

Wearily, Stephan closed his eyes and decided to take a brief snooze, since, at the present moment, it was definitely safer than thinking. His thoughts, he decided rationally, were nearing the danger zone. Then he reached over and set his alarm clock for an hour later; that would give him enough time to study the script once more before dinner.

He rolled over, kicked off his shoes, and shoved his head into the softness of his pillow. Before he dozed off, his last thoughts were of Angela, in hopes that if he dreamed at all, it would be of her and not Celine.

❧❧❧❧

"Doesn't this warm water feel great against the cool of the winter air?" Raine called out to the women from the other side of the pool.

Neither Lynette nor Celine replied, but nodded instead as they continued to swim the length of the pool. They had just turned their twenty-fifth lap and had seventy-five more to go. Celine grimaced at the thought and wished she had kept her big mouth shut. Lynette's favorite activity was swimming, so Celine knew she would have to work hard to keep up with her.

At the turn of their fortieth lap, Raine caught their attention. "When you two calorie counters are done, meet me in the jacuzzi."

The women kept swimming, ignoring his bantering comments. When they finally hit the fiftieth lap, Lynette grabbed Celine's arm and said in between deep breaths, "For the last five laps, I've had a stomach cramp. Would you mind if I join Raine in the jacuzzi?"

Celine smiled in relief. "Would you mind if I joined you in joining Raine?" she asked breathlessly while she pushed aside a wet strand of hair from her face.

"Last one to the jacuzzi has to swim fifty more laps." Lynette giggled as she climbed out of the pool quickly, with Celine on her heels.

Raine opened his eyes from his brief siesta when he heard the women slip into the water. He glanced at them and raised his eyebrows in suspicion. "Don't tell me you've already finished one hundred laps?"

"Yes," Lynette teased. "Aren't you impressed by our stamina and outstanding endurance?"

Celine was beside herself with laughter. "I am."

"Lynette, didn't your mother tell you it isn't ladylike to fib?" Raine scolded.

Celine came to Lynette's defense. "Oh, it's true, Raine. We really did swim one hundred laps," she said with a sheepish grin. "Lynette swam fifty laps and I swam fifty laps and, by my addition, that adds up to one hundred laps."

"If I've said it once, I've said it a million times. . .women, harumph!" The women laughed heartily, and Raine leaned back and watched them sitting opposite him in the tub. He had always felt so blessed that his wife and sister were such good friends.

In no time at all, the three of them felt and looked like prunes. Once they climbed out of the water and darted for the bathhouse, fighting the cool evening air, they wasted no time in changing out of their swimsuits and going back to the cabin.

After Celine artfully applied her makeup, she went over to her suitcase and rummaged through it, her stomach rumbling as she stared at her dress options. *After all those laps in the pool,* Celine told herself, *I deserve an appetizing dinner.* Once again, she gazed at the clothes in the suitcase. Secretly, she wanted to dress her best since she would be meeting with Stephan after the play, but she knew that was silly since Stephan was engaged.

Raine tapped on her door. "Ce?"

"Yes, come in," Celine said.

He opened the door slightly and peered around it. "Dress warm for the play. It could get pretty chilly later, and even the outdoor heater lamps won't keep you warm if you don't dress properly," he warned.

"Okay, Dad," she replied in a child's voice.

"Don't be smart with me, you little brat," he retorted, then chuckled as he closed the door.

Minutes later, she finally decided on her attire for the evening, and she reached down and pulled out her neatly pressed white corduroy pants and a lovely green and white angora sweater. They fit the mood of the Christmas season and would be appropriate for the cool winter air. She also laid out her gloves, scarf, and white down jacket. "Now if this doesn't keep me warm, nothing will," she muttered as she began to dress in the layers of clothing.

After Celine was dressed, she brushed out her long hair with much care. Suddenly she felt extremely stupid for even being concerned about looking nice for Stephan's benefit. He was another woman's man, and that crushed all the hopes she had of furthering a relationship with him. She shook off the feeling of depression that was trying to make her miserable. There would be other Stephans out there, and someday she would find Mr. Right and settle down and have a family. As she reviewed her reflection in the mirror, she felt burdened to pray. "Lord, my future is in Your hands, since I certainly don't trust myself with it. Please guide my walk with You."

"Are you ready yet, Ce?" Raine called through the door.

Celine snatched up her jacket and purse and opened the door. "I'm ready when you are."

"Good," Lynette drawled, "because I'm famished from those one hundred laps we swam." She giggled and winked at Raine, then turned back to Celine. "I'm so hungry I could eat a mule—oops, I mean a horse."

Celine grinned and put her arm around Lynette's shoulders. "You really know how to beat a subject into the ground, don't you?"

"I'm sorry, Ce, I couldn't resist," Lynette said with a grin.

"Okay, okay, ladies. Can we go now?" Raine begged as his stomach growled. Food was the only thing on his mind.

❧❧❧

Stephan stretched out his long frame and yawned, trying to awaken himself fully from his deep slumber. He rolled over slowly and focused his eyes on the clock. "What?" he exclaimed as he shot out of bed. How did he ever sleep that long? It then dawned on him. He must have unconsciously hit the alarm button off and fallen back to sleep. He usually did that only when he was going through a stressful situation.

Now he didn't even have time for dinner since he had to review the script one last time before the play. Still slightly groggy with sleep, Stephan picked up the script and reviewed it. When he got to the part where Joseph was leading Mary on the mule, he smiled and thought of Celine. He had wanted to eat his dinner with her and her family but, due to his stupidity, he had blown his chance.

Maybe it happened for the best, he tried to reason. The less time he spent with Celine, the better. "Lord," he prayed, "please help me through this situation with Celine."

He dropped his script on the couch and went over to the kitchen nook and opened up his small refrigerator. The counselors and teachers at the retreat had cabins with a few extra amenities, like a small cooking area and a large living room with a fireplace. As he viewed the contents of the refrigerator, he decided to polish off the potato salad and ham slices that Heidi, the retreat's cook, had given him earlier.

Heidi was a gem. She was a little woman with a big heart who always made sure that he and the other staff members had enough goodies stocked in their refrigerators. In fact, her chocolate chip cookies were the best this side of the Mississippi. Not only was she a great cook, but she was a good listener too.

After Stephan had finished eating, he cleaned up the cabin and loaded the fireplace with a few logs for later. He had decided it would be a relaxing place to talk about old times with Celine after the Nativity play. Earlier, during his sleep, he had had pleasant dreams of Angela, and that seemed to help him regain control of his feelings toward Celine. It somehow helped him to put their chance meeting into perspective instead of being overwhelmed by it. Also, he knew that tomorrow would be the last he would probably ever see of Celine, and his thoughts clung to that old saying, "Out of sight, out of mind." A wave of relief washed over him, and he felt safe and secure with his emotions controlled once again. He walked back into his bedroom, dressed in his costume, and headed for the outdoor amphitheater.

⮞⬥⬥⮜

After dinner, the three Harts strolled around the retreat's property. Lynette busily chattered about the camping trips her family used to take when she and her brothers were growing up. Celine and Raine chuckled as Lynette rambled on. She had a talent for telling stories about her family's adventures that would make anyone want to listen. She also had a tendency to exaggerate and embellish on the original stories, and that was what made the adventures worth listening to. "And the wolf and I became friends—"

"Whoa, Honey," Raine interrupted. "I can't believe the wolf made friends with you so easily, as if it were a cuddly puppy dog."

"Dear, dare you question me? You know yourself how animals are naturally drawn to me."

Celine let out a loud squeal and patted Raine on the back. "You should understand that, dear brother," she interjected as she suppressed another giggle. "Remember, you were drawn to Lynette."

"Very funny." He smiled sarcastically at his sister, then made a quick move to grab her.

But Celine, anticipating her brother's move, dodged him quickly, and she sprinted ahead of them to avoid the "wrath of Raine." When she was a safe distance from him, she yelled back, "Lynette, I really enjoyed your story. See you both at the play."

❧❧❧

Celine arrived early at the amphitheater so she would be able to save a couple of seats in the front. As the place began to fill up with people, she kept a watch out for Raine and Lynette. She knew if Raine had his way, Lynette and he were probably still exactly where she had left them, under the moonlit sky, whispering sweet words of love to each other.

Celine sank back against the bench and gazed up into the crystal-clear evening sky. *How wonderful it must be to love and be loved by the right person,* she thought dreamily to herself. *One day, I pray, it will happen to me.*

A few minutes before the play began, Celine spotted the two lovebirds. She waved her hand until they saw her. When they reached the seats and sat down, Lynette squeezed her arm. "Thanks for saving a place for us."

Celine nodded. "No problem. . .I had a feeling you'd be late," she said with a twinkle in her eye, then leaned over to her brother. "Did you get lost in the woods, Raine? Or were you simply stargazing?"

"Aren't you kind of pushing it, Ce? I still owe you for that animal crack you made earlier," he countered with a smirk.

Lynette held up her hands. "Quiet, you children. The play's starting."

At that moment, the music started and the curtain opened. The costumes and the props on the stage were all so elaborate and professionally done for a small production. Celine was truly impressed with all the work and time the organizers and the staff must have put into the Nativity play. The picture that they had painted seemed so real that Celine felt like she had actually been transported to the little town of Bethlehem.

The actors and actresses had prepared well for their parts, and they acted out their roles with grace and ease. When Celine spotted Joseph, she was amazed at how comfortable Stephan seemed playing his character's part. He made her almost forget that he was really Stephan and not Joseph. Celine marveled at all of the talents God had bestowed upon his life.

At that moment, she had such an intense desire to get to know more about this intricate man. *Why do all the good men have to be taken?* she wondered dismally.

When the play came to a close, all of the performers lined up on stage and started singing "Joy to the World," with the audience joining in with exuberance.

It was a night of celebration in true remembrance of Christ's wondrous birth, and Celine knew that the angels in heaven were rejoicing along with them.

When the stage curtain was drawn, Celine turned to Raine and Lynette. "I'm going to find Stephan, so I'll see you both later."

"Don't you want a couple of chaperons to tag along with you, little sister?" Raine teased and smiled a lopsided grin.

"No, big brother, I don't. Besides, Stephan and I are just friends and only friends, so don't let your curious mind wander."

Raine turned to Lynette. "Honey, Ce smoothly gave us the brush-off. Aren't you going to say anything?"

"Yes," Lynette drawled. "Have a good time, Ce." Lynette then grabbed Raine's hand. "Come on, Honey, let's go and get lost in the woods again."

Raine's eyes twinkled. "You've got me wrapped around your little finger."

"And vice versa, Dear," she whispered as she snuggled up to him.

"I think this is my cue to leave," Celine smiled. "Have fun, you two." Then she turned and made her way to the backstage area.

As Celine entered the room where all the cast members were celebrating among themselves, she felt nervous, and she chided herself for it. She didn't spot Stephan right away, who stood on the far side of the large room, talking to a friend.

Stephan waved her over and excused himself from his friend, then he watched her weave her way through the crowd. *She's definitely the loveliest woman in the room,* he noticed with appreciation.

When she reached him, she flashed him a dynamic smile that sent tingles throughout his body. *Great, Stephan,* he thought, half-annoyed with himself. *You're really controlling your emotions well, aren't you?*

Now he was having second thoughts about inviting Celine over to his cabin. Maybe she would settle for talking right where they were.

"You did an excellent job in portraying Joseph," she said sincerely as she touched his arm. "I was impressed, Stephan."

He grinned. "It's my favorite part of the retreat. I enjoy acting," he confessed.

"You've come such a long way since I knew you in high school." She blushed slightly. "I'm sorry. I must sound repetitive, huh?" He shook his head, so Celine continued. "It's probably because I can't believe you're the same person I once knew."

"I know it's hard to believe." He chuckled. "My sisters still comment about it, from time to time, even after all these years."

Celine glanced around the room, searching for some empty chairs, but didn't see any. "Stephan, do you want to stay here and talk or did you have another place we could go?"

Suddenly, Stephan didn't want to have the remainder of their talk in a room full of noise. He wanted peace and quiet and a place where they could sit down. "How about if we go over to my cabin and talk there?" he suggested, against his better judgment.

Before answering, she hesitated slightly. *What could it hurt?* "That sounds fine."

When they entered the cabin, Stephan switched on the lights and immediately headed for the fireplace. "Make yourself comfortable," he said over his shoulder, "while I light the logs so we can get some heat in this icebox."

Celine shed her white jacket and gloves and slung them over the corner of the couch and sat down. She noticed that his cabin had a few more luxuries than hers.

When the fire was lit, Stephan turned around and saw Celine nestled cozily in the folds of the couch, browsing through one of his hiking magazines that he had brought with him on the retreat. She looked like an expensive Christmas package in her exquisite white and emerald green sweater.

Celine met his gaze. He was embarrassed; she could tell. It was as if he had just been caught with his hand in the cookie jar.

"I'm sorry," he apologized and coughed nervously. "I didn't mean to stare. It's just that you look so beautiful sitting there."

Celine replaced the magazine on the coffee table, then looked back up at him. "That's okay," she replied unsteadily, not knowing what else to say. She hadn't been ready for that kind of compliment and instantly felt her face blush with color.

"Would you like a soda or mineral water to drink?" he asked, changing the subject swiftly.

"Soda's fine," she murmured.

He went to the refrigerator and pulled out a couple of cans of soda and flipped the tops open. He handed her the soda, then positioned himself on the couch next to her.

"Thank you," she said as she took a sip and glanced at him while he was looking toward the fireplace. The firelight flickered across his face, accentuating his high cheekbones and rugged jawline. It made her want to impulsively reach out and touch his face. Why did she have to be so attracted to him? She glanced away and took another sip of her soda.

"Celine," Stephan broke the silence. "Tell me more about what you've been doing since our high school days."

"First off, please call me Ce. . .all my close friends do," she insisted as she readjusted herself on the couch so she would be facing him. "Well, I guess I could start with my career. I'm a writer," she paused slightly when she saw his eyes widen in surprise, "and that pretty much fills up my time."

"What kind of writing do you do?"

"Until today, I wrote romance novels for Pennington Publishers."

"Pennington. Wow, I'm impressed," he marveled. "You must be extremely good. But what did you mean by 'until today'?"

She smiled. "Stephan, God spoke to me through your message earlier today in class," she explained. "I know God has given me the gift of writing, and now I want to start writing inspirational novels."

Stephan sat back against the soft cushion of the couch. He was so overwhelmed when he heard this, and his emotions were threatening to cloud his common sense. But, at this special moment, he didn't care. Without thinking, he leaned over and pulled Celine into his arms.

Celine was startled. She didn't know how to react, but she could feel the electricity in the air and, ironically, she didn't even try to pull away.

"Ce, you're an incredible woman," he whispered softly into her ear.

She nestled herself against him. She felt so comfortable. It was almost like she belonged there.

He continued to hold her in his arms, telling himself that it was only a friendly hug, that's all. So why then was his heart pumping so wildly? As his better sense crept back in, Stephan quickly loosened his hold.

Celine tilted her head up and gazed into his clear blue eyes. Her golden hair spilled gently over her shoulders, and her face was radiant. Stephan lost himself when he met her gaze and, without hesitation, he pulled her back to him as his mouth claimed her soft lips. Uncontrollably, tremors shot through his body.

Never before had Celine felt so drawn to a man. It wasn't just physical—it was spiritual too. They both shared a common interest, and that was serving the Lord. Stephan's love for Christ warmed her heart, and she respected him greatly for it. She laid her head against his chest and was helplessly lost in the moment. It was like a dream. . .a wonderful dream. Then, all of a sudden, the name hit her mind like an arrow piercing her heart—*Angela!* Instantly, Celine's mind became alert, and she twisted out of Stephan's warm embrace.

Yes, it is like a dream, she thought sadly. *An impossible dream.* Waves of shock flowed through her body. How could she have let this happen?

When she pulled away so suddenly, Stephan looked flustered. He was at a loss for words and felt ashamed of his actions. What must she think of him now?

"Ce, I. . .I," he stuttered as he searched for the right words to say. "I don't know what came over me." He reached out and touched her hand, but she pulled it away. "I'm so sorry."

Celine was confused and didn't know how to reply. She knew one thing, though—she had to leave. "Stephan, you don't have to say anything," Celine stated as she stood up hastily and put on her jacket. "I'd better be going."

Stephan stood up and walked over to her. "Let me at least walk you back to your cabin."

"No, I'll be fine," she said as she opened the door and walked out into the cool winter evening.

He touched her arm and pleaded, "Ce, I don't want you to walk alone. Please, let me walk with you. Believe me; I'll behave."

Celine turned away, then said in the calmest voice she could muster, "Good night, Stephan."

A troubled look crossed his face as he stood there and watched her walk away, not once looking back. He rubbed his face with his hands and took one last look at the small figure, disappearing into the darkness of night.

He had never felt so lousy. He wanted to crawl under a rock and forget that this night had ever happened. His behavior had been inexcusable, and he would have felt better if Celine had slapped him in the face for acting that way.

Chapter 6

Celine walked back to the cabin, the tears rolling down her face. She felt much like Belinda, the character in her novel—an emotional mess. Why did Stephan have to kiss her? Why did she have to respond? Why did she have to be so attracted to him in every possible way? Why did he have to be engaged? As she opened the cabin door, the questions were spinning around like a whirlwind in her mind.

To her dismay, Lynette was still up, reading on the couch. "Hi," Celine greeted her and headed for her room to avoid any conversation.

But Lynette didn't let her get away that easily. "Ce, are you all right?" she asked in a quiet voice, in hopes of not waking up Raine. "Have you been crying?" she persisted as she stared at Celine's tearstained cheeks.

"I'm fine," she replied and tried to smile. "Good night."

Lynette jumped up from the couch, caught Celine's hand, and pulled her back to the couch. "Ce, did Stephan hurt you?"

Celine wiped a tear from her eye and shook her head. "No, he just kissed me."

"What? I don't understand. Then why are you crying?" Lynette asked.

"He's engaged to be married," Celine replied sullenly.

Lynette squeezed her hand to comfort her. "Oh, I'm so sorry. You really like him, don't you?"

Celine nervously twirled a piece of hair around her finger before replying. "Stupid, isn't it? It's my own fault. I shouldn't have gone over to his cabin." Celine stood up and whispered, "Don't say anything to Raine about this. I know he would probably overreact and end up saying something to Stephan."

"My lips are sealed," Lynette promised. "Good night, Ce."

Celine nodded and slipped into her room. She felt so exhausted and emotionally drained as she changed into her nightgown. Before she shut off the light, she reached over and picked up her Bible from the nightstand. She randomly flipped to a page and started reading. "Trust in the Lord with all thine heart; and lean not unto thine own understanding. In all thy ways acknowledge him, and he shall direct thy paths." Proverbs was the book of wisdom, and in chapter three, verses five and six, she could feel that her heavenly Father was trying to tell her not to worry, but to trust Him. As she gave her burden to the Lord, she felt her turbulent thoughts start to calm down. She switched off the light and pulled the warm blanket up under her chin. Her head found the softness of the pillow and, in minutes, she was fast asleep.

172

Early the next morning, Celine woke up to the melody of birds singing outside her window. Ignoring the morning chill, she hopped out of bed and dressed quickly. She slipped on her running sweats and tiptoed quietly out the doorway.

As Celine rubbed her eyes, she recalled her fitful sleep, and she knew she hadn't slept more than three hours the whole night. Once her eyes focused clearly to the light of day, she glanced around and took in the forest's beauty.

A quiet hush surrounded her, and she could see the sunrise trying to peek through the tall evergreen trees. She felt as if she were the only one awake in the whole camp. As she started her jogging, the brisk, cool air awakened her senses, and the grogginess she had felt earlier disappeared. She could feel that the temperature was going to be cooler that day, and she had heard that the forecast for tomorrow was for a few snow flurries. Fortunately, the retreat would be over before then, and she would be safely back in her warm and cozy abode with good old Queenie.

A squirrel scampered quickly across her path and scurried up the closest pine tree. Celine could easily get used to taking her morning runs in this wonderful atmosphere. As she jogged past the lodge, her mind was elsewhere, and she didn't notice Stephan descending the steps.

He didn't miss her, though, and his eyes caught sight of the small figure, jogging ahead. He knew this probably would be his only chance to talk to her privately, so he decided to get her attention. "Ce!" he yelled out, hoping she could still hear him. He had to explain his actions to her and make things right.

When Celine heard her name called, she stopped abruptly. As she turned around, her left foot slipped on a rock, throwing her off balance. The next thing she knew, she was sitting on the dirt road, embarrassed and upset with herself for being so clumsy. When she saw Stephan rushing to her aid, she felt like crying in humiliation.

"Ce, are you okay?" he asked in a concerned voice as he bent down by her side.

She rubbed her ankle and felt a small twinge of pain but knew it was nothing major. "Yes, I'm fine. It's my pride that's hurt," she complained.

"It's my fault you fell," he acknowledged as he helped her to her feet. "If I hadn't yelled for you, this wouldn't have happened."

"Well, I can surely say this, Stephan, wherever you go, action follows," she commented wryly. A little smile formed as she imagined how silly she must have looked when she tumbled to the ground.

Stephan chuckled at her statement. "I'm happy to hear that your sense of humor has returned."

"What did you need, Stephan?"

"We need to talk, and right now would be the perfect time for it."

"I guess you wouldn't let me take a rain check on it, would you?" She gave him a pleading look, but he remained firm.

"You're right, I won't," he replied and flashed her a grin. "Let's go and sit down on the steps of the lodge."

Celine followed him begrudgingly and sat down next to him on the cold cement steps.

"Ce," Stephan began slowly, "I'm going to share a story with you, and all I ask is that you let me finish before you comment."

Celine nodded in agreement to his wishes and remained silent.

"The story is about a young, rebellious teenager in high school who had a deep crush on his classmate, who happened to be the most popular and prettiest girl in school. Since he was a nobody, he knew in his heart that there was no way this lovely young lady could ever return his feelings. So, he kept quiet about it and locked away his feelings for her in his heart. Graduation day was the last time he ever saw her until, ten years later, he bumped into her by chance. Or was it by chance?"

He paused and glanced over at her. Celine could feel his gaze upon her, but she refused to look up. Instead, she continued to stare at her sneakers and nervously fiddle with her shoestring.

After a few seconds of silence, he continued. "By that time, he was engaged to be married, but when he saw her again, the locked-away feelings he had for her so long ago surfaced once again, without warning. One night while he was talking with her, his emotions got the better of him, and he overstepped the boundaries of their friendship."

"Stephan," Celine interrupted, "you don't have to explain any further. I really appreciate your sharing with me why last night happened, but let's put this episode behind us like adults."

"Yes, aah, let's do," he agreed. He somehow expected a different reaction from her. Maybe he had wished she had felt the same way for him back then and was secretly hoping she would admit it. But how foolish. What difference would it make? And why did it matter? He was engaged to Angela.

"I'll see you later," she stated woodenly and got up from the steps. "I'm going to finish my jogging before breakfast."

"Okay, see you later."

With that reply, she left him as she did the night before and, once again, he sat there quietly and watched her disappear down the road. *Why does life have to be so complicated, Lord?* He stood up, dusted himself off, and walked back to his cabin, not feeling much better than he had the night before.

❧❦❧

After her run, Celine jumped into the shower and let the warm water massage her tight muscles. Then she dried off and changed into her white dress slacks and a soft mohair sweater, quickly French-braided her hair, applied some rouge and lip gloss, and was set for breakfast. She picked up her schedule and reviewed the list of classes and activities scheduled for after church. She was still debating whether or not she should attend Stephan's late-afternoon class. In her heart, she knew that the less she saw of him, the better.

Her mind drifted back to the story he had shared with her earlier. When she had heard that he had had a crush on her back then, she had almost spilled her heart out to him, but the simple fact that he was engaged had kept her quiet. No matter how she felt now, she must be silent about her feelings toward him because it would only bring problems for both of them.

With that decided, Celine went to breakfast and had French toast, bacon, and fresh fruit. Raine had a mountain of thick buttermilk pancakes with maple syrup. When breakfast was over, everyone headed over to the lodge's sanctuary.

The morning service started off with Stephan leading the people in song and worship. Celine avoided looking in Stephan's direction because when she did, her heart ached.

Through most of the service, Celine kept her eyes glued to the pastor and listened intently to his sermon. When the service was over, she edged her way quickly through the crowd to the back doors.

"Ce, wait," Stephan's voice called from behind her. She turned and saw him a few feet away. He was dressed in a handsomely tailored suit that made him look as if he had stepped out of a men's fashion magazine.

"At least this time when you turned around, you didn't fall," Stephan remarked with a wink and flashed her a friendly smile.

She ignored his comment and changed the subject to something neutral. "I enjoyed the song service, Stephan."

"I'm glad. Thanks."

"I have to catch up with Raine and Lynette, so if you'll excuse me. . . ," she said politely and started for the door.

"Wait," he said and reached over and caught her wrist. "I wanted to ask you if you would consider going horseback riding with me in about an hour?"

Celine started to open her mouth, but Stephan didn't give her a chance to speak. "If you say yes, I'll make sure that you get the tamest horse in the stables, and believe me there will be no mules this time," he stated with a chuckle.

Celine mulled over the idea briefly and, once again before she could reply, Stephan spoke up. "And I promise that I won't talk about anything personal. Believe me; I'll be the perfect gentleman."

She couldn't help but smile at his detemination. "Well," she drawled, "I can't refuse then. I'll meet you at the stables in an hour."

"Great!" he exclaimed. "I'll see you then."

❧❧❧

Stephan arrived at the stables a few minutes early so he could have Joe saddle up the horses before Celine arrived.

Celine was a little late, so she ran from her cabin until she reached the small ledge that overlooked the stables below and she spotted Stephan, perched on the fence below. He looked like an advertisement for a men's cologne, with his beige cowboy hat cocked to one side, chewing on a piece of hay.

"Stephan," she called down to him while she reached for her camera. "Smile."

He glanced her way and tilted the brim of his hat farther back and smiled broadly.

She clicked the picture, then ran down to the fence to greet him. "I hope you didn't mind me taking a picture of you."

Stephan lowered himself off the fence. "That's fine, but it's hardly fair," he commented. "You'll have a picture of me, but I won't have one of you."

"Well, it doesn't matter because I'm not a famous singer like you are and, besides, now I'll be able to prove to my friends that I know Stephan James." She grinned sheepishly.

"You really know how to make a person feel special."

She strapped her camera over her shoulder and sidestepped his remark. "I wanted to take some pictures of the horses and scenery, so I hope you don't mind if we stop here and there along the trail."

"No problem," he answered, then led her over to Joe, who was standing by the horses. Stephan watched Celine as she strode slightly ahead of him. She was graceful in everything she did, even walking.

Joe greeted them cheerfully. "I heard you wanted the wildest beast here," Joe teased playfully and winked at Celine.

"Yes, do you have any black stallions, Joe?"

"No," he said as he looked at Stephan and grinned, "but I do have a rowdy mule you can ride."

"You told Joe?" she accused Stephan, and he nodded. She gave him a stern look, fighting back a smile. "Shame on you."

"Ma'am, don't be angry with Steve for sharing your little adventure with me," Joe chuckled heartily. "It isn't every day that someone finds a mule hiding behind a horse's clothing."

"I bet the whole retreat knows the story, thanks to you." She threw Stephan a look of annoyance.

He laughed. "Come on, Celine, mount your horse," Stephan urged, anxious to hit the trail.

Joe helped her up on a gentle-looking Appaloosa. "Her name is Daisy, and she's the sweetest little filly you could ever ride," he informed.

"Thanks, Joe," she said gratefully. "I really appreciate it."

Stephan threw a large brown saddlebag on his horse, Lightning, and jumped on. "Ce, I thought we could ride the path that runs parallel to the stream. Then we could have lunch at the spot I took you to yesterday."

"That sounds wonderful," she replied, *and romantic,* she added to herself. She would have to keep a close watch on her emotions—that was for certain.

The sky was overcast as the horses ascended the side of the hill behind the lodge. The cold air nipped at her nose, and the wind rippled through her golden hair.

"See that clearing up ahead?" Stephan pointed his finger and Celine nodded. "I'll race you to the end of the clearing, which will lead us to the path along the stream."

"Okay, you're on. I'll count down," she called out excitedly. "One, two, three. . .go!"

The leaves and dirt flew under the horses' hooves, and the cool wind splashed against Stephan and Celine's faces as both of their Appaloosas bolted forth. Daisy and Lightning raced neck and neck until seconds before the imaginary finish line, when Daisy had a burst of energy and shot out ahead of Lightning, winning the race.

"Whoa, Daisy," Celine said as she pulled back on the reins and reared Daisy around to meet Stephan. She sat up straight and put her nose in the air haughtily. "Ooh, I feel so good."

Stephan grinned. "You braggart. Let's have a rematch, and I promise you, I'll beat the horseshoes off of you."

She laughed. "Mere words you speak, young man. You know I would win again," she said confidently, her eyes sparkling with mischief.

Stephan's head went back, and he roared with laughter. She watched a dimple form on his face, giving him a cute boyish look. It reminded her of their younger days in high school.

"Okay, woman, since you won't let me race you again, how about if we make like a tree and leaf for the stream so this hungry man can eat lunch?"

"Make like a tree and leaf?" she repeated, then grinned. "Is that Pine Cove humor?"

"No, it's just plain Stephan humor." He chuckled.

Celine smiled as she gazed upward, exclaiming, "Forgive him, Lord, for he does not know what he says."

"Boy," he drawled as he wiped his hand dramatically across his forehead, "I feel like you just rescued me from getting zapped by a lightning bolt from heaven."

"Don't thank me," she giggled compulsively. "Thank the Lord for having a sense of humor too."

They laughed as they rode toward the stream. Stephan enjoyed being with Celine so much that he didn't want to think about having to say good-bye to her tomorrow morning. His feelings for her were real, and he knew that when this weekend was over, he definitely had to sit down and reevaluate his feelings for Angela.

He had to be honest with himself. It certainly wasn't fair to Angela if he had feelings for another woman, and he had better make a decision on his engagement with Angela before he made a rash move in the direction of marriage. It was a holy sacrament, and he didn't want to make a mistake.

When they arrived at the spot where they had been the day before, they dismounted and set up lunch. Stephan grabbed his saddlebag off Lightning and pulled out a neatly folded red-checked tablecloth.

"Would you help me spread this on the ground?" he asked.

"Sure." She took one end and they laid it out on the grassy ground that was littered with fallen leaves. "Stephan, ever since class I've been wanting to ask you something."

"What?" he asked curiously as he positioned himself across from her.

"When you changed from singing rock and roll to Christian music, was it a difficult adjustment?"

"Why do you ask?"

"I'm afraid that I'll fail making the change from my old style of writing to inspirational writing. I even had a dream last night that I couldn't make the switch over," she explained in a worried voice.

"Ce, can I ask you a question?" She nodded and he continued. "How well did you write before?"

"Well, good enough to have my last novel hit the best-seller list," she replied modestly.

Stephan's mouth dropped open in amazement. "Remember one thing about your ability to write—God gave you the gift. Before, you weren't writing under His guidance and direction, but now you will be and, believe me, God will pour ideas into your head for your books," he responded confidently.

"Are you sure?"

"When I first changed over to singing Christian songs, I felt the same way. I had trouble in the beginning, I have to admit, but that was because I wasn't trusting God to work through me. In time, though, I did learn to put my life into God's hands, and then He poured songs of life into my heart to share with everyone who wanted to hear."

Celine relaxed a little. "Thanks for sharing that with me. I don't feel quite so afraid now. Trusting God is the key, isn't it?"

He nodded, then grinned handsomely. "Are you hungry now?"

"Yes, I'm starved."

"Good," he said as he unpacked the food. "I hope you like cold chicken, fresh fruit, and French bread. Heidi, the retreat's cook, packed it for me. It's some of last night's leftovers."

A few yards from their picnic, a blue jay landed on a low branch and hungrily eyed their lunch.

"He looks hungrier than we are," Stephan observed as he pointed to the blue jay. He broke off a piece of bread and threw it in the blue jay's path.

"I think you're right," Celine responded quietly as she saw Mr. Blue Jay quickly swoop down and carry off the delicious morsel. She then eyed the two pieces of chicken that Stephan had placed on her plate. "It does look yummy."

"What more could we ask for?" he replied contently as he dished some sliced fruit onto her plate. "We have the beauty of nature surrounding us, good, nutritious food to satisfy our hunger, and each other's company to enjoy."

His words sound a little on the romantic side, Celine thought and quickly interjected, "One more thing could have made this perfect, and that would be if our sweethearts could be here to share this wondrous place with us." She paused and met his gaze. "I know you must miss Angela."

He nodded slowly, caught off guard by her remark. "Yes, I do." His reply was brief; no more was mentioned about the woman Celine so envied.

When Celine had said "sweethearts," it had abruptly snapped him out of dreamland and brought him back to reality. *Who is her sweetheart? Are they serious? How long have they dated each other?* These questions were on the tip of his tongue, but there was no way he could ask her any of them because he had promised he wouldn't talk about anything personal.

He sighed inwardly as he looked down at his half-eaten piece of chicken that suddenly wasn't very appealing. Why was he so upset over this newfound information? This is what he had wished for originally; that way Ce would be off-limits. Instead of relieving him, the news bothered him intensely. *Double standard,* he silently scolded himself. He could have a fiancée, but she couldn't have a boyfriend. How selfish and stupid he felt.

"Stephan?"

"Huh?"

"It looked like you were off in dreamland," she remarked, secretly hoping he would let her in on his thoughts.

"No, quite the opposite."

"What?" Celine questioned.

"Oh, nothing," he shrugged.

By the expression on his face and the tone of his voice, Celine knew better than to pursue it any further, and so she changed the subject. "Stephan, do you still live in southern California?"

He nodded. "I have a house in Rolling Green Heights. Have you heard of the area?"

"Heard of it?" she repeated in astonishment. "I grew up there. My parents still live there."

Stephan smiled broadly. "Little did I know when I was younger that I'd be able to afford a house in the same area that the Hart family lived. I had heard from some kids back then that you lived in a wealthy part of the city, but I never knew where it was," he mused.

"Well, now you do," she winked at him.

"Do you still live in the same area?"

"Now that question does fall under the catagory of personal." She paused and grinned. "But I'll let it slide this time. I live a short distance from Rolling Green Heights. A few years ago I bought a town house in Canterbury Corner; it's located about a mile from South Coast Plaza."

"That's the huge shopping mall off Bristol Street, isn't it?"

"That's the one."

"It looks like we've both been fortunate, Ce. God has truly blessed us."

"I know, and I'm so grateful," she remarked sincerely, then started to gather up the two empty plates. "The lunch was super. Thank Heidi for me."

"Ce, uh. . . ," he hesitated, "my band and I are booked for a concert next month at the Irvine Amphitheater, which isn't far from where you live, and I was wondering if you'd like to come."

"Are you kidding? Of course I would," she voiced enthusiastically.

"Fantastic!" He ripped off a piece of paper towel and pulled out a pen from his saddlebag. "Give me your address, and I'll have my manager send you four tickets with backstage passes for after the concert."

She accepted the paper and pen and jotted down her address, then handed it back to him.

"Thanks," he said, then looked at his watch. "I really don't want to cut this time short, but I have to get back and change for my class."

"That's okay," she replied and helped him gather up the tablecloth and leftovers.

"Will you be at class?" he asked in a hopeful voice.

"I'll be there," she assured him, reinforcing it with a 100-watt smile that made him want to reach out and hold her in his arms and never let go. Only in his dreams, and really not even there.

Chapter 7

After Celine and Stephan rode back to the stables, they parted company, and Celine strode back to the cabin to change. When she walked into the cabin, she heard a soft moaning sound coming from Raine and Lynette's room. She walked over and peeked around the open door. She saw Lynette curled up on the bed.

"Lynette," she whispered.

Lynette rolled over to face Celine. Her face was locked in a grimace.

"Hi, Ce," she said with a groan.

"What's wrong?" Celine asked in concern.

"It all started this morning when I felt queasy after I dressed for breakfast, but then in a matter of minutes the feeling went away. Then after church, Raine and I were going to take a dip in the whirlpool and the queasiness hit me again. So Raine brought me back here to rest."

"Where is he now?"

"He's at the lodge's office, checking to see if there's a doctor in the area," Lynette answered and moaned again.

Seconds later, they heard the door to the cabin open. Raine came rushing into the bedroom. "Ce, I'm glad you're here," he said in a frantic voice. "I couldn't reach the doctor in town, so we are going to have to pack up our gear and stop at the first hospital we see on the way home."

"I'll go and pack my things then," Celine responded.

"But what about Gramma Em, Raine? She's expecting to see us before we leave," Lynette reminded.

"Honey, I've already called Gramma Em while I was at the lodge, and I told her about the situation." He patted her hand lovingly. "Don't worry. She understands."

When they were packed, Celine threw her gear in the back of the car and then turned to Raine. "I have a quick errand to do, but I'll be right back."

He winked at her and smiled, "Sure, go ahead."

As she ran to Stephan's cabin, she had a feeling that Raine knew where she was going by the way he smiled. She could read him like a book. She laughed. It looked like he could read her just as well.

When Celine reached the cabin, she knocked on the door several times, but Stephan didn't answer. She must have just missed him. She really wanted to say good-bye. Reaching into her purse, she grabbed a piece of paper from her small notebook and a pen and wrote a quick note:

> *Dear Stephan,*
>
> *I'm sorry I had to miss your class, but Lynette has become ill, and we have to get her to a doctor. I truly enjoyed getting to know the new Stephan, and I'm looking forward to seeing you in concert next month.*
>
> *God bless you,*
> *Ce*

After she had finished scribbling down the note, she slipped it partway between the door and the weather stripping.

When she arrived back at the cabin, Raine and Lynette were ready to go. Now they only had to drop the cabin key off at the office before heading out for the hospital.

As they were turning onto the main road to leave the retreat facility, a sleek red sports car pulled into the retreat's entrance. Celine could only imagine that it probably belonged to the owner of the property.

The red car steered up to the lodge's entrance and parked. A stunningly attractive brunette got out and walked into the office. "Excuse me, Miss." The woman tapped her fingers on the counter impatiently.

"Yes, may I help you?" the receptionist asked.

"My name is Angela Brady, and I was wondering if you could tell me where I could find Stephan James?"

"I'm not sure where he is at the moment, but I can tell you the location of his cabin," she offered.

"That's fine; thank you."

"Here is the map, and here," she circled the location, "is where his cabin is."

Angela took the map and wasted no time in finding Stephan's cabin. When she reached up to knock on the door, she noticed a piece of paper stuck in the door-jamb. She pulled the paper free and opened it up to investigate its contents. Hurriedly, she skimmed over the words. *Who is Ce?* she wondered as her face burned slowly with anger. She looked around and then tucked the note in her purse. She knocked on the door a couple of times and, when no one answered, she walked back to the lodge.

⸙⸙⸙⸙

During the class, Stephan's eyes kept glancing toward the back door, hoping to see Celine walk in. But, to his disappointment, she never showed up. When the class was over and all the questions were answered, Stephan picked up his notes and headed out to the hallway.

He was seriously pondering the thought of walking over to Ce's cabin to see why she didn't show up. Then he thought again. Would that be wise? He'd probably see her at dinner, anyway.

He went to push open the main door of the lodge, but stopped when he heard his name called. The voice was all too familiar to Stephan and before he turned around completely, he said, "Angela?"

"Surprise, Darling," she greeted and then reached up and kissed him.

"What are you doing here?" he asked politely, trying desperately to hide his annoyance.

"Darling, I came up here to give you a lift home."

"Ange, I don't need a ride home. You know I drove up with the band in the van," he said as he raked his fingers through his hair in exasperation. He instantly felt guilty for feeling that way.

Angela locked her arm through his and led him out the door. "Hon, I didn't mean to upset your plans, but I missed you so much," she purred, then kissed him on his cheek. "Let's go to your cabin, and we'll talk this out." She started to lead him up the road.

"Do you know where my cabin is?" Stephan asked.

She nodded. "The receptionist gave me a map."

Stephan dug into his pocket and pulled out his cabin key. "Here, take this and wait at the cabin."

Angela eyed him suspiciously. "Why?"

"I have a quick errand to do," he explained, then seeing her displeasure he quickly added, "I'll be right back, Ange."

Stephan made a dash for Ce's cabin. He didn't even know what he was going to say, but he knew he had to see her. When he reached the cabin, he rapped loudly on the door a few times, but no one answered. He turned around and noticed there was no vehicle parked in their space. *They didn't leave, did they?* he thought to himself in dismay. Ce would have at least said good-bye. Maybe they went to town.

As he walked back, he decided to stop at the office to check and see if the Harts were still registered. "Hi, Betty," he greeted.

"Hello, Stephan. What's up?" she asked as she got up from her desk and walked over to the counter.

"Are the Harts still registered in cabin seventeen?"

She shook her head. "You missed them by about half an hour."

"They checked out?" he asked in a shocked voice.

Betty nodded.

"Did they leave any messages?"

"No, I'm sorry, they didn't."

Feeling discouraged, Stephan walked back to his cabin. He couldn't understand why Ce hadn't even said good-bye. *Maybe,* he picked up his pace, *she left a note on the door.*

But when he reached the cabin door, a disappointed expression crossed his face as he saw no note. He walked in and saw Angela sitting on the couch.

"Ange, did you see a note on the door when you arrived?"

"No," she replied innocently. "I didn't see one."

Stephan couldn't suppress the disgruntled look that appeared on his face. His eyes went to Angela. "I'm going to change for dinner, then you and I are going to go to the office so we can get you a cabin for the night."

"You don't have to bother, Darling," she replied smoothly as she stood up and wrapped her arms around him. "I'll stay here and sleep on the couch."

"No need to, Ange. There's a cabin some guests vacated a day early so you'll be able to stay there." Stephan gently twisted out from her grasp. With a sigh, Stephan walked into his room, closed the door, and changed for dinner.

⁓❦❧⁓

"Raine, I see a sign on the right for a hospital at the next exit," Celine said.

"Good; we'll stop there."

Celine turned around in her seat and said quietly, "Lynette, we're almost there."

Lynette nodded in between groans. "I feel so nauseous."

"Don't worry. Once you get to the doctor's, you'll be feeling fine in no time," Celine reassured and prayed that she was right.

Raine drove up to the hospital's emergency entrance and dropped off Celine and Lynette so that he could park in the garage. By the time he made it back to the waiting room, a nurse had already taken Lynette to be examined by a staff doctor.

"Will you please sit down?" Celine asked. "You're making me nervous." She watched her brother continue to pace the floor.

"I can't help it," Raine expressed, still pacing. "I wouldn't be so worried if she hadn't passed out on me earlier."

"Lynette didn't tell me that she had passed out," Celine stated in a troubled voice.

"She probably didn't want to worry you," he surmised as he finally sat down. "Lynette passed out by the whirlpool, and fortunately I caught her before her head hit the concrete."

"Oh, now I'm really worried."

A nurse appeared around the door. "Mr. Hart, your wife will be out in a minute."

"How is she?" he questioned anxiously.

"I think I'll let your wife tell you herself," the nurse replied and smiled. "While you're waiting, you may pay the bill at the billing office around the corner."

After the nurse closed the door, Raine threw Celine a puzzled look. "What was that all about?"

"Your guess is as good as mine," she said, also perplexed over the nurse's response.

As Raine wrote out a check at the billing window, Lynette walked out into the waiting room. She looked radiant and was smiling from ear to ear. Raine spotted her and went over and hugged her tightly.

"You look great," he commented. "What medicine did the doctor give you to cure you so quickly?"

"Oh, the usual medicine for morning sickness—two crackers and a glass of soda," she giggled.

"Morning sickness?" Raine and Celine both vocalized their surprise loudly.

"Uh-huh," Lynette replied gleefully.

"I'm going to be a daddy?" Raine asked, as if the information wasn't sinking in.

"That's right, Honey." She smiled up at him, her eyes twinkling. "We are going to be parents." They had tried for two long years, so this was news to celebrate, Celine knew.

"Congratulations, you two," Celine cut in. "Now, if you don't mind letting go of Lynette, Raine, maybe I could give her a hug too."

Raine grinned and reluctantly let go of his wife. Celine embraced her sister-in-law warmly. "Everyone will be so excited when they hear the good news," Celine remarked.

And then Lynette chattered about what to name the baby, depending on whether it was a boy or girl. In fact, she kept talking about names all the way home.

Celine, though, had trouble staying with the conversation as her mind kept straying back to the stolen moments she had spent with Stephan. In only a few hours, he had touched her heartstrings on every level. But he was another woman's man, and she knew that she would have to lock away her special feelings for him and let them fade into memories of a beautiful place in time.

❧

The next day was dismally cold with a few flurries. Stephan helped the guys in his band pack the van with the equipment and gear. When they finished, he left them to drive home with Angela.

"Honey, you look really tired," Angela commented. "You even have dark circles under your eyes."

"I didn't sleep well last night," Stephan stated and sighed wearily. He leaned his head back on the soft leather headrest. Ce's strange departure had given him a headache all night long, so sleep had not come easily to him. He still didn't understand it. After all they had shared, why hadn't she even made an attempt to say a simple good-bye? It didn't make one ounce of sense. It was like she had just vanished into thin air. Did it even happen—their meeting of chance? Was she just a vision of lost memories? *No!* he shouted silently to himself. Her smile was real, her laughter was intoxicating, and her eyes sparkled like the stars on a crystal-clear night. Yes, Celine was very real and had placed an impression upon his heart that would never be erased.

"Darling," Angela raised her voice, "aren't you listening to me?"

"Sorry, Ange. What did you say?"

"I was asking you if you'd like to join my parents and me for dinner tonight at the house," she repeated impatiently.

"I can't tonight, Ange," he apologized. "I've got too many things to do." He tore his gaze away from the window and turned to her, giving her his full attention. "But how about coming over to dinner at my place tomorrow evening?"

"That sounds nice, Darling," she remarked as she looked in her rearview mirror and changed lanes, exiting the freeway.

"There are some things we have to talk about tomorrow evening," he added.

"And what are they?" she asked as she arched her eyebrow.

"I'm too tired to go into everything now."

"Okay, we'll wait."

Stephan knew he couldn't continue the engagement, not when he had strong feelings for Ce. He didn't know how he would approach Angela on the subject, but he knew he couldn't postpone it because it wouldn't be fair to her.

He glanced over at Angela, behind the steering wheel. She was truly a beautiful woman, and he didn't want to hurt her, but their personalities were definitely diametrically opposed. Now he clearly saw that there had been a lot missing in their relationship and, until this past weekend, he had been blind to it.

Being with Ce for a couple of days had opened his eyes and made him realize that there was something more he needed from a permanent relationship.

His attraction to Ce was different from his attraction to Angela. He had been drawn by Ce's childlike faith in God and her gentle and caring spirit. She had a way, just by listening, of showing a person she really cared. Through her dry wit and carefree attitude, she also had a special way of making a person laugh and smile. Celine had all the attributes that he had been looking for in a potential mate. He wanted his future wife to desire a close walk with God, like he himself wanted.

With Angela, it had been a chore to get her to go to church. She didn't want to know the Lord in a deeper way, and that frustrated him. He thought she would change, but she hadn't and, many times, she made it very clear to him that God wasn't her first priority.

With Ce, though, he could see her love for God shine forth, and he knew in his heart that she desired the same things he did.

The car rolled up his driveway and Angela gave him a pleading look. "Darling, are you sure you can't join us for dinner tonight?"

"I'm sure," he responded and fought back a yawn. "Thanks for driving me home," he said and leaned over and kissed her cheek. "I'll see you tomorrow."

"Fine, Darling," she said and waved out her window as she backed down the driveway.

Stephan opened his front door and headed straight for his bedroom. A long, hot shower was what his tired bones and overworked mind needed.

⊱❄⊰

When Raine and Lynette had dropped off Celine the evening before, she had wasted no time in picking up Queenie at Mrs. Kay's. Ironically, she had mused, Celine had really missed that crazy cat.

The next morning, she awoke to the unwelcome noise of her neighbor's German shepherd barking loudly outside her window, and Queenie joining in the racket by meowing on the windowsill. In between yawns, she cracked a smile. She didn't need an alarm clock with Queenie and the town crier, Fido, around to wake her up in the mornings.

She rolled out of bed slowly and then marched downstairs and fixed a cup of lemon tea. A few minutes later, like clockwork, Queenie sauntered into the kitchen and parked her furry body directly in front of her bowl and meowed, looking at her mistress expectantly.

"And dare I ask what you want, Queen Esther?" she questioned, then bent down and took the bowl from underneath her feline friend. After she had poured some cat munchies into the bowl and given it to Queenie, she picked up her cup of tea and headed for her study to start work on her new book.

Celine sat down at the desk and flipped open the notebook that was filled with character outlines, plot and location information, and, of course, pages of dialogue. She turned on the computer and started the tedious work of revising the old outline. As she typed on the keyboard, she marveled at the myriad of ideas that God was pouring into her head to write about. Stephan had been right. She grinned—she had to trust God all the way, not just part of the way.

Celine became so engrossed in the new Brad and Belinda that she worked straight through lunch before she decided it was time for a break. She showered and changed into a sweater dress and headed out to the local deli to get a bite to eat. After she ate a delicious ham-and-cheese sandwich, she walked across the street to a row of shops.

Excitement stirred in her as she spotted the Lighthouse, a Christian bookstore. She hadn't been in a Christian bookstore for a long while, and she knew it probably had to do with guilt over her secular novels. Now she felt free and renewed because she was really doing what the Lord wanted her to do.

She wandered between the book racks, looking at titles. She picked up and paged through a handful of books. One book, entitled *Growing in Christ,* caught her eye, and she decided to buy it as well as a young adult mystery.

After she paid for the books, she headed home, suddenly feeling anxious to do some reading and take a break from writing for the rest of the day. She also had a new desire to read the Bible. Silently, she thanked God for renewing her spirit.

When Celine walked in the door, she heard the phone ringing and rushed over and picked up the receiver. "Hello," Celine said.

"Hi! How's my favorite sister doing?" her cousin asked.

"Super, Bill," she replied sweetly. "It's great to hear your voice. How are you doing?"

"Well," he drawled, "it's so good, that I'd like to take you out to dinner tonight."

"You're in town?"

"Yes, our company is having a convention at the Westin Hotel," he explained. "I'll have only tonight free, so I wanted to get together with you, if it's possible."

"I'd love to go," she gladly accepted. "Do you want me to pick you up at the hotel?"

"No, I have a company car at my disposal, so I'll pick you up at six o'clock."

"Great," she responded cheerfully. "I'll be ready, Bill."

After Celine hung up, she spent a few moments reminiscing about her dear cousin. Celine had always had a soft spot where Bill was concerned. He was an only child, and when he was growing up, he had always wanted to have a sister. Long ago, when Bill was staying with the Harts, he had asked Raine if he would share Celine with him so he could have a sister too. Raine, at the age of ten, gladly obliged Bill and gave him the okay. So, from that day on, Bill had treated Celine like his very own sister.

Over the years, Bill had always kept in contact with her, and whenever he was in town, he would take her out to dinner, usually at one of the best restaurants, and treat her like a queen. When Darrell had left Celine brokenhearted, Bill had been there to comfort her and help pick up the broken pieces. He was a friend to her as well as a brother, and God knew she greatly appreciated his attention and friendship.

≈❈❈≈

Stephan held the phone receiver for a few seconds before he dialed for assistance.

"Hello, can I help you?" the operator asked.

"Yes, I'd like the number for Celine Hart in Costa Mesa."

"Just a moment, please," she replied. "Sorry, Sir, it's an unlisted number."

As Stephan replaced the receiver on its cradle, he knew his only other option was to drive over to Ce's place. Her abrupt departure from the retreat made him feel very uneasy, and he wouldn't rest until he knew that she was all right. Without another thought, he stuffed her address into his pocket, grabbed the keys to his car, and headed for Ce's town house.

Within fifteen minutes he reached the cobblestoned entrance to Canterbury Corner. He pulled over to the side of the street and glanced down at the address in his hand—77 Oaktree Drive. He wished he had brought a city map with him.

He looked up and saw a woman walking up ahead with a dachshund on a leash. He opened the door and walked over to her. "Excuse me, I'm lost and I'm looking for a friend's house on Oaktree Drive," he explained. "Could you by chance tell me where the street is?"

"Of course, young man. I also live on Oaktree. By the way, what is the house number?" the woman inquired.

"It's seventy-seven," he said as he bent down to pet the dachshund. "Hi, pooch," he said as the dog hid behind the woman's legs.

"She's a little shy around strangers," she explained. "Now, 77 Oaktree is where Celine lives. So, are you a friend of hers?" she questioned as she looked him over.

"Yes. You're her neighbor then?"

"That's right. My name is Mrs. Kay," she said as she held out her hand to shake his. "And your name is?"

"Stephan James."

"What a nice-sounding name," she replied with a smile. "Now, Celine's house is easy to find. Take this street until it ends at the tennis courts, then turn right, and Celine's place is the second town house on the right."

"Thanks for your help."

"You're quite welcome," Mrs. Kay replied as she tugged on the leash and continued her walk.

With Mrs. Kay's directions, Stephan found the town house easily and parked his car across the street. But, before he even had a chance to open the door, he saw Ce coming out of her home, walking arm in arm with a man.

Startled and disappointed, Stephan reacted quickly. He grabbed his sunglasses and slithered down into his seat. He felt really bad for spying on Ce. *Talk about being at the wrong place at the worst time.* Stephan, ashamed of himself, continued to stare at the couple.

The man was tall and good-looking and seemed to be a few years her senior. He opened the door to a new town car, and Ce, who was dressed in a burgundy evening dress, slipped into the passenger seat.

Stephan sighed loudly, then frowned. It didn't take much more detective work to figure out that this was the man she had called her sweetheart that day by the stream at Pine Cove.

After their car pulled away, Stephan started up his car and headed for home. *At least one thing was worth the drive to Canterbury Corner,* he told himself, *and that was seeing that Ce was all right and safe at home.*

Chapter 8

Bill took Celine to Chez Marie, the most popular French restaurant in the area. The pheasant in a delicate cream sauce, along with the wild rice, was delicious, and Celine enjoyed every morsel. It was only once in awhile that she would dine so extravagantly.

While there, they were seated in a small room with only one other couple, who occupied a table nearby. It was a beautiful library room, just one of the many different rooms to choose from in the restaurant. The walls were lined with floor-to-ceiling bookcases filled with a wide variety of famous books. Celine was tempted to take a break from her chocolate mousse pie to examine all the interesting reading material.

"Ce, I've waited all evening to share some very important news with you," Bill announced with a certain cheerfulness in his voice.

"You got a promotion?"

"No, better. I've asked Sherry to marry me, and she's said yes," he said, smiling broadly.

"Oh, Bill, I'm so very happy for you," Celine said as she reached across the small candlelit table and squeezed his hand. "Have you set a date yet?"

"Sort of. Sherry wants it to be in late spring," he said and then grinned. "I also want to ask you a question."

"Ask away."

"Since etiquette says that you can't be my best man since you are a woman, Sherry and I want you to be the maid of honor in our wedding."

Celine's eyes grew moist as Bill covered her hand with his. "I don't know what to say."

"Say yes."

"I feel so honored," she wiped her eyes. "Of course, I'll be the maid of honor, Bill."

"You've made my day," he declared warmly. "Thanks, Ce."

After they finished their calorie-filled dessert, Bill drove Celine home. At thirty years of age Bill was finally settling down. Celine wondered if it would ever happen to her. First it had been Raine to tie the knot; now it was Bill. When would her turn come? She suddenly felt very lonely.

❧❦❧

The next few days breezed by. Ce had bravely fought the crowds of holiday shoppers in the stores and had bought the last of her Christmas presents. As she was leaving the mall, she stopped to view a beautiful Nativity display in front of one of the stores. When she saw the figurine of Joseph, she instantly thought of Stephan, who had played the part so marvelously that special night under the stars. Why did he have to be taken? "All the good men usually are," she mumbled under her breath. As she walked away from the display, Celine left her thoughts of Stephan there, also.

As she drove home, she reprimanded herself for being so glum. This was a joyous time of the year, and here she was behaving like Scrooge. While thinking of past Christmases, she wiped away the frown that had been on her face and replaced it with a smile. Every year her father had read the Christmas story in the book of Luke. It was a family tradition and the very essence of Christmas. This year, the Christmas festivities were to be held at Raine and Lynette's home. Celine was glad of that, since her kitchen wasn't set up for preparing such a grand feast.

While getting ready for Christmas, Celine had also worked diligently on her writing. She was so ecstatic on how well her book was progressing, and she knew that it was only a matter of time before it would be completed. The more time Celine spent on writing about the lives of her Christian characters, the more she began to study God's Word. She could see how God was using her book to draw her closer to Him and, for the first time in a long time, Celine felt a great desire in her heart to learn more about God on a deeper level.

As the days passed by, she could feel that the void in her life that she had felt for so long was starting to ebb away. She could feel God filling that empty spot with His love, peace, and joy. It was a wonderful feeling, and what better time for it to happen than at Christmas.

Celine had waited to tell her parents about her new book and the changes in her life because she didn't want to steal any of the excitement from Raine and Lynette's news of a baby Hart on the way. *One surprise at a time,* she rationalized thoughtfully.

On the day before Christmas, though, Celine dialed her parents to share the good news. She couldn't hold back any longer. "Hi, Mom," she greeted, then paused. "Is Dad home? I have some news I wanted to share with you both."

"Yes, your dad came in the door awhile ago, but I don't know if I can pull him away from the newspaper," her mother commented kiddingly. "I can hear him in the other room, holding a conversation with the sports section, and it seems pretty serious."

Celine laughed. "Mom, go to the garage and find Dad's crowbar, and pry him away from the paper, and get him on the phone, pronto."

Her mother chuckled. "Now, how is it that I never thought of that before?" she joked, then placed the receiver on the counter and went to fetch her husband.

"Hi, Honey. How's my favorite daughter?" her father asked cheerfully.

"Dad, I'm your only daughter," she stated wryly.

"Well, that doesn't stop you from being my favorite, now does it?" he teased.

"Now, Chase," Samantha interjected, "stop teasing Celine. She has some important news she'd like to share with us."

"Okay, okay. Don't pick on me," Chase moaned. "What's the news, Honey?"

"I guess I could have waited until tomorrow when I would see you in person, but it's been a couple of weeks now, and I couldn't wait a day longer to share it with you."

"Don't keep us in suspense, Dear," her mother pleaded.

"I'm not writing any more novels for Pennington Publishers. I've started writing inspirational novels instead."

"Honey, that's great!" her father exclaimed.

"That's a wonderful Christmas present, Dear," her mother responded joyfully. "What made you change over?"

"I'll share all that with you tomorrow, okay?"

"What about your contract with Pennington?" her father asked.

"Karen Matlin, my agent, is handling all that. She called yesterday and told me that there wouldn't be any problems getting out of it because of a clause in the contract."

"Well, that's a relief," her father replied. "We're very proud of you, Honey."

"We sure are," her mother chimed in.

"Thanks, I'll see you tomorrow evening, and we'll talk some more about it."

After the good-byes, Celine replaced the phone and leaned back in her soft recliner chair and smiled. *Anything is possible with God,* she rejoiced silently with her eyes closed. She was a happy woman and a very thankful one too.

♪♪♪

For the last few weeks, Stephan had been too busy preparing his new material for his upcoming concert to have much time to dwell on his unexpected feelings for Ce. He had hoped that, with time, he would think of her less and less. But, to no avail, the sweet thoughts of her lingered in his mind.

It was just yesterday that he had made sure that Nelson Smith, his public relations manager, had sent four concert tickets to Ce's address. Stephan had decided in his heart that if she didn't show up at the concert, it would be a sign for him to put her out of his mind and to stop pursuing any further contact with her. He wanted to use wisdom in all areas of his life, including this delicate one concerning Ce.

Stephan snapped himself out of his deep thoughts when he heard the band's van park outside his home. Without wasting time, he went and opened the door and greeted his friends. Today he was especially anxious to rehearse with the band a new song that he had written a few days prior. He had wanted it to be ready so he could sing it at the concert. Ce had been the inspiration behind the song, but no one would ever find that out. The song was to be dedicated to all the single men who were searching for the perfect women to be their wives. His thoughts instantly went to Ce. He knew that whoever would be so fortunate to be her husband would be one very blessed man.

While the band was setting up, Stephan reflected back to the not-so-memorable night when he had explained to Angela that he couldn't go through with their engagement. He hadn't been prepared for her hysterical sobs and desperate pleas. He had felt like a real heel, and it had grieved his heart to the point where he had almost given in to her request of reconciliation, but he had been stopped by a small inner voice that was saying a resounding no.

That evening had ended with a loud bang, literally. Stephan winced as he remembered Angela's hand, flying across his face, sending a cracking sound echoing off the living room walls. Before he had time to recover from the shock of the cold sting of her slap, Angela had stormed out of his home in a fit of anger.

In retrospect, Stephan knew that it was better to take a slap on the face than to go through with a marriage that he now knew was not meant to be. Stephan grabbed his microphone and, for the duration of the band's rehearsal, he tucked away his thoughts concerning his personal life. There was always time later to analyze the chain of events that were currently affecting his life.

⪻✥⪼

After the Christmas holidays had passed and the new year had been ushered in, the only thing that was on Celine's mind was her book. When she heard the mailman drop the mail into her box, she jumped up from the couch and walked outside. Quickly sorting through the mail, she frowned when she didn't see anything from the Christian publishing house. She had sent a letter with an in-depth outline of her book for their review and was expecting to hear from them any day now.

Her eyes strayed to the last envelope in her hand. Its return address, although local, wasn't familiar to her. It didn't look like a bill, either. She ripped it open, pulled out its contents, and stared in amazement at the tickets she held in her hand. Stephan hadn't forgotten to send her the tickets for his concert. Over the last few weeks, she had tried hard to get him out of her mind, and now the thought of seeing him both excited and upset her.

Quickly, she ran inside the house and up the stairs to her bedroom. She pulled out the bottom drawer of her vanity desk, picked up a handful of pictures, and carefully sorted through them until she found what she was looking for. Her heart raced as she looked at Stephan, sitting on the fence in the picture she had taken at the retreat. She inhaled a sharp breath, for she hadn't looked at it since the day she had picked up the developed film.

As she continued to stare at the picture, she debated whether she should give the tickets away, thus making it easier for her to forget about him, or keep the tickets and risk having her feelings tampered with. She laid the tickets down on the desk and shoved his picture back into the drawer. She had a week to decide, so for right now, she would put the problem on the back burner.

She walked into her neatly decorated study, sat down at her desk, and grinned at her computer. At least one thing was going smoothly in life. She had only a few more chapters to edit, and Brad and Belinda's story would be complete. She had felt confident that the editor at White Dove Publishing House would like the outline that she had sent, but it was the waiting for a reply that was the hard part. Celine was not known for her patience, but God was working with her in that particular area.

The sound of the doorbell, echoing up the staircase, interrupted her thoughts. She hadn't been expecting anyone, so she couldn't imagine who it was. She hurried down the stairs and opened the door, and a smile formed on her face when she saw Mrs. Kay standing on the doorstep with a large plate of homemade cookies.

"Hi, Dear," Mrs. Kay greeted. "I hope you don't mind an interruption from your work, but I was baking cookies and thought you could use a few on that skinny frame of yours."

Celine chuckled softly and took the plate of peanut butter cookies Mrs. Kay handed to her. "Can you come in and help eat these?" she asked.

"No, I have to get back and feed my babies," she replied, then added, "I forgot to ask you if your gentleman friend ever found you that day."

Celine raised her eyebrow questioningly, "What?"

"A few weeks back a young man asked for directions to your place," she explained. "I think he had said his name was James something."

"James?" Celine repeated. "I don't know a James," she said and stopped as a thought hit her. *Could it have been Stephen?* "Could James have been his last name?" she asked. "Does Stephan James ring a bell?"

"Hmm. . .yes, that was the name. So he was a friend of yours?"

"Yes," Celine said with a smile.

"Good. I felt kind of bad after I had given him directions because, after all, you can never tell if they are really a friend or not," Mrs. Kay responded.

"Well, he is definitely a friend, so no need to worry," Celine said. "Thanks for the cookies."

"Don't forget to give one to Queen Esther," Mrs. Kay said and winked, then headed down the steps.

After Mrs. Kay left, Celine remained standing by the door, with her eyes fixed on the mailbox. She knew that it was no coincidence that she received those tickets the same day that Mrs. Kay shared about Stephan's stopping by earlier. At that moment, she made her decision to go to Stephan's concert.

She still didn't understand, though, why he had dropped by. She must have been out that day, but why didn't he leave a note? Her curiosity was running high. She would have to ask him about it after the concert. She hoped Angela wouldn't be hovering over him, and Celine could talk to him for a few minutes.

❧❦❧

When Stephan's band and stage crew had finished setting up their equipment on the stage, they all gathered around for the group prayer. They had a short while before the opening band was to perform, so Stephan and his band used that time to get ready spiritually. Stephan had been nervous not knowing whether Ce would show up or not and, right before the opening group went on, he peered out at the crowd. He had sent Ce front-row seats, so there was no way he wouldn't see her if she were there. Until seconds before the performance began, he stood off to the side but saw no sign of her.

Trying desperately not to be affected by her "no show," Stephan walked backstage and sat with his band until their cue to perform. He felt stupid for even thinking she would show up when she hadn't even bothered to say good-bye at the retreat. He felt like he was chasing after the wind. What a major fool he was.

When Buddy, his stage manager, gave the cue, they all took their places in the center of the blackened stage. Usually, Stephan felt a rush of excitement when he stepped out on the stage to perform, but tonight he didn't feel anything. *Dear Lord,* he prayed silently, *please help me to overcome this disappointment.*

Then the lights flashed on, and the audience roared and clapped loudly. Immediately, Stephan's eyes went to the four empty seats in the front row. As the band began to play its opening number, he took his microphone off the stand, put Ce in the back of his mind, and started to sing.

Halfway through his second song, his heart raced when he spotted Ce, walking down the aisle with her brother and his wife and another young man. As they sat down, he caught her eye and winked. Her eyes sparkled as they tangled with his, and then she winked back. He almost messed up his next line because his mind was stuck on Ce's dynamic, sensuous smile. Dressed in a daintily flowered dress with matching pumps, Ce looked exquisitely feminine, romantically delicate, and extremely young. He silently thanked God that Ce had made it after all.

Dazed, Celine sat back in her seat and soaked up the heavenly music. Throughout the concert, Stephan would stop in between songs and share about Christ and how serving the Lord had changed his life. She saw that he was adept at motivating the crowd into worship and praise, and she was extremely glad that she had decided to come and share this moment with a crowd of believers.

When Stephan and his band, Voices in the Light, finished their last song, they thanked the audience for coming, then disappeared off the stage. While the crowd went crazy with clapping for an encore, the stage lights dimmed. Celine joined in with the crowd and waited for Stephan to reappear on the stage. Suddenly, a spotlight isolated Stephan onstage, and the music played softly in the background when he started to speak.

"I want to share with you one last song I wrote a couple of weeks prior to this concert," he began, "and I want to dedicate it to all the single guys out there in the audience who are searching for that special woman to share their life with."

Celine sat glued in her seat as the lyrics of the song started to slowly sink into her heart. She noticed that Stephan's eyes were fixed on her, and if she hadn't already known that he was engaged, she would have sworn that he was singing it to her. Feeling her cheeks burning at the thought, she transferred her gaze to the others in the band. Unfortunately, it didn't help much when the words of the chorus rang through her mind.

"So here I sit and patiently wait for the day when God will bring me my help-mate, but meanwhile I'll continue to do the work of the Lord. . . ."

As he continued to sing, Celine tried her utmost not to read into the song's lyrics. When the song finally ended, Stephan and the band waved good-bye once again, and the crowd exploded into a deafening roar of applause. Celine had had no idea how incredibly popular Stephan and his band were.

"Ce," Lynette leaned over, "would you like us to wait here while you go backstage?"

"No, please come with me," she pleaded, suddenly feeling quite nervous about seeing Stephan again.

"Ce, you go alone, and we'll wait here," Raine insisted. "And take your time." He smiled.

"Well, okay," she mumbled and stood up. "But I won't be long."

With her backstage pass in hand, she gave it to the guard, and he opened the door. He ushered her down a long hallway and opened the door to a large room full of people. She scanned the room and silently wondered if Angela were there. No doubt she probably was. Celine stopped when she heard her name called.

"Over here, Ce."

She turned around and saw Stephan through the crowd and smiled. He had a can of soda in his hand and beckoned her over. She quickly made her way to him.

"I'm happy you could come," Stephan said when she reached his side. "How did you enjoy the concert?"

"It was absolutely fantastic. Now I can see why you gather such a crowd. Your music is inspiring," she complimented sincerely. "Thank you for the great seats."

"It was my pleasure," he said as he took a sip of his soda. "Can I get you something to drink?"

"No, thank you. I can't stay long."

A disappointed look crossed over his face. "I see you came with your brother and sister-in-law and another friend," he commented, hoping he would find out who the third party was.

"Yes, and the other friend is Lynette's younger brother, Andrew."

"Oh."

"Stephan," she began hesitantly, "I was talking to my neighbor awhile ago, and she told me that you had asked her directions to my place. How was it that you never stopped by then?"

Stephan was caught off guard by her question and shifted his feet nervously before replying. "When I came by that day, you were just leaving."

"Why didn't you leave a note or stop by again?" she questioned with curiosity.

"Let me be honest with you, okay?" he said as he set down his soda on a nearby table. "I only stopped by your house because I was worried about you."

"What do you mean, you were worried about me, Stephan?" she asked in a confused voice.

"What was I supposed to think when you left a day early from the retreat?" he said defensively. "You didn't say good-bye or even leave me a note."

Celine couldn't believe what she was hearing. "Stephan, I left a note on your cabin door," she remarked. "Didn't you see it?"

"What? I can't believe it," he exclaimed in disgust. "I should have known. The thought had entered my mind, but I didn't think she'd stoop that low."

"Excuse me," Celine interrupted, "but what are you talking about?"

"Angela."

"Angela, your fiancée?"

"Yes, she must have taken the note off the door before I arrived back at the cabin," he explained, his voice tight with anger.

"What was Angela doing at the retreat?" she asked.

"She came up right after you left. She thought she'd do me a favor and drive me home in luxury the next day instead of my having to drive back in the van with the band."

The pieces started to fit. "So you think Angela took my note off the door?"

"It doesn't really matter what I think now. The point is I didn't know what had happened to you," he emphasized.

"Please don't get angry at her or say anything to her about it," she urged. "When she read the note she probably wondered who I was, and she could have possibly taken it the wrong way."

"Ce, it doesn't matter. The day after I came home from the retreat, I broke off my engagement with Angela," he confessed and searched her face for a reaction.

Celine's heart skipped a beat and then she dared to ask, "Why?"

"It's a long story, but to break it down in short form, there was something missing from our relationship," he explained honestly.

"I'm so sorry." She didn't know what else to say. His confession had startled her. What she had secretly hoped for was now a reality—Stephan didn't belong to another woman.

"Ce," he said as he took hold of her hand, "would you like to go out to dinner sometime?"

Instantly she blushed, feeling like he had read her thoughts. "That would be really nice," she said softly, all of a sudden feeling shy and overwhelmed with the turn of events.

"How does this Wednesday sound? Say seven o'clock?"

"That's perfect," she agreed and reached into her purse for a pen. "Let me give you my phone number in case there's a change in plans."

"Here," he stretched out the palm of his hand, "write the number on my hand."

"I feel like I'm back in high school." She giggled as she wrote her number on his hand. "I'd better get back to my family now. I'll see you on Wednesday then."

He nodded and smiled at her warmly. "Thanks for coming tonight."

"It was my pleasure," she said as she turned to go. When she reached the door, she turned to wave, but he had already vanished into the crowd of people.

Chapter 9

The next few days went by too slowly for Celine. She enthusiastically greeted Wednesday morning's sunrise when she thought of spending the evening with Stephan. No longer could she deny her deep feelings for him. The fact that he wasn't involved with Angela anymore helped Celine to be open and honest with herself about the way she had felt about Stephan ever since the retreat.

She stretched lazily and scooted Queenie off her bed, then she showered and changed into her sweat suit and made her way to the park for her morning run. She had so much energy that she ran an extra mile with ease.

Ever since the concert, her mind had been stuck on one thing—Stephan. She had a hard time even concentrating on her book. For a moment, her thoughts strayed to Darrell, and she was surprised that ever since the retreat she hadn't thought about him at all. She was completely amazed and knew without a shadow of a doubt that it was the Lord who had healed her wounded heart.

❧❦❧

Stephan stood in his walk-in closet for what seemed to him to be a good half hour, grumbling under his breath at his indecisiveness about what to wear. He didn't want to dress up too much, yet he didn't want to be too casual. Finally, when he was sick and tired of debating back and forth, he chose an outfit. After he got dressed, he looked at his watch and grimaced, then made a dash for the door and went over to Celine's.

When Celine heard the doorbell ring, she took one more glance in the mirror, sprayed some perfume behind her ears, and headed downstairs. She felt like a young girl going on her first date. In hopes of calming her nerves, she stood in the hallway and inhaled a deep breath, then she exhaled slowly and opened the door. When she saw Stephan peering through a few dozen pink baby roses, she flashed a brilliant smile.

"Ce, you look lovely," he said admiringly as he handed her the flowers. She had dressed in a navy blue linen sheath dress, accented by a single strand of pearls around her neck.

"Thank you," she said shyly as she took the flowers. "Come in while I put these in a vase, then I'll get my coat so we can leave."

"Take your time; there's no rush."

"Make yourself comfortable in the living room. I'll be right back."

Stephan sat down on a soft leather couch and surveyed the elegant room. In front of him, resting on an Oriental rug, was a glass table with an arrangement of dried flowers in a jade-colored vase. The room was filled with plants, and the walls were graced with tasteful oil paintings. Suddenly, he felt something against his leg. He looked down to see a calico cat simultaneously purring and rubbing her chin on his pants.

"I see you've met Queen Esther," Celine noticed as she walked in. Queenie purred louder at the mention of her name.

"Is that who this attractive female is?" he grinned as he reached down to stroke Queenie's chin.

"You didn't know that I had such a gorgeous roommate, did you?" she said wryly as she sat down next to him on the couch. "Maybe you'd rather take her out to dinner instead of her blah and homely roommate?"

"I think our culinary tastes would be an immediate problem." He chuckled. "In fact, I know we wouldn't get along in that area."

Celine laughed. "Well, then, I guess you are stuck with me." She stood up. "Shall we go?"

"Yes, let's do." Stephan followed Celine out and opened the passenger door of his car for her. "I made reservations at Yen's Dynasty West. I sure hope you like Chinese food," he said as he started up the engine.

"I've been to Yen's, and I love their food."

"Good," he said and hesitated slightly. "Ce, I know I probably have put you in an awkward position."

"What do you mean?"

"I mean with your boyfriend." He paused. "I don't want to cause any problems by asking you out."

Celine threw him a bewildered look. "What boyfriend? Do you know something I don't?"

"I saw you walking arm in arm with a man the day I dropped by to see how you were."

"What are you talking about?" she asked, still confused.

Stephan ignored her question and asked boldly, "Wasn't he the reason why you left the retreat early?" He knew he was jumping to conclusions, but he had to know.

"Wait a minute," she responded haughtily as it dawned on her who he was talking about. "The man you saw me with that day was my cousin Bill, and furthermore, the reason I had left early from the retreat was due to the fact that Lynette had become ill, and we had to get her to a doctor. And, may I remind you, this whole misunderstanding stems from you not receiving the note I had left for you, which was not my fault."

"You're right, and I am sorry," he apologized as he steered the car onto the freeway. Casually, he let his arm rest along the top of Celine's seat. "Well, I still don't know if you have a boyfriend or not," he remarked and inhaled a deep breath when she turned toward him. Her long hair dusted his arm, and her blue eyes sparkled with amusement. The fresh, sweet scent of her perfume heightened all his senses until he wanted to lift his hand from behind her and touch the silky softness of her hair. The sound of her voice brought him slowly back to reality.

"If I had a boyfriend, Stephan," she retorted, "I certainly wouldn't have accepted this dinner date with you."

"I guess that answers my question pretty clearly." He smiled ruefully. "By the way, what was wrong with your sister-in-law that day?"

"She had a bad case of morning sickness," Celine explained. "She's pregnant and didn't even realize it."

"So you are going to be an auntie?"

She nodded. "Yup."

"I know you'll make a good one. . .but, better yet, you'll make a fantastic mother someday."

Celine was touched by his comment. Suddenly she caught herself wondering what Stephan's children would look like. Beautiful—no doubt about it. Her thoughts were disrupted when Stephan wheeled the car into the restaurant's parking lot.

Once inside, the hostess promptly led them to a table by the window and, to their delight, they had a perfect view of the majestic ocean. The restaurant was built on a cliff high above the sandy beach.

Celine watched the waves gently breaking against the shore with the brilliant evening moon casting its reflection upon the waters. "Stephan, I could sit here all night and be content to gaze out this window," she admitted dreamily.

"I agree to a point," he said and looked deeply into her eyes. "The view of the ocean is awesome, but I'm more content to look at the view across the table, which is even more captivating."

"Oh, how many times have you said that line before?" she countered with a playful grin.

"Ce, I'm serious," he remarked.

Celine could tell by his expression that he meant what he said.

"Stephan—"

"Ce," he interrupted smoothly, "I've never been with someone with whom I really felt free to be myself and open up completely to, without fear of rejection. But with you I do. For some reason, I'm not afraid to share my heart with you."

"I have those same feelings about you," she confessed. "And it's wonderful but scary at the same time."

"I know what you mean," he agreed as he took a drink of his tea. "After dinner I was wondering if you would like to take a stroll on the beach with me? The restaurant has steps outside that lead down to the beach. It's well lit, so we can't stumble in the darkness."

"With my luck, I'll stumble anyway," she chuckled softly.

"But I'll be there to catch you." He grinned.

"The beach looks so inviting, I can hardly wait," she responded with delight. A rush of excitement surged through every inch of her body. The prospect of walking along the sandy, moonlit beach with Stephan more than appealed to her—it emotionally charged her whole being. Never before had she felt so happy and content to be with a man as she was now.

Their dinner arrived, and Celine ate her sweet-and-sour chicken heartily, and Stephan devoured his beef chow mein along with his wonton soup. To go along with tradition, they ended their meal with fortune cookies.

As Celine read the strip of paper from inside her cookie, she started to giggle uncontrollably.

"What does yours say?" he asked with interest.

"Well, it's not too original, but it seems appropriate. It says, 'I will meet a tall, dark, and handsome man today and have dinner with him,' " she said as another giggle escaped from her lips. "It's a smart cookie, huh?"

"Well, I don't know about that," he chuckled. "What would have happened if I would have gotten your cookie?"

Celine laughed at the thought. "Okay. Now what does yours say?"

"My cookie is smarter than yours," he teased as he picked up the small piece of paper to read. "It says, 'I'll dine under the stars with the most beautiful woman in the world.' "

"Stephan, stop kidding around and read me what it really says."

"I read what it really said, scout's honor," he said as he handed her the piece of paper to read.

She quickly read it and, to her amazement, that was exactly what it said. She glanced over at Stephan and saw a Cheshire cat grin etched on his face. "Okay, how did you do it?"

He laughed. "You saw right through me." He sighed, then paused, baiting her deliberately.

"Stephan!"

"Hmm, I guess I'll have to tell you my secret. I'm good friends with the manager here, so I took advantage of the position and asked him to give me some special cookies, if you know what I mean." He smiled and winked playfully at her.

"Clever, very clever." She grinned. "But tell me, don't you think the-most-beautiful-woman-in-the-world bit was a little ridiculous?"

"Not to me it wasn't," he declared honestly. "It might be a bit forward of me to say this, but to me you are exactly what I wrote for the message in the cookie."

Celine blinked twice, stunned by his sincerity and touched by his openness in sharing his feelings with her. "You flatter me and, truthfully, I'm astonished that you see me that way."

He leaned forward, grabbing her hands gently in his and whispered, "I see your beauty on the outside, and I marvel at it. But it is the beauty on the inside that intrigues and draws me to you."

"Excuse me, Sir," the waiter interrupted. "Is there anything else I can bring you tonight?"

"No, thank you," Stephan said as he reached for his wallet. "I'll pay the check now."

Celine was glad for the interruption; it gave her burning cheeks and racing heart a rest. Stephan's compliments had overwhelmed her and sent her heart dancing on cloud nine.

After he had settled the bill, he helped Celine on with her wrap and ushered her out the side exit leading to the steps.

"Stephan, I forgot I have high heels on," she groaned.

"Why don't we both shed our shoes and go barefoot?" he suggested.

"That sounds like fun," she said as they reached the bottom of the steps.

After they removed their shoes, they ventured onto the cool sand. The gentle, rhythmic swish of the waves, ebbing and flowing on the shore, provided background music for their stroll.

"Doesn't the sand feel good under your feet?" he remarked as they walked toward the edge of the water.

"It's heavenly, and to think that God created all this for our enjoyment," she marveled.

"It is incredible," he agreed.

Celine ran ahead and twirled around in the sand like a ballerina. "I feel like a kid again," she exclaimed joyfully.

Stephan watched her in amazement. She was a rare jewel, and he was becoming addicted to her presence. He caught up with her and took her hand in his. For a few moments, they walked in silence, side by side, enjoying the soft melodic sound of the waves rolling in. The evening sky was crystal clear and brilliantly lit by the silvery moon, and the many stars were scattered across the black velvet sky.

Stephan stopped and turned to Celine. He didn't say anything at first but simply looked at her. Her heart began to race. Stephan softly caressed her face with his hand, then lifted her chin up. "I can't quite explain the deep feelings that are churning inside of me, but I can say that there is no other place in the world that I'd rather be right now than here with you."

He lowered his head and slowly their lips met. His soft and tender kiss was quickly warmed by their mutual passion. They melted against each other and Stephan encircled his arms around her and pulled her closer.

Celine felt like she was standing on the clouds instead of sand. It was a moment that she didn't want to end.

Stephan was intoxicated by the sweet taste of her lips and the warmth of her response. This was a woman with whom he could spend a lifetime. His feelings for her overwhelmed him, and he knew if he were smart, he'd better keep a tight rein on them for now so as not to frighten her away. He had to admit that he was falling hard for her, and the realization that he felt love for her startled even himself. Everything was moving so quickly.

Reluctantly, he loosened his hold on her. "Ce, I didn't expect this to happen." His eyes didn't leave her face, so beautifully framed by the moonlight.

"You're not the only one," she said breathlessly. "But I'm not sorry it happened."

Stephan's eyes lit up. "You're not?"

"No, I'm definitely not."

"Where do we go from here?" he asked cautiously.

She grinned sheepishly. "How about asking me out on another date?"

"That could be a good start." He chuckled as they headed toward the steps. "Could I be so forward as to think you would except a dinner invitation at my place tomorrow evening?"

"That is a little presumptuous, but I think I will overlook it and accept your gracious and most inviting offer."

Stephan grinned as he pulled her into his arms and gave her one last kiss before they walked back up the stairs.

❧❦❦❧

That night, when Celine slid into bed, she was mildly annoyed with herself for accepting Stephan's dinner date so quickly. Her mind told her to take things slowly, but her heart wanted to be around him twenty-four hours a day. Could it be love? Her heart skipped a beat at the mere thought of it. How silly—one date with him and she was thinking she was in love with him. What nonsense—or was it? She rolled over and punched her pillow. One thing she definitely knew was that her feelings for him were strong and unlike any she had ever experienced before, including the ones she had had for Darrell.

A thought entered her mind, and it scared her. Could Stephan be completely happy with her for a lifetime, if that were the situation? After all, after two years he had discovered that there was something lacking in his relationship with Angela. Would that happen between her and Stephan?

She rolled over again and buried her head in the fluffy softness of the pillow. She was jumping ahead of the situation. For peace of mind, she would just have to take their relationship one day at a time. "Oh, Lord, help me to use wisdom and not jump ahead of things," she prayed. "I'm a little afraid of giving my heart away to someone again. Please help me to not fear this relationship if it is ordained by You."

Hoping to get some rest, Celine switched her mind to "off." Sleep eventually came and so did a night full of dreams.

The next day rushed by quickly and, to Celine's surprise, it had been a day filled with good news, for which she praised God. She had finally received a reply from Lesley Andrews, the editor of White Dove Publishing House. Enclosed was a contract for her first inspirational novel for her to review and sign. Immediately, she called and told her family. Now she was anxiously awaiting the time to tell Stephan the exciting news.

She looked into the mirror and applied a little blush and lipstick, then finished braiding her hair down the back. A few minutes later she was heading for dinner at Stephan's house. She could hardly wait to see him. Everything was going so right in her life, and she was so full of thankfulness to God.

When Stephan heard the door chimes echo through the house, he carefully pulled the small piece of tissue off his chin where he had cut himself shaving. He had been so nervous about the evening that he had practically gouged out a hole in his chin. Fortunately, the bleeding had stopped. He rubbed some aftershave lotion onto his face and neck, then headed for the front door.

When he opened the front door, he caught his breath. There Celine stood, dressed in an elegant black dress with a full skirt and a leopard print belt accentuating her small waist.

"Am I too early?" she asked as she noticed his bare feet. "Or am I overdressed?"

Stephan followed Celine's gaze and put his hand on his forehead. "I can't believe I forgot to put on my socks and shoes," he said with embarrassment. "I was so preoccupied with fixing dinner that I was late in getting dressed."

"It doesn't matter, Stephan." She smiled and walked inside. "Besides, you look cute without shoes. I could go as far as saying bare feet become you."

"Okay, okay." He sighed and gave her a crooked grin. "Don't overdo it, young lady, or I might purposely burn the dinner." He chuckled as he took her arm and led her into the living room. "Have a seat while I go and find my shoes."

Celine sank down in a large, coffee-colored sectional sofa and recalled being intimidated when she first saw the outside of Stephan's house as she drove up. It reminded her of an hacienda nestled in the hills of Spain. Large palm trees lined the circular driveway, and potted red and pink geraniums graced the front of the house. The red-tiled roof and the terra-cotta-tiled entrance set off the picture-perfect home. The interior, with woven rugs on the floors, earthen-colored wall hangings, and potted palms and plants went along with the Spanish theme.

"I thought we could start off the evening with a bottle of sparkling grape juice," Stephan said as he entered the room carrying a tray with glasses and a bottle.

"Your home is beautiful," she said appreciatively as he began to pour the sparkling liquid.

"I've worked hard to attain this place," he stated as he handed her a glass. "After my mom died, I decided I owed it to her memory to be 'someone in life,' foremost to God, then to my future wife and children." He leaned back against the sofa. "Until my band was really successful, I worked two jobs and had long hours. All I wanted was to save for my future family. I wanted to give my wife and children what my dad didn't have a chance to give my mother, sisters, and myself. That has been the major driving force behind my success."

"I admire you so much," she remarked sincerely.

"Tell me, how is your book coming?" he asked, changing the subject.

Celine smiled broadly and her blue eyes danced with excitement. "I'm glad you asked. Today I received a reply on my book from White Dove Publishing House."

"What did they say?"

"They sent me a contract, so I think they liked it," she stated cheerfully.

"I knew you could do it," he exclaimed happily. He set down his glass on the low coffee table. "Now that news certainly deserves a congratulatory kiss." His eyes twinkled mischievously as he leaned over and kissed her with warm tenderness. There was a chemistry between them that couldn't be denied. Stephan put his arms around her and hugged her tightly.

Celine was happily lost in the deliciousness of his kiss. It was full of passion, and she knew his feelings for her were as intense as hers for him.

Stephan nestled his head against her shoulder, seeking to bury himself in her lovely neck forever. "Ce," he murmured softly, "as silly as this may sound, I truly wish that this moment would never end."

She snuggled up against him even closer, loving the feel of his strong arms around her. "It's not silly," she replied in a sultry voice. "It's romantic."

"Aha. . .I'm falling for a romantic." He chided as he kissed her softly on the cheek, sending shivers down her spine. "I should have known that all you writers think alike."

She chuckled softly at his remark. "Would you mind if I use this particular scene in one of my romance novels?"

"Only if you give me the credit for thinking of it," he grinned.

"How about if we collaborate on my next book?" she suggested teasingly.

"On one condition," he said seriously.

"What?" she raised her eyebrow.

"That you'll have to then collaborate with me on some of my songs."

"Are you serious?" she asked incredulously.

"Very," he said, then threw the question back at her. "Weren't you?"

"Well, I—"

"Ce," he interrupted, "I know you weren't serious, but I really think it could give us each some fresh, new material."

"It might work," she said with some reserve. "It would mean a lot of long hours together," she smiled.

"That, my dear, is the best part of the idea." He grinned.

Celine's mouth kicked upward at the corners in an amused expression. "Why don't we put the idea on the back burner for now?"

Stephan jumped up. "Speaking of back burners, would you like to join me in the kitchen while I check on dinner?"

"I'd be delighted, as long as you don't put me to work," she said as she took hold of his outstretched hand, "because tonight's my night off."

"You can sit and watch me do all the work," he promised as he led her into the kitchen.

"Umm, it smells delicious in here. What's cooking?"

"It's my specialty, Hawaiian chicken," he boasted as he slipped the chef's apron on and tied the strings around his waist.

"Does it taste as good as it smells?" she asked.

Stephan grabbed her by the waist and twirled her around, then gently put her down and kissed her lips softly. "Yes." He winked playfully. "It does taste as good as it smells."

"Stephan," she giggled, "you naughty boy. I meant the chicken."

"And I meant you," he breathed against her cheek, and she pushed him away. "Weren't you supposed to be checking on dinner?"

"I am."

"Stop joking around," she pleaded. "I'm hungry."

"So am I," he said as he reached out to pull her to him.

Celine pushed him away. "Stephan James," she announced loudly, trying to sound serious, but a small giggle escaped from her lips. She was enjoying all of the attention.

"Okay, my dear lady, I shall grant your request and check on the food." When he realized it was ready, he dished the chicken onto each plate. Once all the food was carried into the dining room, they sat down and said grace.

"I don't think I ever want to cook for you," she commented as she took another bite of the wild rice and chicken.

"And why is that?" he frowned.

"Because I honestly can't compete with such culinary talent," she explained.

He smiled and put down his fork. "Can I tell you the truth? This is the only meal I can cook decently," he confessed.

"Sure," she drawled, voicing her disbelief.

"You don't believe me?"

"No, I don't."

"Well, you can ask my sisters to verify it. They taught me how to make this meal because they couldn't stand my other cooking."

"Really?"

"Yes. You see, I usually eat out or have frozen dinners at home. I'm a very simple eater and very easy to please."

"So does that mean you'd like anything I would cook for you?" she tested him.

"Believe me, I would eat anything prepared by your beautiful hands."

"Boy, you sure know how to butter up the girls, don't you?"

"The only girl I care to butter up is you," he expressed genuinely.

She flushed a crimson red, then changed the subject. "The dinner was very tasty. And I'm impressed, even if it is the only meal you can prepare." She smiled sweetly.

"Thank you, M'lady," he said in an English accent and then bowed before her. "Shall we adjourn to the living room for our after-dinner tea?"

"That sounds delightful, Sir James," she said as she matched his English accent with ease.

"My, my, you have that accent quite good, m'lady. Where did you acquire it?"

"I acquired it, my good fellow, on one of my sojourns to London."

"Ce," he said as he reverted back to his normal voice, "this night isn't even over, but I'd like to say that this has been one of the most wonderful evenings that I can remember."

They sat down on the sofa and he continued. "You are the most interesting, not to mention, the most beautiful woman I have ever known."

He touched her face softly with his hand, and Celine could tell by the look in his eyes that he meant every word.

"I'm flattered, Stephan. This night has been equally as wonderful for me too," she confessed as she reached out and squeezed his hand.

"My feelings for you are serious. Ce, I—"

She quickly placed her finger on his lips to silence him from saying more. "Stephan, not that long ago you broke off an engagement," she reminded him. "Shouldn't you take your time before getting involved seriously in another relationship?"

Stephan felt like kicking himself as he listened to her speak. He had said too much, too soon, and had jumped the gun. Now he had probably blown it. "Does that mean that you just want to be friends?" he inquired, not particularly wanting to hear the answer, afraid that it would be negative.

Celine chose her words carefully. "Not necessarily, I—"

The sound of the door chimes cut her off in midsentence. "Now who could that be?" he muttered. "I'll be right back."

Seconds later, Celine heard the front door open and could hear the muffled voice of a woman talking to Stephan in the entrance hall.

"Keep your voice down, Angela. I have company."

"Who is it? The woman you so conveniently dropped me for?" she accused.

"Angela, what did you come here for?" he asked impatiently.

"Don't be snappy with me, Darling. I was at a party at the Thomases' and I thought I'd drop by after it had ended, since I was only around the corner from your house."

"Well, thanks for dropping by, Angela," he said as he opened the door, but she ignored the hint to leave.

"The Thomases had invited you tonight. Why didn't you come?"

"I had other plans."

"Can I meet her, Stephan?" she asked pointedly.

"That's the real reason you stopped by, isn't it?" he demanded. "You saw an unfamiliar car in the driveway, so you presumed there was a woman here, right?"

Celine got up from the sofa and moved closer to the entrance hall. She knew that the woman's voice belonged to Angela. So she put two and two together and went back and picked up her purse from the coffee table. Then she headed for the front door, definitely not prepared for the scene she was about to witness.

"Angela, this is the third and last warning I'm going to give you," Stephan stated in an agitated voice. "Please, leave now."

In an instant, Angela moved forward and wrapped her arms around his neck and kissed him, catching him completely off guard.

As Celine entered the hallway, she saw the embrace and her mouth dropped open in shock. Stephan's back was to her, but Angela's eyes were on her, piercing through her like daggers.

"Aren't you going to introduce me, Darling, to your guest?" Angela purred innocently.

"There is no need," Celine blurted out as she stepped around them. "I was just leaving." She reached for the doorknob, but Stephan blocked her attempt to escape.

"Ce, you don't understand," he tried to explain.

"Oh, so this is your friend from the retreat," Angela commented with interest.

"Angela, please, stay out of this."

In a flash, Celine opened the door and made her way to her car. Stephan hurried after her and, before she could slip into the driver's seat, he took hold of her arm.

"Let go of me!" she ordered shakily, putting a hand out to ward him off.

He released her instantly. "Please let me explain," he pleaded.

She looked him squarely in the eyes, fighting back the tears that were threatening to fall. "Stephan, think about what I said earlier," she said, then slid into her car. "You need to make sure your relationship with Angela is truly over before you start another one." Without another word, she started the engine and shut the door.

Stephan knocked on the car window, but she ignored him. "You've pronounced me guilty without giving me a chance to prove my innocence," he yelled through the glass in exasperation.

Celine looked straight ahead and pulled down the driveway. She dashed a hand across her eyes as she stared out her car window. Why did she have to make matters worse by crying? She instantly recalled Stephan's last words. Maybe she had been too harsh on him. Her stomach was twisted into one large knot. She hadn't even given him a chance to explain. No, she shook her head, the scene had looked clear to her. They were in each other's arms and kissing, no less. How else could she take it? *But then again,* she thought carefully, *it didn't fit Stephan's character.*

"Lord," she cried out, "I don't know what to think. Show me if I'm wrong."

Chapter 10

Once inside her home, Celine ran upstairs to her room and flung herself onto her bed. Queen Esther followed her up the stairs and jumped up next to her onto the bed, purring softly as she nuzzled up to her. Celine picked up Queenie and buried her face in her soft fur. Why did the most wonderful night of her life have to turn out so disastrously?

Celine glanced over at her answering machine; the message button was blinking red in the darkness. She put Queenie down, walked over, and pressed the replay button. One message was from Lynette and the other was from Stephan.

"Ce," Stephan's voice came over the machine, "I think I deserve a chance to explain what happened tonight, but I will not do it over this stupid machine." There was a brief pause. "Can you meet me tomorrow at noon at the Blue Moon Cafe? Please think about it. We need to talk."

The machine clicked off and Celine lay back down on the bed and stared at the ceiling. He did deserve a chance to explain, and she would be there tomorrow to hear him out.

☙❧

The next morning, while Celine finished feeding Queenie, she glanced at her watch and realized she had enough time to do a few errands before she met Stephan at the restaurant. On her way out the door, she heard the phone ringing, so she rushed back in and grabbed the receiver. "Hello," she answered.

"Honey, do you have a minute?" her mother, Samantha, asked.

"Sure, Mom. What's up?"

"I'm afraid I have some bad news," her mother said in a shaky voice. "Celine, it's about Bill."

"What about Bill, Mom?" Celine asked in concern.

"He's been in a car accident in San Diego."

Panic struck Celine's heart instantly. "How badly has he been hurt?"

"It doesn't look good." Her mother started to cry. "Sherry called from the hospital and said that Bill has been asking for us."

"Oh, Mom," her voice quivered, "I've got to go see Bill right away. What hospital is he at?"

"He's at San Diego General. I've already checked on a flight that we could take in about an hour. I called Raine at work, but he can't get away."

"Is Dad coming?"

"Yes."

"Oh, Mom, this is so terrible," Celine said as she started to cry. Celine's family was the only family that Bill had left. His mother, Samantha's sister, had died a few years ago, and Bill's father had left his wife and son when Bill was only ten.

"We'll be there in thirty minutes," her mother said.

"Okay, I'll be ready."

"Honey?"

"Yes, Mom?"

"Start praying."

છજીજ્ર

Celine didn't stop praying until they walked into the intensive care unit where Bill was. The unit nurse brought them over to Bill, and Celine gasped when she saw him. Her eyes filled with tears as she saw him lying there with tubes in his nose, a gauze bandage around his head, and his upper lip bruised and swollen. "Lord," she whispered, "please help me to be strong for Bill."

When Bill looked up and noticed that they were there, he smiled weakly. "You came. . .I knew you would," he said in a raspy voice. "You just missed Sherry. I told her to go home and rest."

Celine swallowed hard, trying desperately to hold herself together. Her mother grabbed her hand and squeezed it tightly.

Chase, her dad, spoke first. "Bill, we love you like a son, and we know you'll pull through this," Chase said as he walked over and gently rested his hand on Bill's shoulder. "We'll be with you every step of the way."

"Honey," Celine's mother addressed Bill tenderly, "we're going to stay here in San Diego and be with you until you're better and ready to go home."

"You all are so dear to me," Bill said as a single tear rolled down his cheek. "You're my family, and I love you all so much."

Celine could no longer hold back the tears. She walked over to Bill's side and took his hand in hers. She looked at him and began to weep. "Bill, please make it, please," she begged.

Bill looked up at her tenderly and said softly, "Sis, you've always been so good to me. Do you know how many times I've thanked God for giving me a special sister like you? Countless times, dear Celine," he said, then winced in pain.

Without hesitation, seeing the pain on his face, Celine pushed the nurse's button. Immediately the doctor and nurse came rushing in. The nurse ushered Celine and her parents from Bill's room to the waiting area. "We'll keep you informed of his condition," the nurse said.

"Mom, Dad. . .Bill's going to make it, isn't he?" Celine asked in a petrified voice.

"Sure he will, Honey," her father assured her.

Celine sat down on a chair and wrung her hands together nervously.

"Celine."

Celine turned and saw Sherry, Bill's fiancée, walking toward her.

Celine rose and greeted her warmly. "Sherry, I'm so sorry this has happened."

"It looks so bad, Celine," Sherry said, then began to cry. "I love him so much. I don't know what I'd do without him."

Chase and Samantha came over and greeted Sherry and helped her to a seat. "He'll make it, Sherry," Samantha tried to console her.

Sherry's expression looked grim. "You know Bill's a hemophiliac?"

"Yes, why?" Celine asked.

"Bill has internal bleeding, and the doctors have done all they can to stop the bleeding, but his chances of pulling through this are very slim," Sherry said, then lowered her head into her hands. "I can't believe this is happening."

Celine put her arms around Sherry. "There must be something they can do." Sherry just shook her head.

Celine looked at her parents through her tears. Her mother mouthed the word "pray," and Celine did just that. "Dear God, please stop the bleeding," she pleaded.

"Excuse me," the nurse appeared. "You can go back in, but only one at a time and for a few minutes each."

"You go first while I try to collect myself," Sherry said to Celine.

Celine walked into Bill's room and saw that his eyes were closed. Fear paralyzed her momentarily. "Bill. . .Bill," her voice cracked. She reached for his hand. "Bill, please wake up."

His eyes slowly opened. "Celine," he said and squeezed her hand gently. "Please don't look so sad. No matter what happens, I'm not afraid. God is with me, Ce."

"Bill, you're going to make it," Celine choked out.

"Sis, bend down here," he ordered softly and Celine leaned forward as tears spilled down her cheeks. Bill softly brushed her brow with his lips. "I love you dearly," he said with infinite tenderness.

"Oh, Bill, I love you too," she whispered, then said, "Sherry's waiting to see you."

"Good. Have her come in, okay?"

"I'll go and get her right now," Celine said as she bent down and kissed his cheek. As she left the room, she turned and saw a single tear roll down Bill's cheek. The tears rolled down her face as she turned to go and get Sherry.

While Sherry was with Bill, Celine and her parents waited for her return. As the minutes passed by, Celine's stomach twisted into tiny knots. When Celine saw Sherry walk through the doorway, leaning against the nurse for support, she bolted from her chair.

"Sherry." Celine reached out her hand.

The nurse released Sherry and said sympathetically, "I'm so sorry." The nurse then looked over at Celine. "Make sure she gets home safely."

Celine could only nod. She was numb with the realization of what had happened. Celine's parents were immediately by Sherry's side for support.

"Bill didn't make it." Sherry sobbed and leaned heavily against Celine. Celine held her tightly; grief overwhelmed her. The two women wept together, silently sharing each other's pain and loss.

❧❅❧

After the funeral, Celine flew home with her parents, still in a daze over Bill's death. Celine was fighting with the grips of depression. She had repeatedly asked God why it had happened, but she received no answers, or at least that is what she had thought. Maybe God had given her an answer, and it wasn't the answer she had wanted, so she rejected it. She didn't know; her thoughts were hazy and clouded with grief.

She hadn't slept much over the past few days. Everything had happened so quickly, and she had drained herself trying to comfort Sherry. She had felt so sorry for her and didn't know what else to say or do, but she knew she had to leave Sherry in God's hands.

When Celine arrived home, she was exhausted and went directly to bed, knowing that the only answer for her now was sleep. She reached out and grabbed her pillow and scrunched it up under her head. She shut her eyes and tried to shut out the questions in her mind. The shrill sound of the phone made her jerk up quickly. She hesitated in answering but then reached for the phone.

"Hello," she answered in a hoarse voice.

"Ce, is that you?"

"Yes."

"Where have you been?" Stephan asked. "I've been trying to get ahold of you for days."

"My cousin, Bill, died," she choked out. She really didn't feel like talking.

"Oh, Ce, I'm so sorry," he expressed with compassion. "Can I come over and see you?"

"No, I'm not in the mood for visitors," she said bluntly.

"Ce, I know how you are feeling right now," he empathized. "Remember, I lost two people who were very dear to me, so I understand your pain."

"Stephan, I appreciate your sympathy, but I really want to be by myself right now, okay?"

"Okay," he replied. Knowing that Ce was hit hard by her cousin's death, Stephan knew not to force himself upon her at this time. "Can I call you again some other time?"

"Whatever," she said as her voice quivered. "I have to go now. Good-bye."

After Stephan hung up the receiver, he sat by the phone and silently said a prayer for Ce. He so desperately wanted to rush over to her side to comfort her, but he knew she would only reject him. He wished there was something more he could do for her, but maybe the best thing was to wait a few days, then give her a call back. Yes, that was what he was going to do.

Meanwhile, Celine fell back onto her bed and sobbed softly against her pillow. She had so badly wanted Stephan to come over and hold her tightly and tell her everything would be all right, but pride had kept her from doing so. He had hurt her terribly when she saw him kissing Angela that night, and she couldn't seem to get that scene out of her mind. And now, she was grieving and torn inside about the loss of her beloved cousin. It was all too much to handle, and she felt like she was sinking into a pit of despair. Her pillow was moist with her fallen tears. The more she thought about never seeing Bill again and what Sherry must be going through, the more she cried.

"Dear Lord, I can't go on like this. My heart is feeling so much pain that I can barely handle it. Please help me to understand all of this," she cried out. "Please forgive me for being so angry," she sobbed. "It's just that I miss Bill so much."

Celine slid under the covers and closed her eyes once again. In the quietness of the night a Scripture, John 14:27, floated around in her mind. As she repeated the words, she felt a calm peace fall over her. She softly spoke the Scripture out loud. "Peace I leave with you, my peace I give unto you: not as the world giveth, give I unto you. Let not your heart be troubled, neither let it be afraid." She quietly thanked the Lord as she wiped a tear from her cheek.

As Celine lay there, she was instantly reminded that God knew what it felt like to see a loved one go through pain and die, for He had experienced it with His very own Son. He knew what she was feeling with the loss of Bill. Celine was also comforted to know that Bill was in heaven with Jesus, and that someday she would see him again.

≈❈❈≈

A few days later, Celine finally switched on her computer. It had been almost two weeks since she had worked on her book. She studied the screen for a few moments, then typed in a single name. Guilt hit her square in the jaw as she stared at Stephan's name on the screen. Celine felt rotten about the way she had treated him over the phone. During their brief conversation, she had let her emotions dictate her attitude, and now she was the one suffering for it.

Celine pushed back her chair on its rollers, picked up the phone, and dialed Stephan's number but, to her frustration, it was busy. Then she glanced back at the computer screen and erased Stephan's name and knew instantly that if she didn't talk to someone, she wouldn't get any work done. Knowing she needed some good motherly advice to help her put some sense into all the different emotions she was feeling over Bill and Stephan, she picked up her car keys, ran out of the house, and drove over to her mother's.

"Mom, does a person ever get over losing a loved one?" Celine asked.

"Honey, do you remember when your grandma died?"

Celine nodded. "Yes, I think I was in my first year of high school," she recalled.

"Well, when my mother died, I was overcome with grief to the point that I could barely function," her mother admitted.

"You seemed to handle it pretty well as I remember," Celine said.

"That's what it looked like from the outside. You see, Honey, I held all my grief inside and didn't let anyone see how much I was affected by my mother's death," she confided. "I didn't even share my pain and grief with God, and that was my biggest mistake."

"What do you mean?"

"It took me three months of silent grieving to finally realize that I was self-ishly holding onto my feelings and was not dealing with the fact that my mother would never come back. That's when I turned to God and unloaded all of the feel-ings that had been bottled up inside of me," she said as a warm smile appeared on her face. "And that's when God started to heal my heart. He replaced that area that was consumed with grief with warm and loving memories of times spent with my mother. From that moment on, I was on the road to recovery, and God was holding my hand all the way."

Celine leaned over and hugged her mother. "Thanks for sharing that, Mom. I know now that I have to give this to the Lord and let go."

"It's hard to let go, but it's the only way to get over a loss as deep as this," her mother said gently.

"I know you're right, Mom."

"Why don't we have some lemon tea in the kitchen?" her mother suggested.

"That sounds good," Celine said and followed her mother into the kitchen and sat down at the large oak table. "Mom, there's something else I need your advice on."

"What, Honey?"

"It's about Stephan," she began with reservation. "Does it sound stupid to say that I think I've fallen in love with him?" she asked impulsively. "I mean, it's been only a short time that we've been reacquainted with each other, but I really feel so happy and comfortable when I'm around him."

Samantha smiled at her daughter. "Honey, if you're stupid, then so was I. I never told you, but I fell in love with your father only a few weeks after I met him, and do you know what? On the fourth week of dating, your father told me that he loved me and then asked me to marry him."

"I didn't know that," Celine said. "But then there's the episode with Angela," she said, then gestured with her hand in exasperation. "I'd like to believe that there's a logical explanation about what happened that night with her. Stephan had said that their relationship was over, but how can I be sure?"

Her mother gave her the cup of lemon tea, then sat down at the table. "Honey, that is something you'll find out in time. There is always a risk in loving someone, because you take the chance of being hurt or rejected, as you well know." Her mother paused in thought, then continued. "But it's worth all the risk if the person you love loves you back. Remember, also, that with love comes trust, and if you believe you love Stephan, then give him the benefit of the doubt and let him have a chance to explain about the Angela episode."

"You make it sound so easy, Mom," she replied. "You haven't seen Angela— she's gorgeous."

"Is Stephan the type of man who's only interested in what a woman looks like on the outside? If he is, I'd drop him like a hot potato."

"No, no. . .I know he's not, Mom."

"Then you know what to do. Go and talk it out with him."

"I will. Thanks, Mom. I feel so much better now."

"That's what mothers are for," her mother said and reached over and hugged her.

Knowing that she was less than a mile away from Stephan's house, Celine decided to stop by on her way home. Silently she prayed that he would be home. But, when she pulled up to his home, she noticed his car in the driveway along with a half-dozen other cars. Either he was having band practice or a party of some sort. Disappointed, she turned the car around and headed for home.

❧✿❧

The next morning, Celine was awakened by the shrill sound of the phone. Rubbing her eyes, she glanced at the clock by her bedside—nine o'clock; how did she oversleep? She reached over and picked up the receiver. "Hello," she answered in a groggy voice.

"Ce?"

Celine sat up straight in bed when she recognized the voice. "Hi, Stephan."

"I hope I'm not calling at a bad time."

"Oh, no," Celine said, stifling a yawn. "I was just getting up."

"The reason I called was to invite you to a barbecue at my house this Saturday. My sisters are throwing a birthday party for me, and I'd really like you to be there," he explained.

"That sounds like fun," she responded cheerfully. "You can count on my being there."

"I can?" he said in a surprised voice.

"Sure," she said softly. "Stephan, I'm really sorry I wasn't able to meet you that day at the Blue Moon Cafe, but that's when I heard the news of Bill's accident."

"Oh, I understand," he expressed sympathetically.

"And I also want to apologize for my coldness to you over the phone when you called. I was still so very upset over Bill's death."

"You don't have to apologize, Ce. I know you were hurting and experiencing a great deal of pain," he acknowledged. "Tell me something, though. . . ."

"What?"

"Would you have met me that day at the Blue Moon Cafe?"

"Yes. As it was, I was going out the door to meet you when I received the call about Bill."

"Will you still give me a chance to explain about Angela?"

"Yes. That's why I'm coming to your barbecue on Saturday," she confessed.

"Thanks. I'll see you then," he said in almost a whisper, then said good-bye.

ꙮ

Celine spent the next few days hunting for a special gift for Stephan's birthday. She hadn't a clue as to what to buy him, but she wanted it to be unique and different from the usual birthday gifts. Finally, the day before the barbecue, Celine found the perfect gift—an electric blue baseball jacket that she then took to a shirt shop and had them stitch in gold thread, on the back of the jacket, "Stephan James and the Voices in the Light." When she saw the finished product, she smiled, knowing Stephan would definitely like it and that he would look great wearing it.

Celine was feeling a little nervous about going to the barbecue, and she almost wished she was going to see Stephan alone, instead of at a big party with his friends and relatives. Suddenly, she wondered if they would have any time alone to talk, and she muttered under her breath and scolded herself for being such a worrywart. Things would work out, and she just had to trust that Stephan would explain about the episode with Angela.

Chapter 11

It was half past seven, and Stephan was pacing the ground nervously.

"Hey, Steve," Mike, one of his band members, called from the patio door. "It's your birthday bash. Try to enjoy it."

"Don't worry about me." He tried to produce a smile. "I'm having a great time."

"Sure," Mike chuckled as he walked over and patted him on the back. "I believe she'll show up, so stop worrying."

"I feel like a kid, waiting for her to come," Stephan confessed in a quiet voice so only Mike could hear.

"You've really fallen hard for her, huh, Steve?"

"I guess you could say that," he admitted.

"Well, my friend, it happens to the best of us," Mike chuckled.

Stephan grinned. "You make it sound like a disease."

"It is. It's called love," Mike replied humorously. "And it's the best disease you can catch."

"I don't know," Stephan sighed. "It makes me feel like a nervous wreck." Then he caught his breath as he saw Ce step through the patio doorway with a big red box in tow.

Mike followed Stephan's gaze. "I told you she'd come, Steve." Mike grinned as Stephan moved to greet her. Stephan's pleased gaze wandered from her soft golden hair, to her gorgeous red sweater dress, to her lovely manicured hands that held the big red box.

Celine stood there, feeling as if all eyes were on her. "Happy birthday, Stephan. I'm sorry I'm late," she apologized and handed him the gift.

He smiled handsomely. "I forgot to tell you no presents," he said as he took the box. "Would you mind if I opened up this package later tonight?"

"That's fine with me." She flashed him a sweet smile.

"I want to introduce you to my sisters and friends," he said as he took hold of her hand and led her to the far side of the beautifully landscaped yard. They stopped at a large table where a group of people were eating.

"Hey, gang. I want to introduce you to Celine Hart, an old school friend of mine."

Everyone turned toward her and they all said hello in unison.

"The pretty girls on the left are my sisters, Joan and Ann Marie. They're with their husbands, John and Matt."

"Glad to meet you all," Celine greeted them.

"Stephan," a voice called out from the other side of the yard, "there's a phone call for you."

"Ce, wait right here. I won't be but a moment."

"Yes, have a seat with us, Celine," Joan insisted.

"Thank you, I will." She sat down on an empty seat next to Ann Marie.

"Stephan was sharing with us earlier that after many years you both met again at the pre-Christmas retreat," Ann Marie commented and Celine nodded.

"I bet you were surprised at how much he had changed since your high school days," Joan interjected.

"To tell you the truth, I barely recognized him."

"Stephan is a living testimony of how God can change lives around for the better," Joan remarked.

"I know." Celine smiled. "It's so wonderful."

Ann Marie spotted Stephan coming out of the house and leaned over to Celine. "Stephan is simply crazy about you."

"And you are all he talks about," Joan whispered quickly before Stephan arrived at the table.

Stephan eyed his sisters suspiciously and turned to Celine. "Did you learn anything from the gabby twins?"

Celine laughed. Joan pursed her lips together in a pouting look, and Ann Marie rolled her eyes.

"Celine, ignore our dear brother. He thinks all we do is talk," Joan remarked with a grin.

"I'm just saying it like it is," Stephan chuckled.

"Stephan, don't be so hard on your sisters. They were talking about how proud they are of you." Celine smiled and winked at Joan and Ann Marie, who were smiling broadly.

"You won't win, Steve," John voiced loudly. "Women always stick together."

"You can say that again," Matt chimed in.

"Come on, Ce." Stephan extended his hand out to her. "Let's get something to eat before it's all gone."

"Haven't you eaten yet?" she asked as she took his hand.

"No. I was waiting for you to arrive so we could eat together," he admitted as he squeezed her hand. "So in other words, I'm glad you came, or I would have starved at my own birthday party."

Celine saw laughter in his eyes and giggled. "Not on your birthday?"

"Yes. If you didn't come tonight, I was all prepared to go on a hunger strike," he teased and stopped in front of a long table of home-cooked food. He handed her a paper plate, and they made their way down the table.

"Stephan, I really enjoyed talking to your sisters," she said as she dished out some pasta salad onto her plate. "They are very sweet and ahh. . .very informative." She smiled, her eyes were dancing with mischief.

"Okay, what did they tell you?"

"How about if I tell you later when the crowd thins out a little?" she suggested. "That is, if you want me around that long."

"I want you here until there's no one left except you and me," he stated in a low and husky voice. "There are a few important things that I have to discuss with you."

Celine raised her eyebrow with interest. "Sounds fine with me," she said as she followed him back to the table where his family group was sitting, talking among themselves.

Celine could tell how close the family was and how much Joan and Ann Marie adored their brother. She also realized that the loss of their parents had brought all of them close together. Long ago, Celine had decided that she would never marry someone who wasn't close to his family or didn't have a loving relationship with them. *Stephan passed on that test,* she thought happily to herself as she continued to listen to Stephan talk to John and Matt.

By the time everyone had finished eating, Joan ushered all the guests into the living room for cake and punch. The night air had turned cool, and Celine welcomed the warmth of the house. She sat down next to Stephan on the leather sectional since he insisted he wouldn't have her sit anywhere else, and besides, that's where she wanted to be.

Joan and Ann Marie brought out the birthday cake and held it under Stephan's chin.

"Hey, old man. Do you think you have enough wind left in you to blow out all those candles?" Dean, his drummer, yelled out jokingly.

"Somehow that statement makes me feel ancient, Dean," Stephan remarked dryly, then looked over at Celine. "Can you help this old guy blow out the candles?"

She laughed. "Sure can." She was having such a great time. All of Stephan's friends and family had treated her so kindly, and she really felt at home and accepted by the group.

As the crowd cheered Celine and Stephan on, they blew hard and all the flames went out. Ann Marie cut the cake and Joan passed out the pieces among the guests. As Celine was ready to spoon a piece of German chocolate cake in her mouth, she felt someone from behind the couch tap her on the shoulder. She put her plate down on the table, turned around, and grinned as she saw a blond, curly headed cherub with big green eyes peering over the couch at her. It was Ann Marie's little girl, Jennifer, whom she had met her earlier, along with Stephan's other nieces and nephews.

"Hi, Jennifer," Celine greeted her. Jennifer didn't reply but motioned Celine with her finger to move closer. Celine obeyed without question.

Jennifer then cupped her tiny hands around her little mouth so no one else could hear. "Are you going to be my auntie?" Jennifer asked in a whisper.

Celine's face turned bright red with color as she replied softly, "Why do you ask, Honey?"

"Because Mommy said you and Uncle Steve are gonna get married."

"She did, did she?"

"Yup, and Auntie Joanie said you were going to make the prettiest bride ever."

"Oh, is that so?" Celine grinned, amused at how Stephan's sisters were more sure of their relationship than she and Stephan.

"Uh-huh. . .and I was wondering if I could be your flower girl," Jennifer asked shyly.

"Honey, if that day comes, I'd be honored to have you as my flower girl," Celine said and watched two dimples form on her little face. "But let's keep it a secret between you and me, okay?"

"Okay," she giggled. "See you later, Auntie Celine," she whispered.

As Jennifer ran off to play with her other cousins, Celine could only stare after her. "Auntie Celine," she repeated to herself slowly. It seemed to her like Joan and Ann Marie were confident that she and Stephan would soon be married. The thought startled her, yet at the same time she was deliriously happy that his family had already accepted her after only one meeting. It seemed hard to believe. Celine turned around and sank into the softness of the sofa.

Stephan cut short his conversation with Mike and turned to Celine, eyeing her flushed cheeks. "I don't suppose you'll tell me what my little niece was talking to you about?"

Celine shook her head and grinned.

"And may I ask why not?" he questioned, hoping his niece didn't say anything out of order.

"It's top secret."

"You're baiting me."

Celine leaned over and whispered, "Can I tell you later when we are alone?"

"I guess I don't have a choice." He frowned, his brows creasing together. "It seems like we are going to have a lot to talk about later," he mused.

"Yup," Celine agreed, imitating a little girl's voice, making Stephan chuckle.

Chapter 12

The evening passed by quickly, much to Celine's surprise, and she had a sneaky feeling that Joan and Ann Marie were trying to get everyone to leave early so she and Stephan could be alone. She had to laugh at those two hardworking cupids, and she wondered if Stephan had caught on to what they were up to.

Stephan and Celine said good-bye to his family last and, on their way out the door, little Jennifer came up to her and motioned for her to bend down.

Jennifer planted a big kiss on Celine's cheek, then whispered, "I'll keep it a secret," she smiled. "Bye, Auntie Celine."

Celine kissed her on the cheek. "Thank you, Dear."

Stephan threw her a questioning look as if to say, "What did Jennifer say now?" but she ignored him until he shut the door and they were finally alone.

"Quiet. . .oh, how I love quiet," he remarked softly. "I've been waiting all night to be alone with you. Not to mention the days before when I've wanted to be with you."

As they moved back to the living room, Celine asked, "Would you like to open your gift now?"

"I thought you'd never ask," he grinned as he walked over and picked up the package. With great anticipation, he ripped off the paper and opened the lid; then he pushed aside the tissue and lifted out the jacket carefully. He was quiet as he held the gift in his hands and examined the gold stitching on the back.

Celine ventured to break the silence. "I hope it fits."

"Ce, you shouldn't have been so extravagant," he said as he slipped his arms into the jacket sleeves. "It fits perfectly."

"It looks great on you," she exclaimed with delight.

"It feels great too. Thank you for your thoughtfulness," he said as he strutted across the room, modeling it. "I love it."

Celine grinned. He looked like a kid with a new toy. "I'm glad, Stephan, because it took me awhile to find a gift for you."

"I think you've started something, though," he remarked. "Now my band members will want one just like it." He shed the jacket and positioned himself next to her on the sofa. "I have so much I want to say to you," he expressed.

"Go ahead," she urged, feeling his anxiousness. "You're the birthday boy, so I'll give you the floor."

"I think a good place for me to begin is with Angela," he said and took a deep breath and gathered his thoughts. "When Angela and I were first dating, I was really mesmerized by her because she seemed so perfect in every way, and her life was so together and organized. But after awhile, I started noticing that she wasn't that at all. I guess you could say it was mostly a facade. I realized then that I fell for her outward beauty and sophistication, and I really hadn't taken the time to look into who Angela really is.

"When we got engaged, it was her idea, not mine. I agreed to it only because I really didn't think I could do better. I did enjoy being around her, and I had grown accustomed to having her in my life." He paused briefly. "That was, until I saw you again after all those years. I'll be honest with you. When I talked with you that day by the stream, I was overwhelmed with feelings I didn't even understand. It was like there was an instant bond between us. I could have been perfectly content to spend the rest of the retreat talking to only you."

Celine smiled at the thought as Stephan continued. "That night, after the Nativity play, I wasn't sure if I should ask you over to my cabin because I was engaged to another woman. But it's like she didn't even exist anymore, and that scared me. You had made such an impact on me that I didn't know if I could trust myself around you. When I finally decided to invite you over after all, well. . .you know what happened. I didn't mean to kiss you, but I lost control of my emotions for a few minutes."

"I guess you weren't the only one," Celine remarked wryly.

He smiled. "When you left my cabin I felt like a real creep, and I knew you probably thought I was a womanizer."

"The thought did enter my mind briefly," she admitted.

"Well, I wanted to run after you and explain, but that was a stupid idea because I didn't even know what to say," he confessed. "Later that night, I had a good amount of time alone to think about everything, and it finally dawned on me why I felt so different around you than I did with Angela."

Stephan took her hand in his and looked into her clear blue eyes. "The difference was that we had Christ in common. I love the fact that you want to serve God with the same intensity that I do. That was the major factor that had been missing in my relationship with Angela." A smile appeared on his face. "Now, I'm not going to say that you aren't attractive, because you are, in the extreme sense of the word, but it seemed that when I was with you at the retreat, I was looking at you more with my spiritual eyesight than with my natural eyesight."

"What about the night you and Angela were in each other's arms in the entranceway?" Celine asked. "To me it didn't look like you were using your spiritual eyesight," she chided.

"Ahh. . .that's another reason I like you so much. Your delightful wit always keeps me on my toes." He chuckled.

"Well?" she prodded.

"Hold on for a minute. I'm almost to that part," he grinned. "The night after I arrived home from the retreat, I broke off my engagement to Angela. After I had been with you for just that short period of time, I knew I couldn't ever be happy with Angela. So the next evening I was honest with her, and she slapped me hard and walked out—not that I can blame her.

"That was the last I saw of her until that evening when you were over. She dropped by and told me she had been to a party down the street and wanted to know why I hadn't come. I said I had company, and she asked if she could meet you. I told her to please leave, and the next thing I knew she was kissing me." He looked at her apologetically. "That's when you came in and, may I say, you looked a little miffed."

"Go on." Celine ignored his comment.

"Well, after you left and I came back inside the house, Angela slapped me again and told me very explicitly what she thought of me, which I will not repeat."

Celine chuckled softly. "Do you feel better now that you got that off your chest?"

"Only if you tell me that you believe what I have shared with you."

"I believe you, Stephan."

"Phew, I'm glad that part of the evening is over."

"Now that we've cleared the air, what's next?" she asked as she relaxed and leaned back in the soft folds of the sofa.

Stephan had been waiting for this moment for a lifetime, actually, as ridiculous as it sounded. He slipped off the sofa and fell on his knees to the floor in front of Celine.

"What are you—" she began, but Stephan put his finger to her lips to quiet her.

He took her hands in his once again and squeezed them tightly. "Celine Hart, I want to grow old with you. I want to share my life, my dreams, and my heart with you. I want to be the father of your children and the grandfather of our children's children. To put it short, I love you and I can't see living my life without you by my side."

The tears spilled over her cheeks, and her throat was tight with emotion. She stared silently at Stephan as she watched his eyes become misty. "Stephan," she started, as she wiped a tear from her cheek, "you are a dream come true. . .and my prayer has been answered. I love you more than I've ever loved anyone, and I want to be by your side for the rest of my life."

Stephan pulled her to him and encircled his arms around her. Their lips melted against each other, and they were caught up in the rapture of their new-found love.

Stephan gently pulled back and whispered, "Will you marry me, Miss Hart?"

Celine looked happily into his eyes. "Yes, Mr. James. I'd be ever so delighted to accept your proposal."

He glanced upward and said, "Thank You, Lord." Then he turned to Celine. "And thank you, my love." He got up from the floor to sit next to her. "By the way, before I forget, what did Jennifer say to you earlier?"

"It's funny you should ask." Celine laughed. "She asked me if I was going to be her aunt."

"What?" Stephan asked incredulously.

"That's not all," she continued. "She wants to be the flower girl in our wedding."

"What did you tell her?" he asked in an amused voice. He couldn't believe the boldness of his little niece.

"I said sure but to keep it a secret." She giggled.

"So now it comes out in the open. You knew you had me wrapped around your little finger all the time."

"Well, I don't know about that. I guess you could say it was a heavenly guess." She smiled lovingly at him then whispered, "Can I ask a favor of you, birthday boy?"

"Anything."

"Would you mind if we take a drive down the street and share the good news with my parents?"

"Let's do. I want to meet my new family," he said as he leaned over and kissed her. "Do you think Raine and Lynette will be happy about us?" he questioned.

"They'll be estatic, believe me," she assured him. "They'll be relieved to hear that I won't be an old maid." She laughed.

Then Celine stood up and Stephan helped her on with her coat and, in turn, she helped him on with his new jacket.

"Ce, how does two children sound?" he grinned.

She nodded happily. "I like the sound of that."

"And if we have a boy, we can name him after Bill, your cousin," he said softly.

Tears formed in Celine's eyes. "Oh, Stephan, that's a wonderful idea." She hugged him tightly and said softly, "You are too good to be true."

Stephan kissed her, then looked down at her. "And you, my darling, are my gift from above."

DINA LEONHARDT KOEHLY
Dina and her husband, Craig, have two daughters. She is a California native and lives minutes from Disneyland, Knotts Berry Farm, the beach, and the mountains. She thinks it's an ideal spot for fiction writers.

Dina was blessed to be raised in a family that had two sets of grandparents who were strong Christians and were both married for over fifty years. Her passion for writing love stories stems from the fact that she has had the privilege of seeing so many wonderful marriages in her family succeed because the foundations were built on the Rock, Jesus Christ. Dina invites you to visit her at her web site: htt://www.koehlywrites.homestead.com.

Better than Friends

Sally Laity

Dedication

To Gloria. . .kindred spirit, treasured friend.
Special thanks to Jo Frazier and Wendy Lynch.

*Who would have believed
That people as different
As the two of us
Could ever have seen eye to eye
On anything. . .
Much less fall in love.
All my life
You were the complete opposite
Of all my dreams, my fantasies.
We shared nothing in common. . .
Or so I thought.
How strange to discover
That in reality,
You and I were kindred spirits. . .
Alike, yet different,
The two sides of one coin.
Now I finally can admit,
To myself and to the world,
That even before my heart
Found its way back to you
We were destined for something
Beyond mere friendship. . .
Something infinitely better.*

Chapter 1

Muted blue and mauve from the early evening sky filtered in through the bay window and mingled with the soft indoor lighting.

Collapsing another banker box, Callie McRae added it to the stack she had piled along the kitchen wall of her new condo apartment, then rubbed her hands on her jeans and released a whoosh of breath. "Well, that was the last carton. Ready for a break?"

"You don't have to ask me twice." Willowy, redheaded Trish Porter stretched a kink out of her back and plopped onto the nearest rattan chair in the breakfast nook. She drew up one knee and wrapped her slender arms around it. "Moving. Who needs it?"

"Hey, this was your idea," Callie chided as she filled two tall glasses with citrus drink and brought them to the smoked-glass table. She handed one to her best friend, then sat opposite her.

Trish crinkled her nose. "Only partly. You're the one who was griping about driving up the mountain every day and wanted to live closer to our boutique. And you must admit this place was a steal."

"You're right, both counts." Callie sipped her drink, letting her gaze wander over the marbled peach and silver countertops and oak cupboards in the cozy room, which was already her favorite part of the apartment. Even the apricot floral wallpaper would have been her choice. Noticing that the coordinating bustle valance above the sink was off center, she rose and went to straighten it, then repositioned the philodendron and coleus on the shelves of the plant window.

"Well, Girl, if you can handle the rest on your own, Phil would probably appreciate having some supper pretty soon."

Callie turned with a smile. "Sure, go on. Thanks for helping—and for covering the shop for me while I moved. I owe you."

"Like the song says, that's what friends are for, right?" Trish's blue eyes twinkled with her silly grin as she walked to the door and opened it. "But don't think I won't need you there tomorrow. The order from Chic Petite should arrive fairly early, and we've been running that sale ad in the paper. We'll probably have a good turnout."

"Right." Watching her friend hurry down the front walk, Callie waited until Trish drove away, then closed the door. She turned with a sigh and went back to the kitchen, where she put a skinless chicken breast into the toaster oven to broil and dumped leftover lunch salad into a bowl.

A few hours later in her mirrored ivory and mint bathroom, Callie stripped out of her jeans and T-shirt and took a shower, letting the hot spray soothe her weary muscles. Then, donning her robe, she curled up on the sofa with a cup of herbal tea to watch the ten o'clock news.

In the middle of the local report, music filtered in from the adjoining apartment as someone played a loud, intricate run up and down the frets of an acoustic guitar.

Callie suddenly realized that she hadn't so much as inquired about who occupied the other half of the condo when the opening had popped up. She'd just signed the lease and moved in. She gritted her teeth and turned the TV volume up a notch as she settled back against the floral upholstery, hoping every night wasn't going to be like this.

☙❧❧❧❧

Not a cloud marred the clear California sky the following morning as Callie unrolled her steam curls and finger-combed her medium-length, chestnut hair into its normal tousled style. Her face still glowed from jogging in the ever-present Tehachapi Mountain breeze, so she added only the barest hint of blush to her cheekbones and a scant application of mascara to the dark lashes surrounding her brown eyes.

After draping tiny multicolored beads around her neck above her gauzy ivory peasant dress, she chose matching dangly earrings and spritzed on some L'Air du Temps before hurrying off to work.

She couldn't help the pride that swelled within her as she pulled up behind La Femme Fashions, the fashion boutique in which she and Trish had invested nearly all of their life savings. The Victorian-style shop occupied a prominent end spot of the newly erected Windy Hills Plaza, situated across Highway 58 from the thriving mountain community of Tehachapi.

Callie found the back door unlocked and could already hear Trish humming from one of the dressing rooms. "Hi," Callie called as she let herself in. "I'm here."

"Morning," Trish answered, her bubbly voice cheery as always. In a jade shirt-waist, she emerged from dressing room three, a lambs' wool duster in her hand. She gave the shuttered rose-colored door a swift once-over. "Coffee's on."

"I know. I smelled it when I came in. I need some too, after the night I had."

"Really?" Trish stopped dusting in midstroke and turned, curiosity sparkling in her eyes.

"Apparently, whoever lives next door is into guitars. And guess when he chooses to practice. It took me forever to fall asleep after the music finally stopped."

"Oh, no. Well, assert yourself. Half of that condo belongs to you, you know. Go tell the dope to cease and desist."

"I might have to."

"Hey, if the guy gives you any problems, I'll send Phil over to read him the riot act."

Envisioning Trish's big, brawny husband of four months instilling fear in some unsuspecting neighbor, Callie chuckled. "Thanks, but it's my problem." She went to the urn and filled a mug with coffee, adding a smidgen of cream before sampling it.

"The ad looks pretty good," Trish said, offering Callie the current issue of the *Tehachapi News* already folded open to the right page. With a smile, she gripped her duster purposefully and went out to the main room.

Callie checked the copy. The girl who normally handled the boutique's advertising account at the newspaper office had done her usual splendid job. The sale notice took up half of the third page and caught the eye immediately. Intending to call the editor later and express her appreciation, Callie set down her cup and walked out into the showroom.

Trish had already finished the new displays in the windows that flanked either side of the U-shaped entrance, so Callie went to the register and checked the tape, then straightened the surrounding counter area in preparation for the store's opening in fifteen minutes. Already, several cars occupied the nearest parking spots in anticipation of clearance bargains. Callie knew a busy day lay ahead.

≈≋≋≈

Maneuvering her teal LeBaron up the curved incline to the Spanish-style duplex after work, Callie couldn't help but notice the sapphire Corvette convertible parked on the street in front of her neighbor's apartment. *Fitting for a guitarist,* she decided. Inserting the key into her lock, she grimaced at the other door in the sheltered entry.

As if she'd rung the bell, it opened. A tall, lanky man with sandy shoulder-length hair and a couple days' growth of beard leaned out. A lazy smile added a twinkle to a pair of dark cobalt eyes. "Hi, Neighbor."

Appraising muscled arms and the tank top which barely stretched across his solid chest, not to mention the ridiculous shredded jeans she couldn't believe had ever been in vogue, Callie was surprised that he wasn't wearing an earring. She offered a reserved smile as the notion that he looked vaguely familiar pricked her consciousness.

He registered a look of shock himself as his deep-set eyes narrowed. He stepped out with a frown. "Caralyn? Caralyn McRae? I don't believe it."

Hearing her name pronounced in that deeply modulated voice reminiscent of years gone by, Callie's spirits plummeted. How could she be living next door to Lex Sheridan, of all people? That chapter of her life had ended years ago. She closed her eyelids and breathed out to a silent count of five before opening them again. "Yes," she answered numbly. "But I go by Callie now."

He sputtered into a mirthless laugh. "Well, there goes the neighborhood."

"Funny," Callie said, elevating her brows. "My sentiment exactly." Turning on one heel, she presented her back to him and unlocked her door.

Lex snickered. "Well, Callie," he said, giving slight emphasis to her name, "no doubt we'll be crossing paths from time to time, now that we live in such close proximity again."

"Not if I see you first," Callie muttered under her breath.

"What?"

"I suppose."

"Well, then, I'll see you around."

With a toss of her hair, Callie went into her apartment. She hung the slim strap of her shoulder bag on the oak hall tree and slipped off her sandals, then padded to the bedroom. A little sore from lifting cartons and boxes for the last two days, she knew a good workout would loosen her muscles. She changed into rainbow spandex Danskins and fastened her hair back with a pouf clip.

In the smaller spare bedroom, which housed her exercise equipment, Callie started out on the stationary bike. Before the first five minutes had passed, she found herself pedaling furiously at the idea of having signed a two-year lease on the apartment right beside that of His Royal Highness, Alexander Sheridan III. Growing up in Bakersfield's Starlane Heights a mere few houses away from his and sharing the same school bus stop from kindergarten through high school had been more than enough to last a lifetime.

Callie recalled the undisciplined ruffian who had been a thorn in her side since they had first laid eyes on each other. From painting her brand-new bike— tires and all—a bright hot pink, to kidnapping her dog, Patches, for a day and a half, Lex Sheridan's brainless pranks knew no end. It mattered little that the paint turned out to be the harmless poster variety or that Patches seemed his perky little self after he mysteriously reappeared in her fenced backyard the next night. Callie could not abide so much as the sight of Lex Sheridan again, even after a four-year liberal arts course at Bible school, plus another four years of working and scrimping to invest in her own business. What fates had caused him to move forty plus miles away from home and take up residence in the Tehachapi Mountains? And why, oh why, did it have to be right next door to her?

Far too steamed to remain indoors, Callie decided to switch to the cross-country ski machine out on her deck instead. She grabbed a bottle of mineral water on her way past the fridge and exited through the sliding glass door. Her present state of mind spoiled any enjoyment she might have found in the magnificent mountain view, but she did notice it was a refreshing change from much of the residential and industrial scenery she'd been used to. Steep mountains, their tree-dotted slopes reaching to the sky, rimmed the entire Cummings Valley. They framed the swiftly growing Stallion Springs community and the Sky Mountain Resort, which nestled against the hilly western rim not far down the road from her.

Setting her drink on the snack table nearby, Callie stepped onto the footpads and closed her hands around the handle grips, starting off at an easy, steady pace, hoping the regulated motion would calm her frazzled nerves.

᠗᠑᠖᠕

Lex Sheridan stood at his cluttered white tile kitchen counter and wolfed down a jelly donut and a huge glass of milk. Returning to the living room, he flopped down on the black leather couch, then removed the stub of a pencil from above one ear and filled in several measures of chords on the music manuscript paper on the coffee table in front of him. One side of his mouth drew upward in a smirk. Caralyn McRae. Little Miss Prim and Proper—who not only spent most of her time with her nose in the air whenever he was around, but even worse—gave a whole new meaning to the word pip-squeak. There ought to be a law against short people. At twenty-six now, two years his junior, she hadn't changed a bit. She was a living portrait of Yesterday.

Laying his pencil aside, he searched among the paper rubble for the phone and dialed his fiancée's number. Waiting for her to answer, he envisioned lithe, leggy Brenda Harding. He filled his lungs and smiled. *All women could take lessons from her in style and grace,* he assured himself. *And optimism.* Brenda was an upbeat person, always ready for a good time. Disappointed when there was no response, he replaced the receiver and lounged back against the couch.

A muffled thump sounded from the other side of the shared wall. Lex sighed, knowing Caralyn must have caused it—perhaps even deliberately. He knew he was harboring uncharitable thoughts toward her, but for some reason she possessed an uncanny ability to bring out the absolute worst in him. In truth, he realized she had been smart to steer clear of him over the years, for he had always derived a kind of perverse satisfaction from heckling the girl. Maybe if she would have just cried once and gotten it over with, he might have felt guilty and looked for someone else to provoke. But she would merely cross her arms, stick out her bottom lip, and flounce off—which only made him want to try all the harder. Maybe it was that spirit of hers that had challenged and fascinated him way back then.

Having her a single common wall away now was tough to swallow. All things considered, there was just no getting around it. Certain individuals in this world functioned much better when separated by vast distances, and he and Callie McRae headed that list.

Lex ran a hand through his hair and forced himself to concentrate on the music. In view of the present circumstances, it seemed almost comical that he had volunteered to compose a friendship song for the upcoming Friends Day at New Life Fellowship. He had expected to have it done already but had yet to put the finishing touches to the arrangement so the other guys in the ensemble could practice it. He stared at the half-written piece, then unfolded his long legs and stood. Maybe a drive out to the desert would clear his mind. He grabbed his sleeveless denim vest and checked his pants pocket for his keys.

⟨❦❦⟩

Callie heard the sports car drive off, and along with a flash of relief felt, at the same time, suddenly alone. Setting aside the mystery novel she'd been reading, she picked up the receiver on her transparent acrylic phone and dialed Bakersfield.

"Hello?" came her grandmother's crackly voice.

"Hi, Gram, it's me."

"Oh, Callie, Honey. We were just talking about you. All settled in, are you?"

"Yes, pretty much. I miss you and Gramps already, though." Blinking back threatening tears, she allowed her mind to form a sweet picture of the slight, older woman, the wonderful "mother" who had held Callie together after her own parents had died in a plane crash when she'd been barely four. Never one to follow fashion trends, Gram had an assortment of homemade cotton dresses that she always wore around the house. To this day, she sewed all her own clothes and baked homemade goodies. Callie almost imagined she could smell fresh bread right through the telephone wire.

"Gramps thought maybe we'd drive up and see your place one of these days, as soon as I feel a little more chipper."

"That would be nice, Gram. Just make sure you're up to it, okay? Stop trying to do so much all the time. Take it easy for a change, like the doctor said." She paused with a silent sigh. "Well, just thought I'd let you know I love you, so you wouldn't think I've forgotten about you."

"That's real sweet, Honey. We love you too."

"Ken didn't happen to call yet, did he?"

"No, not yet. But I have your number written right by the phone to give him when he does. You take care, now."

"I will. Bye." As Callie hung up, it was all she could do not to cry. *Must be too many childhood memories all at once,* she surmised, added to the fact that her fiancé, Ken Vincent, was out of town until tomorrow night and unlikely to call. There could be no other logical explanation for her blues. She shook off the peculiar teariness with a determined sniff and flicked on the TV.

Inside, she hoped Ken wouldn't find out just yet that she'd moved. He'd been upset enough when she'd invested in La Femme with Trish in the first place, since it was forty miles from home. And now when he learned she'd found a place in the mountains while he was away, he was going to be furious.

Chapter 2

The mountain breeze swished over the wild grasses as Callie jogged along the hilly route she'd chosen. It seemed cool for May. Thin morning sunshine glistened on patches of snow on the higher mountain peaks, making the splashes of spring wildflowers on the surrounding hills all the more delicate against the azure sky. Callie let her gaze drink its fill of brilliant orange poppies and blue lupine as she bounded over the open field behind her home.

No sign of life came from the adjoining apartment, she noticed upon reaching the landing of her elevated deck. She cast a scornful look at the other unit as she went up the steps and turned the key in her lock, then went inside to shower and dress. Perhaps the high and mighty Alex Sheridan, of the wealthy Sheridan household, had never had to do a day's work, but her own lifestyle had been far less privileged. Gram and Gramps McRae owned their sprawling Spanish colonial home outright and had few bills to speak of, but they believed in being frugal and had passed their convictions on to Callie, encouraging her to earn whatever spending money she desired. It was a lesson she appreciated immensely, for along the way she had learned not to squander her hard-earned funds.

In her kitchen, Callie spooned some yogurt and strawberries into a bowl and hurried through her morning devotions as she ate. The selection for today, she noted with some chagrin, centered on the story of the Good Samaritan. When she finished reading, she bowed her head. *Lord, I know I should pray for Lex Sheridan. Heaven knows he could probably use it, but I'm sure he passed the point of help years ago. Mostly I just want to keep out of his way now. Please help me to hold my tongue when he's around and not make things any worse than they already are. And, somehow, just get us both through this.* With her conscience somewhat appeased, Callie smiled to herself.

She arrived at the boutique ahead of Trish. After starting the coffee, she went to check the dresses and blouses in the petite section, arranging the various sizes in groups of neat precision on the hangers.

"Hi, Callie," Trish called moments later from the back room. "You're early today." Brushing wrinkles from her yellow, straight skirt, she emerged through the curtained French doors that separated the office area from the remainder of the store.

Callie shrugged an almost bare shoulder in the string-gathered neckline of her Aztec blouse. "I guess I'm expecting a repeat of yesterday. That was quite the turnout."

"Sure was. Eliminated a good half of the old winter stock, I'd say. But we needed the room." She cocked her head to one side and stared at Callie, concern darkening the blue of her eyes. "Something wrong?"

Callie grimaced. "I guess you could say that."

"What is it?"

"I met my neighbor."

"And?" At Callie's lack of response, Trish lifted her hands palms up in a prompting gesture.

"It's Lex Sheridan." She paused and took a breath. "Can you believe it, Trish? Lex Sheridan, of all people. Honestly, what did I do to deserve this? That guy is like my own personal plague."

A disbelieving smile widened her friend's lips. "Do tell. Well, this should add an interesting twist to your otherwise drab existence." Moving nearer, she gave a comforting pat to Callie's arm before picking up some empty lingerie boxes and carting them to the storage closet.

"I just want to wake up and find out none of this is happening," Callie said almost to herself. Then as Trish's last comment registered, she frowned and went after her. "Do you really consider my life boring?"

Trish scrunched her oval face in an obvious attempt to remain serious as she plucked imaginary lint from her white short-sleeved sweater. "Well, with Ken, 'Mr. Excitement' himself, looming on your marriage horizon, what else should a friend think?"

Stunned, Callie raised her chin but didn't answer. Stepping to the small rest room next to the closet, she fluffed her curls and checked her lipstick. When she came out, she saw Trish at the front door turning the Open sign outward.

A handful of customers entered and began browsing through the sale racks. *Ken's not boring,* Callie affirmed, becoming distantly aware of a teenager waiting at the register with some earrings from the clearance basket on the counter. *A little predictable, maybe, and even reserved. But he's reliable and trustworthy. That should count for something.* Drawing a deep breath, she put on a smile and went to wait on the frizzy-haired younger girl. "Will this be all?"

"Mm-hm. I'm glad they were still here." She handed over her selection along with a five-dollar bill.

Callie smiled as she rang up the merchandise and bagged it, then gave the girl the change. "Come back again."

All morning long, Trish's remark grated on Callie's nerves. It came as a surprise that her friend did not seem to consider Ken much of a catch. She'd never so much as hinted at it before. Five-foot-eleven with medium build and glossy brown hair, Ken, with his levelheadedness and staid demeanor, seemed to Callie a refreshing change from today's run-of-the-mill egoists. Oh, well, why did it matter what Trish thought anyway? Ken would be back this evening from that St. Louis convention, and Callie was looking forward to seeing her fiancé. Once he got over the shock of her move, she was sure he'd approve of her new surroundings.

"Whew!" came her partner's voice from behind. "Finally, things have slowed down."

"Oh?" Glancing around the shop, Callie noticed the absence of customers. "Probably after lunch we'll have another rush."

Trish eyed her curiously, then started in with her usual third degree. "You sure were quiet all morning. Tell me again about that neighbor of yours. What's he been up to these last few years while you and I were busy going to college and slaving away to save up for our dream? Still cruising around in that red Datsun ZX?"

"No, now he's got a shiny dark blue convertible—which clashes with my car, by the way, and I have no idea what he's been doing. Nor do I care." Callie shook her head for emphasis.

"Too bad." Trish's expression looked crestfallen.

"You should see him," Callie said with disdain. "His hair is long, his clothes are a mess, and he could use a good shave."

"Hm. Well, neatness is only now coming back into fashion, you know, and so are more conservative haircuts."

"Yes, well, I don't know why we're even discussing the jerk." Rolling her eyes, Callie headed for the back room. "I'm going to lunch."

❧❀❧

Callie stifled a yawn as the phone rang later that evening. She picked up the receiver. "Hello?"

"It's me. Ken. I just got back."

"Oh." From his terse greeting, Callie didn't have to guess at his mood. "Um, hi. It's good to hear your voice," she said tentatively.

"Is it?"

"Yes. I missed you, you know." She paused. "I guess you got my new number from Gram."

"Yeah." He exhaled an impatient, angry breath. "Why did you do this, Cal?"

"Please, don't be mad, Hon. You know I've been wishing I didn't have to drive so far to get to the store every day, and Trish's landlady mentioned this really nice place to her. I know you'll approve once you see it." Already hating having to defend herself, she took a different tack. "Anyway, it wouldn't have been such a shock if you'd have called more often." She gave a nod, futile though it was, since he couldn't see it.

"Well, you know how busy a convention can get. Besides, I hate what hotels charge for outside calls."

Feeling as though her fiancé didn't consider her worth spending some pocket change for, she grimaced. "Did you have a good time, at least?"

"Yeah, not bad. I'm pretty tired, though. Since it's late already I thought I might as well wait 'til tomorrow night to come see you."

Callie felt a prick of mild irritation, but since his tone had lost much of its sharp edge, she felt herself relax. "Sure. Whatever you think is best. My grandparents can give you the directions I wrote out. Love you."

"Me too. Tomorrow night, then."

Flopping back dejectedly against the couch, Callie emitted a sigh and hung up the phone just as music throbbed her way again, this time from an electronic keyboard. In no mood now to put up with another aggravation, she clenched her teeth and rose, deciding now was as good a time as any to declare war. She marched out her door, straight to his, and pressed the doorbell twice.

Lex appeared in seconds, barefoot and in a ponytail.

"Must you play that thing so loud?" She planted a fist on either hip in exasperation.

He grinned, strong white teeth flashing against his perfect tan. "Now, is that any way to greet a neighbor?"

Callie pressed her lips together.

"Who is it, Sweetheart?" called a husky female voice from inside.

"Just the gal next door," he tossed over his shoulder, then looked back at Callie innocently. "You were saying?"

Astounded that some woman would actually keep company with Lex Sheridan, Callie nevertheless bristled at his condescending demeanor. "I'd appreciate it, *Mr.* Sheridan, if you would keep your music down to some reasonable volume at night so a person could hear herself think."

"No problem." He gave a wave of his hand. "I wouldn't want to disturb your peace of mind or deprive you of your beauty sleep. I'll switch to the earphones."

Prepared for an argument, Callie felt speechless at his acquiescence. She swallowed. "Oh. Well, um, thanks."

"Anytime." He winked mischievously as he closed the door.

Staring momentarily at the leaded-glass panes at eye level, Callie turned and went back into her apartment.

❦❧

Just as she finished putting on her gold hoop earrings the following evening, Callie heard her fiancé's usual rapid knock at the front door. She slipped into her sandals and ran to answer.

Ken didn't quite smile when she drew open the door.

"Hi, Honey," she said brightly, praying he'd warm to the idea of her move once he'd had time to get used to it.

His gray eyes looked stormy and cold behind his navy wire-rimmed glasses as he stepped inside, but he reached for Callie. Drawing her close, he planted a kiss on her lips. "Missed you, Angel."

"And I missed you." She resisted the urge to tousle Ken's silky brown hair, knowing he hated to have it mussed. Instead, she contented herself with nuzzling against him.

He tossed an assessing look around. "So this is it," he said flatly.

Callie drew in a nervous breath. "Yes. I'll give you the grand tour, if you like, starting here." Turning, she made a wide motion with one arm. "This is the living room, as you can see. And down this hallway are two bedrooms. Come on; I'll show you."

Returning after he had seen it all, Ken put an arm around Callie's waist, his studious face serious as he gave a begrudging nod. "Well, as much as I hate to admit it, you've made a decent choice, at least. I think I'll adjust to living here once we're married. We'll have to get some bookcases, of course, and I'll need a side of the spare room for my computer and stuff. Otherwise, it'll do fine." He pushed his glasses up the bridge of his nose as he studied the view out the window. "It's gonna be a drag driving down the mountain to the office every day, though, once fog season hits. I knew I should never have let you open a business way up here."

That last rather chauvinistic statement piqued Callie. Then, envisioning her airy home cluttered up with heavy books and her exercise room turned into an office, Callie fought another twinge, one of selfishness. This was supposed to be what she had wanted, had planned for, wasn't it? Perhaps soon after they married they'd get a house suitable for both of them. She forced a smile. "You'll get used to it, I'm sure."

"Probably. Well, ready to go to dinner?"

Within half an hour, they were making their way down the line of entrees at Shelby's Buffet, a casual eatery in Tehachapi which Ken liked. Subdued evening lighting and quiet instrumentals gave the establishment a more intimate atmosphere than it had during the normal daytime bustle.

Callie chose baked haddock with her small garden salad, and as Ken took his usual fried chicken, Trish's comment from earlier that day rang in her ears. She knew he'd place a huge baked potato on his plate with all the trimmings, while she passed them up for steamed broccoli. She'd never really thought about it before, but now she realized she could have named every single item that would occupy his tray before they'd even entered the restaurant.

Coming to an available tapestry and vinyl booth with their selections, Callie slid into one side and Ken took the other. Knowing Ken frowned on praying in public himself, she said her own quick silent prayer. When she met his eyes, he smiled.

"You're looking especially lovely tonight."

"Thank you." She drizzled some low-cal dressing over her tossed greens. "How was St. Louis?"

"Gray and cool. One day was fairly nice, but we never got out of the convention center to enjoy it. Seminars and lectures from mornin 'til night." He bit into a buttered roll.

"Didn't you even get to ride up in the Gateway Arch while you were there?" She watched him chew slowly and swallow.

"Nope. A couple of the guys tried to, but as luck would have it, the thing was closed for maintenance."

Returning her attention to her own plate, Callie concentrated on the melodic harp and piano song currently playing, purposely tuning out Ken's recounting of computer software demonstrations and tax accounting shortcuts he'd picked up at the convention. By the time they had finished eating, a dull ache throbbed in her head. She found herself hoping he was still tired from the trip and would just drop her off at her apartment, since he had a long drive back down the mountain. But he eliminated that possibility at her door.

"Gonna put on coffee while we watch the news?"

"Sure. Why not?" While Ken seated himself on the couch and flicked channels with the remote, Callie switched on the coffeemaker, then took some pain medicine before going to sit next to him.

Ken put his arm around her shoulders and pulled her closer. "Ah, this is what I've been missing." Bending his head, he lowered his lips to hers.

She relaxed and warmed in his embrace.

"And now for an update on the earthquake that shook Barstow a few hours ago. . . ," the newscaster droned.

Ken pulled back. "That's not even a hundred miles from here. Did you notice a trembler before I arrived?"

She shrugged. "Not especially."

He shook his head. "One of these days I think we'll be in for a really good one. Wait and see."

With an indulgent smile, Callie rose to pour the coffee. She watched from the counter as Ken flicked through the rest of the cable lineup as if she had no preferences whatsoever.

Trying to envision a whole life like this brought a strange emptiness and loneliness. Callie couldn't help wondering how long these ignored emotions of hers had gone unrecognized—and if they'd go away.

Chapter 3

Callie opened the garment box just delivered by UPS and folded back the protective tissue. "Trish!"

The overhead lights reflected off her friend's coppery waves as she came into the office from the salesroom. "What is it?"

"The shipment arrived from that preview of Danielle Hemingway's a few weeks ago. I just had to show you this." Holding up an exquisitely embroidered blouse of crystal blue satin, Callie perused the long sleeves and high rolled neckline while awaiting her partner's response.

"Wow! How gorgeous! You said that show was classy. Now I believe it."

With a smile, Callie picked up the next item, a tucked peach camisole which matched exactly the hues of the broomstick pleated skirt beneath.

"Think I'll snag this one for myself," Trish said with determination as she reached for the top. "It'll go perfectly with my new white suit. Listen, I have a customer out in the other room, so—"

"Sure. I'll look over the rest. Maybe we can fax an order later this afternoon or tomorrow. This is going to be a great line to carry."

As Trish returned to the showroom, Callie ran her fingers over the elegant beaded silver trim on the shoulder and bodice inset of a white jacquard dress with matching silver belt. She wondered if Ken would like it, then dismissed the notion. They never went anywhere requiring dressy attire. Still, one never knew when something like that might be an asset. Deciding to purchase it for herself, her gaze lingered on it as she hung it and the rest of the assortment on padded hangers and returned to the desk to peruse the catalog that had accompanied the order.

Deciding exactly which articles and how many of each size and color to purchase took most of the day. When Callie arrived home, she kicked off her shoes and went at once to change into an exercise outfit, tying her hair off her face with a coordinating scarf.

❧❦❧

Lex took off his earphones and relaxed against the couch, satisfied with the arrangement of the new song. He had yet to title it and write lyrics, but he had some ideas floating around in his brain and felt confident that one of them would probably be workable. As he rested his head against the back of the couch and closed his eyes, a strange sound carried from the adjoining deck. Sawing? Grabbing the last jelly donut from the open box on the table, he slid open the patio door and went out.

He peered around the edge of the privacy wall and saw Caralyn McRae on a cross-country ski machine. Her face was turned away, so he took advantage of it and let his eyes rove over her trim figure. If he knew anything about her, she'd probably work herself to death to stay that way. He suppressed a laugh. "My, my. Aren't you the dedicated health nut."

Callie's head snapped around, but she didn't miss a stride as her gaze came to rest on his half-eaten donut. "I suppose I should expect that kind of remark from someone who's clogging his arteries with excess fat and empty calories. You have jelly on your face, by the way."

This time Lex did laugh. He popped the remainder of the sweet into his mouth and wiped away the offending sticky glob.

Hiking her chin a notch, Callie turned her attention to the distance as she maintained a measured pace. "Honestly, have you nothing better to do than stand there gawking? More practice on that loud guitar of yours or something?"

"Why? Do you like music, McRae?"

"No." She let out a frustrated breath. "Yes. But only when I choose to listen to it."

"Actually, I just came out for some fresh air," Lex said, sliding his hands into the pockets of his sweatpants. "Or do you have objections to that too?"

"Not at all." Glancing at her watch, Callie stepped off the machine, grabbed a towel from the floral chaise nearby, and draped it around her neck. "I'm finished anyway." With a toss of chestnut curls, she went inside and shut the sliding door. The vertical blinds swished into place, then closed.

Lex shook his head and stared momentarily at the mountain splendor mirrored against the glass, then sighed and went through his own door to change clothes.

An hour later, he pulled into an available parking space at the unassuming Spanish-style building owned by New Life Fellowship, a relatively recent establishment nestled in a shaded glen on the west end of Tehachapi. Not quite four years old, the simple yet functional structure with its contemporary mode of worship appealed to a growing number of younger individuals and new families, and was gaining popularity each month. Lex took marginal pride in having helped found the little church. Grabbing his guitar and the folder of music, he bounded up the stone steps.

"Hey, Lex." Doug Farmer, a rake-thin twenty year old, was already seated amid his prized blue and chrome Pearl drums. He lifted a stick in greeting, interrupting the random patterns he'd been tapping out across the skins while adjusting the pitch.

Raul and Manuel Perez, on bass guitar and keyboard, looked up at the same time. "Hey, Man," they said as one. Eighteen, and identical twins with coal-black hair and eyes, the wiry pair bore such close resemblance to one another that few could tell them apart, an asset they played to great advantage around the awestruck fairer sex.

Lex opened the guitar case and took out his Yamaha APX 20, then passed the manuscripts around. "Think we can start putting this together. But I need some input on it, so feel free to be honest."

∾∾

"Oh, my goodness. . . ," Trish said, stretching out the entire remark and letting it dangle. At the window, she fingered the skirt on one of the mannequins and peered outside from behind it. "You have got to see this hunk. Come here, Callie."

Marveling at her friend's dreamy tone of voice, Callie rose and crossed the room, but she couldn't resist a jibe. "I must say, that is an odd statement to be coming from a married woman."

Trish blushed slightly, coloring her fair skin up to her hairline as she fluttered a guilty hand. "Hey, I'm only married, not dead. I can still see. And that guy is gorgeous. See him? The one over by the music store?" She swung her intent gaze back toward the man.

Callie followed Trish's direction, and her mouth dropped open. "Trish. That's Alex Sheridan."

"Our Alex Sheridan?" Trish asked, swinging around to face Callie. "Beanpole Alex Sheridan? I thought you said he looked a mess these days."

"He does. Look at that hair. Those jeans."

"Those shoulders," Trish swooned. "That car."

Callie rolled her eyes and shook her head slowly as she returned to the register, where she'd been tagging a rack of new dress slacks. She would never understand how any woman could consider unkempt, useless Lex attractive when southern California had handsome and eligible males at every turn. Resuming her seat, she forced her attention to the task her partner's summons had interrupted.

Suddenly, Trish skittered across the room to the counter and seized a handful of receipts, examining each with infinite concentration.

"Something wrong?"

"Wrong? What could be wrong?" Trish asked in a high voice. "He just happens to be coming this way, that's all."

The electronic chimes over the door went off, and Callie's gaze flew across the open space and locked onto dark blue eyes. She blinked and looked down.

"M-may I help you?" Trish managed, setting the sales slips aside.

From the corner of her eye, Callie saw Lex's head tilt as he gaped at her friend. "Aren't you—"

"Yes. Trish Hudson. . .only my last name is Porter now."

He gave a nod. "This your place?"

"Yes. Callie's and mine."

"Hm. Not bad."

Callie felt the warmth of the surprised glance he flicked her way and determined all the more to ignore him completely. "I think I'll finish up in the office," she said, cool and composed. She stood and headed toward the French doors.

"How can I help you?" she heard her partner ask Lex.

"I'm looking for a gift. Have any jewelry?"

"Right over here."

As Callie turned the doorknob, the electric motor of the display case whirred on, and she knew that the horizontal shelves had rotated to a different level of rings, watches, and earrings. She closed the office door and sank into the chair at the desk, intending to remain there until every item in the room had been inventoried—or Lex Sheridan had left—whichever came first. She reached first for a carton of new scarves and accessories that needed price tags, then the tagging gun.

Shortly after the chimes sounded again, Trish swept into the office. She leaned back against the door and blew out an exhilarated breath.

"He's gone?"

Her partner nodded.

"Well, did he at least buy something?"

Trish gave her a slow smile. "Yeah. That nice silver and turquoise necklace you picked up in Arizona, and the matching earrings."

With a shrug, Callie grimaced. "Nice taste, anyway. I'll give him that."

"Who do you suppose they were for?"

"How should I know?" Callie frowned. "Could we please find something better to talk about?"

Neither spoke for a moment. Callie went back to her task.

"Imagine. That rich, handsome guy still available. Surely some gal's hot on his trail, wouldn't you say?" Trish asked casually, moving to the water cooler. She dispensed some into a paper cup and sipped it.

Callie shot her partner a weary look.

"I'm not wondering for myself," Trish added.

"Well, I'm sure I don't know. And even more sure that I don't care. Besides, don't you think it might upset Phil just a little to have you interested in some other man?"

Trish looked abashed as she dropped her used cup into the wastebasket. "I'm perfectly happy with my husband. And if you must know, I was wondering about you."

"What?" Callie asked, shocked.

"A girl could do a lot worse than Lex Sheridan."

Laying aside the scarf she was about to tag, Callie moistened her lips and stood. "Trish. You seem to have forgotten one little detail. I'm engaged. I am not looking to replace my fiancé. Not now, not ever. Whoever Lex Sheridan happens to have dangling on his string is of no concern to me whatsoever."

"Then why are you so defensive every time I mention his name?"

Callie went blank. "How should I know?" She finally scowled. "I just don't want his name creeping up all the time. Now, if you'll excuse me, I have some things to finish up in the salesroom."

On her way, she glanced at Trish, who remained beside the cooler tapping an index finger against her pant leg, a stupid smile on her face. Callie doggedly kept going. "And anyway, that has to be the dumbest thing you have ever said. Ever!"

With a shake of her head, Callie shut the door against her partner's peals of laughter.

Chapter 4

Lex hesitated on Brenda's doorstep, enjoying the lilting melody from her piano. She was always more relaxed when she was unaware of an audience, and the notes flowed smoothly from the keys, lingering in the mild evening stillness long after she finished the song. Lex waited momentarily, then rang the doorbell.

In seconds she answered. "Oh, it's you, Darling." Her hand paused midair as she ceased patting her already flawless hair into place and stepped aside. "Come in."

He entered the quaint studio apartment, which was tastefully furnished with antiques, and bestowed a light kiss on Brenda's upturned lips. "It's such a nice night; I thought you might like to go for a drive."

"Is the top down?" she asked, peering around him toward the car.

"Yeah. But it's not cold out."

She scrunched her heart-shaped face into a pretty pout. "I'll have to get a scarf."

Hands in his jean pockets, Lex watched her cross the homey living room in her normal graceful, fluid way. Tall and slender, Brenda showed obvious years of classical dance training.

She removed a wisp of silk from a breakfront drawer in her hallway and returned. The aqua watercolor roses in its print mirrored the hue of the silk blouse she had paired with her gray dress slacks.

Lex let his gaze drink in the perfection that was uniquely Brenda. Her honey blond hair had just been trimmed to its usual stylish, swingy length and glistened alongside braided gold earrings and a matching gold chain resting on the contours of her slight collarbones. He smiled and ran his fingers over the curve of one soft cheek, then as the scent of her perfume drifted up to him, he bent his head and kissed her.

"What was that for?" she asked, her voice teasing and seductive as she slid her hands around his waist.

"You just looked tempting. . .as always." After another kiss, Lex eased her gently away and turned her toward the exit. "Your chariot awaits."

After closing the car door for Brenda, Lex slid into his own side and started the engine. Out of the corner of his eye, he saw her tie on her scarf. He knew without looking that her jaw would be rigid. Brenda did not like convertibles. More than once, she'd broached the subject and suggested he replace the car with a coupe or sedan—or at the very least, use her Honda whenever they went out. But finally she'd given up. Now she would simply cover her hair and force a smile. He took her hand and lifted it to his mouth for a kiss, then pressed the accelerator and pulled away.

"Where are we going?"

"Nowhere in particular. Maybe for some dessert in Lancaster or Palmdale. I just wanted to be with you."

She turned a smile his way, one rife with meaning. "You wouldn't have to miss me so much if you'd just let me name a date, you know."

"Yeah." Lex inhaled deeply and released the breath. Much as he fully intended to marry her one of these days, now just didn't seem quite the right time. His parents both seemed eager for their eldest son and heir to wed; and, in fact, had introduced him to Brenda, hoping to encourage him to settle down. The daughter of one of the area's leading defense attorneys, she moved in all the proper circles. The thing was that Lex no longer felt comfortable in them. Not since he'd given his heart to the Lord four years ago and gotten involved at New Life Fellowship.

The lights of Lancaster and Palmdale glittered like sequins in the darkness and blended together under the night sky as the car crested the final hill overlooking the Antelope Valley, then began its descent. Just a few short years ago, both towns had been quiet desert communities, but now that a freeway connected them to Los Angeles, they both teemed with growth. One after another, new housing developments and shopping centers had sprouted to accommodate the influx of people seeking more reasonable housing as well as relief from the smog.

Lex reached for Brenda's hand. "Beautiful, huh?"

She nodded. "It's always been one of my favorite sights. Why don't we just hit one of the nightspots for a drink?"

"Come on, Hon. You know I don't go for that stuff anymore."

Brenda pursed her lips and averted her eyes. "Well, you can have your boring old coffee, and I'll have a cocktail."

" 'Fraid not. You know the kids at church look to me as an example. I wouldn't want it to get back to them that I go to bars while speaking out against the evils of alcohol."

With a sigh of defeat, she turned her head toward the desert landscape illuminated in the glow of the city lights. "Really, Lex. You've gotten so stuffy since you got *religion*. You're no fun at all now."

Her comment saddened Lex. *Religion*—or more accurately, a personal relationship with the Lord—had brought him the only true joy and peace he had ever known. He prayed daily for his fiancée and hoped that in time she would accept Jesus also.

"Well, after we get married, I don't intend to restrict my friends to your narrow views. I plan to keep some liquor on hand to offer them when they come to visit me. And, of course, we'll have to give our fair share of parties."

"We'll see." Lex pressed his mouth together and turned onto the freeway. Nothing he'd ever said to her about his faith had gotten through yet. She couldn't see that true Christianity wasn't a mere religion or list of beliefs, but a way of life that had its core centered around a person, the Son of God—that every decision he made now he checked out first on his knees. But in time she'd see it was the only way to have lasting satisfaction and real peace in life.

"Could we live over here after we get married?" Brenda asked suddenly, breaking into his thoughts. "It would be much handier for me, since I teach dance at the Academy here. And it's so much livelier than Tehachapi."

Lex cocked his head. "Never gave it much thought. I'd be kind of far from the church."

"That's silly. There are churches all over the place."

"Maybe. But not ones that need me." Pulling into a parking space outside Casa de Miguel, his favorite Mexican restaurant, he turned out the lights and hurried around to assist Brenda.

❦

Callie jogged past the golf course and through the covered bridge on her way home a few nights later. The early evening air was breezy but mild, and off in the distance, a hang glider hovered above the mountains. She stopped and ran in place for several minutes, watching as it caught a thermal and spiraled upward. She wondered how it must feel to soar so freely on invisible currents, high above the noise and clatter of the world. She'd been so used to the ever-present drone of traffic and industry down in Bakersfield, it had taken some time to become accustomed to the stillness of the mountains. But already she loved the peace. Turning around, she continued on her route.

A songbird warbled in a California live oak along the way. Fascinated, Callie searched the dark green branches trying to pinpoint its location and discover the species.

So intent was she in her quest, she never even saw the uneven rock directly in her path. Her foot landed awkwardly and twisted, throwing her off balance as a stab of pain shot through her ankle.

As she sprawled into a heap, she fought the urge to moan. Sitting up and drawing several slow, deep breaths, she brushed off her hands, then rubbed her injured foot. *Dummy,* she thought with a grimace. *The first rule of running is to watch where you're going.*

Checking ahead of her, Callie realized she still had a considerable distance to go before she reached the condo. Behind her, the hilly terrain blocked from her view anyone who might have been in sight. She'd have to make it on her own.

After a few minutes' rest, she ran her tongue over her lips and struggled to stand. But the instant she tried to put weight on her ankle, she yelped and sank back down. It was too soon to attempt that feat. She'd wait awhile and try again.

The faraway drone of an engine grew gradually louder as it headed her way. She recognized the familiar expensive purr of the sports car and resisted the urge to confirm what her mind already suspected. Ignoring the sharp jabs of pain, she composed her expression to one of casual indifference as she effected a relaxed pose in the grass and tried to look engrossed in the view.

The vehicle downshifted and crested the knoll, then its musical horn sounded with "You Are My Sunshine" as it slowed to a stop abreast of her.

"What have we here?" Lex Sheridan asked incredulously. "The little health nut actually wasting precious time sitting in one spot? Winded? Out of breath?"

Callie didn't even have to look at him to know he wore a smirk. She raised her nose. "Just enjoying the fresh air, thanks."

"Ah. Well, then I won't distract you. You're almost out of daylight anyway. See you around, McRae."

She nodded. For the briefest second, she considered asking for his help but changed her mind. The last thing she needed was to be beholden to Alex Sheridan. But as the beginning notes of that idiotic tune blared again and he drove away, she sighed. "Well, that was brilliant."

Letting out an exasperated breath as the crown of the next hill swallowed the Corvette from her sight, Callie managed to get up again. She began hopping on one foot. But each hop jarred her other ankle, and before she'd gone six yards she eased back down to the ground. *Oh, Lord,* she prayed. *If I hadn't been so proud, I might at least have gotten a ride home. What am I going to do now?*

Dusk didn't last long in the mountains, Callie discovered. And sitting here wasn't getting her any closer to home. Steeling herself against the discomfort she knew was ahead, she started crawling on her hands and knees, biting her lip against the pain.

In his apartment, Lex strained his ear to hear the usual sounds from next door, but it was dead silent. There wasn't even a light on yet; he knew from making an unnecessary trip out to the car to get music he didn't need. She should have been home by now. Oh, well, he'd forgotten to pick up some milk anyway when he'd passed the convenience store. He might as well make another trip.

The minute the headlights picked up curly, chestnut hair, his jaw went slack. *Sitting again?* he thought, perplexed. He skidded to a stop, spraying gravel onto the side of the road. "What do you think you're doing?" he asked as she looked his way.

"I. . .um. . ."

"Are you okay, McRae?"

She moistened her lips and looked nervously about, then met his gaze without answering.

"Get in. I'll give you a ride home. You know it's not safe to be out alone after dark. Especially with the prison on the other end of this valley."

"Thanks, but I—"

Shaking his head in grim finality, Lex got out of the car. He stomped over to her and started lifting her under her armpits.

"Ow! Be careful," she gritted through her teeth. "My ankle."

"What?" Releasing his hold, Lex bent and scooped her up bodily. Despite the fact she was so little, he couldn't help but notice she felt amazingly solid in his arms. But he dismissed that notion and glared at her until she looked at him. "Boy, I really must have done some number on you when we were kids. You little dope, what were you planning to do, sit here by the road until tomorrow morning or the day after, until Trish reported you missing?"

"I don't know."

"Women." Emitting a disgusted breath over the concept that any person— and this one in particular—could hold grudges forever, he deposited her on the car seat as gently as his anger would allow. He couldn't believe a young woman who by all appearances seemed bright would knowingly refuse help when she needed it most. No telling what could have happened to her if some unsavory character had come by instead of him. It wasn't unusual for a bear to wander down from the more secluded and wooded areas of the mountain. "Would you like me to run you to the hospital in Lancaster?"

"No, I don't really think it's that bad."

"Your choice. Well, I'm on my way to the store. Do you need anything while we're there?"

She gave a sideways glance at him and shook her head.

"Okay. You'll be home in a few minutes then." Without so much as another look at her, he got in and drove the rest of the way in angry silence. This gal possessed an incredible knack for making him furious.

Callie chewed the inside of her lip until Lex came out of the store, a bag in each arm. He didn't even acknowledge her presence after he put the purchases into the trunk and got back into the car. She was almost afraid to look at him, knowing his jaw was set and his eyes blazing. She swallowed hard.

When they drew up in front of the condo, Lex got out and came around to her side.

"I–I can probably—"

"Be quiet, McRae." He swept her up unceremoniously and strode up the walk to her door. "Gimme your key."

His tone was not one to challenge, so she dug into her pocket and handed it over. Once the place was unlocked, he carried her inside, flicked on the light switch, and set her down on the living room sofa. On one knee, he took her swollen foot between his hands and raised it, examining it closely. He barely touched the outer edge of her ankle with his thumb as he eased off her shoe.

Callie winced and stiffened.

"Stay here. I'll be right back." He went out and in seconds she heard the trunk of the car slam shut. Then he returned with one of the sacks and took it into the kitchen. She heard him getting ice from the fridge. When he came back into the room, he propped her foot up on two throw pillows and put an ice bag against the swelling. "Keep this on your ankle for awhile. Is your store open on Saturdays?"

"Yes."

"Well, call Trish and tell her you won't be in tomorrow. Maybe Monday, if you stay off your foot, but even then you'll have to take it real easy."

"But I have to—"

Lex narrowed his eyes, and the sparks from them silenced her. "You're going to stay put tomorrow, McRae, or so help me, I'll go let the air out of your tires right now. It's up to you."

Pressing her lips together, Callie dutifully held out a hand, and he gave her the phone.

It rang only twice before her partner's cheery voice came over the wire. "Hello?"

"Hi. It's me."

"Callie?"

"Yes. Listen, Trish." She drew a calming breath. "You're going to hate me, but I had a little mishap while I was jogging."

"What? Are you okay?"

"Yes. I'm fine, but my ankle isn't. I don't think I'll be able to come to the shop in the morning. If I stay off of it, I should be in on Monday. I'm really sorry."

"Hey, well, an accident is an accident. I can get by without you for a day. With your move and all, I'm getting pretty good at it lately." She giggled at her own barb, and then her voice softened. "You're okay? Truly?"

"Mm-hm. I really owe you, Trish."

"Yeah, I know. One of these days I'll collect too. Count on it."

"I will. Bye."

Lex took the phone and put it beside Callie on the glass end table. "There, now. That wasn't so hard, was it?"

She didn't dignify the remark with an answer but kept her eyes fastened on his hands which were clenched at his sides. Had they really been so gentle only a few minutes ago? Taking control of her wandering thoughts, Callie flicked a gaze up at him.

One corner of his mouth curved and he chuckled. "You have got to be the most stubborn female I've ever known." He took her hands, turned them over, and shook his head. Lex headed into the bathroom, and Callie heard him turn on a faucet and open cabinet doors. He returned with a warm washcloth and sponged the scratches. After dabbing on peroxide with a cotton ball, he added some soothing ointment. "I'll get you some pain medicine, then I'll go home for awhile. But you'd better still be on this couch when I come back."

Chapter 5

Despite the throbbing in her left ankle, Callie sat so still she almost didn't breathe. She reached for the remote control and clicked on the TV, hoping to take her mind off the pain. When she came across an old film already in progress on the movie classics channel, she settled back and found herself drawn at once into the funny love story. It seemed everyone in the production could see that Lucille Ball and James Ellison were made for each other—that is, everyone but them. Smiling inwardly, Callie assured herself that in real life things didn't happen that way.

Halfway through the movie, Callie heard Lex's footsteps outside, and, as he entered, she turned off the TV. He placed a tray he'd brought with him on her lap without a word before turning his attention to her propped foot. "How's it doing?"

"A little better, actually. It's still throbbing, but not as bad as it was." Looking down at the snack he'd brought, Callie's eyes came to rest gratefully on a cup of tea. She took a sip and allowed the soothing warmth to penetrate her being. Assessing the other offerings, she knew it would take all she could do to eat the grilled cheese sandwich, what with the abundance of cholesterol and fat to consider. But she had to admit it looked and smelled delicious. She figured she could undo the damage with added exercise later on.

Hesitantly, she picked up half of the sandwich and took a bite. She had serious doubts that her gratitude would so easily excuse the custard-filled donut off to one side, but perhaps if she ate slowly enough he'd be gone before she got to that.

Lex removed a rolled elastic bandage from his pocket and started at the arch of her foot, wrapping the long strip into a secure figure eight. He pinned the end with the silver clips, then stood. "Well, there's not enough discoloration for it to be broken. If you just stay off it this weekend as much as possible, you should notice some improvement by Monday. Now, where are your pajamas, or whatever it is you sleep in?"

"What?"

"Oh, come on, McRae. Let me save you from hobbling around, at least for tonight."

Callie could not fault his logic, but that didn't make it any easier for her to reconcile herself to this new helpful side of Alex Sheridan. Nevertheless, she did need some assistance at the moment, so she heard herself acquiesce. "In my second dresser drawer, left side. Anything will do."

With a nod, Lex strode down the hall to the bedroom. He couldn't help but notice the contrast between her apartment, with its fresh, airy decorating scheme, and his own stark white walls and heavy furnishings. Not even her bedroom furniture broke the mood of the rest of the place. Obviously from a quality manufacturer, the natural rattan was a nice touch. A fluffy comforter and matching decorator valance in a watercolor light green and peach had the same ivory background as the vertical blinds. Framed prints on the walls echoed the soft pastels. Caralyn McRae had very feminine taste, and he found it surprisingly pleasant and restful here.

He drew open the drawer she had specified, and his eyes flared wide. Neatly folded lay a classy assortment of all kinds of wispy things with spaghetti straps and ruffles and lace. Imagining how pretty and feminine she must look every night, he had to suppress a smile.

Put a lid on it, Sheridan, he reminded himself. *She's short, remember? A guy has to break his back just to bend down and look at her. And you're merely the errand boy for the evening—not to mention engaged.*

Expelling a lungful of air, he chose a white satin nightshirt with lacy ruffles around its scoop neckline and sleeves and set it on the bathroom counter. A quick check confirmed that her short terry robe hung on the hook inside the door. Then he went back to the living room. "Okay," he announced. "Bedtime."

"Hey, I can put my own self—"

Her words drifted off as he swept her up and carried her to the bathroom. "Give a yell when you're dressed." With that he left, closing the door on his way.

Back at the couch, Lex noticed the sandwich was gone, but the donut remained. With a shrug, he gulped it down almost whole and set the tray on the table by the entrance.

Glancing in the mirror, Callie wondered if the abundance of color on her cheeks was from sunburn or embarrassment, then quickly discarded either possibility. Her dangling ankle ached profusely as she stood on her good foot with her left knee bent. Quickly as she could, she peeled off her ruined Dior sweats, freshened up and brushed her teeth, then changed into her nightie. Inching over to her robe, she tugged it down and put it on, tying the belt as snugly as possible. She opened the bathroom door and looked at her bed a mile across the room. Much as she would have preferred to hop to it on her own, the mere thought of the pain she'd have to endure ended that inclination. "I'm ready," she called out.

In seconds Lex strode in from the hall. He flipped back the comforter and top sheet, then came and swept her up effortlessly and carried her to the bed, where he put her down as if he were handling the world's most expensive porcelain. "Okay to use your spare pillow to prop your foot?"

She nodded and lay back while he elevated her injury and then covered her.

"That's it, then. There's some pain medicine and a glass of water here on the bedside table. Anything else I can get you before you go to sleep?"

"No, I don't think so."

"Well, I'll be off. If you need any help in the morning, call me. I put my number there by your phone. Night, McRae." He turned and started down the hall.

Callie swallowed. "Hey, wait," she called.

His returning footsteps sounded, and he peered around the doorjamb.

"It. . .it was. . .nice of you to help me. Thank you."

His even brows rose high on his forehead as a disbelieving smile quirked over his mouth. "All part of my penance. Past wrongs, and all that sort of rot. Sleep well."

Callie couldn't help smiling in return as he left. She struggled out of her robe, then settled back against her pillow and tried to get comfortable as she heard the front door close after Lex.

Who would have expected His Highness, Alex the III, to take it upon himself to see to her welfare? The memory of the granite expression and the hard set of his jaw when they'd been in the car rose to taunt her, and so did the gentleness of his touch, the kindness in his tone. If he hadn't been truly concerned, his talent was going to waste in the music business. He should go to Hollywood and try to break into acting.

She plumped the pillow beneath her head and lay back down as her thoughts drifted on unchecked. Some women would probably consider Lex the perfect romantic lead for a movie, with his smoldering blue eyes, the mischievous grin, the muscled arms, and quiet strength that only added to his appeal. She, on the other hand, knew what he was really like—the complete opposite of everything she considered ideal in a man. Crossing her arms determinedly, Callie gave a little huff and forced her mind in Ken's direction. Ken! He should hear about her accident.

Wincing as she leaned over for the phone, Callie took a deep breath and dialed her fiancé's number.

"Hello?" came his pleasantly intoned voice.

"Hi, Honey. It's Callie."

"Funny, I was just about to call you, Cal. What's up?"

"Not too much. I just thought I'd better let you know I won't be driving down to Bakersfield for church on Sunday."

"Too far already? And you haven't even been there a week."

"No, it's not that. I've had a little mishap. I sprained my ankle and have to stay off it for a couple of days."

"Oh." Disappointment colored his voice. "See? I knew if I left you all on your own up in the boondocks, you'd get into trouble."

"What? It had nothing to do with my being here by myself, Ken. It was just an accident. It could have happened anywhere."

"I see," he said grudgingly. "Well, you're okay, then, aren't you? I'll come up after church and take you for a drive. How about that?"

"Sure, I'd like that. I'll see you when you get here."

"Okay. Take care, Cal. Love you."

The hasty click on the other end of the line made any reply unnecessary. With a sigh, Callie replaced the receiver and settled back, becoming more irritated by the second. *He sure was concerned,* she thought facetiously. *Couldn't ask enough questions about my injury. But how like him to jump on the chance for an I-told-you-so.* Callie clenched her teeth. Oh, well, she'd probably called at some inopportune time, when he had his nose buried in a tax reference book or something equally dull. He'd undoubtedly be more thoughtful when he came up the day after tomorrow.

⁂

Lex punched his defenseless pillow so hard that a seam bulged to near breaking. He ordered himself to relax. Laying his head into the depression his fist had made, he tried to put Callie McRae out of his mind. How could anyone who seemed so bright on the surface have such a hidden stubborn streak? She might have done serious injury to that ankle if he hadn't come along.

Yeah, same old Caralyn. She might have curbed that childish inclination to stick out that bottom lip of hers, and possibly resisted the impulse to cross her arms, but her nose had been raised so high it was a wonder the thing hadn't popped out of joint. Imagine a tiny girl like that out there in the dark alone. What was wrong with that wimp boyfriend he'd seen ringing her doorbell a few nights ago? He shouldn't be letting her run loose like that anyway.

Lex did have to admire her spunk, though. From experience, he knew she was in considerable pain, yet she'd barely uttered a sound the whole time he'd been with her. Only the minuscule crease between her slender eyebrows gave any indication of her discomfort. And, he had to admit, it did seem kind of gratifying to see her with grubby knees and hands, with those soft brown curls in windy disarray. Come to think of it, he hadn't checked her knees to be sure they didn't need some salve too. Oh, well. It was a miracle that she'd allowed him to help her at all, after all the pranks he'd pulled on her when they were kids. But then, she'd always been the perfect target.

Lex suppressed the urge to chuckle as a few incidents came to mind. But once they started, an amazing number of them paraded by—an endless line, in fact, of thoughtless deeds. His initial humor swiftly dissolved to guilt. As the conviction grew too strong to ignore, he soon realized he could never feel comfortable in his relationship with Jesus until he started building a bridge between him and his new neighbor. He grimaced at the thought of her hostility. It wouldn't be easy.

Lex slid out of bed onto his knees.

Chapter 6

Despite a few sleep interruptions during the night to take more pain medication, Callie awakened fairly rested the following morning. By early afternoon, she noticed that although she still couldn't put her full weight on her ankle, at least it was possible to get from one room to another on her own.

It felt strange to be at home on a Saturday, normally the busiest day of the week at the shop. But she had to admit that it was a treat to be free to enjoy the glorious spring day. Through her open windows, she could hear the gentle breeze ruffling the wild grasses beneath the clear sky, while birds chirped their joyous songs across meadows and treetops.

With a sigh, Callie took her Bible and a tumbler of iced herbal tea out onto the deck and lowered herself onto the chaise. She gave a brief prayer, then smoothed out her mauve velour sweats and opened to the leather bookmark for her current reading, in Second Chronicles. Alternately fascinating and tedious with its accounts of righteous kings and wicked kings, Callie read it every year on her way through the Bible.

She lingered today, as always, over the passage where King Hezekiah, of Judah, pleaded with God for his life to be spared and was granted an added fifteen years. It seemed beyond belief that after being the recipient of such a miracle, the king—who had once been dedicated to the spiritual welfare of his people—hadn't lived those extended days in thankfulness and praise but instead became proud and exulted in his own accomplishments rather than in God's goodness.

Pride was responsible for many a downfall, Callie mused, and it was a factor even in her own life. Just last night, her conscience had pricked her as she lay in bed. She knew she should have been more appreciative of Alex Sheridan's ministrations, yet she had resisted all but a grudging, mumbled thank you. But, her other half reminded her, the opinion of him that she harbored inside had been acquired over many years. One good deed seemed less than sufficient reason to change it.

The sliding door on Lex's side opened just then, and Callie held her breath while he came out to the edge of the deck and paused at his banister. Apparently unaware of her presence, he yawned and stretched, his long tanned arm visible from her position. He inhaled deeply and turned, then leaned to peer around the dividing lattice. Shirtless, his blond hair still mussed, he quirked a half-smile and flicked a gaze at her foot. "How is it this morning?"

"Afternoon," Callie corrected. Immediately, she felt waspish as his expression hardened. "It's, um, feeling better."

"Keeping off it?"

She nodded. For a fleeting second, she expected him to say more, but a resigned look settled over his features and he merely gave a hint of a polite smile.

"Well, see you around, McRae." Stepping out of sight, he returned inside, and she heard the door slide closed.

Callie released a breath. *Well, that was sure sweet of you, Girl*, she thought. *What a display of gratitude. Maybe you don't have to act like the two of you are best buddies, but you're both grown up. It could be possible he's trying to extend an olive branch your way. You might at least give the guy the benefit of the doubt.*

Settling back in the chaise, she opened her Bible and tried to read another chapter. But her mind refused to cooperate, and the words ran together before her eyes. When she heard the Corvette drive away shortly after that, an oppressive silence settled around her.

❦❦❦

"Missed you this morning at church," Ken said as he helped Callie hobble to his green Volvo the next afternoon. "You'd have liked the sermon."

"Oh?"

"Yeah. It was about how managing our lives is like gardening, cultivating new ideas, weeding out negative influences, that sort of thing." Reaching the car, Ken opened the door for her.

"Interesting concept." Callie sat and gingerly positioned her bandaged foot, then reached for the seat belt while Ken went around to his side. "Where are we going?" she asked as he got in and turned the key.

"Ridgecrest, and possibly Apple Valley."

Callie quenched the wish that he'd have said they'd be taking the Kern River Canyon to Lake Isabella. It was out of the way, she knew, and they were getting off to a late start. But still, the winter rains had added welcome volume to the lake after several years of drought had severely depleted the water level. It would have been refreshing to see it for herself. She inhaled slowly and watched the road ahead. "Getting rested up after your trip?" she asked after several minutes of silence passed.

"Hm? Oh, yeah." Ken reached over and squeezed her hand. "You know, Cal, I've been thinking. It's silly for you to have your money invested in that dinky little shop in a place like Tehachapi. You should be in Bakersfield, where I could look after you, and all that."

His proprietary tone irked her, and the passing spring green landscape lost its luster as she drew her hand away. "What do you mean, look after me?"

"You know. If you had to go running, at least you'd be on level roads with sidewalks. You'd never have tripped and hurt yourself."

Callie raised her chin. "I didn't trip. I wasn't watching where I was going."

"What's the difference? You wouldn't have to pay attention if you were on flat land."

"Ken, I don't want to talk about this. I'm very happy in partnership with Trish, and the business is doing fine."

"Maybe."

"Ken," she warned, frowning at him.

"Okay, okay." Raising one hand in concession, he shrugged.

Callie observed her fiancé across the seat. His neat, navy-checked shirt with its button-down collar and sleeves rolled to the elbow, a birthday gift from her last year, went well with his fair skin. Dark hairs on his arm curled over the brown leather band of the watch she had given him for Christmas from the shop. No doubt about it, from his impeccably groomed head to the toes of his shiny wing-tips, Ken looked every inch the self-reliant young executive.

Ken glanced in the rearview mirror, then passed a slower vehicle as he turned north. Steering into the right-hand lane again, he brushed a lock of hair away from Callie's eyes and smiled. "I just care about what happens to you. I love you."

"I know," she said on a sigh. "I love you too. I just don't want to argue about anything today."

"Then we won't. Let's just enjoy being together. After all, I don't get to see you every night now that you moved up here, which is taking some getting used to, I might add." He paused. "Now that you've got the store off the ground, have you given any thought to setting a date?"

Callie shrugged. It did seem different now that they lived in different towns. She had time on her hands nearly every night. And he didn't even phone that much, now that it involved long-distance expense. But that seemed a poor reason to jump into a major decision involving lifelong commitment. "I'm just not ready yet."

"Well, think about it, will you? I don't like all the space you put between us."

"I will."

❧❀❧

Lex's headlights picked up the green Volvo parked on the street behind Callie's car when he came home from dropping Brenda off after church. He pulled up and stopped in back of it. When he turned off the ignition, angry voices carried from outside the condo, where Lex could see his neighbor and some guy in glasses glaring at one another on her doorstep.

"But it doesn't make sense, Cal," came the man's voice. "I wish you'd see it my way for a change."

With her arms crossed, Callie tapped a fingertip against her forearm as Lex had seen her do dozens of times in their past encounters. "I don't agree. You knew I had this chance, and you could just as easily have said something back then, before Trish and I formed the partnership."

"Guess I figured you had brains enough to come to the smart conclusion on your own," the man replied stubbornly.

Hesitating as long as he could without appearing obvious, Lex took his guitar case from the passenger seat and strode up the walk.

"That is the most chauvinistic thing you have ever said to me. I can't believe you're so—so—" Callie's dark eyes flashed in Lex's direction, and she clamped her lips together.

He cleared his throat as he approached them. "Everything okay here?" he asked in a casual tone.

The man snapped his head around and peered through his wire glasses. "Yeah, Pal. Buzz off."

"Sorry. I live here." Ignoring the pair, Lex inserted his key into the lock and let himself in. But after setting the instrument down, he left the door open a crack.

"Maybe you'd just better go, Ken," came Callie's voice. "This discussion isn't accomplishing anything."

"Well, I think it is, and I have a few more points to make. You might as well hear them so you'll get the whole picture."

Lex curled his fingers inward just listening to the guy's belligerent attitude.

"Look," she reasoned. "It's been a long day. I'm tired, I have a headache, and my ankle's sore. I just want to go back inside and be by myself."

"Not 'til I've said a few more things."

"Come on, Ken," Callie groaned. "Give it a rest. It's pointless. You're not going to change my mind."

"You seem awfully sure of that."

Having reached his limit, Lex stepped outside and tapped the man's shoulder. "I believe the lady asked you to leave, Friend."

A good three inches short of Lex's over six foot height, Ken glowered over the tops of his glasses. "Butt out."

"I will. Just as soon as you trot down to that crate at the end of the walk and take off." Already Lex's fists ached to rearrange the guy's preppie face. "Or do you need some help?"

Ken shot a look at Callie, then back at Lex. He let out a disgusted snort. "There's not much reason to hang around here. That's for sure." Turning on his heel, he stomped to the Volvo, got in, and slammed the door.

Lex heard Callie release a pent-up breath as the car drove away. She swallowed, and a faint rose tint crested her cheeks in the porch light as she raised her lashes. "I'm sorry. That was my fiancé, Ken Vincent. He's not usually like that."

Lex shrugged. "A guy should know when he's worn out his welcome—however temporarily that might be."

A small smile softened her lips.

He glanced down at her foot. "Need help getting in?"

"No. Thanks, though, for asking. I'm fine, really." She peered down the road as the taillights from Ken's car mounted a distant hill, then disappeared. "We were just having a bad day."

He gave a nod. "Well, night, then. Take care."

Callie lifted a hand in a wave as Lex turned and went inside. A beam of light illuminated the stoop just before his door closed.

She glanced down the empty road once more and grimaced. Ken sure had been in a strange mood. He'd never acted as though he owned her before. She couldn't help but wonder if this were a new side of him just being revealed, or just his frustration over her hesitancy to set a wedding date.

Not even tempted to put on the ten o'clock news, Callie freshened up and dressed for bed early, knowing it would feel good just to be off her foot. Turning on a lamp, she took the most recent issue of *Brides* magazine out of the stack on the far end of the counter, then hobbled back to the bedroom to change. Moments later, after plumping her pillows behind her, she relaxed against them and opened the magazine, leafing idly through the pages. She hadn't even decided whether she wanted a big wedding or a smaller, more intimate one, let alone in which season of the year to plan it. But this two-year engagement had to come to an end sometime. Everyone expected it. Once she and Ken were married, things would settle down. After all, there'd be no reason to argue over jobs or places of residence.

As she perused various wedding gowns and formal wear among the glossy pictures, a tea-length dress in delicate pink chantilly lace captured her attention. Callie lost herself in its simple, yet elegant, design. *The identical versions in ivory and white are equally lovely,* she mused, *and the style would be suitable for anytime of the year.* A turn of the page brought a more modern off-shoulder fashion into view, and her eyes lingered on the cut and draping of the whispery embroidered chiffon over satin. Deciding finally that the decision would present more difficulty than she had anticipated, she closed the book and put it aside.

Soft guitar music, moody and slow, drifted from next door, and for once Callie lay back and listened. She didn't recall Alex Sheridan's playing any instruments during their growing-up years, but then she'd never inquired after any of his possible interests either. All she had cared about was keeping out of his way, lest he yank her hair, tape a "Please whistle" sign on her back, or flip her schoolbooks out of her grasp. Now, despite his appearance as a member of some rock band, the enchanting melody that hovered, breathless, on the spring night belied that impression. Apparently somewhere along the way Lex had acquired some actual talent.

Thinking back on the evening, it had been kind of a shock when Lex had "invited" Ken to leave. No doubt she could have accomplished the same thing herself eventually, but still, it had come as no small relief not to have to do so. And the flabbergasted look on Ken's face had been comical, almost priceless. Oh, well, she decided, once her fiancé finished sulking he'd be over their difference of opinion. Things would get back to normal.

Callie switched off the bedside lamp and stared up at the ceiling as the lilting music caressed her ears.

Resting within the canopy of a huge weeping willow, Callie sat up and blinked her eyes, more refreshed than she'd ever felt in her life. A breeze played across the long fronds like an angel harp, plucking notes and chords in a melody that rose and fell like ocean breakers against the sand. Above the boughs, a great bird dipped and soared in perfect time with the tempo of the sweet, swelling refrain.

She stood, reveling in the feel of the cool sand beneath her bare feet, and ran down to the water's edge, where the salty breeze rustled her long skirt about her like a frothy cloud of mist. Idly, she tried to hold the fragile snowy satin in place with one hand, aware suddenly that in her other she held an exquisite arrangement of flowers, white and pure. The time had come, she knew. He would be here soon.

Brushing a fold of filmy tulle away from her eyes, she scanned the seashore, trying to pick out his dark head in the distance. Finally she saw him hurrying her way, arms opened wide. She smiled and started running toward him, hoping to shorten the distance by half.

As he drew near, she flung herself into his embrace. They had waited forever for this moment.

The ocean paused, motionless, while their lips met in a joyous kiss. Afterward, the waves swirled around their feet, bubbles of white foam that tickled their skin. Callie raised her lashes, eager to fill her vision with his darkly handsome face.

But the eyes that smiled down at her were not gray but deep blue. And the head bent so tenderly above hers was not dark, but sun-streaked and sandy—as Lex smiled at her!

Callie's heart stopped for a breathless instant. She gasped and drew in a huge draught of air. Panting, she gulped another.

Bolting upright, she clutched the sheet to her breast and swallowed as she tried to still her breathing.

Could it be? In the strange netherlands known as sleep, could she actually have dreamed of Lex Sheridan? She must have lost her mind.

But the tumultuous feelings that had stormed within her in her dream would not go away.

Chapter 7

Callie made her way cautiously to the back door of the shop Monday morning, favoring her ankle. Though still tender, the swelling had gone down, and she found she could walk on it with care. "Trish?" she called out, entering the office. "I'm here."

Almost at once, a French door opened and her redheaded partner rushed in from the salesroom as Callie sat down at the desk. "Welcome back. How is your foot?" She peered across the cluttered desktop. "Did the doctor say you could resume your normal life already?"

"I didn't see a doctor, actually."

"What? Why not? How do you know you should be out on it then?"

Callie gave Trish a wry smile. "Because it feels better. Trust me." Leaning over, she placed her purse in the bottom desk drawer.

"Well, how in the world did you manage to get home that night? You did say it happened while you were jogging, right?"

"Yes." Hedging, Callie cleared her throat. "I. . .um. . .had some help. Somebody came by."

"Oh. Well, that's a relief. I'm glad there are still strangers in this world one can trust. Who was it?"

For the first time she could remember, Callie found Trish's normal inquisitiveness somewhat overbearing. She fussed with one of the tiny pleats down the front of her mauve blouse. "It was, um. . ." She averted her gaze. "Alex Sheridan." No longer able to avoid the inevitable, she looked up.

A most annoying smile widened Trish's face as a smug expression brightened her eyes. "Oh. Well. No wonder I'm having to drag all the lurid details out of you. So are you going to tell me the rest of it now, or do I have to die of curiosity?" Grabbing a folding chair along the wall, she tugged it close to the desk and plopped onto it. She rested her chin in her upturned palm and grinned.

Callie mentally counted to ten, then exhaled. Too late to hope Trish would give up for lack of interest. "It's no big deal, really. He just gave me a ride home, then bandaged my ankle and left."

"Yeah, right. And our bid on that oceanfront property in Arizona was accepted too."

"Come on, Trish. Maybe he was a Boy Scout out looking for a good deed; I don't know. He just happened along after I fell." Purposely, Callie omitted that he had, in fact, *happened by* twice before she got home and once more afterward. And she didn't allow her own mind to dwell on his concern that seemed entirely sincere or how gently he had ministered to her injury. A flash of her unexplainable dream surfaced, but she dismissed it as quickly as it had come.

Trish stared long and hard, then with a sigh, perused the nails on her right hand. She blew on them before rubbing them lightly against her dove gray blouse. "I suppose Mr. Personality came rushing right up to be at your side."

A flush started upward over Callie's face as she focused her attention beyond her partner's slender frame. "Well, he. . .um. . .came yesterday and took me for a drive."

Trish coughed and got up, crossing to the coffeepot. She poured herself a cup and took a sip. "Let's see. . .you were hurt on Friday, right? And—"

"Come on," Callie interrupted none too patiently. "I'm a big girl now. I don't need anyone to hold my hand or kiss my boo-boos better. Anyway, Ken has another life, you know."

Swallowing a mouthful of the rich brew, Trish nodded slowly.

"Why is it that you don't like him all of a sudden?" Callie asked.

"I wouldn't say it's all of a sudden, exactly," her friend admitted. "It's just—now that I'm married, I see things differently from the way I used to."

"Like what?"

"Like a person's idiosyncracies. Like faults that will never go away but will forever be a part of that someone which somebody else will have to live with. That kind of thing."

Callie pondered the statement momentarily before speaking again. "I love Ken."

"I'm sure you do. But—" Turning away, Trish set down her empty mug.

"But what?" Callie said, prompting her. "You might as well finish what you've started. Who knows, perhaps what I'm imagining you mean might be worse than your answer."

Trish exhaled and swiveled on her heel, meeting Callie's gaze. "Look, I don't hate the guy. He's decent enough. He's bright and successful. But. . .personally, I don't think you're *in* love with him. Besides, the guy has no lips."

"Excuse me?" Realizing her mouth was gaping, Callie shut it. Only the life-long friendship she had known over the years kept her from taking offense at Trish's judgmental remark.

"You asked." Trish straightened matter-of-factly and checked her watch, then started toward the salesroom. "Time to open. Anyway, you'd better take it easy today. If you handle the phone and stuff back here, I can look after whatever customers happen to come in."

Callie gawked after her partner's departing back and reached for the delivery log to see if any shipments might have arrived in her absence. Then, suddenly thirsty, she rose and hobbled over to the coffeepot.

But Trish's comments hung suspended in her thoughts even as she downed a whole cup black and poured another to take to the desk.

❧❧❧❧

Lex smiled when Brenda's voice came on the line. "Hello?"

"Hi, Love," he answered. "Listen, it's Mom's birthday. I was wondering if you'd like to be in on the celebration. They're having a little family barbecue tonight. Nothing elaborate."

"Sure. Sounds lovely. When shall I be ready?"

"An hour good enough?"

"I'll do my best."

"Mm," he teased. "Like you have a problem looking beautiful."

"Maybe not for you, anyway," she said on a light note. "See you in awhile."

Lex showered and changed into tan jeans and a red open-necked sport shirt. It had been weeks since he'd visited his parents, and he was looking forward to the evening.

Brenda's bright floral skirt and white silk blouse, Lex decided upon seeing her when he went to pick her up, complemented both her lustrous tan and his own clothes. He reveled in the knowledge that the two of them blended in so many ways. His mother and father thought a lot of Brenda. They had met her during business dealings with her parents years before he and she ever actually met, and it was through their urging that the two began dating. When he and Brenda finally announced their engagement, both families had been pleased.

Turning onto the circular drive of his parents' hacienda, as he'd laughingly named their sprawling Spanish-style home in Bakersfield, he admired the manicured grounds that during his childhood he'd always had to be careful not to damage. One of the city's leading building contractors, Lex's father, Alexander Sheridan II, kept his residence picture-perfect as a prime example of his skill. Each Christmas the display of brilliant-colored lights that adorned the property drew hordes of cars through Starlane Heights, a development "In the Sheridan Style," as the company motto proclaimed. Though the other homes in the development were slightly more modest in comparison, all showed the quality of the Sheridan touch.

"Well, we're here," Lex announced, pulling up before the triple garage alongside the ivory stuccoed dwelling. He got out and went around to Brenda's side.

"I'll probably need my sweater," she said, accepting his hand. She reached inside and removed it from her seat back.

Going in through the side gate, they could already see several people clustered near the gazebo and others at the pool. Blue-green underwater lights glowed softly against the dusky sky, accenting the irregular contours of the tiled, scalloped edge. Japanese lanterns outlined the entire backyard, their glowing orbs casting circles of color along the grass and sculptured shrubs.

"Oh, Lex, Dear," his mother gushed, coming toward them. "And Brenda. We're so glad you both could make it."

Lex smiled and wrapped an arm around her compact, motherly form as he bestowed a kiss on the top of her silver blond hairdo and inhaled her expensive perfume. Beneath his fingers, the rich texture of the sparkly plum-colored ensemble she wore bespoke its elegance. "Happy birthday, Mom."

"Yes, happy birthday," Brenda echoed. She also leaned forward and hugged her.

"Your parents should be here shortly," his mom told her with a bright smile, then looked up at Lex. "This started out just for the family, but you know how things get out of hand once your father lets the word slip. Oh, excuse me, I see Dwayne and Evelyn Shore arriving." Giving Lex's arm a squeeze, she nodded to them both and took her leave.

Lex swept a glance to the huge, built-in barbecue which took up a good portion of an alcove along the back wall of the house. His father, in chef's apron and hat, attended a huge slab of beef on a rotating spit. He grinned and waved a spatula.

Lex waved back, extending the greeting to include a few other familiar faces. "Let's have a seat, shall we?" he said, guiding Brenda by the elbow to some vacant lawn chairs near the water. He grabbed two cups of punch as they passed a table laden with finger foods and beverages.

"I love this place," she breathed, her eyes shining as she drank in the surroundings. "It's just the thing I hope to have someday. I'll love playing hostess to all our friends."

Lex offered her a drink, then sank into the chair beside hers. Recognizing the bite of alcohol in his first taste, he poured the remainder of it on the grass and set the cup down as Brenda sipped hers with obvious relish. He let his gaze wander idly about the grounds.

Situated prominently on the highest elevation in the development, the hacienda occupied three choice, oversized lots and had a sweeping view of the country club golf course. But despite his parents' affluence, Lex knew they were well liked by their neighbors and respected all over town.

He tried to picture himself living once more in such a setting, raising a family of restless boys who were forbidden—as he and his younger brother had been—to touch anything lest they mar the perfect beauty. He'd have much preferred some sturdy swings or a fort, or even a tree house to romp in. But lacking those, it somehow seemed easier to expend his boundless energy in other directions. *Which had been unfortunate for poor Caralyn McRae,* he thought with chagrin.

"Oh, there's Mom and Dad," Brenda remarked, swinging her legs over the side of the chaise. "Think I'll go say hi."

"Sure," Lex said. "I'll go to the car and get the gifts we brought for the birthday girl." He waved and grinned at the newcomers, pausing to give Brenda's mother a hug and shake her father's hand on the way to the gate.

When the meal was at last ready to eat, Brenda and Lex found a spot in line and started filling their plates with the succulent beef, roast potatoes and corn, garden salad, and rolls. Lex reached for a Coke, while Brenda accepted more punch, then they took seats at one of several round linen-covered umbrella tables scattered about the lawn.

Both sets of parents joined them. Mrs. Harding, a delicately boned, reserved woman of rare beauty not unlike her daughter's, chose the chair next to Brenda. Mr. Harding, a commanding presence anywhere, took the one next to his wife. He rested one of his fine, soft, attorney hands, as well groomed as the rest of him, on the tablecloth beside his plate. "I'm so glad this is a grand night," Lex's mother said as she chose the next spot. "They said it might rain again."

"Oh, I think it'll stay mostly in the mountains, Muffy," Lex's father declared. "It's getting too late for showers down in the valley." Tugging out a chair, he put his brimming plate on the tablecloth and sat, and he and the others started right in eating.

Lex quietly bowed his head for a brief prayer of thanks, then sliced off a chunk of meat. "How's business?" he asked his father.

"Booming, as always. Sure glad Jeff decided to jump in and help," he said pointedly. "Though it was your place, as the oldest."

"Yeah, I know. But he's the one with the interest in building, remember? I wouldn't have been much use in the company."

"Nonsense. Anybody can learn a trade. It's not like you're a moron."

Lex emitted a silent sigh as he watched his father eat in his usual hearty fashion. His skin, tanned and leathery from years in the California sun, glowed a rich bronze. Lex knew his father's greatest joy had always been to work right alongside his men, setting an example of dependability and quality they followed with deepest loyalty. And since Lex's younger brother, Jeff, had gone into construction right out of engineering school, it released Lex from the burden of guilt he'd felt since choosing music as his field. "Where *is* Jeff, anyway?" he finally asked.

His father swallowed. "Finishing up on a job site over in the southwest part of town. He should be here pretty soon."

Awhile later, after the buffet table had sat idle for ten minutes in a row, a serving girl hired for the evening wheeled out a huge sheet cake ablaze with lit candles. Everyone rose and sang "Happy Birthday." Lex's mom made a wish and blew out as many of the flames as humanly possible, then laughed as those around her came to her rescue and finished the job.

"Sure wish I could see inside some of those presents," Lex's father teased, eyeing the stack while he cut the cake and passed it around. "Hurry up, Muffy, and eat."

Blushing, she chewed a dainty portion. "No matter what they contain, the thing that would make me happiest is to hear that my oldest son will be taking this lovely young woman for his wife." She inclined her head in Brenda's direction. "I'm getting anxious for some grandchildren to spoil."

The laughter that followed made Lex feel warm around his collar. He shifted in his chair, then got up and brought over a small wrapped gift, which he handed to her. "All in good time, Mom. In the meantime, I hope you like this."

He watched her unwrap the box and lift the turquoise necklace and matching earrings from the enclosed tissue paper. He almost missed his mother's delighted response as he recalled his own surprise at discovering that the little fashion boutique where he'd bought the jewelry had belonged to Callie and Trish.

☙ ❧

"I had a really lovely time, Darling," Brenda said on her doorstep two hours later. A few light sprinkles misted the night air from scattered clouds above as she snuggled close and turned up her face. "Want to come in?"

"Naw. It's late. I'd better go home. I'm supposed to go with the guys to L.A. early tomorrow morning to look at some new amplifiers for church."

"Whatever." Her shoulders sagged as she gave a sniff of disappointment.

Lex smiled and brushed his mouth across hers. "Hey, I'm leaving as much for your benefit as my own, you know."

"Why? You don't have to," she murmured meaningfully.

"Yes, I do. There's a little matter of right and wrong at stake here."

She grimaced and held the diamond solitaire on her third finger up to him. "I already belong to you. I don't see what difference a dumb ceremony makes."

"It makes all the difference." He kissed the tip of her nose and grinned sheepishly in the glow of the outside light.

"So you say. Well, why don't we at least start making some concrete plans, then? When do you want to get married, Lex?"

He thought for a moment. Brenda felt warm and inviting in his arms. And right. His parents loved her. Hers seemed to look forward to having him for a son-in-law. They all wanted grandchildren in their lifetime. But yet— He expelled a deep breath. "I'll have to get back to you on that."

Resignation drew her eyebrows into a frown as a harsh note made its way into her voice. "Know what? I'm beginning to wonder if you ever will." Taking her key out of his grasp, she unlocked her door and went inside without another word.

Hands in his pockets, Lex stared after her as the door shut in his face. Her comment replayed itself in his mind as he trudged back to his car.

Chapter 8

U nable to sleep, Callie got out of bed and slipped into her robe, leaving the ends of the belt untied and dangling loosely for comfort. She didn't bother to turn on a light as she pulled on a pair of knitted scuffies and went out to the kitchen. She took a bottle of Perrier from the fridge and sipped the sparkling water as she opened the back door and stared outside.

Storm clouds from earlier that evening had drifted off, and now a full moon frosted the treetops and occasional faraway rooflines in glowy, glistening white. A pair of crickets chirped in regular cadence, calling first from one side of the house and then the other. But aside from their chorus, even the wind was quiet. The whole week had been unseasonably mild, indicating the possibility of an early summer.

Deciding it was much too nice a night to waste, Callie stepped onto the wooden deck and lowered herself onto the chaise, her hands crossed over her abdomen as she gazed up at the few stars visible beyond the roof overhang. Life was so relaxing here that she doubted she'd ever willingly live in the city again. She supposed Ken was still mad about their difference of opinion the other night. He hadn't phoned for days, which was unusual for him, and confirmed her suspicions that he still hadn't forgiven her for daring to express an opinion which differed from his. *Surely he wouldn't always be so bullheaded,* she assured herself. Once they were married, they'd have more time together and would be able to communicate more fully about their feelings.

It had been that way earlier in their relationship, back when they couldn't spend enough time together, back when he'd call just to hear her voice, back when it was important for him to know how she felt about one thing or another. How had they drifted to this near-married state they were in now, where they'd grown so comfortable with one another that little things no longer seemed of any value? It was a mystery.

She sighed and closed her eyes, breathing deeply of the clean mountain air.

Callie had nearly drifted off to sleep when she heard the adjoining patio door slide open on its tracks. She held her breath and listened as Lex strolled outside. She could make out his silhouette beyond the edge of the divider. The far end of the banister creaked beneath his weight as he sat down and leaned against the side support. Callie waited, unmoving, hardly breathing, wondering whether to let him know she was there as he stared off into the distance.

A sudden flicker of her ridiculous dream surfaced in her mind, and she pushed it away by concentrating on the moment.

Lex was toying with something resembling a straw or pencil, and from time to time he broke off a chunk of it and tossed it. When he rid himself of the last piece, he rubbed his hands on his pant legs, then slid them into his pockets.

Watching him, Callie noticed that his head was drooping listlessly, his shoulders sagging. The posture seemed so unlike his usual confident demeanor, she couldn't help but feel curious. As she drew a deep breath for courage to speak up, a gnat or mosquito brushed past her upper lip. She sneezed and waved it away.

Lex stiffened, then resumed his resigned pose as he exhaled, the sound akin to that made in disgust.

"I guess you can't sleep either," Callie finally said.

"You're right." He peered off in the other direction, the outline of his profile and strong shoulders gilded by the moon.

"Nice night to be restless, though." Callie berated herself for not being more eloquent.

"Yeah." After a few silent seconds, he moved to the near side of the railing into plain view. "How's the ankle?"

"Just about normal already. You were right to make me stay off it."

"Guess there's a first time for everything."

His bitter tone was no less than she had coming, of that she had little doubt. She'd barely said a civil word to him since she moved in. "Bad day?" she asked at last.

"You could say that."

"Worse than mine a few nights ago?" She hoped her light tone would put him at ease. The two of them had never carried on a normal conversation in their history, not as far back as she could remember.

He chuckled and cocked his head. "How is Prince Charming, anyway?"

Callie felt a giggle bubble up inside of her, and she didn't bother to hold it back. "Actually, I think I'm still banished from the kingdom, if you must know."

"I can relate to that; believe me."

"Is that right? The. . .um. . .woman whose voice I heard at your place the night I complained about your music?"

He sniffed and adjusted his position a little. "Yep. My fiancée, Brenda Harding."

"Need to talk?" Callie's mounting interest shocked even her, yet somehow in the semidarkness it seemed safe to be open with Lex. He couldn't really make out her face, nor she his. And since they had no designs on each other, it provided enough freedom for honesty, she reasoned.

He inhaled a huge draught of air and slowly let it out. "She wants to get married."

"To you, or somebody else?"

He snorted. "Me. Of course, you probably doubt her sanity."

Callie ignored the barb. "Why should I? Do you love her?"

The query hung in limbo for a timeless moment.

Lex regarded his neighbor steadily without answering. He opened his mouth to reply, then thought better of it. And even he wondered at the proper response. "Our parents want us to get married too. Now."

"Hm. That makes it tough." She paused, then raised her head his way again. "You are engaged, though?"

He nodded. "For a couple years already. It seemed a good idea at the time."

"Doesn't it now?"

Lex considered the question briefly before he responded. Surprisingly, Callie's voice and her relaxed pose emitted sincerity, and Lex felt no pressure to reply in haste. "I don't know. Sometimes I think it does. Other times. . ."

Callie lowered her legs to the deck and sat upright. She reached for the beverage bottle beside her and took a drink. "Oh, sorry, Lex," she blurted. "It's Perrier. Could I offer you some?"

He shook his head. "Don't suppose you have anything revolting on hand, like maybe some soda."

"There's Diet Coke in the fridge. Revolting enough?"

"Well," he said with mock resignation, "guess it'll have to do. But stay put; I'll get it." Swinging a leg around the partition, he crossed to her side of the deck and went in. When he returned with a can in his grip, he took the other of Callie's two chairs and extended his legs comfortably.

They sat in companionable silence momentarily, then Callie spoke. "How. . . um. . .did you meet your fiancée? Brenda, was it?"

Lex nodded. "Friend of the family. Our parents have known each other forever." He leveled his gaze her way. "How'd you meet what's-his-name?"

He saw her teeth glisten as she smiled. "I was taking a night school course in business management. He gave a lecture on finance one evening. He's a CPA. He still teaches a class one night a week."

"Ah." Lex drained the remainder of his drink. "You're engaged too, right?"

"Yes. And my fiancé hates it that I'm living up here. Says he doesn't like the distance between us. Know what's really funny?" She waited 'til he shrugged. "He wants to get married now too. So we're in the same boat, you might say."

Lex watched the way the silver moonlight reflected upon her tousled hair and brightened the white of her robe, making it appear almost iridescent in a blue-white sort of way. For the second time in a week, he considered Callie's CPA boyfriend a numbskull for living almost fifty miles away from this next-door neighbor of his. For all her independence, she appeared tiny and vulnerable in the pale glow of the night, someone who should have another person looking out for her. *Oh, well,* he thought. There was nothing he could do about that. He stretched and yawned, then got up. "Well, I should go back where I belong so you can turn in. Thanks for listening. . .and for the soda."

"No trouble," she breathed. "Good night."

"Night." He stood rooted for a second, until he reminded himself to get going. "See you, Callie." As he closed his door, he heard the adjoining one slide shut. And he pictured Callie in that airy place of hers, wondering if she felt as lonely as he.

❧❀❧

The next morning, Callie awakened so early she managed to put in a full session on her rowing machine and exercise bike before she showered. She got to the shop way ahead of Trish's normal arrival time. After unlocking the back door and setting the coffeemaker in readiness to start, Callie took a seat at the desk. She'd fallen behind in her Bible reading the last few days, so she drew her purse-sized New Testament from her purse and read several chapters in Matthew, through the Sermon on the Mount, then closed the book and reclined against the springy chair back in thought.

Gram was one of the "peacemakers" the Lord called the children of God, Callie decided. How often her grandmother had calmed the waters young Alex Sheridan had so constantly kept stirring long ago. Funny, now those memories seemed somehow remote, part of another time, another life. Somewhere along the way, Lex had changed. But part of her couldn't help wondering if it had been a mere surface change or one that went deeper and would last. That undoubtedly would take time to figure out.

"Hello," came Trish's breezy greeting as the door opened and she came in. "What, no coffee on yet?"

Callie jumped up. "Oh. Sorry. I got here so early I thought I'd wait for awhile to start it brewing, but it's all ready to go." Hurrying to the cabinet, she clicked the On button and listened as the machine spurted to life.

"What are you doing?" Trish asked, hanging her shoulder bag on a wall hook, followed by her cardigan.

"Nothing much. Just having my devotions."

"Hm. You look preoccupied or something." Her steady perusal made Callie uncomfortable.

"Oh. Well, let's see." Callie forced a light tone. "I was just trying to decide which individual I know demonstrates which Beatitude. I figured Gram fit the peacemaker category, for obvious reasons, and Gramps the pure in heart. He never could see any wrong in anyone."

"What about me?" her partner asked with a half-smile.

"Let's see. . .meek is still available."

Trish snickered. "Somehow I don't quite fit the job description."

"Well," Callie sighed, trying to be serious, "there doesn't seem to be a helpful but nosy category. Sorry."

Jutting out her chin, Trish pouted in mock offense. "Oh, well. Guess I'm just a leftover, then. Pity."

Rising, Callie went around the desk and gave her partner a hug. "Just remember, everyone can always use one of those friends mentioned in Proverbs whose wounds are faithful. You've never let me get away with anything. I appreciate that."

"Oh, well. That does sound a little more like I have some purpose for being here on this earth, anyway. Anytime you need to be shot down, just let me know."

Callie grinned and reached for the feather duster. "Guess I'll go spruce up the salesroom while you have some coffee."

"Wait," Trish said suddenly, turning from the urn to face Callie. A spark of mischief glinted in her eyes. "Surely there must be some verse or proverb that describes that neighbor of yours, isn't there?"

Remembering her dream and the quiet chat she and Lex had shared last night in the moonlit darkness, a discomforting warmth threatened Callie's cheeks. Only by sheer determination did she manage to squelch it and maintain her composure as she met Trish's gaze. "Probably. It'll come to mind, in time, I'm sure."

"Right." Raising her cup, Trish took a cautious sip of the hot liquid.

"By the way," Callie said evenly, "you can wipe that smug expression off your face. He's engaged." But having made the announcement, instead of the satisfaction she had expected to feel, in its place was a hollow emptiness.

Chapter 9

After work the following Saturday, Callie drove down the mountain to Bakersfield. For the first time in her life, as she turned onto Starlight Drive, the sight of the sprawling Sheridan place at the end of the crescent did not seem as intimidating as it once had. The thought struck her as odd, since for years she had never so much as allowed her gaze to wander in that direction. But maturity—or something she could not name—had apparently changed Lex for the better, and now the family residence no longer gave her the feeling that someone was lurking inside its gates waiting to pounce on some unsuspecting passerby in general—or her in particular.

After parking in the driveway at her grandparents' house, she pushed the trunk release button and retrieved her travel case.

The warm glow from the street lamps bathed the dove gray stucco structure and glinted off the tile roof as Callie approached the front door and let herself in. "Anybody home?"

"In here, Honey," came her grandmother's voice from the kitchen.

Like a magnet, the delicious aroma of fresh cinnamon buns drew her through the L-shaped living and dining rooms done in navy and burgundy to the room beyond, where she found her two favorite people in the world sitting at the rectangular kitchen table. She tried not to notice how their shoulders were beginning to stoop with the passing years. She could not bear the thought of living without them entirely someday.

"Hi, you two," she breathed, bestowing a hug and kiss to each before taking the chair Gramps had reached over and pulled out for her. She filled her eyes with their beaming faces. "Hope you don't mind some overnight company. It feels like I've been gone for a semester at Bible school and just come home for Christmas. I've sure missed you."

"I know the feeling. And you're more than welcome to come anytime you want. You know that." Gramps gave her hand a squeeze with his work-roughened one, and his broad grin amplified the network of lines crisscrossing his face. "Getting settled in your new place, are you?"

"Oh, yes. That didn't take much time at all, really. You'll have to come up and see it when you can."

"That's still in the plans, Honey," Gram said. "Don't give up on us. Oh, we were just about to have our snack. Would you join us?"

"Sure, but I can help myself."

Her grandmother stayed her with a pat on the arm. "Stuff and nonsense. I've got to keep moving, or I stiffen all up. Besides, I don't get to do for you now that you're living away from home again." Blinking telltale moisture quickly from her narrow blue eyes, she got up and crossed to the hutch, returning with three cups and saucers. Then, bringing over the pot of tea and a plate of sticky buns, she eased her frail-looking frame back down to her chair.

Callie watched the light from the kitchen chandelier play among her grandmother's white curls as the older woman removed the quilted tea cozy. The gnarled hands trembled slightly as she poured the rich brew into the cups and passed them around with the cinnamon rolls.

"These look delicious, Gram. I'm pretty sure I could smell them all the way down the hill!" Then, imagining how many extra half hours she would have to pedal on her stationary bike for indulging in the rare confection, she closed her eyes and bit into the cloudlike softness.

"I'm surprised you're free this evening," Gram said. "Shouldn't you be out with Kenneth, as usual?"

Callie grimaced as she swallowed. "I'm afraid he and I have had a little falling out. He did not appreciate my. . . um. . .*underhanded* move up to the mountain."

"That right?" Gramps asked. His eyes, the same shade of blue as Gram's, crinkled at the corners as he tried not to smile. "Could've sworn we had this conversation already."

"Yes," Callie said, fighting to contain her own grin. "You did warn me that he might be annoyed about the idea. But it's not as if I purposely waited for him to leave town long enough for me to skip out, you know. The opportunity just arose, and I took it. I don't regret it in the least."

"Oh, well," Gram said in her soothing tone, "I'm sure the two of you will work it out in time."

"Yes, or so I hope." Callie sighed. "That's why I've come, actually. I plan to call him later. And we'll probably go to church together tomorrow."

"Well," Gramps said, "how are things going for you otherwise? Store okay? Have good neighbors?"

Sipping her tea, Callie almost choked. She struggled to recover her breath. "Everything's fine." She looked from one overly curious face to the other, then giggled. "You are not going to believe who my neighbor is. Lex Sheridan."

"Now that *is* something," Gram finally said as the statement sank in.

"Hope he's not up to his old tricks," Gramps said.

Callie shook her head. "No. At first I expected him to start right in again with that nonsense, but he seems to have changed. He seems much quieter now. More settled down."

Gram toyed absently with an apron pocket. "I always did have a soft spot in my heart for that boy, in spite of his mischief. I thought he just needed somebody who'd treat him special."

The remark surprised Callie. She mulled it over momentarily without answering.

The older woman refilled her cup before meeting Callie's gaze. "I bumped into his mom at Albertson's grocery store one day not too long ago, and she mentioned that he'd gotten quite religious over the last few years. That might account for the change in him."

"Lex?" Callie asked in astonishment. That would have been the last thing she'd have imagined. "Well, all I know is he seems helpful and considerate now. Even thoughtful. I guess we've both grown up at last, huh?"

"Happens to the best of us," Gramps said with a chuckle as he ran a hand through his thin silver hair. "Could be the Lord wanted to give you and young Lex a chance to make up to one another for the wrongs of the old days."

"There weren't any on *my* part," Callie shot in.

He gave her an indulgent smile. "Oh, now, you probably could've taken time to see the humor in some of his doings, instead of always getting on your high horse and turning up your nose at him. You know that only added fuel to the fire."

Gram's expression mirrored the same thought.

Feeling a sudden need to change the subject, Callie gulped the last mouthful of her now-tepid tea and stood up. "Well, thanks for the snack. I'll just put these dishes into the dishwasher and turn in now, if the two of you don't mind."

"Not at all, Hon," Gram said, giving Callie's hand another pat. "You just go on and make yourself at home. Your bed's always ready."

In her old bedroom moments later, Callie felt twelve years old again as she stared between the frilly pink curtains to the darkened backyard. No matter how often she went away, the room always stayed the same. Her five Madam Alexander dolls reigned over the twelve-by-twelve kingdom from a walnut shelf high above the rose-skirted dressing table. And in one corner, the oval wicker bed Patches had once occupied still looked as though he'd scamper in at any moment to play with his worn blue ball.

With a sigh, she turned down the ruffled rose spread and floral top sheet on the walnut twin bed. Then she lay down with the bedside lamp still burning, working up courage enough to dial Ken's number. He'd never stayed mad so long before, and she dreaded having to defend herself once more because of her move. But when she could no longer postpone the inevitable, she reached for the pink phone on the nightstand.

Surprisingly, his "Hello" sounded almost pleasant and gave her hope that he was mellowing.

"Hi, Sweetheart. It's me."

"Oh. Cal." There came a definite cool edge to his voice, which made her own anxiety return.

"How are you?"

"So-so. Busy. Just got in, in fact, from dinner."

"I just thought I'd let you know I'm at Gram's tonight. I was hoping we might go to church in the morning."

"Sure. Whatever. I'll pick you up at the usual time."

"Good. I'll see you then. Love you. . . ."

"Yeah. Bye."

Callie clenched her teeth at the brush-off. Tomorrow they'd better do some real talking.

❧❦❧

The house seemed eerily quiet after her grandparents left for the little church where they'd been members for as far back as Callie could remember.

When Ken came by an hour later, hazy June sunshine made her don sunglasses. And despite his somewhat dutiful kiss, something about his rigid demeanor sent off an alarm within her. She felt like a scolded puppy as she followed his stiff, brusque walk to his car, and when he opened the door for her, the courtesy seemed more mechanical than thoughtful.

She settled the skirt of her jonquil sundress about her while Ken went around to his side and got in.

He barely looked her way.

Callie cleared her throat. "So. How've you been?"

"Fine."

Automatically, he turned the key and the engine of the Volvo sprang to life. He shifted into reverse.

"Wait," Callie blurted. "I've changed my mind."

He looked at her with exasperation. "What are you talking about?"

"It's pointless to go to the service with you in this mood. The mannequins at the store have more life in them." Clutching her purse, she grabbed the door handle.

"Wait." He let out a deep breath. "You're right. I'm being too hard on you. You made a mistake and will have to live with it, but I shouldn't hold it against you forever. You do have a lease, and all that. We'll just have to make the best of a bad situation."

Callie was sure he hadn't meant what he'd said in quite the way she was taking it. After all, he loved her, didn't he? They'd just have to get through this. She inhaled slowly for patience. Searching his face, she noticed his countenance appeared to have eased, so she released some of her own tension and ventured a smile.

He grinned back.

For a split second, Callie's gaze lingered on his mouth, and the thought flashed into her mind that Trish was right. Ken did have very thin lips. She swallowed and gave herself a mental shake for being ridiculous as Ken backed out of the drive and started toward church a mile away.

During the standard formalities of the first half of the service, with its assorted anthems and congregational responses, Callie had to force her mind to concentrate. She gazed purposefully at the pastor, the Reverend Elliot, in his proper ministerial garb. Somehow it did seem to fit in with the austere interior of the thirty-year-old building with its dark woodwork and ornate pews.

"How can we not care for this world we call our home," he was saying, the rich modulations of his voice echoing through the sanctuary, "when the lives of our very children depend upon our making it a better place for them to dwell?"

His smile made Callie think of the Cheshire cat. No matter how many times she came here to worship with her fiancé, where dozens of prominent and mon-eyed families were counted among its membership, Callie found it lacking. She had yet to feel as though she'd been in God's presence, much less had received anything in the sermon that drew her closer to the Lord. She found herself longing for the life and fervor of the little church she'd attended all through her childhood with her grandparents. She didn't even know the benediction had been pronounced until Ken nudged her.

"Great sermon, huh?"

She smiled at him, then nodded to some familiar faces as they made their way to the door.

In the car, Ken turned on the oldies station. "What are you hungry for?"

"Oh, I don't know. A good salad, I suppose."

"Then we'll hit the Garden Spot, just for you."

❧

"How's the chili?" Callie asked, trying to recapture Ken's attention from the view of attractive office buildings right outside the restaurant window.

"Not bad." He crumbled a few saltines into his bowl and spooned the rich mixture into his mouth. But his gaze drifted just as quickly back to where it was.

Looking over her spinach greens at her fiancé, Callie realized he was avoid-ing her eyes. For twenty minutes already they'd eaten in near silence, with him replying in monosyllables to her every attempt at conversation. She had the dis-tinct impression that until she groveled at his feet and repented in sackcloth and ashes for her unspeakable conduct and attitude—which allowed her to relocate without consulting him—nothing would ever be the same between them.

"I've always liked the food here," she tried again.

"Hm? Oh, yeah. Me too." He perked up for a second as he waved to some-one he knew across the room. Then he reverted to his morose, mechanical eating motions.

Callie shoved her salad aside, no longer interested in food or in prolonging the day. She blotted her lips on her napkin. "Think I'll head on up the hill while it's early."

"Might be wise."

Later that night, Callie tossed and turned in her own bed. Ken had expended some effort to be pleasant during church and on the short drive they took afterward. Yet nothing between them had truly been resolved. And lunch had been a complete wipeout. It was almost as if he'd convinced himself to be polite for a certain period of time, and when that limit was reached, it was back to the silent treatment. Didn't he even miss her? Or care about her happiness?

Low keyboard music drifted from next door, a melody Callie did not recognize as she strained her ears to listen. Emitting a sigh, she found herself pondering the concept that Lex had, in his mother's words, become religious. She would never have imagined that of him, not in a million years. Still, a major change had come over him from the way he used to be.

Her thoughts continued on. Religion in itself didn't truly alter a person—after all, Ken was religious, in his own way, and considered himself a Christian. But he didn't think anything of being overbearing and cold, even to the woman he supposedly loved.

If Alex Sheridan had actually found the Lord and had had a real change of heart, that would explain a number of things. She had noticed something different in his eyes when he had come to her aid that night, and now that she thought about it, it was easily identified. Peacefulness. If the restless lion that once had been inside Lex had indeed been tamed, the Lord had performed a modern-day miracle.

Turning onto her other side, her diamond snagged the lace edging on her pillowcase. Callie tugged it off and let it drop with a clink into the coaster on her nightstand.

And she wondered if Lex's fiancée appreciated the man whose engagement ring she wore.

Chapter 10

Where's Brenda *this* week, man?" Raul Perez asked as Lex removed his Yamaha from the guitar case for the brief practice session before the service. Coal-black eyes sparking with mischief, the teenager elbowed his twin and smirked.

"Headache," Lex said unceremoniously. But not even *he* believed this evening's excuse. *She could have used more imagination,* he thought bitterly, *and come up with something original.* Their relationship was at the point where he came to church alone more often than not. His prayers seemed to be falling on deaf ears, but he held to the hope that some of the simple, yet deep sermons Pastor Phil had preached in Brenda's presence would in time bring on a change of heart and cause her to find the Lord.

Doug did a percussion roll across his drums and ended with a tap on a cymbal. "Come on, guys, we're wastin' time."

Thankful for the diversion that effectively turned the twins' attention to something other than himself, Lex ducked his head and slid the guitar strap over his head. "Before we go over tonight's choruses, why not give the Friends song a couple run-throughs? Next week is the special service, you know."

"Good idea," Manuel Perez said at the keyboard. He played a sequence of chords in the key of F as introduction.

With the bookkeeping and new orders for the month caught up, Callie flipped through the new *Brides* magazine while her partner waited on a customer out in the salesroom. Unable to decide on her own bridal attire, Callie figured the next best thing would be to focus on her matron of honor.

She appraised the jade French silk attendant's gown on the current page, deciding it would look lovely against Trish's red hair in the event of a fall or winter wedding. But on the other hand, the peach blush tea length dress in lace, which had caught her eye in the last issue, would be equally stunning, and much more appropriate for late summer. With a sigh, Callie closed the magazine and sat back in the chair.

Setting a definite date would appease Ken. Once he could see the end of this separation, things would smooth out between them again. She imagined his delight in hearing she was complying with his wishes.

August, she figured, would be as good as any other month. And it was enough weeks away that she'd have plenty of time to plan the event. Picking up the desk calendar, she considered all the Fridays and Saturdays, settling on the sixteenth. From that day and forevermore, her name would cease to be Callie McRae.

The mere idea of actually making that commitment began to take on ominous significance. As a Christian wife, Callie was more than aware that she'd be relinquishing some of her own independence for all time and giving precedence to her husband's decisions. That would take as much grace as the Lord could provide, but she did not doubt that with prayer and determination, she'd make Ken a good wife.

Idly, she jotted "Callie Vincent" and "Caralyn Vincent" on the notepad by the phone, then beneath them, "Mrs. Ken Vincent." She wondered how long it would take to get used to thinking of herself that way.

❧❦❧❧

Lex parked some distance from La Femme Fashions on the odd chance that Callie would go out for lunch. Unaccountably restless for the past week, he attributed it to nothing more than concern for her. She hadn't come home after work on Saturday and was gone all day yesterday as well. He assumed she'd driven home to Bakersfield, where she'd have time to talk things out with that boyfriend of hers and settle that minor skirmish they had going on her doorstep.

Catching sight of Callie's car as it emerged from behind the complex and headed toward town, Lex started the Corvette and followed at a distance. When the LeBaron turned onto the parking lot at Shelby's Buffet, he smiled and did the same. But he stayed outside for several minutes until he was satisfied she wasn't meeting someone.

When he went in, he made a few quick selections from the line of entrees, then scanned the dining area until he spotted her hair. Nonchalantly, he headed over to the booth and stopped. "Well," he said, manufacturing a look of surprise with raised eyebrows, "looks like they let just about anybody in here."

Callie's fork stopped in midair, lettuce dangling from the tines, but her smile appeared sincere. "So it would seem. Hi."

"This seat taken, by any chance?"

She shook her head and gestured for him to join her.

Lex set down his tray and slid into the opposite side. "Excuse me a sec." He bowed his head for a moment, then met Callie's wide brown eyes. "How's everything?" he asked, slicing a chunk of chopped sirloin and then sampling it.

"Just fine. No complaints."

He nodded. "Go away for the weekend? I noticed it was pretty quiet on your side."

She stopped chewing. "You keep tabs on your neighbors?"

"Not all of them," he answered evenly as he buttered a roll.

"Well, as it happened, I went home to see my grandparents. Gram's arthritis

282

has been bothering her, and I kind of missed them both anyway."

"Ah."

"How was your weekend?" A teasing glint shone in her eyes. "You must have gotten in lots of practice, without having to worry about the volume."

Lex chuckled. "Right. I did. Actually, I've been working for awhile on a new song for a special service coming up at our church this coming Sunday, kind of an Invite a Friend day. If you don't have any plans, you and what's-his-name—"

"Ken," she supplied.

"Right. Ken. You and Ken are welcome to fill my quota."

He wished she wouldn't stare at him that way, as if he were an alien from some faraway galaxy. But then she smiled, and he felt more at ease.

"And what church might that be, if you don't mind my asking?" She popped a piece of radish into her mouth.

"New Life Fellowship, over on the east side of town, off Willow Springs Road."

"Yes. I've heard of that one. Somehow, I believe it's a little out of our league, but it's nice of you to invite us."

"Oh, come on, Callie. Don't make judgments without checking it out yourself. Give it some thought, okay?" He paused. "Or I'll have to run all over town to find someone else to fit the bill. You wouldn't want me to have to do that, would you?"

Callie had to laugh at the sight of Lex's sheepish expression. "Tell you what. I'll mention it to Ken, okay? But don't count on his agreeing to it. He prefers his church services to contain a certain level of starch and formality. I don't know if he'd go for a radical new format."

"Then again, he might. It's only an invitation. He. . .uh. . .over his little—" Lex gestured meaningfully in the air.

"More or less." Callie sipped her iced tea, debating whether to elaborate, then threw caution to the wind. "Would you. . .hate it. . .if Brenda decided she needed to relocate to someplace within reasonable driving distance?"

Lex ate his roll with slow deliberation. "Not if it was something she felt she needed to do. I'd rather she didn't, of course, but it would be her decision. Why? Is that the problem?"

Callie nodded. "He refuses to see my side. I'm. . .wondering if it would help if I set a wedding date. At least that way we'd be together more, instead of having this distance between us."

"Well, I don't know the guy, that's for sure. Who knows, he might go for it. But I'd probably do a lot of praying before I suggested it. Make sure it's what *you* want. That's all I can say."

❧❦❧

Callie dashed into the office and stowed her purse in the desk drawer, then hurried into the main room. "Sorry I'm late," she said breathlessly. "I wasn't watching the time."

"Oh, think nothing of it." Trish's tone contained just enough sarcasm to make Callie cringe. "I was just about to eat the African violet here, that's all."

"Well, I'll take over now. Go have some lunch. And don't hurry back," she added after her departing partner. "I'll be fine."

I'll be just fine, echoed her thoughts. *As soon as I figure out what on earth to do.* How had things gotten so complicated? One day everything was settled and almost boring, and the next, everything was in chaos.

Make sure it's what you want. Lex's statement still reverberated in her mind. Callie refused to think about how simple that suggestion was. Or how easy it was becoming to open up to him about her problems. What *did* she want?

Moving to the cash register, she took a piece of scrap paper and made two columns, labeled Pros and Cons. She tapped the pencil against her lips and stared off into the distance.

"I love Ken and he loves me," she wrote on the Pro side. "I think," she added under the Con. Did Ken truly love her, or was she merely a convenience for him, someone he could count on not to make waves, to keep the bills organized, the laundry done, their entire day-to-day existence routine?

There was a time she could have answered that question in a heartbeat. But that was way back in the beginning of their relationship, when she'd been starry-eyed and infatuated with the handsome professor at night school. Back when she had hung onto his every word and took every comment to heart. The initial fluttery warmth she'd felt whenever he was near, the tongue-tied awkwardness, had mellowed over time. Now going out together had become comfortable—too comfortable—almost habitual. And lately he seemed like a stranger, someone with whom she had to weigh everything she said. And part of her wondered which man was the real Ken Vincent.

With a sigh, Callie wadded up the list and tossed it into the wastebasket.

The electronic chimes went off just then as an elderly lady entered the store and began making her way among the various racks of merchandise.

"Let me know if there's any way I might help you, Ma'am," Callie said with a smile, and received a pleasant nod. When two other women also came in, she decided to present a more efficient and businesslike atmosphere and get busy.

※※※

Later that night, in the evening stillness, Callie took a bottle of Perrier out onto the deck and did a session on her cross-country machine. *Ken, sweetheart,* she imagined herself saying the next time they were together, *I've decided we should get married. In August. What do you think?* Picturing the undisguised delight she knew beyond a doubt he'd display, an apprehensive sensation washed over her. *Mrs. Ken Vincent.*

Then she envisioned all the heavy books and bookcases he'd be bringing along, the huge desk where he'd bury his nose for hours in order to keep on top of the constantly changing tax laws. Would he wave her away more often than not so she wouldn't be a distraction? Or would he make the most of their time together, listening to music in front of a crackling fire, watching the occasional romantic movie classic with his arm around her? *Surely there'd be times like this,* she told herself, when they would sit outside after a busy day and enjoy the sounds and smells of nature. Everything would work out.

Then another thought jolted her. Did he even *like* children? The subject had so rarely come up and then been dismissed so quickly, she honestly didn't know. Even with the shop to run, she planned to make room in her life for a baby or two. Would that upset Ken? She tried to imagine him bouncing a curly headed toddler on his knee.

With astonishing clarity, she realized Lex was right. Before she voiced to Ken any thought regarding marriage in the near future, she needed to do some serious praying.

❧❦❧

Lex only finished half of the donut he'd just taken out of the box before he didn't feel hungry anymore. Callie. Married. Well, he reasoned, that would relieve him of the burden of looking out for her. It was for the best, actually. If he had any brains, he'd encourage her along that route.

He should take the plunge himself too. Brenda was more than ready. Everyone thought the two of them were right for one another. And once they were man and wife, he'd have all kinds of time to win her to the Lord. It was definitely something to consider. Didn't the Bible say something about the conduct of the believing mate drawing the unbelieving one to salvation?

In fact, once the weddings were over, they might even make a fairly decent foursome—him and Brenda, Callie and Ken. Once they all got to know each other, they might discover they had similar tastes and could do things together. California was a huge state, and he'd never taken time to go to all the attractions the tourists flocked to see. Might be a lot of fun.

Optimistic again, he grabbed the remainder of the donut and finished it. But inside, he felt a compelling need to do some praying of his own.

Chapter 11

Over dinner a few nights later at Shelby's, Callie looked across the table at Ken, who was engrossed in the list of weekly entrees in the acrylic holder as he ate his fried chicken. She cleared her throat. "Feel like doing something different this Sunday?"

A blank expression came over his face for a second as he swallowed and looked at her. "Can't. I'll be out of town."

"Oh? You never mentioned it."

"I was going to later. Aunt Phoebe asked me to run her up to Pismo to see her sister. You can come with us, if you like. Of course, she wants to go early, so you'd have to spend the night in town on Saturday."

Callie pictured Phoebe Jenson, the domineering spinster with whom her fiancé boarded. Since the moment they were introduced, Callie knew her engagement to the woman's sole nephew made the older woman feel threatened, and Callie felt ill at ease around her. It wasn't so much what Phoebe said as it was the subtle way she elevated her chin and peered down her nose whenever she looked Callie's way. And her smiles seemed more a baring of her piano-key false teeth than a show of warmth or humor. Too, the woman was prone to car sickness and always required the front seat. Not that Callie minded being the backseat passenger, but it did leave her feeling like a ten year old.

And Phoebe's sister, Irene, was even worse, always fluttering about and squinting over her reading glasses to be sure no one chipped her precious teacups. Callie could think of a lot of places she would rather go than on this particular outing with the Jenson sisters.

"How about it?" Ken asked, breaking into her musings. "I'm sure Aunt Phoebe would love to have you along. She's always asking after you and wanting to know when we plan to get married."

"I'll bet," Callie muttered under her breath. With a polite smile, she took a sip of ice water, then set down the glass. "Oh, I think I'll just pass. It's been kind of a busy week at the shop, and I'd like a day to kick back. Maybe next time."

"Oh well, whatever." Picking up a chicken leg, he bit off a chunk, then rotated the laminated holder around to the dessert photos with his other hand.

Do try not to look so disappointed, Hon, Callie thought as she forked some salad into her mouth. But the mild offense she usually felt at having been slighted was strangely missing. In its place was actual relief. She'd wanted to go to the Friends

Day service with Lex and his fiancée, and instead of hassling her, Ken had just made it possible. A tiny smile teased the corners of her lips.

❧❧❧

Lex ground his teeth together and stormed out of Brenda's house to his car. Women could be so stubborn. For the third time in a row, Brenda would miss the Sunday service, and he was getting increasingly weary of having to make excuses for her to his friends. Bad enough to have to fabricate a story for her absence on a regular week, but Friends Day? He would have thought she'd enjoy that. All the special music, the potluck afterward—and the sermon probably would go along with the theme of the day too. It was no big deal that he wouldn't be bringing anyone new to church, even if the whole thing *had* been his idea in the first place to bring in some welcome new faces.

Jamming the key into the ignition, he started the engine and tromped on the accelerator. The squeal of the tires jarred him back to reality, and with some chagrin, he eased up on the gas and drove home at a more reasonable speed.

Lights were on in Callie's place, he noticed as he parked on the street behind her LeBaron. He hadn't checked with her to see if she and Mr. Prep were planning to go to the fellowship with him. Not that there was much chance of it, but the least he could do was follow through, let her know the invitation had been on the level. He glanced at his watch. Eleven. He probably shouldn't bother her. She might be dozing or something. But still, tomorrow was Saturday, and he had to drive to Pasadena in the morning. He did need to know her plans. Taking a deep breath, he rang her doorbell.

"Who is it?" came her voice from inside.

"Me. Lex."

He heard the chain lock slide, and then the door opened. "Hi." Dressed for the hour in her white robe and blue knitted slippers, Callie smiled.

Lex couldn't help noticing she looked sleepy and utterly charming. His words tumbled out in a rush. "Sorry to bother you. I know it's late. But I won't be around tomorrow and thought I'd check to see if you were planning to come to church."

"Oh. Well, yes, actually. But it'll be just me. Ken is otherwise occupied."

The announcement caught Lex off guard, and he felt a flood of elation course through him. Somehow he held it in check. He gave a businesslike nod. "Good. I'll. . .uh. . .see you on Sunday then. Say 10:20?"

"Sure. See you then. Good night."

"Night." He stayed there as the door closed and the lock slid into place again. Then, with a surprisingly light step, he went over to his own side.

❧❧❧

"If Brenda Harding is anything like her voice," Callie muttered to her reflection on Sunday morning, "she'll probably look like a million dollars when Lex introduces us." She tried on and discarded half a dozen outfits before finally settling on her magenta crushed silk with tiny white hearts and white accessories. She eyed herself critically as she applied some blush and spritzed on cologne, wondering all the while if she should wear sandals instead of the white sling-back heels she had on.

The doorbell sounded, ending her debate. She grabbed her Bible and purse and went to answer.

Sporting a trendy suit and tie, his hair shiny and pulled back, Lex didn't look half bad, she decided. Then aware that the assessment had been mutual, she felt her cheeks warm as they went down the front walk. "Should we. . .um. . .take my car, so there'll be room for three? Or shall I just drive myself?"

"Neither. The 'Vette will do."

Callie didn't see how but shrugged and got in, sinking into the rich leather upholstery as Lex closed the door after her.

"There's a scarf in the glove compartment, if you need one," he said as he took the driver's seat and started the engine.

"I'll just take my chances," she said lightly. She thought she saw a look of surprise flash in his face but wondered if it had been her imagination.

Unaccountably nervous, Callie didn't attempt to make conversation on the drive, but when they pulled into the church parking lot without having made a side trip to get Brenda, she looked questioningly at Lex. "It's just the two of us?"

"Brenda couldn't come today. I hoped you wouldn't mind. I think you'll enjoy the service."

Callie gathered her Bible and purse while Lex opened her door. While he opened the trunk and took out his guitar, she let her eyes roam the neat, ivory-stuccoed building with its cedar shake roof. Obviously well cared for, it fairly teemed with people already milling around.

"Lex is here!" Two young boys, one a towhead, the other of Oriental descent, broke off from the crowd and came running. They latched onto him as Callie watched.

"Hi, guys. How's it going? Oh, Callie, I'd like you to meet two of my best buddies, Mark and Danny," he said, indicating each with a tap on the head. "Did you bring friends with you today?" he asked the boys as he ruffled their hair.

"Sure did," they said at the same time.

"I brought two," light-haired Mark announced proudly.

"Say, that's great." Lex gave each lad a hug with his free arm. "Well, we'd better go in. It's almost time to start."

Seated in the second row from the front moments later, Callie felt somehow at home in the cozy sanctuary with its pews of light oak. Behind the pulpit a wooden cross, backlit against the off-white paint of the interior walls, gave quiet significance to the place of worship.

Dozens of introductions still buzzed in her mind along with a blur of friendly faces. She didn't even feel alone, despite the fact that Lex was one of the musicians on the platform and wouldn't occupy the vacant spot beside her until after the end of the musical portion of the service. Again and again, her gaze found its way to him. He looked so right there, and the unmistakable admiration of the entire church body toward him was not something she could ignore. She almost felt as though she'd never truly seen the tall, compelling man with the guitar before. He was nothing at all like the young Alex Sheridan she once knew.

"And now," he said, his voice and smile interrupting her rambling thoughts, "we have a special song for you to learn. One written especially for this day." His eyes swept over the congregation. "All of us here at the fellowship want to welcome the visitors who've come to worship the Lord with us for the very first time. You don't have to become a member here to fit in, you know. If you know Jesus, you're not only friends, you're much more. You're part of the family. That's what this song is about. It's called, 'Better Than Friends.' We'll run through the music twice so you can get a handle on it, and then I'll let you in on the words. Ready?"

Callie watched as Lex used an arm to indicate the meter to the other guys in the ensemble, and then they broke into the melody. Even though the tune was coming forth at a much livelier tempo, she recognized it instantly as one she'd heard through the condo walls on several occasions.

On the third time through, Lex stepped close to the mike, and grinned, and his rich baritone voice reverberated through the sanctuary. Callie listened, enraptured:

Once in sin's darkness,
  Lost and alone,
Hopeless and friendless,
  Nowhere to turn...
We heard God whisper,
  Come unto Me,
Give Me your heart
  For you're precious to Me.

Now we're better than friends,
  We are family;
We've been washed in the blood
  Of the Son;
We are better than friends
  Through the Savior...
He made us whole,
  We are one.

"Think you can try it with me next time?" Lex asked with his usual smile. He nodded to someone in the back of the auditorium, and a movie screen lowered into place behind Lex. Seconds later, the lyrics were flashed onto the stark white background from an overhead projector. He started the band on the introduction, then motioned for everyone to sing.

Callie joined in with all the other voices, amazed at how easily they all had picked up on it. And the subtle message in the words warmed her. It did seem as if everyone present was part of the same family. She hadn't had that feeling for quite some time, not since she'd gone to her old childhood church or attended Bible school. Glancing around at some of the people nearby, she smiled.

All too soon, the song service came to an end, and instruments were set aside. Lex slid into the pew beside her, and a hush fell over the gathering as the young, redheaded pastor stepped up to the pulpit. Of medium height and build, the minister looked out across the congregation, his face beaming. He gestured with a freckled hand toward the musicians, who occupied the first row, just in front of Lex.

"Well, that was a treat, wasn't it? I'm sure we'd all like to extend our thanks to Lex Sheridan for that great song we cornered him into writing. At the potluck after the service, be sure you let him know how much we appreciate him. And now to continue on with our friendship theme, please turn in your Bibles to the book of Psalms. We'll be seeing what God has to say about being a friend."

❧❀❧

"You should try some of Mrs. Perkins's fried chicken," Lex said as he helped himself to a leg quarter.

Callie perused the array of crisp, meaty parts arranged on a cut-glass platter. "It does look scrumptious," she admitted. Surprising even herself, she gingerly placed a golden brown chicken breast on her plate, then gestured with her head toward the remaining people in line. "You were right—there's plenty of food for everyone. I nearly asked you to take me home, since I hadn't brought anything."

Lex chuckled. "Eating's one thing church folks do best, you know. I'm sure you know our theme song, 'When the Rolls Are Served Up Yonder, I'll Be There.' "

He looked perfectly serious, but the way his eyes twinkled made Callie laugh. Grasping the salad tongs, she filled the larger section of her Chinette plate with tossed greens. Her arm brushed Lex's as he reached for a roll, and a pleasing jolt of static electricity sparked through her.

"Sorry. The carpet," he explained. "The social hall's famous for shocking unsuspecting folk. Keeps us awake, though."

The tiniest of doubts made Callie wonder if the carpeting were all at fault. But she dismissed the idea before she could dwell on it. Reaching the beverage table, she took some iced tea.

Lex snagged some fruit punch and used the paper cup to indicate a pair of empty chairs at the far end of the tables, where the other three musicians were already delving into their food. "Mind sitting with the guys?"

"Not at all."

"So, Callie," one of the Manuel twins said as Lex pulled out a chair for her, "you have to put up with having this guy for a neighbor, huh?" He nudged his olive-skinned brother.

Callie wondered how anyone could possibly tell them apart as she compared their cheerful grins. "I mostly grit my teeth and take it one day at a time," she quipped.

Lex slanted her a wry glance as he slathered butter on his roll. "Actually, she keeps pretty busy. She's not home very much."

Surprised that her neighbor seemed to be keeping pretty close tabs on her, Callie sent him a sideways glance and listened to the good-natured banter that went on for the next several minutes.

"You say Brenda will be around again next Sunday?" Doug asked suddenly, drumming a straw on the paper tablecover. "We're starting to forget what she looks like."

"Yeah, man, it's been awhile," one of the twins piped in.

Callie noticed the subtle whitening of Lex's knuckles as he gripped his fork. "Far as I know," he grated. "She'll come when she comes."

Watching the surreptitious glances being swapped among the others across from her, Callie concentrated on her salad. But part of her wondered why the jovial atmosphere had taken such a chilly turn. She chanced a glance Lex's way and saw a muscle twitch in his jaw as he stood. "About finished?"

Callie stopped chewing and looked at her half-eaten food. "Um. . .yes. Guess I took a little too much." She wiped her mouth on the yellow paper napkin while Lex took her plate and strode toward the refuse can at the end of the long open room. "Excuse me," she said as she got up. "Nice to have met you all."

She could have sworn one or both of the twins smirked, or at least kneed each other smartly under the table as they nodded. "Come again," Doug said with a parting wave.

Callie knew it was a tribute to her good physical condition that she was able to keep pace with Lex's long strides once she caught up with him. Automatically, he opened the car door for her before going around to his side.

The ride home would have been silent, if he hadn't started a CD of classical guitar music partway there. "I. . .um. . .liked your church," she finally ventured. "It wasn't much like I expected."

Her comment calmed Lex a little. He eased his grip on the wheel and felt some of his anger drain away. He forced himself to relax as a half-smile tugged at a corner of his mouth. None of this had been Callie's fault. He didn't even know why today's ribbing by the guys had gotten to him in the first place. He should have been used to it. That and having Brenda snub the church—and him—more and more often.

"I guess I shouldn't have been so quick to judge without seeing for myself. It's one of my worst faults, but I'm working on it."

"Glad you had a good time."

"And the friends' song. . .I liked that too. I recognized it, actually, from hearing you practice."

"Have I been too loud again?"

"No, not at all. Sometimes not loud enough, really." She smiled. "You've quite a talent."

He shrugged a shoulder. "Thanks. I just enjoy being able to use it for the Lord."

"I know how you feel. It was a great service. Music, sermon, even the food. Thanks for taking me."

"Anytime, Callie." Surprisingly, Lex knew he meant it. He guided the car up to the curb at the condo and turned off the engine.

"Would you like to come in for a soda or anything?" she asked as she got out.

The invitation was quite tempting, but Lex could think of a few good reasons why it would be wiser to refuse. He removed his guitar case from the trunk. "I can't today. But thanks."

As they went up the sidewalk and opened their separate doors, Lex was really glad Callie had gone to the Fellowship today—and even more glad Brenda hadn't. And despite the shock of that realization, he couldn't help but notice he felt very little guilt over the fact he was beginning to enjoy Callie's company over his fiancée's.

Chapter 12

Callie looked up from the blouse rack as Trish emerged from the office with some folded gift boxes.

"All stocked up again," her partner said, depositing the stack under the counter. "Are those the new arrivals you just hung?"

Callie nodded. "The delivery was one short, though. I'll call the warehouse about it later. They're usually quick about making amends."

"Yeah."

A short silence followed. Feeling her friend's gaze, Callie looked up to find Trish staring at her. "Something wrong?"

She shrugged. "I was just wondering the same thing. You've hardly said a word since you got here an hour ago. Have another fight with Mr. Perfect?"

"Why would you think that?" Callie hedged. "I haven't even see him since Friday. Everything's fine."

"You skipped church? Let me get a red pencil and circle yesterday on the calendar!" Trish teased, making a point of rummaging through the utility drawer in search of one.

"Actually, I went to church in town. At New Life Fellowship, in fact." Callie confessed. Then knowing Trish wouldn't let the matter rest without finding out everything there was to know, she diverted her attention to the dress slacks beside her and positioned the hangers meticulously. "They were having a special Bring a Friend day. I. . .um. . .went with Lex." She couldn't help glancing back toward the register.

Trish's mouth gaped, then slid into a most irritating smile. "You two actually have a truce or something since he came to your rescue that night? Or. . ." The words trailed off significantly.

Callie closed her eyes for a second, then raised them to the ceiling. "Honestly. Why I ever tell you anything is beyond me. Lex and I get along perfectly well these days. After all, we are both adults, now. No sense dwelling in the past. And for your information, he invited Ken *and* me to go with him and his fiancée to the service. . .only Ken couldn't be there."

"Hm." Trish cocked an eyebrow. "Well, what's *she* like, then, this mystery woman who's snagged the cutest hunk around?"

Unable to prevent the rosy warmth already creeping over her face, Callie took an uneven breath. "Her name is Brenda Harding, but. . .um. . .she. . . Well, Brenda wasn't there either," she finally blurted out.

Trish leaned forward, resting her elbows on the counter. "Do tell."

Callie threw up her hands in disgust. "Trish! Will you stop it, for heaven's sake?" Shaking her head in frustration, she stomped into the office, giving the French doors a little too much help to shut. She leaned against the water cooler and rubbed her temples. *Calm down. Just because she is making a big deal out of nothing doesn't mean you have to add fuel to the fire.* After dispensing some water into a paper cup, Callie sipped it slowly.

Trish turned the knob and cautiously came into the room. She gave a self-conscious shrug. "Hey, look. I'm sorry. I was just teasing you, like always. It didn't used to get to you before."

The statement hit Callie full force. Slightly embarrassed, she nodded, then crossed the room and gave her friend a hug. "You're right. I'm sorry too. I don't know what's come over me. I just have a lot on my mind lately."

Completely serious now, Trish tilted her head in concern. "Need to talk? I won't poke any more fun."

"Thanks, but no. I've. . .decided on an August wedding, and I'm just trying to figure out when to tell Ken."

"Oh. That *is* a lot to think about." Trish moved to the desk and sat down. After rooting through the various piles of forms and receipts, she opened the Expenses log and began filling in a column. But making only a few notations, she looked at Callie. "I sure hope you know what you're doing."

"I do. And I'd appreciate some input on the gowns I'm considering. They're in the *Brides* magazine in the drawer. I put bookmarks at the pages."

Her gaze never wavering from Callie, Trish took out the periodical and opened it, then focused her attention on the colored pictures indicated. "Hey, I can see you in the off-shoulder one. It's you. The other one's way too traditional."

"Think so?" Callie moved around to her partner's side and peered at the illustration. "The tux on the male model is perfect, don't you think?"

"Well. . ." Trish made a face. "It's perfect, all right. But not for Ken. I could see it on *someone else,* though."

"Hey, don't start it," Callie said evenly. "The decision has been made, and I'm quite happy with it."

Trish raised a hand as if vowing never again to butt in.

⊱✿✿✿⊰

Returning home from the convenience store with a quart of rocky road ice cream and another of mocha almond fudge, Lex stopped at Callie's and debated whether to ring the doorbell or wait till they ran into one another. He'd caught a glimpse of his neighbor coming back from jogging, around sunset, but before he'd had time to take the earphones off at the keyboard and dash to the door, she'd already gone inside.

He slid a hand into his pants pocket and let his gaze wander to the darkening hills off to the west. The sun had sunk below the tree line nearly an hour ago, and now the sky was fading into a rose-purple glow, silhouetting the jagged treetops. Just as he made up his mind to press the bell, he heard her telephone ring. It helped make up his mind. He turned and went into his own place.

Shortly after stowing the mocha in his freezer and then changing into some sweat shorts, Lex jabbed a spoon into the container of rocky road and went out onto his deck. He smiled at the unmistakable sound of Callie's cross-country machine. Passing up his usual spot on the banister, he peered around the edge of the lattice as he dipped into the frosty dessert. "What do you know, just the person I wanted to see."

She smiled but kept up a regulated stride.

"Care for some ice cream?" He gestured with the container.

"Thanks, but no. Never touch the stuff."

"Really? You don't know what you're missing," he said with a grin.

"Oh, yes, I do. About ten zillion calories. If it was nonfat frozen yogurt, now, I might be tempted."

He made a disgusted face. "Sounds too healthy, if you ask me. My system would probably go into shock if I tried that."

"You could be right."

Even in the semidarkness her expression was amiable, he decided. Friendly and soft. *That Ken whatever-his-name-is is a lucky guy. I hope he knows it.* Lex cleared his throat. "Say, I wanted to ask you something. I have four tickets to a Christian concert in Lancaster next Thursday. Suppose you and Ken would like to double with us? Brenda and me?"

"I don't see why not. It sounds like fun. I'll check with him, but I'm sure he'll agree."

"Great. Oh, it's kind of a classy affair—or at least last year's concert was. Maybe we can have dinner later too."

Callie gave a consenting nod and looked at her watch, then stepped off the treads and draped a towel around her neck. She blotted one cheek on a corner of terry cloth.

The curls that framed her face looked damp, Lex noted. Brenda never would let anyone see her unless she'd assessed herself in a mirror and found everything just so. Yet here stood Callie, a sheen of perspiration on her upper lip and forehead, her hair slightly wet and in disarray, looking incredibly—

"What time does the concert start?"

"Huh? Oh. Seven-thirty. We'll probably use Brenda's car."

Callie nodded as she sipped some Perrier and then lowered the half-empty bottle. "Sounds like fun. I'm looking forward to it."

"Yeah. Me too."

"Who'd you say will be performing?" Ken called out from the living room on Thursday as he waited for Callie to finish getting ready.

She scrunched her hair and then applied a light mist of styling spray. "I didn't even ask." She stepped back to view her reflection in the full-length bathroom mirror. The white jacquard dress that had caught her eye some weeks ago at the shop fit perfectly. As the last touch, she added glittery silver earrings to match the sequined accents on the shoulders and belt, then pulled on some white heels. Grabbing the small evening bag lying on her dresser, she went out to the other room.

Ken flicked off the TV and looked up as she approached. He gave a low whistle and stood. "You look incredible, Cal. Is that a new dress?"

"Thanks. And yes. I ordered it from a fashion show not too long ago." She walked into his open arms and raised her lips for his kiss.

He gave her two, then held her close. "I sure wish we didn't have to live with a whole mountain range between us."

Callie rested her head against the shoulder of his navy pinstripe suit while he caressed her cheek. "Well, maybe it won't be for much longer. As a matter of fact, I—"

The doorbell chimed. She started in surprise and drew away to answer it.

Lex, resplendent in a striking black suit and silk tie, and a tall, graceful woman stood arm in arm on the doorstep. His eyes flared wider as he swept an appreciative glance over Callie.

It barely registered, for in that same split second, she was already absorbing his companion's flawless appearance—the way the exquisite royal blue creation the young woman wore complemented her silver blond hair and gave quiet elegance to her willowy frame.

"Hi, Callie," Lex said with a warm smile. "I'd like you to meet my fiancée, Brenda Harding. Brenda, this is my neighbor and longtime friend, Callie McRae."

"How nice to finally meet," Brenda said, extending her hand. An assortment of delicate, tasteful rings adorned her manicured fingers. "I've heard so much about you."

Still mildly amazed the day had actually come when she'd be labeled Alex Sheridan's friend, Callie found his fiancée's touch on the cool side, but managed a smile. "And I you. So nice to be able now to put a face with your name. And I'd like to introduce my fiancé, Ken Vincent." She gestured with one arm in his direction as he came near. "He and Lex have sort of already met."

Brenda gave him a dazzling smile, Callie noticed. During the ensuing handshakes, not to mention the reserved eyeings the two men gave one another, she stepped over to the couch to retrieve her evening clutch. "Shall we go?"

Returning to the door, she saw Lex turn and start down the walk with his fiancée. Callie realized that his hair wasn't merely slicked back this time. It had been cut into a most attractive trendy style, close in back, longer on the top and sides, and very neatly combed in place. Awed by the change, she smiled and took a more leisurely second look.

Callie's heart swelled as the entire musical cast blended together in a moving rendition of "People Need the Lord," a personal favorite of hers for some years. The song never failed to move her, and seemed a crowning touch to a more than enjoyable two-hour program of instrumentals and vocals performed by a collection of newcomers in the field of Christian music. She could hardly wait for the last note so she could jump to her feet and applaud. But incredibly, the singers continued right into "How Great Thou Art" and gestured for the audience to stand and join in.

"Folks," the pastor of the host church said at the close of the song, "we'd like to thank all the young performers who took the time to make this evening a special time of testimony and fellowship. And thank you all for coming to tonight's program. If you enjoyed it, please spread the word. There are still some tickets for the remaining two performances tomorrow and Sunday, and it would be a shame for them to go to waste. Now, let us close in prayer."

Callie needed time to revel in the glorious music which had, in her estimation, come to an end much too soon. She barely heard the voices around her as the throng filed into the aisles and out to the parking lot. She latched onto Ken's hand and followed his lead as they accompanied Lex and his fiancée to the car.

"Well, I don't know," she heard Brenda say. "Some of those songs just seemed way too emotional. I mean, how can anyone really get excited about the afterlife? It's so bizarre. I don't even like to think about it."

Callie's attention perked. Especially when Ken's voice chimed in.

"I know just what you mean," he said. "Seems like people would do better to concentrate on getting all they can now. Enjoying life while it lasts. Sure, we should be decent and all that, go to church, help those in need whenever possible. Death comes along soon enough, and if we've done our best, everything should work out okay for us."

"Do you actually believe that?" Lex asked incredulously. A less than pleasant expression darkened his eyes.

"Of course," Brenda affirmed. "And you'd do well to adjust your thinking to the way it used to be too, back before you got tangled up in all that religion of yours. After all, it makes more sense to make use of the time we do have than to waste it trying to convince people they're worthless and sinful and need salvation. That's so old-fashioned."

"Exactly what I was thinking," Ken remarked with a grin at Brenda.

From the corner of her eye, Callie saw Lex staring her way. She suddenly became aware that her mouth was agape, and closed it as she met his gaze. She gave a confused shrug as she hastened her pace to match Ken's. This had been the most he'd ever said regarding matters pertaining to faith. Now as she thought back, anytime she'd mentioned the Lord he'd just sat quietly and given a nod of his head as if he agreed. The realization was quite unsettling.

"Well, I for one am absolutely starved!" Brenda exclaimed. "Where are we going to eat, Darling?" She tilted her head toward Lex.

A little more than half an hour later, lilting light classical music from a string quartet blended with quiet conversations around the linen-covered table for four at the sprawling, new Les Amies restaurant in Palmdale. Flickering candle-style chandeliers and table tapers cast a soft glow around the expansive interior of the mirrored room, one half of which had floor-to-ceiling windows overlooking the city. Callie admired the colorful array of neon and gaslights in the distance as she sampled her *poulet l'orange.*

"So, Ken. Do you like being a CPA?" Brenda asked him across the table as she cut off a chunk of her filet mignon.

"Of course. I've always enjoyed working with exact numbers, making columns balance, that sort of thing. I find it challenging."

"I feel the same way about dancing; isn't that odd? Taking one's body to the limits of grace and beauty, expressing inner emotions."

"You should have gone into it professionally," Ken told her. "You certainly have the beauty and grace you just spoke of, and I can only imagine how easily you'd lose yourself to the emotions of dance. We'll have to go to the ballet in L.A. one of these days. I mean—" He cleared his throat and shifted in his seat. "The four of us, of course." He gave Callie an indulgent smile.

"Yes," she said, returning it. She looked at Brenda. "Lex says you run a dance academy. Have you any gifted students?"

She grimaced, the look somehow out of place on her usually composed face. "One. A little eight-year-old girl named Kim of Oriental descent. But her interest seems to be waning already. So few girls have the dedication it takes to devote themselves to dance. Once they reach a certain age, other interests creep in. It's a shame."

"Brenda performs with her students during the holiday recitals," Lex said. "You two will have to come with us this year and watch her display her talent."

"Say," Ken shot in as he nudged Callie's arm, "good idea, huh, Sweetheart? We just might take Lex up on that."

Callie met Lex's eyes. She'd caught him studying her several times during the meal, and though she tried to remain nonchalant about it, it was beginning to unnerve her. She blotted her lips on her napkin and lay it beside her plate as she rose. "Excuse me for a minute, would you?" Spying the rest room sign, she did her best to head toward it at a normal pace, even though at the moment she was more than aware it was an escape and she wanted very much to run.

Inside the Victorian Rose wallpapered haven, Callie sank onto a wine velvet chair and leaned her head back, eyes closed as she inhaled the rose air freshener which permeated the confined space. Her insides were fluttery, her temples throbbed, and no two thoughts tumbling around in her brain made the slightest logical sense. This night she'd been looking forward to all week—and which she'd expected to be an especially romantic outing with Ken that would end with her announcement that she'd set their wedding date—had turned into a comedy of errors. Now she just wanted it to end.

She took a slow, deep breath and got up. She washed her hands at the sink and freshened her lipstick without once meeting her own gaze in the mirror. There'd be plenty of time to face herself later and figure out what in the world was happening. Lifting her chin purposefully, she returned to the table.

Ken and Brenda were sharing a laugh as she approached. "Oh, Cal," Ken said as he noticed her, "Brenda has been telling us some hilarious anecdotes about life at the dance academy. By the way, we took the liberty of ordering dessert already. I figured you wouldn't want any. Hope you don't mind."

"Not at all." With a polite smile, she resumed her chair, where she made it a point not to look at Lex again.

Chapter 13

Callie barely slept at all that night. She lay for hours staring at the darkness. The muted whirring of the ceiling fan above her bed mingled with the sound of the wind rustling through the trees outside the window in an airy murmur that kept her awake.

Part of her was angry and truly mortified at the way her fiancé had carried on with Brenda Harding. And the fact that Lex had barely spoken a word all the way home made his own irritation more than plain as well. But the other part of her wanted to laugh hysterically to vent her frustration and get it completely out of her system.

She had never seen Ken so animated, so full of life, in all the months they'd been together. Where had that studious, complacent, almost stuffy man she'd grown so accustomed to been all evening? She would never have recognized him on this date. Even after they'd arrived back at her condo and he'd come in for coffee, he had done nothing but talk about Brenda and ballet and how the four of them should make going out as a foursome a regular thing. He hadn't even turned on the TV to catch the late news on cable. With a troubled sigh, Callie turned over and tried to go to sleep.

When it seemed as though she had dozed off only a minute ago, the alarm jarred her awake. Callie opened one eye and peered unbelievingly at the hour. With head aching and bleary eyes, she dragged herself to the shower and turned the spray on herself without waiting for it to warm up. By the time it finally did, she felt awake. Hurriedly, she dried off, then chose a sundress in a bright strawberry floral print, hoping the cheerful pattern would perk her up in the middle of the day.

"Well, you're looking chipper this morning," Trish said when Callie arrived at the shop.

"Thanks. Anything exciting happening?"

"No, not so far. The UPS truck is making the rounds already, though. Maybe he'll have something for us too."

"That would be nice." Callie poured herself some coffee and stifled a yawn. It was going to be a long day. A very long day. Gathering a bunch of fashion circulars and order blanks, Callie spread them out on the desk and stared at them, trying to decide where to start.

Several hours later, as she was finishing her lunch at Soup and Salad Haven, someone tapped her shoulder. She looked up into Lex's eyes.

"I was at a table across the room when I noticed you. Mind if I sit down?"

"Not at all. I've only got a few minutes left, though."

"No problem." He set his tray on the Formica table and resumed eating.

Callie let her attention wander up the striped sport shirt he had on, meeting his gaze as she sipped her iced tea. "That was. . .um. . .quite the date last night, wouldn't you say?"

A curious half-smile tweaked his mouth as a chuckle rumbled out. "To say the least." He looked away.

"I really was surprised at Ken's behavior. I had no idea he was going to. . . Well, I'm just sorry."

"It wasn't your fault."

Neither spoke for a few seconds.

Lex bit off a corner of his grilled toast and chewed it thoughtfully. "Strange," he finally said, shaking his head in wonder.

"What was?"

"Those two. . .the way they hit it off."

Callie agreed but saw no point in responding. She had no idea where this conversation was leading and wasn't all that positive she wanted to find out. Just to be on the safe side, she changed tactics slightly. "It was a lovely concert."

"Yeah. I thought so too."

She watched him spoon up the remainder of his chili. For some reason she felt awkward, unable to think of a way to keep the conversation going, and he didn't seem his usually talkative self either. She swallowed her last mouthful, then glanced at her watch. "Well, I'd better get back. Trish is probably starved."

He nodded and tossed his napkin down beside his bowl. "I'll walk you to your car."

Outside, Callie blinked in the dazzling sunlight as she dug into her purse. She located her sunglasses and keys just as they got to the LeBaron.

"Guess I'll see you later," Lex said. He took a step away, then turned.

Callie was still struggling with the locked car door when his big hand curled around hers. She let go and looked up in surprise as he turned the key easily, then dropped the key ring into her palm. He took hold of her upper arm.

"Callie, don't go yet. I—"

Her heart fluttered crazily, and she felt color flood her cheeks at his undecipherable expression.

"You. . .uh. . .have something on your cheek."

Her hand flew to check it, but she felt nothing out of the ordinary.

"Let me," he said, leaning closer. He cupped the curve of her cheekbone with his hand and gazed at her without speaking.

Callie stood mesmerized, unable to move, not altogether sure she wanted to. But as he dipped his head slowly toward hers, her heart stopped for a brief eternity.

"Cara," he murmured as he brushed her lips with his.

The shock of his action and the use of her childhood nickname brought her back to reality. "I–I can't believe you did that!" she cried. Wrenching open the car door, she collapsed into the seat and sorted frantically through the keys for the ignition one. Finding it, she shoved it into place and started the motor.

Lex backed away a few steps as if in a daze, his face a colorless mask.

Callie never looked at him as she pulled away, but she knew it would be a good long time before she would ever forget his expression. Moments later, pulling into her spot behind the shop, she couldn't remember how she'd gotten there. And one look at her watch made her wonder if she'd broken the land speed record on the way. Pursing her lips in irritation, she got out and headed for the entrance.

"You okay?" Trish asked from just inside the back door.

Callie breezed past without stopping. "Yes. Fine. I'm fine."

"Oh. Just wondered. You look a little flushed."

Branding her friend with a sizzling glower over her shoulder, Callie threw her purse into the desk drawer and slammed it shut.

Trish cleared her throat. "Well. . .um. . .guess I'll go to lunch then. See you." Snagging her handbag, she dashed out.

After the sound of her partner's car engine faded into the distance, Callie got up and checked the salesroom. No one was there. *Just as well,* she thought. For two cents she'd have turned the Closed sign around and locked up, but 1:15 in the afternoon was fudging a little too much. Instead, she returned to the desk and sank onto the chair, leaning her throbbing temples into her cupped hands. *Lex, how could you? What were you thinking?*

The clock on the wall ticked audibly in the stillness, each beat like another turn of a screw, tightening her nerves until she thought she'd go mad. What she would give for her stairstepper right now, or her Exercycle. A pair of hand weights, even—anything to rid herself of the frenzy building within. But the possibility of having something so tempting in her grip about now would have caused an intense urge to send them crashing through the plate-glass windows.

The door chimes bonged.

Filling her lungs with a fortifying breath, Callie pasted on a bright smile and went to meet the customer.

⁂

It was pitch-black outside when Callie parked her car in front of the condo. After work, she'd driven aimlessly for some time, finally ending up on Interstate 5. Jolted by the sight of a Pasadena exit sign, she took the turnoff and made a U-turn, then kept the speed limit all the way to the Lancaster/Palmdale turnoff and home.

Lex's convertible was in its usual spot, but his place was shrouded in darkness.

With a small sigh of relief, she locked the LeBaron and went inside.

The next morning Callie was dressed for work and out the door before six. Lips pressed determinedly together, she marched to the car, knowing even as she went that it couldn't become a pattern. She wouldn't be able to avoid running into her neighbor indefinitely. But at least the escape worked now, today. She'd take the rest of the days one at a time and stretch out the success as long as possible.

The entire shopping center looked deserted when she arrived. After starting a pot of coffee and making a valiant attempt to have her morning devotions, she closed her Bible and sat back, fingers laced together over her abdomen.

Her thoughts drifted unbidden to yesterday, despite all her effort to fix her mind on work, Trish, her grandparents, and even the weather. She finally relented and gave in.

It wasn't exactly a kiss, she rationalized. *It was a. . .fluke. A silly fluke. Nothing to get so worked up about.* Lex Sheridan surely hadn't planned it. He couldn't have. Anyway, they were both adults—and *engaged to other people*. In all likelihood, he had already forgotten the incident, and so should she. It would never happen again. With that conclusion, she pressed a fold of her honey-colored jumpsuit between her fingertips and took a deep breath, drawing whatever comfort she could from the easing of her mind.

Callie had the shop dusted and tidy, the new orders ready to be mailed, and was entering the last of yesterday's receipts in the ledger when Trish arrived.

Her friend gave her a quizzical look. "Been here for awhile?"

"Mm-hm."

"Need to talk?" She slid her purse into a cubbyhole near the desk, then straightened her lime green shift.

"Not really," Callie said brightly. "Coffee's made. I was just about to have some. Can I pour you a cup?"

"No, thanks. Think I'll have some herbal tea for a change. Did you look over the new ad?"

Getting up from the desk, Callie handed Trish the pasteup on her way to the coffee machine. She poured some for herself, then dispensed hot water into a mug for Trish, adding a tea bag from the flavored assortment. Returning, she set the cup before her partner.

"Thanks." Trish closed the paper and looked up. "Listen, do you mind if I take off early today? I. . .um. . .have an appointment."

"No problem."

"A doctor's appointment." A peculiar smile lit her friend's eyes.

Callie recognized the sparkle immediately. "Are you saying what I think you're saying?"

Trish nodded. "The home pregnancy test was positive. Now I want it to be confirmed so I can get started right in on vitamins and stuff."

"Oh, Trish!" Swooping her friend up in a big hug, Callie squeezed extrahard. "I am so happy for you! I can't tell you how much."

"Yeah, well, it's taken me long enough. Maybe you'd better finalize your wedding plans while I can still fit into something classy, huh? It wouldn't do for the matron of honor to waddle down the aisle in a one-size-fits-all tent."

Callie's giggle was lost in Trish's as they hugged again. Then she sobered. "Hey, maybe you need to take it easy now. Don't overdo. We could even hire a salesgirl part time."

Trish flopped her hand. "Don't be ridiculous. I'm fine. Never felt better." She checked her watch. "This last half hour, anyway. I was a little queasy earlier this morning."

"Well," Callie said teasingly, "that's supposed to be part of the fun, isn't it?" She snatched up the duster and hung it on the hook by the French doors as she darted through to the salesroom, unable to miss the wad of paper that hit her right between the shoulder blades.

❧❦❧

The door chimes bonged again as the last stragglers from the half-dozen afternoon customers finally meandered out of the shop. "Come back soon," Callie called after them.

The door closed.

She straightened the counter near the register and then began arranging the earring cards on the swivel case. She didn't turn as the chimes sounded again. "I'll be right with you."

No one answered.

A peculiar inkling stood the fine hairs on the back of her neck on end. She swallowed and swung around.

"Hi." Lex stood there, his hands in his pockets, a sheepish look of guilt drawing his brows together above the bridge of his nose.

Callie remained frozen in place.

"Callie," Lex said, starting across the room, "I came to apologize for yesterday. I—"

"Don't." She raised a hand. "Don't. It's over and done with, I know it didn't mean anything, and now let's just both forget it and go on as if nothing happened. Okay? We'll just go back to where we were before yesterday occurred and just keep being friends."

His mouth gaped as he listened to the rush of words, and a half-smile twitched a corner of his mouth. "Hey, I had this big, humble speech prepared. Been memorizing it all day too. Sure you don't want to hear it?"

"What's the point?" she said, unable to restrain her own wry smile. She sincerely hoped the illusion she was trying to put forth—that of being relaxed and nonchalant—was holding up. "I don't want to stop being friends, do you?"

He shook his head. With a look of profound relief, he ran his fingers through his hair. "Well, good. Good. I just want you to know I really am sorry."

"Fine. It's already been zapped from my memory bank." She gave a firm nod.

So did he. "Well. . .I won't bug you then." Sliding a hand into his pocket again, he turned toward the door. "See you, Callie."

"Right. See you."

Not even watching him drive off, Callie gave the pencil drawer meticulous attention as she tried to ignore the lingering scent of the same musky aftershave Lex had worn yesterday. Then she sank to the chair.

Cara. She sighed. At least he hadn't called her that again. Unable to shut out the unbidden remembrance of the way Lex had whispered her name, Callie tried to subdue a rush of guilt as she refocused her thoughts in some safer direction.

Maybe tonight would be another good opportunity to drive down to Bakersfield and stay at Gram's. Spend Sunday with Ken. She picked up the phone and dialed his number.

Chapter 14

Lex cupped the back of his head in his palms and stared up at the dark ceiling. Another restless night like the last few, and he'd be worth next to nothing. But then, what did that matter? Compared to just about everyone else he knew, he'd done nothing with his whole life up 'til now. His younger brother, Jeff, was well on his way to taking over management duties at Dad's construction firm in the future. Brenda all but owned the dance academy where she spent most of her time and was passing on her talent and inspiration to younger girls. Callie and Trish had invested their life savings into what appeared to be a flourishing shop.

And what was he? A musician. Because of the generous inheritance he'd received after Grandfather Sheridan's death, he'd felt no pressure whatsoever to make something of himself. In fact, he recalled with a twinge of shame, the first thing he'd done with the legacy was try to waste it. He had driven to Vegas and hit as many nightspots and casinos as possible in three days and nights. But as Murphy's Law would have it, he only doubled what he was trying to throw away.

It was only by the purest stroke of luck that Brenda hadn't been free to come with him, especially in light of the fact that there were so many handy little wedding chapels sprinkled liberally throughout the place. They could have gotten married on impulse and then stayed on indefinitely, having fun until they were broke.

When Lex had finally tired one night and gone to his room, he emptied his pockets on the mirrored dresser. There among his keys, wallet, and assorted change was a gospel tract some squeaky-clean religious fanatic on a street corner had handed him with a smile. Lex had smirked and sat down on the bed to read it, hoping it would give him a good laugh, if nothing else.

But the opposite had happened. He saw himself sitting on the throne of his life, his own big ego making all the decisions in whatever way suited him best, without thought of anything or anyone else, much less God. Quickly looking up the quoted verses in the Gideon Bible on the nightstand beside the bed, Lex realized beyond a doubt that if he died that night he was not ready to face his maker. And worse, he was destined for eternal punishment, separated from God forever. That night he bowed his knees in prayer and confessed his need of the Lord.

Early the next morning, he'd purchased a leather-bound Bible of his own. Then, throughout the long homeward drive, he thought about his newfound faith and wondered how long it would take to satisfy the intense hunger inside of him that yearned to learn all there was to know about God. He could hardly wait to begin going through the study outlines the bookstore clerk had pointed out inside the new Bible. Already, Lex felt eager to tell everyone he knew that there was truly something satisfying in finding the Lord, but first he had some serious studying to do.

There had been many changes in his life since that fateful night. He no longer sought good times in smoky, liquor-reeking bars. He'd gotten involved at the newly formed New Life Fellowship and even managed to arrange with Dad for a crew to build the church and social hall. He did whatever the pastor asked of him, as far as providing music for the song portions of the services and performing ample special numbers. But what if God had some actual plans for his life? Was it too late now to think about preparing for the ministry or to find something to do with his time on earth? Something that counted for eternity? What would Brenda think if he even suggested such a possibility?

The opportunity to find that out presented itself on an afternoon drive after church that Sunday.

"You're pretty quiet, Darling," Brenda said, placing her hand lightly atop his on the steering wheel.

"I have a lot on my mind."

"About us?"

"In a way."

"Well, what is it? Maybe I can help."

Lex let his gaze meander over her feminine features for a moment, the sleek, straight nose he'd always thought was charming, the silken, honey gold hair that never seemed out of place, the clear green eyes that seemed clouded now with concern.

There was a scenic parking area coming up. Lex steered onto it and cut the engine. They got out of the car and walked around to the front, where he slid his arm around his fiancée and hugged her to his side. The two of them leaned against the warm hood of the Corvette and gazed over the spectacular expanse of the San Joaquin Valley, which sprawled at their feet in misty splendor as far as the eye could see.

Brenda raised her tempting mouth to his. He'd known her forever now. She felt right. She was perfect, so perfect—except for one thing.

"What were you thinking back there?" she breathed.

He filled his lungs slowly, then just as slowly let all the air out. He held her tighter, wondering how to broach the subject. "About life," he finally said.

"What about it?"

There was a smile in her eyes as she tipped her head back and looked up at him.

"That I'm wasting mine."

Her slender eyebrows dipped toward each other as she eased away a little. "What makes you say that?"

"It's the truth." Lex slid his hands into his pockets and switched his attention to some vague portion of the hazy scene before them. "I want to do something different. Better. Something that—I don't know. Lasts, I guess. Something for God. Maybe even in the ministry."

Up until the last phrase, her smile had remained. But now it drooped, and a frown took over. "You mean like be a preacher?" she asked incredulously. "You're actually considering burying your nose in that dusty old Bible of yours and then living your whole life around stuffy people who don't know how to have a good time?"

"Maybe," he said evenly. "I don't know what He wants of me yet. But whatever it is, I think I should do it."

Brenda stiffened and crossed her arms as she rested her weight against the front fender. "I thought your future would have me in it."

"I never said it wouldn't."

"Oh, really?" She let out a little huff. "Well, I can tell you right now that I for one do not intend to plan *my* life around religion. I'm too young. There's too much to do. I want to have fun and enjoy every minute. I want to go places with someone who's fun to be with. Try new things. The last thing that appeals to me is showing up for church three times every Sunday, going to prayer meetings, and rolling bandages with the ladies' aid society once a week."

Lex absorbed her words as a deep sadness began to make its presence known. "And what about when life is over, Brenda? What then?"

"I don't want to think about that."

"But wouldn't you want to have peace? To know where you'll end up?"

"I'll just find out when I get there, just like everybody else, I guess."

Lex put a hand on her shoulder and felt her stiffen under his touch. "It doesn't have to be like that. The Bible says we can know where we'll spend eternity. . . ."

"Yes, well, I couldn't care less. It's morbid to think about."

"That's not entirely true. Actually, when you find the Lord it's more of a peaceful feeling. A joy. Events and circumstances begin to make sense, and you see things in a whole different light."

Brenda raised her chin, a hard glint in her eyes as she turned them his way. "Well, that is one light I have absolutely no interest in finding. And if you must know, I expected you to get tired of all this religious nonsense ages ago. After all, everyone's on the same road, you know. Some people take one turn, and some another. But eventually we all get to heaven."

"That's not what God's Word says. Jesus is the only way."

"And I think that's the most narrow-minded thing any religion ever declared."

Lex met her gaze straight on. "It's the truth, Brenda. All of us either accept it or reject it. And when we die it's too late to decide differently. There are no second chances."

"So *you* think. I do not happen to agree." She took a few steps away, placed her hands on her hips, and swung back. "And furthermore, Lex Sheridan, I will *never* agree. So just in case you've been expecting me to come around to your way of thinking, I can tell you right now not to hold your breath. Because *it's not going to happen. Not now, not ever.*"

He didn't respond. A heavy weight pressed down on his insides, crushing him, making him feel like someone had just punched him in the gut. But if he had any last doubts, they vanished as Brenda slid off her engagement ring and held it out.

"I think you've made your choice," she said icily. "And now I've made mine."

He averted his gaze. "I don't want the ring. Keep it."

"What's the point? It no longer has any meaning."

"Maybe not. But perhaps someday you'll look at it and remember that it was given in love. . .by someone who wanted you to know an even greater one and will pray that you find it. I do love you, Brenda."

She pressed her mouth into a thin line as she closed her fingers over the diamond. "But not the way I need to be loved. I want to go home now."

With a nod, he opened the door for her, then went around to his side. Somehow, he'd known for some time that this day would come. But that didn't make it any easier to swallow.

❧❦❧

Callie idly turned her diamond solitaire around and around on her finger, wondering how to announce to Ken that she'd decided on an August wedding. Wondering if she wanted to. Wondering if she should.

"You seem distracted today," Ken said, guiding the Volvo around a sharp curve.

She looked at him and smiled. "I guess I'm just tired."

"Been busy at the store?"

She nodded. "We ran some good specials last week, and it brought in dozens of new customers. Some even said they'd heard about us from a friend. It was encouraging, to say the least."

"I know the feeling. We've been bogged down doing quarterly tax returns for self-employed people. Sure wish somebody would teach folks how to keep good records, so we wouldn't get stuck with having to unscramble piles and stacks of unrelated receipts and things."

"That would get tiring." She averted her attention to the oil wells flanking both sides of the undulating country landscape. The huge pumps chugged up and down, up and down, in perpetual motion, dragging the rich crude from far beneath the earth to waiting storage tanks. *How like my life,* she decided. *Wake up, go to the shop, come home, go to bed. . .but try not to think about the future or make a concrete decision.*

"Did you enjoy the sermon today?" Ken asked.

It took Callie several minutes even to remember the subject, since the pastor had rambled on so during his discourse that she'd found herself stifling a yawn or two. "Oh, yes. Pressing ever onward toward the goal. What are your goals, exactly, Ken?" Having voiced the question, Callie discovered she was more than curious to know as she appraised her darkly handsome fiancé, who was intent on navigating the curving road.

"I guess someday to have a partnership in an accounting firm. Vincent, Whoever, and Whoever, Certified Public Accountants. Has a nice ring to it, don't you think?"

Callie nodded. "And how do I fit in?"

"Perfectly. I need someone with a beautiful smile and personality to help entertain all the fabulously wealthy clients who'll beat down our door just to deal with us." He grinned.

"After I put in a full day at the shop?"

"Perhaps you'll tire of that venture one of these days and put some of that talent you possess into decorating my elegant office and our glamorous home," he said on a droll note. "After all, I do make enough money to support us."

She searched his face as he drove. "Take care of the house and the kids, is that it?"

"Kids!" He tucked his chin. "Who needs kids? Years of crying, whining, snotty noses, and band concerts, followed by rebellion and then being ignored while they traipse around the world to 'find themselves.' Give me a break. I think the two of us will be more than sufficient. We don't need that complication."

"You're really serious, aren't you?"

"You bet I am. I've worked too long and too hard to get where I am right now. I'm not about to give all that up to coach Little League on Saturdays."

"Funny how this never came up before," she mused more to herself than to him.

Ken turned a quizzical expression on her. "You were planning on a brood of Vincent offspring?"

"Well, yes. Kind of. Isn't that what marriage is all about? Loving, sharing, creating life. . ."

"For peons, maybe. But there are enough people in the world as it is. Too many in some places. Why add to the problem? With what we'd save not having to pay for one kid to go through college, the two of us could tour Europe and the rest of the world, go wherever we pleased. Be free. Answer to no one."

No one but God, she thought. A charming picture of two sweet little boys at New Life Fellowship flashed to mind. And one of a new baby girl in a long white christening dress at today's service. In both cases, the proud parents had beamed lovingly at them as if they were the most priceless of treasures. And soon Trish, too, would know that joy.

"But I suppose it's for the best we're not getting married right away after all," Ken said, breaking into her thoughts. "I'm going to be meeting with two other accountants I know this week who are interested in breaking out with me and forming a partnership in the not-too-distant future. And if it goes through, it'll take awhile to get everything set up and then on its feet, without having to commute from the mountain every day."

"So you don't especially want to hurry to the altar?"

"Not at the moment. By the way, Cal. Think your neighbor and Brenda would be interested in taking in another concert two Saturdays from now? I can pick up tickets anytime."

"I'll have to let you know." Relaxing against the back of the seat, Callie recalled the last occasion the four of them were together.

And a tiny part of her couldn't help wondering if the new partnership was the only reason Ken wasn't anxious to get married.

Chapter 15

It wasn't until three days later that Callie's path intersected with Lex's. She didn't know if he'd gone away for a few days or what, but the few times she did see his car parked out front, not a sound carried from his side of the condo. And having no reason to bother him, she didn't, but went on in her usual routine. Now, after she finished half an hour on her cross-country machine, she toweled off, then reclined in the chaise on the deck to cool down in the balmy heat of the July night.

"Can I interest you in a cold drink, Neighbor?" Lex said, peering around the lattice, the hand nearest her extending a chilled can of Diet Coke.

"Sure. Sounds great."

He swung a long leg over the partition and delivered the soda with a grin as he plunked down on the other chair with his own can of Coke Classic.

"You've been keeping busy lately," Callie remarked for no reason in particular.

"Kind of. Running errands for New Life."

She nodded and sipped the carbonated beverage.

"I've been wondering something, though."

Callie met his gaze.

"I heard it from somewhere that you'd gone to Bible school. That right?"

"For all the good it did me, yes." She took another gulp. "Trish and I both went to Liberty University, in Virginia. We wanted to get away from California, and that school offered the courses we were interested in—business management, and so forth."

"But you didn't care for the Bible part, or what?"

Callie could tell from his sincere expression that he truly was interested. She saw no reason to be less than honest. "Actually, the Bible courses were wonderful. It just wasn't at a time in my life that I appreciated them." She smiled wryly and shook her head. "I mean, look at me now. Engaged to a man who apparently has no interest whatsoever in spiritual matters—even the church I attend with him teaches only surface baloney, like weeding bad habits from the garden of your life. And have I grown at all in the Lord? I doubt it."

Not a muscle in Lex's face moved. He didn't even appear to blink.

"Why?" she finally asked.

He shrugged and cocked his head back and forth. "I've just been thinking lately about getting some training."

"What kind of training?"

"Bible. Maybe some ministry courses. I don't know."

This time she was the speechless one.

His mouth slid into an easy grin. "You think your life shows a lack of depth? I have absolutely nothing to show for mine. My brother will be the one to take over for Dad one day. And here I sit, doing what? Nothing. Zip." He leaned forward, his elbows on his knees, and gazed despondently out at the hills.

"I don't quite agree with that, Lex," Callie said gently. "From what I saw at your church, you fill a vital need there. Music is a valid ministry too, you know. People who never take time to read the Bible or even go to church regularly can still be blessed by the message in a song. And I've seen at least half-a-dozen young boys hanging onto your pant legs at the Fellowship. Obviously, they look to you as some kind of wonder hero. . .or an example, at least."

He didn't turn his head her way, but his eyes did shoot her a sideways glance. "When did you learn how to pass on such wise thoughts at just the right time?"

She felt herself blush. "Who am I to know how 'right' a suggestion of mine might be? You're the only one who knows if the Lord is trying to tell you something. My point was that He can use all of us right where we are. He's given you a lovely talent, and He had His own reasons for doing so. Why not put that to more use? Ever think of opening a music store and giving lessons to some of those less-than-affluent boys who might face some tough temptations in the coming years? Unless their minds are pointed in some other direction, who knows what might happen to them? Maybe that's why the Lord put you there in the first place."

Some of the perplexity in Lex's face seemed to ease as he appeared to be taking her words to heart. His countenance became much more cheerful. He swung her an appreciative smile and straightened his shoulders. "That thought never once entered my brain. And it's definitely worth thinking seriously about. Do you know what? I'm afraid I've given you far too little credit up 'til now."

She laughed lightly. "I aim to please. Need a friend? Call Callie, and all that."

His gaze made a slow circuit of her face. "Friend. Right. I'll tell you one thing, Callie McRae. You're better than a mere friend. Much better."

At the peculiar spark in his eyes, Callie knew she should say something before the flame beneath her skin ignited her cheeks. "Considering our less than amiable past, I'll take that as a compliment."

Lex drained his Coke and slowly stood, a half-smile barely in check. "You can take that as many ways as you like." With a wink, he saluted her with the empty can, then went over to his side.

❧❦❧

"My, don't we look bubbly today," Trish teased as Callie arrived at work the next day.

"Must be this nice morning," she answered evenly, stowing her purse in the drawer. "Ever see such a perfect one in your life?"

"Once or twice."

"How was your doctor's appointment?" Callie asked, hoping to change to a safer subject.

Her partner pinkened ever so slightly. "About what I anticipated. We really are expecting. I'm fine, and now I have to load up on iron and extra vitamins and stuff."

"Oh, well, I'm glad everything checked out okay. I'm really happy for you and Phil." Callie grabbed the feather duster and breezed out into the salesroom just as the phone rang.

"It's for you," Trish called.

Callie returned, taking the receiver from her friend. "Hello?"

"Hi, Cal. It's me. I was just wondering if Sheridan and his fiancée were interested in making it a foursome at that concert. I'll be going by the ticket office today on business and decided to check with you."

"I never thought to ask. I've barely seen Lex at all lately."

"Oh. Well. Guess I can do it another time. Try to find out, though, would you?"

"Sure. Love you."

"Me too. Bye."

She handed the phone back to Trish's waiting hand, meeting her nosy smile. "Nothing exciting. Ken just wants to double with Lex and Brenda to a country concert."

"Ken actually gets along with Alex Sheridan?" Trish asked, her pitch high in wonder.

If Trish only knew, Callie thought to herself, then shrugged. "In a passable way. We doubled with Lex and his fiancée to a Christian concert in Lancaster last week, remember?"

"Oh, right. And with this little secret of mine, I forgot to ask how things went."

"They went fine. The music was great, the dinner afterwards was delicious. . . your average date."

"Then why do you have that guilty look on your face, I wonder?"

Callie glowered at her partner. "You know, Trish, every once in awhile I ask myself why I bother to tell you anything."

Trish laughed even as her fair cheeks turned rosy. "Because you know it's impossible for me as your very best friend in the world to help you unless you come clean. When you only tell me half of something, that's when we have a problem."

"Believe me, my friend, when I have something to tell you, you'll be the first to know. Until then you'll just have to trust me."

"Oh, well. If that's the best you can do, I suppose I'll have to make do."

Callie gave her partner's hand a squeeze. "Good."

۶❧❀❧۹

When Callie pulled into her parking spot on the street in front of the condo, Lex drove up right after her.

"Hi," he called. "Have a good day?"

"Pretty good. How about yours?" She watched him remove the guitar from the trunk, then waited on the walk while he fell into step with her.

He clamped a hand on her shoulder and applied some friendly pressure as he grinned. "I've been thinking a lot about what you said the other night—that a person doesn't necessarily have to be a minister to serve God, that one can use the gifts and talents the Lord has given him to reach others."

"It's just something I believe."

"Well, I had never once thought about it one way or the other, until now. All I know is the more I mull it over in my mind, the more inclined I am to believe the thought came from the Lord. I've never felt so sure of anything in my life before."

"And what was Brenda's reaction?"

An unmistakable dark look crossed Lex's face for a split second, and when it passed, Callie wasn't altogether certain she'd seen it.

"Actually, I haven't mentioned it to her."

"Oh." For some reason, Callie felt the subject was not one to pursue. Reaching her door, she gave a wave. "Well, see you." Fumbling with her key, she suddenly remembered Ken's phone call and turned around. "Oh, Lex, I almost forgot."

At his partially open door, he raised his brows.

"Ken was wondering if you and Brenda would like to double with us to another concert a week from Saturday."

He smiled. "Thanks for asking, but I'm afraid we can't. Brenda. . .can't make it."

"Oh. Too bad. Perhaps another time, then."

"Yeah. Night."

Later, as she curled up in her robe and watched a movie on TV, Callie heard soft music drifting from the adjoining unit. She muted the television sound and strained to listen. Moody and slow, it was only loud enough to make out "Better Than Friends." It brought back very pleasant memories of Friendship Day at New Life Fellowship, and Lex's comment of the evening before. She closed her eyes and let the remark warm her like a velour blanket, afraid even to wonder at the strange new sadness that seemed to lurk behind his smile at the mention of his fiancée.

۶❧❀❧۹

Lex strummed the guitar absently as he went over the events of the day in his mind. Surprisingly, the details of obtaining a music studio were already falling into place. All he lacked now was the right spot for it, but he'd already checked

315

out and dispensed with half the available listings the real estate agent had shown him. There was still a goodly number of properties yet to see. One of them would surely be perfect. When and if he found it, he'd tell Callie.

And who would have believed that Doug, Manuel, and Raul would agree heartily with the idea—to the point that they'd volunteer to pitch in whatever time for lessons they could swing around their working hours. This had to be of the Lord. And as the pastor had told him after practice tonight, a person could take all kinds of Bible courses by mail. Maybe *all* of his dreams would work out.

Well, most of them, at any rate. The initial pain Brenda's rejection had caused was slowly ebbing. He was trying not to take it personally; after all, the realization that she was rejecting the Lord was far more disturbing than the fact she had canceled their planned marriage. All he knew was that a strange peace filled him. The hard part would be informing his parents about the breakup. But that would pass eventually too. He had more important things to concentrate on now than merely blubbering into his Coke. Brenda was a survivor. A fun person. In no time at all, she'd have some other guy interested. And in the meantime, Lex would keep on praying for her.

He fingered a run up the frets and took the song again from the top, singing under his breath. And a whole bunch of more than pleasant recollections of Friendship Day at church paraded through his thoughts. Who would have believed he and Callie McRae would end up friends after the miserable way he'd treated her in the past? Too bad he hadn't known then what a refreshingly honest person she was. Maybe he'd have beaten Ken Vincent to the punch.

That thought shocked him, and he stopped playing. How could he be entertaining those ridiculous notions when he'd only just broken up with Brenda? It wasn't as if Callie were even free. *Put a lid on it, Sheridan,* he reminded himself. *Before you wreck the friendship too.*

Lex propped the guitar upright against the side of the couch and went out to the kitchen, where he'd put a whole box of fresh jelly donuts when he'd come home. He poured a glass of milk and removed two sweets, setting them on the counter. Then as a twinge of guilt assaulted him for thinking first of junk food, he opened the fridge and rummaged around for the makings of a salami sandwich to have first.

Chapter 16

Lex nodded thoughtfully as he swung one more appraising glance around the vacant building unit. Tucked between two other small enterprises in the Tehachapi business district, the former mortgage and loan office already sported several small closed-in cubicles that, after a few minor alterations, would do adequately for practice/lesson rooms. Already Lex could picture them in use. And the roomy open area would provide ample space for music racks, display cases, and instruments. "I don't need to look any further. This will suit me fine."

"Great." Vic Torrence's confident smile looked right at home on his jovial, oblong face. "Well, let's head back to my office, then, and write up the deal. Mr. Ames, the owner, has already agreed to make whatever modifications might be required inside, including replacing the carpeting. I've found him quite easy to work with."

Lex led the way out to the curb, where he'd parked behind Vic's jade Mercedes. For someone who appeared less than ten years older than he, Vic Torrence had all the earmarks of a successful real estate agent. He had a friendly, outgoing way about him, and one trait Lex liked even more—an aboveboard honesty and a desire to satisfy his clients. The neatly dressed sales agent strode to his vehicle and pulled out of the parking spot, with Lex following the Mercedes to the realty office several blocks away.

A dozen phone calls and what seemed like two dozen forms later, Lex found himself the new official tenant of a soon-to-be opened studio of music in downtown Tehachapi. Mr. Ames had suggested a contractor to put in the added soundproofing and structural requirements, and Lex had already spoken to an interior design consultant he knew from church who seemed more than ready to help with coordinating the decor. The next order of business was to drive down to Bakersfield and obtain the license and other legalities. Now that he was actually getting into the thought of his new vocation, it was hard to contain the mounting excitement.

Cresting the overpass to the freeway, Lex glanced toward Windy Hills Plaza. Rolling hills blocked the distant shopping center from view, but it was all he could do not to go there first and gush about his new lease to Callie. The fact that more and more often lately she was a large part of his thoughts was something he was struggling with. He knew he was on the rebound from Brenda, and he had no right to entertain designs on someone who was not free, despite Lex's very real conviction that Ken Vincent was definitely not good enough for her.

In an effort to refocus his attention in a safer direction, he shifted in his seat and popped a classical guitar CD into the CD player.

᳁᳁᳁

Callie tore off the register tape of the day's sales and took the cash drawer back to the office while Trish dimmed the Tiffany lamps and set the salesroom in order for the night.

"Wanna come over for supper tonight?" Trish asked.

Callie smiled over her shoulder. "Sounds nice, thanks. But I have some things I need to do at home."

"Something I might help you with?"

" 'Fraid not." Paused in the open doorway, her arms supporting the register drawer, Callie studied her friend as she repositioned a Louis XIV chair and then stepped back to look it over. "Can I ask you a personal question?"

"Sure." Trish turned, then started toward her. "I've never had secrets from you, you know."

"That's one thing I've always appreciated about you."

"What is it?"

Callie hesitated, wondering how to word the query. "Was Phil happy that you're pregnant? Does he want other babies?"

"He was ecstatic, and yes, eventually we plan to have bunches of them."

"He likes kids, then?"

"Likes them! When he's around his nieces and nephews, they all but worship him. He can't spend enough time keeping them entertained. It's fun just to sit back and watch them together."

With a smile, Callie lowered her gaze.

"Why do you ask?"

"No reason. I was just wondering." Then, as she turned toward the desk, she stopped and swiveled to face Trish. "Ken says he doesn't want children. That they'd be an inconvenience."

Trish raised her light brows. "You two never talked about it before?"

"No," Callie admitted with a sheepish smile. "Ridiculous, isn't it?"

"What do you talk about?"

"Sometimes I wonder." Callie sighed and set down the drawer. "We used to talk about anything and everything, back in the beginning. What we did all day, what we dreamed about at night, who we ran into, our hopes and dreams. . ."

"But not anymore?"

She shook her head. "Now he tells me about the latest advancements in accounting and how he plans to form a partnership with some other CPA pals, how silly it is for me to be in business. Surface stuff. Most of the time we don't talk at all. He hardly even calls now that I live up here. I have to ask myself if he's noticed I'm not around. Is that. . .what it's like to be married?"

A soft smile illuminated Trish's whole face. "It sure doesn't have to be. Phil's such a romantic at heart that he still phones me on his lunch hour just to say he loves me. And whenever something funny happens on the job he can't wait to tell me about it. And I'm the same way. I still tuck little secret notes in between his sandwiches and under his pillow. I look forward to waking up every morning just so I can feast my eyes on that sunburned face of his. . .and anticipate going home every evening just so I can feel that big heart of his against my cheek. I don't remember what life was like before he came along. He's made it ten times better, that's for sure. I wouldn't enjoy a day that he wasn't a part of."

"Won't children kind of. . .disrupt all that?"

"Are you kidding? I can't wait to have a little rough-and-tumble daddy's boy or two curled up on our laps at night, wanting to be read to or taken for horsey-back rides. Watching him grow up to be some lucky little girl's hero. Or watching Phil treat a daughter like a princess, the way he does me."

Callie sighed. "That's how I always felt. Remember how we always planned for our kids to grow up together and be best friends, the way we were? Well, I guess that wasn't meant to be, after all." She walked around the desk and sank into the chair, then got out the ledger book, opening it to the bookmark.

"Listen, Kid," Trish began, "no woman should feel compelled to settle for less than she wants. It's not too late to change your mind." At Callie's expression she raised her chin and spoke more forcibly. "I know you feel you love Ken. But there are lots of kinds of love in this world. . .and some of them change over time. It happens so slowly that we aren't even aware of it until something makes us stop and take note. You've been my best friend all of my life, Callie, and I know things about you that you don't even know about yourself. Like how you deserve some-one who's really special. Someone who loves you for the unique person you are, who will accept whatever changes in life help you to grow, and whose love won't cool down. And forgive me for saying this, but Ken is not that man. He doesn't bring out the best in you. . .he stifles it. And now he says he'll never accept some sweet little replica of you that the Lord sends your way? Puh-leeze. You need to think this through before it's too late."

Callie swallowed. Try as she might, she couldn't fault Trish's words. Any of them. Her and Ken's engagement—though once born out of love—had dimin-ished gradually. Time had watered it down until there was nothing left of the original relationship but one they both took for granted. They no longer worked at it—it was habit. Convenient. Now they were finding more things to differ over than agree on. And both of them seemed to fare amazingly well apart from the other. Was that what she wanted in marriage? For the rest of her life?

Trish's hug brought her back to the present. "Listen, you can let the receipts go 'til tomorrow. Why don't you go home and pray about things and work through the problem?"

Callie mustered a smile. "Maybe I'll do just that. Tomorrow's another day. And I do need to do some heavy thinking." She took a deep breath. "Thanks, faithful friend, for the wise advice. You always come through when I need you most."

"Shooting you down, though, it seems to me," Trish said wryly.

"Maybe. Maybe not. Could be you're 'the wind beneath my wings,' like the song says. I'm going home to pray. See you tomorrow, okay?" Taking her purse out of the desk, she waved and left Trish to lock up.

≈✸✸≈

Callie had hardly ceased praying for wisdom since she had left work and started home. And though some of her petitions were beyond being expressed in words, she lifted them all up to the Lord anyway to sort out and handle. Of one thing she was certain—she now knew Ken was not part of God's will for her life. Not anymore. She was not sure he had ever truly been. But she did have feelings for him, perhaps always would. And hurting him was something she didn't want to do. What she needed now was wisdom for the next step. Wisdom that matched the incredible peace that pervaded her.

The beeper sounded at the five-mile mark on Callie's Exercycle. Raising a corner of the towel she had draped around her neck, she blotted her face and stepped down, then went directly to the shower. She stood motionless in the warm spray, enjoying its soothing and refreshing presence, feeling almost as if it were cleansing away a film of uncertainty that had enshrouded her for months. When she stepped out and wrapped a fluffy towel around herself, she felt much lighter.

Half an hour later, she carried a tossed salad with chunks of chicken breast into the living room and turned on the TV.

The phone rang before the picture flashed completely on. Callie clicked off the remote and picked up the receiver. "Hello?"

"Hi, Cal. It's me. Did you find out about the concert?"

Always a warm greeting, she mused with a sad smile. She moistened her lips and reined in her wayward thoughts. "Hi, Ken. I did mention it to Lex, but he said Brenda wouldn't be able to make that day."

"Oh. Figures." Ken let out a huff of disgust. "Oh, well. Maybe another time."

"Won't we still go?" Callie asked out of pure interest.

"Naw. It's sure to be a sellout by now anyway."

"I suppose." She paused. "Ken. . .are you coming up here on Friday? We need to talk."

"Sure, I guess. See you then, okay? Gotta run."

"Fine. See you then." Hanging up, Callie wondered if he'd even noticed the absence of her habitual endearment. And, for that matter, if he'd notice *her* absence later on. No matter. In the natural process of life, the time had come for them to part. She no longer had the slightest doubt.

She reached for the remote, but the phone jingled again. She stifled a giggle and picked it up, wondering what earth-shattering reason Ken would have for making two long-distance calls in one night. "Hello?"

"Hi. It's Lex. Are you busy?"

"No. No, not at all." Forcing down a rush of warmth that threatened to envelop her, Callie relaxed against the couch back.

"Good. I didn't want to bother you or anything, just wanted to pass on some good news."

"What kind of good news?" She had an inkling it would be unwise to invite him over to tell her in person, but for one fleeting second, she didn't care. "Why don't you come over for a soda, and tell me about it?"

"Sure I'm not catching you at a bad time?"

"Positive."

"Great. I'll bring the donuts."

She giggled and hung up. In seconds she heard Lex's footstep outside. She opened the door.

Standing there on the welcome mat, he almost glowed, looking about to burst as he came in. "I did it, Callie. Prayed about what you said, found peace about it, and decided to go ahead with the music studio idea."

"What?"

The enthusiasm in his voice, his face, his bearing, was hard to resist. Tangible, incredible, radiant. . .touchable.

Callie didn't even try to stop her smile or question the wisdom of her reaction. She hugged him. "Oh, Lex. That's wonderful! I just know it'll be perfect for you. I wish you every success."

She felt his strong arms close around her, pressing her against his solid, muscular chest. Then he swallowed and eased her away. "Thanks. I just wanted you to be the first to know. I've already found a spot I like that the landlord will renovate to my specifications, and better yet, the other guys in the ensemble have offered to help out with lessons and things. Already the details seem to be falling into place."

"I couldn't be happier for you, Lex. I mean that."

"Thanks. So anyway. . .I had to tell you." He grinned, shifted his weight from one foot to the other, then shoved a bag at her. "Here. I know you don't eat junk. I brought you a croissant. Is that acceptable?"

Lex watched a slow smile tremble on her lips as she closed her fingers around the paper sack. "Perfect. I'll get the soda. You like Coke Classic, right?"

He felt almost dazzled by Callie's shining eyes. He inhaled the wake of soap and perfumed shampoo she left behind as she hurried out to the fridge. And he tried very hard to ignore how soft she felt for the second or two he'd held her.

When she returned with a tray, he took one chilled can of soda and a donut, which she'd set atop a napkin, and she helped herself to the diet drink and the almond croissant.

"Would you mind if we prayed?" she asked, taking a seat on the couch and curling her legs under herself. She reached for his hand.

He bowed his head, grateful that her voice rang clear. He couldn't think of one thing to say.

"Dear Lord, it's hard to know where to start to thank You when You work miracles in our lives. But we are so grateful for the new direction Lex is taking, for the way You've already begun working things out for him. We ask that You continue to lead his steps day by day, and glorify Yourself in this new venture that we know is of You. We love You and praise Your name. Thank You for the refreshment too, and this wondrous friendship. In Jesus' name, amen."

Looking up, she smiled.

And Lex had to remind himself to breathe.

Chapter 17

Callie wasn't exactly looking forward to her usual Friday night date this time, but she dressed with care in a swingy, pearl gray jersey with a Belgian lace shawl collar, praying all the while that the Lord would grant her wisdom and the right words to say. She'd seen Ken really angry only three or four times she could recall and sincerely hoped tonight would not make the fifth. She spritzed on some perfume and added silver earrings.

All too soon she heard his knock.

She manufactured a bright smile and swung the door open. "Hi."

"Hi." Ken gave her the typical peck on the lips. "Ready?"

She nodded and snatched a light wrap from the oak hall tree on her way out.

"Man, the traffic up the mountain was awful," Ken grumbled. "One long string of eighteen-wheelers and campers blocking both lanes. There should be a law that keeps the slow vehicles in the outside one."

"There is, isn't there?"

"Well, someone should enforce the dumb thing." He closed the door after her, then went around to his side.

Callie felt her nerves start to tighten. She clasped her hands together in her lap to keep them still and stared straight ahead.

"Any preference?" Ken asked as he inserted the ignition key and started the engine.

The question caught her off guard. He'd always been the one to choose. "Well, you seem to like Shelby's."

"Fine. Shelby's it is."

It seemed to be everyone else's choice too, Callie noted as they entered and she saw the line waiting to be served.

Ken grimaced. "Aw, who needs this? Let's go to Domingo's instead. We haven't tried Mexican for awhile."

Domingo's, with its subdued lighting and Spanish decor, would provide slightly more privacy, Callie knew. And a table for two in a cozy corner opened almost as soon as the hostess had taken their names after their arrival. Callie smiled and accepted the menu from the darkly handsome young waiter, and within moments they'd ordered. Then while they waited for their food to arrive, she dipped a warm tortilla chip into the hot sauce and bit off a corner, hoping that by keeping her hands busy the fluttering in her stomach would calm also.

"You know," Ken said, after sipping water from the goblet in front of him, "I've been doing quite a lot of thinking about things lately."

"Oh?" She dipped another chip and nibbled it while the current recorded mariachi song ended and another began.

"Yeah. And I'm glad we're eating here. It doesn't seem as though we're on display. I like these little booths. Makes it easier to talk."

Callie nodded. Ken seemed in a strange mood. Distracted, nervous, not quite meeting her eyes. "About what?"

"Us, actually." His gaze flicked to hers for a second, then away. "Surely you've noticed things don't seem quite. . .the same since your move."

She opened her mouth to reply, but their orders arrived just then. She leaned back while the chicken quesadilla was set before her. The fancy dollop of guacamole and sour cream, off to one side with the slivered black olives arranged just so, seemed especially artistic this evening.

Ken sliced at once into his enchiladas as the waiter departed. He forked some into his mouth and chewed slowly, then swallowed. "You know, Callie, I think a lot of you. A lot. We've gotten along well together for the most part, up until just recently."

"True." She toyed with a portion of her quesadilla, twisting the stringy melted cheese around the tines of her fork before sampling a mouthful.

"And I really don't want to hurt you," Ken went on. "It was never my intention. I hope you believe that."

"I feel the same way."

"You do?"

"Of course."

He tugged at the collar of his striped sports shirt, leaving the knot of his tie slightly off center. "But, well, even you must agree that the distance between us has been more of a detriment to us than a blessing. I don't mind admitting it's a pain having to drive all the way up the pass every time I want to see you. And since you're adamant about staying up here—as adamant as I am about remaining down in the valley. . ." The words trailed off significantly.

"You want to break up?" Callie fought a ridiculous urge to burst out laughing. It took several sips of water to alleviate the desire as she tried to stay composed.

Even in the golden glow from the little table candle, Ken's complexion took on a reddish tinge as he looked everywhere but at her. "Mind you, I'm not saying I don't have feelings for you, Cal. We've had a lot of wonderful times together. But I don't know. . .lately we seem to be growing further and further apart. We don't want the same things; we don't share the same goals. . .do you know what I'm saying? Maybe it's time we stop and take time to consider other relationships."

Callie patted his hand. "As much as I hate to admit it, I think perhaps you're right."

"Y–you do?" His eyelids snapped up, and he stared right at her.

She nodded and continued eating.

"You don't hate me?"

"Why should I? Maybe we were only meant to be friends. I have feelings for you too. As you said, we've had a lot of great times together, Ken. More than anything, I want you to be happy. And it would take an absolute dunce not to see that you aren't happy engaged to me."

His look of surprise and relief erased years from his age. He shook his head in wonder.

Callie worked off her engagement ring and placed it in Ken's palm, then closed his fingers over it.

"I. . .wouldn't mind at all if you kept the ring," he said.

She just smiled. "Don't be silly. I know it was your mother's. It's only right that it should go to the wonderful girl you meet who'll be everything you've always hoped for."

"Think she exists?" he asked on a droll note.

"Yes, I do. I really do. Take my word for it. A man as fine as you will never go to waste."

"Leave it to you to say the right thing. I suppose I half expected you to dump your supper all over me and call me names. This is amazing."

Callie tilted her head. "I can't see what that would accomplish. Especially when I truly just want to wish you well. To thank you for everything. I have no regrets."

"Know what?" He grinned. "Neither do I. None whatsoever. Aunt Phoebe tried to prepare me for this event, said she'd seen it coming. Wait'll I tell her it turned out to be a mutual, *amiable* parting of the ways."

"Yes, do tell her that. She's quite a lady. I'm sure she'll be more than relieved to have you back."

Ken laughed lightly, then noticed Callie's empty plate. "Can I buy you dessert?"

"Why not? I would really love some flan."

Back at home after bidding Ken a fond good-bye, Callie stayed in her dress and heels and strolled out onto the deck. At the banister, she rested her forearms on the smooth wood and leaned her weight on them as she surveyed the hills and meadows, alight with the glow from a three-quarter moon. The world was so quiet, with nothing to break the stillness but the occasional hoot of an owl or a flutter of feathered wings. Not even the crickets were chirping.

"Nice night, huh?"

Callie's heart tripped over itself as Lex moved into view. "I didn't know you were home. Your car isn't out front."

"Yeah, I know. Doug borrowed it for some heavy date or other. His is in the shop."

"Oh."

Neither spoke for a timeless moment, then Lex cleared his throat. "You're home pretty early for someone who only goes out once a week."

It must have been the weird turn of events or something; Callie couldn't be sure. But the laugh she'd managed to contain all evening at Domingo's finally shook her shoulders. "He dumped me." She turned and saw Lex shaking his head.

"What a jerk. First time I ever saw that guy I had him pegged as a nincompoop."

"Oh, now, come on. Ken's a fine man. We've just grown in different directions. Better we find out now than later on, way down the road of matrimony."

"Yeah, right." He moved to the outside edge of his railing and took his usual perch.

Callie plucked a climbing rose from the trellis and breathed in its sweet perfume as she resumed her relaxed pose. "I might have expected *you* to be out on a heavy date of your own," she finally said.

"And I probably would be too," he said evenly, "if she hadn't dumped me."

The flower slipped from Callie's fingers. "You're kidding, right?"

"Nope. Scratch one fiancée and one diamond. I'm history. Since last Sunday, actually."

Callie sputtered into a real laugh, and he entered right in. By the time their mirth subsided, she was wiping away tears. "I'm sorry. I don't mean to be rude. It just kind of struck me funny."

He gave a nonchalant shrug.

"I guess this makes you and me a couple of losers, Sheridan."

"Looks that way, McRae."

"Will your parents skin you alive?"

"Probably. How about your grandparents?"

She thought for a minute. "I don't suppose they'll care that much about it. They just want me to be happy."

"And are you, Callie?"

She shrugged. "To be honest, I'd have to say yes. . .happier than I've been in quite some time. And Trish will be thrilled. She's never really approved of Ken."

"The guys at church never saw what I did in Brenda either. Guess I can see where they were coming from now."

"Funny how some things work out, isn't it?"

He chuckled.

Callie straightened the kinks out of her back and yawned. "Well, I guess I'll turn in. See you, Lex."

"Yeah. Night."

The sliding door masked whatever he said after that. But Callie had the strange impression he'd added "Cara." She chewed the inside corner of her lip and went to change for bed.

Chapter 18

Callie awakened early, more rested and refreshed than she'd felt in ages. She pulled on a jogging suit and ran out to take advantage of the cool air before returning home to shower and dress and head off to the shop. Lex's Corvette was still not back, she noticed as she drove away. And at the remembrance of the offbeat conversation the two of them had shared last night in the moonlight, she smiled.

"Good morning," she all but sang on her way into La Femme.

Trish looked up from entering yesterday's sales into the ledger. "Callie?"

Nothing her partner could say today would dampen Callie's mood, so she ignored the good-natured barb and looped the strap of her purse on the arm of the desk chair with a big smile.

"I take it you worked things out with Ken."

"That's right. He and I have decided to go our separate ways. . .just like you've been hoping."

Trish laughed. "Well, at least I don't see any bandages or bruises."

"No. It was a friendly parting. Bordering on comical, you might say."

"How so?"

Callie poured herself some coffee and tugged the folding chair over to the desk. "You'll never believe it. There I was, getting dressed for the Big Breakup Date. . .praying my little heart out that he wouldn't be hurt or get mad—get the picture?"

"Yes, yes, and?"

"And he dumped me. Is that amazing or what!" Callie giggled despite herself.

Trish tucked in her chin and sat back, her hands folded over her tummy. "You're putting me on."

"No. He had this big speech all prepared. . .ever so gentle and placating. Saved me the trouble of having to be the one to do the dirty deed. Amazed even me. Ken can be quite eloquent at times. It's a gift."

Trish's smile bubbled into a giggle, then she sobered. "And you're okay, Callie? Really, I mean."

She nodded. "It's something I've seen coming on ever since the move, to be truthful. Things never were the same after that for either of us. I have peace about it, and I'm sure that one of these days he'll find someone more along the lines he's hoping for."

"And you?"

"And me, well, I'm just going to take things a day at a time while I enjoy my newfound freedom."

"It sure looks good on you. If you ever take a turn for the worse, need a shoulder, and all that—"

"Thanks, Pal. But I'm fine. What's on the agenda for today?"

"The new shipment of sleepwear should arrive from Hemingway's. Other than that, it's business as usual."

"Good. I'll go dust the shop before it opens." Grabbing the feather duster, Callie floated into the main room, humming as she went.

Lex parked outside of La Femme Fashions for a full half hour as lunchtime approached. Then mustering his courage, he gulped down his trepidation and strode to the front door. He hated the way the chimes reverberated like a gong in the quietness—and almost changed his mind when Trish popped out of the back room.

He watched a perplexed frown ripple her forehead. "Lex. Can I help you?"

"Callie around?" he asked casually, slipping a hand into his pants pocket.

"Sure. I'll get her." Returning to the French doors, she went through them and closed them after herself. A few seconds later, Callie appeared in her place.

"Hi." She crossed the room toward him in a flowing white jumpsuit, her dark eyes wide, questioning.

He fastened his gaze on the gold chain at her throat. "Hi. I was wondering— oh, it's probably stupid. I shouldn't have come." Waving a hand in a gesture of dismissal, he turned to leave.

"Don't be silly, Lex. What did you want?"

He stopped at the door and looked back over his shoulder as he let out a breath. "Thought you might like to see my studio. But now that I've said it, it sounds really dumb. It's not like there's all that much to see. Yet."

"I'm honored that you'd even ask me. I'd love to see it. It's my lunch hour anyway. Just let me grab my purse."

He nodded and watched her go back to the office, where he heard her make some light comment to Trish just before she emerged again, smiling as she approached him. "Should I take my car?"

"No reason to. I'll bring you back after I feed you. Fair enough?"

"More than fair. Let's go."

Neither of them spoke more than a syllable at a time on the drive into town. But the atmosphere seemed charged, as if an invisible electrical storm was gathering overhead, waiting to spark. Reaching the store, Lex parked at the curb and got out.

He took out the shiny new key he'd barely used yet and unlocked the door.

And he watched Callie's face as she went in and swept a leisurely glance around, then retraced it with her feet, touching, looking.

She swung back and smiled. "It's perfect, just like you said. I suppose the back rooms will be where you give lessons, right?"

He nodded. "I'm having new carpeting put in, of course. Remember Erin Fleming at New Life? She's an interior designer, and she's going to help with all that."

"Well, hold out for what you want. Don't get talked into something you're not really happy with." She lowered her lashes and blushed. "Sorry. Listen to me. You don't need anyone making up your mind for you."

"Hey, I'm always open to good advice from a friend."

She looked up at him and held his gaze for the space of a heartbeat. "All the same, a friend should know when to butt out."

Lex couldn't resist tweaking her chin. "Yeah, well, that time will be a long time coming, I can tell you that. So what are you hungry for?"

Over pasta salad at Mama Alberto's Pasta Palace, Callie relaxed, enjoying the homey polkas and ballads from Lawrence Welk recordings. They took her back to her childhood as she recalled listening to the orchestra on Saturday night television with her grandparents. "How long do you think it'll take before you open for business, Lex?" she asked between songs.

He shrugged a shoulder in a noncommittal way. "A couple months, anyway. I suppose it depends on the contractor. Tomorrow I'll drive to L.A. and check out some music supply stores and catalogs, figure out how many new instruments I'll need. I have a couple old guitars I'm planning to let the first students use. It'll save them a few bucks."

"That's thoughtful. Not that it surprises me, mind you," Callie was quick to add. "Will you have any keyboards?"

"Not in the beginning, unless someone requests one. I'm gonna start small." His eyes made a slow journey over her, finally locking on her eyes. "I don't suppose you'd be interested in coming with me to church this Sunday. . .or were you planning on visiting your grandparents?"

Callie hadn't made plans for the weekend yet. She was aware of the warmth of Lex's perusal, and more than aware of his presence, and how much she enjoyed it. But there was no denying they'd both just broken up with people to whom they'd made commitments that would have been binding forever. "Friends?" she finally asked, knowing he'd catch the deeper meaning behind the simple word.

He didn't answer right away but seemed to be considering one, almost like a move in chess. He nodded with the hint of a smile. "At first." His gaze did not release hers, and she knew he also was trying to find the fragile balance between the yesterdays and the tomorrows.

She also knew Lex was a man worthy of her trust. Perhaps Gramps had been right. The Lord was giving them this second chance, hoping they'd get it right. And if they took their time, maybe there truly would be something beyond mere friendship in store for them. In any case, it would be her purest joy to find out for sure. She returned his smile. "I'd like that."

✲✲✲

Lex slipped smoothly into the pew beside Callie after the end of the song service as Pastor Dan Granger stepped up to the pulpit.

"Nice to see more and more familiar faces each Sunday," the redheaded minister remarked, with an all-encompassing glance over the filled sanctuary. "I hope you all brought your Bibles along. I've found studying today's topic an interesting experience, and you might also. First, let us pray."

Callie experienced once again the feeling of being at home in the small, friendly church. It seemed a stark contrast to the one she'd attended with Ken, almost as though she belonged here and had only been away for a week or two. Hearing Pastor Dan's "amen," at the closing of the prayer, she raised her head.

The minister reached into a pocket in his suit jacket and pulled out a crisp twenty-dollar bill. Smiling at the young boys who occupied the front row, he held the currency between his hands and tugged just hard enough to make it snap. "Sounds good, huh?" He grinned. "Looks good too, right? Bet it would cover a couple fun hours at the video arcade."

The kids snickered and shifted in the seat.

"Too bad, though," Pastor Dan went on with a sad shake of the head. "It's fake. Phony. Counterfeit. Not worth the paper it's printed on." With that, he tore it in half and let the pieces flutter to the carpet. "As we go through life, we'll come across quite a few things that seem good, look wonderful, feel right. . .and some of them will even fool us into believing they are. At least for a time. But *hopefully*," he drew the emphasized word out slightly, "eventually, if we look closely enough, we'll be able to tell the difference.

"I'd like for us to look at a few counterfeits in the Bible. The counterfeit god in Exodus—which the Israelites fashioned for themselves while Moses was speaking face-to-face with the God of creation, the counterfeit disciple, Judas Iscariot—whose love of money was far greater than his loyalty, and the counterfeit Christians, Ananias and Sapphira—who thought they could get away with lying to God and the church. There are other good examples, of course, but with the Sunday roasts to consider, we'll concentrate today on just the three I mentioned. Turn with me to Exodus, chapter thirty-two. . . ."

Callie found the passage and gave the sermon serious concentration as Pastor Dan began his discourse. She grasped quickly the parallels he was so adept at pointing out. But soon enough, her mind drifted to her own life's experiences and some less than wise occasions when she'd misplaced her trust. She recalled a few quick decisions that had proved disastrous. It was all true. Everything the minister said.

Sometimes a near-perfect appearance hid serious flaws just beneath the surface. A person needed to seek wisdom from the Lord in order not to be deceived—in all areas of life. Even love. Ken had seemed perfect at the start. She never had a doubt about him. And yet, looking back on things now, she could see that her own stubbornness and pride had kept her from seeing the truth. Only by the Lord's mercy had she been prevented from making a huge mistake. Humbled by the realization, she took a deep breath and tuned in to the voice from the pulpit once more.

Lex hunkered down into the collar of his open-necked casual shirt. Pastor Dan had zeroed right in on him! On everything he'd ever done! Not only from way before he'd come to know Jesus as his Savior either. Sure, he'd turned around and set out on the right path, but that hadn't stopped him from taking a wrong turn now and again. Even after an untold number of great and powerful sermons about seeking God's will and then following it, he'd escaped making one of the most stupid choices in his entire life. Escaped by the skin of his teeth! How could he have presumed God would bless a union with someone who didn't believe? The passage concerning the lack of fellowship between light and darkness was perfectly plain, but he'd ignored it completely. Well, from now on things would be different. He'd turn all areas of his life over to God's leading. Especially the one regarding a life partner. He observed Callie in the edge of his vision and felt an indescribable flow of warmth and peace, almost like a blessing. He sent a silent prayer of thanks aloft.

"That was one deep sermon," Callie murmured when they exited the car afterward. "I needed that lashing, sorry to say."

Lex ran his fingers through his hair. "I thought he aimed the whole thing at me!"

She laughed lightly. "Well, then, it must have done its work. Maybe everyone felt it. Sure gave us a lot to think about."

"Yeah." Reaching her door, he met Callie's eyes. The light shimmering in the brown depths was almost blinding. He cleared his throat. "Would you come with me again tonight?"

"I'll look forward to it."

"So will I." He had no plans to kiss her. He knew she needed time, needed things to progress slowly. But she didn't move. And her beautiful lips parted ever so slightly.

As if she were true north, his mouth felt drawn like a compass needle to hers. But somehow he managed to keep the kiss soft, brief, and then draw away.

Her lashes fluttered open, and she smiled. "See you later, huh?"

You'll be seeing a lot of me from now on, he thought. "Yeah. Church starts at six."

⌘

September had to be the most glorious month in all the year for weddings. The sky was so breathtakingly blue; the billowy white clouds magnificent against the deep hue. And the ceaseless mountain wind paused to take a breath before whispering through the long grass.

The scalloped neckline of the chantilly lace tea gown skimmed Callie's shoulders, accenting the string of pearls Lex had given her, making her feel especially elegant and feminine as she adjusted her wide-brimmed hat in the mirror. She smiled as Trish handed her the bouquet, white roses and cymbidium orchids atop a white Bible, with slender white and silver ribbons trailing from the bottom of the arrangement.

"Nervous?" Trish asked. Her own nosegay of peach and white roses shook ever so gently in her fingers.

"I'm trying very hard not to be." Callie assessed her friend's appearance in the empire-waisted apricot lace they had chosen. Although Trish was quite vocal about her pregnancy, she had not yet started to show. The color of her ensemble and hat accented her fair complexion.

Strains of keyboard music drifted through the open window.

"Guess it's time," Callie said.

She followed Trish out of the room and onto the lawn of Sky Mountain Resort, where everyone she and Lex loved had come to witness their simple wedding. Looking across the sea of heads that turned her way as she stepped outside, her eyes sought and found Lex's deep blue ones filled with love and admiration as they beckoned to her. She drank in the sight of him in dove gray tails as she walked up the white runner sprinkled with white and peach rose petals. When she reached his side, his hand closed around hers, and he smiled tenderly.

The perfect day, the well wishes, soft keyboard music, and sacred vows all blended together in life's most spiritual harmony. And though it passed all too quickly, Callie knew she would always look back on the memory with joy, treasuring the special day that would always belong to her and Lex.

Even now, checking their baggage at the airport, and waiting to board the American Airlines jet on the first leg of the month-long tour of the British Isles her new husband had arranged after finding out her most secret dream from Trish, Callie feasted her eyes on his strong profile. Her heart swelled within her.

Someone lay a hand on her arm, and she turned to see a dear old lady with a cane smiling at her. "Congratulations, Dear. I hope you'll both be very happy."

"Thank you."

"Yes, congratulations," another stranger said.

Callie stifled a frown, wondering if newlyweds had a special aura that made them stand out so obviously. She flicked a glance to Lex, but he seemed to be holding a grin in check.

"Every happiness," a third person said cheerily a few minutes later.

She gave a polite smile and a nod in return, then slid another look at Lex as the ticket agent handed over their boarding passes. "My goodness," she remarked.

"Everyone seems so. . .friendly."

"Don't they though?" Lex picked up the carry-on bag.

"Think I'd better hit the rest room before we board, if you don't mind."

He nodded.

After Callie washed her hands with the scented liquid soap, she put on a light touch of lipstick, then checked her hair. Her tousled curls had fared well enough during the drive to Bakersfield even with the top down on the Corvette. But she rearranged a few of them with her fingers anyway, then turned slightly to make sure no stray loose hairs were clinging to her navy traveling suit.

That's when she saw it—the rough sketch of a wedding cake taped to her back, with the words "Congratulate me!" emblazoned across it for all the world to see. Even as she rolled her eyes, the humor of it struck her, and she laughed. After removing the paper, she folded it and tucked it into her purse as she began plotting Lex Sheridan's demise.

Ever so calmly, Callie strolled out to the black vinyl and chrome seats in the waiting area and stopped toe to toe at Lex's.

She almost lost it at the look of supreme innocence which rose to meet her eyes. But somehow she hung onto the ragged edges of her composure and eyed him without wavering, even though it was almost impossible to keep a straight face. Her foot began a rapid tapping as she crossed her arms. "Tell me. Is it starting all over? Is this a sample of what I'm going to have to deal with all the rest of my life?"

Out of the corner of her eye, Callie could see the bystanders chuckling good-naturedly and whispering behind their hands. But that all vanished to insignificance as Lex flashed a guilty grin that melted all her resolve.

He rose and drew her into his embrace, planting a kiss square on her mouth. "No. I swear." His right hand rose in Boy Scout oath fashion as if to add credence to the statement.

Callie felt a light laugh coming and didn't try to subdue it as she shook her head slowly back and forth, all but oblivious to the strangers around them as her pulse throbbed in unison with his. "What am I going to do with you?"

Lex grinned and kissed the tip of her nose. "I'll tell you, Cara, my love. You are going to do everything with me for the rest of your natural-born days. Everything your sweet little heart desires. And more."

"And I suppose you expect that one little promise to vindicate you from your whole wild and thoughtless past, right?"

He tipped his head to one side and searched her face. "Not altogether. I thought it would take one of these too." He lowered his lips to hers in a tender kiss. "And one of these." One slightly more passionate followed. "And maybe a few of these. . ."

"Excuse me, Sir," a voice cut in. Callie heard it only from far away. "I believe your flight has been called."

Lex snatched up the travel bag in one hand and captured Callie's in his other. "Come on, dearest wife. I have a small piece of the world to show you."

The joy and anticipation the two of them shared seemed an almost tangible thing to Callie as she and Lex walked hand in hand up the airplane ramp. Yesterday's memories no longer cast shadows. They vanished completely in the blazing brilliance of a lifetime of tomorrows.

SALLY LAITY

Sally spent the first twenty years of her life in Dallas, Pennsylvania, and calls herself a small-town girl at heart. She and her husband Don have lived in New York, Pennsylvania, Illinois, Alberta (Canada), and now reside in Bakersfield, California. They are active in a large Baptist church, where Don teaches Sunday school and Sally sings in the choir. They have four children and twelve grandchildren.

Sally always loved to write, and after her children were grown, she took college writing courses and attended Christian writing conferences. She has written both historical and contemporary romances and considers it a joy to know that the Lord can touch other hearts through her stories.

Having successfully written several novels, including a series co-authored with Dianna Crawford for Tyndale, three Barbour novellas, and six **Heartsong Presents** titles, one of this author's favorite things these days is counseling new authors via the Internet.

Golden Dreams

Kathleen Yapp

Dedication

To THE GROUP,
Ron and Betty Jo Freeman,
Stu and Aura Monfort,
Bob and Betty Spicer,
who shared a weekend in the mountains
with Ken and me,
explored a gold mine and ate apple pie,
laughed with us until we cried,
and will be our dear friends forever.

Chapter 1

The click of a rifle being cocked stopped J.L. in his tracks.

He was about thirty feet inside the entrance to a gold mine in the Laguna Mountains of southern California, and intense darkness hindered his vision of the ten-foot-wide tunnel in front of him. But he knew someone was there, with a gun, someone who could see him clearly silhouetted in the sunlight that streamed into the mine behind him.

Not moving, J.L. listened for a sound to tell him where the person was now, and he heard it—small rocks and gravel being crunched beneath the feet of that someone who was approaching him from the front, although it sounded like the sound was coming from behind him too. Even though it was cool inside the mine, his heart speeded up and sweat exploded on the back of his neck.

Then he saw the rifle barrel, aimed at his chest, and his body stiffened. Dropping the envelope he was carrying, he quickly raised his arms and yelled, "Don't shoot!" But a bullet ripped from the gun, splaying the dirt and gravel behind him; and J.L. dove to his left, losing his Stetson, and scrunched himself against the shadowed, rocky wall of the mine.

He started breathing again after ten seconds when he felt no pain, saw no blood, and knew he wasn't dead.

"Are you all right?" a woman's frantic voice called out through the darkness.

J.L. stayed where he was, not about to be suckered into showing himself, even though the voice sounded genuinely concerned.

But when he saw her not five feet from him, the Winchester still pointing at him, he lunged, fiercely gripping the rifle and shoving it skyward; at the same time his powerful arm circled her waist and yanked her against him with all the delicacy of a bull squashing a chicken.

The gun fell to the ground, and he kicked it away, the barrel clacking loudly over rough dirt before it crashed into the opposite wall.

"Are you crazy?" the young woman gasped.

"Only when someone's using me as target practice," he growled through clenched teeth.

"I wasn't shooting at you."

"Really? Who else is in this tunnel?" He was there to talk with the mine's owner. How had he stumbled into World War III?

"There was a mountain lion behind you, but I missed him."

"Right." J.L. laughed scornfully, looking down into fierce, luminous eyes that challenged him and quickened his pulse.

"It's been attacking dogs and cattle in this county," she explained, wrestling to free herself from his viselike grip, "but so far he's eluded trackers."

"I didn't know California had mountain lions." J.L. relaxed his grip on her as he decided she wasn't all that dangerous.

"Over five thousand, and they're becoming more aggressive and losing their fear of humans because their habitat is being developed."

Her voice was low and smooth, like rich cream, and he liked the sound of it. He also liked the sheen of her long blond hair and the curve of her full lips.

Suddenly he let her go, wondering what a woman so beautiful, wearing dungarees and a green pleated blouse, was doing in so rough a place as a gold mine, carrying a loaded gun. "So you're a committee of one to catch this carnivore?" he asked.

She quickly stepped away from him, placed her hands on her hips, and shook her head. "Hardly, but this morning one of the men who works here told me he heard an animal digging on Level Two. I brought the rifle, thinking I might find the cat, or some other animal, that had decided to set up house in this mine and wouldn't like the idea of being dislodged. When I heard the crunch of your boots, I came looking—"

"And found me."

"And the lion behind you."

J.L. let out a big sigh. Those were the other footsteps—paw steps—he had heard. "Could we go outside?" he asked, leaning over to retrieve his cowboy hat, which he brushed off but kept in his hands. "I'm getting claustrophobic in here."

"Sure."

Picking up the rifle, Lindsey Faraday led the way out of the tunnel, her heart still pounding erratically. When she had first heard the sounds, she hadn't known whether it was a stranger in her mine who didn't belong there or the animal she hunted. All the men who worked for her had gone home for the day. Santiago, her foreman, was still in town. It was too late in the afternoon for tourists to be dropping by.

Finding two intruders in the mine had been a shock, but her daddy had taught her how to shoot when she was just a teenager, and she rarely missed when she aimed. She wasn't at all a hunter, but she did enjoy knocking tin cans off a fence behind the mine office. Today, all the years of practicing had paid off.

The cat she had seen must have been close to two hundred pounds, and there was little doubt in her mind that it had been looking for something to eat. Even though she hadn't killed it, she had scared it away and saved this man's life.

And what a man he was. Now that they were out in the sunshine, she could see him clearly for the heart-stopping, big guy that he was, all six-feet-something, two-hundred-muscled pounds of him. She almost dropped the rifle from pure admiration.

The only word for him was rugged. From thick, unruly dark hair the color of wet earth that surrounded a chiseled face that belonged on Mount Rushmore, to his broad shoulders and formidable chest that filled every inch of a blue western shirt, to his powerful legs encased in blue jeans. Rugged. Even his expensive but scuffed boots sent a message of strength.

Whoever he was, his hard, solid body reminded Lindsey of the rock walls of her mine, his voice of the deep shafts.

"Am I lucky to be alive?" he asked with a questioning look from intense brown eyes behind pronounced lashes. He jammed the hat onto his head, leaving a shock of hair dangling across his forehead.

"I don't mean to brag, but I can hit a target at two hundred yards," she told him.

"You didn't hit the mountain lion."

"I scared him away."

"That's not the same as hitting."

"Look," she said, miffed at his ingratitude, "there were a few problems in between, namely the darkness and you."

"You took an awful chance."

There was no smile in his dark, assessing eyes, nor the defined creases down his cheeks, and his generous mouth pulled taut across a determined jaw made clear his annoyance at being shot at.

"I apologize if I scared you," she grumbled.

"More than scared. You took five years off my life."

"Which you might not have had if I hadn't pulled that trigger."

"Am I supposed to thank you?"

"That would be nice."

They stared at each other a moment, each recognizing in the other a stubborn streak that didn't give ground easily.

J.L. shrugged. "Then I thank you."

It irritated Lindsey that he didn't appreciate what she had done for him, but she wasn't about to get into a full-blown argument over it. "You were trespassing on private property, you know," she said.

"I have business here."

"And what might that be?"

From his serious expression, Lindsey guessed he was a man who always put business first. "I'm looking for Lindsey Faraday," he said.

She took a deep breath and let it out slowly, wondering what he wanted with her and already deciding that whatever he was selling, she didn't want any.

They hadn't gotten off on even ground, which was too bad because she didn't like confrontations. Getting along was better.

"I am Lindsey Faraday," she told him, "and I really am sorry about what just happened."

J.L. stared. For the first time since he could remember, he was speechless. *She* was Lindsey Faraday? *She* owned the Lucky Dollar Mine? He had been expecting a tough old gal with stringy gray hair, skin like sandpaper, baggy clothes, and a voice that could skin a mule at twenty paces.

Lindsey Faraday was a far cry from that. With the sun shimmering through her long, honey blond hair that hung straight and floated behind narrow shoulders, there was a childlike innocence about her that was enhanced by intelligent, diamond blue eyes and a petal-small mouth.

She was tall and slender, and she made him think of undulating leaves on a weeping willow tree, and words to describe her came easily to mind: memorable, feminine, intriguing. Warm. She had felt warm in his arms, the very opposite of the cold, hard steel of the gun she had been carrying.

"I'm pleased to meet you, Miss Faraday," he managed to say without his voice cracking like a lovestruck teenager's; and he whipped his hat off his head, gave her a quick bow in respect, and stepped back, trying to keep his eyes from wandering over every exquisite inch of her. He considered himself a gentleman, after all, who did not put undue importance on a woman's physical appearance. What she was inside—her character, her motivations, her intelligence, her love of God—those were more important than superficial beauty.

"Let me introduce myself," he went on. "I'm Jonathan Logan Brett, and I'm an attorney from San Diego." He smiled just enough to produce two adorable dimples in those otherwise hardened cheeks, and Lindsey couldn't help smiling in return as she shifted the rifle from her right hand to her left and put out her hand to meet his, which he took and kept in his.

What kind of lawyer wears a black Stetson, leather-corded bola, and boots big enough to squash a cobra? she wondered, noting also the robust and tanned look of him that told her he spent as little time as possible indoors behind a stuffy desk in some glassed-in office.

"I have business to discuss with you," he said, releasing her hand, which allowed Lindsey's heartbeat to return to normal—almost.

"Business?" she asked.

"Yes. On the floor of the mine is a paper you need to see, Miss Faraday, which I dropped when I put my hands up and requested, politely, I thought, that you not shoot me."

Lindsey grinned. "Which I didn't."

"That's true." His eyes glanced at the rifle she still held. "If I get that paper from the mine, you won't shoot me, will you?"

"Not unless you prove to be more dangerous than that mountain lion," she teased back.

"I'm a kitten," he promised, and Lindsey knew that was pure fallacy. Everything about the man was full grown and disquieting: the way he stood, the rumble of his voice, the set of his shoulders, the way he looked at her that made her skin tingle in the nicest way.

She watched him stride across the rough and graveled ground and disappear into the mine, her mind finally focusing on what kind of business a lawyer from San Diego might have with her.

Chapter 2

When J.L. returned, Lindsey expected him to give the paper to her. Instead, he said, "Can we talk this over in your office?"

He looked around the hilly, rather barren grounds for such a place, and Lindsey felt a rush of apprehension. *Does he think I'm going to need to sit down after I read this?* She could not imagine what serious business he could have with her. She was scrupulously up to date on all her bills, wasn't being sued by anyone, and, as far as she knew, there was no long-lost relative who had recently died and left her a million dollars, unfortunately.

She studied J.L. Brett and tried to think the best. *Maybe he's drumming up business—wants me to make out a fancy will or open the mine for public investment.*

As if reading her mind, J.L. tapped the envelope. "You'll know when you read this. It will take only a few minutes, and I'll be glad to answer any questions you might have."

With a nod yes, Lindsey pointed behind her to a dilapidated wooden square of a building with a tin roof, about forty feet away. "My office is over there."

As J.L. looked at the building, Lindsey began seeing it through his eyes. It wasn't much, just some timbers that seemed to lean into the mountain behind it and had seen better days—a hundred years ago, maybe. There were a few windows, not too clean, she realized with a dash of embarrassment, and a metal smokestack that was bent and had also seen better days.

Some manzanita bushes, but no flowers, grew across its front, and two huge oak trees guarded either side, their branches spreading over the top of the office and embracing far enough above the roof not to be in danger of catching fire from wayward sparks released from the potbellied stove within.

He might as well know I don't go in for frills, she thought, and started walking toward the building. J.L. fell in beside her, his gait smooth and powerful, she noticed, like a cougar sure of its territory.

There was an aura of manliness about him that exuded self-confidence. He gave the impression of a man who knew who he was, what he wanted in life, went after it, and most always got it. But what was he after now?

She liked the fact that he had not been ashamed to admit that he had been afraid when she was shooting at him. And he didn't seem to be arrogant, just determined.

As they strode toward the office, he didn't make small talk, but his eyes swept over the terrain, taking in everything around him. *Idle curiosity, or was it more?* she wondered.

In the one-room mine office of dusty file cabinets and technical equipment scattered around the floor and on rickety tables, he gave Lindsey the envelope and she took from it the single sheet of paper and began reading it.

J.L. watched her, for reaction, and his pulse quickened as he realized he was attracted to her. She was more than interesting, more than beautiful. She was. . . intriguing. Why was she here, in this rough, bleak place—a delicate rose in the midst of rubble?

She was almost an enigma, a woman who looked like an angel but could shoot a powerful weapon of destruction. A woman who certainly would win men's attention, yet was separated from them by a life's work in a remote mountain.

Even the scent of her was different: not that of expensive French perfume but of what? Yes, talcum. That white, soft powder that goes on every baby's bottom and soothes. On her it smelled every bit as intoxicating as if it cost a hundred dollars an ounce. *Intoxicating. That's what she is,* he thought, starting a mental list of her attributes that already included intriguing, stunning, and intelligent.

His admiration soon turned to concern as he saw the expression on Lindsey's face range from disbelief to anger. He knew he had a fight on his hands.

"This is garbage!" she declared, her eyes flashing fire when she looked up at him. She crumpled the letter in a ball and tossed it at him.

"Excuse me?" He grabbed the paper before it fell to the floor.

"Garbage," she repeated. "Ridiculous. Untrue." She strode behind a gray metal desk and threw herself into a sturdy, straight-backed chair.

"Why do you say that?" J.L. questioned. He had not expected that reaction to the facts. Hooking a well-used wooden chair near the desk with the toe of one boot and deftly turning it around so it was facing Lindsey, he sat down in it and wondered just how much she really knew about the running of the mine. She probably had a business manager. He would talk to him.

With undisguised animosity, Lindsey stared at him. "My daddy, Mr. Brett, would have never borrowed thirty thousand dollars and then not repay it."

J.L. met Lindsey's stare with conviction in his own. "My client has a Note and Deed of Trust, found in the papers of her recently deceased mother, that says William Faraday, your father and then owner of the Lucky Dollar Gold Mine, borrowed a great deal of money from her in 1985 and never paid it back."

"No, he didn't."

Add stubborn to the list, J.L. thought.

"And I know that," Lindsey went on, "because we worked together for many years before he died, running this mine." The words were sharp, like bullets exploding from the rifle she had been carrying. "He would have told me if he had had to borrow that much money."

While J.L. wondered just what she meant by "worked together. . .running this mine," he watched her with the practiced eye of a court attorney used to determining if people were lying under examination. Lindsey Faraday looked straight at him with eyes that did not blink. Her breathing was heightened and her small, narrow hands were locked together on the desk in front of her, although he was sure they would like to be pummeling his chest instead.

Still, he could swear she was telling the truth, as she knew it. But she was wrong about her father. She had to be.

"The Lucky Dollar was used as collateral," he told her.

"Impossible."

Stubborn and tenacious, he expanded the list of her qualities that had started out loftily the first moment he had seen her but was deteriorating into more negative ones as she refused to accept the truth of what he was telling her.

"Do you have proof the note was repaid?" he asked.

"I don't need proof for a loan that was never made."

"Yes, you do."

Lindsey watched J.L. sit forward and slowly, meticulously, unfold the letter from his law firm, pressing out with long, wide fingers, lightly sprinkled with the same dark hair that covered his head, the creases she had made when she had wadded it up. There was danger in his silence, in the methodical way he worked on the letter, like a wild animal skillfully and patiently stalking its prey. Even so, Lindsey was not prepared for the strike.

"If you don't repay the loan voluntarily, Miss Faraday," he said gently, but with his eyes locked to hers, "the Lucky Dollar will be sold to raise the money."

"Foreclosure?" she screamed. Every muscle in her body went taut, and she leaped to her feet. "How dare you come onto my property and tell me I'm about to lose the most precious thing in my life. My father and I struggled for years to make the Lucky Dollar produce enough gold and silver to provide us with a comfortable living, and no two-bit cowboy lawyer is going to change that."

J.L. stood up too, surprised at the vehemence of her challenge. He was used to people getting angry with him over legal matters, and he knew how to control his own reactions when they did. Even name-calling didn't push him over the edge, because when a man's temper is lost, so is his ability to make the kind of decisions that win cases.

Now, however, this ravishing, stubborn, exasperating woman was stirring conflicting emotions in him: He wanted to insist she just do as he said, pay the money, and get it over with. He also wanted to tell her he was sorry and ask her out to dinner.

"Our discussion is over, Mr. Brett!" Lindsey declared before J.L. could decide which direction to take and, walking out from behind the desk, she strode deliberately across the room and was almost past him before he reached out and captured one arm.

"I'm not leaving here, Miss Faraday, until I know what you intend to do about this."

She whirled to face him, and he gave her just as fierce a look as she was giving him. "Is there someone else I should talk with?" he asked. "Someone who handles your business affairs?"

He knew he had made a tactical error the minute the words were out of his mouth, as temper raged in her eyes. "So, Mr. Brett, you're a chauvinist as well as a bully."

J.L.'s mouth dropped open.

"No one knows the details of this mine more than I do," she informed him hotly with a determined lift of her chin. "I need to look through my father's papers again."

Is she stalling or desperate? J.L. pondered, and he saw signs of both in her fiery blue eyes, watching him expectantly for his answer, a determined woman, resolved not to give up a large sum of money without a fight, which he certainly understood and applauded. He also saw a flash of desperation, like a cornered wild animal not sure how to escape. He wasn't quite able to figure her out, but he would have to if he were going to secure for his client what was rightly hers and what she so urgently needed.

"All right," he said finally, as though he were commuting a death sentence, knowing the power he had over her made him number one on her shoot-at-dawn list. "Three days to come up with proof of repayment."

"Which is what?"

"A Full Reconveyance. But the fact that no such document was ever filed with the County Recorder, and my client still has the Note and Deed of Trust—"

"I'll look anyway," Lindsey insisted. *Time,* she thought. *I need time.* Not that she thought that would do any good, because when her father died she had thoroughly gone through everything of his, and there had been no evidence that such a serious transaction had taken place. But how was she going to convince J.L. Brett and the client he represented of that?

She spun on her heels and, straightening her shoulders, walked to the door and opened it with a flourish, allowing the bright California sunshine to burst into the room. She was dismissing him. She hoped he realized that. She never wanted to see him again, despite his rugged, handsome face and deep, rumbling voice. She was getting more agitated by the moment, and who could blame her? She was being threatened.

She wasn't expecting him to move with the force of a tornado across the room and stop so close to her that she had to put her head back to look up at him. He pushed the door shut.

"Are we going to settle this peaceably, Miss Faraday?"

Each word was punctuated clearly with the warning that they had better do just that, but Lindsey stood her ground against his formidable size and scowling eyes. "Probably not," she retorted, "since your client wants what is mine."

"What is hers."

"According to you."

J.L. Brett shook his head emphatically. "According to legal documents."

"That I have not seen yet." Lindsey knew she had a temper. It was something she wanted the Lord to help her eliminate, now that she was born again. Though she had a new life in Christ, just a few months old, sometimes the old life roared into action and she struggled against it, like she was doing now, standing toe to toe with this maverick lawyer who wouldn't take no for an answer. While she had never totally lost control with another human being, J.L. Brett just might be the first.

"I shall be happy to show you those documents," he pressed.

"Another day, perhaps." She yanked open the door. Her voice had risen ten decibels in ten seconds.

"They're in my truck." He pushed the door closed.

"Then go get them!"

When Lindsey saw every muscle in his body expand and his jaw turn to stone, she suspected that J.L. Brett was not used to taking orders. And, when a hand big enough to crush a cantaloupe tore the old door open with such force the old hinges ripped from the frame, she knew it.

He stood there, stunned, holding up the huge piece of wood with one hand. Then, with a grunt of frustration that was actually a growl, he let the door crash to the floor and stormed down the path toward the parking lot, nearly running into Santiago Ramirez, her foreman, who was coming toward the office.

Santiago gave Lindsey a concerned look, and she knew he was seeing flaming cheeks and one angry woman.

"Trouble, Boss?" he asked tentatively.

"No more than a hurricane, flood, and earthquake all put together," she declared, wishing she had something to throw at the departing figure of J.L. Brett. In less than fifteen minutes, the man had threatened her livelihood, destroyed the door of her office, and made her more furious than any person she had met in her life. "Add to that tidal wave."

Then she kicked the door and howled as pain shot through her foot.

Chapter 3

When J.L. opened the door of his burgundy pickup truck, he nearly tore it off. Hurling himself into the driver's seat, he yanked a yellow legal pad from his leather briefcase and a gold ballpoint pen from the pocket of his shirt, and scrawled across the top of the paper in huge, bold letters, LINDSEY FARADAY. Down the left side he put "stubborn, temperamental, uncooperative," saying the words through his teeth as he wrote them, then added "defensive" and "unrealistic" with a flourish.

Leaning over the steering wheel, he stared at the list and took a half-dozen deep breaths before he felt under control again.

"Why did I let that woman get to me?" he asked himself out loud. Tossing the legal pad onto the seat beside him, he slumped back and closed his eyes, feeling like he had been caught in a revolving door that was still going around.

He had lost his temper, which was unprofessional, immature, and against his Christian conscience, and which certainly had not persuaded that feminine ball of fire that his client's claim was legitimate.

Jamming the pen back into his pocket, J.L. reached inside his briefcase and took out an envelope that held copies of the Note and Deed of Trust his client had found in her mother's estate. Looking at it he said, "I hope your contents do a better job of convincing Lindsey Faraday than I did." Then he got out of the truck and, with giant and purposeful steps, he walked back on the path toward the office, fully expecting the beautiful Miss Faraday to meet him halfway with her rifle aimed at his chest.

But she didn't. She was still in the office, talking with a burly Hispanic man who was under six feet tall but had the shoulders of an ox connected to the body of a bull.

When J.L. walked in, both Lindsey and the man, whose hair was jet black and wiry and whose deeply lined face told the story of a hard life, fixed dark looks on him that made him feel about as welcome as a rattlesnake at a picnic.

"I have the papers you wanted to see," he said, holding up the envelope and feeling the acute embarrassment of an adult who had behaved childishly.

Neither Lindsey nor the man spoke or moved.

Clearing his throat, J.L. went on, with true sincerity, "I'm sorry about the door."

The man looked down at the wood on the floor.

Lindsey Faraday stepped forward and, to J.L.'s amazement, gave him a tiny smile as she took the envelope and said, "I apologize too. Getting angry never solves a problem."

J.L. nodded his head in agreement. "I'll pay for the damage."

"You don't have to. The door was old. We've needed another."

"I'd feel better if I did," he insisted gently.

For a long moment they looked at each other, uncertain if this were a truce, then Lindsey said, "All right."

She gestured toward the big man beside her. "This is my foreman, Santiago Ramirez."

J.L. stepped forward and thrust out his hand. "J.L. Brett." The other man hesitated but gave him one of the strongest handshakes he had ever received. A warning, no doubt, that Lindsey Faraday had a protector. "I'm an attorney from San Diego," J.L. clarified.

"That so?"

The look he received was a questioning one and just short of a scowl, and J.L. had the feeling that the man had not been told about the "situation." He wondered why not.

"So, you run the mine for Miss Faraday," J.L. said in supposition.

Lindsey frowned, and Santiago chortled, the lines around his eyes and mouth softening. "No one runs nothin' for Miss Lindsey, Señor. She, and she alone, keeps this mine going."

J.L. cocked his head and looked at Lindsey. "I see."

Pride flashed back at him from bright blue eyes, and Lindsey turned to Santiago and said, "You'd better check out that jump hole on Level Nine tomorrow. The timbers around it are starting to rot." She gave him a warm smile that J.L. wished were for him.

"Will do, Boss. Did you find an animal in the mine when you checked it out today?"

The starting of a grin turned up Lindsey's mouth. "Yes and no, Santiago." She glanced at J.L., and he knew she was talking about him. He had never been called an animal before, and he decided he and the lady mine owner needed to get a few things straight. Insulting him was not going to get her debt cleared.

Lindsey's attention was back with her foreman. "The mountain lion was there."

Santiago drew in a sharp breath. "On Level Two?"

"No, he wandered into the entrance, just behind Mr. Brett." Now she did grin. "I thought they were together at first."

Very funny, J.L. thought.

"I shot at him but missed, and he got away."

The foreman's forehead deepened into a frown. "He might return, especially if he's been in the mine before. There was another strike last night, over at Miller's ranch. One calf dead, another maimed."

"Oh, no," Lindsey cried.

"Could be the same cat."

Lindsey nodded, and J.L. felt the hairs on the back of his neck stand up. He could have been a victim too, if this woman he was battling hadn't been there with a rifle.

"I'll tell the boys to keep an eye open for him," Santiago said. "The authorities think he might be a 'transient.'"

"What's that?" J.L. asked.

"A lion newly on its own, twelve-to-eighteen months old, no longer hunting with its mother, needing to establish a territory of its own," Lindsey explained. "Let's keep a lookout for 'scrapes,'" she said to her foreman.

Before J.L. could ask the question, Santiago answered, "That's a no trespassing sign a lion leaves around his home range, usually a pile of debris he's urinated on to warn off others."

Lindsey patted his arm. "Thanks for telling the boys about this, Santiago."

"Sure, Boss." He glanced over at J.L., then back to Lindsey. "Will you be all right?" he asked her.

"Just fine, thanks."

"Okay."

He left the room with the force of a small storm, the old wooden floorboards vibrating under his weight, and J.L. muttered, "Interesting man."

"That he is," Lindsey agreed. "He's worked at this mine for over thirty years and is invaluable to me."

"And protective." He moved closer to her.

"Always." She stepped back.

"But you're the boss." It was a statement rather than a question, and Lindsey was glad he understood that fact. In his eyes she saw respect, and her fierce resentment of him softened.

When a warm smile from him drifted over her, weakening her knees, she walked briskly to the potbellied stove that had been there as long as the mine had, she suspected, and closed the door that didn't really need closing, but she did it anyway. It was something to do to keep her away from J.L. Brett, to quiet the tremor of her hands, to distract her mind from this compelling lawyer who stirred her up, shortened her breath, and made her forget the real reason he was there.

That this tall, muscled, all-American male watching her now with growing interest should make her heart flutter infuriated her. He was threatening her with the loss of her golden dream. He insulted her with his stubborn insistence that her father had been negligent in fulfilling a contract. He exasperated her with the certainty that he would not go away until the problem was solved, probably to her detriment.

So why was she attracted to him?

Of course she recognized how good-looking he was, how developed and manly his body was. Certainly she had to admit he had dark, compelling eyes, and a strong mouth that would thrill a woman with its kiss. Undoubtedly, he was intelligent and successful. Beyond argument, he was a lethal combination of brains and brawn, sensuality and sensitivity. She wasn't stupid, or made of ice, after all.

She was, however, a woman who did not think a lot about men in "that" way, for her life had always been focused on the mine, and the dream she had shared with her father to find the mother lode.

Living forty-two-hundred feet up in the mountains, with mostly tough old miners and a few stray dogs for company, she had been somewhat isolated from many of the activities that other young girls grew up with. But she had never minded. Her father and the Lucky Dollar had been her whole world.

She had always expected to fall in love someday, get married, and have a family, but the men she had met around town and at university had shied away from a woman whose passion was a gold mine in a remote mountain.

She couldn't help it. The mine was, indeed, her passion, her love, always there, always demanding but faithful, always holding out to her the promise of even more satisfaction to come. And it was enough for her, or had been, until two months ago, when two major events entered her life: She became a Christian and met a man who wanted to marry her.

"How did you come to run this gold mine?" J.L. asked, interrupting her thoughts as he eased himself down on one corner of her desk, his hands laced together casually in front of him, one leg dangling, giving the appearance of his belonging there, in her office, on her desk.

Lindsey fought to overcome emotion with reason. The man was not interested in her; he wanted to know about the mine. He wanted to know the whereabouts of the thirty thousand dollars that he insisted belonged to his client.

Stabbing him with a look of impatience, she said, "I really don't have time to chitchat about my personal life, Mr. Brett," and she took out the papers he had brought her and started to examine them.

But he slid off the desk, came over to her, and laid his large hand on her small one, stopping her from reading them.

J.L. didn't want her to look at the copies of the Note and Deed of Trust that would prove his case. Not yet. They would ignite her ire again. For just a few minutes, he wanted to talk to her calmly, hear the melodic rhythm of her contralto voice, and have her smiling at him rather than regarding him coldly as the enemy-of-the-month.

She aggravated him one minute and fascinated him the next with her combination of intelligence and naïveté, and he wished he were getting to know her under any other circumstance than what he was. "Please tell me about you and the mine," he urged her. "I really would like to know."

"It isn't a very exciting story," she began, moving away from him. "I was eight years old when my daddy brought me to this mine. He was a successful stockbroker then but gave it up to pursue a new life. To find the mother lode was his dream and is now mine. I've grown up here, among crusty miners who'd rather work for far less than they're worth than make twice as much doing something else."

Her eyes filled with passion. "Mining gets in your soul, Mr. Brett. It becomes something you *have* to do." She stared at him. "Can you understand that?"

"Of course. That's how I feel about my work. As long as there are people being exploited, held down, kept from their rights and freedoms, I want to represent them."

"For a staggering fee, of course," Lindsey quipped.

J.L.'s eyes narrowed at the slur. "Believe it or not, I don't take advantage of people needing help. Winning a case for someone who can't win on his own gives me tremendous satisfaction."

"And is this client you currently represent one of those poor unfortunates who needs your expertise to win her her rights and freedoms?"

"Oh, yes. She needs the money your father borrowed."

"Allegedly borrowed," Lindsey corrected, deciding that was enough small talk for the day. She held the papers up and ran her eyes over them.

They were copies of the originals, as she had thought they would be, but they looked authentic enough. Her thoughts dashed to and fro looking for answers, frantic, as though she were being sucked into a whirlpool from which there was no escape.

She still clung to the belief that her father would never have left the mine in such jeopardy, and her loyalty was fierce, so she would fight hard to prove it justified.

Thirty thousand dollars. She almost laughed out loud. It might as well be thirty million. She didn't have either.

She looked up at J.L. and said firmly, "I suggest you talk with your client again, Mr. Brett, because these documents cannot be true."

"And I suggest you look through your father's papers again, Miss Faraday," he countered firmly.

Lindsey gave him a long look. He was so sure of himself, of his legal case, so smug and unbending. But he was wrong. She knew he was. She, after all, knew what kind of man her father had been.

"You gave me three days to prove my case," she reminded him pointedly.

"That's right."

"And I give you three days to be sure your client is not deceiving you."

J.L. expulsed a breath. "Why can't you see reason?"

"Oh, I do, Mr. Brett. And I just hope you can too, because I guarantee you're going to have the fight of your life on your hands before you foreclose on my mine!" She promised this with all the sweet menace of one person handing another a lighted stick of dynamite, burning an inch from the end.

Turning away from him, she walked over to the open doorway, wanting him to understand that their conversation was ended. He followed her.

"You could make this a whole lot easier on all of us," he said, standing close to her, "if you'd just cooperate."

"How? By giving you what's not yours?"

His eyes narrowed, but he walked away without another word, and Lindsey wished the door were still intact so that she could slam it on him.

Chapter 4

The first thing J.L. did when he got out to his truck was to take out his list on Lindsey Faraday and underline the words *stubborn* and *temperamental*. Then he added "sassy."

But when he started to put the yellow tablet back in his briefcase, he paused, then wrote on the opposite side of the page "loyal." He looked at it a long time and thought how lucky William Faraday had been to have a daughter who believed in him so much.

He wrote the word "beautiful" too, but the letters were small.

Three days, J.L. thought. *I'll see her again in three days,* and he was definitely glad he would, despite their tempestuous beginning and knowing that the skirmishes weren't over yet. For personal reasons as well as professional, he wanted to be with her.

She was different from any woman he had known, not just because she was trying to make it in a business dominated by men, but because she was a striking contrast between courageous and vulnerable, hard and soft. She was irritating and antagonistic, but he had also seen moments of lightheartedness and caring. He wanted to know her better.

As he headed his truck south and west toward San Diego, she stayed in his thoughts, like a romantic sonata, and he wondered what it would be like to go out with her. What would they talk about? What interests might they share?

Then he chuckled softly. "Right, Brett. I'm sure the lady is going to walk into the arms of the very man who has depleted her business by thirty thousand dollars."

Yet, he believed he could win her, because one of his strengths was the power of persuasion. If he could move juries and judges to his way of thinking, certainly he could convince this stubborn, tenacious, temperamental, uncooperative, defensive, sassy woman to share a pizza with him on a Friday night.

So, he decided, with a big sigh, *I'll ask her out, but not until this legal problem is settled. It wouldn't be ethical to do it sooner.*

He began to whistle, something he rarely did, and he smiled, knowing he would win this case against Lindsey Faraday, even though, for awhile, they would be adversaries, a situation he did not want but could not avoid. The real challenge would come afterward, in turning an adversary into a friend.

❧❀❧

J.L. pulled into the downtown parking lot across from the eleven-storied building where his law practice was located, got out of the truck, and walked briskly across the busy street. The fresh air felt good. He would take it over air-conditioning any day, just as he would find almost any reason to be out of doors instead of inside.

His thoughts of Lindsey, as he strode through the gleaming lobby of his building with its marbled floor and brass accoutrements, were whether or not she could actually pay the money owed his client. There was certainly no doubt that she didn't want to pay and that she would fight him all the way to keep from paying.

The heavy elevator door closed, and he pushed the button that would take him to the top floor. His research into the Lucky Dollar had revealed a gold mine that was still bringing in enough gold and silver to support its owner and a few employees, but to J.L.'s personal observation, the mine and its environs hadn't looked all that prosperous.

Still, he remembered reading that there remained more gold in those mountains than was ever taken out in its heyday and up to the present.

I wonder if she pays her employees dirt and keeps the big bucks for herself, he pondered as the door of the elevator silently slid open on his floor. He stepped out into a gargantuan reception area where his dusty boots sank into plush, forest green carpet and where the heavy woods and beveled glass were every bit as impressive as the tall man who walked among them.

Didn't she tell me herself that her miners worked for far less than they were worth? He allowed himself one last thought of her before he approached the moon-shaped walnut reception desk standing on a white alpaca rug.

"Almost time to go home, isn't it, Mrs. Larson?" he addressed the attractive, middle-aged receptionist who was busy at her desk, examining several envelopes of airline tickets. Her ivory, double-breasted suit and stylishly smooth brown hair added another touch of elegance to the already stunning surroundings.

She looked up at him and smiled broadly. "Yes, Sir, it is about that time. Has it been a good day for you?"

He had been gone since early morning but knew that between Mrs. Larson and Heather Davenport, his executive secretary, the office couldn't be in more capable hands.

"It was an. . .unusual day, Mrs. Larson, but good," he answered, as all other business he had conducted paled in comparison to his experience with Lindsey Faraday at the Lucky Dollar Mine.

"I'm happy to hear that, Sir. All's right with Brett and Associates too."

"As I knew it would be. Is Mr. Packard on his way to Chicago?" he asked, looking at the airline tickets she held in her hand and referring to his newest associate, a recent graduate of the Harvard Law School.

"Tomorrow. I have his tickets here."

"How long will he be gone?"

"Two days."

"That should wrap up the case."

In the law firm of Brett and Associates, there were four associates, three men and a woman, all from different parts of the country and each specializing in a different field of law from civil and criminal cases to corporate and tax situations, from handling sensitive business for the rich and famous of all southern California to solving the dilemmas of the most humble of working people.

J.L. was the maverick amongst them, preferring the "unusual" cases, the ones that espoused a cause or were for people or groups who could not afford the high price of a competent attorney. In truth, it was the associates who brought revenue to the firm.

Turning down a hallway, he entered his secretary's office, on the other side of which was his own office.

Heather Davenport was there, as usual, working diligently at her desk, a gorgeous, dark-haired woman whose immaculate appearance and competent manner matched her skills as a professional secretary. In her late twenties, Heather, a college graduate with a major in English, was logically minded, dedicated, unemotional, and kept J.L.'s business running smoothly at all times. She was invaluable to him.

She was also in love with him, a fact he knew and regretted because his feelings for her involved only respect for her skills as a secretary and a general liking because she was easy to work with.

Some of his friends thought he was crazy for not dating her, but he was not about to get into those murky waters, mixing business and pleasure.

Because of Heather's careful attention to the day-to-day detail of his practice, he was free to involve himself in other areas, being a man who had learned early that much of a business's success could be the result of having talented secretaries.

"Good afternoon, Heather," he greeted her cheerfully, noticing the strong scent of her perfume that he had never liked. He much preferred the gentle hint of Lindsey Faraday's talcum.

"I'm glad you're back, Mr. Brett," she enthused, jumping to her feet and following him into his office. "You have messages."

"Fire away." With a circular toss of the wrist, he threw his Stetson toward a large Remington bronze of "The Cowboy," where the hat landed square on the horse's head. J.L. smiled. "What's the most important?" he asked over his shoulder, dropping his briefcase onto a green three-seater couch. He went to a small niche in the corner where he opened a nearly hidden refrigerator and took out of it an old-fashioned sarsaparilla in a dark brown bottle. He was addicted to the stuff, but only if it was icy cold. Taking a long, thirsty drink while thumbing through some papers on his desk, he listened to Heather's precise recitation.

"Senator Billings called about that government fraud case you're handling.

The television station wants to set up a time tomorrow afternoon for your interview about the Flores trial. Joe Blyden over at the courthouse wants you to represent his daughter, who's being sued for sexual harassment."

J.L. stopped rummaging and looked up, surprised. "*She's being sued?*"

"Yes, but Joe said it's a smoke screen. The man wants her job and can't get it any other way than to get rid of her first."

"I'll call Joe later. Anything else?"

"Your mother wants your advice on a birthday present for your father. Next Wednesday's the big day."

"Okay. I have something in mind."

"And Dr. Phillips, the veterinarian, reported that Thunder, your stallion, is fine. He just has a mild stomach upset that's not serious."

"Great. Let's call the senator first. Then schedule a meeting with Angela, Jeffrey, and Gordon for ten A.M. the day after tomorrow. Tell them I want updates on all their cases. See if you can arrange the TV interview for five o'clock tomorrow afternoon; at two I'm meeting with those Warner factory workers. What their boss expects from them harks back to slave labor."

"Try not to get beat up, like the last time you were involved in management versus labor," Heather warned with a frown, and J.L. groaned, remembering the pain.

"I'll call my mother and the vet when I get a chance. Does that do it?"

"Yes, Sir." Heather made notations on her steno pad, then started to leave, but J.L. waved his hand to stop her. "And don't stay late again tonight, Heather. I know you must have a life outside this law firm."

She blushed and fluttered her eyelashes at him. "I don't mind working late, Mr. Brett."

"Then I'll have to mind for you." He glanced at his watch, hardly believing it was nearly five o'clock. "Fifteen minutes and you're out of here."

"Will you be leaving too? You need rest and relaxation as much as the rest of us."

J.L. shook his head no. "I want to go over my notes for that court case I'm trying tomorrow at eleven."

Heather sighed and shook her head as though he were impossible to reason with. "By the way, did you get out to the Lucky Dollar Mine?"

"Yes."

"Did you meet the woman who owns it?"

"Yes."

"What is she like?"

"She's. . ." J.L. searched for the right word while walking over to the floor-to-ceiling window. He stared out into the spring blue sky dotted with fluffy clouds scudding their way over bustling San Diego and a shimmering Pacific Ocean in the distance. What was the exact adjective he could use to describe a woman he couldn't stop thinking about?

"She's what, Sir?"

"Different."

"How?"

"Oh, she's young, for one thing. I hadn't expected that. And argumentative. Spunky, actually. Smart. Pretty." He turned around and gazed at Heather who had a frown on her face. "She's not going to give up the money easily."

"Uh-oh."

"Anyway, that's for another day." J.L. closed the conversation, and Heather, knowing his ways, left the room, closing the heavy door behind her.

With a dozen other things to sort through, J.L.'s thoughts, nevertheless, stayed with Lindsey Faraday. He had not expected so much resistance from her to his client's demands, but he was getting it. Lindsey's fierce belief in her father's innocence touched him and warned him not to let personal admiration sway his professional duty. While he always enjoyed a challenge, he did not look forward to making someone suffer because of legal action taken against them, and it looked like that was exactly what was going to happen with Lindsey Faraday.

He spent the next three hours making phone calls, reviewing his notes for the next day's court case, which he expected would only last an hour at most, and further arranging his thoughts for his afternoon meeting with the factory workers. All the situations should not have taken long to complete, but he had trouble concentrating because a willowy blond kept drifting into his mind. This aggravated him to no end but finally brought him to the decision that he would go back to the mine first thing the next day and fix the door he had torn from its frame. It was the least he could do.

Chapter 5

After J.L. Brett left Lindsey's office, she worked for nearly two hours, going through the files of the Lucky Dollar Mine, searching for any paper that would show that her father had borrowed thirty thousand dollars back in 1985 from a woman named Francesca Owens. She found nothing, and was encouraged. Surely the whole situation was a mistake. All she had to do was prove it.

"You're working late, Boss." She heard Santiago's familiar voice behind her and, turning, Lindsey saw her foreman standing just inside the door, frowning. Glancing at her watch, she was surprised to see that it was half past six. "It's been a long day, hasn't it?"

"Sure has. I checked out that jump hole on Level Nine like you told me to, and it won't be a problem to replace those timbers around it."

"I'm glad. There's always something, isn't there, Santiago, to keeping a mine safe?"

"That's the truth."

Lindsey went to her desk and gathered some papers into a manila folder that she then placed in the center drawer. She locked the drawer with a key.

"We're not in trouble, are we, Boss?" Santiago surprised her by saying.

Lindsey stiffened, knowing he was referring to J.L. Brett's visit. While she was tempted to ask Santiago if he knew anything about a loan her father had received from a Francesca Owens, she decided against asking, knowing her father had done all his own bookkeeping and would not likely have confided in the foreman. Also, if she could help it, she didn't want to involve Santiago in the problem or have him worrying whether or not he would have a job in a few months' time.

Even if he did know something about it, word of mouth would not help. She needed hard proof that the loan had been repaid *if*, as she still doubted, it had been made in the first place.

"Mr. Brett and I have some legal business that is tedious, Santiago," she answered him. "That's all." She smiled, hoping to reassure him and knowing he was concerned for her, just as he had been for many years.

In a way, Santiago Ramirez *was* the Lucky Dollar Mine. He had been a vital part of it for as long as she could remember, and before that even. When her father had purchased the mine, Santiago had offered to stay on and oversee it in return for reasonable pay and permission to continue to live, with his wife Maria and their five children, in a sturdy four-room cabin, made of weathered logs and at the end of the property, that they had occupied for many years, through several changes of ownership of the mine. Since William Faraday had known little about gold mining, he had quickly agreed to the suggestion, and Santiago had become a part of their lives.

All through her childhood and teen years, Lindsey had followed the big man around like a hungry puppy, asking countless questions, listening to his every word, amassing from him a formidable knowledge of gold and silver mining.

"You know you can always count on my help, don't you, Boss?" Santiago asked her now.

Lindsey walked over to him and patted his bulky, hairy arm. "Of course I do."

"If you have any trouble with this Brett fella, you just let me know."

"Oh, I can handle J.L. Brett, Santiago."

He gave her a doubtful look.

"You and Larry, Pete, and Sanchez just keep the Lucky Dollar producing as healthily as it is," she complimented him lavishly, "and maybe even find that elusive mother lode, then J.L. Brett won't be a problem."

They walked to where Santiago had propped the torn-off door against the wall. "I'll bring in a new one tomorrow," he promised. "Will the office be safe tonight without it?"

"There's not much to steal, Santiago. Besides, I don't lock it half the time anyway."

The foreman chuckled. "That's what I like about living in this area. People leave you alone."

"You're right."

They walked outside together. "Why don't you meet me on Level Two tomorrow around nine o'clock?" she said. "I didn't find the animal the men reported hearing there, but I want to check more closely for evidence of some kind."

"It could be that mountain lion."

"I know, but I sure hope not. Good night, Santiago."

Lindsey took a deep breath of fresh air and watched her foreman saunter down the path toward his humble home that stood a quarter of a mile away. What a charming place it was, surrounded entirely by purple and blue wildflowers, the path to its front porch bordered every spring with the hundreds of yellow daffodils that had been lovingly planted by Maria, Santiago's wife.

How often she had gone there, Lindsey remembered, to play with Santiago's children who now were grown and living elsewhere, or to share a meal with this important family. But not tonight. Tonight she just wanted to get home, take a shower, relax with a good book, and hope she could quell the nagging feeling that was growing in her mind—today her life had taken a turn from which she might never recover, an unexpected turn caused by J.L. Brett and his client that was going to upset the life she had been content with for so many years.

Leaning against one of the posts that held up the slanted roof of the mine office and listening to the night silence that enveloped her, Lindsey contemplated the fact that she wasn't a millionaire by any means but was able to support herself and her employees by doing something she loved—mining.

What would she do if she lost the Lucky Dollar? Teach? She could, for she had a degree in mining engineering. Work at some other mine? No, she only wanted to be at the one her father had owned, into which he had put the last years of his life.

Was that all she wanted? To work? Was it time for her to settle down and get married?

There was a man waiting for her to say yes—Lance Robards, a successful restaurateur from La Jolla with whom she had had six dates. She had met him while attending a birthday dinner for a friend of hers, held at one of his elite restaurants. He had seen her across the room, was intrigued (his word, not hers) by her, struck up a conversation with her when the celebration was over, invited her for a walk along the beach the next afternoon, took her to a concert in San Diego four nights later, and the dating began.

On their second date he said he was in love with her; on their third date he asked her to marry him, assuring her that he always made up his mind quickly and that they were perfect for each other.

But Lindsey was far too practical a woman to leap into marriage so quickly, and while she hadn't said yes to Lance's proposal, she hadn't said no either. She just wanted to get to know him better.

Lance was an attractive if not handsome man, with a short, stocky build and curly blond hair. Lindsey liked the green hue of his eyes but did not care for his pencil-thin moustache. He was easy to be with, good-natured, generous, romantic, and considerate. Those were his sterling qualities.

There were two areas, though, that concerned Lindsey and made her cautious. First of all, he could not fathom her love of the Lucky Dollar and, while he listened patiently when she talked about it, she wondered if he would want her to continue running it were they to be married.

Secondly, and even more troublesome, was Lance's disdain for Christianity. He impatiently claimed the church was out of touch with the real world, its precepts based on nothing more than archaic commandments, and that most supposed followers of Christ were hypocrites. He had been surprised when Lindsey boldly told him she had just given her heart to the Lord and considered the church a bastion against evil and a nurturing place of love and encouragement.

Lance, ever the diplomat, backtracked a little, and asked Lindsey to explain her beliefs to him, which she did, though she felt totally inadequate doing so since it was all so new to her. No one in her family had ever been a Christian, or even a nominal churchgoer, so Lindsey knew she was a baby Christian who had a long way to go to grow into spiritual maturity.

I wonder how J.L. Brett feels about God? she thought suddenly. *Is he a Christian?*

She meandered down to the small parking lot and got into her car, warning herself not to think of Mr. Brett in any other way than the threat that he was. He was not a new friend. He was not someone she should get to know personally. He had a job to do, and that job was to dispossess her of a great deal of money and perhaps even sell her beloved gold mine.

As Lindsey drove to her home in Majestic, population 1,300, with only ten streets running through its 150-year-old environs, she prayed to her heavenly Father for guidance in her dilemma. Prayer was an act new and thrilling to her. To think that she could actually speak to the God who had created the universe, as intimately and often as she had spoken to her own father.

"Dear Lord, I don't know what tomorrow holds, or where the truth lies about this loan to my father, but You know. Lead me in the way I should go. Give me wisdom. . .and patience. In the name of Jesus, I pray."

The last part of her petition, for patience, meant she knew she would need to hold her sometimes volatile temper when it came to dealing with J.L. Brett. He was an exasperating man who was too sure of himself, too unbending.

After she had showered and put on a nightgown, a terry cloth robe, and old, floppy slippers, and had read ten pages of a book, Lindsey was ready for bed. But she could not stop thinking of the contemplative scrutiny of J.L. Brett, gazing at her earlier that day, making her aware of herself as a woman as she had not felt for a long time, even with Lance.

What had J.L. seen when he had looked at her so? Did he find her pretty or plain? Could he see beyond the minimal makeup to the soul that lay within her? Did he care what kind of person she was?

She hadn't looked her best today. Her hair had been wild and unstyled. She had been wearing dungarees and a work shirt. Even though J.L. Brett had been dressed casually too, there was a sophistication about him in the way he expressed himself and moved that told her he was probably used to women who wore satin and lace and smelled like rose gardens.

Lindsey turned out the light and closed her eyes, willing herself to stop thinking about that varmint lawyer. The sooner this problem was settled and he was out of her life, the better she would like it.

Chapter 6

J.L. knew he had given Lindsey three days to find some evidence to negate the claim that there was money owed his client. So when he showed up at the office of the Lucky Dollar the very next morning, he told himself it was not to pressure her with the case but merely to fix the door that he had ridiculously broken.

No one was around, so he put the broken door into the back of his truck to haul it away and decided to just go ahead with the repair. He also noted that there was coffee brewing in a blue tin pot on the potbellied stove.

With tools in hand, he replaced the old splintered frame, attached new hinges, and hung the thirty-two-inch-wide door that he had bought, and then started to paint it.

While he worked, he whistled, having a sense of comfort that the lady would be well-protected behind this rugged door. Protected from what or whom he did not know, but at least she wouldn't be vulnerable because he had lost his temper.

"How's it going?"

The deep voice came from behind him. Turning around, paint brush in hand, J.L. saw Santiago Ramirez, the mine foreman, watching him with a serious expression and his arms folded over his wide chest. His old blue jeans were held up with green suspenders, and the sleeves of his lightweight, woolen, black shirt were rolled up to the elbow. There was a chill in the morning air from the altitude, but J.L. found it refreshing even though he was in short sleeves.

"Good morning," he greeted Santiago cheerfully. Motioning toward the door he said, "I thought I'd better fix it since I'm the one who destroyed it."

"Nice door."

"Yep. Should last a few years."

J.L. put the finishing stroke of dusky brown latex enamel paint on the door, then squatted beside a jar of soapy water and began cleaning his brush in it.

"I'll have one of the men put the knob and lock on later," Santiago offered.

"I'll do it myself, if you don't mind," J.L. countered. "I'm sure your guys have other things to do."

Santiago shrugged and said, "Okay."

J.L. wiped his hands on a piece of rag and asked, "Is Miss Faraday coming in today?"

Santiago looked at his watch. "Should be here by eight. It's ten to now."

"Great. Is there any chance I can get a cup of that coffee brewing on the stove?"

"Sure."

Santiago went into the office, returning moments later with a paper cup filled to the brim. He handed the steaming liquid to J.L., who smelled it coming and took a deep draft, finding it to be just what he had expected: miner's brew, strong enough to walk by itself. Knowing the foreman was waiting for him to spit out the awful stuff, he exclaimed, "Now that's what I call a cup of coffee. Thanks, Santiago."

The foreman frowned. "If you want more, just help yourself."

"Will do."

J.L. swished the brush in the soapy water again and said casually, "You're a man of many talents, Santiago. Does Miss Faraday pay you what you're worth?"

He could tell from the way Santiago's eyes narrowed almost shut that the man was wary and might not answer at all.

"Why do you want to know?" Santiago grunted.

"Because I help employees get fair treatment from their employers. If you're not paid enough, or working conditions are poor—"

Santiago jutted his chin out in a defiant gesture. "Miss Lindsey is good to us."

"Is she?"

J.L. captured Santiago's gaze with his own, wondering how much of the man's declaration was truth and how much was loyalty. He took another gulp of coffee. "Are your wages comparable to what other mine workers make, Santiago? Do you have health benefits and a pension plan?"

"You should be asking me those questions," a feminine voice interrupted, and J.L. turned to see Lindsey Faraday in the doorway, holding a briefcase with both hands, her right side just inches from the newly painted door. From the frown that creased her narrow forehead, she either had not had her first cup of coffee of the day, or she was not happy to see him.

J.L. jumped forward, grabbed both her arms, and pulled her away from the door.

"What are you doing?" she yelped, her gleaming blue eyes sparking as she fell into his arms, her hands clutching him for support.

"Keeping you clean."

J.L. turned her around, holding her waist, and pointed toward the door. "Fresh paint."

"Oh."

Lindsey regained her balance and stepped away from J.L., looked at the door and at the paint stains on his Levis and hands, and at Santiago, who shrugged his shoulders and said, "He was here when I got here, Boss."

She looked back at J.L. "Penance, Mr. Brett?"

He nodded without a word. She was doing it again, taking his breath away with her long, straight hair flowing down to her shoulders and her feisty blue eyes matching the shade of the cotton blouse she wore. Her dungarees were black today, as were her low-heeled boots and her mood.

Lindsey walked back to the door, inspected it, and then turned and gave J.L. a smile of three on a scale of one to ten. "You've gone to a lot of trouble for us, Mr. Brett, and I thank you for it, especially since I am partially to blame for the door being torn from its hinges."

"You are?"

"You wouldn't have pulled it off if you hadn't been angry with me," she surprised him by saying. "Isn't that true?"

J.L. nodded cautiously. "But you didn't make me lose my temper. I did that all by myself."

Lindsey acknowledged the truth of that statement by nodding her head, then her smile disappeared and was replaced by an annoyed expression.

"While I thank you for the door, Mr. Brett, I do not thank you for trying to stir up trouble with my employees. Why were you asking Santiago about how I treat my people?"

"I'll explain over breakfast."

Lindsey shook her head. "I don't eat breakfast."

"That's a bad habit. It's important to get the metabolism started in the morning."

"I work better on an empty stomach."

"The experts don't agree."

"The experts don't have my stomach."

As though an imaginary line had been drawn between them, they each stood their ground, and Santiago looked from one to the other before shaking his head in puzzlement and leaving the office.

"Now, about breakfast," J.L. began again.

"No," Lindsey said firmly, and meant it.

"It's not a personal invitation," he assured her, trying to fool himself. "I have to wait 'til the paint dries before I can put in the door handle and lock."

"One of my men will do that."

One of her men, J.L. thought. *One of her men. She is surrounded by men.* That bothered him.

"Santiago offered the same help," he said, "but I told him I'd rather complete the job myself."

Lindsey walked over to the desk and set her briefcase down in the middle of it with a decided thud, then began extricating papers and folders, trying to calm her frustration.

She didn't want him here, reminding her of the loan. Didn't want him asking questions of her employees, insinuating she wasn't fair to them. *Is that how he gets business, by dredging up trouble?* she wondered.

"I'm sure you have far more important things to do, Mr. Brett, than play handyman," she said flatly.

J.L. looked at his watch. "Not 'til later this morning, when I have to be in court."

"Humph," Lindsey grunted, taking some of the papers over to a nearby file cabinet that had more than its share of dents in the sides. She opened the top drawer. "Evicting a little old lady from her family home?" she quipped.

J.L. chuckled. "Fighting for proper living conditions for migrant workers. Bigger cabins. Better facilities."

"Bravo," she said.

Lindsey was shocked at herself. She wasn't a mean person, but she was being mean to him and just couldn't help it. Everything about him irritated her. Well, almost everything. He was wearing a red short-sleeved shirt, and she had noticed the muscles along his forearms tense and ripple as he had grabbed for her and held her, and the heavy forest of dark hair on his arms that she had felt beneath her fingers had only reminded her of how masculine he was.

She began plopping papers into any old file she came to, not even realizing what she was doing.

"All of that sounds far more important than fixing a broken door," she said, feeling a little short of breath.

"More important perhaps, but not more enjoyable." His husky voice sent shivers down Lindsey's spine, and she didn't dare look at him after that remark. She didn't have to. She remembered the shine of his hair and its smell of recent shampoo, both of which she had noticed when she had been in his arms.

His shoulders were broad.

His hands strong.

His waist trim.

Lindsey slammed the file cabinet shut and J.L. jumped.

"Something wrong?" he inquired, figuring, *Here it comes, the order to get off her property, the call for Santiago to draw and quarter me, the whistle for the marauding mountain lion to come and have me for breakfast.*

"Not one thing."

"Ready for breakfast, then?" He was, above all, a persistent man and an optimist.

"Not today, thanks." Lindsey strode over to him. "Let me help you with your tools. I'm sure you must be going."

J.L. got the message and decided not to annoy her any more than she already was, but he sure would have to underline "temperamental" on his list of her faults.

He leaned down to pick up a screwdriver at exactly the same moment Lindsey reached for the same one. They bumped, straightened quickly, and

Lindsey screamed. Her hair was caught in one of the metal buttons of his western shirt.

Lindsey's head was practically on his chest, and she was so off balance that J.L. had to put his arms around her to hold her up. Their bodies pressed together and drew apart as she fought desperately to get away.

"Do something!" she ordered.

"I will if you stop squirming," he promised, trying to hold her steady with one arm while his bulky fingers worked through the silky texture of her hair to untangle her from his shirt button. "Stop fidgeting."

"I can't help it; you're hurting me."

"Not intentionally."

"I'll bet. Ow!"

Lindsey's scalp felt like it was being jerked from her head, and her hands clutched J.L.'s arms, feeling the strength that supported her helplessness, while her ears, so near his chest, heard the rapid beating of his heart and knew it matched her own.

She made the mistake of turning up her head just as J.L. looked down. His dark eyes captured hers and their gazes held. Her lips opened and their faces moved slowly toward each other.

"Hold very still," J.L. whispered.

Lindsey obeyed as his arm around her waist pulled her firmly against him and the fingers of his other hand worked the hair loose that was caught, but stayed long enough to meander through the thickness of it. His face touched its softness and an almost inaudible groan escaped him.

Lindsey closed her eyes and felt his lips brush the curve of her cheek. His mouth was soft and moist and her skin tingled, and the sensation raced through her like a laser beam. His lips touched the corner of her mouth and Lindsey feared her knees would give way. Her fingers gripped his supporting arm, and she turned into his kiss that was gentle and fleeting and left her wanting more.

Chapter 7

The kiss was light and over in a second, but J.L. knew he had wanted it to happen. And when he looked deeply into Lindsey's eyes, he saw in those mesmerizing blue diamonds the same acceptance of this crazy moment in time that they had been given.

Tiny wheat-colored lashes swept around the bottom of her eyes, and long, gently curved lashes defined their brilliance as she gazed up at him in silent surprise.

Without thinking, he brushed the back of his fingers across Lindsey's cheek, and she did not recoil, but he wondered what she would do if he tried to kiss her again.

Deciding he would be wise to retreat with his limbs intact, he straightened up, still holding her near, their eyes never leaving each other's. Hands on her waist, he held her lightly until her gaze lowered, in embarrassment, and the moment was broken.

Lindsey struggled to regain her composure, caught off guard by what had happened, confused that so simple a kiss could tumble her emotions and make her moan with pleasure. Or had that sound come from him?

Now safely on her feet and with her hair free, rational thought returned to her mind, but her cheeks were still warm from his touch and she realized: *I just kissed the enemy.* Her heart skipped a beat. *How could I have done that?*

J.L. cleared his throat. "I think it's time for breakfast."

"No." Lindsey stepped away from his hands.

"Yes." J.L. firmly took her elbow and, despite feeble resistance, ushered her through the new door and down the path to his truck.

Snooks and Bones, two scraggly dogs of indiscriminate parentage, tagged after them, cavorting at their feet, hoping for a pat on the head and a kind word. But neither Lindsey nor J.L. had room in their thoughts for anyone but each other, and they were both thinking the same thing: *That kiss should never have happened. Why did I enjoy it so much?*

When they reached the gravel parking lot and a burgundy, half-ton, 4 x 4 pickup with oversized tires and gray-and-burgundy striping down the sides, Lindsey considered the truck that was not all that clean, and observed dryly, "I assume you're a successful lawyer, Mr. Brett, but you dress like a cowboy and drive a truck. Why?" She suspected there was another side of him that wore a tuxedo and drove a red Porsche.

J.L. laughed softly and opened the door for her. "Don't tell me you're more impressed by a man's possessions than by the man himself?"

Lindsey gulped. "Certainly not."

"Then that was just an idle comment and not meant to put me down for my choice of clothes or vehicle?"

Those diamond eyes that he had eulogized rounded into twin circles of fire. "I wasn't doing that."

"I didn't think so."

He watched her get in, closed her door, then strode around to the driver's side and slid behind the wheel, putting the key in the ignition. Turning to her he said, "Even though you're wearing dungarees instead of a frilly dress, I still think you're beautiful."

"What?"

His eyes twinkled. "And though you work in a dirty mine and let your hair hang loose and wild, that's no sign you're less feminine than any other woman."

Lindsey's cheeks flamed with indignation. "I don't really care whether or not you like my wardrobe and hairstyle." She flung the words at him, and her hand reached for the door handle.

J.L. chuckled and brought the engine to life, driving off before she could escape. "Just making an observation, Miss Faraday, not a judgment."

Lindsey sat tensely in the seat, staring straight ahead, while J.L. expertly maneuvered the pickup onto the narrow country road and headed toward Majestic, the nearest town, about two miles away. She said not a word but once did surreptitiously glance over at him and notice how strong his hands were as they gripped the leather-covered steering wheel, how in control he was of this powerful machine, and, at the moment, of her.

Suppressing a deep sigh, she returned her gaze forward and knew she was in trouble.

Without being guided, J.L. took her to her favorite restaurant, a cheerful and homey place with sunlight dancing through spotless windows where blue-and-white gingham curtains carried their colors through to the blue wooden benches and white wicker plant holders from which tumbled healthy green philodendron.

The smell of the place was of freshly baked cinnamon rolls and glazed donuts the size of pancakes, and the crowd of happily chattering adults and giggly teen-agers spoke well of its reputation for fine food.

Lindsey perused the menu and battled her self-will that yearned for one of the cinnamon rolls dripping with white icing, instead of choosing something sensible and healthy. Whenever she was upset, she usually ate something gooey, rich, and fattening; and right now, sitting across from J.L. Brett, the enemy, whose kiss had nevertheless been devastating, and who had told her she was beautiful despite the fact that she wore dungarees and worked in a dirty mine, she felt the temptation to abandon common sense.

With amazement she listened to J.L. order "a Denver omelet, double order of bacon, hash browns, a blueberry muffin, and the largest orange juice you have." *How can he have such a gorgeous physique when he eats all that gook?* she wondered, knowing she would gain two pounds just watching him eat it all.

"I'll take a bran muffin and tomato juice," she said, overcoming temptation; and the waitress, a young girl of about nineteen, her dark hair in a curly ponytail, wrote down the orders while gazing in admiration at J.L. as though he were Tom Cruise and Rhett Butler in the same body.

"Coffee?" she asked with an eager child's voice.

"Yes, please," J.L. answered with a winning smile, and the girl fell over her feet scurrying away, without asking Lindsey if she wanted any.

She soon returned with a full pot of steaming coffee that looked too heavy for her to carry. When J.L. gave her another million-dollar smile that brought out the two dimples in his cheeks, her body went limp, she gave him a goo-goo smile, giggled nervously, and poured the coffee way too fast, over the cup and saucer, onto the table.

J.L. and Lindsey both gasped, and the waitress did too, and grabbed the nearest cloth napkin and frantically tried to mop up the scalding liquid. But when her pencil fell into the cup and she anxiously tried to retrieve it, the cup tipped over, sending the scalding liquid running off the table and onto J.L.'s lap.

As the waitress reached to clean up the table, she tipped the pot in her hand, and more coffee plummeted out.

Lindsey and J.L. both scrambled out of the booth. Lindsey missed disaster, but J.L. didn't. Most of the mess went on him, staining his jeans even more.

"Oh, no," the girl screamed and dashed away to get a towel, which she brought quickly and thrust at J.L., who pressed it carefully against the soaked material. A busboy came to work on the table.

"We'll move," Lindsey told the distraught girl with a straight face. She didn't want to laugh. She tried very hard not to laugh, but a snicker escaped from behind her hand, and J.L. glared at her as they seated themselves in another booth.

"I don't see what is funny here," he said.

Immediately Lindsey forced an innocent expression to her face. "Neither do I," she fibbed, and told the waitress, "Could you bring the gentleman a clean towel, please?" She turned to J.L. "If you put water on those jeans right away, they'll be okay." She paused. "Was it hot?"

He looked at her as though she were daft. "Of course it was hot. Coffee is always hot. That's what the swirls of steam mean."

"I see."

The girl brought the towel, J.L. excused himself to go to the washroom, and Lindsey chuckled to herself over the mishap. *How fortunate J.L. was wearing blue jeans rather than dress slacks,* she thought as she watched the unhappy girl explaining to her supervisor what had happened. Lindsey felt sorry for her, knowing that waiting on such a handsome male as J.L. Brett had unnerved her.

When he returned to the table, Lindsey asked, "Everything all right?"

"Yes," he said sharply. "Is this the only restaurant in town?"

"No, but it is one of the best."

She nodded toward the waitress who was sniffling into a tissue, and J.L. understood her silent suggestion and immediately got up and went over to the girl, gently touching her arm while assuring her that no harm had been done.

Lindsey felt the power of his charisma and the sincerity of his gentlemanly gesture, even from a distance and, when the waitress gave him a beatific smile of adoration, she was not surprised.

He probably is a nice guy, she thought for an instant, but then changed her mind. *No, he's trouble.*

J.L. returned and slid into the booth. "This is her first day," he reported with a look of sympathy. "I asked for coffee for you." He grinned. "You did want some, didn't you?"

"Yes, Mr. Brett," Lindsey answered tentatively, and kept her eyes glued to the young waitress who, this time, did a perfect job pouring it into Lindsey's cup.

"Thanks, Tina," J.L. said, and the girl fluttered her eyes, blushed, and managed to move on to the next table without having an accident.

"On a first-name basis already?" Lindsey quipped after the girl had gone.

J.L. gave her a long look. "That's more than I can say for us, isn't it?"

Lindsey took a long sip of the very good coffee before murmuring, "I don't see any reason for us to get more familiar."

J.L. captured her gaze. "Don't you?"

There was an awkward silence in which both of them wondered what would really happen if they forgot they were on opposite sides of a legal case.

"So," J.L. finally broke the contemplation, "how many employees do you have?"

Lindsey eyed him suspiciously. "Why do you want to know?"

"Just curious."

Lindsey shook her head in disbelief. "This has to do with what you were asking Santiago about his wages and benefits?"

J.L. returned her direct gaze. "In a way, I suppose."

"Ask another question. I don't want to argue over a meal. It's bad for the stomach."

"Who says we're going to argue?"

"A good guess since we don't seem to be able to say two words to each other without disagreeing."

"I don't have that problem with anyone else."

"Neither do I."

They both drank from their cups.

J.L. took a deep breath and let it out. "Does it get very hot up at the mine in the summer?"

Lindsey's eyes narrowed. "Yes, it does."

"Do you think it will rain today?" J.L. picked up his fork as their meals arrived.

"No, it will not rain," Lindsey returned sharply, looking at her paltry muffin, wishing it were a gooey cinnamon roll, "and why are my employees of interest to you?" *Better to understand the enemy than ignore him,* she now decided.

J.L. took a man-sized bite of omelet, chewed it thoroughly, and swallowed it, never taking his eyes off Lindsey, then answered, "Because a lot of workers don't make adequate salaries or receive the benefits they should."

"Were you thinking about representing my employees against me, Mr. Brett?" She tore off a chunk of her bran muffin and popped it into her mouth, without even adding soft butter.

"Do they need representing?"

"Certainly not." She glared at him. "The Lucky Dollar isn't a wealthy mine, but I do everything I can to provide for the four people who work for it." Her voice was steady, her gaze sure, because she knew she was a good employer.

"So, you have health coverage?"

"Yes, of course."

"And a pension plan?"

Lindsey hesitated. "I will have. Someday soon. That costs a lot of money."

"Every worker needs a secure future, especially if he's not highly paid. Social Security isn't enough to live on for most people."

Lindsey knew the truth of that, but she was miffed that J.L. was pointing it out to her. "I want my employees to be fully protected. Right now, though, every dollar is earmarked for salaries or mine operation." And a pitiful amount in savings, she could have added, knowing J.L. Brett would be shocked to learn what that was and also what a tiny salary she took for herself.

"Let's get back to enjoying our breakfast," J.L. suggested. "I don't want to upset you."

Lindsey's eyes blazed. "How can I not be upset when you're trying to take a great amount of money from my company *and* stir up trouble with my employees?"

"Now wait a minute, that's not fair," J.L. complained, leaning forward and reaching for Lindsey's hand. She quickly withdrew, accidentally knocking over his coffee, which knew where to go and ran directly off the table, onto his lap.

Chapter 8

"Not again," J.L. howled. People turned to look, Tina hurried over with another towel, the busboy shuffled over to attend to the table, and this time Lindsey laughed out loud.

"Let's get out of here," J.L. growled, whipping some bills out of his wallet and thrusting them into Tina's hands. "Here you go, kid." He held the door open for Lindsey, but she tugged at his arm.

"Don't you want to. . . ?" She glanced demurely downward.

J.L. assessed the latest damage. "Oh. . .yeah," and he strode off, again, to the washroom.

"He'll be okay, Tina," Lindsey assured the girl, who looked like she had lost her last friend.

"He called me a kid," she blubbered, burst into tears, and ran out the front door.

J.L. came back, a watermark all too discernible on his jeans. "I'm starving. Where else can we eat?"

They had an uneventful breakfast at the Apple Orchard coffee shop, talking only of national news and the latest books they had read. With a little effort, they managed not to get into another argument and they were both glad, because when they finished and went outside, it was one of those balmy, sunny days when one is glad to be alive and wants only to be happy.

On the way to the truck, the song of tiny birds chirping madly in nearby trees caught their attention and J.L. said, "Maybe we should play hooky and enjoy this day."

Lindsey quickened her step instead of slowing it.

"Playing hooky is for children, Mr. Brett. Besides, you have to be in court, and I have a Full Reconveyance to find."

The words were a little sharper than she had intended but true enough, and only her finding some proof that the loan had either been paid or had never been made in the first place would get J.L. Brett and his client out of her life. And that's what she wanted, wasn't it?

"How about a short walk, then?" he suggested. Lindsey resisted but finally allowed him to talk her into a few more minutes with him.

They strolled past the Majestic Hotel, built in 1897, and went into an antique shop when J.L. saw a piece of Victorian cranberry glass he thought his mother would like. At the cider mill, he insisted on checking out the many shelves of specialty candies, nuts, syrups, jams, and jellies.

"In the winter, the locals sit around the parlor stove and sip hot apple cider and converse over the events of the day," Lindsey told him after he had bought her a bag of licorice buttons.

"That's great."

"Do you really think so?"

"Yeah, I do."

"Things move slowly in Majestic compared with San Diego," she admitted.

"Nothin' wrong with that. There's a time for fast and a time for slow." His gaze drifted over her hair and settled on her lips.

"It's a quiet town, a quaint place," she said, starting their walk again, which was better than standing still and gazing into his hypnotic eyes. "Streets A, B, C, and D run parallel to Main, and First through Fifth cross east and west. One can walk through it in half an hour, if you don't stop to look in the pretty shops or to have a piece of warm apple pie."

"Majestic is well-known for its apple orchards, isn't it?"

"Yes, and for its history that really began when gold was discovered in 1869. The earth around here has given up thirteen million dollars worth over the years."

J.L. whistled through his teeth. "I guess it was a real boomtown once."

"Yes, indeed, with six hotels, four general stores, a dozen saloons, two stage lines to San Diego, and thousands of miners, all with dreams of hitting it big."

"I like the way it's evolved."

"You do?"

"Yes. It has personality. This morning I drove around a little before coming to the mine."

Lindsey was stunned. She remembered Lance thinking the town was horrible. "What do people do for entertainment?" he had asked, and when Lindsey had asked if he would ever open a restaurant there, he had gaped at her as though she were mad and responded, "Not in a thousand years."

Then he had gone on to say the hotel was too small for his taste, the cider mill and antique shops looked depressingly unprofitable, and not even sampling the biggest slice of apple pie in Majestic, at the Green and Yellow Cafe on Second Street, had impressed him. "Way too much sugar," he had groaned, and Lindsey had sighed and felt a little miffed at his lack of appreciation for her town.

But J.L. liked Majestic, and this inched him one notch higher on Lindsey's approval ladder.

"Do you live in town?" he asked.

"On the outskirts, but it's not far from here."

"Do you want to show me?"

Lindsey shook her head no. "I have to get back to the mine. This is way later than I normally start work." Besides, showing her home to J.L. Brett was too personal a gesture for her. It wasn't as though they were starting to date and would ever mean anything to each other.

"Actually, I have to get back too," he said, "but I'll put the knob and lock on your door first."

"Santiago can do that," Lindsey suggested.

"Santiago didn't break the door."

They were at the truck and J.L. started to open the passenger door for Lindsey just as she reached for it herself. Their hands collided on the hard, hot metal of the handle, and Lindsey froze.

"Thank you for having breakfast with me," J.L. said softly in her ear, his body too near, his scent triggering a response in Lindsey that unnerved her. It would be so easy to turn, just one slight turn, and she would be in his arms; and he would kiss her again, she knew he would, and a part of her would relish it.

She yearned to be a woman desired and cherished, the awareness welling up from deep inside her where it had been held down by years of hard work, determination to fulfill her father's dream, and the lack of any man to ignite her passions. Would there be passion with J.L.?

Stepping back abruptly, full length against his muscled chest and legs, Lindsey jerked the door open and slid onto the seat. What was the matter with her, having romantic fantasies about this man who was here to destroy her life?

She stared straight ahead when he closed the door, then walked around the front of the truck and got in beside her. She stared and tried not to let the sound of her breathing be heard.

He sat there, leaning his arms on the steering wheel, and she knew he was battling strange feelings too, and the silence and inactivity stirred Lindsey's impatience as she tried to control a crazy urge to fling herself into his arms.

Thankfully, just as her nerves reached the end of their tether, he started the truck and drove to C Street where he turned right, onto the narrow road that led to the mine.

"I'll come out and see you in few days, Lindsey, to get things straightened out."

"Please call for an appointment first," she answered stiffly, trying to put him off. She had to keep him at arm's length, or she would make a mistake and give him her heart—a mistake she knew she would regret.

She was unprepared for the soft chuckle that resonated through the cab of the truck. "No, Darlin', I'll just show up," he said, "because if I call, you'll find some way to electrocute me through the phone lines."

"What an interesting thought."

"Why are you so anxious to not like me?"

Lindsey couldn't help sighing. "The circumstances that have brought us together make it impossible for me to like you and your greedy client."

A frown moved his heavy eyebrows down to a vee. "You shouldn't judge people you don't know. My client is an honorable person, and I'm really a nice guy. In fact, I love children, and haven't kicked a dog since I was ten and was being bitten by one."

"How touching."

"So, can we be friends?"

"I don't see how."

"Certainly not enemies."

There was a twinkle in his eyes that Lindsey couldn't believe. Why wasn't he put off by her standoffish attitude? "Adversaries is a better word," she said. "That's all we can be to each other."

J.L. chuckled and said, "How wrong you are, Miss Faraday," and he continued driving down the road toward the mine, the mine that had brought them together, and the mine that would very likely keep them apart.

Chapter 9

For five days, J.L. didn't come back to the mine. He didn't even phone for five days, and Lindsey wondered why. Was he simply giving her more time to find a way to defend her position, or had he told her she was beautiful, taken her to breakfast, and been fun to be with just so he could find ammunition to enable him to win his case for his client?

She didn't want to think that. She was not a cynical person by temperament, but she was fighting for her life now, her dream, and her father's. *I won't allow myself to be attracted to him,* she decided, *and I won't spend any more time with him than what is absolutely necessary.*

The phone rang.

"Lindsey? Hello. This is J.L. How are you?"

"Hi." The sound of his voice, so deep and rich, familiarly speaking her first name, carried through the receiver and washed over Lindsey like warm milk, soothing her anxious feelings, toying with her decision to have as little to do with him as possible. It was not going to be easy to keep this man at bay, but she knew she had to if she was going to win against him.

"I'd like to see you this afternoon," he said. "Would two o'clock be all right?"

Lindsey didn't hesitate. "I'm afraid not. I have tourists going through the mine." She sounded stiff when she wanted to sound self-confident, as though hearing from him meant nothing at all, and seeing him was of no importance to her.

"How long will the tour last?"

"An hour or so."

"Fine. I can be there at three-thirty or four."

Lindsey squelched a sigh. The man was tracking his prey and not about to give up. "That won't work either," she told him.

"Oh?"

"I. . .I have a meeting with my attorney." That was the truth. She had a friend who was a lawyer, and the day after her breakfast with J.L., she had called him and asked him for advice and also to check on the track record of one J.L. Brett of San Diego. "I'm sorry, but it really will be impossible to see you this afternoon."

"This evening, then. You just name the time."

"No. This evening is not good either."

There was no immediate response from him, and Lindsey wondered what he was thinking, what he was planning.

Finally he said coldly, "Lindsey, I'm not asking for a date. This is a business meeting and one we have to have. It's in your best interest as well as mine."

"That's highly questionable," she retorted, the steel in his voice infuriating her. She didn't like being told what to do, even though she knew he was right: They had to see each other for legal reasons, if for no other. "Why don't you just drop me a letter, and I'll answer with one?"

"Fine." The word was sharp.

She started to hang up, breathing a sigh of relief. She had done it—fended him off for now. Hopefully, her lawyer friend, John Gregory, would have a brilliant idea on how she could defeat this self-assured adversary. There had to be a way she could keep her mine. Then she heard J.L. call her name. "Lindsey?"

"Yes?" She quickly brought the receiver back to her ear.

"Thanks for not electrocuting me through the phone." He laughed softly. "Good-bye, Beautiful."

He hung up, and Lindsey stared at the phone for more than a minute before putting it down. He had called her beautiful again, and he shouldn't have, for she was sure she was not at all beautiful to a sophisticated man like him.

❧❈❧

For the next hour, Lindsey went through, again, every file that might possibly have anything to do with a loan made years ago. But she found nothing and was therefore frustrated and not in the best of moods when it came time to take the small group of tourists through the mine.

She wished she didn't have to conduct tours in order to help pay the bills. The Lucky Dollar gave up enough minerals each month to support her and her employees, but mining expenses were astronomical and the money went out as fast as it came in. She needed tourist revenue, so she met the strangers with as good a smile as she could muster, determined to do her very best to bring to them the excitement and history of this fascinating place.

When she led the group into the Lucky Dollar, a tingle of anticipation raced up her back and over her shoulders as the rocky, sedimentary walls surrounded her. Even though she had entered this tunnel a thousand times before, the thrill she now experienced was as deep and wondrous as it had been that very first time she had been brought there, at the age of eight, by her father.

On that unforgettable day, she had clung tightly to his smooth, cool hand as he had led her along, only a little afraid when the light from the outside world faded, and the unusual darkness that comes from being underground began to engulf them. She knew she was safe as long as she was with her daddy, holding his hand.

But he wasn't there anymore, and today, as she faced seven eager people staring expectantly at her when she stopped them a ways inside the mine, she knew she was in the hands of another Father, a Father she could not touch or hear but whom she knew loved her and who had promised never to leave or forsake her. He would be her Father forever, for eternity, but He was also interested in every day of her life, every moment. He was there right now, His Spirit within her, caring, able to guide her. "Thank You, Father," she whispered in the muted darkness of the mine and in that moment felt His presence and His peace.

"Ladies and gentlemen," she addressed the three married couples and the small fidgety boy, tugging at his mother's slacks and whining for a piece of gum, "welcome to the Lucky Dollar.

"This is an actual working mine. Gold, silver, and platinum are being extracted from it today, as they have been since the year 1870 when the mine was discovered and registered."

The little boy got his gum and threw the wrapper down on the ground. Without a frown, Lindsey picked it up and stuffed it into the back pocket of her jeans.

"Let me remind you to stay close to me as we move along," she instructed, and was interrupted by the sound of someone running toward them. Everyone turned around and saw a tall, ruggedly built man approaching. It was J.L.

He was dressed in a business suit, white shirt, and tie, and looked more ready for a day in the office than a tour of a dusty mine. His hair, tousled over his forehead, softened the sharp planes of his face, as did the triumphant smile that, to Lindsey, was actually a smirk.

He held out a ticket to her. "A man in the office said you'd just started the tour and that I could still make it."

He wasn't breathing hard after his run, and he stared right at her with intense brown eyes and an innocent expression. Lindsey wondered how she could trigger a cave-in that would fall only on him and not anyone else. "I hope I haven't missed anything," he said.

Without returning his smile, Lindsey took the ticket from him and remarked, "No, we've just started, but I was telling the folks to stay close to me—"

"No problem."

"And do exactly as I say."

"Yes, Ma'am." His eyes were twinkling.

Lindsey looked at the rest of the group, because it was infinitely easier than looking at J.L. Brett, who was making her dander rise because he had blatantly come here when she had expressly told him not to. Obviously, he was a man who did not take orders well.

"Please do not wander down any of the side tunnels to explore on your own," she told them all. "There are eleven levels to this mine and numerous holes that drop hundreds of feet into a black abyss. There is danger here, but respect that danger, and you won't get lost or hurt."

"Or abandoned?" J.L. quipped, and the others made nervous sounds and glanced at the walls that entombed them, while Lindsey hurriedly said, "Certainly not," although it was an intriguing idea if it meant getting him out of her sight.

Lindsey began to walk, and J.L. fell in beside her, much to her dismay. "It will be dark in many places where we don't have electricity," she warned, "so walk carefully. We have left it this way so you can get the true feeling of a mine in its natural setting."

As the natural light diminished, Lindsey turned on a heavy-duty flashlight and used it to guide them along the dirt path ahead.

In a few seconds, they reached their first stop, where Lindsey flipped on a single light bulb that illuminated the surroundings. The tunnel here was fairly wide and well over six feet in height, and she noticed that the top of J.L.'s head was only inches from the rocky ceiling. And his tightly muscled body was only inches from her own.

She took a step to her right and directed her flashlight along the rocky wall. "Geologists tell us that at the dawn of creation, this area of southern California was a seabed, and that enormous pressure deep within the earth finally heaved it upward to form this mountain range."

She could feel J.L.'s eyes surveying her.

"When this occurred, the seabed tilted from the horizontal to approximately 82 degrees, and cracks and crevices occurred in the rock. Hot gasses, solutions, and molten rock surged up from down below and filled those crevices, and because it was virgin rock it was heavily mineralized. When it cooled, it formed the quartz veins in which the gold, silver, and platinum lie."

She was unprepared when one of J.L.'s strong hands surrounded hers that held the flashlight and directed it to another part of the wall.

"Is that a quartz vein?" he asked in resonant tones that reminded her of thick, dark, hot fudge sliding over a mound of rapidly warming vanilla ice cream. She was the ice cream, trying to stay firm, but knowing she would soon melt if she stayed too close to him.

She quickly withdrew her hand from his grasp.

"Yes, it is a vein," she told him and the others in a voice that quivered, to her consternation. "It runs from here clear through the mountain and widens out to between two and three feet on the other end. Notice the color. That means there's a mineral there. Every mineral has its own color, and a miner will say that quartz with color has a 'kindly' look, while one without color is 'hungry.' This one is kindly."

Lindsey stepped aside so the others in her group could move closer to see what she was highlighting with her flashlight. A tourist asked a question, which she answered with authority; and J.L. asked, with undisguised admiration in his voice, "Do you really know this much about mining, or have you memorized a speech?"

Lindsey thought of all the years she had spent getting a college degree and exploring these tunnels with her foreman, Santiago Ramirez, and other miners, learning every square inch of the miles and miles of it.

"Let's just say I have a retentive memory," she said, moving away from J.L., for he made her uncomfortable. She was used to being around men, had been surrounded by them most of her life; but none had made her feel the way he did, strangely aware of her own femininity, or lack of it. Not even Lance made her respond so.

Self-consciously, she tucked behind her ear an errant strand of pale blond hair that had fallen out of her ponytail, then she started to move on. But J.L.'s arm shot out in front of her, blocking her way, the palm of his hand flat against the wall.

"I think there's more to your knowledge of gold mining than a good memory," he said. "Tell us, please, how a young and charming woman like yourself knows so much about it."

"Yes, tell us," several of the tourists echoed his request.

He was too close to her. In the semidark, without even touching her, J.L. assaulted Lindsey's senses, and she grappled with the horrible truth that he was unbelievably appealing to her.

"I have a degree in mining engineering," she finally said, not at all at ease talking about herself, "from the Colorado School of Mines."

"A prestigious school," J.L. said. "What subjects did you have to take?"

"Physics, chemistry, mathematics, civil, mechanical, and electrical engineering."

He whistled. "Impressive. Four-point-O grade-point average, I'll bet."

"Three-point-eight, actually."

"Slipped up somewhere, hmm?"

"Let's just get on with the tour, Mr. Brett."

"Of course." He lowered his arm. "Now that I know that you know what you're talking about, I'll pay more attention."

To what? Lindsey wondered. *Me or the mine?*

"Miss," a heavyset woman in a snug-fitting pantsuit addressed her, "how do you get the gold out of these rocks?"

"I'll explain it at our next stop," Lindsey said to the woman, which she did, reciting by rote the facts she had given hundreds of times before, that miners drilled alongside the quartz vein where possible, in the softer sedimentary rock, enabling explosives to be used to bring out the quartz, also known as ore.

"When we get outside, to the stamp mill," she promised the attentive woman, "I'll show you how the gold is extracted from the ore."

But that's forty-five minutes from now, Lindsey realized, as her stomach tightened. Her palms were already wet and her breathing shallower than usual. Her head was even throbbing a little. Was she coming down with the flu?

Chapter 10

The tour continued along narrow tunnels, down stairs and ladders, around corners, descending gradual paths leading further and further into the bowels of the earth, and always, Lindsey was aware of the presence of J.L. Brett.

Only when the group emerged into daylight some time later did Lindsey feel more at ease, the bright, warming sunshine a relief from the intimate darkness of the tunnels and the intimate closeness of J.L. Brett.

He was standing away from her now, talking with one of the other men, and she began to breathe normally as she showed the people the unique Cornish stamp mill, not in use at the moment, and the mortar box in it, in which the ore from the mine was placed, after having been precrushed in a jaw crusher.

"The mill has two stamps, each weighing over a thousand pounds, that act like giant hammers," Lindsey told the fascinated group, "crushing even further the ore that has been mixed with water, and to which quicksilver is added. When it is fine enough, like sand, and looks like muddy water, it is known as 'slurry,' and is passed through a screen and over an amalgam plate that, before the mill is started, is cleaned with cyanide and coated with silver nitrate and quicksilver. The quicksilver on the plate picks up the bright gold and silver by a process called amalgamation. . . ."

For another ten minutes, her voice droned on about the quicksilver trap, the percussion table, and the concentration tank, all further steps in the laborious process of removing gold from ore. She stopped short of getting into the refining of the gold.

"How much gold do you get per ton from this mine?" one of the men asked.

"Anywhere from one-and-a-half to four ounces, which is quite respectable for this day, plus other minerals—namely silver and platinum. And to answer what is probably your next question, the mill can process ten tons of ore in a twenty-four-hour period. We often keep it operating for ten to twenty days at a time, and it's scheduled to start up again late this afternoon."

Lindsey's eyes moved over the group but stopped when she came to J.L., who gave her a nod of respect for her knowledge and began to applaud, while the others heartily joined in. Lindsey smiled.

"I might add that mining costs are horrendous, so there isn't as much profit as one might expect, considering the figures I just gave you." She gestured around the area. "Most months we barely meet expenses and salaries."

She wished she could direct them to the small museum she had been working on for months, but it wasn't nearly ready for the public yet. There still remained a mountain of data and physical apparatus from the early days right up to the present to organize and display. Time and funds were the constant hindrances to the museum's completion.

"This ends our tour, ladies and gentlemen, but I'll be happy to answer any of your questions."

Some of the group headed for the parking lot, and two men stayed behind to ask Lindsey more questions, which she easily answered, but there were none from J.L. He just stood there and watched her and the men.

Later, when the tourists had gone away, but he had not, he walked with her to the mine office and Lindsey said, "I have to be leaving soon." In response to his raised eyebrows she explained, "I have an appointment with my attorney. Remember?"

"Yes, I do, and I hope it's not for awhile yet, because we really do need to talk about this case against you."

Lindsey sighed impatiently and pushed ahead of him, ignoring his attempt to open the door to the office for her. Once inside, she retreated behind her desk and sank down into the old, squeaky chair.

J.L. sauntered into the office behind her, shrugged out of his suit jacket, dropped it on a nearby and dusty (she noticed with dismay) table, and loosened the knot in his tie—all movements that Lindsey found terribly appealing. His hands fascinated her. They were so deliberate, with a strong personality of their own as they moved from one task to another. She remembered the feel of those hands on her skin. . . .

J.L. did not sit down but stood in front of Lindsey's desk, those masculine hands at his sides, and went right to the heart of the matter: "Did you find the Full Reconveyance?"

"No, I didn't. Maybe my father destroyed it once the loan was paid back," she suggested, grasping at an unlikely straw, "or lost it."

J.L. shook his head no. "The county recorder would still have a record of the transaction. She doesn't. I inquired."

Lindsey smiled in defense. "I'm not going to worry about it because I know this is all a mistake."

"It's not a mistake."

"It's a mistake that I shall straighten out in time."

"Just so you realize there is a time limit."

Despite her nonchalant attitude, she knew very well that this was a serious problem, even though a part of her refused to believe what was happening: Her world was crumbling around her, the light disappearing just as it did whenever she entered the mine.

She unsnapped the top button on her red paisley blouse and folded up the cuffs of the long sleeves. She was feeling claustrophobic in her own office.

J.L. silently watched every movement. He liked watching and listening to Lindsey Faraday. She was a lethal combination of brains and beauty—someone to respect and learn from, someone to take in his arms and kiss as he suspected she had never been kissed before.

He wondered how long he could keep from doing that. Not until the legal matter was settled, he had decided, but it would be tough waiting. So tough, in fact, that he had prayed about it just that morning. He had asked the Lord to give him the strength to do the right thing.

"Did my father and Francesca Owens know each other well?" Lindsey asked.

"My client has a diary in which her mother admits to being in love with your father. How he felt about her is not revealed, and it's a mystery why Francesca Owens did not do anything when the loan came due and wasn't paid back."

"Maybe she never wanted the money back," Lindsey snapped. "If she truly cared for my father, do you think she'd be pleased with your forcing me to repay the loan now?"

"My client needs the money."

"And my employees need jobs!" Lindsey contended, suddenly standing up to face him. "They have families. Two of them have young children; one is expecting another baby. I have to—" She broke off when emotion choked her, and she struggled to regain composure. Finally she said in a low voice, "Never mind. I'll work things out myself." She hugged herself at the waist and stared at the floor.

"Will you?" J.L.'s words were soft. He wanted to tell her there was another source who could help her.

"Yes," she said, forcing herself to calm down. "I've taken care of my people until now. I'll continue to do so, somehow, with God's help."

J.L.'s eyes opened wide. "Are you a Christian, Lindsey?"

"As of a few months ago."

He smiled. "Then trust in God to guide you. You're part of His family now— His child. He cares what happens to you."

Lindsey looked into J.L.'s eyes, more distressed than relieved to learn that they shared a common faith. If he was also a Christian, how could he be threatening her livelihood as he was? And if God was indeed her heavenly Father, could she trust Him to always care for her?

She had trusted her father implicitly, believed him when he said everything he did was for her. Well, he had done one thing that was turning out not to be good for her at all. Would God be more reliable?

"I'm more concerned here for my employees than I am for myself," she told J.L. "I don't want anyone else but me running the mine."

"You're assuming that new owners would want to bring in their own people."

"It's a strong possibility, wouldn't you say? Especially with Santiago, at his age."

"Perhaps."

J.L. put his hands down on the desk and leaned forward. A nagging feeling was being born that told him she couldn't pay the thirty thousand dollars. Having seen the mine, its buildings, equipment, and environs, he suspected the Lucky Dollar was barely paying for itself and its employees. Could he really take it away from her, even for his client?

He respected her reluctance to simply take his word for the loan's having been made and not repaid. Thirty thousand dollars was a lot to give up when one wasn't certain that one had to. Even the legal documents he had hadn't convinced her.

He wanted to help her but couldn't. He represented someone else.

"You won't be losing your home in Majestic if the mine is sold, will you?" he asked, genuinely concerned.

She shook her head. "No, but Santiago has a simple cabin on the edge of the property that he's lived in for more than thirty years. I couldn't stand to see him lose it."

"Then just pay the thirty thousand dollars, Lindsey, and no one has to lose a job or a home."

Easier said than done, Lindsey could have said, but didn't. She still wasn't about to let J.L. Brett know she didn't have that kind of money. If it turned out she did have to repay the loan, perhaps some miracle would come along in the months before the foreclosure. The banks might lend her the money; she had an excellent credit rating. The mother lode might be discovered in the Lucky Dollar. She might be struck by lightning, and then it wouldn't matter at all.

In frustration, she stuffed her hands into the back pockets of her jeans and stared out through a nearby open window, past a few of her men who were getting the stamp mill ready for operation, and looked beyond to the rugged hills behind and above the mine.

It was May, and the mountain air was losing its crispness to soft breezes, one of which now floated into the room and fanned the heat of her cheeks.

Wildflowers filled the surrounding hills—golden California poppies, vibrant pink rose mallows, blue cowslips and lupine, yellow and purple and white blossoms bobbing on slender stalks, scattered in kaleidoscopic profusion over rocky ground that one would not think could grow anything. But they were there, hardy, returning every year, brilliant, scented, and presenting a dazzling contrast to the bleakness of the mine and the land around it.

The earth was alive with spring while her way of life could very well die.

Lindsey had to get outside, into the clean air where she could breathe and look up and see the sky, while her eye could travel 360 degrees and see only her property. . .*her property*.

"Excuse me," she mumbled to J.L. as she rushed past him and out the door.

She practically ran along the gravel path, up the hill, paying no attention to Snooks and Bones, the mongrel dogs, who now gamboled around her feet so that she almost tripped on them.

When she reached the field of flowers, she threw herself down in them, sitting cross-legged, and smelled their perfume, and fought the tears.

She could hear the voices of Santiago and Larry shouting to each other by the stamp mill, and saw the mine and its rambling buildings and machinery below in the near distance. Why did she love it so? It was dirty and ugly and demanded far too much hard work for the little reward that it gave.

But it was her heart and soul, giving her treasured memories of her father and their days together. It was challenge and heartbreak, stubborn, but with a rare burst of generosity such as the significant vein they had found just two years before.

To give it up willingly, to move on to another life, another endeavor, to marry Lance Robards, would be one thing. But to have the mine ripped from her against her will, would take her very life along with it.

She let out a long, slow sigh and leaned back on her elbows, stretching her legs out and closing her eyes, feeling the sun's warmth seep into her skin. The wind gently lifted the ends of her hair. She absorbed the absolute peace of the place in an effort to still her heart from surging to and fro for solutions.

She heard J.L. settle down in the flowers beside her, knew he was near her, but she did not open her eyes.

Chapter 11

I s this your special place?" J.L. asked.

Lindsey nodded silently, not wanting to put words to the truth that she had many times sought out this hill, this bumpy ground, this glorious expanse of sparse grass and stones and flowers that belonged to her.

"I have one too. It's on the beach, about a mile from my house in La Jolla, a crescent-shaped stretch of sand that's hidden by shrubs and boulders." He sighed deeply. "My soul expands in that place when I feel the wind whip over my face and the salt spray get on my skin, and I can taste the ocean. I feel God there in His nature."

Lindsey slowly opened her eyes, sat up, and turned her head to look at him. She knew what he meant about sensing God somewhere other than in church. She felt His strength in the rugged depths of her mine, His caring in the delicate wildflowers that beautified this very hill.

She wanted to ask J.L. about his faith, but she was hesitant to. It was all so new to her, and she had much to learn, but she didn't know if she should ask questions of the man who might destroy her golden dreams.

He was sitting there with one leg stretched out in front of him, the other bent, his arms leaning over his knee, and he was staring at the sign that hung above the entrance to the mine. It wasn't much of a sign, she had to admit, just a hunk of wood that someone a long time ago had carved with block letters announcing the location of the Lucky Dollar.

"It's the last mine around here, you know," she said in a voice that was faraway, as though she were talking to the wind instead of to him. "There were at least twenty-five of them in Majestic in the 1870s. What a boomtown it was. The Lucky Dollar was the best."

He glanced at her. "In what way?"

"It's yielded almost four million dollars during the past century, but there's a whole lot more gold and silver in her, just waiting to be dug or blasted out."

Unwanted twin tears escaped her clouded eyes and zigzagged down her cheeks as she was overwhelmed with how much the mine and the men who worked it meant to her. She started to brush the tears away, but J.L. was there already, one of his fingers gently catching the tears as they fell.

"There's nothing wrong with caring," he said softly, his eyes soothing her with their understanding. His touch made her feel better, protected somehow, as though he understood how she felt, and approved.

She returned his look, and her heart slowed in anticipation as he leaned over her and his fingers held her chin. Then she felt the moistness of his mouth when, after long exquisite seconds, he kissed her gently, like a feather touching velvet.

The kiss was sensitive, and J.L. stayed against her mouth, savoring the sweet nectar of her lips, almost unbelieving of her willingness to share this sublime moment when their hearts touched.

He thought it would end soon, that she would push him away, but what he felt was a tremble that fluttered from her lips to his, and an almost inaudible murmur of satisfaction.

The kiss ended, but only long enough for them to gaze into each other's eyes with wonder, and then his arms reached out and gathered her against him, and a new kiss, one of more depth, took the place of the first and built in intensity as his lips searched for yet more of her sweetness.

He felt her hand grip his shoulder, then plunge into the thickness of his hair, and his hand tightened at her waist.

The thunderous sound of two, thousand-pound stamps suddenly roaring into action, beginning to crush a ton of ore beneath them, jolted Lindsey and J.L. apart. They sat bolt upright in their field of flowers and stared down at the massive machinery.

When J.L.'s heart began to slow, he laughed outright. "I thought it was an earthquake," he admitted, running an unsteady hand through his thick shock of hair.

Lindsey grinned and yelled above the noise, "I thought your kiss had moved the earth for me."

They laughed together then, until J.L. thoughtfully gazed at her and, with a featherlight touch, stroked her forehead with the back of his fingers. "May I move the earth again?"

Lindsey, blushing, shook her head no and turned away from him, pointing down the hill. "Santiago probably started the mill to protect me."

J.L. grinned, disappointed with her decision, but knowing she was right. What had he been thinking of, kissing her that way? "Yes, he is staring at us, isn't he? I'm disappointed he thinks you need protection from me."

"It is a little silly since I'm a grown woman and can take care of myself."

"I'm sure you can." J.L. reached down and pulled from the ground a delicate pink blossom that he planned to place behind Lindsey's right ear. But his action was checked by the rambunctious interruption of Snooks and Bones, bounding up to them. The two dogs, one weighing a healthy forty pounds and the other a skinny brown runt worthy of his name Bones, were rewarded for their persistence when J.L. scratched their ears and wrestled with them, ignoring the damage they were doing to his suit pants. He petted them with a man's firm hands, which they adored and demanded more of.

Lindsey watched him, admitting to herself what an incredibly attractive man he was in many ways, with his deep, rich voice that mesmerized, his dimpled smile, and his generosity in representing people who could not afford attorney fees. He was even kind to animals. Still, was that any reason to lose her head over him? Absolutely not!

The sad truth was that she suspected she already had lost her head over him, or was fast on her way to doing so.

"You're spoiling my dogs," she said.

"I'd rather spoil their mistress," J.L. countered, rising to his feet and extending a hand to help her up too, which she accepted.

"I don't need spoiling. I need to be left alone, with my life intact."

"Lindsey, I'd love to do that, but I can't. Facts are facts." He kept her hand and started them down the hill, the dogs following, but then Lindsey pulled away from him, knowing she had crossed a dangerous line when she had let him kiss her. She had never intended to do that, and all the reasons why she could not get close to J.L. Brett came flooding into her mind, allowing her to put up an emotional wall between them.

"You don't trust me, do you?" he asked.

"Should I?"

"Of course you should."

"You're asking too much. I don't know you or what kind of man you are. What makes you tick. Why are you a champion of the unfortunate when there's no money in it?"

"Is this curiosity about a man you're starting to care about?"

Lindsey forced out a breath. "No, Mr. Brett. It's just an explanation of why I won't care about you."

"Even if I tell you why I am the man I am?"

"No." She meant it. She had been foolish to give in to his kisses, to let him rouse her feelings. She and he were in combat. She had to stand against him, not melt into his arms.

They were back down the hill now and walking toward the lot where J.L.'s truck was parked.

"I was beaten up when I was six years old," he started, despite her not wanting him to, "because I wouldn't voluntarily give my lunch money to an older boy. I did not enjoy the experience, and I never forgot it. When I was ten, and big for my age, I went after some boys who had taken the football of a friend of mine, a Mexican boy who was little. I won because of my size. In junior high, my opponents also were big, but this time I won by using my brain to defend a new girl who was being taunted because of her red hair."

Lindsey couldn't help being intrigued. "What did you do?"

"Not do—say. I lied through my teeth and told the bullies that her dad was the police chief and ate junior highers for breakfast, none of which was true, but I learned something: Brains can be more effective than brawn in getting what you want. That's when I decided I enjoyed helping people who could not help themselves."

Lindsey murmured, "And did all these friends properly appreciate your help?" She could just see him on a white horse, riding to the rescue of the beautiful red-head in distress, who then lavished him with grateful kisses.

"The girl gave me a whole bag of homemade chocolate chip cookies, one of the best payments I've ever received."

A rush of admiration made Lindsey silently study J.L. Brett for a moment. "Does your present client have red hair?" she asked softly, admitting to herself that the world needed attorneys who cared about bringing justice to those who couldn't obtain it for themselves.

J.L. leaned back against the door of the truck, grinned, and shook his head no; and Lindsey wished he were defending her instead of prosecuting her. It would be better to have him on her side.

With grudging appreciation, she gazed into his eyes, and he returned her gaze, their smiles slowly disappearing as velvet thoughts about each other moved into their heads, thoughts that saw good more than bad and gave birth to respect that went beyond physical attraction.

"If I don't hurry, I'll be late for my appointment with my lawyer," she said.

J.L. nodded, approving. Maybe if she heard the facts from another attorney, she would believe it, and they could get the matter settled. "Do remember," he said to her, "that you need to decide soon what you're going to do."

There it was, the gentle threat, and Lindsey didn't like the sound of it. "All right, all right," she replied sharply, "I understand. Would the amount have to be paid all at once?"

"Yes."

Her breath quickened. "And if I don't?"

"Then I file a Notice of Default with the county."

"After which?"

"You'll have a three-month reinstatement period to cure the default. If you fail to do that, public notice will be given and the mine will be sold to the highest bidder."

Lindsey whirled around, her back to J.L. She felt sick to her stomach.

So it was over, the dance between them, the vying for position, like two wrestlers circling each other, waiting for their first chance to contact. She had tried to avoid the situation, denying its existence. She had tried to avoid J.L. Brett, the man, but had failed at that too.

She had kissed him, had been in his arms, had felt for one or two crazy moments that he really cared for her. Didn't he? If so, it didn't deter him from doing his job of getting a whole lot of money from her for his client. The most frightening thought was that J.L. Brett did not strike her as the kind of man who would waste his time on a case that wasn't foolproof.

She was going to have to fight for the Lucky Dollar with every means she had, and she would before she'd just hand it over, but the idea of repaying thirty thousand dollars was about as possible as California never again having an earthquake.

"There's one thing you should know about me," Lindsey said, turning around and looking J.L. straight in the eye. "I honor my commitments. I pay my debts. If, and I say *if* this debt of my father's is legitimate, then it shall be paid, no matter what it takes to do so. But if this proves to be just somebody's idea of a way to get their hands on some quick money, you are going to have the fight of your life on your hands. Do you understand, Mr. Brett?"

J.L. gave her a rakish grin. "Yes, Ma'am."

Lindsey spun around and strode away, back along the path toward the office, and shouted over her shoulder, "I'll be in touch." She longed for J.L. to follow her, stop her, take her in his arms, and tell her there had been a terrible mistake, that she was safe, her mine was safe, her workers were safe.

But instead, she walked on, and heard the sound of J.L.'s truck starting up. Slowly it moved out of the parking lot, the big tires mercilessly crunching the gravel beneath them, and Lindsey kept walking until she got to the office. Inside, she threw herself into her chair behind her desk, put her head down on her arms, and wept.

Chapter 12

I'm a fool to jeopardize my objectivity by falling for Lindsey Faraday, J.L. told himself as he drove away from the mine, but he knew he was drawn to her goodness, her determination, and that innocent, soft beauty that with one look melted his rough edges.

His euphoria at having held Lindsey in his arms was still fresh in his mind, as was the taste of her lips on his. Yet, an unwanted suspicion crept into his brain: *Did she give herself to me so I would ease up on the legal case and persuade my client to drop the demand?*

"No!" he said out loud. "Lindsey's not that kind of woman. I know that! I know that? I've been with her only three times. That hardly makes me an expert on the workings of her mind and heart."

He pounded the steering wheel with the heel of one hand and decided he had better watch his step before he made a crucial error in handling this case for his client.

❧❦❧

By the time Lindsey lifted her head from her desk, it was nearly dark. The sky outside was gray, and the stamp mill was still making horrendous noise as it went about its job of grinding rock into dust.

She stood up, hastily wiped the now-dried tears from her face, went outside, and said good night to Santiago and the men. Then she drove to her little house in Majestic, determined to forget what had happened between herself and J.L. Brett.

While she could not satisfactorily explain why she had kissed him—and enjoyed it—one thing she knew for certain: She was not interested in a quick fling or having an affair. She looked forward to a physical relationship with a man, but she wanted it only in marriage, surrounded by commitment and genuine caring.

She did not know, of course, how J.L. felt about such things. He seemed to be a Christian, so perhaps he shared her ideals, but she didn't know him well enough to be sure. What if kissing her had been nothing more than a pleasant diversion for him, or a way to soften her attitude and eventually benefit his client? That horrible doubt locked into Lindsey's mind and taunted her while she drove right through a stop sign.

"Dear Lord, I need Your guidance," she prayed. "I'm not experienced in the ways of men. I haven't dated anyone for quite awhile, and now I have Lance wanting to marry me but my heart is responding to J.L. Help me, God, to make wise decisions."

Arriving home, she picked up the evening paper on the front porch and went inside her two-bedroom, one-storied house that had been there for over forty years. She tossed her purse on the couch and sank down into her favorite chair to glance at the headlines, but her mind was not on current events. She was drowning in a sea of contradictory feelings for J.L. Brett.

She didn't want to be with him, but she did. They weren't right for each other because they were so different. He was a brainy lawyer. She worked with her hands, in dirt. He made his living by the power of his words, persuading jurors and judges to his way of thinking. She was a worker, not a talker, and was not at all clever at bantering words with aggressive men.

He was experienced with women. That was obvious from the way he touched her. She, on the other hand, was relatively inexperienced with men. He roused strange new feelings in her that were as dangerous as dynamite ready to explode, and because Lindsey knew she couldn't avoid being with him, she also knew she could get emotionally hurt.

How can I protect myself? she asked herself as she took a shower, changed clothes, and waited for the only lawyer in town, who happened to be a friend of hers, to come to the house for their appointment. She really needed his help.

❧❧❧

John Gregory, tall, lanky, thirty-eight years old, and balding, looked at the copies of the Note and Deed of Trust that Lindsey handed him. "These appear to be in order, but they aren't proof the loan wasn't repaid. I'll check with the county recorder's office. But I must tell you, Lindsey, if Jonathan Brett is against you, there's little chance of your winning the case."

"Why do you say that?"

"Because he has a reputation in the legal field for being tough and shrewd, also completely honest, and only takes on cases he totally believes in."

Lindsey sighed and poured them both glasses of iced tea. They were standing in her kitchen. "Is it true he likes to represent people who can't really afford a high-priced lawyer?"

"Yes. They say he works for pennies when he could get thousands from important people who want him every day of the week. He lets his associates handle the high-profile cases while he takes on the world for those who can't protect themselves."

"He sounds too good to be true," Lindsey grumbled, skeptical.

"He's a man of high principles."

"Who strikes me as being a maverick. I mean, John, how many lawyers do you know who go around dressed like Wild Bill Hickok?"

He chuckled. "He is different, I'll grant you. A throwback to a century ago, when he should have been born, so he could have tamed the West. He raises horses, I'm told, and would rather be riding in the hills than attending a social event."

Lindsey carried two small plates, on which sat store-bought chocolate cupcakes, into the cozy living room where she directed John to a long, comfortable-looking, ten-year-old couch upholstered in a faded floral pattern. Two imitation Tiffany lamps, on either end of the couch, cast a cheerful glow about the room, and Lindsey sat down in a cane-backed chair in front of the fireplace.

"Do you think this client he's representing is also highly principled or just moneygrubbing and after my mine?" she asked him, taking a bite of the cupcake and licking the frosting off her lip with her tongue.

"From what I've been told, J.L. Brett wouldn't be involved in anything that isn't strictly on the up-and-up."

Lindsey's heart sank. "Isn't there a loophole somewhere, John? A statute of limitations or something that will keep Mr. Brett's client from foreclosing on the Lucky Dollar?"

"I'll try to find one."

"Please let me know the minute you have any information for me."

"Will do." He finished the cupcake, wiped his fingers on the napkin, and stood up. "How about dinner one night this week?"

Lindsey knew he had feelings for her. He spoke to her every time they ran into each other in town and had even asked her out a few times. She had always said no, and he had accepted rejection as a gentleman, but she wondered if he would think her coming to him now was an open door to something personal developing. She hoped not. It was all she could do now to cope with the threat to the mine, the pressure of Lance Robards to deepen their relationship, and her irrational feelings for J.L. Brett.

"I think I'll pass on the dinner, John, but I do so appreciate your helping me. I'll expect a bill from you." She gave him a winning smile and walked him out to his car, satisfied that someone wiser than herself in matters like these was now on her side. She even allowed herself to feel optimistic that John would find the answer to saving her mine.

He drove away with a wave, and Lindsey gave a big sigh and turned back to the home she had lived in for many years. It wasn't an impressive house by any means, just a square wooden building needing a fresh coat of pale green paint, with a small porch in the front, weeds growing up between the flagstones, and a little grass around its four sides.

The backyard was a good size. At one end of it was a building, misnamed a garage, that just barely accommodated her Jeep Cherokee and a lawn mower.

Inside, the house was welcoming, if not glamorous, and, while the decor might not thrill an interior decorator, there was a warmth and casualness about it that suited Lindsey just fine. "It's a house of character," she had often said proudly.

Translated, that meant there were things that needed repair and furnishings that could just as easily have come from a yard sale as from a fancy department store.

More important than glamorous furnishings, she felt, was to be surrounded by things she treasured: a music box her father had given her on her twelfth birthday that played Brahms, an arrangement of silk flowers from Santiago, a picture of her and her father, in a silver frame, grinning over the largest gold nugget they had ever found in the Lucky Dollar.

There was no picture of her mother, Alicia, a world-renowned concert pianist, although Lindsey had several, including an especially nice one showing her playing at the Royal Albert Hall in London, wearing a stunning, white satin evening gown. The picture was kept in a drawer, not on a shelf.

Lindsey pulled off her dusty cowboy boots and trudged wearily into the kitchen to wash the glasses and plates she and John had used, her feet relishing the rough feel of the well-trodden braided rug on the wooden floor. Whoever came up with the phrase, "Home Sweet Home," certainly knew what he or she was talking about, Lindsey decided. She loved her home, the natural acreage it was on, and the interesting small town in which it existed.

Above the sink were three black-and-white pictures of the Lucky Dollar at the turn of the century. Lindsey paused in her dishwashing to gaze in adoration at the sights she had seen a hundred times before but never tired of.

Her life had been a good one, filled with simple pleasures and simple friendships, hard work, some rewards. The thrill of being allowed to try, sometimes doing well, other times failing. But that was what it was all about—good days and bad days.

Outside, a few male cicadas began their night singing, and Lindsey finished her chore and went back into the living room where she collapsed onto the comfy old couch and took off the end table the large Bible she had bought the week before, from which she read a few chapters every evening. Instead of opening the Book right away, she clasped it against her chest and closed her eyes.

"There is so much about You I don't know," she prayed to God in a whisper. "I know this is Your Word to me. Give me the desire to read it, and help me to understand why You love me and want me for Your child. This Bible tells me You are my Father, and that You want to give me abundant life, and that if I will acknowledge You and trust You, You will direct my paths."

Lindsey gazed up at the picture of her father and her on the fireplace mantel. "I had a wonderful father, Lord. He loved me more than anything, and took care of me, and gave me a wonderful life. But now he's gone, and he's left me a problem I need to solve."

Lindsey's eyes filled with tears. Her heart ached from missing her father. If any child ever adored and trusted a father, she had hers. William Faraday had been her whole world.

"My father's gone, dear Lord, but I have You." Lindsey smiled as an unusual peace settled over her. She tucked her feet under her and rested her head on the back of the couch, letting her thoughts roam over her life, her family, the mine, her friends, J.L. Brett. They stopped with him, with a recollection of dark, probing eyes but a happy, dimpled smile that could make her forget the harsh realities of life.

She wondered about love. What exactly was it? Did she need it to be complete? Her father had loved her mother, once, and look at the pain he had suffered. Lindsey had decided very young that man/woman love was not as important as people claimed it was.

So when J.L. had taken her into his arms and kissed her, she had been surprised at how much she had liked it, and how far different his kisses were from those few Lance had given her.

Lance was a passionate man, and so was J.L.; but Lance seemed intent on pleasing himself, whereas J.L. had approached her with more tenderness, more in exploration as to what would please her as well as himself.

"I can't think of him," she said out loud. "I won't think of him," and she fell asleep, still clutching the Bible in her hands, while the world outside darkened and surrounded her house. Inside, though, she was warm and protected, for the moment.

⁂

The days went by, a week exactly, and then Lindsey heard from John. "I couldn't find anything to show that the loan was ever repaid, Lindsey. I'm afraid Brett's client has legal claim to thirty thousand of your dollars."

Lindsey didn't cry; she just went dead inside. "Thank you, John," she said quietly and hung up the phone.

For days after that phone call, she hardly said a word to anyone, and the men at the mine worried about her.

She knew she had to call J.L. and tell him the situation, and she did try to do so several times, but every time her hand reached for the phone, she felt sick to her stomach and just couldn't do it. It would be like digging her own grave.

Another week went by, a week of agony when all she could think of was losing the Lucky Dollar. She also couldn't stop thinking of J.L., her thoughts a crazy mixture of good memories and bad. He was two sides of a coin to her, one where she'd win, the other where she'd lose.

She really expected him to call or come to see her, but he didn't, and she wondered why. How long would he wait for her to contact him?

Had she been right in figuring he didn't take their romantic interlude seriously, or was he backing away from the case because he didn't want to hurt her?

She hated all the mental gymnastics she was going through these days and longed for times past when running the mine had been her only concern. Oh,

397

what she wouldn't give for her life to be like that again, with her father alive, and them sharing their hopes for the future.

It was on a day when Lindsey already had a headache that the official-looking envelope arrived from the county. Tearing it open with dread, Lindsey's worst nightmare came true: A Notice of Default had been filed with the county by the law firm of Brett and Associates. She had ninety days to pay J.L.'s client thirty thousand dollars. If she did not, the mine would be sold.

He didn't even wait for me to tell him whether or not I could pay the money, she at first fumed, but then had to admit he had given her more than enough time to contact him. Only she hadn't, and he had acted.

Leaping to her feet, she slammed the letter down on the desk. "He didn't have the common decency to let me know he was going to file," she grumbled out loud. "The snake in the grass. The despicable snake in the grass. Well, he can't do this to me!" and she stormed out of the office, ignoring the dogs as well as the cheerful greeting of Santiago as he passed by her.

Her foreman stopped and watched Lindsey plunge, stone-faced, down the path toward her Jeep. *Someone's in a whole lot of trouble,* he thought, and just knew it was J.L. Brett.

Chapter 13

Lindsey did not obey the speed limit in driving the sixty miles southwest to San Diego. Later she would berate herself for being foolish, but now all she could think of was seeing J.L. Brett, face-to-face and telling him a thing or two.

Don't lose your temper, she told herself, concerned over a trait she had battled all her life and had been praying, since her conversion, would come under God's control. *Temper never solves anything. Just ask J.L. Brett how a man can hold a woman in his arms one day and then legally move to take away her livelihood the next?*

Fortunately, it wasn't rush hour as she distractedly drove her sturdy Jeep through the downtown area looking for Fifth Avenue where many prestigious businesses were located, and for the building in which the arch villain, J.L. Brett, worked.

She breezed, unseeing, through the sophisticated lobby, rode the silent elevator to the top floor while rehearsing just what she was going to say to a certain lawyer. She stepped out into a magnificent reception area of walnut woods, beveled mirrors, and Oriental flower arrangements, but she was barely aware of her surroundings. Her thinking was focused on one thing only—confronting J.L. Brett.

He had betrayed her. He had kissed her in a way she had never been kissed, scratched the ears of her dogs, and then walked away to file his contemptible Notice of Default.

He deserved to know just what she thought of him. *Just don't lose your temper,* she warned herself one last time.

"I'd like to see J.L. Brett," she stated to a middle-aged receptionist who answered politely, "Your name, please?"

"Lindsey Faraday."

"I'll see if Mr. Brett is in."

Lindsey felt like charging down the twin halls that led to the right and left away from the reception area, banging on every door until she found the scoundrel. But she was, after all, she told herself, a civilized person, with manners, and she would not be rude to J.L.'s employees when it was the man himself who would receive her indignation.

The receptionist hung up the phone, gave Lindsey a sincere smile, and said, "If you'll take the hallway to your right, Miss Faraday, Mr. Brett's office is at the end of it."

Lindsey took a quick breath and said, "Thank you." Then she covered the distance in record time and burst through the door.

A stunning young woman with sleek, raven hair brushed softly behind her ears rose from behind a large oak desk, the top of which was unbelievably uncluttered. Her skin was flawless, her nails expertly polished, and her stylish suit showed nary a wrinkle.

"Miss Faraday?" she asked with cool appraisal.

"Yes." Lindsey moved swiftly to the desk. "I'd like to see J.L., please."

Heather Davenport eyed Lindsey's yellow Wrangler jeans, simple yellow blouse under a brown suede jacket with fringed sleeves, and well-worn brown boots that left no doubt she worked in the out-of-doors, far from the city. Was her style of dress what Mr. Brett had meant when he had said she was "different"?

Heather came around her desk to stand closer to Lindsey and saw shining golden hair, vivid blue eyes, soft skin. She knew then Mr. Brett's terse comment involved more than a physical assessment. There was something palpable about Lindsey Faraday, an intensity that blended with an unmistakable naïveté that would always cause someone to give her a second look.

"I'm Heather Davenport, Miss Faraday, Mr. Brett's executive secretary."

Lindsey's gaze shot to the double doors behind the secretary's desk. "Is *he* in there?" She said the pronoun as though J.L. were a runaway plague.

Heather knew her duty and acted on it. "Mr. Brett is not able to see you now, Miss Faraday."

Lindsey glanced down at the telephone board. One of the lines was lit up. "I'll take only a moment of his time, Miss Davenport," and before Heather could stop her, she surged forward, flung open one of the doors with only a quick knock. There he was, the snake.

"Bingo," she cried out.

J.L. glanced up as Lindsey charged into the room. "I'll call you back," he said into the phone, and started to get up, but Lindsey was already behind his desk with her hands on his shoulders, pushing him back into his chair.

"Is something wrong?" he asked, not mistaking the sparks in her eyes that resembled a volcano about to erupt.

"Now why would you think that, J.L., just because you filed a Notice of Default against my mine?"

"You knew I had to do that sooner or later, Lindsey. I waited as long as I could."

"Did you?"

He started to get up, but she pushed him back down.

Heather, still standing at the door, unable to tear herself away from the drama unfolding, sprang forward and asked, "Mr. Brett, shall I call security?"

J.L. glared at her as though she were daft. Security? She thought he needed protection from a hundred and twenty pounds of soft woman, albeit a woman who was bent on intimidation? "No security, Heather. Just close the door behind you when you leave."

Heather reluctantly made her exit but stayed on the other side of the door, her ear to the wood. She had never seen anyone treat J.L. Brett that way, and her curiosity demanded she learn all she could about the situation.

"You really are something else," Lindsey leaned over him to within inches of his face. "First you tell me I'm beautiful—"

He thinks she's beautiful? Heather frowned.

"Then you kiss me among the flowers—"

Flowers? On the ground? Heather clasped a hand over her mouth to stifle an exclamation.

"Then you have the unbelievable gall to file a Notice of Default on me when you know I'm trying to find proof that that ridiculous loan was paid back. You tried to soften me up so I'd give your client the money without a fuss."

"That's not true, Lindsey." J.L. slid the chair back on the plastic mat and rose to his feet, towering over her, his expression concerned. "Holding you in my arms had nothing to do with the legal problem between us."

"Didn't it?"

"Have you forgotten that we both felt the earth move?"

Heather gasped.

"It was just a game you were playing with me, wasn't it—the passionate kisses?"

"Oh," Heather moaned from the other side of the door. She had been yearning for three years for J.L. to kiss her passionately, or any other way.

"I wouldn't play games with your emotions, Lindsey. I'm not that kind of man."

"Ah, yes, I know of your sterling reputation as a man of principle." She leaned toward him. "But maybe people don't know you as well as they think they do."

J.L.'s eyes darkened. "I'm sorry this is hard on you, Lindsey, but the law is the law. Your father borrowed money; it has to be repaid. End of case."

He reached out to her, but she backed away, around the corner of his desk, past a well-worn western saddle and lariat that had once belonged to Will Rogers. With her hands firmly planted on her hips, she said, "You'd do anything to get what you want for your client, wouldn't you?"

"If you're saying I manipulate people, you're wrong, Lindsey."

"I don't think so. You're unethical."

Heather's eyes widened.

J.L. reached out and grasped Lindsey's hand.

She struggled to be free. "Let me go, you brute."

Heather gulped.

"Not until you calm down."

"I'm never going to calm down because you. . .you are unscrupulous as well as unethical."

"Hey, wait a minute."

"And dishonest."

"Whoa!" J.L. felt heat around his collar.

"You should be reported to the Bar Association."

"Miss Faraday, you're out of line."

"I have a right to be. You used me."

"I kissed you, and you responded."

Heather ground her teeth.

"If you don't let go of me within five seconds, J.L. Brett, you'll be sorry."

"I said I'm not going to let you go until you calm down so we can talk about this rationally."

Lindsey kicked him in the shins. Both of them.

"Ow," he howled.

Heather's eyebrows shot up.

"You're crazy, you know that?" He leaned over and rubbed his legs. "This isn't the way differences are solved by mature adults."

"I'm just defending what is mine," Lindsey declared as she whirled around and started for the door.

J.L. limped after her. "Just pay the stupid money," he yelled.

Lindsey stopped, turned, and stared at him. *He's lost his temper,* she thought in amazement. Then she smiled smugly. *I'm so glad I didn't lose mine.*

Since she was in total control of herself, she now looked around J.L.'s office. It was spacious, decorated with deep-seated chairs and a couch, rugged oak furniture, and cowboy memorabilia sprawled on tables and shelves. Through the huge window behind his desk she saw a breathtaking view of sunny San Diego. Hanging on the walls were oil and watercolor paintings of forests and waterfalls and Half Dome in Yosemite, portraying the personal likes of this man who loved the outdoors.

It was a sumptuous office, expensively furnished, and far different from her dilapidated one at the mine. Lindsey wondered if it would make any difference if she told J.L. the reason she wasn't paying the money immediately to his client was that she barely had thirty thousand dollars in the bank, and that some of that was retirement money for her employees, which she would never touch.

No, he wouldn't understand, she decided, *not with all the money he obviously has if this office is any indication. Thirty thousand dollars probably means nothing to him, but giving that much away is an impossibility for me.*

Frustration at being hounded ended Lindsey's speculation and renewed her determination to fight the injustice being thrust upon her. She bravely stepped closer to J.L., looked up into his blazing eyes, and issued an ultimatum: "You tell your nameless client to meet me in court, Mr. Brett. This whole thing is a setup. There never was a loan."

"What?" J.L. raged. "Are you accusing me of being party to a deception?"

"Why not?"

"You're loony. Irrational."

Heather's mouth was agape. She had never heard J.L. so upset. "You put that down, Lindsey," she heard him warn.

Lindsey had picked up a cloisonné vase and was holding it between her hands. It was cool and elegant. It belonged to J.L. Brett. She wanted to throw it. Needed to throw it. Shouldn't throw it. She desperately wanted to control her temper, but she was growing angrier by the moment and her body demanded she do something physical to relieve its tension.

"Don't you throw that," J.L. warned, starting menacingly toward her. "That would be childish, unproductive, and—"

She threw it.

"Ridiculous!" he roared.

Heather quaked at the door.

The vase shattered into three large pieces and a dozen smaller ones, and Lindsey felt infinitely better.

"You're going to pay for that," J.L. shouted at her, his face rigid.

"You'll get that the same day you get my mine," Lindsey yelled back. She yanked open the door to leave his office and literally ran over Heather, who was leaning on the other side of it.

The secretary scrambled as fast as she could to get out of the path of Lindsey's tornado exit. Good thing, for J.L. didn't see her there and slammed the door. A huge, glass-framed picture that hung behind her desk, on the same wall as his office door, crashed to the floor.

Heather's suit was wrinkled. Her hair was mussed. She had broken a fingernail. But she had heard it all and still couldn't believe it. Even though Mr. Brett had told Lindsey Faraday that she was beautiful and he had kissed her passionately among the flowers, she had kicked him in the shins and broken a priceless vase. Heather sank down onto the chair behind her desk and decided that this fiery young woman was Enemy Number One and would never get by her again.

Chapter 14

The morning after her confrontation with J.L., Lindsey felt utter shame. How could she have stormed into his office that way, confronted him so rudely, accused him of unethical conduct, and then smashed an expensive vase? How could she have lost her temper when she had been so determined not to lose it?

I guess this is what the Bible calls being a carnal Christian, she thought while listlessly buttering a piece of cold toast in her kitchen, *doing things you don't want to do and not doing things you should do. I hope there's an answer for it in the Scriptures.*

She poured milk into a bowl of cornflakes, added some banana slices, and ate at her kitchen table while staring out the window at the riot of daffodils that grew along a broken-down wooden fence. Now she understood the Old Testament story spoken by the prophet Nathan about a man who had only one little lamb, his children's pet, and was forced to give it to a rich man who had guests to feed but wouldn't take from his own many flocks to do so.

J.L. Brett and his ruthless client were trying to take what little she had, and she couldn't let them do that—not just for her sake, but for the sakes of those conscientious, deserving men who worked for her, and especially Santiago, who had given three decades of his life to the Lucky Dollar.

Still, I shouldn't have lost my temper, and I was rude to J.L.'s receptionist and secretary, she thought as she washed the few dishes she had used for her breakfast. *What a mannerless creature they must think me to be.* So, before going to the mine, she wrote them both a warm note of apology, which shocked Heather, who never mentioned it to J.L.

Life moved on. Lindsey's bank turned down her request for a loan. She applied at another and another, with no success. The fourth bank, in the next county, was in no hurry to make a decision and Lindsey struggled to maintain hope.

Could she ask for help from her talented and wealthy mother? No, for Alicia Faraday had never shown much interest in Lindsey, not even wanting custody of her when the divorce had taken place. Yes, they spoke to each other once or twice a year, usually by phone; but only rarely had Lindsey seen her mother in person, and she had too much pride to turn to her now.

How about her maternal grandmother? Unfortunately, they were not close enough for her to ask such a huge favor since her Grandmother Mathis blamed the breakup of her daughter's marriage on William Faraday for wanting a silly gold mine and giving up a lucrative career in a prestigious stock brokerage to get it. She conveniently ignored the fact that her daughter had a dream also, to play the piano around the world, away from her family.

What am I to do? Lindsey pondered day after day. Her responsibility for her employees, and especially Santiago and his wife, Maria, weighed heavily on her, and a solution eluded her.

She remembered J.L.'s words more than once: "Trust in God to guide you. You're part of His family now—His child. He cares what happens to you."

She wanted to trust. She was trying to trust, but the waiting was hard.

Lance was not as sympathetic as she had hoped he would be when she told him of the situation one night when they were having dinner at one of his restaurants.

"Maybe it's meant to be. . .that you'll have to sell the mine. Then you can marry me and be free of that responsibility."

Lindsey frowned. "It's a joy, not a responsibility, Lance, and I don't want to be free of it. Even if I have to sell it, I would still wish I were running it."

"I don't understand that." He played with the fine hairs of his blond moustache.

"I know." The tiny hope that had come to mind while they were eating, that Lance might loan her the money, was extinguished.

"I love you, Sweetheart," he said, reaching for her hand and raising her fingertips to his lips, "and admire your intelligence and spunk in running that dirty old mine, but that surely can't be something you want to do the rest of your life. You wouldn't want your children growing up around that dangerous place, would you?"

"Why not? I did and loved every minute of it. My father taught me to be careful, and gave me responsibility, and the miners took me under their wings—"

"That's another thing: I worry about you up in those hills, alone, with just a bunch of crusty old men around."

"You mustn't worry," she assured him. "They're my protectors as well my employees. Not one of them would ever hurt me."

"You don't know that."

"Yes, I do. I know my men. They're hardworking and faithful, and I'd trust them with my life."

Lance laid her hand down and reached inside his suit jacket. "It's just that I love you so much, Lindsey. I don't want anything to happen to you." He took something small from his shirt pocket and handed it to her. "Open it, Sweetheart."

Lindsey hesitantly took the blue velvet box from him and slowly opened it, knowing what was inside, and she was right—it was a diamond ring, large and flashy and expensive, she was sure. It was pretty, she supposed, but it wasn't something she would have chosen for herself.

"Lance, you shouldn't have done this."

"Yes, I should have, and I know you haven't said yes to my proposal yet, but I'm an optimistic guy." He winked at her. "I know you will someday and soon. I wanted you to see the ring, Lindsey, and think about it. Maybe it will help you make up your mind."

Lindsey just smiled, knowing she liked Lance and was enjoying getting to know him, but also knowing she was not at all sure their friendship would mature into love.

At home that night, reading her Bible before going to bed, she turned to the fifth and sixth verses of Proverbs 3 that she was trying to memorize: "Trust in the Lord with all thine heart; and lean not unto thine own understanding. In all thy ways acknowledge him, and he shall direct thy paths."

She lifted her face upward and closed her eyes. "I know I'm Your child now, Lord, and that You care for me. Help me to let You guide me, and not get in the way."

❧❧❧❧

It was six weeks after the episode at J.L.'s office, on a Sunday afternoon, six weeks that had tried Lindsey's patience and wits and had, despite her best efforts, made her snappish toward almost anyone who crossed her path.

The men stayed as far away from her as they could. Snooks and Bones ducked their heads and put their tails between their legs when Lindsey approached, having been yelled at a couple of times when they never had been before.

Even Santiago walked on eggs around her, and more than once Lindsey chided herself for a display of temper she seemed less and less able to control.

It was hard for her to relax, to greet each day with the joy and enthusiasm she once had, for there was no telling how long she would even own the Lucky Dollar.

"I trust You, Lord," she said every day, but that trust didn't manifest itself in her behavior.

When she asked her lawyer friend, John, to do her one more favor, to find out how much the Lucky Dollar was worth, there were tears in her eyes. "I guess I'm going to have to sell it," were the hardest words she had ever spoken.

Today, Lindsey was curled up on a wicker chair on her front porch, her bare feet tucked beneath her. She should have been at the mine an hour ago but just hadn't been able to get herself going.

She wasn't daydreaming. She had given that up weeks before. She was still struggling with how she could repay her father's debt without having to sacrifice the mine.

Her mind in a whirl, her emotions frayed; she gazed over the peaceful slope of scrubby grass, tall pines, and rocky ground that made up the five acres of property she owned. She appreciated the fact that she had so much land. It gave her a peaceful, uncrowded life. But was it a complete life? The question suddenly came to her.

She listened to the quiet, to the leaves of the oak trees rustling in the early morning breeze. No sound here of blaring music from a neighbor's stereo. No monotonous drone of cars on a freeway. No man talking to her, either, sharing his day and dreams.

Tears spilled over her cheeks as she remembered the wonderful talks she had had with her father, on this very porch, in this very chair. They had laughed together, planned together, shared the love of the Lucky Dollar. All this had given her a growing up she wouldn't trade with anyone else's.

She had been blessed to live in this simple place, learning to work hard and care deeply. The people she knew in Majestic were down-to-earth, honest folk, earning a living in a way they liked, not pressured to live up to someone else's standards. They weren't terribly sophisticated, but they were genuine. They didn't move fast, but they accomplished much in preserving a meaningful life that many of those people on the most prestigious streets in San Diego could only dream about.

She heard someone approaching, and looked up to see Santiago lumbering up the path, his shoulders sagging and his face wearing an expression of dejection.

"Hello, there," she called out to him. "Come sit. Can I get you some coffee?"

The old foreman shook his head no and gave her a half-smile as he sank down in the nearest chair.

"There isn't trouble at the mine, is there?" she asked.

"Nope. The mine's fine, and the men are working. Larry is singing his fool head off 'cause his Susy is pregnant again. You know how he gets."

"Yes." Lindsey laughed, then sobered. "But something's wrong, Santiago. I can see it in your eyes."

"You're right." He fidgeted in the chair.

"Well, if it's not the mine or the men, what is it?"

"It's you, Boss. Something's going on you're not telling me about, and I want to help." His words were filled with concern. "What can I do?"

Lindsey sighed and closed her eyes for a moment, then admitted, "I'm up against a stone wall, Santiago," and she told him everything about the loan, but not about kissing J.L. in the flowers and attacking him in his own law office.

Santiago frowned. "Don't you think I had a right to know about the mine, Boss? After all, I've given my life for the Lucky Dollar."

Lindsey reached out and grasped both his hands. "The only reason I didn't tell you was that I didn't want you to worry about losing your job and house, in case whoever buys the mine brings in his own people."

Her blue eyes misted with tears and she whimpered like a wounded animal, "Oh, Santiago, what am I going to do? I have less than two months to pay back J.L. Brett's client or I lose the mine. I have enough money in one account to satisfy the loan, but I've been saving that for my employees' retirement, and it would be hard to build it up again before one of the men needs it. Also, I have a few thousand in a general account, but it's not enough, and it's earmarked for everyday expenses."

Santiago was quiet for a long time, thinking. "I never heard of your father getting such a loan," he said at last, "but we'll think of something to do 'cause I know the Lucky Dollar is your whole life, just as it was your daddy's. You've both been real good to me and Maria. You're like family."

Lindsey heard the pathos in his voice and wanted to hug him and assure him that everything would be all right. But she couldn't do that, for she had no idea of how to get out of the terrible trouble she was in.

Chapter 15

In the law office of Brett and Associates, things were not much better than at the Lucky Dollar. For weeks J.L. had been like a wounded bull—cross, abrupt, a perpetual scowl on his face, giving sharp orders to Heather and little more than grunts to his associates.

"Mr. Brett is getting on my nerves," Angela Baines said to Heather. Angela handled all the tax cases for the firm and was normally calm, deliberative, and never raised her voice. She was thirty-nine years old, extremely intelligent, married to a pediatrician, and had been with J.L. for five years. She had never seen him in this state of mind.

"He's normally not moody," Heather defended her boss.

"He's moody now."

"Or temperamental."

"He's temperamental now."

Heather suspected the reason was that scrawny mine owner who had gotten him to make passionate love to her in a field of flowers. Despite Lindsey's handwritten apology note, Heather thought her little better than an unsophisticate.

Angela's complaint wasn't the only one to come to Heather's attention. Every associate had, more than once, asked her what was wrong with their normally cheerful boss.

Heather decided to take action. She didn't appreciate being abruptly spoken to either. She marched into J.L.'s office, wishing he would leave his cowboy taste at home and decorate with more style. She was actually embarrassed, sometimes, to take people into the room.

Not that J.L. had poor taste—far from it. Growing up in his affluent family, he knew about fine furniture, accessories, and art. J.L.'s home in La Jolla, where the firm's Christmas party was held every year, demonstrated his acute understanding of what was culturally stylish. Heather loved that home. She could see herself as mistress of that home.

Here at the office, though, he stubbornly held to an informal atmosphere. "My clients feel more comfortable sitting on my down-to-earth furniture than they do on that expensive designer sofa we have in the reception room," he'd said.

"May I speak with you, Mr. Brett?"

"Certainly, Heather."

He did not look up from peering at one of four volumes of *California Reports* that were sprawled, opened, over his mammoth oak desk, near a half-dozen sheets of yellow legal paper showing his illegible handwriting.

"Are you working on your Lucky Dollar case?" she asked.

He gave her such a scowl, she actually took a step backward, amazed that her no-nonsense boss, who was always the epitome of coolness under pressure, had been changed by this case, or this woman, into an emotional inferno.

"I. . .uh. . .have something. . .uh. . .difficult to say," she began her mission.

"Yes?" J.L. whirled his chair around and grabbed a book that said *American Jurisprudence II* from the shelf. He riffled quickly through the pages, found what he wanted in thirty seconds, and rapidly added it to his notes.

"People are beginning to notice, Sir," Heather said.

"Notice what?"

"Your behavior."

He paused and gazed up at her with a squint. "What about my behavior?"

"It's. . .it's unusual."

"Unusual?"

"Testy."

His eyebrows raised. "Someone's told you this?"

"Several someones."

"Told you I'm testy?"

"And moody, and distracted, and. . .and not nice to be around," she concluded bravely.

"I see. Well, that's too bad." J.L. lowered his eyes and began flipping through his notes, but then the full meaning of Heather's words struck him—he was behaving badly toward his employees, something he abhorred, especially since it wasn't their fault.

He knew he owed Heather and the others an apology for being a jerk these days, and he also knew why he was acting that way—it was because of one feisty little blond who had more temper than good sense, more stubbornness than flexibility, and more ways to turn his stomach into knots than he thought any woman could.

Her whirlwind visit to his office had clarified an error in his judgment—he should never have kissed her, held her. It had been unethical to do so because they were on opposite sides of a legal battle. He certainly hadn't planned to do so, but there was just something about Lindsey Faraday that drew him to her every time they were together.

Her accusations to him, that he was using her feelings to advance the case of his client, had hurt deeply. Of course, she was wrong in thinking that, but once he had cooled down, after she had left his office, he had understood how she could have come to that conclusion.

All right. Can't I think the same thing? After all, she didn't pull away from me. She kissed me in return, looked at me with a warm, accepting expression. Couldn't she have been hoping I would convince my client to drop the case once I became involved with her? So, she owes me an apology.

Also, she conveniently forgot that he had given her more than the allotted time to bring him hard evidence that the loan had been repaid. Didn't she appreciate that? He had had no choice but to file a Notice of Default. Her racing into his office, upsetting his receptionist and secretary, had been uncalled for.

He stood up so suddenly one of his hands overturned a pencil cup on his desk, and pens and pencils skittered across papers and onto the floor. Heather gaped at him, and he recognized her disappointment in him.

"Heather, I'm very sorry for my conduct of late. I will do better, I promise, with you and the others." He gave her his best smile, but inside, the guilt he felt over making others suffer for his own misconduct raked his conscience.

I need to see Lindsey Faraday, he decided, then just as quickly decided he should stay away from her—far, far away. *Let the law take its course, then I'll deal with the intriguing owner of the Lucky Dollar and how we feel about each other.*

As though his thoughts had produced her, there was a knock on the open door of his office, and both he and Heather looked over to see Lindsey standing there. She was wearing a simple cotton dress, rosy pink in color, with short sleeves and a skirt that brushed the tops of her knees, and J.L. wished at that moment that he were an artist so he could capture her loveliness on canvas.

"No one was at your secretary's desk," she said haltingly, "and I need to see you, J.L."

Quickly, he walked over to her. "Yes, of course, come in." He wondered what was in the box she carried in her arms. "Would you like some coffee? Or tea?"

"Tea would be nice."

As Heather started out the door to accomplish a task she did not welcome, Lindsey laid a hand on her arm. "Heather, I'm sorry about the last time I was here. I know I was rude to you. I hope you'll forgive me."

Heather, surprised at the apology, hastily mumbled, "I suppose so."

"Good." Lindsey gave her a smile. "I assume you got my note."

"Well, uh. . ."

"Note?" J.L. asked, puzzled.

"Miss Faraday wrote me an apology," Heather explained.

"I see." His attention stayed on his secretary a moment as he wondered why he hadn't been told this, then he turned to Lindsey. "Why don't we sit down and you can tell me why you've come." He directed her to a conversation area near a window where she sat down on a burgundy and hunter green upholstered chair, and he seated himself on a matching couch to the side of her.

The fact that Lindsey was here, seated only a few feet from him, made his throat dry, and his breathing quickened as the sun shining through the window beside her fell over her long, straight hair hanging down her back, giving it the appearance of spun gold.

It hadn't been easy staying away from her these past many weeks. He had thought of her often and even though she had behaved badly the last time she had been here, she was still a woman he respected and admired, and a vigorous male attraction tempted him to forget his own advice about not pursuing her until their legal differences were settled.

"I can't stay long," she said, looking into his eyes at the same time she extended the box to him.

"What's this?" he asked.

"A replacement for the vase I broke."

J.L. gulped. His vase had cost fifteen hundred dollars. He hoped Lindsey had not spent that. He wouldn't accept it if she had.

Slowly he opened the box and took out a piece of porcelain that amazingly resembled what had been broken, but even a quick look told him it was not worth a tenth of what his had been.

"I know it's not as good as yours," she said, leaning forward, her fingers touching the side of the vase and accidentally brushing his, "but I had to bring you something."

"No, you didn't," he said gently.

"Yes, I did," she insisted. "I behaved abominably."

"You were upset."

"An understatement of fact."

"I should have notified you that I was filing the Notice of Default."

"I knew it was coming. Just not when." Her gaze drifted to the green wool carpet.

He leaned toward her. "That wasn't the whole problem, though. You thought my kissing you was only a ruse to get what my client is asking for."

Slowly Lindsey looked up and her eyes met his, questioning, shimmering blue and moist, and J.L. had to tense every muscle in his body to keep from drawing her into his arms and telling her she was special to him, very special.

"Yes, that's what I thought."

He took a deep breath and let it out slowly, wanting to touch her, hold her hand, convince her his feelings for her were genuine, but he couldn't—not yet.

"Lindsey, let me be honest with you," he said. His voice was soft. "I'm attracted to you. . .a lot. I have been since day one when I met you. But we're on opposite sides of an unfortunate situation and, until that is settled, it isn't ethical for us to have a relationship."

"I understand."

"Do you?"

"Yes, because I'm battling the same inconsistency with my own feelings. There are things about you that I like, but then you're threatening my livelihood and those of people I care about. It's hard to separate the two men and, to tell the truth, I can't right now. Anyway, there's another man in my life. He's asked me to marry him."

Heather entered the room with the tea and heard the last words of Lindsey. *J.L. kissed her passionately, but there's another man who wants to marry her?* she thought, incredulous. *What do they see in her, anyway?*

She set the tea things down with a little thump and whirled around, leaving the office. More than ever, she disliked Lindsey Faraday and the power she had over men's feelings.

J.L. struggled with his own feelings, having just heard that there was an important man in Lindsey's life. He hadn't expected that, not the way she had kissed him. How could she care for someone else when he was pretty certain that she had feelings for him? He hoped she wasn't using him the way she had accused him of using her—to get her own way in this legal mess.

"So, there's someone else," he stated, hoping she would give him details.

"Yes, but I didn't come here to talk about him. I came to apologize for my behavior and to ask if it's too late to stop the sale of the mine? I mean, would your client accept monthly payments instead of a lump sum?"

The expression on Lindsey's face was so hopeful, bordering on desperation, that J.L. saw the truth of the situation and sucked in his breath, feeling like he had just been kicked by the meanest bull this side of the Rio Grande.

"You can't pay the thirty thousand, can you?" he asked her.

"I didn't say that."

"All right, then the answer to your question is no. My client needs the money as soon as possible. All of it."

"But wouldn't a monthly amount be better than waiting three months to sell the mine, then going through an escrow period of who knows how long, not to mention the risk of it falling out of escrow and causing even more delays?"

"You need to pay the entire amount, Lindsey."

She stared at him a moment, then rose to her feet. "I see. Well, let me assure you that if, indeed, this is a legitimate claim, then the money will be repaid. . . somehow. . .whatever it takes."

He stood up too and couldn't help reaching out to take her arm. "Lindsey, can you pay the money?"

She moved away from him, breaking the contact, and walked toward the door. He moved quickly to get in front of her. "Lindsey, tell me. Do you have the thirty thousand dollars to pay my client?"

She looked directly into his eyes. "No, I don't. I have no assets to sell. Every piece of equipment I own is used to mine the Lucky Dollar. There! Are you satisfied? Go back to your barracuda client and tell her she's won." The air sizzled with her frustration.

"Why didn't you tell me this the first day I came to you?" J.L. asked sharply.

"Because I never thought I would have to pay it. But I will. As I said—whatever it takes!"

She pushed around him and walked stiffly out of the office. J.L. watched her go and felt a part of him go with her. Deep anguish ran through him that he and his client were pushing Lindsey to the wall, and she most likely would lose the mine that, he knew well enough by now, meant the world to her.

Closing his office door before an interested Heather could ask him any questions, J.L. began pacing. He was angry with Lindsey's father for not having paid back the money and with the system of justice that demands reparation even if it means punishing a law-abiding, hardworking person who just happens to be taking the brunt for someone else's mistakes. He wondered if Lindsey's great loyalty to her father would waver now.

For the first time in his successful law career, he was torn between the two sides. He believed in the rights of his client, no doubt about that, but he also felt sick inside that Lindsey was going to suffer because of those rights. He was legally bound to do all he could to bring about a positive resolution for his client, but in the process, he would be destroying Lindsey Faraday in the name of justice.

Finally settling down at his desk, he glanced over at the coffee table and saw the teacups sitting there, the liquid now cold and untouched. He, though, was not untouched. Every fiber of his being was touched by the predicament of this woman he had just met, and he wanted desperately to help her, but how?

Slumping in his chair, he thought of Lindsey a long time until an idea formed in his head. Then, sitting up straight, he grabbed the phone and dialed a number written on a legal pad in front of him. It was the home number of Santiago Ramirez.

"Mrs. Ramirez? This is J.L. Brett. Is Santiago there? I see. Could you have him call me as soon as he comes in, please? It's important that I talk with him before I go out of town on business. Let me give you my numbers of my home and cell phone. Thanks a lot. I look forward to meeting you too."

He put down the phone and smiled. He felt better. He was going to help Lindsey.

Chapter 16

I wish you'd forget about my birthday party," Santiago said with sincerity when he found Lindsey making out a grocery list late one afternoon at her desk in the office.

Lindsey looked up, tired. For the past week, in anticipation of potential buyers looking over the place, she had driven herself and the men relentlessly to complete projects she had let go for too long. Even so, there was no way she would deprive Santiago of his party.

She gave him one of her thousand-dollar smiles. "What would my employees and their families think if I canceled one of the Lucky Dollar's oldest traditions? Not to mention the fact that they'd miss tasting my marvelous chili."

Santiago chuckled. "You don't like to cook."

"But my chili recipe is prizewinning good. Yes?"

"Yes, but with so much on your mind, I hate to see you go to a lot of trouble just for me. Remember last year what the Mahoney baby did to your best chair?"

"I remember, and this time I'll be prepared with disposable diapers in three sizes."

They both laughed, and Lindsey stood up. "Santiago, this may be the last party I'll have for you here at the mine." Her voice quivered. "Don't deny me this very small way of saying thank you for all you've meant to my father and me through the years."

Lindsey saw moisture well up in Santiago's eyes, and she quickly turned away so he wouldn't know she had seen. His emotion was her emotion. She would miss him terribly. "Besides," she sighed, "we need a party around here to lighten our spirits. I know you're as down about selling the mine as I am."

"But we still have some time before that happens. Maybe God will send a miracle, and you'll find the money."

Lindsey smiled. "I believe in miracles, Santiago, I really do, but I'm not just sitting back waiting for one to deliver us. Every minute I'm thinking of where I can find that thirty thousand."

"You don't know anyone who could loan it to you?"

"Afraid not."

She came around the desk and gave him a shove toward the front door. "In the meantime, Sir, you go home and relax and get ready for your party tomorrow. There's going to be good food, good friends, and good music, and if that doesn't take our minds off our troubles, I don't know what will. Off with you now," she ordered, pushing his bulky body out the door. "I have a party to get ready for."

Santiago obeyed, a grin on his face.

❦

The next morning, Lindsey dragged herself out of bed, woefully lacking the energy she needed for the coming day. She had to buy groceries, clean her house, cook chili, and prepare other food for an onslaught of twenty-two adults and wiggling children who would be invading her home and yard at one o'clock for Santiago's party.

She was tired before she even started—tired in mind as well as body. Giving this party for Santiago, probably the last one, was breaking her heart. Then there was the mine. She had never worked so hard as she had this past week to get the Lucky Dollar in prime condition *if* that terrible day came when she had to sell it. At least if she could get top dollar for it, she could give her well-deserving employees severance pay to ease their disappointment.

Sleepily easing herself into a blue cotton top, well-worn shorts, and floppy sandals, she made a quick trip to the grocery store. Then, back in her kitchen, she became annoyed when a hard knock on her front door interrupted her unpacking of the hamburger, Spanish onions, chili beans, and assorted spices she had purchased. She hoped it wasn't one of her employees' wives, coming to graciously offer to help. She wanted to do this party all by herself this time, this last time for Santiago.

She opened the door.

"Hi. I'm here to cook the chili for you."

It was J.L. Brett.

Before Lindsey could stop him, he walked in, with a large grocery bag in one arm and a comment: "I heard cooking is not your forte and, since it's mine, I'll take over."

"I beg your pardon?" Lindsey questioned, wondering who could have betrayed her by telling him that secret. "Thanks, but no thanks. Good-bye."

He didn't get the message, however, and kept right on walking, through her living room, into the kitchen.

She ran behind him, through her house, having to admire his straight back encased in an olive green, short-sleeved shirt and his narrow hips and long, well-built legs clothed in olive green walking shorts.

With his intimidating height and powerful carriage, he would look impressive striding down the center aisle of a magnificent cathedral, wearing ministerial robes, she thought. *Or across the south lawn of the White House, followed by news-hungry reporters. Or along the deck of a battle cruiser, shouting, "Fire the torpedoes!"*

Wherever his feet touched, it was territory claimed.

But not in her house!

"Why are you really here?" she yelled at his back, and almost ran into him when he stopped abruptly.

"I had to see you."

"Your client has died?"

He turned around and scowled at her. "That's not funny."

Crossing her arms over her chest, she gave him a firm look. "I don't think it's funny either, for you to force your way into my house and disturb my plans for the day."

He flashed her a smile that would melt the Sphinx. "I didn't force myself in. You opened the door, and I'm not disturbing. I'm helping."

"I don't need your help."

"Of course you do." He began to remove bottles and packages from the brown bag and plunked them down on the kitchen counters beside Lindsey's supplies. "I didn't bring hamburger. I assumed you had it."

"Of course I have it. But—"

"Great. Let's see. Here's the chili beans, Tabasco, tomato sauce, Spanish onions, the chili bricks, chili powder—I put one tablespoon of chili powder per pound in my basic recipe."

"One tablespoon?" Lindsey gasped. "I use only one teaspoon."

"Oh, good chili needs more." His look was recriminating. "Gives it a real bite."

"That's too hot for my taste."

"Hot is good."

"Not for me."

He grinned. "How do you know 'til you've tried it?"

Lindsey's blood began to boil. "I don't need your advice on how to make chili," she said sharply, "and what makes you think I'm cooking up a batch today, anyway?"

"Because Santiago's birthday party is this afternoon, right?" He began to rummage through the drawers for utensils.

"Yes," she conceded, "but you're not invited."

"Santiago said I could come."

"He did not."

"Did too. And not only did he invite me," J.L. went on in a disgustingly cheerful banter, pulling out a wooden spoon, a spatula, and a six-inch-long knife that he laid on the counter beside the sack, "he said I would be welcome."

"What?"

"I guess he was speaking for himself and not the hostess."

"Most definitely."

Lindsey was almost in shock. Why would Santiago invite this man to the party when he knew how she felt about J.L. Brett and this horrible legal situation?

"Before you decide to fire the man," J.L. said, washing his hands in the sink,

417

"you should know that the main reason he invited me was so that I could talk to one of your men who works at the mine."

"About whether or not I properly pay him and provide adequate health insurance?"

J.L. chuckled. "No. It's a family matter."

"Santiago thinks you can advise him?"

"Yep. More comfortably here at the party than in my office."

That conclusion made sense, but Lindsey was still thoroughly puzzled why her devoted foreman was suddenly so chummy with the "enemy," and she mutely watched J.L. whip open the door beneath the sink, find the paper towels, and wipe his wet hands. Then he faced her. "Do you have an apron?"

Lindsey's eyes bugged wide. "Now just one minute," and she grabbed his left arm as he started opening one drawer after another in search of the garment.

Her reaction to touching his skin, to feeling the strong mat of hair that covered his forearm, jolted her. It was like touching fire that then raced through her body, leaving her limp. From simply touching him. She was in trouble.

She dropped her hand as though scalded. "I cannot keep you from attending Santiago's party since he invited you himself, but I do not want or need your help. Please leave my house."

Ignoring her tirade, J.L. searched until he found the drawer that held aprons and pot holders. From it, he took a well-used white terry cloth apron with a deer on the front, tied it around his waist, and said, "This will do, don't you think?"

Lindsey refused to smile, even though the rugged hunk of a man before her looked deceptively domesticated and docile, which were definitely two words she would never use to describe him.

"You're a regular Betty Crocker," she declared, then glanced at her watch. "When you came in, you said you had to see me. Are you wanting to remind me that the ninety-day deadline's almost up, then the mine will be sold and you'll be victorious?"

J.L. frowned and shook his head no. "Lindsey, I'm not insensitive to what you're going through."

"Really? You're giving a good imitation."

"I've been more than lenient with the time I've given you to prove the loan was repaid."

"That's true." She was going to say more, but she felt tears spring into her eyes, and turned her back on him, not wanting him to see her emotion. Her nerves were frazzled these days, and every time she thought of losing the mine, she got either mad or sad.

She felt him come up behind her, close. "Talk to me, Lindsey," he pleaded, his voice low and gentle beside her ear.

She didn't want to talk with him. She wanted him out of her house, out of her life.

"Have you found any way to raise the money you need?" he asked.

"No, but I'm not giving up. We're mining every day. I can hope—"

"You've tried the banks?"

"Of course."

"Relatives with money?"

"There's no one."

"Friends?" Instantly she thought of Lance, and just as quickly dismissed the thought. She had too much pride to ask him for money. Besides, if he gave it to her, she would feel more than obligated to marry him, and she was pretty sure Lance was not the right man for her.

"I. . .don't think so," she answered J.L.'s question. In ultimate frustration, she said, "So, file your notices in the newspapers, Mr. Brett. Put up a 'For Sale' sign on my property. Sell. . ." Her voice broke. "Sell the Lucky Dollar."

He moved toward her, but she put up her hands to keep him at a distance. "I know what you're thinking, that I'm silly about the mine. After all, it's just a piece of property, a thing, a possession. But to me, the Lucky Dollar is the embodiment of my life with my father, the days and months and years I spent with him growing up, learning the business, having him proud of me, being loved by him unconditionally. How can I give that up?"

With a gentle touch, he reached out and pulled her into his arms, and while she at first resisted, it was infinitely easier to give in and let her face rest on his broad chest while the tears she could not prevent rushed down her cheeks.

Chapter 17

Silent moments passed, and Lindsey grew content in J.L.'s arms, for they circled her like a safe haven that would protect her from anything bad happening to her. Of course the idea was ludicrous since it was J.L. himself, representing some nameless client, who was taking away her peace.

She pulled away from him and looked around the kitchen—anywhere other than into his eyes that she suspected would be filled with concern and would melt her heart.

"I'm going to be fine," she assured him with more pluck than she actually possessed at that moment.

"Good girl." He lifted her face with one of his hands and gazed at her. "I care about what happens to you, Lindsey. Can you believe that?"

Lindsey's pulse raced and she tried to answer as steadily as possible, "I'm not sure, J.L."

"Please try."

She gave him a tiny smile. "I will."

"Great, because believe it or not, I don't want to see the mine sold away from you any more than you do. I know how much it means to you."

Lindsey wanted to believe him. It would be so comforting to do so. His sentiment seemed sincere, but could she trust him? After all, she could not forget that he had kissed her intensely at the mine, and still had filed a Notice of Default against her.

"It might be that God has a better plan for your life than running the mine," J.L. suggested. "Have you thought about that?"

"My pastor brought up the same idea last Sunday," she told him honestly, "but I'm resisting it."

J.L. squeezed her arms, then let her go and turned toward the living room. "Did I see a Bible on one of your tables?" he asked.

"Yes. Why?"

"There's an obscure couple of verses in the Old Testament, written by the prophet Jeremiah, that fit your situation perfectly."

He walked briskly out of the kitchen and into the living room where he found her Bible, whipped skillfully through the pages, then handed it back to Lindsey.

"Jeremiah 29:11–13," he said.

Hesitantly, she took the sacred Book from him, surprised at his familiarity with it. Slowly, her eyes lowered from his face to the white pages before her.

"Why not read the verses out loud?" he prodded, and when Lindsey found the reference, she did just that, in a quiet manner, still in awe that the very words of God were available to her, and everyone, to read and inspire.

" 'For I know the thoughts that I think toward you, saith the Lord, thoughts of peace, and not of evil, to give you an expected end. Then shall ye call upon me, and ye shall go and pray unto me, and I will hearken unto you. And ye shall seek me, and find me, when ye shall search for me with all your heart.' "

Lindsey looked into J.L.'s eyes as the tremendous impact of those words settled in her brain. "Do you really believe that, J.L., that God cares so much about each one of us?" she whispered.

J.L. nodded yes. "His promises are everlasting, Lindsey, and He is faithful in keeping those promises."

"How do you know that?"

"Because it's happened in my life. I'll tell you about it someday."

How could Lindsey argue with that? J.L. seemed to have strong faith, just as she hoped to have, and a thorough knowledge of the Bible. Was it that knowledge that gave him his confidence in God's faithfulness?

She closed the Bible, laid it down, and walked back into the kitchen, her heart suddenly stabbed with the realization that she had always thought her father was faithful to his promises too. He had told her the mine would be her inheritance forever—*forever*. For her and her children and grandchildren. His promise was about to be broken. How could J.L. be so sure that God would not also break a promise?

"Thank you for showing me that," she said to J.L. when he joined her in the kitchen. "I'll. . .think about it."

"You won't be sorry to put your trust in the Lord, Lindsey."

"We'll see," she countered, a stubborn part of her old nature still not able to totally grasp this new relationship she had with the God of the universe. "For now, you'll have to excuse me. I have lots of chili to make and other tasks to complete before Santiago's party."

"I'll help."

Before she could stop him, J.L. went to the refrigerator and took from it six pounds of hamburger meat and put them next to the stove.

"J.L., I really don't need your help."

He stopped unwrapping the meat and clucked his tongue. "You know, Lady, the first day I met you, I put down on my list that you were uncooperative. You were then, and you still are."

Lindsey stabbed him with a look of unbelief. "You have a list on me? That says I'm uncooperative?" She picked up one of the Spanish onions and gripped it fiercely. "How else do you describe me?"

"Stubborn. Temperamental. Defensive. Unrealistic."

"Ooo!" Her howl resounded through the tiny kitchen and she raised her hand to throw the onion, but J.L. snatched the vegetable from her hand and tossed it into the sink.

"I added loyal and compassionate to it."

"Wonderful."

"And I'm sure I put down beautiful. And intriguing."

"Oh."

"And intoxicating."

"Really?"

"As well as stunning and intelligent."

"My, my."

With a move that caught her off guard, J.L. reached out for Lindsey and pulled her against him, lowering his mouth until his lips hovered tantalizingly over hers.

"In other words, Lindsey Faraday, you're not like any other woman I've ever known." Then he kissed her, intently, his arms sliding around her waist in an eager possessiveness that sent Lindsey's senses exploding into awareness, heightened by the salty taste of his hungry lips on hers, the scent of his cologne, and the feel of his muscled arms as she clutched them for support.

"J.L., we can't do this," she whispered, her cheek next to his. "You were the one who said we should wait to start a relationship until this legal problem is solved."

"Yes, I did say that, didn't I?" He kissed the tip of her nose. "And I should take my own counsel." He stroked her cheek. "Why, then, do I find it practically impossible to stay away from you?" His look was tender. "But I have to, don't I?"

"Yes."

He straightened, took in a lungful of air, let it out, and released her. "Okay, you're the boss. I think I'll get to work on something less volatile than you," and he put cooking oil in each of the three Dutch ovens.

Lindsey eyed him skeptically. "*If* I let you stay and help, do you promise to put in only one teaspoon of chili powder per pound of meat?"

J.L. looked pained. "You don't know what you're missing."

Lindsey laughed out loud. "Yes, I do."

"How about a compromise?"

When Lindsey reluctantly agreed, J.L. winked at her, and she sighed. "I'll start on the salad." Gathering together the lettuce, celery, tomatoes, and hard-boiled eggs gave her time to get herself under control, but there was something she had to say that J.L. had to hear.

She paused from her work and waited until he was looking at her, then she said decisively, "I must be honest with you, J.L. I'm powerfully attracted to you, now, but if the Lucky Dollar is sold and my employees are out of work, and I end up losing the dream of my life, I'm not sure I'll want to have anything to do with you."

Forty minutes before the party was due to begin, Lindsey collapsed on the back porch swing, holding a frosty glass of lemonade in her hand, and took a deep breath.

She was ready, amazingly, despite the interruption of J.L. that morning. He had helped her not only with the chili (his recipe was better than hers, she had to admit), but also with setting up the tables and chairs on the lawn. Together they had hung gaily-colored balloons on several tree branches and arranged red plastic plates, silverware, and napkins on the red-and-white-checkered tablecloths covering the tables. J.L. had even tried on one of the funny hats to be given to the children in attendance, and Lindsey had tried, unsuccessfully, to pin the tail on the paper donkey tacked to an ancient oak tree.

They had made it a point not to talk of anything personal, and the time had passed quickly and comfortably.

Then she had shooed him away so she could clean the house, which he had offered to do while she showered and changed clothes, but she had declined.

"I do have something I need to buy in town," he had said then, "but I'll be back soon," and off he had gone.

Thinking about their morning together, Lindsey realized that working with J.L. had been fun. He had been patient, diligent to detail, and had seemed to enjoy getting things ready as much as she had.

Closing her eyes now, hoping for a few more minutes of peace before the onslaught began, Lindsey heard the crunch of gravel as someone came along the path from the front of the house to the back. Thinking that some of her guests were arriving early, she opened her eyes and saw J.L.

"Do the caterers have everything ready?" he joked, the twinkle in his eyes warming her heart.

"Yes, indeedy. They've come and gone, leaving me nothing to do."

"Except talk to your first guest. Me."

"I can handle that." But no sooner were the words out of her mouth than Lindsey wondered if she had spoken too soon. J.L., tall and tanned, had changed into brown brushed denims and a forest green western shirt with embroidered circles on the yoke. A snakeskin belt wrapped its way around his trim waist and ended in a matching buckle with his initials on it. Between snakeskin boots and a green paisley Apache tie lying jauntily around his neck, he looked anything but a man to be handled.

Lindsey swallowed hard.

"I'm glad you approve," he said with a wink, coming up to the swing and taking from behind his back the biggest bunch of red tulips she had ever seen in her life.

"Oh, J.L.," she gasped, "they're gorgeous."

"I thought you could put them on the tables. Didn't I see some glass Mason jars in one of your cupboards?"

"Yes, you did. What a perfect idea. Thank you so much."

She smiled warmly at him and sniffed the flowers as he eased himself down on the swing beside her.

"I approve of you too, Lindsey," he said, the brown of his eyes deepening. "You look. . .incredible in that blouse," and with two fingers he reached out and carefully felt the material of one billowy, long sleeve that ended in a cuff of ruffles and lace. "You remind me of a cool, delicious dish of mint ice cream."

"Do I?"

Lindsey sat very still as he touched the high, banded-lace collar of the blouse, trimmed with tiny ribbons. When she had bought the blouse, she had wondered if it were too feminine for her. Though it went perfectly with her black dress jeans, it was quite a change from the plain western shirts she usually wore at the mine.

"Can I help you put those flowers into water?" he offered.

"No, I'll be just a minute. Why don't you sit here and enjoy the solitude? There won't be much of that for the next few hours."

J.L. chuckled while Lindsey hurried into the house, willing her heart to stop pounding. But how could it, when she knew J.L.'s eyes were watching every step she took?

Chapter 18

I'm sure the party will be a success, Lindsey," J.L. said, when they set the last Mason jar of glorious tulips in the center of the table where Santiago would sit.

"Your chili will help."

"I hope so. I got the recipe from my father."

"Is he a chef?"

"No. Chili is the one and only dish in his entire cookbook."

Lindsey smiled. "Tell me about your family."

They went back to the swing and sat down together. J.L. began the swing moving slowly and said, "I have a lovely, elegant mother and a somewhat pompous father, both of whom I adore, no brothers or sisters, but a big Labrador I call Brute, and a house in La Jolla."

"Do you get on well with your parents?"

"Pretty much, although more so with my mother."

"Tell me about her."

J.L.'s expression became contemplative, and Lindsey recognized love and respect in his gaze. "She's a special woman, regal but unpretentious, who cares about people, as you do, and won't put up with rudeness or unkindness. She feels she has the right to know about every woman I go out with and gives me her opinion of them, whether I want it or not."

Lindsey giggled. "She sounds delightful."

"She is, and precious to my father and me."

"What is he like?"

J.L. snorted softly. "Dad is a handsome and charming guy. People like him instantly, which he takes advantage of when he's raising huge amounts of money for charity."

"Does he do that for a living?"

"No. He plays with corporations—buys up small ones, improves management, then sells them for good profit. He thrives on having and making money. It's his *raison d'être*."

"Which you don't approve of?"

"Oh, I wouldn't say that. We just have different goals. I respect my dad, his drive, and sense of fair play. He's a hard man to do business with, but an honest one. He's given me his self-confidence."

Lindsey smiled and offered him some more lemonade from the pitcher she had brought out after arranging the tulips. "Do you get your compassion for people from your mother?"

J.L. thought about that a moment. "Yes, I think I do. You'd like her, Lindsey."

"I'm sure I would."

He shifted on the swing and faced her more directly, his leg sprawled across the seat. "What's your mother like, Lindsey? I've heard you talk about your father but never her."

Lindsey looked away from him. "That's because she's barely a part of my life."

"Oh?"

"She gave up my father and me to pursue her concert career. I've never understood that. Of course, my father didn't make their life together easy when he gave up his own career as a stockbroker and bought the Lucky Dollar. Mother hated the place on sight and only came here once. The marriage ended shortly thereafter."

"I'm sorry." J.L. reached out and took her hand. "Have you missed her?"

"I did unbelievably the first year, then it got easier."

"Do you hear from her?"

Lindsey looked off into the distance. "Through the years, she's faithfully sent me birthday and Christmas cards with hastily scribbled notes saying she looks forward to seeing me soon, but soon never comes." She shrugged. "I've gotten used to life without her."

J.L. doubted that were true. He couldn't imagine a full life without the presence of his mother, and he was sure a woman as sensitive as Lindsey needed one too.

"So you and your father came to Majestic."

"Yes, and loved it because the pace was slow, and the people were friendly. They didn't care how big our house was or if we were wearing the latest fashion. I loved the mine too, because I could run through the tunnels, and hold real gold in my hands, and only had to wear a dress on the occasional Sunday when we'd go to church."

"I would like to have known your dad," J.L. said somberly.

"Everyone liked him. He was a happy, positive-thinking man—and infinitely patient with me." She tucked one of her feet underneath her and turned to face J.L. "He used to tell me over and over, 'Someday, Pumpkin, you and I are going to find the mother lode.'" She gulped back a sudden lump in her throat. "Obviously we didn't find it since your client's relative had to lend him. . ." She choked on the words.

It was all J.L. could do to keep from reaching out and taking Lindsey into his arms. The war raged inside him, one side saying to hold Lindsey and never let her go, and the other warning him to stay away from her until the legal mess was settled.

He loved holding her, smelling the sweetness of her perfume, touching her skin, nuzzling her shiny hair. He had never had trouble before choosing directions, making tough decisions that needed making, but with Lindsey Faraday, it was tearing him apart to deny his feelings for her that grew stronger every day despite disagreements, harsh words, and even a kick in the shins.

There was so much about her to admire: her intelligence, loyalty to others, compassion, how hard she worked, and a whole lot of other things that added up to one strong but vulnerable woman he wanted in his life, maybe even permanently.

⤜⭒⭒⤛

The party was a roaring success, as was J.L.'s chili, and the man himself. Lindsey could not believe how well he fit in with everyone.

The men found him unaffected and down-to-earth and genuinely interested in their everyday lives. The women were charmed by his rugged good looks, urbane conversation, and appreciation for their beautiful children. The eight children themselves, ranging in age from four months to fourteen years, found him a willing partner for baby talk or games of ring toss or touch football.

Lindsey didn't chide Santiago for inviting him, for she wanted nothing to spoil this last celebration they would share.

"This is the best party of them all," the guest of honor said, looking very handsome in a startling white, western bib shirt and new black denims. His dark hair was slicked back, and the bushy brows above his eyes were wetted down to keep them under control.

"I'm glad you think so," Lindsey responded, "because it's for the best foreman anyone ever had." She gave him a hug, and when he apologized for inviting J.L. without telling her, she told him it was okay.

J.L. walked up to them. "Happy birthday, Santiago."

The two men shook hands vigorously. "Thanks, Señor Brett."

"Call me J.L. Is your friend here? The one you want me to talk with?"

"He's late, but he'll be along. I'll get you when he comes."

"Great."

Santiago walked off, and J.L. smiled down at Lindsey, the laugh lines around his eyes telling her he was more used to smiling than frowning. "I'd say your party is a hit."

"It does look that way, doesn't it?"

Maria, Santiago's wife, paused on her way to one of the picnic tables with a tray full of French bread. "Are you two having a good time?" Her eyes skirted from Lindsey to J.L., where they rested long enough to give him homage, not that Lindsey blamed her.

"We're doing great, Mrs. Ramirez," J.L. answered her with one of his melt-women-into-the-ground smiles. "I'm glad you and I got to meet."

"Me too." Turning to Lindsey she said, "Thank you for this party for

Santiago. He is thrilled with it. You are so kind," and she leaned over the tray of bread and kissed Lindsey's cheek.

"Believe me, Maria, it is little enough to do for all that Santiago, and you, have meant to me through the years."

Maria went on her way, delivering the bread to hungry people who were everywhere—in the house, out on the grass, talking, laughing, playing games, and eating all they wanted.

"Nice woman," J.L. summarized.

"The best."

"She thinks you're number one."

"How do you know that?"

"She told me. When does the entertainment start?"

"Wait a minute," Lindsey said, her eyes widening. "What do you mean she told you? When? Where? *Why?*"

"My, my, so many questions," J.L. teased. "Oh, I see some guys setting up now. What do they play?"

"Country western," Lindsey answered distractedly, not wanting to stray from finding out what Maria was up to.

"Darlin', that's my favorite kind." J.L. clapped his hands enthusiastically. "Maybe I can join them."

"What do you mean?"

"I play a pretty good guitar."

"J.L., I don't think so—"

"Don't worry. I'm not shy. I have my instrument in my truck. I'll go get it and sing a few songs to warm everyone up for the main event." He gave her a wink. "And I won't even charge you." He strode off, and Lindsey ground her teeth, realizing that this man was unstoppable once he set his mind to something.

His musical ability surprised her and pleased her guests to no end. He sang a couple of Clint Black and Alan Jackson songs with a clear voice that was easy to listen to and got everyone tapping their feet.

It was unbelievable how he stepped right into the lives of these strangers and had them eating out of his hand. They loved his chili. They loved his music. They loved him.

The question that haunted Lindsey was how to keep herself from loving him too. If this were the real J.L. Brett, he was everything in a man she could possibly want. But if he were deceiving her for his own purposes, it would be cruel to lose her heart to him as well as her mine.

A small voice chided her for continuing to mistrust J.L., but Lindsey couldn't help it. A lot was at stake here.

She saw the object of her contemplation across the yard, standing with Santiago and Pete Donaldson. J.L. was listening intently to what Pete was saying.

More apprehension fell over Lindsey that Santiago seemed to like the very man who was tearing the Lucky Dollar away from her. Even though she knew J.L. was just doing his job, representing someone with a legitimate claim against the mine, it still felt personal to her, as though he himself were the cause of her misfortune. Her temper flared.

Moving toward the house, she said good-bye en route to some of the guests who were leaving. In the kitchen, she found a tray of leftover food on a counter and worked furiously for the next ten minutes putting things away, yanking plastic bowls out of the cupboard for storing the remaining chili and salad, and fiercely tearing food storage bags from their box for the French bread.

"It isn't fair," she muttered angrily. "It just isn't fair."

"What isn't?"

She whirled around to see J.L. standing there, with Santiago beside him. She felt like yelling at them both, but she couldn't without spoiling Santiago's party, and she could never do that to him.

"All these leftovers," she fibbed, gesturing toward the pile of plastic bags and colored bowls. "I'll be big as a house if I have to eat them all myself."

"But we'll both still love you, won't we, Santiago?" J.L. kidded.

Santiago agreed.

Lindsey heard the word "love" and dismissed it as a figure of speech. There was no way J.L. Brett could love her on the one hand and be destroying her on the other.

Maria came into the room and slipped her hands around her husband's waist. "I knew I'd find you in the kitchen sneaking more to eat." She turned to J.L. "You make great chili, J.L., but not as good as Lindsey's. It's a little too hot."

They all laughed, especially J.L. and Lindsey when they exchanged a secret look, and he winked at her. Then Santiago shook J.L.'s hand and ushered Maria out the door, and Lindsey kept smiling as she heard them go—but wouldn't have been if she had known that Santiago and Maria had decided that J.L. Brett was the perfect man for her.

Chapter 19

Around five o'clock, after most of the guests had gone, J.L. leaned back against one of the kitchen counters, folded his arms across his chest, and just stared at Lindsey. She was so heart-stoppingly beautiful, so nice to people, so good and decent and plucky.

The list he had started on her when they had first met now had many words on it to describe her, a few negative ones, but mostly positive words that explained why, this day, his mouth had gone dry every time he had seen her and heard her voice saying encouraging things to the guests.

Just how close am I, he wondered, *to falling in love with her? Or has it already happened? How does one know?*

He saw the frown on her face now, and asked, "What's wrong?"

"Nothing," Lindsey insisted in a high falsetto voice, scooping up used plates and utensils and throwing them into a huge, plastic garbage bag. But J.L. could feel the animosity racing across the room from her to him and wondered what had triggered it.

He watched the muscles in her back tighten up and the way she avoided looking at him. After a few minutes he said, "What happened to the friendship we had this morning, Lindsey?"

"I don't know what you mean."

"Yes, you do. Tell me the truth, please."

Lindsey raised her head and looked him straight in the eye, "I'm trying, J.L., I really am, to be civilized over the fact that in a short time my life will be turned upside down. . .by you."

"This is not a personal fight between us, Lindsey."

"It feels like it."

"You're making it that way."

"I know, and you're just doing your job, but you've intruded yourself into my life, and I feel like everything is slipping out of my control. The mine is going. You have Santiago, as well as Maria, eating out of your hand, and all my employees and their families think you're Mr. Wonderful."

"But you don't."

She lowered her eyes and went back to her cleanup work, knowing she could not answer that question to his face, and not wanting him to see how really upset she was. She felt like that mountain lion she had shot at in the mine. He wanted all other lions to know this was his territory. Well, she had territory too, and J.L. had invaded it, conquered it, and, worst of all, was on the way to conquering her as well.

She understood why her friends and employees thought he was terrific. She did too.

As the party had progressed, she had been aware of a growing resentment toward J.L. and how easily he fit in with the people she loved. Of course, none of them except Santiago knew what was about to happen to the mine, but that didn't alter her sense of betrayal, that "her" people were slipping over to the enemy camp, and she was being left alone to struggle against the encroaching danger.

"I can't be a good sport about losing my mine," she said, "especially since I don't feel the claim against it is valid."

"Lindsey, you've seen the evidence."

She heard the censure in his voice, and it was like a twig snapping in her spirit. Try as she would, she couldn't prevent the law from taking from her what she didn't want to give. She could kick, scream, and protest all she wanted, but J.L. Brett had the upper hand.

"Fine," she snapped. "Sell the mine. Fire my employees. Laugh all the way to the bank with your—"

"That does it!" J.L. roared, interrupting her tirade. Reaching out, he grabbed her hand and yanked her toward the door. Plastic dinnerware flew to the floor as he announced, "It's time you learned the truth."

"About what?" Lindsey struggled to be free of him, but her effort was useless.

"About who is going to get the thirty thousand dollars."

"I know who—your client!"

"You need to understand the circumstances."

They were outside now and he was pulling her along the path toward his truck.

"J.L., let me go. I have to clean up from the party."

"Later."

Lindsey saw that Santiago and Maria hadn't left the property yet but were quietly talking with some folks beside a rose hedge. They looked up when they heard Lindsey and J.L. coming.

"Let go of me," Lindsey ordered between gritted teeth.

"If you behave yourself and come with me without fuss, I will."

"All right," she promised, but the minute he let go of her, she turned on her heels and started back for the house.

"Hey, come back here," he yelled, then charged after her.

"I have work to do, Mr. Lawyer."

"That's the trouble with you, Miss Faraday—you don't think of anything but work. Well, it's time you saw that there are other things in life more important."

"Such as?"

"You'll see."

"I'm not going anywhere with you, J.L. Brett." Lindsey dug the heels of her boots into the soft earth and clamped her arms across her chest in determination.

J.L. scooped her off the ground and dumped her over his shoulder.

"Put me down!" she shrieked. "What do you think you're doing?"

"You're going to meet my client, Lindsey girl," came the determined answer, as J.L.'s lengthy strides took them past a gaping Santiago and Maria and friends.

"I am not going anywhere with you!" Lindsey squirmed as much as she could, beating her hands against his back while her head bobbed up and down.

"Yes, you are."

Lindsey could not believe how fast he moved despite her fighting him with all her strength. "Santiago! Maria!" she screamed for help, but neither of them tried to stop J.L. *They'll answer for this,* Lindsey vowed, especially when she saw a smile on Maria's face.

They were almost to J.L.'s truck when she heard a familiar voice.

"Lindsey!"

She gasped, and squirmed around over J.L.'s shoulder just enough to see Lance staring at her, incredulous.

"What's going on here?" he demanded to know.

"I'm kidnapping Miss Faraday," J.L. answered roughly. "Excuse us, please," and he strode around Lance, whose mouth dropped open.

"Help me, Lance," Lindsey pleaded, stretching her arms out toward him. They were at the truck now.

Maria and Santiago hurried up to them, staring at the scene she and J.L. were making. She felt like the star attraction in a grade B movie. It was degrading.

"Put her down," Lance told J.L. "Right now." The words were more a plea than an order, Lindsey noticed with a sinking heart. Lance was no match for J.L.

"Exactly my plan," J.L. declared, bending powerful thighs so he could open the passenger door. "The party's over," he said to Lance, "if that's why you've come."

"It isn't. I'm here to see my fiancée."

J.L.'s body went rigid, and Lindsey heard a slight intake of his breath just before he unceremoniously slid her off his shoulder, but held onto her arm.

"Your fiancée?" With raised eyebrows, he turned to face Lindsey.

Before she could disclaim Lance's rash statement, he stepped closer to J.L. and said firmly, "Who are you, and what do you want with Lindsey?" His eyes narrowed; and Lindsey thought he might actually be bold enough to challenge J.L. but, before a confrontation between the two men arose, she said, "Lance, this is J.L. Brett. He's an attorney and—"

"J.L. Brett? Of Brett and Associates, and the San Diego Bretts?" The light that sprang into his eyes and the transformation in his face from concern to awe puzzled Lindsey.

"One and the same," J.L. answered him, releasing Lindsey's arm and extending his hand to Lance. "Your name, Sir?"

"Lance Robards."

"Robards, Robards." J.L. tried to recall the name.

"I own the Trivoli restaurants, in La Jolla as well as San Diego." Lance stuck out his chest in pride. "You may have dined at one of them."

"Can't say that I have."

"Heard of them, at least."

"Sorry."

Lance's crestfallen look almost made Lindsey laugh, but he quickly recovered. "Then you must come for dinner one night, as my guest."

J.L. smiled as Lindsey frowned over Lance's fawning. Why did he think J.L. Brett was such a big deal?

"I'd be happy to. . .uh, Lance, was it?"

"Yes. Lance Robards. R-o-b-a-r-d-s."

"I'll remember."

"Perhaps tonight?" Lance suggested, looking at the expensive watch on his wrist. "We could all go together. I'm sure you'd find something you'd like on our sophisticated menu. I have extraordinary chefs."

J.L. shook his head. "Sorry, can't. Miss Faraday and I have some business to take care of."

"Now?"

Lindsey moved away from J.L. and slipped her arm through Lance's, a move that brought an immediate rise to Lance's shoulders. "Lance, Mr. Brett is attorney for the party claiming the Lucky Dollar owes her thirty thousand dollars."

Lance's eyebrows rose. "I see."

"He thinks I need to meet the person. . .tonight."

"Tonight?"

"Right now, as a matter of fact," J.L. jumped in, giving Lance a manly slap on the back. "So, if you'll excuse us, Robards, we'll be going."

"We're not going anywhere," Lindsey insisted.

"You need to meet her, Lindsey. It will make you feel better."

"Ha! How could anything make me feel good about giving up thirty thousand dollars or selling my mine?"

"Trust me." J.L. gestured with his hand, palm up, toward the passenger door, as though he were directing her into a golden chariot.

Lindsey hesitated.

"Maybe you should go, Sweetheart," Lance suggested, his eyes dashing from Lindsey to J.L. then back to Lindsey. "I'll come back tomorrow night, and we'll. . .talk."

"Go ahead, Boss," Santiago said. "We'll warm up some chili for Mr. Robards so he won't have driven all this way for nothing."

"Good idea, Santiago," J.L. exclaimed, gently taking Lindsey's hand and leading her to the door of the truck. "Do you like your chili hot, Robards?"

Lance grimaced. "Certainly not."

J.L. chuckled in Lindsey's ear. "Figures."

She gave him a scowl and got into the truck.

Chapter 20

I didn't know you were engaged," J.L. said sharply to Lindsey as they drove into San Diego.

"And I didn't know your family was prominent society."

"Have you set a wedding date?"

"Now I understand why, since you were born with the proverbial silver spoon in your mouth, it's easy for you to ask me to pay your client thirty thousand dollars. Just like that."

"You told me you were attracted to me."

"Since you've never had to scrounge for money—"

"Could we talk about the same thing, please? How serious are you and Lance Robards?"

"I don't want to talk about it."

"Great. Are you going to marry him so you can get the money to save the mine?"

Lindsey gasped. "How can you think I would marry a man I don't love just to get my hands on his money—"

"Aha, so you don't love him."

"I didn't say that."

"Yes, you did."

The smile on J.L.'s face was so maddening that Lindsey wanted to slap it off.

"I'll bet you're not even engaged."

When she refused to answer him, he went on. "Robards probably just said that to let me know you were off limits, like the mountain lions do when they leave scrapes to define their territory."

"Oh, please, I'm not a piece of property to be fought over."

"No, you're not. Are you going to marry him?"

Lindsey clasped her hands together until they turned white and then stared straight ahead. Why should she answer such a personal question? Actually, she couldn't answer it. She didn't know herself.

"He's not right for you," J.L. informed her.

She jerked her head to stare at him. "You don't even know him."

"I've met men like him. They're interested only in themselves."

"Really?"

"Does he approve of you owning and running the Lucky Dollar?"

"No comment."

"I'll bet he wants you to give it up if you get married."

"No comment."

J.L. began to whistle. "No comment necessary, m'lady. Lance Robards is a nerd, and you're too smart to marry him."

Lindsey ground her teeth and stared at the floor, praying they would reach their destination before she strangled Mr. Know-It-All Brett.

"My client's name is Mindy Carson," he said as he turned the truck into a poor neighborhood where houses were run-down and the grass, if there was any, was brown and patchy. The words were the first ones spoken by either of them for ten minutes. "She's very nice. You'll like her."

Lindsey groaned. "I will like the person who is going to take my mine away from me? You're out of your mind."

J.L. chuckled softly and said, "We'll see."

Lindsey turned away from him in the seat and stared out at the run-down neighborhood. She couldn't get over Lance's deference to J.L. Quickly enough he had forgotten her being forced against her will to go with J.L. and shamelessly had begged the wealthy, influential man to patronize his restaurants. She had been embarrassed for Lance, who hadn't the common sense to be embarrassed for himself.

She also felt uncomfortable with J.L. thinking she was engaged to Lance when it was neither officially true nor likely to be. The more she was with J.L., the more she realized her feelings for Lance were not strong enough for marriage. But J.L. was just so sure of himself, he needed a blow to his ego to bring him in line. She wished she hadn't slipped and intimated she didn't love Lance. She was fond of him, after all.

The truck stopped in front of a tiny, yellow stucco house whose sidewalk was cracked and where two lonely daffodils sat in a dry patch of ground that at one time had been a garden before the weeds had taken over.

"We're here," J.L. announced.

Lindsey already understood one powerful reason why Mindy Carson wanted her money, and wanted it all—to find a better neighborhood in which to live. This one was depressing. It even looked dangerous.

"Maybe she isn't home," Lindsey said.

"She probably is. She doesn't go out much."

He opened the truck door for Lindsey to get out, and together they walked up to the rickety wooden porch badly in need of a paint job. As they came to the front door, Lindsey brushed a cobweb from her arm, and J.L. knocked.

"Who is it?" came a female voice from inside.

"J.L. Brett, Miss Carson. May I see you?"

"Of course. Give me a minute."

They waited and heard a lock on the other side of the door being fumbled with. Finally the voice called out, "Please come in."

J.L. opened the door for Lindsey, and the two of them stepped into a narrow and dark hallway with fading flowered wallpaper and plain brown linoleum on the floor.

At the end of the hallway was a young woman, very pretty, with light brown hair softly framing a round, pale face—and sitting in a wheelchair.

Her frail body looked almost like a child's in its simple shirtwaist dress, and her eyes looked tired, even though there was a lovely expression on her face that showed no irritation at being interrupted from her evening's activity.

"This is a surprise visit, Mr. Brett," she said.

"Yes, Miss Carson. I'm sorry for the time, and that I didn't call first, but it was a last-minute decision to come."

"That's perfectly all right. Let's go into the living room where there's more light, and you can introduce me to your friend."

Lindsey's mind was whirling. *Surely this can't be the woman who wants my money?* Immediate compassion rushed out to her as Lindsey wondered why she was incapacitated.

Mindy Carson expertly turned her chair around and moved it into another room, and Lindsey and J.L. followed.

The small but immaculate living room was filled with soft light and old furniture, but not much of it, for space was needed to accommodate the wheelchair.

"Miss Carson, I'd like to introduce you to Lindsey Faraday, the owner of the Lucky Dollar." J.L. turned his gaze to Lindsey. "Mindy is the client I represent," he said softly. "It was her mother who loaned your father the money."

"I see," Lindsey said softly.

Mindy exclaimed, "How nice to meet you, Miss Faraday." With a genuine smile enhanced by lovely white teeth, she extended her hands, which Lindsey awkwardly took, feeling suddenly uncomfortable at being here with the woman about whom she had thought unkindly. Mindy's eyes brightened. "It must be exciting to have a gold mine," she assumed.

Lindsey glanced at J.L. before smiling weakly at Mindy and saying, "It is. I love it. One never knows what the ground is going to give up from day to day."

Mindy nodded enthusiastically. "Maybe someday I can come and take a tour of it. Could I get my wheelchair through the tunnels?"

"On the main level, yes," Lindsey answered as calmly as she could, knowing there weren't many weeks left for them to do that. "We'll give it a try." It was obvious that Mindy Carson did not know that the Lucky Dollar was probably going to have to be sold in order to raise the money with which to pay her.

"Please sit down," Mindy suggested, "and let me get you something cool to drink. I have iced tea or lemonade."

"Please don't go to any trouble," Lindsey said.

"It will be my pleasure. I don't get many guests to fawn over."

"Lemonade, then."

"Iced tea," J.L. requested, and Lindsey suppressed a sigh. They couldn't even agree on what to drink. Were they always going to be on opposite sides?

In looking around the humble lodgings of Mindy Carson, it was easy to see why this charming young woman needed the money she had discovered was owed her mother's estate, and Lindsey began to understand why J.L. had been so unrelenting in his demand for the thirty thousand dollars.

Mindy soon returned with frosted glasses of tea and lemonade for them and herself, and a plate of homemade oatmeal raisin cookies, which she graciously offered her guests.

"Tell Lindsey how you happen to be in a wheelchair," J.L. suggested, and Mindy explained, in a straightforward manner devoid of self-pity.

"I'm a paraplegic because of a motorcycle accident that happened three years ago. My bike slid out from under me and I fell over a cliff. Crashed about forty feet down." She gave a little laugh. "The bike was totaled, and I didn't do much better."

Lindsey admired the young woman's candor.

"I've always been a bit of a daredevil," Mindy went on. "Try anything once; that's me. Was me. Like most people who ride motorcycles, I was convinced that nothing would ever happen to me. I was an excellent rider. I'd had my own dirt bike since I was ten years old, and the bike I was riding the day of the accident felt like an extension of my own body."

Lindsey shuddered, wondering how the trauma had changed Mindy's life, and J.L. supplied part of the answer. "Mindy was going to San Diego State at the time, majoring in art and history but, because of months of recuperation in the hospital and several required operations, she had to drop out."

"What do you do now?" Lindsey asked.

"I stuff envelopes for a company in San Francisco. It doesn't pay much, but at least I can afford to feed myself. My mother left me this house, and when I get the money from the Lucky Dollar—" She stopped. "I'm sorry, Lindsey. I'm sure that's a lot of money for you to part with, but it will be a godsend to me."

"Mindy needs it for more surgery and medical equipment to help her get around."

"I want to be a teacher someday, but I need a van that's converted for wheelchair use so I can drive myself and not have to depend on others."

"Do you have family nearby?" Lindsey asked, hoping she did.

Mindy looked down at her hands but said nothing.

J.L. spoke up. "Mindy was married to a man who didn't understand the vows that said, 'For better or for worse, in sickness and in health.' After the accident, he divorced Mindy as soon as he could."

Mindy looked up into Lindsey's eyes. "It was hard for him to be married to a woman confined to a wheelchair. He's active in sports. . .and other things."

Lindsey wanted to put her arms around the young woman. Even though they had just met, she already liked and respected Mindy Carson. She was real, a fighter who wanted to support herself and didn't ask for pity from others.

"Is there a chance you'll walk again?" Lindsey had to ask.

Mindy's face brightened. "Yes, eventually, but it will take a lot of money, and time."

"And patience," J.L. added. He turned to Lindsey. "So you can see why Mindy needs all the money at once, not small amounts over a period of time. That money will help her recovery."

"Yes, I do understand, now," Lindsey admitted, and her eyes were soft when she looked at J.L.

She leaned over from her place on a lumpy, upholstered couch and squeezed Mindy's hands. "Your mother helped my father at a time when he desperately needed it. I'm happy to be able to repay the debt." And, strangely enough, she meant it. Mindy Carson deserved another chance.

☙❧☙

Driving home after their visit, neither J.L. nor Lindsey spoke for awhile, but then Lindsey broke the silence. "Mindy has really suffered these past few years, but look at her positive attitude. I like her determination to take care of herself. I'm sorry I was so resentful of her."

"Don't be hard on yourself." J.L. reached over and patted her hand where it lay on the seat. "You were fighting for your life too."

"Well," Lindsey gave a wan smile, "you won't have to fight me anymore, Mr. Brett. You can start procedures to sell the mine as soon as you want. Mindy needs help now." She paused, and her eyes suddenly flashed. "I will, of course, still try to find the money on my own."

J.L. pulled her hand up to his lips and kissed her fingertips, slowly. "I hope you do. Believe that, Lindsey. And I respect you for honoring your father's debt."

Lindsey liked the feeling of self-respect that flooded through her, as well as the distinct pleasure of having J.L.'s admiration, but she still wasn't sure how it all would end. What if no buyer were found for the Lucky Dollar? She asked J.L. the question.

In answer, he put a cassette tape in to play. "This is one of my favorite songs. Listen to the words, Lindsey. They'll give you the answers you seek."

Lindsey listened as a rich baritone sang, "Great is Thy faithfulness! Great is Thy faithfulness! Morning by morning new mercies I see. All I have needed Thy hand hath provided. Great is Thy faithfulness, Lord, unto me! Pardon for sin and a peace that endureth. Thy own dear presence to cheer and to guide. Strength for today and bright hope for tomorrow—blessings all mine, with ten thousand beside!"*

Her eyes filled with tears. New as she was at being a Christian, she did believe that God would give her strength and hope. She had to trust in His faithfulness to guide her. After all, she was His child. He loved her.

When they arrived at her house, there was a package resting against the front door. It was small and wrapped exquisitely in gold foil and black-and-gold netting and silk ribbon.

"I wonder what this is?" Lindsey questioned, turning the package over and over in her hands while J.L. unlocked the front door with the key she had given him.

In the darkness that had come with the night, she could not see the set of his jaw harden or note the jealousy that narrowed his eyes. She did not know what was in the package, but J.L. suspected.

Chapter 21

L et me check the house and then I'll go," J.L. said to Lindsey, holding the door open for her.

"Out here we don't worry about people breaking in," she told him.

"The advantage of living in a small town. Still, you can never be too careful."

"You're right. Thank you."

J.L. walked quickly through each of her rooms to be sure there was no unwanted visitor, and to give Lindsey a chance to open the mysterious package.

"Oh, how sweet," he heard her murmur. He finished his inspection and joined her in the living room. She held up an exquisite half-ounce, tear-shaped bottle of perfume with a crystal dove on the top for him to see. "It's from Lance. L'Air du Temps." She said the name with awe and tipped it over so the stopper would absorb some of the delicate floral and spice scent that she then dabbed behind her ears. "Mmm, it smells heavenly."

It ought to, J.L. thought, knowing the deeply romantic French scent, in its handblown Lalique crystal bottle, cost around $110.00 a quarter-ounce. He often bought this very perfume for his mother. Old Lance was lavishing quite a gift on the woman he hoped to marry. *Must have figured it would impress Lindsey, and it is.* J.L. wished it weren't.

He leaned over close to her face, her shining hair touching his forehead. "You wear it well," he whispered, feeling a rush of emotion at her nearness and the tempting scent of her, but he stood back without taking advantage of the situation.

As he watched Lindsey's enchantment with her gift, turning the bottle around and around so that it caught the dazzling light from the table lamp, frustration knotted his stomach at the thought of Lance romancing Lindsey while he, J.L., lost out because of some antiquated ideal of ethics.

He doubted Lance Robards truly understood the woman he was pursuing. Lindsey was not ordinary. She was unique, exquisite, compassionate, charming, and courageous. She was also vulnerable at the moment, and J.L. prayed she would not be tempted to find the money to pay Mindy by marrying the shallow, self-interested restaurateur.

Wait for me, Lindsey, he told her with his eyes and with his heart. *Wait for me, and I'll marry you myself.*

❧❀❧

"Lindsey, I need to talk with you," Santiago said, lumbering into the mine office two weeks after Lindsey's fateful meeting with Mindy Carson. His shirt was wet with perspiration from working on the sixth level of the mine where Lindsey had found some water seepage the day before and had sent him to check it out.

"I can't talk right now, Santiago. I've learned about a new bank in Escondido where I might get a loan for the Lucky Dollar." Her eyes were bright with excitement. "But look at all they want to know: business loan application, three years' tax returns, three years' balance sheets from the mine, list of outstanding debts, assets, liabilities." She picked up one paper after another on her desk and waved them at him. "I'm surprised they don't require a day-by-day account of my life from the moment I was born."

Santiago chuckled.

"Can we talk when I get back?" she asked, slinging a black patent-leather purse over the shoulder of her green linen business suit and taking up several file folders into her arms. "I'm on my way to the bank now and after that to see Mindy Carson in San Diego." She had told him about Mindy. "What's the situation on the water?"

"We found the problem," Santiago answered, following her brisk walk out the door. "The men are working on it now. But I really need to talk to you."

They reached the parking lot and Lindsey got into her red two-door Cherokee. "I'm sorry, Santiago, but I must fly." She gave him an apologetic smile. "Later?"

He shrugged. "Sure, it can wait, I guess. It's probably not a good idea anyway."

Lindsey turned on the ignition, shifted into gear, and the tires of the Jeep kicked up some gravel as she drove away.

Santiago watched her go. Then he stuffed his hands in the pockets of his jeans and shuffled slowly back to the mine.

❧❦❧

It was long after dark when Lindsey got home and remembered she had promised to talk to Santiago. "Oh, well, it's too late to call him now. I'll see him tomorrow." She went to bed but couldn't sleep because she kept comparing J.L. with Lance.

She had seen her would-be fiancé several times since he had come to the mine, and she had thanked him profusely for the perfume. More and more, however, he had succeeded in turning her off. His continual put-down of Christians and his unwillingness to understand what the mine meant to her made her wonder why she even spent time with him.

The main goal of his life was the acquisition of things and position and reputation. Though he was, basically, a nice man, there was not enough depth to him to interest her.

J.L., on the other hand, was a whole different story. While he wasn't against the wealthy life he had inherited and was living, the joy in his life came from doing for others. It gave him power and respect, to be sure, but that's not why he did what he did. His motive was simple: If people needed help, he wanted to be there.

In her darkened bedroom, Lindsey pulled the covers up to her chin and gazed through the tall window at the moon outside. It splashed a benevolent path of silvery light across her bed and focused her thoughts on J.L. She had told him, "You won't have to fight me anymore. . .sell the mine as soon as you want. Mindy needs help now. I will, of course, still try to find the money on my own." She murmured out loud, "I sure hope this bank in Escondido comes through for me."

Snuggling deeper into the covers and closing her eyes, she recounted how much she admired J.L.—his strength, his humor, his rugged manliness that thrilled her heart. Did he really want to start a relationship with her when their legal situation was settled? She hoped so. Oh, how she hoped so.

ᕷᘓᘓᕷ

The next morning, Lindsey was glad to see Santiago already in the mine office when she arrived. He had made coffee, and she drank deeply from her first cup and said, "Okay, Santiago, what did you want to talk with me about?"

The big man eased himself down into the chair in front of her desk and took a deep breath. "You look nice, Boss," he said.

"Thanks." She felt comfortable in a cool and feminine cucumber-colored jumpsuit of rayon and polyester, a paisley scarf around her neck. "I may be going back to the bank in Escondido this afternoon. Surprisingly, they said it might take only twenty-four hours to make up their minds on my loan request. The other banks took a week or two."

Santiago bent forward, leaning massive, hairy arms on the old wooden desk. Taking a deep breath, he said, "You don't have to wait for that bank, Boss. I have the thirty thousand dollars."

"Mmm?" she answered distractedly, for she was pulling papers out of the file drawer in her desk.

"I have thirty thousand dollars, and you can have it to pay back the loan, and the mine won't have to be sold."

Lindsey's hands froze in midair, holding a manila folder with a red label on one corner. Looking up and into Santiago's eyes, she could tell he was nervous, and also thought she had heard him wrong. "What did you say?" she questioned.

"I can lend you the thirty thousand."

"Lend me. . . ?"

"Maria and I have been saving a thousand dollars a year ever since I started working at this mine."

"That's admirable, Santiago."

"I don't want the mine to be sold. I don't want to look for another job."

"New owners might keep you on."

"Might and might not. I don't want to take any chances, and I don't want to work for anyone but you. Better yet, you can have our thirty thousand dollars in exchange for a partnership in the mine."

Lindsey's mouth slowly opened wider and wider, and she offered no dissent.

"I'm getting up in age, Lindsey, and I want to know there will be money for Maria and me when it's time to retire. Right now, the mine isn't producing a whole lot more than what keeps all of us living a fairly decent life, but there's always that chance that we'll find the mother lode, or at least another big strike.

"You and your father have been good to me and Maria through the years. You and the Lucky Dollar are like family to us. So take the money. Keep the mine, and give me a shot at a good future."

Lindsey exploded out of her chair and charged around the desk, flinging herself into his arms. "Oh, Santiago, you're a lifesaver. What a brilliant plan—for the mine as well as yourself. Yes, yes, yes. Let's do it. Let's keep the Lucky Dollar... together."

An unbelieving grin began on the heavy lips of the old foreman and expanded into a broad, incredulous smile, then into a deep belly laugh.

"Really, Boss? You like the idea?"

"Oh, Santiago, it's perfect. I'd be thrilled to know that after more than thirty years of faithful service to the Lucky Dollar, it would give you back a safe and comfortable retirement. How wise you and Maria were to save your money a little each year."

She backed away now, a little embarrassed at how she had overwhelmed him, but still wanting him to know how thrilled she was with his suggestion. "You *are* the Lucky Dollar, Santiago," she told him. "You belong to each other." Her eyes glistened with tears. "Are you absolutely sure you want to do this? There is always the chance that the mine will fizzle out today, tomorrow, next year."

He was still smiling. "I know that, and Maria knows that, but we want to stay where we are, in that house where we raised our children, and I want to keep working the mine. I figure I still have a good ten years left in me, and I'd feel like a million dollars walking through the tunnels, knowing a percentage of them belong to me."

He got serious then. "I've never owned anything much in my life, Lindsey, except that beat-up old truck I drive. I don't even own that house that you let me live in. It would make me proud to have a part of the mine to show for a life's work and to leave to my children. I want them, and Maria, to be proud of me."

Lindsey began to cry. "Santiago, you are so precious. I know for a fact how proud your children, and Maria too, are of you already. You're a good man, a faithful, hardworking man."

Santiago stepped back and stuck out his hand. "So, is it a deal?"

Lindsey did not hesitate for a moment. She pushed her hand into his and said, "Yes, Sir. We'll get John Gregory to draw up papers after we figure out what a fair percentage would be for you to own in exchange for your money."

"It doesn't have to be much—"

"It has to be fair," Lindsey insisted, pointing a finger at him.

"Okay, Boss."

"Partner," Lindsey corrected firmly, then wiped her eyes and stared at her foreman. "Santiago, you have made me a very happy woman."

Later that morning, Santiago appeared back in the mine office with a cashier's check for thirty thousand dollars. "But, Santiago, we haven't signed any papers yet," Lindsey said.

"We shook hands. That's enough."

"We're still going to write this up legally, though," Lindsey told him.

"I know, but I wanted you to have this as soon as possible," he countered. "Now your heart can be at ease."

Lindsey gave him an enthusiastic kiss on the cheek. "How does it feel to be a lifesaver?" she asked him, and Santiago just grinned from ear to ear and stuck out his barrel chest even further than normal.

❧❦❧

Lindsey drove to San Diego, singing. On her way to J.L.'s office, she smiled at every person she passed, even Heather, who looked at her warily, wondering if anything would be broken today because of her visit. It pleased Heather to announce, "I'm sorry, but Mr. Brett is not here. He's in Los Angeles on a case."

"When will he be back?" Lindsey asked, disappointed. She had been looking forward to seeing the expression on J.L.'s face when she handed him the check for thirty thousand dollars.

"Day after tomorrow."

"I see."

Reluctantly, Lindsey took an envelope from her purse. "Please give him this, then, and tell him who it's from." She added, "Have him call me, please. Immediately."

Heather accepted the envelope with a question in her eyes. Whatever could be inside? She hoped it wasn't a flat little bomb that would explode in J.L.'s face when he opened it.

Chapter 22

Lindsey left J.L.'s office in buoyant but reflective spirits. What a totally unexpected way the mine situation had been resolved. Everyone was a winner: she was, the mine, its employees, Santiago, Mindy. . .but what about her relationship with J.L.?

He had told her on the day of Santiago's birthday party that, until the case was settled, it was not ethical for him to pursue her. He had also said, "I'm attracted to you. . .a lot. . .I keep wanting to be with you."

As to her part in all this, she remembered telling him that once the Lucky Dollar was sold, she wasn't sure she would want to have anything to do with him. Now that things would soon be settled, she could tell him the truth that she was in love with him—sensibly, rationally, deliriously, wildly in love with him.

How could she not love this man of high principle and singular determination who, at a single touch, could set her mind, heart, and body into a turmoil? One look from those dark, penetrating eyes, and she melted. One word with that voice that was made for Shakespeare, and she soared to heaven.

He cared about the same things she did—people and God. His quiet Christian life showed her a way that was new and uncertain to her, but she knew she could trust him. Trust his judgment. Even if she had lost the mine, she would still have loved him.

Slamming the door of the Jeep after she got in, Lindsey knew her life would be unsettled until she could talk to J.L. face-to-face and explain where she had gotten the thirty thousand dollars to save the mine. *Won't he be surprised?* she giggled in anticipation of their next meeting.

In the meantime, since he was out of town, she decided she needed a vacation and, when she got home, she called a quiet bed-and-breakfast inn she had stayed at before on Santa Catalina Island, twenty-six miles off the southern California coast, and made a reservation for a few days. It was the perfect place to relax until J.L. returned. She wanted to be her best for him when they started their relationship.

❦

J.L. charged up the path to the mine office, flung open the door, nearly taking it off its hinges again, and startled Santiago who was sitting at Lindsey's desk, going over the accounts. Lindsey had wanted him to familiarize himself with the paperwork involved in running the mine.

"Where is she?" J.L. demanded to know.

Santiago rose to his feet and folded his arms across his wide chest. "Miss Lindsey isn't here," he answered firmly, not liking the wild look in the lawyer's eyes.

J.L. placed both hands on the desk and leaned forward on them. "Don't protect her, Santiago. I have to see her. Did you know she brought a check for thirty thousand dollars to my office?"

Santiago shook his head yes.

"So I have to talk with her about it. Where is she?"

"Miss Lindsey's gone."

"Gone? Where?"

"On vacation."

"What?" The word exploded from J.L.'s mouth and he slammed one hand down hard on the desk. A small clock tumbled off one corner and clattered on the floor.

Santiago frowned. "Is there anything else I can help you with, Mr. Brett?"

J.L. took a deep breath and let it out all at once. "She's with *him*, isn't she? I hadn't expected he'd move so fast. The snake. He gave her the money to save her mine and thinks she'll marry him in gratitude. But she won't. She can't. She doesn't love him, I know that. I *know* that!"

He slammed his other hand down on the desk, and a vase with dried flowers in it flew off one side and shattered into a dozen pieces when it hit the floor.

Santiago did not move, nor correct J.L.'s erroneous conception as to where the money had come from. That was Lindsey's prerogative.

"Why didn't I tell her a long time ago that I love her?" he flung the words at Santiago, but he wasn't really talking to him; he was talking to himself. "I started falling in love with her the very first day I met her, when she nearly killed me, shooting at that mountain lion. I'd never seen so spunky a woman. I'd never been so intrigued by a personality. I was attracted to her uniqueness, her spirit, her fire, her vulnerability, her precious Christian faith."

His pacing quickened, and with his long and powerful legs, it took only a few strides to go from wall to wall in the small office.

"I told myself I couldn't pursue her. That it wasn't ethical as long as I was representing an opposing client. But I kept wanting to be with her." He whirled to face Santiago. "You can understand that, can't you? I mean, what man wouldn't fall in love with Lindsey Faraday after five minutes with her?"

Santiago nodded in agreement and began to grin.

"Now I've probably lost her," J.L. declared and, with the flat of a hand, he smacked the nearest wall. A picture fell off and the glass broke on the floor.

Santiago finally came from behind the desk and grabbed J.L. by the shoulders. "Before you destroy this office, I'm going to tell you where Lindsey is. She went to Catalina. To a bed-and-breakfast inn on Metropole Avenue."

A roar like that of a wounded beast shook the little office to its foundation. "She's with him, isn't she? I know she is. Well, while I have a breath in my body, he's not going to seduce the woman I love!"

J.L. whirled around and crashed into an old wooden chair, which splintered and fell to the floor, destroyed. A furious groan accompanied his race to the door, which he tore open but not off its hinges, and Santiago chuckled as he watched the lawyer storm down the path to save his lady love from a fate worse than death, which didn't even exist.

༒

J.L. was an irate and determined man with a mission: Find Lindsey and save her from Lance Robards. They didn't belong together. They saw life from opposite ends of the telescope. Robards was materialistic; Lindsey was idealistic.

He condemned Robards for taking advantage of Lindsey's predicament and buying himself a wife who would never love him and whom he could never satisfy.

J.L. ached for Lindsey who had been so desperate to keep her mine and the jobs of a few people who were dear to her that she had sold herself and her future for money.

All these thoughts churned relentlessly through J.L.'s mind as he drove frantically from the mine back to his home in La Jolla, threw a few things into an overnight bag, and caught a two o'clock flight out of San Diego. He endured the thirty-minute flight, chafed at the twenty minutes or so it took the bus to go from the Airport-in-the-Sky into Avalon, the tiny principal town of fifteen hundred on the island, and walked the short distance to Metropole Avenue where he found the Sunset Inn.

It was a blazing hot day, under a merciless sun (the sun shines 267 days a year on Catalina), and his shirt had dampened considerably during his travels as he pushed himself to reach the inn and confront Robards. He wasn't tired, though. Relentless energy had driven him across the ocean to rescue the woman he loved.

"I'm looking for Lindsey Faraday," he told the pretty blond woman who answered the door at the inn.

"Come in," she invited. "She's not here right now but should be back shortly. She's parasailing."

J.L. followed her into a cheerful sun-splashed living room with windows on three walls through which could be seen a thick green lawn dotted with white, wrought-iron benches, the riotous red and purple flowers of a bougainvillea vine, and a spectacular view of the Pacific Ocean and boats bobbing in Avalon Bay.

The young woman smiled. "Are you looking for a room or only for Lindsey?"

"I'd better have a room," he told her.

"For how many nights?"

J.L. didn't hesitate. "One, to start with. I may go home tomorrow."

"That's too bad."

"Or I might stay longer." *Depending on whether or not I'm wanted for murdering Lance Robards,* he considered. He thought of asking for Robards, but assumed he was with Lindsey, and even if he weren't, J.L. wanted to talk with Lindsey first.

Taking a key from the desk drawer, the young woman started up some stairs and J.L. followed, toting his overnight bag. "We'll put you in the Sunflower Room," she said. "It has one of the finest views of the ocean and a king-sized bed."

She led him into a dazzling room decorated in warm yellow and white, with white wicker chairs and white-and-yellow-striped curtains that did not diminish the view from the large window.

"Feel free to cool off in our pool and have some lemonade and freshly baked cookies until Lindsey gets back," his hostess suggested.

"Sounds great."

J.L. was hot and sweaty and had been knotted up for hours. He needed to relax before he met Lindsey. He didn't want to scare her or do anything he would regret to Lance Robards.

He swam laps for twenty minutes, but even the warm water of the pool did not ease the tension he felt all over his body. He didn't enjoy the soft lounge chair or the lemonade or the sugar cookies.

He paced around the pool, back and forth, not even noticing the pleasant breeze that drifted over the hillside and played with the ends of his hair. He tried to read a magazine but couldn't concentrate, so he sat and stared at the ocean in the distance and waited for the happy couple.

Twenty minutes later, his vigil was rewarded. Looking through his dark sunglasses, he saw Lindsey strolling toward the diving board. Over her bathing suit she was wearing a wrap that, when she reached the board, she unfastened and tossed onto a nearby chair. Robards was not with her.

J.L. admired her slim figure and golden angel hair that hung straight, below her shoulders. She was one beautiful woman, tanned and firm and appealing in a cranberry red suit that had only one strap over her left shoulder. He swallowed hard and rose from the chair.

The water made little sound when Lindsey cleanly dove into it, swam half the length of the pool before surfacing, then did a breaststroke to the end where she looked up and saw a pair of muscular legs leading up to narrow hips and a black bathing suit on a man whose chest was far from narrow and whose face she recognized with shock.

J.L.

He leaned over and extended a hand, and Lindsey eagerly took it. The dream of their being together, finally, flowered deep within her as his strong hand enfolded hers. The relationship they had denied each other through the last torturous months was about to begin, possible now because J.L. had her check for thirty thousand dollars. He had probably already delivered it to Mindy.

As he effortlessly hoisted her up, Lindsey smiled exuberantly, but when her wet feet found the deck, she saw the scowl on his face and she lost her concentration and slipped. One of J.L.'s arms flew around her waist and brought her against the dry, hot length of him. Their skin touching, Lindsey looked into his eyes and he into hers, and she wondered why he wasn't kissing her.

"Lindsey. We have to talk."

Chapter 23

J.L. released Lindsey and gestured toward a white wrought-iron table. Lindsey, unsure of why his attitude was chilly toward her, nodded her approval, and they went over to the table and sat down.

In a flash, J.L. recalled how he had felt just that morning when he had gone into his office and Heather had handed him Lindsey's check for thirty thousand dollars. He had been dumbfounded.

"Did she leave me a note with this?" he had asked his secretary.

"No."

"A verbal message?"

"Nothing."

J.L. had thought for a moment, scratching his chin. *Where did she get the money?* he had asked himself over and over until a light had dawned. There was no other explanation. Lindsey must not have been able to get financing to save the mine, so she had taken the only course open to her—she was going to marry Lance Robards and get the money from him. Mostly for the sake of her employees, whom she loved and hovered over like a mother hen, she was sacrificing her future in order to secure theirs.

Of course, he didn't know this for sure. She might have found another source, but a gut feeling he couldn't deny believed only that.

So he had gone after her, like the cavalry to the rescue. He was going to save her from ruining her life, show her what a cad Lance Robards was for taking advantage of her desperate need, be her hero and carry her off and tell her he loved her and claim her for himself. He was even going to offer to pay the thirty thousand dollars to save the mine. She would then be free to marry him. Him, not Robards.

But all the words he had rehearsed, all the emotions he had yearned to express, suddenly fled him as he faced her here on this island paradise of flowers and ocean and playful breezes, her eyes crystal blue and questioning. His stomach did flip-flops as he suddenly remembered something she had told him just a few weeks before. She had said, "How can you think I would marry a man I don't love just to get my hands on his money?" But she had. The check proved it.

He was angry with her—very angry with her—her.

Until this moment, all his outrage had been against Robards, as though the man had forced Lindsey to accept him against her will. Now, as J.L. sat and

451

looked at Lindsey, aching to take her in his arms, longing to taste her lips, yearning to tell her of his feelings for her, he realized she must have willingly agreed to the plan. She was too strong-minded, too independent, too intelligent to be persuaded to do something she did not want to do.

"If this debt of my father's is legitimate," she had told him once, "then it shall be paid, no matter what it takes to do so." That she would go into marriage for such a wrong reason bothered J.L. For her to put more priority on a possession, the mine, than on the sanctity of a lifetime relationship made J.L. think he might have made a mistake in thinking Lindsey was a sincere Christian.

Still, one small voice urged him to reconsider. Maybe she did get the money from a bank. She deserved the benefit of the doubt, didn't she?

So instead of telling her he loved her and wanted her, he gave her a chance and said simply, "I have the check."

"Good," Lindsey responded with a smile.

"He gave it to you, didn't he?" J.L. asked, "he" meaning Robards.

"Yes, he did. Wasn't it wonderful of him?" "Him" meaning Santiago.

"Wouldn't a bank lend you the money?"

"I tried as many as would even give me an application, J.L. When I called the last one, in Escondido, to let them know I didn't need the loan anymore, I found out that it too was going to turn me down."

J.L. was really put off by her cheerful attitude. *How could she be happy over a forthcoming marriage of convenience? Unless. . .unless. . .she really cared for Robards,* he thought.

"Is this really what you want?" he asked, leaning forward, giving her one more chance to break down and sob out her unfortunate plight and beg him to rescue her.

Instead, she gave him a look of amazement. "Of course it is. How could you doubt it? You know what the mine means to me. This offer was a godsend."

J.L. felt sick to his stomach. Instead of holding her in his arms and telling her he loved her and wanted her desperately, and would she please mark off a few hours on her calendar one day next month so that they could get married, he had lost her. He had waited too long, and lost her.

"Did you give the money to Mindy?" Lindsey asked.

"Uh, no, not yet. I just got it this morning. I've been out of town."

"Yes, I know. Mindy's a wonderful person, isn't she? So genuine and positive. I'm glad it's worked out for her. And the Lucky Dollar."

She leaned over the table toward him, her wet hair hanging within a few inches of J.L.'s hand, presenting a temptation he found hard to resist. "Aren't you thrilled with how all of this has turned out?" she asked.

J.L. sprang to his feet, pushing the chair back with his legs. "Thrilled is not the word I'd use," he growled. "More like appalled."

Lindsey stared up at him through the bright sunshine. "Appalled? What does that mean, J.L.?"

He wanted to grab her and shake her until her teeth rattled. Her unflappable calm in the face of the degrading alliance she had made galled him.

"You want to know what's the matter?" he roared. "Well, Lady, for starters, I can't believe you stooped so low to get your hands on that money—"

Lindsey rose to her feet. "It was graciously offered to me—"

"Graciously? You mean you didn't grovel for it?"

"Certainly not. The offer was a sensible one that I'm thrilled with, if you must know."

"A sensible business deal, in other words."

"Yes, and no one deserves it more than him. He's been so good to me."

J.L.'s eyes almost fell out of his head. "How good?"

"Why, with his time and devotion—"

"Garbage!"

Lindsey plastered her hands on her hips. "I cannot believe your reaction to this, J.L. Why aren't you delighted the money has been paid? That means you've won. What difference does it make where the funds came from?"

J.L. rolled his eyes as though he had been struck by a frying pan. "I thought you were a woman of principle, Lindsey, a woman who would not compromise when it came to her integrity."

Lindsey gasped. "Compromise? You call it compromise to accept the offer of help from a man I think the world of?"

"So you have strong feelings for him?"

"I adore him."

J.L. gaped at her, then stumbled over to the pool and stared down into it.

Lindsey followed him, her temper rising. "This man is one in a million. I couldn't ask for anyone more perfect for a partner."

J.L. whirled around and faced her. "Then you're a fool!" He threw the words at her before he had a chance to think.

Lindsey's eyes flashed. "Santiago has given most of his adult life to that mine, and he deserves a solid retirement. I just hope his partnership in the mine will do that. If you think I'm a fool for giving him that, then you're a heartless man."

She whirled and started to walk away, but J.L. grabbed her wrist and turned her back to him. "Santiago? Why are we talking about him?"

"We've been talking about him all along, J.L."

"Santiago?" J.L. hit the side of his forehead with the heel of his hand. "Santiago gave you the money?"

"I've been telling you that for ten minutes."

"I thought you got it from Lance Robards. That you agreed to marry him—"

"What?" The word exploded out of Lindsey's mouth, and she took two steps backward. "You believe I agreed to marry Lance Robards just to get the money to save the mine?"

"Yes."

"You think I have so little regard for myself? No more dignity than a hopeless beggar? No more respect for the sacrament of marriage? Ooo."

"Now, don't get upset, Lindsey. I misunderstood, that's all."

"Misunderstood? If you knew me at all, you could never have *misunderstood.*"

J.L. reached out and placed both hands on her waist. "I have something to tell you, Lindsey, now that I know you're not really going to marry Lance Robards." He bent to kiss her, but Lindsey slammed both her hands on his hard-breathing chest and gave him a shove—backward, into the shimmering water.

He came up sputtering. "Hey, what was that for?"

"It was my way of saying good-bye, J.L. Brett. I hope I never set eyes on you again. Never hear your disgusting voice. If I could, I'd move off the planet to keep from being within a million miles of you!"

Lindsey spun on her heels and stormed off toward the inn. Ignoring calls from J.L. to come back, she dashed up the stairs that led to her room, threw her belongings into her suitcase, stopped at the hostess's room just long enough to tell her she was leaving, ran the several blocks into Avalon and to the dock, and took the last boat leaving for the mainland.

Seventy minutes later, with the millions of lights of Long Beach magnificently dancing in welcome to the returning vacationers, Lindsey left the boat, got her car from the parking lot, and drove all the way to Majestic, without shedding one tear. She was too furious to cry.

But she did pray. *Oh, Lord, great is Your faithfulness. I thank You for helping me to keep the mine. I also thank You for letting me see just what kind of man J.L. Brett is and keeping me from making a mistake over him. I've always been content with the Lucky Dollar as the love of my life, and that's the way it will be from now on.*

Then she cried.

Chapter 24

Y ou actually accused Lindsey of agreeing to marry Lance Robards, just to pay off the debt of the mine?" Santiago asked J.L., then listened in disbelief to J.L.'s confession. They were standing in the office of the Lucky Dollar the day after the fateful confrontation on Catalina.

"Pretty stupid, eh?"

"It just proves you don't know her very well."

"But I want to, Santiago. I love her and want to marry her."

Santiago smiled. "Then go after her. Apologize as you've never apologized before. She'll forgive you."

"How do you know?"

"I just know. For some reason only understood by God and women, they love us men in spite of ourselves."

"I'm not sure she loves me or will even speak to me."

"Then you speak to her. Don't let her get away or you'll be sorry the rest of your life."

"Good idea. Do you know where she is?"

"Try the mine. She's been sulking in there all day."

"Thanks, Santiago." J.L. stuck out his hand and vigorously shook the foreman's. "I'm glad you're investing in the mine. I think it will do well for you."

"Me too. Now, if you'll excuse me, I've got things to do. Partners are busy people."

With a big grin, J.L. slapped Santiago on the back and ran out the door and down the rocky hillside toward the mine but skidded to a stop when he saw a tawny brown mountain lion, big and stealthy, entering the mine, crouched and cautious, expecting to find something to satisfy his hunger.

"Lindsey," J.L. gasped under his breath.

Whirling around, he sped back to the mine office, grabbed the rifle from the corner behind the desk where Lindsey kept it, checked to see that it was loaded, and, as he raced out, yelled, "Mountain lion!" to Santiago.

When he entered the mine, it was dark and silent and he saw no sign of the cat, nor heard it either.

Where was Lindsey? There were dozens of tunnels she could be in, and he barely knew his way through the main one. What if she were on another level and he couldn't get to her in time? The thought of that huge cat mauling her, drawing blood, made every hair on J.L.'s body stand on end.

He crouched and silently advanced, stopping every few feet to listen and let his eyes adjust to the darkness.

He remembered where Lindsey kept a flashlight not far from the entrance, found it, and turned it on. He had no idea where light switches were, or even if there were some all along the way. Even if the light from the flashlight distracted the big cat, that was okay. Better it attack him than Lindsey. He was bigger than she and he had the gun. She was helpless and unaware that she was being stalked.

Then he heard it—the soft growl. It didn't sound far off, so he inched his way forward as quietly as he could, not knowing if he could surprise the big cat but certain that that might be the only chance Lindsey would have, and he had to give it to her.

J.L. stepped cautiously, wishing he were wearing tennis shoes. Stalking a hungry cougar while wearing a business suit and slick-soled shoes was not an everyday occurrence for him. Fortunately, he had always had good balance and, as he took step after careful step, powerful muscles in his thighs and calves kept him from sliding as the terrain descended further and further into the darkness.

He followed the sounds from the cat down a ramp, around a corner. A sudden flap of wings—bats—startled him and he dropped the flashlight. It went out, and cold, gut-wrenching terror gripped his insides. Frantically groping for the light, he could not even see his own hand in front of his face. He was holding his breath and he had never felt so alone.

Then his fingers connected with metal, and he grabbed the flashlight and turned it on just as he heard a snarling sound followed by a heart-stopping roar and a piercing female scream.

"Lindsey!" he yelled at the top of his voice. "I'm coming!"

He tripped and fell, but still had the flashlight in his hand and, though his skin was torn from scraping himself on the dirt floor of the mine, he got up, feeling no pain in his body but sheer panic in his heart.

He rounded a corner and there they were, in a jump hole where, "in the old days," Lindsey had explained once, "when a miner heard the roar of an approaching mine car, he had to get out of the way, so 'jump holes' were dug out from place to place in the walls for safety's sake."

Lindsey was in such a jump hole now, illuminated by a single lightbulb. She was squatting on a small plank desk whose top was covered with various field tests and measurement equipment, papers and pencils, and a telephone.

In her hand was a long stick that she was using to fend off the cat who was pawing at it from the ground and growling fiercely, baring its teeth.

Instantly, with smooth reflexive motion, J.L. raised and aimed the rifle just as the cat became aware he was there. The big beast forgot Lindsey and leaped for J.L. instead, who pulled the trigger while the animal was in midair.

The awful thud of one bullet and then another, impacting with thick flesh, was amplified a hundred times in the narrow confines of the tunnel. The cat crashed to the floor and an eerie silence followed.

Then Lindsey sobbed and leaped from the table and threw herself into J.L.'s arms. Still holding the rifle, he crushed her against him, burying his face in the lush thickness of her hair.

"Oh, J.L.," she cried, "you saved my life. I thought I was going to die, and all I could think of was that I loved you but had never told you, and how silly I had been to be angry with you over the money. You made an honest mistake, and I blew it all out of proportion. I love you. Oh, I love you."

She was babbling and crying, and J.L. held her close, thanking God that she was alive.

They clutched each other frantically, and not even when they heard the pounding of running footsteps did they separate.

Santiago and two other men tore around the last corner and stopped dead when they saw the big cat lying across the path and Lindsey firmly in J.L.'s arms as though they were attached to each other.

"Are you all right, Lindsey?" Santiago asked frantically.

"She's fine," J.L. answered for her, and Lindsey raised her tearstained face enough to nod agreement to her foreman.

"This is the same cat that's been destroying cattle near here," one of the men said, leaning over the beast, examining it to be sure it was dead. "Here's the peculiar white marking over its right eye."

Santiago confirmed the identity.

Slowly, Lindsey extricated herself from J.L. and walked over to the lion. She fell to the floor on her knees, and amazingly, for someone who had just been threatened with death by this very creature, ran her hand over his beautiful fur.

She addressed it: "I know why you killed those cattle. We humans kept encroaching on your territory, building homes and towns, and your food supply disappeared. What else could you do but survive any way you could?" She sobbed and whispered, "I'm sorry," and then looked up at J.L., and he came to her and helped her up. Santiago and the men picked up the mountain lion and carried it away.

J.L. gently enfolded Lindsey into his arms and whispered brokenly, "If I'd lost you, Lindsey. . ."

She clung to him, and their mutual tears blended on their cheeks.

※※※

Two nights later, Lindsey and J.L. were back in the mine, approaching the third level where the lion had attacked Lindsey.

"I want you to see the place again," J.L. told her, "and not be afraid of it."

Lindsey squeezed his hand and gazed adoringly up at him. "Like getting back on a horse after being thrown?"

"Yeah."

They found the jump hole and stood looking at the desk and scattered instruments silhouetted in the muted darkness. After a few minutes, Lindsey said, "I'm okay," and J.L. put his arm around her and led her away, but not toward the surface.

"Where are we going?" she asked, and then stopped. "I hear music. Why is there music?"

"You'll see," J.L. promised.

They rounded a bend, and Lindsey stopped abruptly and took in a breath.

"It's about time you got here," Santiago said with mock censure. "The beef Wellington is drying out."

Lindsey gaped at what she saw—a table covered with a crisp, white cloth and adorned with lit candles in silver holders placed around a lavish bowl of pink rosebuds, and covered dishes like one gets in a hotel with room service, from which the most delicious odors were emanating. Romantic music from a tape recorder played in the background.

"Thanks for keeping an eye on things, Santiago," J.L. said, shaking the man's hand.

"Anytime," he answered with a wink that Lindsey caught. "Anytime."

With a flourish, J.L. pulled out one of the two chairs and motioned for Lindsey to sit down. She did, in a state of shock.

"We should eat while everything's hot," J.L. instructed, taking the cloth napkin from beside her china plate, shaking it open, and laying it with great flair over her lap.

She laughed. "You're crazy; do you know that?"

"Crazy in love with you," he murmured, leaning over to kiss her on the lips.

Lindsey giggled and looked up at Santiago. "Are you joining us, Partner?"

Santiago grinned. "Can't, Lindsey. I've got things to do." He walked away.

"And so do you," J.L. told Lindsey as he lifted the covers off the four dishes and insisted she begin a dinner fit for a queen.

Lindsey ate the gourmet food hungrily, as did J.L., but they both knew the best was yet to come. Seldom looking elsewhere but into each other's eyes, they ate and listened to the soft, dreamy music drifting through the narrow tunnel while the flickering candles created intimate shadows that danced off the surrounding rocky, sedimentary walls.

"Enjoying yourself?" J.L. asked, rolling part of an artichoke heart into his mouth.

Lindsey nodded her head. "You're very imaginative."

"Thank you."

"And romantic."

Lindsey knew she was living a dream, with this extraordinary man she loved above anything else in this world, even the Lucky Dollar. She got up and went around the table to J.L., who rose to accept her into his arms. They held each other, then J.L. kissed her, and she kissed him back.

"Does this mean we're starting our relationship?" Lindsey asked.

J.L. laughed softly. "I think we started it the first day we met each other, only we didn't know it."

"Or admit it."

He held her face between his strong hands. "Lindsey, I love you more than life. You are everything I admire in a person. You're honest and hardworking, thoughtful of others, loyal—"

"You make me sound like Girl Scout of the Year."

He kissed the tip of her nose. "There's nothing wrong with being good. It shines around you and makes me want to protect you from anything bad."

"Are you saying I need a guardian?"

He gathered her into his arms again. "No. I'm asking if you'll take me as a husband, a husband who thinks you're the most beautiful, enticing, enchanting female he's ever encountered."

Lindsey leaned back and gave him a teasing grin. "Did you put those words on that infamous list of yours that describes me?"

J.L. laughed out loud. "Those and a hundred more like feisty, unpredictable, smart—"

"Maker of the world's best chili?"

He coughed. "That's debatable. Come here, you," and he kissed her long and with great feeling. "I'll be incomplete without you, Lindsey. Please say yes to my proposal."

Lindsey giggled. "What proposal?"

"To marry me." He kissed her.

Lindsey slipped her arms around his neck and looked into dark, smoldering eyes that made her heart dance. "I love you, J.L. Brett, for all the same reasons you gave for loving me." She sighed and caught his lower lip gently between her teeth. "Yes, I will marry you, as long as you don't mind my owning a gold mine."

"Of course not. In case I ever decide to stop working, you can support me comfortably."

Lindsey groaned, then slowly traced the planes and curves of his face with her fingers. "Tell me again that you love me, J.L.," she murmured, her eyes filled with love for him.

He gave her a crooked smile that brought out his dimples, which she adored. "I love you, Lindsey Faraday, today, tomorrow, and forever. I will always be faithful to you."

"As God is faithful."

"Yes," and he captured her lips again and again, with growing fervency, there in the dimly lit tunnel, and neither of them noticed, or cared, that the dinner got cold and the candles burned down.

But the music played on.